VOYAGES OF IMAGINATION

VOYAGES OF IMAGINATION

THE *STAR TREK*® FICTION COMPANION

JEFF AYERS

Based on *Star Trek* and *Star Trek: The Next Generation*® created by Gene Roddenberry
Star Trek: Deep Space Nine® created by Rick Berman and Michael Piller
Star Trek: Voyager® created by Rick Berman, Michael Piller, and Jeri Taylor
Star Trek: Enterprise® created by Rick Berman and Brannon Braga

POCKET BOOKS
New York   London   Toronto   Sydney   Memory Alpha

 POCKET BOOKS, a division of Simon & Schuster, Inc.
1230 Avenue of the Americas, New York, NY 10020

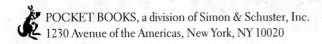
This book is published by Pocket Books, a division of
Simon & Schuster, Inc., under exclusive license from
CBS Studios Inc.

ISBN-13: 978-1-4165-0349-1
ISBN-10:   1-4165-0349-8

This Pocket Books trade paperback edition November 2006

10 9 8 7 6 5 4 3 2 1

POCKET and colophon are registered trademarks of
Simon & Schuster, Inc.

Cover art by Mark Gerber

Manufactured in the United States of America

For information regarding special discounts for bulk purchases,
please contact Simon & Schuster Special Sales at 1-800-456-6798
or business@simonandschuster.com.

This book is dedicated to my wife, Terry.
Having a book published has always been a dream of mine,
but with her by my side, I live a dream every day.

ACKNOWLEDGMENTS

First and foremost, though I dedicated the book to her, I have to say again that without my wonderful wife Terry's love and support, I wouldn't be whole. She is the bright flashlight in an otherwise dark episode of *The X-Files*.

To Greg and Samantha: Thank you for letting your dad have some quiet time on the computer. They are starting to become *Trek* fans and it has been fun to introduce them to this wonderful universe.

Rita Rosenkranz: Thank you for taking a chance on a frustrated librarian who thought that it would be cool to have a guide to all of the *Star Trek* books.

Marco Palmieri: editor extraordinaire and super patient. Thanks for opening up your world to a fan and letting him play with your toys.

Wilda Williams: Thank you for all of the opportunities you have given me. Without your guidance, I wouldn't be published.

John Marshall: Thank you for taking a chance with me, helping me build my résumé and having fun at the same time.

Dan Brown: Congratulations on your success. Thank you for your correspondence and helping me launch my career.

Tom Grime and Scott Rice for their continued support and encouragement.

Gayle Lynds: Your encouragement and support have had a major role in trying to tame this writing bug.

James Thayer: Your friendship and advice have been inspiring and have made me a better writer.

Patrick Yearout: You have taught me so much and forced me to think.

John DeAngeli: first reader and great friend.

The *Star Trek* book group at Barnes & Noble in Lynnwood: Your excitement when I mentioned my little project and then when I actually landed the assignment reinforced the idea that more people might buy the book than just my mother. In addition, a huge thank you to Michelle for helping me transcribe some of my tapes.

My mother, Donna, and my stepfather, Santo: Thanks for having me and trying to understand my obsession with that strange space show, and understanding why I had to write instead of talk to you. Santo, thank you for taking care of my mom. As Spock would say, "Live Long and Prosper."

Trying to find everyone to interview was a major challenge and major thanks are due to the following people who helped me track down others: Richard Arnold, Paula M. Block, Margaret Clark, Keith DeCandido, Kevin (Lifesaver) Dilmore, Dave Galanter, Elisa Kassin, Kevin Killiany, Jacqueline Lichtenberg, Victor Milan, Steve Roby, Amy Sisson, Geoff Trowbridge, Dayton (sorry I stole your book) Ward, Mary Wiecek, and David Wilson.

Thank you to the Timeliners for a terrific new edition of the fiction timeline. And, major thanks to all of the authors who took the time to talk to me. Without all of your input, this project would have never even gotten started.

CONTENTS

STAR TREK FICTION: THEN AND NOW

It started with a television series on September 8, 1966. Forty years later, the *Star Trek* phenomenon includes four spin-off series, ten features films, an animated series, uncounted licensed products . . . and a publishing aspect nearly as old and enduring as the franchise itself.

In 1967, long before the invention of DVDs and TiVo, Bantam Books acquired the rights to publish adaptations of *Star Trek* episodes. Noted science fiction author James Blish was approached to write short stories based on the episodes, working entirely from scripts.

Around the same time, now-defunct publisher Whitman commissioned author Mack Reynolds to craft the first original *Star Trek* novel. Published in 1968, this young adult novel was entitled *Mission to Horatius*, and was Whitman's only foray into *Trek* fiction.

Meanwhile, Bantam continued the increasingly popular collected adaptations by Blish. Before he passed away in 1975, Blish had completed eleven *Star Trek* anthologies, as well as his original novelette, *Spock Must Die!* Writing these books made more money for Blish than any other books he had written during his lifetime. When he died, his wife, Judith, saw through the unfinished *Star Trek 12* and adapted the remaining episodes for *Mudd's Angels*.

During its run, Bantam also published two original *Star Trek* short story anthologies and thirteen original novels, edited by science fiction luminary Frederik Pohl.

Star Trek's animated series debuted in 1973. Inspired by the success of the Bantam adaptations, publisher Ballantine Books acquired the license to publish books based on the cartoon, and tapped Alan Dean Foster to write novellas based on these new episodes, under the title *Star Trek Logs*. Adapting three episodes each, the books did so well that by the time Alan reached *Log Seven*, he had started incorporating original story concepts into the adaptations in order to stretch the remaining four episodes into individual novel-length stories so that Ballantine could publish three additional volumes.

In 1979, Simon & Schuster's mass-market publishing division, Pocket Books, became the official publisher of *Star Trek* books with the release of the novelization of *Star Trek: The Motion Picture*, written by *Star Trek* creator Gene Roddenberry. Editor David Hartwell successfully convinced his superiors that Pocket should publish original novels as well, and in 1981, eighteen months after the publication of the *Motion Picture* adaptation, Pocket published its first original *Star Trek* novel, Vonda N. McIntyre's *The Entropy Effect*.

The program did well for Pocket and then hit a roadblock with the publication of *Killing Time*, the twenty-fourth novel in the line, published in 1985. This marked the beginning of a period during which Gene Roddenberry's personal assistant, Richard Arnold, became involved in *Star Trek* fiction review. All proposals and manuscripts went through Richard, who would review them and pass them on to Gene with his comments. In some cases, Gene would pass comments back to Richard, and Richard would sometimes send the comments on Gene's behalf. This created some confusion over the next few years about whether the comments were coming from Richard or Gene, especially when the nature of those comments strongly discouraged Pocket and its authors from venturing beyond the scope of what was established on screen in any way. Under these constraints, innovative stories and depth of characterization seemed to decrease dramatically over what it had been before.

When *Star Trek: The Next Generation* premiered in 1987, Pocket Books began a series of books for the new show. With the launch of the TNG book line, the frequency of *Star Trek* novels increased to one per month, alternating between the new series and the original. Richard and Gene looked at everything and it all went relatively smoothly until the novel, *Music of the Spheres*, was submitted for approval. Roddenberry took offense to some of the content, and the book, eventually retitled *Probe*, ended up being re-written by another author, though still published under the original author's name.

After Gene Roddenberry passed away in 1991, Richard Arnold lost his role in reviewing *Star Trek* books. Paula Block, already the studio's direct editorial contact with Pocket in matters relating to the novels, became the primary authority on approvals. Slowly, the prior constraints and limitations placed on the fiction began to loosen, though it took several years more for the results to be felt.

With the premiere of *Star Trek: Deep Space Nine* in 1993, there were now three different series with four to six books coming out per year for each. In 1995, with the launch of *Star Trek: Voyager*, Pocket's annual output of *Star Trek* fiction rose to twenty-four mass-market titles per year, plus the infrequent hardcover novel and a newly launched line of digest-size Young Adult adventures.

In 1997, Pocket launched *New Frontier*, the first series of *Star Trek* novels focusing on an original ship and crew. The success of this launch paved the way for further innovations, as Pocket began in earnest to generate *Star Trek* fiction of increasingly greater scope and characterization, experimenting not only with content, but with structure and format. Multi-part stories became popular for a time, anthologies returned, and a line of monthly novellas published as eBooks was launched. Even as Pocket secured the book rights to the fifth *Star Trek* television series, *Enterprise*, new editorial directions were developed to produce authorized continuations of TV series that were ending, such as *Deep Space Nine* and *Voyager*, taking those sagas beyond where their final episodes left off. More original fiction concepts were conceived, such as *Stargazer* and *I.K.S. Gorkon*.

In 2005, following years of declining ratings and box office receipts culminating in the cancellation of *Enterprise*, it was clear the *Star Trek* phenomenon no longer held its audience as it once had. In July of that year, citing reasons both editorial and economic, Pocket reduced the number of mass-market *Star Trek* paperbacks published per year from twenty-four to twelve. Despite the reduced publishing schedule, Pocket continued to innovate, launching two original *Star Trek* fiction concepts, *Titan* and *Vanguard*, that same year.

In 2006, the year of *Star Trek*'s fortieth anniversary, Pocket marked the occasion with a special lineup of anniversary-themed projects for the latter half of the year, even as it continued to develop books for the years beyond.

PART ONE

STAR TREK FICTION

Published by Bantam Books

1 9 6 7 – 1 9 8 1

STAR TREK
(Later retitled STAR TREK I)
James Blish

JANUARY 1967   (136 pp)

 daptations of seven episodes from the first TV series:

"Charlie's Law" (retitled "Charlie X" for television)
"Dagger of the Mind"
"The Unreal McCoy" (retitled "The Man Trap" for television)
"Balance of Terror"
"The Naked Time"
"Miri"
"The Conscience of the King"

STAR TREK 2
James Blish

FEBRUARY 1968   (122 pp)

 daptations of seven episodes from the first TV series:

"Arena"
"A Taste of Armageddon"
"Tomorrow is Yesterday"
"Errand of Mercy"
"Court Martial"
"Operation: Annihilate!"
"The City on the Edge of Forever"
"Space Seed"

STAR TREK 3
James Blish

APRIL 1969 (118 pp)

 daptations of seven episodes from the first TV series:

"The Trouble with Tribbles"
"The Last Gunfight" (retitled "Spectre of the Gun" for television)
"The Doomsday Machine"
"Assignment: Earth"
"Mirror, Mirror"
"Friday's Child"
"Amok Time"

STAR TREK 4
James Blish

APRIL 1971 (134 pp)

 daptations of six episodes from the first TV series:

"All Our Yesterdays"
"The Devil in the Dark"
"Journey to Babel"
"The Menagerie"
"The *Enterprise* Incident"
"A Piece of the Action"

STAR TREK 5
JAMES BLISH

FEBRUARY 1972   (136PP)

 daptations of seven episodes from the first TV series:

"Whom Gods Destroy"
"The Tholian Web"
"Let That Be Your Last Battlefield"
"This Side of Paradise"
"Turnabout Intruder"
"Requiem for Methuselah"
"The Way to Eden"

STAR TREK 6
JAMES BLISH

APRIL 1972   (149PP)

 daptations of six episodes from the first TV series:

"The Savage Curtain"
"The Lights of Zetar"
"The Apple"
"By Any Other Name"
"The Cloud Minders"
"The Mark of Gideon"

STAR TREK 7
JAMES BLISH

JULY 1972   **(155PP)**

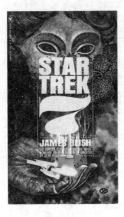

daptations of six episodes from the first TV series:

"Who Mourns for Adonais?"
"The Changeling"
"The Paradise Syndrome"
"Metamorphosis"
"The Deadly Years"
"Elaan of Troyius"

STAR TREK 8
JAMES BLISH

NOVEMBER 1972   **(170PP)**

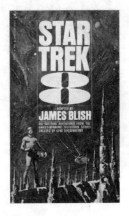

daptations of six episodes from the first TV series:

"Spock's Brain"
"The Enemy Within"
"Catspaw"
"Where No Man Has Gone Before"
"Wolf in the Fold"
"For the World Is Hollow, and I Have Touched the Sky"

STAR TREK 9
JAMES BLISH

AUGUST 1973 (183PP)

daptations of six episodes from the first TV series:

"Return to Tomorrow"
"The Ultimate Computer"
"That Which Survives"
"Obsession"
"The Return of the Archons"
"The Immunity Syndrome"

STAR TREK 10
JAMES BLISH

FEBRUARY 1974 (164PP)

daptations of six episodes from the first TV series:

"The Alternative Factor"
"The Empath"
"The Galileo Seven"
"Is There in Truth No Beauty?"
"A Private Little War"
"The Omega Glory"

STAR TREK 11
James Blish

APRIL 1975   (188 pp)

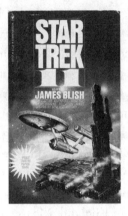

 daptations of six episodes from the first TV series:

"What Are Little Girls Made Of?"
"The Squire of Gothos"
"Wink of an Eye"
"Bread and Circuses"
"Day of the Dove"
"Plato's Stepchildren"

STAR TREK 12
James Blish and J. A. Lawrence

NOVEMBER 1977   (177 pp)

 daptations of five episodes from the first TV series:

"Patterns of Force"
"The Gamesters of Triskelion"
"And the Children Shall Lead"
"The Corbomite Maneuver"
"Shore Leave"

MUDD'S ANGELS

J. A. LAWRENCE

MAY 1978   (177PP)

 Adaptations of two episodes from the first TV series, plus an original story:

"Mudd's Women"

"I, Mudd"

"The Business As Usual, During Altercations"
  The Federation finds competition and begins to lose out on new shipments of dilithium. The *Enterprise* investigates and discovers the miners are sending their deliveries to a new buyer.

Judy Blish (Judith Ann Lawrence AKA J. A. Lawrence, wife of James Blish) remembered, "The first Jim and I ever heard of *Star Trek* was at a Milford Conference in the mid-1960s, when Harlan Ellison bounced in all enthusiasm with the news that finally someone who really appreciated science fiction was to produce a new series, and his plan was to invite all the pros to contribute scripts. That notion fizzled out because writing for the visual media is very different from writing for the reader and many very good writers just don't have the knack. But they certainly did elicit some good stories from Theodore Sturgeon, Harlan himself, and many others who did have it. The next year the series was under way, and we certainly watched it when we could. But believe it or not, we didn't always have television. With all the things Jim and I were doing, we just didn't get around to it for years. I'm racking my brain to remember when we did and when we didn't, since from 1965 to 1968 we lived in New York, Virginia, Brooklyn, and then England. I think we got a TV in England. Meanwhile *Star Trek* was a roaring success. At the time someone approached Jim—I never really knew whether it was the editor at Bantam or Harlan or an agent—and asked him to write a book series from the scripts. He was reluctant, as he had never done such a project and hadn't followed all the episodes. However, as he realized that this series was creating a whole new audience for science fiction, he wanted to participate in that. It was a new venture for him. The studio supplied all the material they could, most importantly the final shooting scripts, and guidelines for the visual details. Occasionally the script was altered in the final shooting, and nobody told him, which caused a ruckus among fans who had seen the different version."

Judy continued, "The hardest thing about it, and perhaps the most fun, was to try to explain why the story happened as it did with some logical explanation, since many of the scripts' logic simply did not hold up when read. He (and then we) was always having to wrestle out an ingenious explanation for something that the producers had glided over. And yes, he did get a kick out of it, and out of the massive fan mail, though he was amazed. While the fans' interest inspired him—there's nothing like knowing someone is reading with interest what you write—I can't say that he relied on the fans for information. He had to work from the scripts, then the book was published, and only *then* could the fans complain, which was too late. Fan response did make him pay more attention to certain kinds of detail, such as costume, which to one who is trying to make sense of the story were not all that vital, but which mattered very much in the presentation. With the later books, there was, obviously, much more input and argument from them, and he/we had to mind all our p's and q's."

Judy started assisting with the books. "How I got involved was that somewhere around the seventh or eighth book, Jim was beginning to feel a breeze from the Angel's wings and an urgency to attend to his own work. He didn't have the energy to do both; he was not very well. Rather than abandon the project, my mother, a long-term professional writer in other fields, and I, who had begun selling my own science fiction (SF) stories, offered to write them, and he would do the quality control on our production. We tried it and it seemed to work okay. (In some of those later stories you can see the fine romantic hand of my mother who was strong on the mushy love stuff.) After Jim died, I told all this to then editor Frederik Pohl, who rather doubtfully allowed me to continue. But he found the result acceptable, [so *Star Trek 12*] has both our names on it. I made a great effort to see the shows I'd missed, and my agent in London arranged screenings at the BBC for me, where I audio-recorded the shows and took a lot of notes. Only the Mudd stories remained, and were supposed to be worked into a novel. Jim had tried, and I tried, but we simply could not come up with a way to combine them. The two actual scripts were fully self-contained stories, told in a strict chronological order that did not allow for interspersions, and it seemed to me that twisting them somehow into a longer story would not do anything to improve them. So instead I offered an original additional story to round out the sequence."

Dorothy Fontana remembers the Blish books. "The James Blish novelizations came about after the first year of the series. Unfortunately, the publishing house chose to jam a number of script stories into each book, thereby causing Mr. Blish—a wonderful writer—to have to cut the novelization of each story down to the barest main plot. Much of the subplot material from each story had to be left out. I know this was not his choice—and it was an unfortunate one, I believe—because his touch expanding the original stories was diluted. They were still good, but there could have been so much more."

Frederik Pohl, editor of the Bantam *Star Trek* line starting in 1972, remembered, "After all the scripts had been done, he sort of retired on the proceeds. Then he developed cancer of the throat and other problems. Judith finished the remainder of his work."

SPOCK MUST DIE!

JAMES BLISH

FEBRUARY 1970 (118PP)

The second original *Star Trek* novel, and the first published by Bantam. The Klingons declare war and it appears that the Organians are not holding up their end of the accord. Captain Kirk decides to send Spock to Organia to discover their whereabouts. A transporter accident renders Spock into two Spocks, each indistinguishable from the other. Like the episode, "The Enemy Within," one of the Spocks is evil, but which one? The evil Spock has clearly learned from Kirk's accident! To make things worse, when the *Enterprise* finally arrives at Organia, it appears to be utterly lifeless.

According to Judy Blish, "The novel came about, I think, because they asked for a novel, and [Jim] tried to think of something surprising, even shocking—at that time, Spock had not picked up the habit of dying—and he had been completely taken by surprise at the fan response to Spock. He, like the studio, had expected the hero figure of Kirk to be the idol, and when Spock gathered a huge following—and a lot of female admirers—Jim was thunderstruck. I too thought Spock more interesting, and after some discussion, Jim began to work it out in his mind, and began to think more about who he was, and so he became the pivotal character.

SF master Frederik Pohl edited the Bantam *Star Trek* novels. He commented, "I acquired the line in 1972. James Blish had told me once that the biggest checks he had ever seen came from those *Trek* novelizations. A number of *Trek* fans wanted to do their own stories and that's why we did *New Voyages*. The truth is, I didn't really pay much attention to *Star Trek*."

STAR TREK: THE NEW VOYAGES

SONDRA MARSHAK AND MYRNA CULBREATH, EDITORS

MARCH 1976 (237PP)

An anthology of eight original short stories and one poem:

"**Ni Var**" by Claire Gabriel (with an introduction by Leonard Nimoy)

A dying scientist makes Spock two separate beings: one entirely Vulcan, the other fully human.

"Intersection Point" by Juanita Coulson (with an introduction by James Doohan)
A strange hull breach causes problems for Scotty and the crew.

"The Enchanted Pool" by Marcia Ericson (with an introduction by Nichelle Nichols)
Spock meets the love of his life, but all is not as it seems.

"Visit to a Weird Planet Revisited" by Ruth Berman (with an introduction by Majel Barrett Roddenberry)
The actors who play Kirk, Spock, and McCoy find themselves in an alternate universe where their fictional counterparts are real.

"The Face on the Barroom Floor" by Eleanor Arnason and Ruth Berman (with an introduction by George Takei)
While on shore leave, Kirk disappears and the Enterprise crew receives orders to abandon the search.

"The Hunting" by Doris Beetem (with an introduction by Sondra Marshak and Myrna Culbreath)
Spock takes McCoy on a unique hunting expedition.

"The Winged Dreamers" by Jennifer Guttridge (with an introduction by DeForest Kelley)
In paradise, shore leave turns to mutiny.

"Mind Sifter" by Shirley S. Maiewski (with an introduction by William Shatner)
A mentally unstable Captain Kirk winds up in a twentieth-century asylum.

"Sonnet from the Vulcan: Omicron Ceti Three" by Shirley Meech
A love poem from Spock to Leila Kalomi.

Sondra and Myrna answered questions jointly. "We owe a debt to Gene Roddenberry, who not only brought us together but also gave a boost to each of our writing careers that ultimately led us to merge them. Sondra had earned her Master's degree in history, with straight-A honors. She was married to a professor, had a young son, and was planning to go on for her Ph.D. to teach at the university level and write culture-changing nonfiction. Then she decided that she was going into the wrong business. Sondra's first real love had always been fiction. She had made a couple of abortive attempts to watch parts of *Star Trek* episodes in reruns, on the recommendation of friends, but had happened to see a couple of episodes with things like some female apparition saying, 'My touch is death . . .' or Kang seeming to blame all evil on some whirling blob in space. *Star Trek* was well into reruns before Sondra gave it one last shot and tuned in to the episode 'Bread and Circuses.' She saw the powerful relationship between Kirk and Spock and the focus on moral and philosophical issues. She was hooked. Some who know Sondra have said that the show would never have been canceled if she had tuned in sooner. Could be. Here was a vision of humankind as it could be and should be, not the plaything of invisible forces, but able to go to the stars, master fate, master themselves, bond with each other or with an alien — as more than a brother. And virtually every other value that she had wanted to teach and write about. When she did understand the impact of *Star Trek*, Sondra realized that as a professor she would reach a few thousand students in her lifetime. But *Star Trek* was reaching tens of millions a day. She decided to change professions.

"Myrna had come to *Star Trek* somewhat earlier but had her hands full with the reading crisis and with editing *The Fire Bringer*—also aimed at changing the world, and to which Gene was a devoted reader. She did steal time to write a *Star Trek* script, 'Triangle.' But at about that time, the show was canceled. It was a different early version, which [we] later reinvented into [our] novel *Triangle*."

When asked about how they write together, they commented, "We've described it as virtually a Vulcan mind-meld. For the most part we can't remember who did what, although we know each other's strengths, and rely on them in each other. We've been known to write a novel, start to finish, in two weeks."

Sondra and Myrna continued, "*Star Trek: The New Voyages* became the first anthology of original *Star Trek* fiction. It may well be the first time that the fan fiction of *any* phenomenon was professionally published. *The New Voyages* became an immediate mass-market best seller. After Bantam editor Fred Pohl chose Marshak and Culbreath's *Star Trek: The New Voyages*, it occurred to him that it would be a nice bonus for fans if Marshak and Culbreath's relationships with Gene Roddenberry and members of the original *Star Trek* cast could make possible an introduction to the first *New Voyages* by creator Gene Roddenberry, and to each story by the members of the original cast. Myrna and Sondra did ask for those introductions, Gene and everyone they asked graciously agreed. It became the first and last book of *Star Trek* fiction with such introduc-

tions. (At a late stage, as they had already asked for nearly all the introductions, Bantam cut the story they had earmarked for Walter Koenig (Mr. Chekov) for space reasons and there was nothing they could do. Afterwards Walter told us that he, too, would have agreed.)"

They explained that none of it could be done without Paramount's consent. While Paramount was aware of the myriad of *Star Trek* fanzines, it would have to approve professional publication of any licensed fiction.

"Given that Paramount had all of *Star Trek* to protect, they would have to be convinced that new original fiction would be impeccably professional and consistent with aired *Star Trek*, and that it would not cut off any future *Star Trek* potential. Moreover, Paramount executives had to be convinced that such fiction would find a major market, and not embarrass them. All of that amounted to moving a mountain. We figured that job was just about Fred Pohl's size. He had called to buy *Star Trek Lives!*—the book on the *Star Trek* phenomenon that later became a bible in the *Star Trek* offices at Paramount. Sondra had started the query package for *Star Trek Lives!* with talented co-author and science fiction writer Jacqueline Lichtenberg. Later Sondra brought in Joan Winston, a television executive who had helped organize and get major publicity for the first *Star Trek* convention. That was before Sondra met Myrna. After *Star Trek Lives!* was in the pipeline, we suggested to Fred Pohl that it was a shame—and a huge missed marketing opportunity—that no new, original *Star Trek* fiction was being published. (Science fiction writer James Blish had been commissioned to adapt the already-aired TV episodes as short stories, and somewhere a short novel by Blish had slipped in—then nothing.) We suggested to Pohl that with the right editing, the best of the fan fiction could be made professionally publishable. Fred hadn't thought anyone would do it professionally enough, but now he knew that they could. Get him a manuscript, more or less instantly—what else was new? When Fred phoned to buy *Star Trek Lives!* he had said, 'When I passed up your *Star Trek* phenomenon book a while ago, I said that the *Star Trek* phenomenon was dead, there'll never be another *Star Trek* book. Guess what? I was wrong. I need your book and I need it in less than 30 days. Can you do it?' Who's going to tell him 'No'? Only a few chapters and an outline had been written for the query package for *Star Trek Lives!* Even those chapters were extensively rewritten and the outline morphed into a largely new shape. The *Star Trek Lives!* manuscript got to Fred on time. It did well. But it was not fiction. . . . *New Voyages* was to become the true mass-marketing breakthrough. It has been widely credited with helping fuel the growing fan phenomenon that led to increasingly massive *Star Trek* conventions and eventually to the revival of *Star Trek* in movies, then in ongoing new formats."

They finished, "We again hustled to get Fred the manuscript for *Star Trek: The New Voyages* in the short required time, before he left on a planned trip to Russia. We have vivid memories—and the occasional flashback—to those days of the birth of new *Star Trek* fiction: We were collecting, editing, and sometimes, at the authors' requests, extensively cutting or partly rewriting some stories or long novellas for fan authors who threw up their hands and said that they couldn't do it, please do it for them. While there was exciting raw material,

fanzines had different editing standards and no great limitations on length. Everything we would send to Fred to show Paramount had to pay off on our promise that it could be extremely professional, marketable, meet space requirements, and leave Fred some options for final choices. Probably that editing or rewriting process was foredoomed to be an example of 'no good deed goes unpunished.' While the fan authors wanted us to do it, it's hard for any writers to let anyone touch a hair on a story's head. Eventually our judgment was vindicated when *Star Trek: The New Voyages* became one of the most beloved books of *Star Trek* fiction."

SPOCK, MESSIAH!
THEODORE R. COGSWELL AND CHARLES A. SPANO, JR.

SEPTEMBER 1976 (182PP)

To investigate a planet with limited technology and have the capability to blend in with the populace, members of the crew have a device surgically implanted that enables the user to successfully mind-link with an inhabitant. The procedure is thoroughly researched and the natives of the planet are specifically screened for compatibility with their Starfleet hosts. An act of sabotage links Spock with a madman who believes he is the planet's messiah, making Spock act irrational and believe he is their savior.

Theodore Cogswell passed away in 1987. He only wrote fewer than forty stories over the length of his career. Charles Spano was an avid science fiction reader as he grew up in the 1950s. According to Charles, "I read every Tom Swift printed (and still have them, the Tom Swift, Jr. series), and every analog (back then it was astounding SF) *Fantasy & ScienceFiction* magazine I could get my hands on. I went through every single science fiction book in the youth section of my public library and watched every SF movie I could when it was shown on TV. There used to be a used book store in the town where I went to college and for one dollar I could get ten books, so I burned through a whole five dollars about once a month and brought home grocery bags filled with Heinleins, Asimovs, Andersons, Pohl, Harrisons, you name it. Now when *Star Trek* actually dared to take some of those ideas seriously and turn them into visualizations, I was easy prey. *Star Trek* wasn't the first TV SF show—I watched *Fireball XL-5*, *World of Giants*, *Tom Corbett*, *SpaceCadet*, *Twilight Zone*, but *Star Trek* handled the SF concepts the way John Campbell would have approved, and Heinlein did put the story in front of the gadgets and ray guns. I remember being in college

and making sure to be home on Friday nights so I could audio tape the shows (yes, audio!). I sat on the floor with a mike up to the speaker of the TV and held my family at bay with a broom and scotch tape so they would be quiet. I think I actually missed the first two or three shows, but after that I was hooked on seeing things I read about actually being portrayed on TV."

As much as he enjoyed reading science-fiction stories, he wanted to write them as well. "I wrote many unpublished and unpublishable things—not *Star Trek*—but I wanted to get into the SF world, and because the future is the touchstone of optimism and the belief that bad as things may be, or could be, there is the chance that in the future things will be better."

How did Charles end up writing *Spock, Messiah!* with Theodore? "It came about as I attempted to write on my own and collected many lovely letters from editors. I read a small article in our local newspaper that Theodore Cogswell was going to speak about something. I had read much about SF writers willing to help younger writers and, of course, the famous Clarion writer's workshops originated near Scranton, so hoping he would be kind and generous like all established SF writers, I called him and asked if I could visit and show him my stuff. Not to be put off by the gruff persona he affected (Ted, if you're reading, you didn't fool me!) he gave me great help. One day, he called me and asked if I would coauthor a *Star Trek* novel which Fred Pohl had asked him to do. Don't ever let anyone tell you that the light barrier is an absolute. Overall I thought the collaboration was enjoyable. The changes and criticisms Ted made improved the story. This began in 1975 and the idea of *Spock, Messiah!* was mine as was the majority of the first draft. The first Arab oil embargo was recent history and militant Islam was making its first stirrings. However, the idea that a fanatical desert leader could arise to threaten a civilization was (is) a staple throughout history. Of course, there was always the 'get Spock' school of *Star Trek* fandom which was beginning to grow about then too. Ted outlined a general plan in accord with Fred Pohl's one injunction: 'Get them off that damned ship.' Thus, a quest was born. Somebody had to be the object of the quest and it had to have sufficient urgency for one and all. The idea of the dop was Ted's and the beshwa itinerants were mine. I knew the *Star Trek* pattern and some of the technical things. Ted helped (ordered, actually and painfully, when I saw those red Xs through my lovely words, ah well) bring the story back to the questing when I wandered off for a chapter or two on irrelevancies. To more directly answer the question, *Spock, Messiah!* was born more because we needed a sufficiently dangerous place where they could not use their technology, which immediately brought to mind a semi-primitive world, and a mind tough enough to take out Spock could only be a fanatic of the first order."

The publication was relatively straightforward. "We wrote the book on contract, cleaned it up, sent it out, Pohl asked for a few minor changes, and we got galleys a month or two later. After we proofed them and made some minor changes, *Spock, Messiah!* was published in September 1976, validating the Bantam theory that there was a hunger for original *Star Trek* novels. I am very proud to have had a small part in expanding the *Star Trek* and SF universe to the level of acceptance it has today."

THE PRICE OF THE PHOENIX
SONDRA MARSHAK AND MYRNA CULBREATH

JULY 1977   (182PP)

The body of Captain Kirk beams back to the ship in a body bag. While the crew deals with the shocking loss, Spock confronts Omne, the being responsible for Kirk's death. To Spock's horror, Omne resurrects Kirk, plus an identical duplicate. Now to save his friend and liberate the double, Spock must sell his own soul.

Sondra and Myrna remarked, "When Fred Pohl negotiated with Paramount for our proposal for new *Star Trek* fiction, the process led to the right to do a package of six *Star Trek* novels. Those six novels were meant to be by leading, established science fiction writers. All but one of the six *were* by already well-known science fiction writers. That one, chosen and edited by Fred Pohl and personally approved by Gene Roddenberry, was our first novel, *The Price of the Phoenix*. We told Fred that we had a

Star Trek novel and asked him to look at it for future consideration. We thought that it was ruled out by the ground rules for the six, intended for 'brand name' sci-fi writers (like Joe Haldeman, for example). We were not then known for science fiction or even fiction. We were honored and very gratified when Fred chose *The Price of the Phoenix* as one of those first six."

They continued, "We made our villain, Omne, 'the man who hated death' mainly because *we* hated death. An appalling waste. Often, an unendurable loss. We asked the question: What price would someone pay if he or she had lost someone he could not lose? What if he could have that person back, but at a price? Say that Kirk is brought back to the *Enterprise* in a body bag. And then Spock discovers that an identical Kirk is *alive.* Omne contends that *that* Kirk is Omne's property. For sale. At a price. What price? 'Merely the usual. Your honor. Your sword. Your flag. Your soul.' The price of the phoenix. Black Omne was way ahead of us. He had invented immortality— and the Kirk he created was *really* identical— to the last molecule and memory."

Sandra and Myrna went on, "When that first of six novels came out, and fans did not respond or buy well, that could have been a significant problem for *Star Trek* fiction. What if too many fans decided that *Star Trek* fiction was not 'real' *Star Trek? The Price of the Phoenix* was next—and would have to turn the tide—or not. Fred had edited it himself. We suggested to Fred that Bantam might want to take out advertising to let fans know that our novel was different. He said, 'It's not necessary. Your names are a seal of quality on *Star Trek* fiction.' We believed he meant it, but we took it

with a grain of salt. Then we learned that he had put money and his reputation where his mouth was. He went out with a massive first printing of a quarter of a million copies. That was gutsy. He was vindicated. *Price* hit the best-seller lists. It soon went into a second printing. All of our books have had many printings, new covers, boxed sets, foreign editions in many languages, hardbacks in some foreign editions, and so on. Some time later, Fred's assistant— and then an editor herself—the wonderful Sydny Weinberg, was walking us to the elevator. She said, 'I really wanted to know a lot more about the Commander (our female Romulan Commander in *Price*), more about the Commander and Spock, the Commander and James, James in the Romulan Empire. I just didn't want the book to end.' 'Oh,' we said, 'We didn't exactly stop there. There's another 150 pages or so of it floating around somewhere in our filing cabinet.' The elevator came but Sydny ignored it. 'You mean you've got the *sequel* to *Price* floating around in your filing cabinet? You're to get it out the minute you get home and mail it to me immediately! Do you promise me?' We did, and we sent it to her. It became *The Fate of the Phoenix.* But not without considerable difficulty."

They had a story to tell: "Once when we were having lunch with Bill [Shatner] and Leonard [Nimoy], Bill had read our then forthcoming novel *The Price of the Phoenix* in manuscript. Bill told Leonard, 'I don't know why Paramount is still looking for a script. *Their* novel, *The Price of the Phoenix*, should *be* the script for the *Star Trek* movie. It would give us a chance to play things no two actors have ever played before.' It was not to be, and we did not put *Price* forward for that purpose. We considered that it was Gene's movie to write, and that probably, despite ongoing conflicts, it would ultimately *be* Gene's. But what Bill envisioned if *Price* were the script *would* have been fascinating."

PLANET OF JUDGMENT

JOE HALDEMAN

AUGUST 1977   **(151PP)**

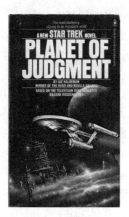

The crew discovers a planet that should not exist. Even more baffling, all of their equipment malfunctions when landing on the strange world. With transporters not available, and a shuttle rescue impossible, how do you recover the stranded men and women on a planet where an alien intelligence is holding them for a higher purpose?

Joe became a *Trek* fan when he saw the original pilot at the World Science Fiction Convention before the series started. Drafted in the summer of 1967, he missed the last two seasons. As for writing a *Trek* novel, Joe said, "When James Blish died, I was in correspondence with [editor] Frederik Pohl. . . . I apologized for being ghoulish, but said, 'Now that Jim is dead, who's going to be writing the *Trek* books?' Fred replied, 'You are.' "

Joe doesn't remember where the idea for *Planet of Judgment* originated. He said, "I'd immersed myself in all of the 'about *Trek*' books — at the time, that was mostly mimeographed fan stuff from Bjo Trimble and friends — and watched the repeats every day for several months, so I just started typing whatever came into my mind, doing a treatment of twenty-some pages. At that time, Paramount required a lo-o-ong outline like this before they'd approve a book. It was way too much hassle, and once I'd finished the first book I had no desire to write another. I'd done it just to see what it would be like to write a book where all the main characters were already known to the readers. Having done it once, I didn't have to do it again.

"The advance of $7,500 was fair for the time, but after I finished the first one I'd made $100,000 for my second actual SF novel, *Mindbridge*, and so I had no financial motivation."

STAR TREK: THE NEW VOYAGES 2

SONDRA MARSHAK AND
MYRNA CULBREATH, EDITORS

JANUARY 1978   (252PP)

 An anthology of eight original short stories and two poems:

"Surprise" by Nichelle Nichols, Sondra Marshak, and Myrna Culbreath
The crew has difficulty planning a birthday party for the captain.

"Snake Pit!" by Connie Faddis
Nurse Chapel must enter the pit to save the captain's life.

"The Patient Parasites" by Russell Bates
The crew encounters an unusual energy being. Written as a screenplay.

"In The Maze" by Jennifer Guttridge
The crew become pawns in an experiment.

"Cave-In" by Jane Peyton
A free-form story involving Spock.

"Marginal Existence" by Connie Faddis
A mission awakens the presumed dead.

"Procrustean Petard" by Sondra Marshak and Myrna Culbreath
A mysterious lure changes the sex of the crew.

"The Sleeping God" by Jesco von Puttkamer
While transporting Singa, a powerful mutant, the ship is captured by a planetary computer.

"Elegy For Charlie" by Antonia Vallario
A poem for the tragically lost Charlie Evans.

"Soliloquy" by Marguerite B. Thompson
A poem about the sheer sadness of Vulcan love.

Sondra and Myrna commented, "Both of us for some years were featured speakers at major *Star Trek* conventions and have heard from many fans we met there, or in our fan mail, how our particular *Star Trek* fiction changed lives, even saved lives. Most dramatically, some told how that fiction pulled them back—from suicide. *Star Trek* touched many people enough that they felt compelled to write it—and *did* write it, even when it could not be published. We knew that *Star Trek: The New Voyages* could unleash that phenomenon. *New Voyages* was the first professional publication for the fan writers, and for some, the only one. For others it became the start of other professional publications. For *Star Trek: The New Voyages 2*, we took up the fight for NASA. Nichelle Nichols had become a friend who visited at Sondra's home. As things developed, Nichelle was under a NASA contract to help recruit women and minorities as astronauts. We left from Sondra's home with Nichelle to go to NASA in Huntsville, Alabama. We learned there that NASA—as its *reward for landing man* on the moon—had been cut off at the knees. Scientists who had helped put footprints on the moon had been reduced to selling burgers. We were outraged. We told shell-shocked scientists at NASA, who believed most Americans *knew* of their plight, and didn't care, that it was not true. If Americans knew they *would* care. That was when we decided to back NASA with an outreach to *Star Trek* fans and to the public, starting with *New Voyages 2*. We persuaded the head of Advanced Long Range Planning for NASA, Jesco von Puttkamer—an authentic German baron who had written science fiction stories in his youth before coming here to join NASA—to write a *Star Trek* novella and an introduction for the second *New Voyages*. Along with our own introduction, it was aimed at getting fans to write and support NASA, bringing the dream of *Star Trek* to the aid of the real space program. Later, perhaps partly because of this, Jesco became a technical advisor to the first *Star Trek* movie."

VULCAN!

Kathleen Sky

SEPTEMBER 1978   (175PP)

The crew heads to the planet Arachne IV to establish if the natives are sentient. A brilliant scientist who specializes in alien species arrives on board and immediately demands to return home. Not knowing she would be working with a Vulcan, she would rather die than start now.

Kathleen was never really a *Trek* fan. "My interest in the show was as a writer. I did up a script outline for the show and my agent sent it to Gene Roddenberry. He liked the outline and said it would make a great episode for the next season. The only problem was that there was no next season. The show was canceled and my outline was put in my files of lost causes. A few years later, Bantam Books asked me if I would like to write a *Star Trek* book. My script outline became the book, *Vulcan!*"

THE STARLESS WORLD
GORDON EKLUND

NOVEMBER 1978　　　(152PP)

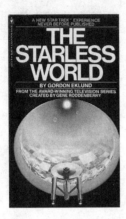

The *U.S.S. Rickover* vanished in the area years ago. When a shuttlecraft from the missing ship appears on the *Enterprise*'s sensors, Kirk must investigate. The single passenger aboard appears to be stark raving insane, claiming to be Jesus Christ. Kirk recognizes the lunatic as Thomas Clayton, his roommate during his first two years at the academy. When the *Enterprise* orbits a mysterious planet, Clayton escapes confinement and makes it to the bridge to begin praying to "Ay-nab." What mysteries await the crew?

Gordon's first comment was, "God, what do I remember of my *Star Trek* novel writing days? I was never really a fan of the show. I only saw occasional episodes of the first two seasons when I was at somebody else's home and it happened to be on. I didn't have a TV of my own. By the third season I had acquired a 13-inch black-and-white set but everyone agrees that was the weakest year. Before writing the books, I think I may have seen other episodes on rerun. Though let me be clear: I always liked what I saw. In actually writing the books I depended on my occasionally indistinct memories of what I'd seen—no video back then—and Bjo Trimble's *Star Trek* (and thank God for the existence of) *Concordance*."

Gordon continued, "I wrote the books because they paid well and I was trying to be a full-time writer at the time with bills and family and all of that. In fact, they paid better (in advances) than anything else I'd written up to then. The neat thing about the *Star Trek* universe for me was that it had room for just about anything you might want to write, though Paramount reps at the time still kept close tabs on all ideas and held power of final approval on all series books as they were written and before they were published."

Gordon concluded, "I think this is my favorite of the two books and the one that engaged me the deepest."

TREK TO MADWORLD
Stephen Goldin

JANUARY 1979   (177PP)

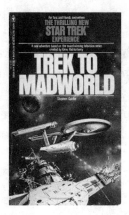

Captain Kirk and the crew race to the planet Epsilon Delta 4 to rescue over 700 colonists who are dying of radiation poisoning. Unfortunately, the *Enterprise* is pulled into a strange void, and the crew finds itself trapped with a Klingon vessel and a Romulan ship. An impish being named Enowil arrives on the *Enterprise* bridge and asks for assistance from the three ships. The reward for help could change the power in the quadrant, but helping could commit all of the colonists to a lingering death.

Stephen became a fan of *Star Trek* when he saw the very first aired episode, "The Man Trap." He had sold short stories in the 1960s and started writing novels in the early 1970s. Stephen said, "I had just signed a contract to write a ten-book series based on some work by Doc Smith. Fred Pohl, who'd bought my first two short stories, was looking for dependable

writers to do *Star Trek*. He wrote to me asking if I'd like to do a *Star Trek* book, and I said yes. My storyline was approved with no problem whatsoever."

Reflecting on writing the book, he said, "This was one of the hardest books I had to write, for a fundamental reason: By definition, a novel is a tale of someone or something undergoing change, and in *Trek*, none of the major characters nor the basic universe [were] permitted to change. I had to do it the way they did on the series, by introducing "guest stars" who *were* allowed to change. But I still felt somewhat hamstrung."

When Stephen received the assignment, he tracked down the previously published novels. He said, "There were very few, and they were very serious. Then I looked at people's favorite episodes, like "Tribbles," "Shore Leave," and "I, Mudd"—all light-hearted and comical. I decided to do the first comical *Star Trek* book. And since I was (and am) a big fan of *Willie Wonka*, I used that as the basic idea to take off from."

While *Trek to Madworld* appears to be Goldin's only *Star Trek* novel, he actually wrote another. Stephen remembers, "In the mid-80s my wife (Mary Mason) and I submitted a 'classic' *Trek* story to the Pocket Books editor at the time, David Stern. It concerned a political change in the Federation government (which had always been based on Gene Roddenberry's 1960s liberalism) to one that, today, would be called 'neo-con' with strong anti-alien prejudices rising to the surface. Kirk would naturally be upset with this, and would end up leading a mutiny that restored the good guys to power once again. David Stern liked the idea, but faced an interesting quandary. Another of his writers, Diane Carey, had come up with a similar idea—and David himself had also wanted to write a book along those lines. His solution was to do it as a three-part book; Mary and I would write the first book, Diane the second, and David the third. All three books were to be written simultaneously (which I foresaw as a big problem, and I turned out to be right)."

Elaborating further, Stephen said, "Pocket Books paid for Mary and me and Diane and her husband to fly to New York for a several-day plot meeting. We talked a lot of things over, and then went to our respective homes to work on the project. The job of being first is the hardest, because you have to point things in the right direction and set things up properly for the other writers to take care of in their portions. We kept asking Diane and David what they needed us to do, and got very little feedback. Paramount [handed] down the dictum (relayed through David) that there is no prejudice in the *Star Trek* universe. This was certainly news to me. As I said to David (who, like me, is Jewish), "How many times have we heard McCoy say something like, 'Spock, you pointy-eared Vulcan, your damn logic will kill us all'? Now let's change a few words there: 'Spock, you hook-nosed Jew, your damn stinginess will kill us all.' And McCoy is a professional man, a college-educated doctor who should be above such things. Even if you try to rationalize it as good-natured banter, there has to be an underlying sense of racial inequity to make it work. David took a big gulp and didn't dispute me, but he [enforced] Paramount's dictum anyway."

The book obviously never saw the light of day. He said, "Despite minimal input from our partners in this venture, Mary and I did an exceedingly rough draft that would need to be smoothed out to bring it into line with what the others were doing. We sent copies to Diane and David, and waited. Eventually we got word that Pocket Books was unhappy and canceled the project—but they paid us for it anyway. I don't know what happened to Diane's or David's books."

Asked about this Federation Trilogy that never materialized, Dave Stern said, "It didn't happen because of deadline issues."

Stephen has since written a four-book fantasy epic called the *Parsina Saga*, and has written two science fiction novels with Mary Mason about female space mercenary Jade Darcy. They are both currently working on the third book in the series.

WORLD WITHOUT END
JOE HALDEMAN

FEBRUARY 1979   **(150PP)**

Captain Kirk and crew discover a hollow, inhabited asteroid. Upon beaming down to this artificial world, the crew is taken captive and discovers that the inhabitants don't believe the out universe exists. Meanwhile, out in space,

Spock pinpoints the wreckage of an ancient Klingon vessel on the surface of the asteroid.

Having no desire to write another *Trek* novel, Joe was forced to because the publisher refused to let him buy out of the contract. He said, "The end result was that I really enjoyed writing *Planet of Judgment*, and finished it in three months. Writing *World Without End* was like pulling your own teeth, and it took nine months. (Oddly enough, I've met people who liked the second book better. I certainly worked harder on it!)" Afterward, "I was fed up . . . and left the *Star Trek* enterprise at about warp factor five, and have never picked up one of the books since I handed in *World Without End*."

THE FATE OF THE PHOENIX
SONDRA MARSHAK AND MYRNA CULBREATH

MAY 1979 (262PP)

irk and crew thought they defeated Omne, but they were wrong. Kirk's doppelganger, James, travels with the Romulan Commander and finds he is falling in love with his captor. Soon, evidence reveals that Omne is alive, but he's now two separate beings, one called Omne and one called the Other, who wears a duplicate body of Spock.

Myrna and Sondra commented, "If immortality is an option, the four who survived the night of the Phoenix—Jim Kirk, James, Spock, the Commander—and the galaxy will have to cope with it, and with Omne, the first immortal who died at the hands of Jim Kirk. If James was not to die, and Jim Kirk was to have the life that had always been his, the friendships that were his, then James needed a life and a fight that was his size. What if he found one in the Romulan Empire, at the side of the Romulan Commander? What if he could only go there as her Princeling? And what if Omne, the man who invented immortality with finality, had *not* died? What if Omne proved to be more complex than merely a villain? What if Kirk had to fight a reborn Omne—now with the mind and powers of Spock to augment his own? What if they clashed with each other across the galaxy, over 'the political and the personal'—including the meaning of the Prime Directive and the fate of the future? Could Spock protect Kirk when Omne could come to Kirk as Spock, himself?"

They talked about the origins of their sequel. "Gene Roddenberry . . . took it upon himself to [review] *The Price of the Phoenix*. *Price* was apparently the only *Star Trek* novel that Gene ever personally [reviewed]. As pressure mounted toward producing the movie, he delegated [subsequent reviews] to someone in his office.

"*The Fate of the Phoenix* . . . was quite

provocative on many levels. But the review comments were very simple and impossible: James must die. The first *Star Trek* movie was then in planning. There could not be a second, identical, real Kirk left alive in the *Star Trek* universe. No way. James must die. Or the novel would not be published. We said, 'Then the novel will not be published.' We refused to kill James. The irresistible force meets the immovable object. Our editors at Bantam backed us, and were basically frantic, wanting the book but unable to budge the resistance. It was a shootout at the OK Corral. Finally, we made a trip out to Paramount to see if something could be worked out. Without giving away too much, for those who may not yet have read *Fate*, we found a way out by getting agreement to an alternative ending that we had written earlier for our private version. James did not die. James just wound up in an unreachable location—with perhaps the last person in the galaxy it was safe for him to be with—and from which, the premise of the book assured the person we had to convince, James could *never* return or be retrieved in his lifetime. *Theoretically*. But this is science fiction and it is never safe to say never."

DEVIL WORLD
Gordon Eklund

NOVEMBER 1979 (153 PP)

The planet Heartland has a dark secret and the Federation has put the entire world under quarantine. Now a beautiful woman has asked Kirk to break the law and take her to the planet so she can see her long-lost father. The inhabitants of the planet appear like miniature demonic beings, complete with the horns on the head and barbed tail. In addition to the creepy alien life, the world harbors a terrible secret that could easily destroy the *Enterprise* and drive the crew insane.

Gordon's second book is "Yet another borrowing of Conrad's *Heart of Darkness* story, a la God knows how many others both inside and outside the science fiction world. There's also, I imagine, a good bit of the John Ford film *The Searchers*, which I'd only just seen for the first time. It's the darker book of the two [*Trek* novels I wrote] and the one with the stronger emphasis on character. Bantam editors told me at the time that they rated my two books as the best yet. It's been too long for me to confirm or deny. In general, I liked writing the books because the characters were already there, I liked them, and I could build on everything about them that had gone before. After the series left Bantam I was unable to connect with the new editors, new publishers, and probably wasn't the right person anyway since I think they wanted fans or writers more into TV plotting and storytelling. I could be wrong."

in time for the arrival of Klingons. Can McCoy cure the "disease" in time?

Jack C. Haldeman II passed away in 2002. According to his brother, Joe, "Oddly enough, he never told me much about *Perry's Planet*. I loaned him all my *Star Trek* research materials and he wrote the book. I was so burned out about *Trek* by then I've never read his book (or any other)."

PERRY'S PLANET
JACK C. HALDEMAN II

FEBRUARY 1980   (132PP)

While investigating a planet, the crew discovers that the colonists do not commit any acts of aggression. Also, the leader of the planet should be centuries old, but appears to be younger than Kirk! The *Enterprise* crew starts collapsing when forced to act aggressively, just

THE GALACTIC WHIRLPOOL
DAVID GERROLD

OCTOBER 1980   (223PP)

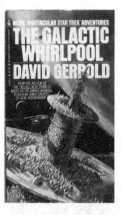

Investigating the area near the center of the galaxy, the crew discovers a giant spaceship that appears abandoned. Research leads to a shocking revelation: The ship originated from Earth. Kevin Riley leads a team inside to meet the inhabitants. While the crew negotiates for peace, Chekov discovers the large vessel must be steered away from its present course, otherwise it will plummet into an immense black hole.

When asked about the novel, David said, *"The Galactic Whirlpool* was adapted from the very first outline I ever submitted to *Star Trek*. It was intended as a two-part episode, so there was more than enough story for a novel. When I did the novel, I expanded it so as to give much more to all the characters involved."

This book references the real star, Wolf 359, which later came into prominence during the Borg battle in the *Next Generation* episode, "The Best of Both Worlds, Part II."

DEATH'S ANGEL
KATHLEEN SKY

APRIL 1981   (213 PP)

A visit to a planet has repercussions for Kirk, Spock, and some of the crew. McCoy has no clue how to bring the crew members out of deep comas. Several days later, the survivors awaken and seem to be in reasonable health.

Ordered to bring a delegation of ambassadors to the space station Détente One to negotiate a peace treaty with the Romulans, problems start immediately when one of the party is murdered. Soon reports of seeing the Angel of Death spook the entire ship. A beautiful SSD officer arrives on the *Enterprise* to capture the killer and soon succumbs to Kirk's charms.

The last Bantam novel was a result of the publisher being pleased with how the author's previous book, *Vulcan!* sold. "I love murder mysteries, so I thought that might make a fun book. Paramount asked that I use a lot of aliens and give Kirk a romance. The result was *Death's Angel*."

The two novels are not her only experience in the *Trek* universe. "Paramount was filming the first *Star Trek* movie and asked me to be an extra in the film. My character was a security officer, so I probably died in the film." Kathleen has retired from writing and lives on a ranch in California and she is very happy to be out of the Big City.

PART TWO

STAR TREK FICTION
Published by Ballantine Books

1974 – 1978

STAR TREK LOG ONE
Alan Dean Foster

JUNE 1974 (184PP)

 daptations of three episodes from the animated series:

"Beyond the Farthest Star"
"Yesteryear"
"One of Our Planets Is Missing"

STAR TREK LOG TWO
Alan Dean Foster

SEPTEMBER 1974 (176PP)

 daptations of three episodes from the animated series:

"The Survivor"
"The Lorelei Signal"
"The Infinite Vulcan"

STAR TREK LOG THREE
Alan Dean Foster

JANUARY 1975 (215PP)

daptations of three episodes from the animated series:

"Once Upon a Planet"
"Mudd's Passion"
"The Magicks of Megas-Tu"

STAR TREK LOG FOUR
Alan Dean Foster

MARCH 1975 (215PP)

daptations of three episodes from the animated series:

"The Terratin Incident"
"Time Trap"
"More Tribbles, More Troubles"

STAR TREK LOG FIVE
Alan Dean Foster

AUGUST 1975   (195PP)

daptations of three episodes
from the animated series:

"Ambergris Element"
"Pirates of Orion"
"Jihad"

STAR TREK LOG SIX
Alan Dean Foster

MARCH 1976   (195PP)

daptations of three episodes
from the animated series:

"Albatross"
"The Practical Joker"
"How Sharper Than a Serpent's Tooth"

STAR TREK LOG SEVEN
ALAN DEAN FOSTER

JUNE 1976 (182PP)

 daptation of one episode from the animated series:

"The Counter-Clock Incident"

STAR TREK LOG EIGHT
ALAN DEAN FOSTER

AUGUST 1976 (183PP)

 daptation of one episode from the animated series:

"The Eye of the Beholder"

STAR TREK LOG NINE
Alan Dean Foster

FEBRUARY 1977   (183PP)

daptation of one episode from the animated series:

"Bem"

STAR TREK LOG TEN
Alan Dean Foster

JANUARY 1978   (250PP)

daptation of one episode from the animated series:

"**The Slaver Weapon**" (Note: This episode was itself adapted by SF author Larry Niven from his own original short story, "The Soft Weapon.")

Alan Dean Foster discovered *Star Trek* during the show's first season. It was the first real SF he had seen on TV since *Outer Limits* and *Twilight Zone*. Having written a number of original SF novels, plus two novelizations (*Luana* and *Dark Star*) for Ballantine Books, editor Judy-Lynn del Rey offered the assignment of adapting *Star Trek*'s animated episodes to prose. Alan said, "She came to me, and I readily acquiesced. Judy-Lynn told me I could arrange the adaptations however I wished. Upon reading the scripts for the animated shows, I didn't see how I could possibly expand a screenplay for a twenty-minute cartoon into a full-length novel. So I decided to structure the books utilizing three scripts per volume while attempting to tie them, however loosely, together as best I could. As the sales of the books skyrocketed, Judy-Lynn came back to me half demanding, half pleading, that I somehow get four books out of the last four scripts. Fortunately, these were among the best that I had to work with, though it was still a difficult job. For one of these last four titles, I incorporated the story from an original *Star Trek* [script] that I had submitted earlier to Paramount. Interestingly, it was returned to me with a note to resubmit it for the following season . . . which never came to pass, as the show was canceled. But at least the story did not go to waste."

Alan came up with the idea of calling the books the *Star Trek* "Logs", after the captain's log that was often used in *Star Trek* to set the stage for an episode or as the connective exposition for different scenes. As to how much freedom Alan had writing the books, he said, "I had pretty much a free hand. Hence the opportunity to insert little fun bits and pieces such as having a smitten ensign chase Uhura around the ship's Christmas tree."

Alan wrote a draft for the *Star Trek: Motion Picture* in 1977. He said, "I wrote the original treatment, based on a two-page suggestion of Roddenberry's titled 'Robot's Return.' I never wrote a screenplay. I was never asked to." As to the longstanding rumor that Alan wrote the novelization for *Star Trek: The Motion Picture*, Alan said, "I had absolutely nothing whatsoever to do with the novelization, and was not asked to write it."

PART THREE

STAR TREK FICTION
Published by Pocket Books

1979 - 2006

STAR TREK NUMBERED NOVELS

1

STAR TREK: THE MOTION PICTURE

(SEE SECTION 10: NOVELIZATIONS)

2

THE ENTROPY EFFECT

VONDA N. MCINTYRE

JUNE 1981   (224PP)

Sent under false pretenses to Aleph Prime, the *Enterprise* is forced to transport criminal scientist Dr. Georges Mordreaux to a rehabilitation colony. A former professor of Spock's, the doctor is accused of murdering several people.

He claims innocence, insisting that the people are not dead, but merely sent back in time. The account is given little credence until an older version of Dr. Mordreaux appears on the bridge and murders Captain Kirk.

The author declined to be interviewed for this book. The editor for Timescape, the science fiction imprint under which Pocket's early *Star Trek* novels were published, was David Hartwell. He remarked, "I had to argue to get *The Entropy Effect* published. . . . It was hard to convince the publisher there was a market for original novels. Vonda took a pay cut to write *The Entropy Effect*. One of her dreams in life was to write for *Star Trek*. At that time, an average advance [for an original novel] was between five and six thousand dollars. For a *Trek* novel, it was three thousand. This weeded out people who wanted to do it for the money and we got authors who needed to care about what they were doing."

David continued, "Vonda corresponded with Gene Roddenberry and George Takei to give Sulu a first name, Hikaru. They both eventually agreed. The success of this novel gave her the plum assignment of writing the novelization for *Star Trek II: The Wrath of Khan*."

#3

THE KLINGON GAMBIT

ROBERT E. VARDEMAN

OCTOBER 1981   (158PP)

When the *Enterprise* arrives at Alnath II, a Klingon colony bent on conflict, the crew discovers a ship of Vulcans with everyone on board dead. Have the Klingons developed a new type of weapon? And, why is everyone on the *Enterprise* starting to act strangely?

Robert had been reading science fiction for about ten years when *Star Trek* first aired. "Up to this time, there had been scant good SF on TV (Science Fiction Theater in the mid-50s is about the best of the lot). I had enjoyed the space opera shows, especially *Space Patrol*, but realized this did not carry the same entertainment value as written SF. When *Star Trek* was being hyped, one of the real lures for me was the list of writers. Theodore Sturgeon, James Blish, Robert Bloch, Jerry Sohl. I did not realize that Gene Roddenberry had written about forty episodes, among them my favorites, on

another show I watched faithfully (*Have Gun, Will Travel*). His sensibilities and knowledge of the way a script could be more than shoot-em-up space opera captivated me from the beginning. I only had a black-and-white TV and often went to my grandmother's to watch *Star Trek* on her color set. In some cases it was years later before I saw some episodes in color. Even in reruns, the shows were superior to most of what passed as SF on the air. (*Invaders?* Naw. *Outer Limits?* Sometimes. *Quark?* A *Star Trek* parody.) Recently a *Los Angeles Times* op-ed piece excoriated *Star Trek* as a worthless venture, but it seems to me that applying 2005 hindsight and values misses what made *Star Trek* so innovative at the time. It wasn't the special effects, the sets, or any of the science tossed in. Who wasn't expecting that red shirt to get killed when they beamed the captain and all the other officers to the planet? What made *Star Trek* important was its optimistic outlook for the future; something still lacking in most televised science fiction. The civil rights movement was gaining momentum. It is a stretch to say *Star Trek* was a major part, but it was certainly a positive factor with its crew's integration and treatment of races, both alien and human. And, for me, the biggest lure was an affirmation that one day we will roam between the stars. Considering how the space program hit the doldrums immediately after the *Apollo* missions, we seem to be in need of this message again in some revitalized form. Which brings up the way I have been using the term *Star Trek*. I am referring to the original series. I watched a significant portion of *The Next Generation* (until the holodeck became the only storyline), fewer of *Deep Space Nine*, none of *Voyager* or *Enterprise*. The stories just didn't make it for me like the gosh-wow original."

Robert had read Blish's novelizations of the original series stories and was not overly impressed with them, despite his admiration for him as an author. "The Bantam series had major authors turning in stories that looked like they had been pulled out of the trunk, dusted off, and the characters' names changed to those of *Star Trek* characters. Not one of those books had the feel of *Star Trek*, no matter what the character's name. The contract for the books migrated to Simon & Schuster, overseen by the inimitable David Hartwell. I had started writing full-time about five years before I heard that he was looking for original stories. How could I pass up the chance? I submitted two proposals and he bought *The Klingon Gambit*. I tried to make the story fit into the *Star Trek* universe and have the crew engaging my favorite baddies. The moral conflict in the original that appealed most to me was between what was expedient and what was right. This is what I aimed for in *The Klingon Gambit*. My story was the first title Hartwell bought but was the third to be published. Roddenberry's novelization of the first *Star Trek* movie became the initial release. And Vonda McIntyre had made the hallowed pulp halls of *The National Enquirer* (among other places) with news that she had killed off Kirk in her book. Riding that publicity, hers was the actual first of the new Simon & Schuster line. Then came *The Klingon Gambit*."

4
THE COVENANT OF THE CROWN
HOWARD WEINSTEIN

DECEMBER 1981   **(191 PP)**

Eighteen years earlier, Captain Kirk helped King Stevvin and his family escape from the planet Shad during a civil war. With this conflict still raging, the Klingons hope to take advantage of the chaos and plunder the weakened planet for tridenite, an efficient energy ore. Stevvin is now dying, and his daughter, Kailyn, is next in line to the throne. To ascend and hopefully stop the war, she needs the ancestral crown that was hidden in the mountain range of a distant planet. Spock and McCoy join Kailyn on her journey, but their shuttle crashes. The three survive, unaware that the Klingons are pursuing them.

Howard talked about how he became a *Star Trek* fan. "I was about seven when Alan Shepard became the first non-canine, non-chimp American astronaut in 1961 (fast becoming ancient history!). I knew nothing about science fiction, but real space exploration captured my imagination right from the start. Five years later, as NASA advanced from Mercury to Gemini, *Star Trek* started without me. I don't know what I was watching in September '66, but it wasn't *Star Trek*. I heard my junior-high pals talk about it at the lunch table, but I must not have been paying close attention, because I confused Mr. Spock with Dr. Spock and Dr. Spock with Dr. Smith from *Lost in Space*. And what little I'd seen of *Lost in Space* had not impressed me, and I hadn't even noticed *Star Trek*. But my friends kept talking about it, so midway through the first season, I watched *Star Trek* myself. My reaction was similar to what I thought about Alan Shepard's *Freedom 7* launch: *Wow!*"

Howard decided he wanted to become a writer after reading the *Making of Star Trek* (Ballantine, 1968) by Stephen E. Whitfield (a pseudonym for Stephen Poe) and Gene Roddenberry. Howard said, "I read it right after *Star Trek* went into syndicated reruns, and I was fascinated by the details of creating and producing a TV series. I was already interested in writing, and that book nudged me toward writing for TV in general and *Star Trek* in particular. I was old enough to appreciate *Star Trek* on two levels—as a fun and cool action-adventure show, and as science fiction allegory. I've always preferred stories that used the speculative freedom of science fiction to examine current events and real-world problems (and over the years, most of my favorite *Star Trek* stories, whether I'm the writer or the audience, have been political or based on issues we're wrestling with right here and now). *Star Trek* was the only TV drama doing that at the time, and I thought, *That's what I want to write!* The

only problem—there was no longer any *Star Trek* for which to write. Talk about crappy timing!"

No one could imagine the resurgence that *Star Trek* would generate, like a phoenix from the ashes. Howard spent his time figuring out how to write and getting his "Starfleet Degree" by watching the reruns. When the animated series appeared on NBC's Saturday morning schedule, Howard knew enough about scriptwriting at that point to give it a shot.

Howard remembers how he landed a screenplay for the animated series. "Back in high school, before I even knew about fanzines, I was writing the equivalent of fanzine stories, which I'd pass around to my friends. I wrote two *Star Trek* short stories, which appeared in *Probe* '70 and '71, the one-shot science/science fiction fanzine, published by students at my high school in East Meadow, New York. Most of those stories were probably pretty awful (I still have them, but I'm afraid to look at them!) but they were good practice. I was in college (University of Connecticut) when the animated series started. By then, in my junior year, I knew I wanted to be a writer, so I figured I had nothing to lose—I went back to those high school short stories, picked what I thought was the best one (the one I'd chosen for *Probe* '71), and rewrote it as a script."

Howard had an agent at that time. He said, "In high school, I'd written a *Mission: Impossible* script and sent it in, without realizing TV shows only accepted submissions through agents. They sent my script back, along with a list of Writers Guild-approved agents. My father recognized the name of a childhood friend he hadn't seen in years (Bill Cooper), called the guy and told him about me. Cooper said he wouldn't mind reading what I wrote, and if he thought it might sell, he'd submit it for me. Which is what happened with my *Star Trek* script, 'The Pirates of Orion'—except that he addressed the envelope to Dorothy Fontana, who'd been working on the animated show but had left by the time my script arrived. The office staff forwarded the unopened package to Dorothy, who shipped it right back to my agent, since she was no longer working for the series. So the script did a cross-country round-trip without being so much as opened, much less read by anybody! Bill Cooper told me to send it back using his name, if the series got picked up for a second season—which it was, and which I did. I was pretty lucky that they bought it, because Filmation (the studio which produced the animated series) only did 6 or 7 new episodes for what proved to be the animated show's final season. Anyway, producer Lou Scheimer called me at my dorm (they had no idea I was 19, which made me feel pretty good) and said they wanted to buy it, but he asked me to change the ending a little bit. Which I was happy to do, even though I was in the process of having my heart broken by my first real girlfriend—ahhh, the bittersweet angst of youth!"

Howard looked back at the success he had as a result of "The Pirates of Orion." He said, "Some people would say I've been milking that one animated script for 30 years now! But it really did open some doors for me—it gave me instant credibility with Pocket Books in '79 when they were just starting their *Star Trek* novel series. It got me invited as a guest to my first *Star Trek* convention when I was 21. It enabled me to meet actors and writers whom I ad-

mired. It's really been a great ride, and it all started with those nasty Orion pirates in 1974."

When asked about the idea of his first novel, he said, "Oh my goodness! I wrote this book 25 years ago—half my life ago! I'm so NOT the same person I was then, and I haven't read this book since it came out. I guess I just wanted to write a good *Star Trek* story and see it published. And this was the first of many times I've gone back to McCoy and his endearingly crusty nobility."

#5

THE PROMETHEUS DESIGN
SONDRA MARSHAK AND MYRNA CULBREATH

MARCH 1982 (190PP)

Outbreaks of violence sweep the planet Helva, where the inhabitants have horns and decidedly satanic appearance. Kirk and his crew must decipher the cause of the unrest. During their investigation, the presence of an antagonistic Vulcan admiral forces Kirk to give up command to Spock, as whatever mysterious force is at work on the planet threatens the *Enterprise*.

Sondra and Myrna commented, *"The Prometheus Design* asks: 'What if the rats were to go and interview the experimenters?' What if, in fact, *we* are the rats in an experiment so vast that the very universe is at stake? What if the experimenters say that they do not have to consider the lives or feelings of the rats, while their own lives and their children's lives are endangered by something worse than cancer? But Kirk, Spock, and a Vulcan, Savaj, who figured out the existence of the experiment, have the nerve, and wit, to get themselves picked up out of the maze. Ultimately they argue, in the teeth of beings that *are* to them as man to rat, that the increase in callousness caused by the experimenters' disregard of the lives of feeling beings is the very thing that *will* destroy their world. Or, perhaps, *our* world. On a personal level, Kirk has to overcome his own worst fault. We wanted to experiment with Spock as Captain of the *Enterprise* and of Kirk. In the end, could Kirk really accept Spock's command—to avoid catastrophe? A professor we respected said that [the themes of] *The Prometheus Design* [were] vital and relevant. . . . Basically, that kind of relevance was what Gene had wanted for all of *Star Trek*, and for *Star Trek* fiction. Gene wrote in his introduction to *Star Trek: The New Voyages*, what had long been his watchword: 'We always believed that there was an intelligent life form out there beyond the cameras.' Relevance, intelligence, and a rousing good story, a dash of sexiness and forbidden fantasy, a view of friendship that says that two can be one, 'two halves that come together to make a whole.' That's the essence of the best *Star Trek* fiction."

#6
THE ABODE OF LIFE
Lee Correy

MAY 1982   (207PP)

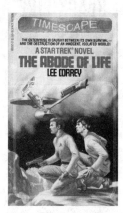

The *Enterprise* hits a spatial anomaly and ends up needing repairs desperately. It manages to reach the planet Mercan, whose inhabitants call their home "the abode of life." Mercans have no inkling of the existence of life elsewhere in the universe. Needing help from these people, Kirk must risk breaking the Prime Directive; otherwise the *Enterprise* will never make it back to Federation space.

Lee Correy was a pseudonym for G. Harry Stine, who passed away in 1997.

7

STAR TREK II: THE WRATH OF KHAN

(SEE SECTION 10: NOVELIZATIONS)

8

BLACK FIRE
SONNI COOPER

JANUARY 1983   (220PP)

A massive explosion rocks the *Enterprise* bridge, killing several crewmen, incapacitating Kirk, and severely injuring Spock. With a sliver of metal near his spine threatening to permanently paralyze him, Spock defies Starfleet orders to find the culprit. Eventually, with Scotty's help, he uncovers the truth, but ends up being declared a traitor and sent to prison before making an escape and embarking on a life of piracy.

Sonni remembered, "I was a fan when [*Star Trek*] first came out. I was always a science fic-

tion fan. I had major surgery when it started and was in the hospital for months and there was *Star Trek*. I was trapped. I would have watched it anyway. When I got home from the hospital, my husband had gotten me a color TV set. I watched it all over again in color and I sometimes got the colors all wrong. It was kind of amusing to see the way I perceived it at first and how I saw it the second time. I was attracted to the morality."

Sonni commented about writing, "*Black Fire* was not the first thing I had written, but was the first novel I wrote. When I lived in New York City as a child, the school system had a special thing for the kids who didn't fit in the classroom setting and were driving the teachers crazy. The kids were absolutely bored and I was one of them. I wrote and spoke in three different languages when I started school. I was a little crazy. They took four of us and let us write for WNYC, a New York City radio station. We did a news show, formed it, wrote it, and did the research. I was nine and it was much better than school. That is how I started writing."

She continued, "I met Theodore Sturgeon a number of years before. I gave him *Black Fire* and he read it. An agent sent it to New York and you know how it is with a book, you write it and forget it since it takes so long to make up their minds. You would go bananas if you thought about it every day. I put it out of my mind. I actually was in Gene Roddenberry's office the next week and I saw the manuscript on his desk. I said, 'What's going on here, Gene? The book was sent to New York, what's it doing on your desk?' He said, 'They actually sent it out to me special delivery to review it.' I said, 'Have you?' He said, 'Yes, you have sold your book.' "

Sonni remembered the editing process. "It

was absolutely horrendous. David Hartwell, who is marvelous by the way, was by far one of the best editors in science fiction at that time, and for a novice it was really an honor to work with him. But he sent a twit to the Bay Area to work with me on the editing. I finally called him up and said, 'I can't work with her. She is absolutely psychotic.' So David and I finished up the editing."

9

TRIANGLE

SONDRA MARSHAK AND MYRNA CULBREATH

MARCH 1983   (188PP)

AT ransporting Ambassador Gailbraith and his followers of the "oneness," Kirk and Spock end up opposing each other when they rescue Sola Thane, a female Federation Free Agent. Somehow, both Spock and Kirk fall in love with her and must fight for their souls against the Totality, a group of humans who have formed a collective consciousness and who have a plan for galactic domination.

• • •

Sondra and Myrna remarked, "Kirk and Spock fall in love with the same woman. They didn't have enough trouble already. She is Sola Thane, a Free Agent of the Federation. The rank is one that starship captains regard as heroic—and lonely. Our novel version of *Triangle* adds, among many other things, the science fiction element of 'The Oneness.' It confronts Kirk, Spock, and Sola Thane with the struggle between individuality and the collective mind—a form of totalitarianism that extends even to the mind and soul. And it has a certain seductive appeal. Eventually the head of the Oneness confronts Sola with the choice of which man she loves she will save or let die—Kirk or Spock?"

Sondra and Myrna have worked together to publish a Phonics Game that is aimed at tackling illiteracy.

#10

WEB OF THE ROMULANS

M. S. MURDOCK

JUNE 1983 (220PP)

AS'Talon, a Romulan, embarks on a secret mission across the Neutral Zone, critical to the survival of his people. Meanwhile, the *Enterprise* computer begins acting strangely. Recently programmed with a personality, it begins to show signs of being in love with Captain Kirk. Chronicling the events after "Tomorrow is Yesterday," the ship's crew badly needs shore leave and the *Enterprise*'s computer system is in dire need of repairs. Instead, a new mission propels them to the Romulan Neutral Zone to investigate what appears to be an incoming Romulan invasion fleet.

Melinda commented, "I discovered *Star Trek* (the original series) in 1969 when I was a senior in college. I immediately loved it, but I had absolutely no idea what it was. I went to college in a small town of 10,000. *Star Trek* was not shown there, to my knowledge, until 1969.

Being my senior year, I was exceptionally busy. One Friday night, I came back from a meeting and switched on my small black-and-white television to a program already in progress. For a minute or two I didn't pay much attention, but soon I was absolutely riveted. The show was marvelous! It had wonderful characters; it was incredibly funny, and so very well written. The show concluded and I never realized what it was. I knew nothing about *Star Trek*, did not know about Spock's green complexion (somehow I accepted the ears without thought) because of my TV, and somehow missed anything that would identify the show. For years I walked around describing this wonderful show, even quoting bits of dialogue, and I never ran into anyone who knew what it was. Some years later, local pressure resulted in *Star Trek* being rebroadcast here in Omaha. I started watching the show and enjoying it, but I still didn't realize that the episode I had loved was *Star Trek* until 'A Piece of the Action' was shown. There it was! The very show! The show was rebroadcast in order, and I actually fell in love with the first episode and was hooked at that time, but when I saw 'A Piece of the Action' I realized I had loved it for years!"

Commenting further, "It's hard to realize now, but back in the 1970s the only *Star Trek* available was what had already been. With only a few channels to choose from, a fan was incredibly lucky to be able to see the series at all once it was canceled. The hunger for *Star Trek* was immense, and it spawned the fan network we take for granted today. From the very beginning, there was something about the series that encouraged creativity. People drew the characters and the hardware and invented their own characters and hardware. They wrote stories and poems and music. They recreated and designed costumes—all to be able to enjoy the world of *Star Trek*. Like many others, I was involved in a fanzine; a one-shot wonder called *Dilithium Crystals*. I wrote a story for that fanzine based upon the idea of what it would be like if the *Enterprise*'s computer fell in love with Captain Kirk—after all, everyone and everything else had fallen in love with him. We published the fanzine and I thought that was the last of it. However, there came a time when, through the fan network, I knew that Pocket Books was actually taking manuscripts from unsolicited authors for new *Star Trek* novels. It occurred to me my story might make a fair novel if I made the original funny idea the complication in a more serious story. I happened to be between jobs and had six weeks to devote to the project, so I did it. I produced a manuscript about the length of the novels that were currently being published. No one was more surprised than I was when I was actually able to produce a complete manuscript. I credit *Star Trek* with teaching me that I have the ability to write a novel, and I will be forever grateful for that. The book also became a writing school. In the course of its history it was expanded and reduced, and each process taught me a great deal. Moreover, since I only had to wrestle with the mechanics and not create a new universe, it allowed me to focus on the nuts and bolts of writing, to my edification."

In terms of the idea behind the novel, "The original story of the computer falling for Kirk and how it might react (I consulted a computer designer about what was possible—he said, given the *Enterprise*'s capabilities, anything that was logical would work), the systematic elimination of rivals, Spock's annoyance, and

so on were just fun. When I needed to expand the story, I had to look for more. I had used the Romulans as they are portrayed in the original series—I really am not fond of what they have become—because I enjoyed them. The plague and so forth were not based on anything specific that I could recall. I knew I needed a desperate situation, which would make a fairly minor computer malfunction into a life-threatening situation. The Romulans would never be able to admit vulnerability and so would react militarily, as was their wont. Also, at this time there was very little done on the Romulans, and it was fun to extrapolate. I used only what had been filmed and a very little in Roddenberry's book as canon and tried to build their world as a logical outgrowth of that information."

Melinda wrote the initial novel in six weeks. She remembered, "I typed a clean copy and sent it off to Pocket Books. I heard nothing. Every six months I would send a query letter. I received polite but evasive replies; most of them signed by different editors. Almost three years went by, and I was beginning to feel more a staple of Pocket Books than the editors who worked there. One day, out of the blue, I was contacted by the current editor asking if I could enlarge the book, since the novels now being published were longer than the story I had submitted. The words 'buy' and 'contract' were conspicuously absent. Now, I am not a fool. I realized that to expand the book with no assurance that it would be purchased by Pocket Books was likely to mean a lot of work for me that went nowhere. However, I felt I had no more than time to lose, and I might learn something. I started to expand the book. It was a nightmare. Not because the story was difficult to expand, but because, before the days of computers, the only way I could effectively add material was to type up new lines and paragraphs, cut a copy of the manuscript to pieces, and tape in the additions. I kept doggedly on, line by line, and was about two thirds of the way through the book when the editor again contacted me, this time with the magic words 'We would like to buy your book.' There is no impetus to work that can better those words! I finished the rewrite in about another month, and then set about typing a clean copy. I submitted the book, and, I am happy to say, not a word was changed. The only thing that did change was the title. My original title for the book was *We Who Are About to Die*. I still think it is a much better title than *Web of the Romulans*, which is confusing to *Star Trek* fans as it reminded them of the wonderful episode, 'The Tholian Web.' My story had nothing to do with this episode, but I was told that there was a mainstream novel coming out that year with a title similar to mine and the company didn't want the two confused. Of course, Pocket Books alone published more than one title with 'web' in it that same year. *We Who Are About to Die* had a nice classical feel which tied in with the Romulans themselves and the *Star Trek* canon which enjoyed references to the classics. Oh, well."

Melinda continues to write in her little spare time, and has two fantasy novels in the pipeline.

11

YESTERDAY'S SON
A. C. Crispin

AUGUST 1983   (191 PP)

Spock discovers he has a son, a result of his liaison with Zarabeth in the original series episode "All Our Yesterdays." He convinces Captain Kirk and Doctor McCoy that he must retrieve his offspring. Using the Guardian of Forever from the classic episode "City on the Edge of Forever," the three journey back in time and bring Zar back to the present. Having been alone all of his life, Zar has to learn to interact with others. Followed by a sequel, *Time for Yesterday*.

After seeing the episode, "What Are Little Girls Made Of?" Ann Crispin was an instant fan. She wrote her first *Star Trek* story during the summer between the first and second season of the show. Crispin said, "I think I was 15. Thankfully, it has been lost in the mists of time!"

Asked how she came up with the idea for

Yesterday's Son, Crispin said, "I went to a *Star Trek* convention in 1978, and for the first time in many years, I saw the episode 'All Our Yesterdays.' That episode stuck in my mind, and I found myself thinking about it one morning as I drove to work. I found myself wondering what had happened to Zarabeth after Spock left her alone in that ice age on Sarpeidon."

Contemplating it further, she said, "Suddenly an image of a cave painting popped into my head, and the next thing I knew the whole story for *Yesterday's Son* was there, full-blown. I started writing it that night, after work, and I just kept writing. Eventually I sent the manuscript to Pocket Books, and three years later they called with an offer to buy it."

1 2

MUTINY ON THE ENTERPRISE

ROBERT E. VARDEMAN

O CTOBER 1983   (189 PP)

The crew of the *Enterprise* begins to act strangely. In desperate need of repairs, the *Enterprise* will have to be patient. Ordered to transport a Tellarite Ambassador and his assistants to the planets Ammdon and Jurnamoria to stop a war, the *Enterprise* picks up a strange woman passenger along the way from the planet Hyla. Her people have the power of persuasion by just using words, and she slowly convinces the *Enterprise* crew to become pacifists.

Robert commented about his second *Star Trek* novel: "Between the sale of *The Klingon Gambit* and *Mutiny on the Enterprise*, I had changed agents. It came as a pleasant surprise and a problem when Hartwell asked to buy *Mutiny on the Enterprise* about a year later. I worked it out, original agent handled the deal and new agent was good with that ('new agent' then in 1981—I still have the same one 24 years later). The genesis of the plot for *Mutiny on the Enterprise* harkened back to one of my favorite Heinlein books, *Starman Jones*. The idea of an entire planet being one interlocked intelligence appealed greatly (score one for Heinlein—his idea came long before the conceptualization of Gaia). I tossed in a few other elements to add menace to an orbiting *Enterprise* and was satisfied with the result. *The Klingon Gambit* and *Mutiny on the Enterprise* were oddities for me in one respect. Both were published by [Pocket Books] in paperback and then came the hardcover editions from Gregg Press. Hardcover reprints. Doesn't happen often."

Robert had some final thoughts about *Trek*. "The basic concept of *Star Trek* has to be a powerful one to have lasted over forty years. Some of the movies were more successful than others, but there were sequels and sequels to the sequels. Lots of sequels. *Star Trek* has had more reincarnations than any other television show. And novels? I have no idea how many novels have been generated since Vonda McIntyre's *The Entropy Effect*, but they would fill several long bookshelves. And the books are not just a United States phenomenon. Worldwide publication in Spain, Germany, Japan—I don't know where else—has shown a universal appeal. Kudos to Gene Roddenberry for a vision that has engendered decades of enjoyment by millions of people worldwide."

1 3

THE WOUNDED SKY

DIANE DUANE

DECEMBER 1983   (255PP)

The *Enterprise* becomes the test bed for a new propulsion system that transcends warp drive and promises intergalactic travel. The spider-like engineer K't'lk works with Scotty and the tests start hallucinations among the crew. Or are the visions actually reality? Evidence shows that their experiments are destroying the fabric of space. Can they fix the tear and make it back home without going insane in the process?

Diane was a fan of the original series from the start. "I remember having seen the commercials for the premiere on NBC and thinking, 'Hey . . . this is different!' When I saw the first episode, I was immediately in love. I think I should also mention, at peril of letting out a terrible secret, that within a matter of weeks I had it *so* bad for Mr. Spock. He was unquestionably the coolest thing I had ever seen and a real change in my crush material: until then my crushes had mostly had to do with rock groups. I immediately browbeat my parents into letting me get a Spock haircut—which, little and thin as I was then, didn't suit me at all. But even after the hair grew out, I remained lost in admiration of Spock in particular, and *Trek* in general, for the next few years. I was profoundly annoyed when the series was canceled."

Diane had a habit of writing about whatever took her fancy during a given period. "I had been writing fantasy since I was eight or so, with a fair amount of science fiction thrown in—I started reading SF writers like Heinlein at a very early age, so that *Trek* looked like familiar territory to me. By the time *Trek* came around, I was already writing Tolkien-style fantasy—I'd have written Tolkienish fanfic if the idea had occurred to me—and at that point writing *Trek* fanfic was the next step. Mercifully, no one ever saw that early material. It was, not to put too fine a point on it, complete crap. Yet it served some purpose. My old friend David Gerrold frequently said that 'the first million words are for practice,' and I got a whole lot of practice done writing, first all that Trekfic, and later the more developed fantasy which was the antecedent material for *The Door into Fire.* The practice must have done me some good over time, since when *Fire* came out, it got me nominated two years in a row for the Campbell Award. Even at that point, though, it didn't immediately occur to me that I might write a *Trek* novel."

When asked about the concept for *The Wounded Sky,* she commented, "Um. Now I have to confess something else that's likely to get embarrassing. Most writers have a touch of arrogance hidden away somewhere about their persons. Mine is pretty poorly hidden. I was reading some of the other *Star Trek* novels, which were being published in the early 80s, and one of them—I can't remember which one it was—really got up my nose for some obscure reason. I got infuriated. I remember calling one of my friends and shouting down the phone, 'I could write a better *Trek* novel than that while standing on my head in the toilet!' . . . I *told* you I was arrogant. Well, at any rate, I went off about my business with the intention of writing the best *Trek* novel that anybody had ever seen. It took me a week or so to come up with the basic outline—I still have some of the notes from that period: About half the work happened while I was sitting on a bus bench one afternoon at Reseda Boulevard. Then, when I was finished with the outline, I called my agent and said, 'Don, guess what! I'm going to write a *Star Trek* novel!' There was this prolonged pause, and then Don said, 'Do you have to?' I explained that I did have to, and I told him the story I was planning to write. He said that it sounded pretty good to him. There was something of a pause between the time it was submitted and the time it was approved, as Paramount was then in the middle of changing

publishing houses; but about six months after the outline was originally submitted, Pocket bought it. And then I wrote it, and had endless fun doing so. I don't think I realized, when I was outlining, what a rush it was going to be to write for *Star Trek.* Then Pocket published the book . . . and I went on, as I thought, to other things, leaving *Star Trek* behind me. *That* lasted five minutes."

The idea for the novel became one of the first episodes of *Star Trek: The Next Generation.* "When *The Next Generation* was given the go-ahead by Paramount, I think probably every TV writer in L.A. tried to get involved. The problem, in my case, was that I had absolutely no chance to be involved; the word had come down that Roddenberry's office was accepting pitches only from writers with previous live-action TV credentials. I had only animation credentials at that point: It wasn't going to be good enough. At the time, though, we were sharing houseroom with our friends Michael Reaves and Brynne Stephens. Michael was also thinking of pitching, and to my great surprise he came to me one evening and said, 'I've got an idea, but it sounds too much like *The Wounded Sky.* So do you want to pitch with me?' It was an incredibly gracious offer, and only an insane person would have refused. So we pitched together, and the story we sold Gene eventually—after many, many changes—became the basis of 'Where No One Has Gone Before.'

#14

THE TRELLISANE CONFRONTATION

DAVID DVORKIN

FEBRUARY 1984 (190PP)

The first Pocket *Star Trek* novel not to bear the Timescape logo. Sent to the planet Trefolg, the ship takes on several prisoners to transport to Starfleet Headquarters. Members of the United Expansion Party, their primary goal is to invade the Neutral Zone and trigger a war with the Romulans. Called away on another mission to the planet Trellisane, Kirk, Spock, and McCoy are stranded as the prisoners escape their bondage and take over the *Enterprise* bridge. The new rulers of the *Enterprise* send the ship toward the Neutral Zone while Kirk schemes to get his ship back.

David became a fan of the original *Star Trek* during the show's first season. He said, "I'm an old guy." (Laughs) "I was working on the Apollo missions at NASA in Houston at the time, and *Star Trek* seemed like a happy extrapolation of what I was doing on the job as well as being excellent TV science fiction. I think I missed the first couple of episodes of the first season, and then my wife told me about the show and I don't think we missed another episode for the duration of the show's run."

David continued, "After [the first series] left the air and before the first movie appeared, my agent at the time told me that Pocket Books was looking for people to write *Star Trek* novels. As a fan, I was delighted at the chance to write new episodes for a show I loved that had been cruelly murdered in its prime. As a writer, I was intrigued by the idea of writing in someone else's universe, especially one I was so fond of."

David juggled various themes and ideas he had been playing with for a while and thought about how he could incorporate it into the *Trek* universe. He said, "For me, how the plot evolves from the underlying ideas or gimmicks is usually kind of mysterious, and it was in this case. After my outline and sample chapters were approved by Pocket and Paramount, I wrote the book fairly quickly, sent it in via my agent, and no one complained about it or wanted changes. At least, that's how I remember it."

#15

CORONA
GREG BEAR

APRIL 1984 (192PP)

A team of Vulcan scientists sends out a distress signal that takes ten years to reach the Federation. Sent on the rescue, the *Enterprise* arrives upon a seemingly stable situation. To make matters worse, the ship has a new computer that can override major command decisions, making Kirk more irritable than usual. Toss in a reporter overseeing his every move and the situation is quite volatile.

Greg Bear became a *Trek* fan after watching the first episode on a snowy black-and-white TV, while living in Los Angeles. In 1968, Bjo Trimble sent him a batch of film clips to help illustrate her *Star Trek Concordance*, and he was hooked. According to Bear, "In 1977 I was privileged to have lunch (at his request) with Gene Roddenberry, after he read my piece about science fiction films and *Star Wars* in the *Los Angeles Times* Calendar section. We spent about two hours discussing the future possibilities for *Star Trek*, which was then being considered for a new television season. Shortly thereafter, Alan Brennert and I went in together to pitch story ideas to [*Phase II*]—and almost sold one."

In terms of *Corona*, Bear said, "I used my first computer to write *Corona*, which took me about ninety days—and I was given the freedom to write the novel pretty much the way I wanted." He updated the original series technology, "Otherwise, I tried to stay completely faithful to the original show." Bear had some final thoughts on his only *Star Trek* novel. "I used an idea I think James Blish would have been pleased with, the notion of the title character." Greg Bear has gone on to become an award-winning and highly respected science fiction author.

#16

THE FINAL REFLECTION
JOHN M. FORD

MAY 1984 (253PP)

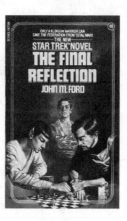

A hot new fiction novel resides on Starfleet's reading list. Called *The Final Reflection*, the novel looks at the life of a Klingon captain. From his early childhood as an orphan to his adult life commanding a battlecruiser, Krenn becomes the reader's lens through which to experience the Klingon way of life. Captain Kirk and the rest of the familiar characters are absent except for the prologue and epilogue (though some make recognizable cameos).

The author declined to be interviewed for this book. His editor, David Hartwell, remembered, "John wanted to write a novel without the other characters in the program. It sold hundreds of thousands of copies."

1 7

STAR TREK III:
THE SEARCH FOR SPOCK

(SEE SECTION 10: NOVELIZATIONS)

1 8

MY ENEMY, MY ALLY
(RIHANNSU, Book One)
DIANE DUANE

JULY 1984   (309 PP)

The start of what became known in later years as "The *Rihannsu* Saga." A Romulan commander learns of a plot that uses Vulcans for horrible genetic experiments, so she commits treason by asking the Federation for help. Captain Kirk and his crew must trust their enemies if they are to succeed in stopping the experiments. Followed by several sequels: *The Romulan Way*, *Swordhunt*, *Honor Blade*, and *The Empty Chair*.

"*My Enemy, My Ally* was one of those story ideas that sort of creeps up on you while you're not looking. As far as I can do, it did this in two pieces. First, the nature of the relationship between the Romulans and the Vulcans had been on my mind for some time as something that needed some investigation: the hints and suggestions dropped during the course of the original-series episode 'The *Enterprise* Incident' was tantalizing. But, along an entirely different line, I was becoming aware of a long-delayed reaction to the frequent portrayal of Kirk as the relentless ladies' man who went cutting a swath—without much resistance—through the feminine contingent of *Star Trek* characters. Somewhere along the line I'd started thinking, 'I wish somebody would drop a woman into this man's path that would give him a run for his money.' As frequently happens with me, these two very different trains of thought somehow wound up, not exactly on the same track, but at least running on parallel ones . . . so that, sometime in 1983, the character who would become Ael put her head in through the door, so to speak, and said, 'I'm available . . .' and the story which would be *My Enemy, My Ally* started to develop. Lest I be accused of writing too rampant a Mary Sue novel (and there are those who'll claim that even *The Wounded Sky* was a "Mary Sue"), I should probably mention at this point that the person on whom Ael was based was my then-editor at Timescape, Mimi Panitch—so the elfin features, delicate build, and raven hair were drawn from life. I can't say a lot about where the plot as such came from—partly because the actual process of plotting mystifies me somewhat to this day. But the outline was accepted for publication, and I got busy. The writing process became a little complicated at that point. My agent, the redoubtable Don Maass, called me suddenly and said, 'Something's come up. They need the book a lot faster than they originally thought. Can you get it to them—' and he named a date which was eleven days away. I kind of gulped and said 'Okay.' The next eleven days were fairly busy, but the book was delivered as promised—

despite such minor hiccups as a huge snowstorm that happened in the middle of it, the car that belonged to one of my housemates catching fire during the storm, and me nearly throwing my back out once while shoveling snow. But everything eventually turned out all right, and a lot of people seemed to like the book."

 # 1 9

THE TEARS OF THE SINGERS
MELINDA SNODGRASS

SEPTEMBER 1984   (252PP)

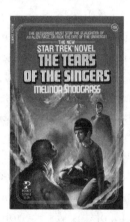

The inhabitants of the planet Taygeta are seal-like creatures known for their beautiful song. In addition, they produce a jewel-like tear when they die. Hunters are commonplace and the killing needs to stop. A spatial rift near the planet has the *Enterprise* investigating along with the Klingons. Captain Kirk has recruited a famous musician to attempt communication with the creatures and Uhura falls in love with him. Can Kirk's shipmates get along with the Klingons, stop the slaughter of the animals, and seal up the rift?

• • •

Melinda was a *Trek* fan from the moment she saw the very first episode in 1966. It was the salt monster episode, "The Man Trap," and she was hooked. She remembered, "I had quit my law practice. My dear friend Vic Milan was suggesting that I try writing as a new career. With his help I got a New York agent, and he took the liberty of telling me about an opportunity to write a *Star Trek* novel. I wasn't one of the 'approved' writers, but I sent in an outline and David Hartwell bought the book. Vic and I spent a lot of evenings kicking around plot ideas for other books. We analyzed *Trek* episodes and realized they fell into two categories—the hard-edged action like 'Balance of Terror' and the soft and fuzzy like 'City on the Edge of Forever,' or 'The Trouble with Tribbles.' I decided to try for soft and fuzzy and I couldn't think of anything softer or fuzzier than baby white seals. I'm also a singer and musician so I loved Uhura, and I knew I wanted to use her and her music. I also knew she was a character who hadn't had a lot of play up to that point. A lot of this was a serious attempt to sell this book."

She continued, "It was a fine experience working with David Hartwell, and he gave me a valuable piece of advice. He told me to use the *Trek* book to launch my writing career, but to never write another one, and I never have." Melinda went on to be on the writing staff of *Star Trek: The Next Generation* during its second season and wrote, among other episodes, "The Measure of a Man" (the one where Data's sentience is judged in a Starfleet court).

#20

THE VULCAN ACADEMY MURDERS

JEAN LORRAH

NOVEMBER 1984   (280PP)

A crewman desperately needs a radical medical procedure available only on Vulcan. Amanda, Spock's mother, has undergone this procedure successfully, and currently rests in stasis. When the *Enterprise* arrives, another hospitalized person in stasis dies under mysterious circumstances. Murder hasn't occurred on Vulcan in almost 5,000 years, so is there a murderer afoot? Can Kirk decipher the culprit before someone else, particularly Amanda, is dispensed? Followed by a sequel, *The IDIC Epidemic*.

Jean discovered *Star Trek* through the 1966 Fall Preview issue of *TV Guide*. She said to herself, "If this is actually as good as it sounds, I'm going to love it." Then she watched the first episode and she was hooked.

Being a fan, there were no media fanzines at that time, so she tried writing scripts. "Of course they weren't bought (I had a hellish time getting around the Hollywood agent problem), but I tried."

For her first *Star Trek* novel, Jean remembered, "At the time, you couldn't get a *Trek* novel published unless you had other professional credentials. Once I had *First Channel* and the first *Savage Empire* book, I figured it was worth a try—and it worked. *Vulcan Academy Murders* grew out of my fannish stories in the *Night of the Twin Moons* universe."

---

2 1

UHURA'S SONG

JANET KAGAN

J A N U A R Y   1 9 8 5   (3 7 3 P P)

On the planet Eeiauo, a decimating plague ravages its population of cat-like beings. Uhura had visited the planet years before and befriended one of the inhabitants. The songs the two of them shared actually hold a secret that the Eeiauoans are willing to die upholding. When the plague crosses over to humans and Dr. McCoy becomes infected, the *Enterprise* crew must solve the mystery of the songs and cure the plague before everyone succumbs.

Janet cannot honestly call herself a *Star Trek* fan. "I'm a science fiction fan and I'm still the kid in the corner with her nose in a book. But I was home from college for the summer and my kid brother sat me down in front of the TV and turned to *Star Trek*. 'You have to watch this,' he said. 'Theodore Sturgeon writes for this show.' I'm still a huge fan of [his]. I'd read and admired SF by a lot of the other writers who wrote those early *Star Trek* episodes, but Theodore Sturgeon was *the* name to conjure with. Kid brothers always know that sort of thing."

She never imagined in a million years that she would write a *Star Trek* novel. "David Hartwell, who'd read my manuscript for *Hellspark* and wanted to publish it, conned me into submitting a proposal for a *Trek* novel. Except for the occasional episode of *Star Trek* shown at a SF convention, I hadn't seen [the show] for some sixteen to seventeen years. My memory was good but it wasn't *that* good. I had to research *Star Trek*. Luckily, by then, you could find a rerun somewhere around the dial almost any night of the week and, by then, we had a VCR. I taped the late night reruns to watch in the morning before I sat down to write, so the voices would be fresh in my ear."

When she committed to David Hartwell, she promised a thirty-page sample and a ten-page outline within the week. She crammed, but was able to finish what he asked for in plenty of time. "When I write, I want to write about something I've never seen before. In those three seasons of *Star Trek*, I never saw them do right by Uhura. I never saw Nichelle Nichols given those few lines that would burn her into your memory forever. But I'd seen a promotional film she made for NASA, where her pure delight at being a 'captain at last' burned her into my memory with those three words. I wasn't about to pass that up—I had to give Uhura the plum role she deserved. In those three seasons, the only children I remembered were dangerous, sometimes deadly. Hell of a way to skew a universe! Since all of the kids I knew were bright and sweet and happy and scrappy and mischievous, I had to unskew the *Star Trek* universe by writing in all the kids in my family and neighborhood. And just because by then my mom was the *Star Trek* fan in the family, I cast her as the guest star for my episode. I didn't think for a minute this would go beyond the thirty-page sample and the ten-page outline but I took the assignment as a double-dog dare. To the very best of my ability, that thirty-page outline was going to read like *Star Trek* sounded. That way, my mom, at least, would get a kick out of reading the teaser for her episode. David Hartwell called and, on the strength of my sample and outline, told me to go ahead and write the book. First, I panicked. Next, I called every friend I knew who was into the show (and some of them are very hard-core) and I asked for their help. They answered my weird questions, they loaned me books (novels, biographies of the actors) and tapes of the movies, and I asked each of them, 'What have you never seen in *Star Trek* that you'd like to?' During the three months I'd been given to write the first draft, I also read every *Trek* novel and bio and I watched a taped episode of the original series every morning before I sat down to write. Total immersion. It had to sound right, even if Mom and now the Trekkers I'd enlisted in the cause would be the only ones to

read it. When I couldn't think what to write next, I looked at the want list and worked out a way to give another Trekker what he or she had always wanted to see."

Janet had problems when she turned in the manuscript. "David Hartwell left Simon & Schuster for Tor and I had an orphan book and didn't know it. Nothing that normally happens in a publishing house to turn a manuscript into a polished book happened normally in those days. I've since talked to *Trek* authors from that same period whose books had it worse than mine did, so I count myself lucky. (But sometimes late at night, I dream of an alternate universe where David edited and Nancy copyedited and the story is clearer and the words are all the right words. . . .)"

Will Janet write a sequel to *Uhura's Song?* "I had so much fun writing the second draft that, between paragraphs, I sketched out not one but two sequels. Both of them had the same guest star: Evan Wilson/Tail-Kinker/my mom. When a new editor took over the *Trek* series, I thought perhaps things had gone back to normal in the editorial offices, so I submitted my outline for the second. To make a long story short, the next two *Trek* editors in a row wanted me to write it for them but [by then the policy was] that *Trek* novelists weren't allowed to bring back their own characters. So, no, there won't be any sequels: *Star Trek* just wouldn't be as much fun for me without Tail-Kinker."

2 2

SHADOW LORD

LAURENCE YEP

MARCH 1985 (280PP)

Prince Vikram studied on Earth for several years and is ready to get back home. Spock and Sulu accompany our friend to his homecoming and shocking events await! Afraid of modernization, the rivals of the prince stage a coup. Now Spock, Sulu, and the prince must not only survive, but must also take back the throne without violating the Prime Directive.

Laurence remarked, "I'm old enough to have been able to watch *Star Trek* when it was first aired on television. I was the type of fan who saw every science fiction film or television show—it didn't matter how cheesy the special effects might be—so naturally I watched *Star Trek* when it first came on and instantly fell in love with it. I especially liked the fact that the cast included an Asian in a professional role rather than as a servant. (Again, in those days, Asian-American actors were cast as houseboys,

valets, or laundrymen.) There weren't as many *Star Trek* novels in those days and they usually centered on Kirk and/or Spock—which was fine because I liked those characters a lot. However, I felt Sulu deserved a story too. What would an Asian be like in the future? For instance, Asian-Americans face new issues that are different than the Asians who stay in their home countries. What would the impact of other worlds and societies be on them? I'm not trying to say that Mr. Spock is an Asian-American, but as a half-human / half-Vulcan, he would understand the dilemma of Asian-American identity. An Asian-American belongs neither to the Asian culture of his or her homeland nor completely to America. Asian-Americans exist on the border between two cultures, which is similar to Mr. Spock's dilemma. This all sounds abstract, but I hope I showed some of that about Mr. Sulu in the actual book rather than just telling readers that."

Laurence reflected on the story of *Shadow Lord:* "I thought it would be interesting if Mr. Sulu visited a world undergoing convulsions similar to the ones that Japan went through during the Meiji era when Japan converted its traditional agrarian society to a technological one. So it was a form of time travel, if you like. I was interested in that period in Japan when the feudal culture gave way to the modern culture. With all its flaws, the feudal culture had a nobility and beauty that the modern culture lacked. With all its virtues, modern culture lacks what I would call the 'grace' of the feudal culture—of course, that's only true if you were a noble rather than a peasant. My favorite movie of all time was *Seven Samurai* and there's that scene where the perfect swordsman cannot win over the gunman. And while Mr.

Sulu fences in the European style, I thought he would also be fascinated by Japanese sword fighting and the samurai in general."

When asked about the publication story, Laurence remembered, "I had to be careful about not expanding Mr. Sulu's background. That meant I couldn't go back any further in his past than the television shows. You can understand what a problem that can present in character development." In those days, the studio was understandably unwilling to allow the licensed fiction to add much in the way of detail to the official "canon" because they wanted to keep their options open for possible plot developments in the movies and television shows. "Vonda McIntyre can tell you the troubles she had giving Mr. Sulu the first name of Hikaru. So I was amused when I saw a novel about Mr. Sulu's daughter. It's a sign, I suppose, that Paramount [didn't] intend to make movies with the original cast anymore and [was] no longer concerned as much about keeping story lines open."

2 3

ISHMAEL

Barbara Hambly

MAY 1985 (255PP)

Spock gets stranded on Earth in the city of Seattle in 1867. Even though he has no memory of who he is, Spock must stop a Klingon plot; otherwise the Federation will never exist! Will he succeed? Can Captain Kirk find his friend and first officer across time and space?

Barbara was a *Trek* fan and hooked from when the first episode aired, "The Man Trap." She actually started writing *Trek* stories during that first season, at the age of fifteen. Her two close friends wrote stories as well. According to Barbara, "It was the equivalent of a media fanzine for three people, since of course none of us knew of the existence or even the concept of organized fandom or zines." There was a show with Mark Lenard the following year, and Barbara was a fan of that, too: "Hence the rather obvious [influence upon] *Ishmael*."

When asked how Ishmael saw the light of

day, Barbara said, "When Pocket Books got the licensing to do *Star Trek* books, the first editor of the line, David Hartwell, phoned all his agent friends asking who among their clients had old *Trek* tales in their bottom drawers—knowing we all did. I dug out *Ishmael* (which I hadn't touched since I was seventeen and which was only about half written), and wrote Dave a letter." Reflecting further, she said, "I don't feel comfortable going into all the ins and outs of the *Ishmael* saga, but the manuscript was in the keeping of about five different editors. Among them they had the manuscript for about two years and I was really rather surprised when it actually saw print."

---

2 4

KILLING TIME

Della Van Hise

J U L Y   1 9 8 5   (3 1 1 P P)

wo novels in a row concern an excursion into the past to stop the Federation from forming. The *V.S.S. ShiKahr*, commanded by Captain Spock, patrols the Romulan Neutral Zone, looking for signs of a possible invasion into Alliance territory. Ensign James Kirk finds himself having nightmares about a different ship; one that he commands with Spock by his side. Welcome to Second History, the results of a Romulan time travel experiment. Now the galaxy will implode unless history gets restored.

The publication of *Killing Time* created a controversy. According to his assistant, Richard Arnold, Gene Roddenberry received a letter from a woman who felt the book suggested a homoerotic relationship between Kirk and Spock. This perceived subtext of *Killing Time* was the source of the book controversy.

Following complaints from Roddenberry, the original version of the novel was recalled. The corrected version ended up in stores soon afterwards. Reputedly, there are over fifty changes from the first version to the revised edition.

Attempts to contact the author for an interview were unsuccessful.

2 5

DWELLERS IN THE CRUCIBLE

MARGARET WANDER BONANNO

SEPTEMBER 1985   (308PP)

To prevent a war with the Klingons and Romulans, the Federation forms the Warrantors of Peace, a group of people, representatives of their species, who are sacrificed if their planet of origin breaks the peace accord. Of course, the entire group is kidnapped. One of them, a human female, befriends a Vulcan woman.

Margaret has been a *Star Trek* fan "from the time of the beginning." The original series aired when she was in high school. She said, "Ooo, my age is showing! I fell in love with Spock, and I've been hooked ever since."

For the story of *Dwellers in the Crucible*, she said, "(The novel) was my attempt to explore the Kirk-Spock friendship from a woman's point of view."

2 6

PAWNS AND SYMBOLS

MAJLISS LARSON

NOVEMBER 1985   (277PP)

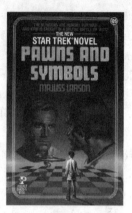

An agricultural scientist working near Space Station K-7 survives a deadly earthquake and finds herself rescued by Klingons. Commander Kang, from the original series episode "Day of the Dove," refuses to release her back to the Federation. Instead, he makes her his consort.

Attempts to contact the author for an interview were unsuccessful.

#27

MINDSHADOW

J. M. DILLARD

JANUARY 1986   (252 PP)

A peaceful planet called Aritani experiences sudden attacks, leaving both barren land and dead bodies in its wake. During the investigation, Spock suffers a traumatic injury, leaving him in a coma and possibly brain dead. Out of nowhere, a mysterious woman appears on the *Enterprise* with a possible, yet controversial cure for Spock.

Jeanne remembers when she became a fan of the original series: "At the tender age of thirteen, I turned on the television and stumbled into the middle of the episode 'Bread and Circuses.' By that summer, when I saw the rerun of 'Amok Time,' I was totally hooked and a hopeless Spock fan."

She had always written stories, even as a kid. "In 1980, I picked up my first *Star Trek* novel, *The Entropy Effect* by Vonda McIntyre and said, 'This is great!' Then I got the idea: 'Hey,

maybe I could do that.' I was absolutely blown away when I got the call from Pocket Books saying they wanted to buy my novel. You know, I really don't remember how I came up with the idea for *Mindshadow*, other than recalling that I wanted to hit Spock where it hurt the most—his mental abilities. I wrote it during one teaching semester where I was unemployed (for unionizing, but it's okay—we got our union and they rehired me, with full back pay). I sent the manuscript off and didn't hear a word for thirteen months, so I figured that was the end of my brilliant writing career. As I said, I was floored when I got the phone call."

#28

CRISIS ON CENTAURUS

BRAD FERGUSON

MARCH 1986   (254 PP)

Horrific computer malfunctions force the *Enterprise* to request aid at a nearby Starbase. When the message arrives that the planet Centaurus has been bombed and thousands are dead, Kirk has to put the repairs aside to help in any rescue and relief efforts. Several crew-members have a stake in the planet, such as Kirk owning land and Dr. McCoy's daughter, Joanna, working on the planet.

Brad was thirteen when the show premiered. He commented, "It was the first time that I saw a show like that that was done right. It wasn't what I was expecting since I thought it would be about guys banging around a ship and having adventures. It wasn't like that."

Brad bought a Macintosh in 1984 and started writing. "I figured I would write a book and try to sell it so I could stuff the computer. Why *Star Trek?* I could have written anything and the deal was I had been reading the novels. There were these spaces in the novels where, in the early Pocket program, Spock would look at his navel, call it good, and move on. They were all Spock books and all 'aren't we wonderful?' books. Once in a while they would throw in a name or a term and that would make it *Trek.* I was very unsatisfied by all of that."

He continued, "I had this thought about the *Enterprise* traveling over land, flying very low over a planetary surface. How do I put the *Enterprise* over this mountain and why would this happen? Karen Haas was the editor at the time and I called her one day and asked her what were they looking for? I mailed her the first fifty pages on a Monday and by Thursday I had a postcard asking where the rest of it was? I had to call her and tell her I hadn't written it yet. I finished the book three months later and I had to wait a year and a half to see it published. I think it sold 300,000 copies. It didn't pay shit but that was okay because my name was on a book."

Brad continued, "I love the cover. I worked in my version of Joanna McCoy, which has

nothing to do with Dorothy Fontana's version. In her version, McCoy would have a daughter, Kirk would fall in love with her, and McCoy would get pissed off. I thought this was very inappropriate behavior for Kirk, so I made her a lot younger and he had known her since she was a little girl. This was because he and McCoy had been friends so long. That was the fun part. You could do anything you wanted to do. Paramount . . . said they loved this book."

Brad remarked that he left room for a sequel that Paramount didn't buy because *The Next Generation* came along and Roddenberry's office began reviewing the books. Richard Arnold was supposed to provide continuity information. "He was supposed to tell you how warp engines worked and this wouldn't happen in *Trek* and this character wouldn't have that behavior." But according to Brad, he went farther than that. "He didn't think this [character] would do that because [the character] didn't strike him that way. He said Gene didn't like the plots. . . . This is why everyone got mad."

#29

DREADNOUGHT!

DIANE CAREY

MAY 1986   (251 PP)

Told in first person by Piper, a recent academy graduate, the story follows the radical seizing of a classified Starfleet warship. The terrorists demand that the *Enterprise* meet at a specified point and bring Piper along. What does she have to do with these potential warmongers? Followed by a sequel, *Battlestations!*

Diane became a *Trek* fan because her dad, Captain Frank Carey, USMC Ret., watched *Star Trek* in the house. "In those days we had only one TV, so I watched with him. Back then, kids watched what the parents watched. Dad was a veteran of World War II and Korea, and he was also a law enforcement officer. He and I used to watch all the postwar productions: *Combat, Wild Wild West, Rat Patrol, Voyage to the Bottom of the Sea,* and all the war movies. I grew up with that military mind-set and a very clear idea of good guys vs. bad guys.

Star Trek satisfied that part of me, plus the comfortable world of heroes and the New World of science fiction and of high adventure with tough choices."

Diane was already a published and best-selling novelist when she decided to try *Star Trek* novels. She said, "At the time they were a little-known but consistent line of novels, publishing only six books a year. Since I was already a published novelist, I decided to give *Star Trek* a try, but also decided that if I couldn't do it a little differently from other novels, I wouldn't bother. One thing that hadn't been done was to look at the *Trek* characters from some new point of view, so I invented a new character and told a first-person story from her point of view. I made her a female, because if I'd made her a male everyone would've said I was trying to do a young James Kirk and outshine the captain. In fact, James Kirk remained the hero of *Dreadnought!*, which was very important. He was one step ahead of my protagonist, Piper, the whole way. I did everything possible to mirror the *Trek* template without exactly copying or mimicking it. My characters were young, imperfect, and clumsy, but they had heart and integrity."

3 0

DEMONS
J.M. Dillard

JULY 1986   (251 pp)

T he inhabitants of the planet Vulcan are starting to act strangely, even Sarek. When the *Enterprise* investigates, a murder both on the planet and aboard the ship alert Kirk to the danger for himself and everyone he cares about. Accompanying them on this mission is a strange woman. Followed by a *Next Generation* sequel, *Possession.*

"I remember the inspiration for *Demons* very well; I was teaching an evening class at the university, and had to stay late for some reason. It was an older building, somewhat gothic and spooky, and near Halloween. As I was sitting grading papers, this image popped into my mind of Spock staring at Sarek and saying, 'That is *not* my father,' in an *Invasion of the Body Snatchers* sort of way. When I first saw the cover for *Demons,* I laughed. I had long, curly red hair (it's still red and curly, just not as long)

just like the character on the cover; my husband still says the artist must have seen a picture of me somewhere."

3 1

BATTLESTATIONS!
Diane Carey

NOVEMBER 1986   (274 pp)

T he sequel to *Dreadnought!* Captain Kirk gets taken into custody by security guards from Starfleet. The experimental transwarp drive has been stolen and Kirk is the number one suspect. Lt. Commander Piper proves to be the only person capable of stopping the conspiracy and rescuing the captain.

Diane remembers when Pocket Books received the manuscript for *Dreadnought!* She said, "Pocket's then-editor called me to tell me, 'You've broken every rule we've got. We love it.' *Dreadnought!* was published and immediately [made] the *New York Times* best seller list. Pocket instantly asked for another book as fast as I could produce one. We wrote *Battle-*

stations! in six weeks, [and it also became a] *New York Times* best seller."

3 2

CHAIN OF ATTACK

GENE DeWEESE

FEBRUARY 1987   (251PP)

The *Enterprise* finds itself in a distant galaxy, thanks to an interstellar gate. Unable to find the gate to return, the ship spends weeks trying to find another way home. Slowly losing power, the *Enterprise* is in imminent danger of becoming adrift, let alone making it back home, and Kirk attempts to negotiate peace with two warring races. Followed by a sequel, *The Final Nexus.*

Like Joe Haldeman, Gene fell in love with *Star Trek* when Roddenberry previewed the two pilots at the World SF Con and won over the entire audience by apologizing in advance, saying that he knew the pilots fell short of written science fiction but that they were the best he'd been able to do given the whims and restrictions imposed on him by the studio. Gene DeWeese said, "And then Roddenberry explained that the first pilot, 'The Cage,' had been rejected as being 'too intellectual,' and he'd had to dumb it down in the second pilot. And it didn't hurt that his approach was such a huge contrast to the This'll-bowl-you-guys-over approach taken by the studio flak who was there to preview *Time Tunnel.*"

Around this time, Gene DeWeese and Robert Coulson had just sold a couple of *Man From U.N.C.L.E.* novels and tried, very unsuccessfully, to write for the second season of *Star Trek.* He said, "Over the next ten or fifteen years, I sold a couple dozen other novels, mostly SF and horror, so when my agent told me that David Hartwell at Pocket was planning to buy fifty or so *Trek* novels, I jumped at the chance."

The basic idea for *Chain of Attack* was the thought that you can get into big trouble by shooting first and asking questions later. He said, "This had been in my SF 'ideas box' for years, and it just seemed to fit into the *Trek* universe. It didn't get purchased, however, for another four years and three or four editors. And one of the first communications I received after the four-year delay was, could I possibly do it in three months instead of the four specified in the contract."

#33

DEEP DOMAIN

Howard Weinstein

APRIL 1987 (275PP)

Spock and Chekov take a shuttle to the planet Akkalla and promptly disappear. The scientific outpost planetside has made a discovery that various people in the government were hushed. Kirk must save his friends and the scientists from the corrupt power mongers and solve the mystery of an extinct race.

The story for *Deep Domain* started swimming around in Howard's head after he went on a whale-watch cruise out of Gloucester, Mass. in the fall of 1984. Shortly afterwards, Howard said, "I was invited to meet with Leonard Nimoy, who was drumming up ideas for what would become *Star Trek IV: The Voyage Home*. He was meeting with all kinds of scientists and writers, 'stirring the pot,' as he said to me. Now, I'd never met Leonard before, and you have to remember I'm a *Star Trek* fan before I'm a *Star Trek* writer. So even at age thirty, I'm a little

nervous about this meeting . . . and I'm also thinking, *This is so cool!*"

At the meeting, they chatted for a couple of hours, and "I got the feeling pretty early in the session that he wanted to do time travel, but was looking for something interesting for the time travel to be about. So I mentioned the whale-watch cruise, and how it got me thinking: 'What if whales, or whale-like creatures on another planet, turned out to be a species with intelligence equal to the humanoids who dominate the planet? What would it do to a culture to learn that, after generations of hunting those creatures for food? At the end of the meeting, I asked if I could try to come up with a more detailed story idea for him. He said, 'Sure,' and gave me his office phone number. After a few weeks, I had an outline done, based on that idea about intelligent whale-like creatures. I contacted Leonard, asked if I could submit it, and was told they already had something cooking, but thanks anyway. So that story that I *didn't* get to submit for *Star Trek IV* became *Deep Domain*."

Reflecting further, Howard said, "At the time that I wrote it, I really didn't know they were doing a story about humpback whales for the movie, so when my outline was sent to Paramount for approval, they asked me to make some changes because I was a little too close to their story—which confirmed for me what they were doing in the movie. I have no idea how much I contributed to the development of the *Star Trek IV* story, but the producers were nice enough to give me a little 'Special Thanks to—' screen credit. That's my favorite *Star Trek* movie, and I think it's quintessential *Star Trek* in the way it combines adventure, humor, character interaction, and a social comment on our own times, so I'm thrilled to be associated with it, even in a tiny way. I also got to visit the set during shooting, and had a great time watching movie magic being made. So *Star Trek IV* will always be extra-special to me, in part because my serendipitous peripheral involvement helped me think of a cool novel to write."

---

3 4

DREAMS OF THE RAVEN
CARMEN CARTER

JUNE 1987 (255 PP)

seemingly routine rescue mission becomes a battle for survival against an unknown enemy. Dr. McCoy slams his head and suddenly thinks he is twenty-three again, with no memory of Starfleet or his friends on the *Enterprise*. The villains dubbed "the ravens" are particularly vile.

Carmen commented, "I started watching *Star Trek* back when it was being aired by NBC, and I was immediately fascinated by the mix of sci-

ence fiction special effects, social drama, and appealing characters. Since I was only fourteen years old at the time, I've spent the majority of my life as a *Star Trek* fan. I've wanted to be a writer even longer than I've been a *Star Trek* fan, so it was only natural to start writing *Trek* fan fiction when the show was canceled and I couldn't get my weekly fix of episodes. Many years later, after having written a few science fiction short stories, I was curious to see if I could write a novel-length manuscript, and *Star Trek* seemed like a fun subject for that writing exercise. I didn't seriously consider submitting the manuscript for publication until I had actually finished the project."

Where did she get the idea for this novel? "I was interested in playing with the ways in which we choose our own destinies, and McCoy seemed a perfect foil for exploring the reasons we make certain choices. Although his back history was never fully revealed in the series, it was relatively well known among fans that the doctor's marriage had failed and that the resulting guilt and bitterness led to his decision to join Starfleet. A bout of amnesia provided the rollback in time to a crucial pivot point in his young adulthood and let me show how and why McCoy played out the hand he had been dealt. When the manuscript was finished, I decided it was publishable and submitted it to an agent who knew me well enough to take the time to read my work. She agreed with my assessment and sent it in to Pocket Books. Through a stroke of good fortune, the editor at Pocket Books was facing an unexpected hole in his publishing schedule so he was willing to look at an unsolicited manuscript. To my surprise and delight, I received an acceptance within a month or two of the submission, with publication of the book itself in less than a year."

Carmen had something else happen as a result of the book's publication. "I think that book is my sentimental favorite because McCoy is just such a fun character. Also, the love of my life is a dyed-in-the-wool McCoy fan and that book contributed to our meeting at a *Star Trek* convention (some fifteen-plus years ago). Can't beat that for a good ending."

#35

THE ROMULAN WAY
(RIHANNSU, Book Two)
DIANE DUANE AND PETER MORWOOD

AUGUST 1987   **(254PP)**

The sequel to *My Enemy, My Ally*, and the second *Rihannsu* novel. A citizen of the Federation has been living a secret life with the Romulans for the past eight years. When a Starfleet officer is captured, Terise LoBrutto must choose between destroying her cover or saving the life of Dr. McCoy. The history of the split between Vulcan and Romulus echoes in

Diane's next book, *Spock's World*. The *Rihannsu* Saga was continued in *Swordhunt*.

Diane explained, "I'd been wondering, both before and after writing *My Enemy, My Ally*, how a Romulan dictionary might play. However, at that point it didn't seem to be economically viable (this was long, long before the tremendous success of the Klingon-language materials with which Marc Okrand was involved). My editor at that point, Dave Stern, suggested that while a dictionary might not work, more cultural information might—assuming that there was also a strong story wrapped around it. This sounded fine to me, but it left me with the problem: if the Romulans/Rihannsu are so secretive, how do we *get* that information? Possible answer: From a "sleeper," a deep-cover agent installed there years ago . . . one who now has to be pulled out. But there are complications, of course. . . . From this line of reasoning came Terise Haleakala-LoBrutto, a character who was a composite of a couple of very old and dear friends (pardon me if I keep their identities private). The title was an homage to Edith Hamilton's great cultural-history books *The Greek Way* and *The Roman Way*, both of which were constantly by me while I was outlining. The outline was promptly approved, and I got ready to start work. And then things started to happen."

When asked why Peter co-wrote the novel with her, she commented, "Because I was late. Because I was incredibly busy. Because Peter was a writer, living in the same house, and right at that moment in time, *wasn't* incredibly busy. (He was between books right then.) . . . That we'd just gotten married was coincidental, honest. Short version of the story: In mid-1986 I accepted an offer from my old friend Robby

London, then VP of Being Seriously Creative at the animation house DiC, to come in and story-edit an animated TV series called *Dinosaucers*. (It's still out there in syndication, I believe.) This was going to involve relocation to Los Angeles from Philadelphia (where I was then living), but the prospect very much appealed to me, as I had never been a story editor before. However, nothing ever runs all *that* smoothly in my life, and sure enough, before the year was out I had met my One True Love, agreed to marry him, gotten engaged at the World SF Convention in Atlanta (where I caught Peter gang-reciting from *Monty Python* with a bunch of friends, and knew beyond all possible doubt that I was marrying the right man), had gone to Los Angeles, started work on the series bible, returned home, and turned the bible in. Over New Year's, Peter joined me in Philly, and we then packed our bags and headed for Los Angeles. Now, normally this by itself wouldn't have made the book late. But the process of getting together the necessary financing for the series ran much longer than it should have, delaying when I could actually get the series off my plate (so to speak) and get busy with novel-writing. Finance that should have been in place in November did not actually materialize until St. Patrick's Day . . . at which point I had until July 1st to provide the producers with sixty-five half-hour scripts. *That* was what made the book late. And it got later and later as work on *Dinosaucers* got more hectic. Finally my (now our) agent Don called Peter and suggested that he should give me a hand. Fortunately, *The Romulan Way* was very completely outlined. So we rented a spare computer (this was well before laptops would have been an affordable option), and for the next two weeks I would go off to work and spend the usual ten or twelve hours in Encino, and then come home and write until I couldn't see any more. Peter, meanwhile, would have been working on the book the night before, and would be asleep until noon or so. He'd get up then and work on it some more while I was still at the office. When I got home I'd read what he'd written and add more material to it—then fall over around midnight. He'd then write all night, wake me up when it was time for me to go to work again, and go to sleep himself. And so it went for two weeks. But when the two weeks were over, there was a book. . . . And to my delight, Peter mastered my style so completely that to this day no one has correctly guessed which parts of the book I wrote and which he wrote. People who should have known better later claimed that this book was one which had been written earlier, and had *Star Trek* elements injected into it 'just to make some fast money.' To which I can only say: (a) If the book was written earlier, why did I bother spending sixteen days of the twenty-one which should have been my honeymoon writing it (in front of witnesses who were in a position to see what was coming out of the computers every day)? And, (b) Why would I bother doing this when I was making much better money working in TV than I was from writing books? Sheesh. . . . Well, it's all been sorted out a long while ago. But that particular writing stint remains . . . memorable. (It was also during that period that 'Where No One Has Gone Before' happened.)"

When asked about his collaboration with Diane, Peter remarked, "*The Romulan Way* was Diane's sequel to *My Enemy, My Ally*, and already very comprehensively outlined. This was just as well for me as an unexpected collaborator, since we wrote the book chapter-about, partly on what should have been our honeymoon! Both Pocket Books and Paramount had already approved that thorough outline, so sticking closely to it meant we didn't have to continually rewrite each other. There wasn't time for that anyway! By the time we finished, I'd written 50 percent of the manuscript, so neither my agent nor the Pocket Books editor (at that time, David Stern) saw any objection to 'equal billing' on the cover with Diane, but I still have no idea how those Colonial Vipers got there. . . ."

36

HOW MUCH FOR JUST THE PLANET?

JOHN M. FORD

OCTOBER 1987   (253PP)

Star Trek meets Broadway in this comedic Star Trek novel. Kirk and the crew tangle with the Klingons, but in a very unusual way.

The planet Direidi has tons of dilithium and the rights to it will go to the group that can show it will use the dilithium most wisely. The aliens of this world believe in songs and take everyone on a gigantic con game.

The author declined to be interviewed for this book.

37

BLOODTHIRST

J. M. DILLARD

DECEMBER 1987   (264PP)

Sent to the Federation outpost Tanis, Doctor McCoy and the crew find two of the three researchers dead, with all of their blood drained. The sole survivor seems too creepy to be believed. Were these benign researchers actually investigating the possibilities of a biological weapon? The "disease" finds its way on board the Enterprise and the crew starts to succumb to its grisly effects.

• • •

Jeanne remarked, "*Bloodthirst* was sparked by a re-reading of one of my all-time favorite novels, *Dracula*. (I've written a series of historical vampire novels under my real name, Jeanne Kalogridis, called *The Diaries Of The Family Dracul*.) Again, I love writing suspense and horror; it was enormous fun to inject both into *Star Trek*."

Jean commented, "More *Night of the Twin Moons*, this time with the common *Trek* idea of making something good and noble appear to be dangerous and possibly even evil, only to turn the tables again in the end and have good and noble save the day."

#38

THE IDIC EPIDEMIC
JEAN LORRAH

FEBRUARY 1988   (278PP)

#39

TIME FOR YESTERDAY
A. C. CRISPIN

APRIL 1988   (303PP)

A sequel to *The Vulcan Academy Murders*. On the Vulcan Science Colony Nisus, aliens from all over the galaxy work in harmony. The *Enterprise* gets called to investigate when a plague devastates the inhabitants. As McCoy races to save lives, he uncovers evidence that the epidemic is tied into the Vulcan philosophy of IDIC—Infinite Diversity in Infinite Combinations.

• • •

A sequel to *Yesterday's Son*. Something is wrong with the Guardian of Forever. Kirk, Spock, and McCoy determine that Zar, Spock's son, can help them by communicating with the time portal. Now the leader of a land in the ancient past of Sarpeidon, Zar learns of a prophecy that foretells his death in an upcoming battle. Can the *Enterprise* three make it back 5,000 years to get Zar and bring him back? And even if they are successful, will Zar be able to heal the Guardian?

• • •

Asked about how she came to write the sequel to *Yesterday's Son*, Crispin said, *"Yesterday's Son* was a top-selling book, so naturally Pocket Books was interested in a sequel. I had deliberately left myself a back door in the story, so I was able to come up with a storyline pretty quickly."

In terms of the writing, Crispin said, *"Time for Yesterday* took longer to write, since it was twice as long, and a much more complicated book, with a more complex plot and a lot more characters."

When asked about any other *Trek* projects on the horizon, she said, "I will not be writing any more *Trek* books."

#40

TIMETRAP

David Dvorkin

June 1988   **(221pp)**

When the storm intensifies, Kirk loses consciousness. When he wakes up, he finds himself surrounded by Klingons who are peaceful and loving. According to them, he has been thrust 100 years into a future where the Federation and the Klingon Empire are allies.

David said, "The basic idea was inspired by a *Black Hawks* comic book I read as a kid. In that one, the 'Aggressor Nation'—very Slavic looking; this was in the 1950s—kidnapped the head Black Hawk, drugged him, and tried to make him think he was in a peaceful future so that he would tell a supposed historian some sort of secret information from his own time. I worked that gimmick up into the novel *Timetrap*. Later, I discovered that there was a remarkably similar James Garner movie, *36 Hours*, made in 1965. (In World War II, Nazis kidnap an American officer, drug him, and try to persuade him that it's really the 1950s and would he mind clearing up some historical details about the exact time and place of the Allied D-Day landings?) As I remember, *Timetrap* went through the writing and publishing processes quickly and easily, too."

A nswering a distress call, the *Enterprise* finds a Klingon vessel trapped in a strange dimensional storm. Kirk and a security team beam over to assist and help the reluctant crew.

4 1

THE THREE-MINUTE UNIVERSE

BARBARA PAUL

A U G U S T   1 9 8 8   (2 6 5 P P)

Arip in the fabric of space has been detected and the *Enterprise* crew investigate. Evidence indicates the race known as the Sackers are responsible. A race shunned by the Federation, no human can confront them without getting violently ill, due to their repulsive appearance. Can our friends overcome their foes and save the galaxy?

Barbara became a fan during the reruns of the original series. "Then I became intrigued by the whole fan phenomenon that had sprung up around *Star Trek*, and I started watching the show in earnest. A couple of friends had written *Star Trek* novels (Gene DeWeese and David Dvorkin), and I decided I wanted in on the fun. By then the cast and the episode plots were so familiar to me that it seemed the natural thing to do. I liked these people and their ship, and I wanted to play in their world."

Barbara reflected, "The story for *The Three-Minute Universe* had to be about something big. I'd been reading some scientific speculation as to what would happen if a rupture occurred between adjoining universes and felt that was a big enough problem for Kirk to tackle. The writing was pure pleasure. I woke up each morning eager to get back on board the *Enterprise* and move on to what happened next. One thing about writing a *Star Trek* novel is that you can pretty much skip exposition if you want. You don't have to introduce all the crew or explain about the five-year mission, and so on. Everyone who picks up a *Star Trek* book already knows all that. So you can plunge right in and get the story rolling on the very first page.

"The publishing process went as smoothly as I've ever seen; no big problems, small ones easily solved, and everything right on schedule. It was a good experience for me from beginning to end."

#42

MEMORY PRIME

GARFIELD AND JUDITH REEVES-STEVENS

OCTOBER 1988 (309PP)

The greatest minds in the Federation are all convening for an award celebration at Memory Prime, the planet with the largest library of knowledge in the galaxy. Kirk and company have the privilege of shuttling many of the scientists and even Spock seems excited (in his own Vulcan way) about discussing issues with several of them. Unfortunately, an assassin lurks under the festivities. And to Starfleet officials, the number one suspect is Spock.

The authors declined to be interviewed for this book. According to an interview that they both did with Kevin Dilmore in 2003, *Memory Prime* was the first book they wrote together, after it was chosen from among three different *Star Trek* novel outlines submitted to Pocket. They write their books collaboratively by passing material back and forth to each other so many times that they forget who wrote the piece by the time it's finished. For *Memory Prime*, they both tried to give every member of the senior crew a turn in the spotlight. They were intrigued to write a *Trek* novel about what was never explained on the TV show and both loved tackling the question of artificial intelligence and developing the Pathfinders.

#43

THE FINAL NEXUS

GENE DEWEESE

DECEMBER 1988 (282PP)

The sequel to *Chain of Attack*. The interstellar gates are back and they appear to be malfunctioning. In addition, when ships move too close to one, a type of madness engulfs individuals aboard the vessels. Since the *Enterprise* is the only known starship to successfully use the gates, Kirk and crew must defy orders from Starfleet Command to save the galaxy again.

Gene said, "*The Final Nexus* just grew out of *Chain of Attack*. I'm sorry to say I don't remember much else about it."

#44

VULCAN'S GLORY

D. C. FONTANA

FEBRUARY 1989 (252PP)

From the writer who contributed several scripts for the original *Star Trek* comes a novel set during the Captain Pike missions. Spock transfers aboard the *Enterprise* and struggles to keep his duties as a Starfleet officer and his Vulcan heritage from clashing. Another officer transfers on board at the same time: a junior engineering officer named Montgomery Scott. A rumor surfaces that may lead to the whereabouts of a large jewel, missing for centuries, that has deep symbolic meaning to the people of Vulcan.

Dorothy commented, "The jump from television writing to novel writing wasn't as abrupt as it looked. In fact, when I first began writing in school, I wanted to be a novelist and all my work was in prose. When I started working in television after college, I read TV scripts and made the famous last words remark: 'I can do

that.' As I began working on TV series, my boss, Samuel A. Peeples encouraged me to try scripts. I did and eventually sold nine stories or scripts to television before *Star Trek* began production as a series in 1966. I never forgot novel writing and continued to do so on the side. A partner and I, Harry Sanford, published a hardcover Western through a small California press in 1964. Later, I was asked to novelize *The Questor Tapes*, using Gene Roddenberry's and Gene Coon's scripts as the basis for the story, which I filled out into novel length. The step to doing *Vulcan's Glory* came later."

Commenting further, Dorothy said, "I was approached by the editor of the *Star Trek* book series, Dave Stern, asking if I had any ideas I wanted to turn into a novel. I thought about it and pitched an idea about Spock's first voyage on the *Enterprise*, with Captain Pike in command. I also thought it would be fun to have a subplot about Scotty's first voyage as well, and a line with some development of the Number One character. The idea was bought and contracts were signed. I first submitted a ten-page written outline, which was approved. I then went about writing the novel, developing it into a full manuscript. One funny thing that happened during the writing—well, funny now—I had been talking to David Gerrold about the joy of being able to write a novel on a computer. He asked me if I backed up, and I said I did—one backup. He told me to back it up three times. I said, 'Oh, David. Come on. What could happen?' He replied, 'Back it up three times.' Wisely, I followed instructions. There came the day when I had just finished a chapter and saved, then started to back up. The back up (of the entire book) went *ziiiippp*— and I thought, 'That sounded too fast.' I checked the file and found that on the hard disk, all I had was the last ten pages I had written! I quickly went to my additional backups and was able to transfer the full novel (about 200 pages at that point) back onto the hard disk and to properly save everything. Three times."

On the path to publication, "There were no hitches in the schedule. I delivered my manuscript; it came back for proofing, and went to press pretty much on schedule. It was a very positive experience, especially working with Dave Stern."

4 5

DOUBLE, DOUBLE

MICHAEL JAN FRIEDMAN

APRIL 1989   (308PP)

The Starship *Hood* receives a distress call from a planet that Kirk's *Enterprise* visited a few months before. Did they accidentally leave someone behind? When several of the crew beam down, they encounter a dreadful secret. Meanwhile, Captain Kirk looks forward to shore leave on Tranquility Seven. Instead, he

will stand accused of treachery and must run for his life. The *Enterprise* can't help, because they have left the planet with another Captain Kirk on board.

Mike remembered, "I watched the original series as it came out. I was eleven and I watched it religiously and loved it and wasn't even sure why I loved it. But I had been a science fiction fan for a few years already and a comic book reader. And this kind of struck both nerves somehow. It was a colorful, action-packed journey of exploration and it really appealed to me, before I had any idea that it was going to be involved with morality or ethics or more complex issues. To me it was just this great science fiction comic book on TV."

He continued, "I had read a few *Star Trek* novels and I didn't expect to write any. I had enjoyed a couple of them. Many of them were not up to snuff, but I enjoyed them anyway. I read Howard Weinstein's *The Covenant of the Crown* and I read Ann Crispin's *Yesterday's Son* and I did enjoy some of the earlier ones, but I didn't have any expectations that I'd write one. I wanted to write science fiction and had written four *Swords and Sorcery* novels and my agent at the time came to me and said, 'hey, do you want to write a *Star Trek* book? They're looking for some new writers.' This must have been about 1986 or so and I said 'hey, yeah. That sounds like fun, putting words in Spock's mouth and Kirk's mouth. Wow! That could be fun.' The first, the very first proposal I gave to Dave Stern, who was the editor in those days, he didn't like so much, it was more of a fantasy kind of proposal. It was fun but it was a little wonky and he set me straight as far as what type of thing I needed to submit. The next thing I gave him he liked a lot. And that became *Double, Double*, which was my first *Star Trek* book."

His first novel had an interesting path to publication. "Richard Arnold was the person assigned from Gene's office to look over the book. In those days there were two levels of approval at Paramount. One level was the licensing department, which we still work with now, and the other level was Gene's office. Gene or Richard Arnold had to review the proposal. We sent the manuscript up to Paramount and Richard responded via fax. For some reason they weren't talking over phone lines. They were only faxing. And faxes in those days were these dinosaurs, these big, cylindrical things that took four to five minutes to send a page. And so we sent the manuscript and the response came: You have to cut Chekov. He had like ten pages of dialogue in this book. And they suggested that we put in DeSoto. Why are we taking out Chekov? So the fax went back to California: Why are we taking out Chekov? And the next day we got a response. Because he wasn't on the ship at that time. So there was a memo on the wall in or near Dave Stern's office from Gene, from years earlier that said we made up the stardates as we went along. They're functions of time and space. Don't worry about them. Don't let them get in your way. But here was this memo saying that he wasn't on the ship at that time. And we sent a memo, send a fax back: How do you know? And the fax came again from California: Look at your stardate. So Dave and I looked at each other and I said, wait a second. You mean we can change ten pages of dialogue or we can change the stardate? So he sent a fax back and said: Well, how about if we change the star-

date? And they sent a fax back saying: Well, that will be satisfactory! So I changed one numeral instead of ten pages of dialogue."

4 6

THE CRY OF THE ONLIES
JUDY KLASS

OCTOBER 1989   (255PP)

A revolution is brewing on the planet Boaco Six, and the *Enterprise* responds. Before Kirk can determine if the Federation can help, a starship with a prototype cloaking device is stolen and begins attacking the Boacoans. Resolution of the conflict will force Kirk to confront aspects of his past, some of which he can't even remember! Follows up on two episodes, "Miri" and "Requiem for Methuselah."

Judy was a fan of the original series when she was young. "I would watch the original *Star Trek* with family, especially my brother, on our black-and-white TV. My older siblings went off to college, and I became more of a fan; there used to be reruns on twice a day during my adolescence. I became a hard-core *Star Trek* geek, knew Stardates of episodes, long stretches of dialogue, and all sorts of arcane stuff. It was kind of a mental refuge from junior high and high school."

In terms of wanting to write a *Star Trek* novel, Judy said, "Some *Star Trek* books that I read back then were well done, but some were not very well-written, I thought, and in others the writing was good, but the writers didn't know the characters or the show that well. I thought: I'm a reasonably good writer with an ear for dialogue, and I know this show and these characters inside out. I was a college student at the time, and I'd noticed that the books kept making *The New York Times* best seller list. So, I thought: I'll write one of these, retire at an early age, prove to my family that my years of devotion to *Trek* were not all a big waste of time. . . . I was on my junior year abroad in Europe, and I'd traveled to France with a friend, but her British boyfriend on impulse hitchhiked across the Channel and joined us, and it became a miserable trip for me; they were all over each other, and I felt embarrassed and like an interloper. So, I went off on my own and sat down in a cafe in Paris and ordered something and began writing: 'Captain's log . . .' It was fun."

For the idea behind the story, "It was a combination of things, and the book combines different elements. I wanted to continue with a situation from the original show, and 'Miri' was an episode I liked, and I felt it was possible that something would go awry there, with children who had lived so long. I wrote the book during my last years as a Sarah Lawrence student and my first year as a graduate student at Oxford. At Oxford I was studying Latin America, and I was not crazy about the Reagan/Bush administra-

tion's policy in Central America. I was opposed to our country funding and largely creating the Contra War, and supporting a death squad dictatorship in El Salvador, and I felt our government should give the Contadora process a chance instead of sabotaging it, and I didn't have all that many forums to talk about these things. I like original-series *Trek* episodes that are metaphors for things that were going on in the 1960s. 'A Private Little War' is basically a pro-Vietnam war episode, and 'Errand of Mercy' is probably the best example of an anti-Vietnam war episode. So, I took my cue from that sort of thing with my plot about Boaco Six. Boaco is the name of a region in Nicaragua. I had a friend who later thought the film *Star Trek VI* was riffing on my book, with the Federation being blamed for a ship destroyed in space during peace negotiations, and so on. It would be lovely if Nicholas Meyer or Leonard Nimoy had read my book . . . but I think it's more likely that they, like me, were simply using *Star Trek* as a metaphor for the final years of the Cold War and for current events—something that *Trek* lends itself to very well. At any rate, I wrote a draft, and a friend of my parents is a *Star Trek* fan and read it, and showed it to an agent she knew. . . . At that time I think many of the books were unagented, but I had an agent who represented it and that helped it get looked at. The editors were helpful. They wanted some changes. They wanted it longer than some of the books had been in the past, and perhaps that was when I added the subplot involving Flint and things from the episode 'Requiem for Methuselah.' Perhaps I have too many different things going on in the book. . . . I was daunted by the prospect of writing a full-length book, and so I made sure I had a lot of different balls in the air, in terms of the plot. But it was very exciting to be nineteen, twenty, twenty-one, and still in school, and to be revising a book, and looking at proofs, and have it come out. . . . I remember very clearly when I first saw the cover art, which I think is lovely, and sitting down on the steps outside near the publisher's office in Manhattan staring at it, incredibly happy. It did make the best seller list for three weeks . . . and while I didn't make all that much money, it was a positive experience, but maybe it set me up to think that writing and getting published would be that easy for me all down the line. There were some years after that which served as a reality check. But writing *The Cry of the Onlies* did prove to some folks around me that fandom and nerd-dom can pay off in the end, if channeled in creative ways."

Judy sold a story "concept" to the the TV series *Star Trek: Deep Space Nine* for $1,000, "Though I did not get on-screen credit for it, [it was] the idea that Garak was the illegitimate son of Enabran Tain, and that was one more reason why he's a double or triple agent and a chronic liar; he has had to spend his whole life pretending not to know that the man who is his patron and a 'friend of the family' is his father. Robert Hewitt-Wolfe was a gentleman and called me a year after I pitched the idea as the basis for an episode to tell me they were using it, tucked inside another episode, and paying me for it."

Judy teaches English at Nassau Community College, and travels frequently to Nashville to demo songs she writes. She was one of the winners of the Songs Inspired by Literature competition in 2004, with her song "Home to Freedom," inspired by Octavia Butler's SF novel *Kindred*.

4 7

THE KOBAYASHI MARU

JULIA ECKLAR

DECEMBER 1989 **(254PP)**

A shuttlecraft accident leaves Sulu and Kirk injured, and Chekov, Scotty, and McCoy trying to repair the vessel, with no hope of rescue. To pass the time, they decide to swap stories of their experiences with another no-win scenario, the Kobayashi Maru test (first established in *Star Trek II: The Wrath of Khan*).

"I began writing at a very young age, both my own fiction and fiction set in other universes like *Star Trek*. I really didn't know there was a market for that kind of writing until much later. When I first made the jump to being a full-time writer, however, I began to think about writing and selling novels. The real spark came after watching the second *Star Trek* movie. I had such a great time brainstorming with my friends about the Kobayashi Maru test—not only what Kirk must have done to pass it, but what all the other main characters would have done when they took it, too. I came up with so many great ideas that night that I sat down and wrote the proposal that became my first *Star Trek* novel."

#48

RULES OF ENGAGEMENT
PETER MORWOOD

FEBRUARY 1990   (245PP)

The *Enterprise* heads to the planet Dekkanar to help evacuate personnel. A revolution has occurred, and to avoid problems, the crew must not show any signs of force. Of course, the path to success is never smooth. A Klingon Commander, attempting to restore his honor, steals an experimental Klingon vessel and proceeds to "help" in the evacuation effort. Can Kirk defeat his enemy with both hands tied behind his back?

Peter was a fan. "[It began] probably halfway through the first season shown by the BBC; that would be—I think—in the very early

1970s. What got me going most of all was that although much of the onboard action took place on the bridge, the use of background comms chatter, and the appearance of random crewmembers at bridge stations and in corridor shots, managed to convey the existence of a much larger ship than could ever be shown on-screen with the special effects then available. There was a constant impression that the *Enterprise* was getting on with the business of a five-year exploration mission whether the camera was watching or not. Though it's fairly commonplace now, I can't remember seeing anything before *Star Trek* which did that so subtly and yet so effectively. A small thing, I suppose, by comparison with people who've said that the show has somehow changed their lives, but it was enough to catch my fleeting teenage attention long enough that I started to notice the stories. After that, I was hooked."

When asked about wanting to write a *Star Trek* novel, Peter commented, "I never actually wanted to write a *Trek* novel: It just sort of happened. At that time, Diane was story-editor on a TV show, we had just gotten married, and what with one thing and another, *The Romulan Way* was late and getting later. We'd given each other literary agencies as early wedding presents. . . . Well, almost; it's just a fun way of describing how my UK agent and Diane's U.S. agent became one another's transatlantic representatives. But a direct result of that happened right after the wedding (which took place at a science fiction convention, though not in any costume more unusual than a morning-coat rig for me and a full-train dress and veil for Diane). The phone rang, and my brand new U.S. agent suggested that if I wasn't doing anything with an urgent deadline, I should help my new wife, whose deadline was extremely urgent. So I went out, rented a PC, and started helping."

When asked about the idea for his solo project, "Dave Stern was pleased enough with my work on *The Romulan Way* that he wanted to know if I had any ideas for a solo novel. When he asked that, my mind went a bit blank. I mean, Wow! He told me not to rush about it, and that if I came up with something good enough he'd make sure there'd be a slot in the schedule for me. Wow! Again. In the event it took about eighteen months, in which I wrote a few comic scripts and a couple of other novels, before I got back to him with an idea. It originated from my first job, in the British Civil Service (think *Yes Minister* . . .); I'd decided to let James T. Kirk encounter one of the toughest opponents in the universe—government red tape. . . . Of course, the proposal was a bit more elaborate than that, but at the back of my mind was the memory that Kirk's character was partly based on C. S. Forester's 'Captain Horatio Hornblower.' Both officers usually operated so far from H.Q. that their actions were virtually independent—though of course they're held accountable for those actions in due course. What if, for once, Kirk had to heed the regulations because someone was right behind him to make sure he couldn't interpret them, 'creatively?' How would he react to such restriction when a routine situation turned potentially dangerous? And what if someone with a nasty mind (me) added an old Klingon enemy with a stolen brand-new secret weapon to the mixture? Well, that's what happened, and Dave liked it a lot. He also liked my other plot twist, which closed the book with Kirk—who as we know bends the rules more often

than he obeys them: How many starships has that man stolen in his career?—doing it once too often and getting demoted to the Training Command desk job where we find him at the beginning of *The Wrath of Khan*. I thought it would be a neat way to explain why 'Desk-Jockey Kirk' whose actions in *The Motion Picture* saved the world from V'Ger was still 'Desk-Jockey Kirk' at the beginning of the next movie. Unfortunately someone at Paramount vetoed that as something which was going to be written in-house. Was it? I don't know; oh, and I don't know what the *U.S.S. Excelsior* is doing on the cover, either. . . ."

#49

THE PANDORA PRINCIPLE

Carolyn Clowes

APRIL 1990 (273PP)

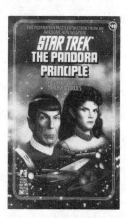

On the planet Hellguard, Spock makes a discovery that will change his life. Years later, the crew of the *Enterprise* finds a Romulan Bird of Prey that appears to be abandoned. The ship gets towed to Earth for further study.

Unfortunately, the ship is a Trojan Horse, and now Spock must probe the mind of his protégé, Saavik, to uncover the secret and possible resolution of the horror now facing Starfleet. This novel tells the backstory of how Spock and Saavik met prior to the events in *The Wrath of Khan*.

Carolyn was a fan from way back in the long-ago. She didn't think of writing a novel until she saw *Star Trek III: The Search for Spock*.

In terms of the idea for *Pandora Principle*, Carolyn remarked, "The idea came from the third film, [Robin Curtis's] performance, and Vonda McIntyre's novelization. Then came the mental and then what if. . . . For a while, it was just a story spinning itself in my head. Then I began writing it down. The publishing process was interminable, as I recall. I submitted some chapters and an outline in the summer of 1985. It was finally published in the spring of 1990. There was a great deal of back-and-forth with Pocket and Paramount over [the] story, then endless revisions. So it took a while to get born."

Carolyn was very appreciative of the fans that wrote to her to tell her they liked the story. "If anyone out there sent a letter, and I didn't answer, that's because I never received it. I appreciate all the kind thoughts and words."

#50
DOCTOR'S ORDERS
Diane Duane

JUNE 1990   (291 PP)

Dr. McCoy opens his mouth once too often, so Captain Kirk decides to teach him a lesson and puts the curmudgeon in charge while he beams down to a planet. When Kirk vanishes, McCoy finds himself truly in command. If his day wasn't bad enough, the Klingons decide to join the party. Does McCoy have the gusto to find his captain and save the day?

When asked about this story, Diane answered, "I like doctors. Some of them, anyway. Having helped train psychiatric residents in my time—'train' involving things like showing them how to talk to their patients, and how not to make coffee by dumping a whole pound of it in the coffeemaker at once—I have a slightly different view of the medical fraternity than some people do. I think I'd always had it in mind to write a McCoy book, one in which the doctor could be seen to do more than just patch peo-

ple up. At the same time, I'd previously been talking to Robert Heinlein about some of the circumstances under which a person could be stuck with command when he wasn't normally 'in the chain.' It became plain, talking to him, that if the circumstances were severe enough, I could fabricate a situation in which it would be legal to do something I'd always wanted to do: stick McCoy in the center seat. So I did it."

#51

ENEMY UNSEEN

V. E. MITCHELL

OCTOBER 1990   (279 PP)

The *Enterprise* takes on another diplomatic party. The Federation Ambassador for this mission has a trophy wife, who happens to have had prior relations with the captain. While Kirk tries to keep her out of his hair and bed, a murder among the diplomats shocks the crew. By all appearances, the assassin appears to be one of *Enterprise*'s own.

• • •

Vicki realized she was a *Trek* fan in junior college. "My sister was taking TV production classes for a year or two in high school, and I had bought some books on various TV shows to give her for Christmas. When I culled the stack, *The Making of Star Trek* got set aside for a later gift, but it was the only book sitting out when I went to grab something to read on the plane to visit my family for the holidays. So I grabbed the book, read it on the plane, and was interested enough to track down the reruns when I got back from vacation. When I discovered I could *not* predict what would happen by seeing five random minutes of an episode (which I could do for any other show running at the time), I was hooked."

What inspired her to write a *Trek* novel? "I've always written, from the time I made stories out of the vocabulary lists in first or second grade. When I started graduate school, my best friend was also a *Star Trek* fan, and we entertained ourselves with starting to tell each othe~ the plots of our own *Star Trek* novels. (For~ nately for the world, these were never ~ ished.) At that time, no one was publishi~ novels, so making up our own stories only way to get new stories. Actual~ writer, the most natural thing in th~ write about something that inte~ most goes without saying that ~ terested in what you're wri~ will be either."

The story of *Enemy U*~ to see print is almost a~ finished reading on~ *Star Trek* novels a~ wall, announci~ it happened, m~ ming for a major reg~

it~
an~
ver~
doin~
mon~
and th~
my age~
gested, ~
Most ~
made the~
address Jo~

vention, and one of the participants was David Hartwell, then editor of the *Star Trek* line, and Jon repeated my comment to David. Like a true editor, David said, 'Tell her to show me.' The idea came out of a discussion with my husband, where we talked about what had and what had not been done in *Star Trek*. The one thing I did not want to do was use an idea that everyone else had already done. At the time, I hadn't seen any murder mysteries involving the *Star Trek* characters, and the idea of a shapechanger as the villain opened up a lot of story possibilities in what is, essentially, a 'locked starship murder mystery.' I sent in the first three chapters and an outline for review while I finished writing the book. Unfortunately, by that time, David Hartwell had left for another job, and the new editor rejected my proposal. By this time, I had finished the first draft of the story and was really in love with the characters and the cultures I had created for it. I decided to rewrite the story, replacing the regular crew and the ship with characters I'd been working on for a small scout ship in a non-*Trek* setting. I rewrote the book and sent it out. After 8 or 10 months, it came back. By then, I had done another rewrite, so I sent that version to nother editor. He had it over two years before came back. About that time, I was talking to ther writer, John Barnes, at our local con- tion. He asked to see what I had been , so I gave him a copy. After about a h, I got it back with a detailed critique e fateful words, 'I've discussed this with nt, and if you make the changes I've sug- e wants to see it.'

of the changes were good ones, so I n and sent the manuscript off to the n had given me, figuring I was in for

another six-month wait. Ashley Grayson called me at work the next week! He said he liked the book and could sell it—but that, whatever I called my lead character, he was Captain Kirk. (Obviously, my rewrite wasn't as good as I thought.) I thought about it for maybe ten seconds before admitting that he was right. He took the manuscript and sent it to David Stern (then editor of the *Star Trek* line), along with a letter pointing out that, despite the names, the book was really a *Star Trek* book. David agreed and promised to buy the book. He and I discussed the characters and where to put it in the *Trek* timeline. I had originally written it in that nebulous post-third season period, but after some discussion, David and I decided it would be fun to play with the early period. Part of this was due to the fact that, in my non-*Trek* rewrite, I had separate characters as science officer and first officer. Putting Gary Mitchell in as the first officer kept meant I would not have to rewrite two separate characters as Spock. We also thought it would be fun to have my half-human telepath character as half-Deltan, because the first movie had just come out and the Deltans seemed like an interesting race to explore. So the book was rewritten along those lines and I sent it in. I didn't hear anything for a while, and then I got a four-page letter filled with what seemed to me to be very off-base requests for changes. I was still studying the manuscript, trying to figure out why I should, for example, repeat on page 42 the same information I had put on page 37 when I got a call from Ashley. He told me that my book was being moved forward to take the place of a book that wasn't going to make its deadline. So I scraped up my nerve and called Kevin Ryan (then David Stern's assistant and later *Star Trek* edi-

tor). We went through the letter and manuscript item by item, and most of his comments were resolved by putting a couple of extra sentences on page 37 (or whatever page I had originally buried the clue) and leaving the other page alone. This was my first experience working with an editor at that level of detail, and it taught me a very important lesson—if your editor thinks something is missing in your manuscript and you think you put it in, you probably better take a good, hard look at what you thought you did and probably make it a little stronger. After that discussion, I quickly made the changes and sent it off. The book still had to make its way past Paramount approvals, but no one seemed worried about that. I even had cover proofs showing what my cover would look like. I was almost ready to relax when I got a call from Kevin. 'I argued with them, and David argued with them, and his boss argued with them, and *his* boss argued with them—but Paramount insists there were no Deltans in the Federation until six months before the first movie.' And, because my book was firmly locked into the printing schedule, I had a month to do a top-to-bottom rewrite, moving the time of the story from *before* 'Where No Man Has Gone Before' until *after* the first movie. Thanks to the help of my wonderful little Osborne computer, I got the book rewritten in time to make the deadline."

5 2

HOME IS THE HUNTER

DANA KRAMER-ROLLS

DECEMBER 1990   (278PP)

A visit to a planet in dispute between the Federation and the Klingons quickly goes from bad to worse. The leader of the planet, Weyland, asks both parties to leave, but we all know how stubborn Kirk and the Klingons can be. For punishment, Weyland sends Sulu, Chekov, and Scotty in "time out of mind." Sulu ends up in 1600 Japan, Chekov finds himself in Stalingrad during World War II, and Scotty arrives in Scotland in 1746.

Dana doesn't think she was ever a *Star Trek* fan. "I came in on the original series in the middle, after I returned to the U.S. from an extended stay in Germany. My mother had been a science fiction reader, and an editor and agent for several of the early SF writers, so I came to it naturally. And being active in the SCA, I knew people like Bjo Trimble, so that was a connection. It wasn't until it went into syndication that

I 'fell for' it. It was during my first marriage, after the birth of my first child, that I had had to quit graduate school because of a difficult pregnancy. So *Star Trek* and the Apollo moon walks were my contacts to a world of science and creativity that I had put on hold. I never warmed up to *The Next Generation*. I still think that *Deep Space Nine* was the best spin-off of the lot. I eventually got interested in *Voyager*, and I think that *Enterprise* had much greater potential, and if it had stayed on the air longer, an arc of the backstory of the Federation would have had legs."

She remembered, "I didn't want to write a *Star Trek* novel. I wanted to sell another book. I had just done a package of choose your own adventure books set in other people's worlds for Bill Fawcett, and sold a couple of short stories to Marion Zimmer Bradley for the *Sword and Sorceress* anthologies, and I ran into some of my SFWA buddies at a Westercon, I think it was, who were working on a contract for Pocket. I used them for a reference, came up with a proposal, and sold it. I am an historian, well, my Ph.D. is in folklore and history/anthropology of belief systems, but I have a solid background as a real-life historian, although that came after I wrote the book. I always wondered what would happen if the characters in *Star Trek* (here the original series) actually got thrown into some other era with no way to get back—no MacGuffins, no escape ladders. . . . So I set up a situation where three characters, Sulu, Scotty, and Chekov, got thrown into their own pasts, Sulu at the battle of Sekigahara in 1600, Scotty at Culloden in 1745, and originally I was going to send Chekov to the Potemkin at the eve of the Russian revolution,

until I discovered that the hero of Stalingrad was a general whose name was almost Chekov, General Chuikov."

She has painful memories of the book seeing publication. "The writing and publishing process was a horror. . . . At one point I was told that the Federation wasn't military, and so I had to excise all the 'aye, aye, sir' dialogue, and then I couldn't use the Klingon language (for the frame story on the *Enterprise* while our three heroes are lost in time), because it hadn't been [used] in the original series, and I had to get permission from Gene Roddenberry himself to use Hikaru as Sulu's first name. Remember that I had already done two successful books in franchise worlds, and I had no problem with the concept. It was the new-rule-of-the-week that was making me nuts. And then the publishers decided that my manuscript was too authentic, and difficult for the apparently stupid fans to understand, and they cut out a whole bunch of historical stuff, and I don't mean dull stuff, but three-hanky farewell letters from the front. *Real* stuff. Still, I'm glad I did it, and I'd do it again in a heartbeat. And I have to give credit where it is due. Despite all the Sturm and Drang, everybody was very nice to me, and very nice to work with. Franchise writing is a business. I think a real 'fan' would have had less trouble, but I suspect would have turned out a less interesting book."

Dana is a knight in the SCA, the third woman to receive that accolade, and the first to win a throne by right of arms. She commented, "I have always had one foot in the past, one in the future, as I have also had one foot in the world of magic and one in the world of logic and science, so I am never bored."

5 3

GHOST-WALKER

BARBARA HAMBLY

FEBRUARY 1991 (273PP)

aptain Kirk is unhappy, since the woman he loves might be staying behind on the planet Elcidar Beta Three. When the crew beams back to the *Enterprise*, it appears that a ghost followed them up in the transporter. Random acts of items breaking and disappearing start to plague the ship. Is the *Enterprise* haunted? And why is Captain Kirk acting so mysteriously all of a sudden?

Barbara said, "Then-editor Dave Stern took the outline for *Ghost-Walker* enthusiastically, but between the time he okayed it and the time I turned in the manuscript, there'd been a change of policy and a change of the approvals procedure. The story is based on Captain Kirk falling seriously in love with an anthropologist whom he's taking to a primitive planet—and she with him—and between the outline being okayed and the manuscript being turned in, someone had decided that there would be *no* serious love interests. I said that was fine with me if they didn't want to print the book, but since I wrote from the outline they'd okayed I did want to be paid for it, and eventually they took it. That was the same story they told me to delete all references to Mr. Spock's pajamas, since at no point on the original show had we seen anyone in the Starfleet jammies I described. . . . I was very tempted to insert a scene of Mr. Spock lolling on his bunk *not* in pajamas, but I restrained myself. They'd only have pulled it out."

The final draft of the novel differs from Barbara's final polish. Barbara said, "they filleted a number of scenes and sub-plots. A great deal of it is not the book I originally wrote. Still, re-reading it, I'm very pleased."

In terms of the idea for the story, she said, "I wanted to do what they used to refer to as a 'bottle-show.' They'd run out of money for a planet set or any guest-stars, so they had to write a show that took place entirely on the ship, with just the main cast—those were some of my favorites. And, I wanted to write an episode that centered completely around Kirk, a character I've always immensely liked."

#54

A FLAG FULL OF STARS
Brad Ferguson

APRIL 1991   (241pp)

The second book in the *Lost Years* saga, the first being J.M. Dillard's hardcover, *The Lost Years*. A Klingon teacher named G'dath teaches young students on Earth. In his spare time, he tinkers with technology and stumbles on a major discovery that he knows the Klingons will kill to utilize. G'dath hopes he can convince Admiral Kirk to help keep the secret, plus keep him alive.

Brad commented, "*A Flag Full of Stars* was a noble experiment which went horribly awry and I've heard all sorts of stories about myself in connection with this book. I haven't heard a true one yet. J.M. Dillard, Irene Kress, and myself put together a proposal and outline and it was all okay. I had the middle book, which was a problem. Then, I had a back operation that went really bad and I couldn't sit in a chair for six months and that was really a problem.

Everything was late and everything was wrong. It wasn't horribly late; as I recall it was about four months late. The first guidance I got back said that I couldn't show Kirk in conflict. They told me to write a book where Kirk realizes his marriage is bad and he had taken a job in Starfleet that he didn't really want. He wants his ship back. But I can't show him conflicted. It made no sense . . . that heroes couldn't be conflicted. You know Kirk ends up doing the right thing and everyone knows this because they saw [*The Wrath of Khan*]."

Brad continued, "I had trouble on everything. I postulated a great quake because you have the line in *Star Trek IV* where Chekov doesn't know where Alameda is. They are in San Francisco and he should know where Alameda is, but he doesn't. Therefore, Alameda disappeared for some reason. Why did Alameda disappear? Because there was a big quake. I made a big deal about the quake and [it got taken out]. I had them in New York and [that got taken out]. So, I did the original draft and three rewrites. Then they finally took the book away and gave it to Jeanne Dillard. I was fine with that. Everybody says I was mad about that and I was not. I was sort of relieved." As a result, the book changed. "The nice Klingon got too nice and the ending got changed. I had a down ending. I killed the Klingon. He died very heroically and the Empire doesn't get his invention. It was really cool. I thought it gave the book meaning."

Brad continued, "Kevin Ryan told me it was still my book and sent me the manuscript to look at and it's all done. I can't change anything. It came the day before I got married. Years later, I was in New York and I went to the Pocket offices about something else. Kevin came from around the desk and we shook hands and apologized to each other. We got along and he bought *The Last Stand*."

5 5

RENEGADE
GENE DEWEESE

J U N E   1 9 9 1   (2 7 6 P P)

or almost a century, a colony from the planet Chrellkan IV has had peaceful relations with its mother world. When rebels take over the colony, the *Enterprise* is called in to settle the dispute and prevent a war. Spock and McCoy beam down, only to be taken as prisoners. When the ship's sensors in orbit register their deaths, Kirk must set his grief aside and handle the dispute without his two best friends and advisors.

Gene said, "Other than the fact that it was a sequel to the original series episode 'Court Martial,' I'm drawing a blank on its origins." He recalled reading a review that seemed to miss an essential story point. "The reviewer thought

one seeming discrepancy between what happened on the ship and what happened on the ground after a beam-down was just sloppy writing and poor copy editing. . . . But the discrepancy was not only intentional, [it was] an integral and vital part of the plot."

5 6

LEGACY
MICHAEL JAN FRIEDMAN

A U G U S T   1 9 9 1   (2 8 0 P P)

routine mission goes awry when Kirk and some members of the crew find themselves trapped underground as the result of an earthquake. Spock is attacked by a giant poisonous creature and fights for his life. When Scotty attempts a rescue of Kirk, the *Enterprise* gets called away by Starfleet Command to rescue a mining colony under attack. Unknown to them, the mysterious attacker of the colonists has a past with Spock and demands revenge.

Mike remembered, "There were two books that I was writing, one right after the other:

Legacy and *Faces of Fire.* I wanted to do a Pike book—I love 'Where No Man Has Gone Before,' but 'The Menagerie' has to be up there, too. I remember that was a Thanksgiving episode and it was stunning and the whole notion that there was a captain before Kirk? How cool is that? It was a great science fiction story aside from many of its *Star Trek* trappings; that out of this tragedy and mismanagement and this whole mess, good could actually come of it. What a wonderful irony that these people who started this zoo and this captive woman can actually do something good for Pike after he's had his accident, and how wonderful that Spock realizes this. So I wanted to include Pike in a book. I wanted to get some insight into him and what's happened to him since the episode. Spock was younger and more reckless; he was the new guy on the block and not the first officer, so he occupied a different place in the pecking order, so it was interesting to do that."

#57

THE RIFT

Peter David

NOVEMBER 1991   **(274pp)**

Captain Christopher Pike and his crew are still reeling from their experience with the Talosians. On the way to Vega for repairs and rest, they encounter a wormhole-like area of space. This rift to the planet Calligar opens every thirty-three years for a period of seventy-two hours. After Pike's encounter, time passes and now it is Captain Kirk's turn to negotiate with their race. Of course, things don't go smoothly. Will Kirk be forced to leave some of his crew behind for thirty-three years?

Peter commented, "I was kind of a late starter. When *Star Trek* was first on, I didn't see the first two seasons. I came across the third season one day while I was channel hopping. I was sitting there watching this guy with pointed ears take off these bizarre big glasses, and he starts screaming. There is this guy wearing a yellow shirt grabbing him and being shot through a distorted lens yelling, 'Spock!' I thought it looked stupid and I turned it off. Several months later, I was channel surfing and I stumbled onto *Star Trek* again. Exact same scene. I got into the James Blish novelizations because a friend of mine recommended them. I started reading them and I didn't realize they were novelizations, I thought they were really cool stories. As a result of the Blish books, I started watching the show in reruns. Then I read in *TV Guide* that there had been an actual gathering of *Trek* fans in New York City. A lot of people don't seem to realize that the article was a major turning point for fandom. It got word out to millions of fans that 'we are not alone.' I went to the next *Trek* convention in New York."

Peter continued, "I had been writing the *Star Trek* comic for DC up until the license expired. I was approached by Dave Stern, then an editor at Pocket, and he said to me, 'I really like your work on the *Trek* comics. Would you be interested in writing a *Star Trek* novel?' I said, 'I have some storylines I was never able to complete. This is perfect because I would love to be able to continue and finish storylines that I was doing in the original series comic.' Dave said, 'Here's the problem. I've got the original series novels scheduled for the next two and a half years. I'm fine with those. If you could write a *Next Generation* novel quickly, I could have that on the stands in six months.' I said, 'Did I say *Star Trek: The Original Series?* I meant to say, *Star Trek: The Next Generation.*' That lead to *Strike Zone.*"

Peter commented about *The Rift*: "They needed a *Trek* novel to fill the hole and they asked me if I would write it. I drafted up three different story outlines and Pocket submitted them without my name on them. I did them in three completely different styles. Roddenberry's office wound up reviewing three story outlines, all by me. Interestingly, I wrote one outline which I thought was fantastic, one that I thought was okay and one outline that was simply a conglomeration of old clichés from previous *Star Trek* episodes. That was the one they liked. Once I got into it, I actually thought I managed to make it a pretty decent book. The outline was the most unpromising thing I ever crafted because it was designed to make the other two look good. It wasn't designed to be the one they picked."

5 8

FACES OF FIRE
MICHAEL JAN FRIEDMAN

MARCH 1992   (307PP)

An abrasive Ambassador is being taken to Alpha Malurian Six to help settle a religious dispute that could escalate to a jihad. On the way, a routine stop to a terraforming colony for a supply run requires Spock to be left behind to help the colonists. One of the colonists, Carol

Marcus, had a history with the Captain, and she doesn't want anyone to know David is the result. When Klingons attack the colony, Spock must use his keen intellect to keep everyone safe until the *Enterprise* can initiate a rescue.

Mike remarked, *"Faces of Fire* pushed the envelope a little because Paramount was very reluctant to approve anything that dealt with Carol Marcus and that whole back story with Kirk and their son David. They would have preferred that we did our own independent stories in space. You know, open the door, go in, shut the door, go out, and it has nothing to do with the continuity. But more and more the only things that were satisfying me were the things that kind of cut into the continuity and *Faces of Fire* did that. It established that McCoy at least knew of that relationship and what came of it and it was fun."

THE DISINHERITED

PETER DAVID, MICHAEL JAN FRIEDMAN, AND ROBERT GREENBERGER

MAY 1992   (261PP)

Uhura finds herself on the *Lexington* under the command of Bob Wesley. A young ensign named Chekov questions his career choice. A mysterious alien fleet devastates planet after planet and the *Enterprise* is called to discover the motivations behind the attacks. When the ship gets damaged during a firefight, Captain Kirk must keep the crew and ship intact while looking for the secret to appeasing the attackers.

Robert remarked, "Carmen [Carter] really liked TNG, and pretty much only TNG, so when David Stern suggested [that the four of us collaborate on] an original series story, she declined. We three continued along, with Mike suggesting the Uhura on the *Lexington* storyline. Interestingly, I got the Chekov and Spock bits and, to be honest, neither were my favorites but I am very pleased with how they turned out. Again, this was an easy story to breakdown and outline. We wrote it and Mike polished it."

Mike commented, "Bob came up with the basic concept. We fleshed it out, we came up with events, certain number of events, divided them as equally as we could, wrote individually, came back, and I did a final polish and that was it. It was fun, too."

---

6 0

ICE TRAP

L. A. GRAF

JULY 1992 (277 PP)

A plague of madness on the planet Nordstral sends the Federation's flagship to investigate. While Kirk and McCoy search for a cure on the space station above, Uhura and Chekov head to the planet below to find a group of missing scientists. Communication with the *Enterprise* is severed, and both groups must struggle to survive as a massive set of earthquakes begins to radically change the landscape.

• • •

L.A. Graf consists of the writing team of Karen Rose Cercone and Julia Ecklar. Karen answered, "I only saw the original show once or twice when it first ran, but fell in love with it during reruns. I forced my family to watch it every day while we ate supper. Hopefully, they've forgiven me by now!"

Julia remembered, "I was too young to watch the show when it first ran on network TV. I became a fan while I was attending boarding school, when a group of students would watch it together. I began attending science fiction fan conventions during high school as well, and quickly realized that *Star Trek* was by far my favorite of the various SF universes. I began writing at a very young age; both my own fiction and fiction set in other universes like *Star Trek*. I really didn't know there was a market for that kind of writing until much later. When I first made the jump to being a full-time writer, however, I began to think about writing and selling novels. The real spark came after watching the second *Star Trek* movie. I had such a great time brainstorming with my friends about the Kobayashi Maru test—not only what Kirk must have done to pass it, but what all the other main characters would have done when they took it too. I came up with so many great ideas that night that I sat down and wrote the proposal that became my first *Star Trek* novel."

Karen responded, "I read a few *Star Trek* novels in graduate school, mostly because my roommate bought and read them. It wasn't until I joined a local writers group and met Julia that I considered writing *Star Trek* myself. I have to say that I probably would never have sent any of my ideas in if I hadn't been part of a group of writers working together on the pro-posal. That really boosted my confidence."

Karen and Julia both answered, "The name for our writers group was LAGRAF, which was short for 'Let's All Get Rich And Famous.' When several of the members joined up for our first proposal, we just turned the writers group name into our pen name. We had originally started out with four writers and we knew that was too many to put on a book cover, especially a *Star Trek* cover. *Ice Trap* was the first proposal we did, and originally had four writers associ-ated with it. It was a bit unwieldy, partly be-cause we were trying to figure out how to divide up the book into four parts and not make it feel choppy or schizophrenic. Based on some other fan writing that we were all doing, we decided that the best way to proceed was to assign each writer a point-of-view character from the crew, and have them write all the scenes that took place in that character's point of view. This turned out to be the smartest thing we could have done, because our individual writing styles became an asset instead of a liability. With different people writing different charac-ters, the 'style' of the writer simply became the 'voice' of the character for the reader. We tried to assign characters appropriately. Julia likes action and adventure scenes, so she got to write Kirk and Chekov (in his role as security chief). Karen Rose has a cooler, calmer writing style so she was originally supposed to do Spock but that proved to be very hard. It's much easier to make Spock seem brilliant when you're por-traying him through the eyes of another char-acter than from inside his point-of-view—kind of like Sherlock Holmes, if you think about it! So Karen Rose took on Uhura instead. The third writer, Melissa Crandall, was very good at

doing emotions so she became the voice of McCoy, and the fourth writer in the group, Wen Spencer, was set to do Scotty. Unfortu-nately, the editor completely cut out Scotty's plot line before we were given the contract. By that time we were committed to our 'one writer, one character' rule, so *Ice Trap* was writ-ten just by the three of us (Julia, Karen Rose, and Melissa)."

6 1

SANCTUARY

JOHN VORNHOLT

SEPTEMBER 1992   (273PP)

The crew of the *Enterprise* has been hunting for the crimi-nal Auk Rex for some time and the pursuit takes them to the mythological planet Sanctuary. When the pirate makes a break for the planet, Kirk, Spock, and McCoy follow in a shuttlecraft. The planet is a refuge for the per-secuted of the galaxy, and once landing on the surface, there is no way off. Can our three friends learn to live among the scoundrels, or will they be the first ever to successfully escape?

John commented, "I grew up as a teenager watching the original *Star Trek* on Friday nights, so I was hooked early on. As the years passed, I watched the movies and the animated shows, plus read a few books, but I was basically a casual fan until *The Next Generation* started. When TNG started, I had been writing a lot but mostly nonfiction and animated cartoons, plus a variety of Hollywood stuff. My then-agent, Ashley Grayson, said he was submitting some story ideas from several of his clients for a proposed series of TNG novels, and he would submit an idea for me if I could write it up in one night. I wasn't even a fiction prose writer when I submitted the outline for *Masks*, but David Hartwell liked it."

John continued, "I started writing *Masks* in January 1989, and it was in stores by that July. *Masks* was the first original TNG novel to make the then-short *New York Times* best seller list at number 11, and it was reprinted three times the first month. It started a string of TNG best sellers that made the *New York Times* list for about ten years straight, and it started a string of thirty or so *Trek* books for me."

John added, "When people ask me 'Where do you get your ideas?' I often cite this book, because it's based on a news story. When the U.S. invaded Panama to kick out Manuel Noriega, the dictator sought sanctuary for a few days in the Papal Nuncio. The U.S. respected the ancient tradition, but they surrounded the church and played loud rock music until they drove him out. Sanctuary sounds good until you realize you're trapped there forever, and I wondered if there could be a whole planet run on

that principle. Voilà, a *Trek* book! This *Trek* book is very classic—it stars the Big Three, Kirk, Spock, and McCoy in a prison-break story from a place that's a lot worse than it appears. Prison-break stories are essentially puzzle stories—how can you escape from a primitive planet that's designed to be escape-proof?"

---

6 2

DEATH COUNT
L. A. GRAF

NOVEMBER 1992   (276 PP)

Patrolling the Andorian/Orion border as a deterrent, the crew hopes to avoid the outbreak of war. A transporter accident is only the beginning as bodies start to pile up and Chekov starts to lose his grip with reality.

Karen and Julia remarked, "Right after we sent in *Ice Trap*, the editors at Pocket suddenly realized they didn't have enough manuscripts lined up for that year and put in a frantic call to all their writers to send in more proposals *fast*.

At the same time, Melissa had decided to leave western Pennsylvania and return to New York where her family lived. We ended up plotting two books simultaneously, and then splitting the writing up into the western PA crew (Karen Rose and Julia who wrote *Death Count*) and the New York crew (Melissa, who wrote *Shell Game*). *Death Count* was the book that taught us to write complete and full outlines for our novels! We wanted to do it fast because Pocket was so desperate, so we just jumped in and started writing. Bad idea! Halfway through, we realized we had a huge plot hole and had to throw away much of what we'd already written. This began the now-honored tradition of L.A. Graf turning in a completely different book than the proposal. Fortunately, our editor liked it better so we didn't get in any trouble for it, but it does make the cover copy editors nuts because we're always asking them to change the back copy at the last minute. If you look at *Death Count*, you'll see the back copy doesn't exactly match what happens inside . . . that's because the cover was done before the book was."

#63
SHELL GAME
MELISSA CRANDALL
FEBRUARY 1993   **(277PP)**

A Romulan space station crosses the Neutral Zone and the *Enterprise* rushes to investigate. The station appears totally without power, and when the crew beams over to the lifeless area, strange images that are almost ghost-like give them a case of fright. Soon the *Enterprise* loses power as well, and when it couldn't get any worse, a Romulan ship arrives and blames Kirk for treachery.

Karen and Julia remembered, "*Shell Game* was plotted mostly by Melissa with just some minor assistance from the rest of us. It was written completely by her and is under her name alone. She was living in New York by then."

Melissa remembered, "I came to *Trek* fandom rather late. I saw one or two episodes when the original *Trek* first aired and wasn't terribly impressed or turned-on by it. Later, as a teenager, when it 'came around again,' I'd developed an interest in science fiction and got mildly interested in the program. My friends and I would roleplay (before roleplaying was big) and write our own stories, but I was never a rabid fan—meaning that my life didn't end if I missed an episode. And, honestly, I watched it just for DeForrest Kelley. When *The Next Generation* raised its head, I watched a few episodes, was again not particularly caught up in it, but came to enjoy it and would catch it when I could. (And they hooked me hard with that original Borg two-parter.)"

She continued, "I wanted to make money as a writer, wanted to get my work out there, and here was an opportunity to do it. It had less to do with *Trek*, per se, than it had to do with me wanting to work as a writer. It was a real learning experience, but I had a great, wonderfully supportive editor and he helped this 'newbie' along."

When asked about her part of the L.A. Graf writing team, Melissa responded, "I co-wrote *Ice Trap* as part of L.A. Graf. There were a number of reasons why I stopped writing with them, the chief one being that I moved away from the area in which we all were living (and this was before the days of lovely accessible e-mail). I was eager to pursue other things and the other members were focused on *Trek*, so it all worked out. No animosity, if that's what you were wondering."

#64
THE STARSHIP TRAP
MEL GILDEN

APRIL 1993   (242PP)

The Klingons attack the *Enterprise* in response to Federation assaults on Klingon vessels. Escaping with a promise of discovering the truth, Kirk and crew head to a secret rendezvous with a respected scientist. At the meeting with Federation personnel, the truth reveals itself. It seems that the Klingons are not the only race to have ships vanish, and it's up to the *Enterprise* to uncover the truth.

Mel replied, "I'm old enough to have been a fan right from the beginning. I was present for 'Nancy the Salt Monster' in September of 1966. I'd never seen a ship like the *Enterprise* before, so wasn't sure that I liked it. But I became more and more hooked as the season went on. My college notes are covered with my drawings of the *Enterprise*. But I am also old enough to remember *Space Patrol*, *Tom Corbett*, *Captain Video*, and *Rocky Jones*. *Star Trek* was just one more in a long line of space shows that I was a fan of. Though I admit, *Star Trek* does seem to have given me an extreme case of fanboy worship. Wanting to tell a story about characters you love is not unusual—that's the primary force behind fan fiction, after all. Each character has a different cadence and style to his/her dialog, and it's fun to reproduce it on paper. Besides, a novel has no special effects budget. You can do things in a novel you could never do on TV or even in a feature film. I never wrote for the *Trek* fanzines, but when I saw original *Star Trek* novels appear in bookstores, I began to think about writing one myself. Of course, until I actually sat down to write a novel of any kind I was intimidated by the novel form. How could any one person write all those words? But by the time *The Next Generation* came around, I had been through the novel-writing experience a few times and knew I could produce a professional *Trek* novel. I pitched an idea to Dave Stern, the editor of the moment, and the rest is history."

When asked about *The Starship Trap*, Mel answered, "I admit that my favorite *Trek* has always been the original, so writing the *The Starship Trap* was a real pleasure. The central idea, the aleph, came from a short story written by South American writer Jorge Luis Borges. The thought of being able to see all of the universe in a point fascinated me. But of course, more needed to be done with the idea if it was to be central to an adventure story. Originally, Conrad Franklin Kent was supposed to be the head of the biggest news gathering organization in the Federation. But I was told that because we had never seen any news gathering organization on TV or the movies, I had to make him something else. Also, I created an icon to flash at the bottom of the main viewscreen when the universal translator was in use. Each of these things seems a logical outgrowth of the *Trek* universe, but Paramount made me take them out. Generally, though, both novel experiences were pleasant ones. Some years ago I heard Norman Spinard say that "The Doomsday Machine" was the *Star Trek* version of *Moby Dick*—a story about a man obsessed with a force of nature that had hurt him in some way. (Now that I think about it, the episode 'Obsession' has a similar thought at its center.) Anyway, after thinking about what Norman had said I decided to write the *Star Trek* version of *20,000 Leagues Under the Sea. The Starship Trap* is the result. Clue: The villain of the piece is Professor Omen. Try reading his name backwards. Hah!"

#65

WINDOWS ON A LOST WORLD

V. E. MITCHELL

JUNE 1993   (275PP)

Exploring the ancient ruins of a civilization proves costly to the crew of the *Enterprise*. Chekov gets teamed with a woman he can't stand, and during the investigation of a strange artifact that looks like a window, both of them fall through it and vanish. While Kirk tries to solve the mystery, he accidentally falls into the portal as well and disappears. When Spock orders scans of the planet, the sensors cannot find any human life. But they have now picked up some strange crab-like creatures.

Vicki remarked, "I sent in half a dozen proposals, and *Windows on a Lost World* was the one selected. The idea started from the combination of three different elements. First was the idea of exploring the artifacts of a very ancient and evil race of beings. Second, there was the image of the alien 'windows' that transformed people into the shape of their creators. Third was the idea of doing something really nasty to Captain Kirk, so that for most of the book he was trying to cope with inhabiting a truly alien body. By the way, the geography of parts of the book are an expanded version of the Columbia River Gorge, and the planet's vegetation is much like the dryland scrub in central Washington and Oregon. I don't remember any real problems with the writing process. When it came time to edit the book, Kevin was swamped with other projects and hired Shawna McCarthy to work on my book. She made a number of excellent suggestions, which improved the final book. The publishing end went very smoothly."

#66

FROM THE DEPTHS

VICTOR MILAN

AUGUST 1993   (280PP)

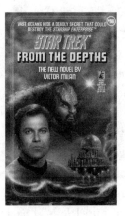

Humans who have genetically altered themselves are living in fragile peace with the natives of the water planet Okeanos. When the

Klingons get involved, the *Enterprise* rushes to settle the now escalating dispute. As the crew enjoys a shore leave, they don't realize that sabotage lurks. And the ambassador brought in to restore the peace decides on a bold plan.

Victor remembered, "I was a fan almost from the outset. Although even today, there are a few episodes I've never seen. I have to add that I'm a classic *Star Trek* fan. I'm not much on later stuff—even the movies allegedly based on the original series, although a couple of them are pretty good. As goofy as some of the original episodes were, I think it had an energy and a conviction not present in subsequent efforts."

After Victor became a writer, it only seemed logical for him to try writing a *Trek* novel. "Even though I got to be fairly cynical about *Trek*, I never lost my little-kid love of it. Fond as I am of the series, I'm a lot less enamored of the totalitarian state it's set in. The Federation is in essence a military regime—no matter what kind of gymnastics the show's producers have put themselves through to deny it. So I wanted to do a *Star Trek* story which would be true to the feel and spirit of the original series, and also more freedom-friendly. So at the end Kirk and the crew and the Discordians of Eris agree to disagree. Also I wanted to see if I could get (and keep) nudity in a *Star Trek* book. And I did. Very first page."

In terms of the writing of the book, Victor reflected, "First, I sold a *Star Trek* proposal to Pocket in the mid-1980s. The basic plot was that reactionary elements within the Federation military conspired with the Romulans to spark an interstellar war. Our heroes and the *Enterprise* of course had to thwart this scheme. Anyway, Pocket accepted it and Paramount

okayed it. Then, before a contract got issued, the editor changed. And the new editor killed it. Oh, well. In the early 90s, possibly goaded by my friend Melinda Snodgrass who had worked on *The Next Generation*, I tried again. This time it happened."

#67

THE GREAT STARSHIP RACE
Diane Carey

October 1993   **(305pp)**

An alien race called the Rey prepares to join the Federation. Discovering the galaxy has many alien races, the new inductees propose a celebration and a race. With ships representing the entire galaxy, the event promises to be historic. The *Enterprise* arrives to participate and so does a Romulan vessel, even though its appearance technically represents an act of war. When the race begins, so does the treachery.

Another title from Diane that sprouted from her sailing exploits. She said, "I was in Fell's Point Harbor in Baltimore, just having finished the Great Chesapeake Bay Schooner Race. I called the then-editor at Pocket and said, 'Hey, how about *The Great Starship Race?*' He said, 'Fine, I'll write up the contract.' I then called my husband and said, 'Guess what, we're doing *The Great Starship Race.*' Greg said, 'Oh, really. And is there a plot?' 'Nope, just a title.' Greg then had to concoct a plot, because, of course, a speed race in space makes no sense. The fastest ship wins, and that's it, because there's no trick and no resistance. Greg cooked up an idea for a relay race, and just for fun we threw in the Romulans."

Diane had a confession to make. "What fans don't know is that the first manuscript for this book was terrible. I was exhausted, the plot was a mess, there was no focus—you name it; it was rotten. The editor from Pocket called to have a long, drawn-out argument, and instead of doing that, I told him, 'What's to talk about? When you're right, you're right. We'll rewrite it.' There was silence on the other end of the phone, until he gulped a couple of times and said, 'I've never had an editorial call like this.' So we rewrote the book in a month and turned out one of the best works we've ever done. It remains one of my favorites."

#68

FIRESTORM
L. A. GRAF

JANUARY 1994   (273PP)

Seems that Captain Kirk always needs to negotiate for peace. The Elasian Dohlman claims the right to mine dilithium from the planet Rakatan. Kirk had a run-in with the previous Dohlman in the episode, "Elaan of Troyius." Regarded as a Dohlman herself, Uhura leads a landing party to help with the dispute. Can Uhura stop a war before a volcano explodes and destroys the entire settlement?

Julia and Karen remarked, "*Firestorm* was sparked, as several of our books have been, by Karen Rose's love of geology. She always wants to have a setting where she can indulge her geological side with exciting events like tsunamis, eruptions, floods, and so on. At the same time, Julia was doing some other writing that involved primitive tribes so we tried to combine these interests into one book. We learned our lesson and outlined well, and the book was written fairly painlessly. One side note is that this was the first book where Karen Rose began using the names of her geoscience students (with their permission) for some of the science characters. That's a tradition that we've continued ever since."

#69

THE PATRIAN TRANSGRESSION
Simon Hawke

APRIL 1994   (278PP)

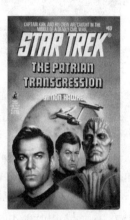

The world of Patria seeks Federation membership, so the *Enterprise* arrives to investigate their application. Rebel attacks with the culprits using Klingon disrupters have started to cause panic. Teaming up with a local police officer, Kirk and Spock must stop the terrorists from causing further damage. Unknown to the Starfleet officers, the police force uses telepathic powers to apprehend criminals and even a harsh thought can be punishable by death.

· · ·

Attempts to contact the author for an interview were unsuccessful.

#70

TRAITOR WINDS
L. A. Graf

JUNE 1994   (275PP)

The third book in the *Lost Years* saga. Chekov is taking classes in security, and Sulu is a test pilot for experimental shuttles. The former physician on the *Enterprise*, Dr. Piper, asks Chekov for help and regrets his decision when he gets thrown into a major conspiracy. Now Dr. Piper is dead and Chekov is on the run. Can Admiral Kirk prove his former crewman's innocence?

Karen and Julia answered, "We had so much fun writing the minor characters (Sulu, Chekov, and Uhura) that we wanted to have a chance to see more of their backgrounds and explore their histories. The *Lost Years* books that had come out previous to *Traitor Winds* had really focused on the main characters. But clearly, things had happened in other characters' lives, especially Chekov who goes from navigator to security chief during that break. So we sat down and figured out how that must have happened, and made a book out of it. (Our original working title was *What Chekov, Sulu, and Uhura did on Their Summer Vacation.*) We also tried to 'connect' some other mismatched plot lines from before and after the lost years (for example, how the Klingons ended up with the Romulans' cloaking technology!). Again, we had learned to outline by then and the book went together well."

---

7 1

CROSSROAD
BARBARA HAMBLY

SEPTEMBER 1994   (274PP)

Kirk and company discover a battered *Constitution*-class starship that, according to Starfleet records, doesn't exist. The crew of the *Nautilus* claim to be refugees from the future, where an evil Consilium has taken control of the Federation. When another starship arrives and de-

mands the *Nautilus* crew, Kirk must decide whom to trust. He must tread carefully; otherwise he might upset the timeline. Unknown to our favorite captain, one of his crew is destined to start the Consilium.

The story is dear to Barbara's heart. She said, "the guest cast—the crew of the *Nautilus* in the story—date back to those first *Trek* tales I wrote with my high school friends. It's still one of my absolute favorites, not only of my *Trek* stories, but of any of my books."

Barbara can't imagine ever writing another *Star Trek* novel. "I've never cared for the other *Trek* shows, or even the films, much. When I think of *Star Trek*, I think of those first two years—I even quit watching the show in its third season, when the writing in so many of the episodes was so poor. Whatever that quality was that drew me, I never encountered it in the little bit of the follow-on works I saw. I wrote those three books as a way of recapturing for myself what it was like, why it was so vital to me that those typed aerograms with synopses of 'City on the Edge of Forever' and 'Operation Annihilate' reached me in New South Wales in the spring of 1967."

Barbara continues to write in several genres. Now a widow, she shares a house in Los Angeles with several small carnivores.

#72

THE BETTER MAN

HOWARD WEINSTEIN

DECEMBER 1994   (268PP)

A mission to renegotiate a treaty proves to be a personal hell for McCoy. First, the Ambassador assigned to the mission used to be a great friend, but a falling out has generated nothing but hatred. Second, something happened on the planet that the doctor refuses to discuss, even with Kirk. Meanwhile, on the planet Empyrea, the council president prepares to force the Federation to leave the area.

When asked about the seed for the story, Howard said, "This one sprouted from a personal seed—my friendships with two pals I've known since I was a kid, both of whom I've long admired and who've inspired me to try to be better than I actually am in some key personal ways. I was also thinking about the theoretical perfectibility of human nature. At our core, people haven't changed much since modern humans first evolved. We still do too many of the same stupid, primitive things for the same stupid, primitive reasons. I find this very disappointing."

Elaborating further, Howard said, "Ever since I first started watching *Star Trek*, I've been inspired by the way the characters make a conscious effort to rise above their human frailties. It's easy to be who we are, ugliness and all . . . it's much harder to be *better*."

Howard also wanted to feature McCoy as the main protagonist, since "the older I get, the more I become like him. He's probably my all-time favorite *Trek* character because he embodies human frailty, he's exquisitely aware of those foibles, he's perpetually conflicted between cynicism and romanticism, yet he plows existentially on, as if to say 'What the hell other choice do I have?' "

#73

RECOVERY

J. M. DILLARD

MARCH 1995   (277PP)

 Admiral Kirk despises his desk job and demands the chance to captain a vessel again. Instead, he is ordered to oversee the testing of an automated medical ship, the *Recovery*. Capable of rescuing large populations without putting any Starfleet personnel in harm's way, the future looks bright for this new generation of vessel. The test-run occurs near the Romulan and Tholian border with Dr. McCoy aboard the prototype. As the test begins, Kirk can't help but remember what happened with M-5 years ago.

According to Jeanne, this fourth book in *The Lost Years* saga came about as follows. "Then-editor, Dave Stern, wanted another book in the series—one featuring Kirk. I asked if I could include McCoy, because I loved writing from the doctor's point of view, and Dave gave me the go-ahead."

#74

THE FEARFUL SUMMONS
DENNY MARTIN FLYNN

JULY 1995 (273PP)

fter the events in *Star Trek VI: The Undiscovered Country*, several members of Captain Sulu's crew, including Sulu himself, are kidnapped by a band of thugs demanding proper payment for their release. Captain Kirk, now enjoying retirement and relations with a young cadet, decides to ignore Starfleet and rescue Sulu.

Denny Flinn had never seen the original series when he was asked by Nicholas Meyer to cowrite *Star Trek VI* with him. He was Meyer's assistant, and with his boss working on a film in Europe, plus a growing writing career, Meyer trusted him enough to write the screenplay. Denny remarked, "I had to sit and screen all five previous films in two days in order to catch up!"

Denny continued, "The first draft of *Star Trek VI: The Undiscovered Country* opened with a sequence that came to be called 'The Round-Up.' When the film was announced, there were jokes in the media about the age of the cast—David Letterman said, 'What are they going to call it? *The Search for Geritol?*'—and I thought we should play them at their real ages, by seeing them all in retirement. Then when Kirk got the assignment—because the Klingons insisted only their old enemy could be trusted—he rounded up his old crew, all of who were anxious to get back into space. In fact, it was very popular, but would have cost an additional 10 or 20 million dollars to shoot, which just wasn't in the budget. Although we stuck with it for a long time, finally it just had to go, and in pre-production Nick—now back from Europe—wrote the conference room scene to replace the whole 'round-up.' I was eventually asked to write the novel version of [the movie], but declined. Then, after the film came out, it occurred to me to use 'The

Round-Up' in novel form, so I came up with another plot that began that way, pitched it to the Pocket Books people, and the rest is history."

The Fearful Summons—so named because it's a sequel to *The Undiscovered Country* and both titles are from *Hamlet*—thus begins with the "out-of-retirement" sequence that was cut from the script of *Star Trek VI*. Denny said, "The writing and publishing of *Fearful Summons* was pretty straightforward. After I wrote the first draft, I got a really good and useful set of notes from the Pocket Books editor."

7 5

FIRST FRONTIER
DIANE CAREY AND DR. JAMES I. KIRKLAND

AUGUST 1995   (383PP)

An experiment goes awry and the *Enterprise* finds itself very far away from home. When a Klingon vessel approaches and the captain claims to have never heard of the Federation or the human race, Kirk heads to Earth for answers. The planet appears jungle-like and huge animals roam the surface. Somehow, the asteroid that wiped out the dinosaurs never struck. Can Spock figure out how far back in the past to travel to guarantee a successful collision?

"My daughter suggested the title *Lost Frontier*, which I still think is better. I finally told Pocket that I didn't want to do anymore "F" books because the fans were confusing my books: *Final Frontier, Flashback, First Strike, First Frontier*—enough, already," Diane said.

A bit of a departure for Diane, she said, "This book was almost entirely real science, written with the advisor Dr. James Kirkland, one of the world's foremost paleontologists. I arranged for Jim Kirk to be sick almost all the way through the book. If they hadn't been 65 million years back in time, they could've cured him easily, but being without his future tech, he stood the chance of dying and leaving his crew in this hostile environment without him to lead them. This book also gave me a prime opportunity: to describe the strike of the asteroid that killed off the dinosaurs. Every writer's dream—and I took it very seriously."

#76

THE CAPTAIN'S DAUGHTER

PETER DAVID

DECEMBER 1995   (278PP)

On a seemingly routine mission, Captain Harriman is forced to kill Demora Sulu, daughter of *Excelsior* Captain Hikaru Sulu. With the planet under strict quarantine, Sulu defies orders and risks his career to find answers to his daughter's mysterious death. Interspersed throughout the novel is the story of the Sulu family.

Peter remembered, "I think the idea of doing a story about Demora came from editor Kevin Ryan. I don't remember pitching a story to them about Sulu's daughter. In terms of constructing the story, it keyed off of Kirk's question that was voiced quite correctly in *Star Trek Generations*, which was, 'When did Sulu have time to have a daughter?' It was almost a challenge to find a reasonable timeline for Demora to have been conceived and been raised by Sulu. That was almost an exercise in putting a

puzzle together, figuring out where Demora was during key points in Sulu's life and what was going on with her at those particular times."

Peter continued, "The original title of the book was *Demora*. Apparently, the *Star Trek* marketing people hated that title. Why, I have absolutely no idea. I may have come up with *Captain's Daughter* for the title, but I absolutely hated it. I also wasn't too wild about the cover art. I thought it was not a good picture of George Takei because they made him look like a horse. Silly me, if the book is called *Captain's Daughter*, I would like to have seen the captain's daughter on the cover! I thought the story was good."

Years after this novel came out, there was an attempt in some circles of fandom to rally support for more Captain Sulu adventures, both on screen and in print. John Ordover decided to have the fans prove that another Sulu novel would be popular. "I said, 'If you can get me a thousand letters by this date, we'll do another Captain Sulu.' And then we only got 800. Why did I do that? Because everyone was telling me how much they wanted a Captain Sulu novel but when we did one, by our most popular writer, Peter David, it did not do very well. You can argue that there were all sorts of reasons, that it wasn't clearly a Captain Sulu novel, that it was this, it was that, the title was wrong. You can give any sort of excuses but the bottom line is our most popular author did a Captain Sulu novel and it didn't sell very well. From which I have to conclude there's a lot of noise being made by a small number of Captain Sulu fans. I was willing to have my mind changed on that. Giving the fans a month, if the demand really exists, you should easily be able to get a thousand letters to me. Not only did we not get the thousand, but a lot of them had taken a petition form to their science fiction club, or something, and had everyone sign it and put it in an envelope. Then when we got a whole stack of envelopes, pretty much on the same day, with the same stamp, the same envelope, and the same exact letter inside—it's just signed differently—we stopped to think: How many people did this really represent and how many people would actually buy it as opposed to just being willing to sign it for a friend? But the bottom line is we didn't make the thousand."

That was not, however, the last word on Captain Sulu fiction. Editor Marco Palmieri noted, "I was already planning a new *Excelsior* novel when all this was going on; I didn't care about how many letters John got. It just seemed silly to let something like that drive an editorial decision. When I developed *The Lost Era* series for 2003, an *Excelsior* novel, *The Sundered*, was the first novel in the set. It sold quite well, and readers can expect still another Captain Sulu novel down the road."

7 7

TWILIGHT'S END
JERRY OLTION

JANUARY 1996   (272PP)

The planet Rimillia will soon be dead. Environmentally unstable, the inhabitants have a bold plan to use gigantic impulse engines to start the planet rotating. Sabotage forces the end of the experiment and the *Enterprise* arrives to help. Scotty must repair the damage if the planet will survive. Meanwhile, Doctor McCoy and Sulu work on bioengineering fauna and Kirk must rescue a kidnapped scientist. The saboteurs see an opportunity and proceed to try to blow up the ship!

Jerry had been writing science fiction stories since he was around five years old. He said, "When *Star Trek* came on, I immediately fell in love with the characters, and I wrote a *Trek* story of my own. I never expected to sell it (and never have), but I wrote it just for fun. Then, years later, when I heard that John Ordover was looking for writers for original series books, I jumped at the chance. I spammed him with outlines until he cried Uncle and gave me the go-ahead for one."

Regarding the story, Jerry said, "It was the collision of two ideas. My optometrist and I like to brainstorm, and about a year beforehand we had a conversation about what life would be like on a tidally-locked planet. Then when I decided to try writing a *Star Trek* book, I was casting about for good ideas that would fit well in the *Trek* universe, and I ran across that one in my notebook. I figured it would make a great engineering challenge for Scotty: to set an entire planet spinning again. John Ordover agreed, and he turned me loose on the novel with very little modification to my original outline. There were some changes required after I finished the manuscript, the most notable being that I had Captain Kirk escape from captivity by getting his captors drunk using alcohol that he and a crewmember distilled from materials on hand, but John didn't like that, so he wanted Kirk to make a bomb out of the alcohol. This was only a couple of months after the Oklahoma City bombing, so I thought the image of Kirk as a bomb-maker was a really bad idea. We compromised on a Molotov cocktail, but I still like my original scene better."

7 8

THE RINGS OF TAUTEE

DEAN WESLEY SMITH AND KRISTINE KATHRYN RUSCH

MAY 1996 (242PP)

A scientist from the Tautee System has made a dreadful mistake. Testing a new energy source on an uninhabited moon, the result of the experiment annihilates the site and the entire surface. Over time, the entire system of nine planets experiences the shock wave from the rift and disintegrates. When the *Enterprise* and the *Farragut* investigate a distress call, they are horrified to discover pockets of survivors scattered throughout the damaged region. The intensity of the waves continues to increase and will soon reach another populated planet. Can Kirk rescue the survivors and close the rift without breaking the Prime Directive?

Kristine refers all questions to Dean, so he responded, "I used to go home from high school in the 60s on Friday and watch *Star Trek*. Not sure if any of us called ourselves fans back then, but I was one. Since I am a professional fiction writer, and I love *Trek*, it just seemed like a natural connection. I felt lucky to get involved back when the novel program was making a change, and got to do an early book in DS9 under the pseudnym Sandy Schofield, then got to do the first original *Voyager*, first original *Enterprise*, and first *S.C.E.* I consider myself lucky to get to write in a universe I love. What fan wouldn't?"

When asked about this novel, Dean replied, "Not a clue how that came out. Really bad memory."

---

7 9

FIRST STRIKE

(INVASION, BOOK ONE; SEE SECTION 12: MINISERIES)

---

8 0

THE JOY MACHINE

JAMES GUNN AND THEODORE STURGEON

SEPTEMBER 1996 (278 PP)

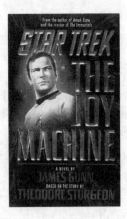

habitants have isolated themselves and refuse any visitors. Two Federation agents sent to investigate never returned. When the *Enterprise* arrives, Kirk beams down to a strange world where everyone works in a hypnotic manner striving for the next payday. Payday enables one to experience total ecstasy from the joy machine. How can Kirk convince the computer that everyone does not want perfect happiness?

James remarked, "Basically, I've been an SF writer since 1948 and have followed *Star Trek* and its various incarnations but have never been a fan. About ten years ago, John Ordover, then the *Star Trek* editor at Pocket and a former student of mine, was a guest at the Writers Workshop in Science Fiction, which I conduct at the University of Kansas. This year he said he had discovered an outline by Ted Sturgeon (famous for two *Star Trek* episodes ['Shore Leave' and 'Amok Time']) for a *Star Trek* episode that had never been turned into a script. It was called 'The Joy Machine' and John asked if I would be willing to turn it into a novel. To honor Ted (who had been a longtime guest writer at the Intensive English Institute on the Teaching of Science Fiction—which I conduct each summer—until his death) and because the Sturgeon heirs would get a share of the royalties, I agreed. *The Joy Machine* is the result. I don't plan to do any more, since I'm busy with my own writing."

The planet Timshel was once the vacation destination of choice. For some reason, the in-

8 1

MUDD IN YOUR EYE

JERRY OLTION

JANUARY 1997 (280PP)

The planets of Prastor and Distrel have been battling each other for centuries. Peace efforts have always failed, so when they declare a truce, the *Enterprise* is called to find out how the two sides settled their differences. When Kirk arrives on the planet, he is horrified to discover the architect of the peace is none other than Harry Mudd. Kirk must tread carefully, otherwise the war could start again, and the *Enterprise* could be caught in the crossfire.

Jerry has fond memories of this title. He said, "After *Twilight's End*, John Ordover invited me to send him an outline for another book. I asked him if there was anything in particular about the original series that he would like to see a book about, and after a little thought he said that he usually told people *not* to write about Harry Mudd, because so many of the proposals for Mudd books were so bad, but he

liked my sense of humor, so he invited me to try a Harry Mudd outline. I felt very flattered by his confidence in me, and excited to be able to write about one of my favorite characters. John liked what I proposed and gave me the go-ahead. Maybe time has just dulled my memory of the revision process, but I don't remember any revision requests at all for this one. It was a joy to write, and I'm still insanely proud of that book."

8 2

MIND MELD

JOHN VORNHOLT

JUNE 1997 (274PP)

Spock receives word from his father that his niece, Teska, will be key to the reunification effort between Vulcan and Romulus. The plan involves her bonding for later marriage with a Romulan boy. Raised on Earth, Teska strives to learn her true heritage and agrees to the plan. The *Enterprise* receives the assignment to escort her and along the way she obtains an image of a murder from a reluctant mind meld.

Spock must now save his niece from certain death as they watch the *Enterprise* head off to another assignment.

"I've written mostly *The Next Generation* novels; but I grew up watching the original series, so my three classic *Trek* books are special favorites of mine. This one stars Spock and his Vulcan niece, Teska, who is gifted at the mind-meld at a very young age. Teska is a stand-in for my daughter Sarah, who was her age when I wrote this book. Trust me, Sarah has pointed ears and can seem quite unearthly at times. Through a mind-meld with a dying victim, Teska is the only witness to a murder, and Spock must protect her from Rigelian criminals. Rigelians were fun to write. . . . I imagined them to be suave criminals, sensual healers, numerologists, and other colorful folk who live on an eclectic planet."

#83

HEART OF THE SUN
PAMELA SARGENT AND GEORGE ZEBROWSKI

NOVEMBER 1997   (245PP)

The *Enterprise* arrives on Tyrtaeus II to install a new library database, replacing the existing damaged one. The inhabitants blame Federation sloppiness for their lifehood being destroyed. While the crew tries to show the inhabitants the truth, a strange vessel shows up on sensors and appears to be heading directly toward the sun. To avoid further problems, the *Enterprise* heads to the star to seek answers.

George and Pam are married and have been writing together for a long time. George reflected on his time as a fan. "We saw the original series in the 1960s, and realized that here was visual science fiction taken from the traditions of its master writers. *Star Trek* derives from A. E. van Vogt's *The Voyage of the Space Beagle*, Eric Frank Russell's *Men, Martians, and Machines*, and from the 1956 movie, *Forbidden Planet*, by Roddenberry's own admission. Seeing this kind of recognition of science fiction in the original series made us fans first, discerning, even critical viewers later. Too few readers today realize that the vast bulk of SF's history is as print—from 1818 to the present—period and everything visual percolates, fairly and unfairly from print, except the skills of the filmmakers."

Pamela commented, "If you're young, and have grown up in a world saturated with science fiction movies, TV, and games, it may be hard to understand how downright original and innovative *Star Trek*—the original series, anyway—was when it first aired. There was simply nothing else like it. It wasn't just science fiction fans who watched it; I knew a number of people, including members of my family, who knew nothing about science fiction but watched this program anyway. On top of that, it actually managed to treat science fiction ideas with some care, attention, and intelligence. Yes, there were the more absurd episodes, which will remain nameless, but there were also some terrific ones, a few of them written by writers like Harlan Ellison and Norman Spinrad who are masters of print SF. That does make a difference."

George talked about the inspiration for writing. "The idea for the novels came from what we call the 'unfinished business' that came to mind in watching the original and new series, and discussing, just for the fun of it, as we pursued our own writing, what might have been, what had been neglected. There was never a jump from watching to writing *Star Trek* novels. We had always known that SF existed in various forms, and we had been writing it for over two decades. We never concocted a novel scenario; we always started with something we would have liked to see developed further. And when the invitation to try our hand came, we had what we needed. *Heart of the Sun* emerged from our desire to have Kirk and company face a genuine unknown. The ideas do in fact derive somewhat from my own novel *Stranger Suns* and also from Arthur C. Clarke's *Rendezvous with Rama*. The writing went well, but the editing was problematic, with the loss of who-is-speaking cues in the dialogue."

Pam added, "I suppose I should add here that in *Heart of the Sun*, as well as in *A Fury Scorned*, we had the fun of casting a few friends and family members as minor characters—as members of the *Enterprise* crew, or in walk-on parts."

#84

ASSIGNMENT: ETERNITY

GREG COX

JANUARY 1998   **(278PP)**

An agent in Romulan space appears to be captured and killed, so Gary Seven (from the episode "Assignment: Earth") must travel into the future to save his comrade. Arriving on the *Enterprise*, Captain Kirk is obviously not happy to see him, or his cat Isis and his partner, Roberta Lincoln. When Seven forces the ship into Romulan territory, negating a rescue mission, Kirk throws him into the brig. Can Seven be trusted? The truth is, if he does not succeed in his mission, the future timeline of the *Enterprise* crew faces serious jeopardy and the death of a beloved crewmember.

Greg remarked, "As a lifelong Trekkie, I suspect the idea of writing a *Trek* novel was always at the back of my mind, but I started out writing other things. I sold a handful of short stories to magazines like *Amazing Stories, Fantasy Book, Mike Shayne Mystery Magazine,* and so on. My first two published books were a nonfiction history of vampire fiction (now sadly out of print) and a young adult pirate novel (ditto). Later on, I cowrote a couple of *Batman* stories with John Gregory Betancourt, which marked my first tentative steps into the whole world of licensed media tie-ins. By that time, I was working at Tor Books, alongside another young assistant editor named John Ordover, who encouraged me to submit a *Star Trek* proposal to Kevin Ryan, who was then in charge of Pocket's *Star Trek* program. Believe it or not, my very first submission to Pocket was an outline for a TOS novel titled *Assignment: Eternity,* which featured the return of Gary Seven and Roberta Lincoln. Aside from the title, the proposal bore little resemblance to my later novel of the same name. (As I recall, it took place on an alien college campus and involved a superweapon designed to kill energy beings. Seven needed to sabotage the project in order to preserve the Organian Peace Treaty. . . .) Any-

way, for various reasons, Kevin passed on the project."

Greg continued, "Three books later, I finally got my chance to bring back Seven, Roberta, and Isis. Why was I so determined to bring them back? Well, the original TV episode, 'Assignment: Earth,' is so open-ended that it just seemed to lend itself to sequels." Not coincidentally, the episode was in fact the backdoor pilot for a possible *Star Trek* spinoff. "I like to think of my Gary Seven novels as coming from a parallel universe in which the *Assignment: Earth* TV series, starring Robert Lansing and Teri Garr, ran for multiple seasons. Also, I have a real nostalgic fondness for all that sixties spy stuff, and Seven and Roberta are pretty much the *Trek* equivalents of *The Man from U.N.C.L.E.* and *The Avengers* (with a good chunk of *The Day the Earth Stood Still* thrown in). Despite my enthusiasm, however, this book went through many mutations on its way to publication. At one point, it was going to be a Picard/Gary Seven novel, but I never came up with an outline that Ordover and I both liked. (The idea was to pit Picard, the staunch defender of the Prime Directive, against Seven, the time-traveling meddler.) Then we played around with the notion of a Kirk/Q novel, but that ended up going nowhere. Finally, I replaced Q with Gary Seven in the latter proposal and *that's* the book that finally got approved! Even then, there were changes. Originally, the bad guys were going to be a bunch of well-intentioned Romulan dissidents, but about halfway through the first draft, I realized this just wasn't working. Although I liked the idea of a book with no actual villains, having three sets of good guys (Kirk, Gary Seven, and dissidents) working in opposition to each other just wasn't generating enough dramatic tension, so I ultimately broke down and turned my good-guy Romulans into a particularly nasty branch of the Tal Shiar. (This is probably a good point to mention that my girlfriend, Karen Palinko, served as the first reader on *The Black Shore*, *The Q Continuum Trilogy*, and *Assignment: Eternity*, providing me with valuable and much-needed input on how the books were progressing. It was Karen who convinced me that, with two heroes already, in the form of Kirk and Gary Seven, I needed an actual villain as well.) Finally, *Assignment: Eternity* contains one of my most embarrassing errors: an eight-foot-long alien tiger that somehow ended up described as eight *meters* long in the finished book. As numerous readers have pointed out to me, that's one big pussycat!"

8 5

REPUBLIC
(MY BROTHER'S KEEPER, Book One)
MICHAEL JAN FRIEDMAN

JANUARY 1999 (267PP)

In the episode, "Where No Man Has Gone Before," Captain Kirk is forced to kill his best friend, Gary Mitchell. Ever wonder about their friendship and adventures prior to that story? Well, wonder no more. In the first of three books, Kirk reminisces about his days as a teacher at the Academy and one of his arrogant students, Gary. Their first confrontation ended up with them coming to blows. Forced to work together on the *U.S.S. Republic*, their budding friendship is put to the test by a demanding captain and a simple mission becomes a rescue operation.

#86

CONSTITUTION
(MY BROTHER'S KEEPER, Book Two)
MICHAEL JAN FRIEDMAN

JANUARY 1999   **(267PP)**

Heading back to Earth to attend Gary's memorial service, Jim Kirk reflects on his time aboard the *U.S.S. Constitution*, when he was the second officer and Mitchell was the chief navigator. Kirk had recently experienced the tragedy aboard his previous vessel, which killed half of the crew. Still finding it difficult to interact with people, his relationship with Gary becomes strained. Forced to assume command when the captain and first officer are stranded on a planet while an alien vessel attacks the ship, his friendship and determination are put to the test.

#87

ENTERPRISE
(MY BROTHER'S KEEPER, Book Three)
MICHAEL JAN FRIEDMAN

JANUARY 1999   **(270PP)**

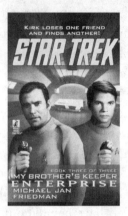

Kirk doesn't look forward to telling Gary's parents the true events surrounding his death. He remembers a situation involving Gary that occurred a few months before. A seemingly routine mission becomes extremely complicated and Kirk loses control of the *Enterprise* to hostile aliens. Scared of losing command and his best friend, Kirk is forced to rely on his Vulcan first officer, a man he barely knows.

Mike remarked, "I liked the Gary Mitchell episode. I remembered a scene in the Tom Cruise movie *Born on the Fourth of July*. He was a Vietnam veteran and he had to go to his friend's house and tell his friend's parents that he had accidentally shot and killed him. That was such a moving scene and I can't imagine how hard it would be to do that. It would be so easy not to. I wanted to show people the pain that Kirk went through afterward. It was a lot of fun and a great opportunity."

ACROSS THE UNIVERSE
PAMELA SARGENT AND GEORGE ZEBROWSKI

OCTOBER 1999   (217PP)

The *Enterprise* discovers a vessel from early twenty-first century Earth with colonists aboard. Can the colonists be trusted, or does Kirk have another Khan-like situation to resolve? Helping them find a place to live with other colonists, the new settlers arrive only to see their new world attacked by a strange creature that appears to be part of the ground, and engulfs anything in its path.

George remembered, "*Across the Universe* went well, with the editing again seeking to keep us to the main characters' viewpoints. I don't recall how the idea was developed, but it was more complex and involved than the final book."

Pam added, "We'd been discussing what might happen if a group of colonists that had set out from Earth to colonize another world, traveling at relativistic speed and aging only two or three decades while a couple of centuries passed, had been overtaken by a more technologically advanced group—in this case, the *Enterprise* and its crew. We actually wanted much of the story to be about the dilemma of these people, how they might acclimate to their encounter with this future civilization and the psychological problems that might cause. I think we were envisioning a darker and more complex tale about people who are slowly aging on a one-way journey, who reach their planetary destination only to discover that the world they thought would be theirs was already settled. In the end, at the editor's suggestion, we ended up writing more of an adventure story. Not necessarily a worse story, simply a different story. Some of the dilemmas our invented characters would have to face are still there, even if they had to be incorporated into a story about an unknown planetary threat."

NEW EARTH
(SEE SECTION 12: MINISERIES)

#95 & 96

SWORDHUNT
(RIHANNSU, Book Three)
HONOR BLADE
(RIHANNSU, Book Four)
DIANE DUANE

OCTOBER 2000   (229PP)
OCTOBER 2000   (220PP)

The Romulan Empire wants the sword that Ael took returned, or they will declare war on the Federation. A peace negotiation between the Romulans and the Federation appears at a standstill without the sword's return. Among the Romulan party is a spy who infiltrated the Empire years ago and almost had her cover blown when she helped McCoy escape. She has a terrible message that she must relay to Kirk, or the entire quadrant will possibly erupt in a major war. The story ends abruptly with a promise of "to be continued."

Diane commented, "The material in *Swordhunt* and *Honor Blade* was originally outlined the year after *The Romulan Way*, and it was always intended to follow more or less directly on *The Romulan Way*'s events. . . . I continue to love *Trek*. Shamelessly."

#97

IN THE NAME OF HONOR
DAYTON WARD

JANUARY 2002   (328PP)

Prior to the Khitomer Conference, the Klingons and the Federation are attempting to negotiate peace. During the talks, Klingon Captain Koloth uncovers a secret that could destroy not only the delicate negotiating process, but could even start a war. With the aid of his nemesis, Captain Kirk, Koloth wants to lead the Federation's flagship into Klingon territory and destroy any evidence of the secret. Not willing to risk his ship, Kirk goes undercover and mercenary to achieve resolution. Trying to lay low, both of them are unaware that the powerful military is after them.

• • •

Dayton started his *Star Trek* writing career by winning a place in each of the first three *Strange New Worlds* contests. When asked about being a fan of the series, he said, "my earliest memories involve being a *Star Trek* fan. I probably would have watched the original show from the beginning, but I was a fetus at the time and TV reception was pretty bad where I lived. I remember watching the reruns on a local television station even before starting kindergarten, and my mom made sure I caught the animated show when they started on Saturday mornings."

Reflecting on writing *Trek* stories, Dayton said, "I don't think there was ever a moment where I consciously decided, 'I want to be a writer!' I did not grow up aspiring to be a writer, it was just something I started playing around with one day. I've always been a big reader, with interests in a great variety of both fiction and nonfiction, and a lot of that reading involved *Trek* fiction, both the professionally published books and fanzines (and later, Internet-based fan fiction). For *Trek*, I was reading and enjoying stuff by Peter David, Diane Carey, Michael Jan Friedman, and so on long before I had any idea that it might be something I wanted to try myself. I hope I don't make those folks feel really old as they read this, but it's no stretch to say that they provided me with the inspiration to try my own hand at writing a *Trek* story. I wrote a few *Trek* stories, the first one sometime around 1992 or 1993, I think."

Dayton remembers getting the call from John Ordover saying he had placed a story in *Strange New Worlds III*, and then, "John Ordover said, 'I think it's time you wrote a *Star Trek* novel for me. Interested?' Well, duh."

Contemplating the opportunity a bit further, Dayton clarified, "I should note here that at this particular point in time (fall 1999), I had no real aspirations to write a full-length *Trek* novel. In fact, I was following advice offered by John and Dean, writing original stories and submitting them to places like *Analog*, *Asimov's*, and so on. I even submitted one of my *Strange New Worlds* entries to the previous incarnation of *Amazing Stories*, which at the time had acquired the license to publish short stories based on *The Next Generation* and *Voyager*. I wasn't having any luck in those areas, but I was keeping after it. Then John went and screwed all that up by asking me to write a *Trek* novel for him. I pitched him a couple of quick ideas via e-mail and he quickly picked up on one he liked, so he told me to go off and write a proposal for it and turn it in to him a month or so later."

For the story, Dayton said, "*In the Name of Honor* started out as me wanting to do a *Trek* riff on *The Great Escape*, my all-time favorite war movie. Pretty much all that survived of that initial idea was a group of Starfleet officers held in a remote prison camp on this backwater planet. My original notes featured the Romulans as the bad guys, and I was asking John if it was better to set the story in the original series timeframe or the TOS movie era, and it was he that suggested I switch the Romulans to Klingons so that we could attempt to tackle 'The Klingon Forehead Question.' That made me go back and revamp my story idea from the beginning, and we tossed ideas back and forth about a reason for the appearance change that would make sense with all of the conflicting evidence and hints that had been provided. We had what I thought was a pretty good reason that fit all the criteria, and which was rooted in the evolving notions of what constituted Klingon honor (hence the book's eventual title). Paramount liked our idea, but ultimately decided that it was a question that should be answered on film, if ever. They did, however, let me keep a lot of the other ideas I had come up with to go with the changes in appearance, and in the end I think Paramount's decision ultimately resulted in a better overall story. Instead of concentrating on the foreheads, I could focus on the honor question and the changes we'd seen in the way Klingons were portrayed on the original series versus the movies and later series."

One last thing Dayton wanted to mention about the novel. "It should be noted that I actually turned the *Honor* manuscript in early. Boo-yah!"

STAR TREK UNNUMBERED NOVELS

ENTERPRISE: THE FIRST ADVENTURE
VONDA N. MCINTYRE

SEPTEMBER 1986   (371 PP)

When he took command of the *Enterprise*, Kirk became the youngest starship captain in history. His first encounters with the crew we have grown to love makes for, as Spock would say, fascinating reading. The thrust of the narrative has the *Enterprise* shuttling circus performers, tossed in with a renegade Klingon, and an encounter with a fascinating alien species.

. . .

The author declined to be interviewed for this book.

STRANGERS FROM THE SKY
MARGARET WANDER BONANNO

JULY 1987   (402 PP)

Three novels for the price of one. The first part occurs just after the original motion picture and has McCoy trying to convince Kirk to read a popular new book called *Strangers From the Sky*. The second part tells the story of the Vulcans' first contact with humans in the twenty-first century. The last half takes place just before the episode "Where No Man Has Gone Before." While Kirk reads this book, he starts to have dreams that convince him he was on Earth during first contact with the Vulcans. Spock starts to believe this also, although no proof exists. All of these threads intertwine into one "giant" novel.

Margaret said, "*Strangers from the Sky* was my desire to tell the Earth/Vulcan first contact story, which my then-editor suggested I wrap in a Kirk/Mitchell/Dehner time travel story to keep it on the same timeline as the other Giant *Trek* novel, *Enterprise: The First Adventure*."

FINAL FRONTIER
DIANE CAREY

JANUARY 1988   (434PP)

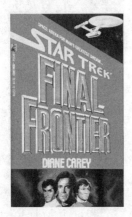

Living on Starbase Two, George Kirk (James T.'s father) and his friend Lieutenant Frances Reed are kidnapped and sent on a secret mission. Their commander, Captain Robert April, is notorious for his unorthodox methods. The colony ship *Rosenberg* has been devastated in an ion storm and the people aboard have little time left. Captain April and his crew are the first voyagers on a new space vessel called a starship. (This particular vessel's fate brings forward the name *Enterprise*.) Followed by a sequel, *Best Destiny*.

Diane received a call from her editor requesting that she write the story of the launch of the *Starship Enterprise* and her first mission under Captain Robert April. She said, "A few days later I got a call asking that I fold in the character of George Kirk. Of course, my response was, 'Who the heck is George Kirk?' Well, apparently this was James Kirk's father. Still later, they asked me to also add the adult James Kirk somehow. Hence the story, the characters, and the framing sequence."

Creating the character of Robert April was a challenge, since there was only a cartoon episode with him in it. Diane said, "so I filled him out, gave him a warm, funny, visionary personality, and made him a gentle and wise counterpoint to the very volatile and action-oriented George Kirk. Either one is inadequate to be the ultimate captain of such a ship with such a mission, and the idea is that somehow James Kirk is the composite of the better qualities of both April and George Kirk, the visionary wisdom with the proactive reactionary hero."

Looking back at the final result, she said, "The question was posed: Is it right to take aggressive action to stop a war from happening? The story is well considered, especially in light of George W. Bush's aggressive actions in the Middle East, with which I firmly agree. The decision to take action to prevent future disaster is one of the most poignant questions of humankind. It manifests itself in that old question: If you could go back in time, would you kill a child who will grow up to be Hitler? Should we force a war to happen now, while we can set the rules, or wait until it happens ten years from now when we have no control over the how and the where? Should we go after terrorists and thug-governments now, or let them live to raise their children to be even worse terrorists, and thus whom our children will then have to deal with? Nobody knows the answer, so any action or inaction becomes arguable."

SPOCK'S WORLD
DIANE DUANE

SEPTEMBER 1988   (310PP)

ORIGINALLY PUBLISHED IN HARDCOVER

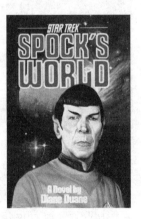

With the planet Vulcan getting ready for a vote on whether or not to pull out of the Federation, the *Enterprise* heads there so Kirk, Spock, and McCoy can give testimony. The

chapters alternate between the *Enterprise* and historical pieces about the planet Vulcan. This was the first *Star Trek* hardcover novel.

"I've always had it bad for Vulcans, as I think I mentioned, and Vulcan history had been an issue for me for quite a while. I'd had a very small run at it in *The Romulan Way*: I was eager to further investigate some of the ideas I'd briefly examined then, but which hadn't been particularly germane to that story. As for the plot proper, there had always seemed to me to be a certain tension between Vulcan and the Federation that was waiting to express itself in concrete terms. I just gave it a chance to do that. If there was a complication in that particular story, it was that I had a massive disk crash when I was very nearly done with it, and my backups turned out to be corrupt. I therefore wound up having to rewrite about sixty thousand words of material during the course of the week before the book was due. However, a lot of it (I think) turned out better as a result . . . and then the book spent eight weeks on *The New York Times* best-seller list, which was satisfying. Yet another happy ending."

THE LOST YEARS
J. M. DILLARD

OCTOBER 1989   (307 PP)

ORIGINALLY PUBLISHED IN HARDCOVER

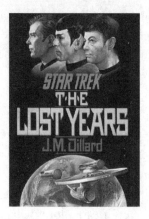

It was decided I'd do the first one—I believe I'd already sent a proposal for the idea before we met. The other writers who were going to do books in the series came as well, and the basic timeline for the novels was decided upon. Because it launched the series, *The Lost Years* was published as a hardcover. The other novels had different problems; one had to be rewritten, another was canceled, so the series as a whole never materialized."

PRIME DIRECTIVE
JUDITH AND GARFIELD REEVES-STEVENS

SEPTEMBER 1990   (406 PP)

ORIGINALLY PUBLISHED IN HARDCOVER

Chronicling the events occurring between the end of the original series and the first motion picture, the crew finds itself separated. Kirk contemplates an admiralty, while Spock takes a teaching assignment on Vulcan. In the meantime, McCoy heads back to Yonada in the hopes of rekindling his relationship with Natira, from the episode "For the World is Hollow, and I Have Touched the Sky." Circumstances will force them together again, though not in the way they had hoped. Projected as part of a trilogy that never materialized.

"The Pocket editor at the time, Dave Stern, gave me call and said, 'We'd like to do a series of novels covering the period of time between the end of the series and the first movie. Come to New York and let's talk about it.' I said, 'Great!'

While on a mission to the planet Talin IV, events go horribly wrong. Engulfed in a nuclear holocaust, the planet dies and the *Enterprise* is nearly destroyed. For violating the Prime Directive and destroying a world, Kirk is thrown out of Starfleet, along with Spock, McCoy, Uhura, Sulu, and Chekov. Left on board the remains of *Enterprise* to try and make her space-worthy again, Scotty believes in his friends' innocence. To reclaim their lives and careers, Kirk and the others go to enormous lengths to return to Talin IV and discover the truth.

The authors declined to be interviewed for this book, but had previously discussed the origins of *Prime Directive* with Kevin Dilmore. After writing *Memory Prime*, Judith and Garfield thought their next novel could deal with Zefram Cochrane and tie in *The Next Generation*. They wanted to write a James Michener-style novel, so they wrote up the outline and Pocket loved it. When Paramount looked at it they immediately nixed the idea, saying it wasn't permissible to combine the generations. So they still had to write a novel to fill an upcoming hardcover slot.

Going through the more memorable phrases in the *Star Trek* lexicon, they both liked "Prime Directive." Thinking about Kirk and having a planet destroy itself by nuclear war, Judith and Garfield wrote up another proposal and had it to Pocket in less than a week.

Starting the book with the aftermath, and the characters devastated by the events they just witnessed, resulted in letters to the authors calling for their heads. It was clear that most of the upset fans had not gotten past the first part of the book. Even with the terrible letters, Judith and Garfield were pleased with the final book. Since the novel covers several months of time, it would be difficult to condense the story into even a two-hour movie let alone a single hour episode, which is exactly what the authors intended.

PROBE
MARGARET WANDER BONANNO

A P R I L   1 9 9 2   (3 4 5 P P)

ORIGINALLY PUBLISHED IN HARDCOVER

Set after the events of *Star Trek IV: The Voyage Home*, the crew of the *Enterprise* heads to the Romulan Neutral Zone to negotiate peace. Meanwhile, the probe that almost destroyed Earth, before being talked out of doing it by humpback whales, heads to the Neutral Zone as well. What does the probe have in mind?

It has long been known that the circumstances surrounding the publication of *Probe* were both difficult and complicated for all concerned. Starting out as a novel by Margaret Wander Bonnano entitled *Music of the Spheres*, the manuscript was rejected by the studio when Gene Roddenberry's office took issue with certain characterizations in the book. This eventually led to editor Dave Stern hiring Gene DeWeese to rewrite the novel—

now retitled *Probe*—despite the fact that the already-printed dust-jacket credited Margaret as sole author.

Beyond that, an objective report of *Probe's* bumpy road to publication is, unfortunately, impossible. All the parties involved have different recollections of those events, as well as different ways of interpreting them, and the various accounts are contradictory. The only consistency in all the versions of the story seems to be that everyone involved wishes that the situation had not deteriorated to the extent that it did, and that the book could have been published to everyone's satisfaction.

BEST DESTINY
DIANE CAREY

NOVEMBER 1992   **(398PP)**

ORIGINALLY PUBLISHED IN HARDCOVER

The sequel to *Final Frontier*. A teenage James T. Kirk has once again defied authority and gotten into trouble. His dad, George, is preparing to go on a mission with Captain Robert April. Reluctantly, he brings along his estranged son, to make amends and also steer his life to a correct path.

Diane said, "Pocket asked me to write James Kirk's first mission in deep space at the age of sixteen. I said, 'Sure, no problem.' The first inclination was to show a perfect young midshipman with all his ducks in a row. Chance, however, put me aboard the Schooners *New Way* and *Bill of Rights* in a crew swap from the ship I was serving at the time. Both these vessels carried crews of adjudicated teenagers, wards of the court, perpetrators of various crimes from misdemeanors to grand larceny. Their sentence had brought them to incarceration aboard these ships, which were licensed by the court system. I was impressed by these troubled youths and their situation, and notice the determination with which they tended their ships. Being at sea, in a closed environment, with officers and orders, had put them in a new direction. I decided they fit the template for James Kirk much better than a kid who never did anything wrong. In fact, the episode 'The Enemy Within' had proven that James Kirk's 'bad' side was very strong and in fact was the part that made him a hero."

RICHARD ARNOLD: IN HIS OWN WORDS

Richard Arnold met Gene Roddenberry in 1972. Why he ended up working with him, he still has no idea. The two began corresponding and Richard visited Gene when he was in the L.A. area. Eventually, he moved to L.A. and became Gene's assistant on a volunteer basis. When the *The Next Generation* got started, Paramount hired Richard to work with Gene. "It wasn't something that happened overnight. It was [my] being there all that time and my loyalty and [my] understanding of his philosophy that helped me get a paid job with him."

Richard discussed the review process as it was when he worked with Gene. "It used to be that the books would be written, they would be sent to Gene, then he would make recommendations with a memo and hopefully they would be fixed. Gene let the books get away from him in the early 80s, allowing Susan Sackett to take them over, while he had minimal involvement."

When Richard became involved in the process, it became his job to read everything. "We had a 72-hour turnaround time as it was, so I wasn't sure how much faster we could do it. After all, we would get it in proposal, then a first draft, then revised, back in final, and then galley, and I had to read all of that plus all of the books going through the process at the same time." There was a perception that Richard himself was commenting in Gene's name. "It was always Gene and it was never me. I would never have done something like that to him. I had far too much respect for him."

Richard continued, "Let me clarify again. I was not doing things behind Gene's back, I was not writing memos without his approval. I was only doing my job and it was [upsetting a lot of] people. So, I was pulled off for a while, but Gene put me back on. Some of my memos got to be over twenty pages long. Sometimes Gene would disagree with me. He said, 'You don't have to win every battle as long as you win the war.' Gene kept saying, 'It's my sandbox. If you want to come in and play with my kids, you have to treat them with respect.' He cared a lot about the characters and the property."

Richard added, "Gene wanted nothing more than [for] the writers to respect the rules that he'd created for writing *Star Trek*, [just like] anyone writing for the show, rules that actually made sense, considering the history and complexity of his universe. Michael Piller once said that the rules that Gene had established only made it impossible to write in Gene's universe if you had no imagination (I loved that!).

"But too often the writers have been more concerned with writing *their* characters, *their* stories, and *their* universes, and Gene's characters and philosophy have far too often had to take a back seat."

SHADOWS ON THE SUN

Michael Jan Friedman

August 1993 **(340pp)**

ORIGINALLY PUBLISHED IN HARDCOVER

et just after the events in *Star Trek VI: The Undiscovered Country*. The planet Ssan's society believes in the time-honored tradition of assassination, but the government in power wishes to eliminate this policy. Needless to say, the assassins are mad enough to kill. Kirk and crew are ordered to shuttle the ambassadors to this dangerous planet. For McCoy, the mission is too personal. When he was studying to be a doctor, he was stationed on Ssan and his experiences are still very painful to recall. In addition, the ambassadors are a married couple—McCoy's ex-wife Jocelyn and her husband, the man who stole her heart away.

Mike remembered, "*Shadows on the Sun* was a hard book to do. It was kind of a painstaking process and I knew from the beginning that it was going to be a sad book." The never-aired but generally accepted backstory about McCoy was that he was divorced, with a daughter named Joanna. Mike explored the question many fans had wondered about for decades: "What happened with his wife?" He answered it by having McCoy come up against "a culture that prizes death as much as he prized life. I did my best to show that that culture had some kind of validity because I didn't want it to be an uneven fight. McCoy had to open up his eyes at least a little bit to this alternative philosophy and so those were the impulses that went into that book. The examination of what it meant to be a doctor and what it meant to preserve life and how an alien civilization might value the opposite point of view. That was one impulse. And the other was to shine a light on McCoy's former wife and what had become of her. It was painful to do it because I knew it was going to end badly, but it was a great book to have done."

SAREK
A. C. CRISPIN

MARCH 1994   **(440PP)**

HARDCOVER

A

The life of Spock's father and Vulcan ambassador examined up close. He married a human woman and had an estranged relationship with his son. Now Amanda is dying and Spock heads to Vulcan to help his parents. Distrust between Sarek and his son arrives quickly when Sarek must leave Amanda's side to handle a crisis that has been growing for some time. Spock must trust his father again and work with him if the threat is going to be neutralized.

Ann was thrilled to write *Sarek* at the suggestion of her editor, who also suggested that the story chronicle the death of Spock's mother, Amanda—an event implied by the introduction of Sarek's wife Perrin in *The Next Generation*. Ann remarked, "I like writing back stories, and it was fun to flesh out Sarek's life for *Star Trek* readers."

FEDERATION
JUDITH AND GARFIELD REEVES-STEVENS

NOVEMBER 1994   **(467PP)**

ORIGINALLY PUBLISHED IN HARDCOVER

A

Captain Kirk reminisces about Edith Keeler and his life when he visits the planet of the Guardian of Forever. When he touches it, the Guardian tells him a haunting tale. Three stories eventually converge, starting with the life of seminal warp theorist Zefram Cochrane and how he ended up adrift in space as an old man waiting to die. The second story takes place immediately after the events in "Journey to Babel." Kirk, Spock, and McCoy have to answer for their hiding of the young Cochrane and leaving him alone to spend his life with the Companion—the life form that took over the dying body of Ambassador Nancy Hedford in the episode "Metamorphosis." The third story focuses on the *Enterprise*-D and Picard's negotiations with a Ferengi who possesses a Romulan vessel and what appears to be an artifact from the Borg. All three stories blend together for one reading experience.

The authors declined to be interviewed for this book.

VULCAN'S FORGE
JOSEPHA SHERMAN AND SUSAN SHWARTZ

AUGUST 1997 (343 PP)

ORIGINALLY PUBLISHED IN HARDCOVER

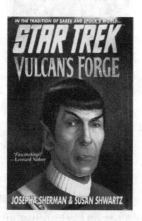

Set a year after Captain Kirk's "death" aboard the *Enter-prise*-B, Captain Spock of the *Intrepid II* rushes his vessel to the planet Obsidian. David Rabin, a childhood friend and now a captain in *Starfleet*, needs help to uncover a saboteur. The book jumps between the present and Spock's past, where he first met David, and reveals the incident that created their friendship.

John Ordover was trying to bring in more SFWA members into the *Trek* field by cornering authors at conventions and asking, "want to write a *Star Trek* book?" Ordover asked both Josepha and Susan separately and they both agreed. As Susan explains, "[I] worked up three stories with no guidance, a matter of about 50-some pages that have gone missing; I was told they were not what was wanted. Okay, I figured, I'd tried. If no one wanted to give me any guidance, fine. I had—and have—other contracts, as well as my work in finance, to eat up my life, so I didn't think anything more about it except to regret I'd never get to write the Romulan Commander played by Joanne Linville. That was a bummer."

Josepha realized she had no time to write a novel by herself, so at a convention she approached Susan and suggested a collaboration. Both of them were Spock fans and wanted to do a Spock story, and John suggested they set the novel on Vulcan. They knew that Paramount was very careful about who gets to write about Vulcan, so they felt honored. They plotted *Vulcan's Forge* while both were guest speakers at Mt. Holyoke, an all-female college. Josepha said, "It was Friday night—cold, isolated, and nothing to do but plot *Vulcan's Forge*. John had wanted something on 'Jews in Space,' and we created David Rabin, a childhood friend of Spock."

Susan was happy with how the novel plotting was going. She wanted to add Romulans, since she had written some historical fantasies set in the Byzantine Empire. "I think of Romulans as Byzantines with pointed ears. After all, the Byzantines did refer to themselves as Rhomaioi, or Romans."

When they submitted their proposal, they were told it wasn't working as a *Star Trek* novel yet. This time, they got feedback and were able to fix it. Susan said, "Once we got the rationale, it made sense. In fact, it made a much, much better plot. *Vulcan's Forge* is a tidily constructed book, with some good dialogue, some solid world-building, a lot of humor, and a number of plot-hooks that would, we figured, enable us to continue things if we got the opportunity."

MISSION TO HORATIUS
MACK REYNOLDS

FEBRUARY 1999   (210PP)

HARDCOVER REISSUE

riginally published by Whitman in 1968, Pocket Books decided to reissue this young adult novel to commemorate Pocket's twentieth anniversary as the official *Star Trek* book publisher. In the story, the crew shows signs of *cafard*, a disease that originates from a person not having enough time off a starship. The crew of the *Enterprise* needs shore leave in the worst way when they answer a distress call that originated from the Horatius System. Trying to

determine the source of the message will send Kirk to three uniquely different planets.

John Ordover commented, "We reprinted that for fun! Paramount has the rights; the original publisher is out of business. It's not going to cost us much to do a facsimile of this. It was selling for $50 at conventions. So why not do a reissue? It was the first *Star Trek* novel ever done and the first one I read."

VULCAN'S HEART
JOSEPHA SHERMAN AND SUSAN SHWARTZ

JULY 1999   (378PP)

ORIGINALLY PUBLISHED IN HARDCOVER

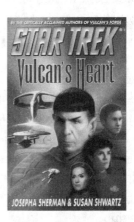

pock becomes betrothed to Saavik. Shortly afterwards, he goes on a secret mission to the heart of the Romulan Empire to assist the Romulan Commander he deceived in "The *Enterprise* Incident." With typical good timing, he begins to experience the effects of *pon farr*. Halfway through the novel, a major shift occurs and the events of the Romulan attack on

Narendra III and the destruction of the *Enterprise*-C are revealed.

Josepha and Susan got to write a sequel to *Vulcan's Forge* as well as a stand-alone novel at the same time. According to Josepha, John wanted to show Spock's wedding, which was established in *The Next Generation* epsiode, "Sarek." She added, "Also, a secondary character in *Vulcan's Forge*, a spear-carrying Romulan named Ruanek, had taken on a life of his own, getting fan mail! So he became a major character in *Vulcan's Heart*."

Susan was ecstatic to write this novel. She said, "I like writing battle sequences, the bigger and more operatic the better, and Narendra III filled the bill. I worked that battle out with a coworker who'd gone to West Point, and gave it a sort of Pearl Harbor subtext." Looking back, she said, "I loved that book, even if it got a few people screaming with rage."

The "rage" stemmed from the decision to marry Spock to Saavik (who was introduced as Spock's protégé in *Star Trek II: The Wrath of Khan*), which divided many readers. Some saw it as a reasonable evolution of their relationship over several decades; others saw it as an inappropriate violation of their earlier teacher/student relationship.

THE EUGENICS WARS
THE RISE AND FALL OF KHAN NOONIEN SINGH, Book One
GREG COX

JULY 2001 (404 PP)

ORIGINALLY PUBLISHED IN HARDCOVER

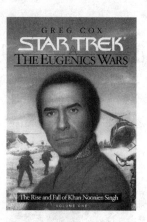

One of *Trek*'s favorite villains gets highlighted in this look at his turbulent life in the late twentieth century. A top-secret experiment called the Chrysalis Project attempts to bioengineer superhumans. Gary Seven, along with his partner, Roberta Lincoln, tries to infiltrate the project and stop the threat from reaching fruition. Real history meshes with *Trek* history.

THE EUGENICS WARS
THE RISE AND FALL OF
KHAN NOONIEN SINGH, Book Two
GREG COX

APRIL 2002   (338PP)

ORIGINALLY PUBLISHED IN HARDCOVER

Picking up the story in 1992, Gary Seven and Roberta reluctantly admit that the children of the Chrysalis Project have grown into superior human beings, and with their superior strength and intellect, spawn plans of domination. Khan's influence spreads secretly across the globe, as he dreams of leading his people to total victory, but some of the other genetically enhanced humans also want to rule.

"At the end of my previous *Trek* book, *Assignment: Eternity*, Spock's historical research turns up the fact that Gary Seven and Roberta Lincoln were instrumental in overthrowing Khan Noonien Singh back during the Eugenics Wars. As God is my witness, that was supposed to be the end of it. I just thought that the

Khan connection made kind of a cute punchline. It made sense, too, since Seven and Khan were more or less contemporaries. I had no intention of going any further with the idea, until John Ordover called me up and asked, 'So, you want to write that book?' Suddenly, I was in the Khan business. . . . The big (and most controversial) question, of course, was how to deal with the fact that the Eugenics Wars did *not* take place in the 1990s that we all lived through. Basically, there were two ways to go:

1. Ignore history as we know it, and describe an all-out, apocalyptic conflict featuring scenes of global destruction a la *Independence Day*, or

2. Go the *X-Files* route and depict the EW as this huge global conspiracy, the true nature of which did not become known to the general public until generations later.

"Ultimately, we went for Option #2, for a number of reasons. Ordover felt very strongly that *Star Trek* should be our future, not the product of an alternate timeline. It also had the advantage of being consistent with the 'Future's End' episodes of *Voyager,* in which Captain Janeway and company visited a 1990s that seemed to be unaware of the existence of the Eugenics Wars. (Of course, you can argue that those two *Voyager* episodes were erased from the timeline anyway, but temporal paradoxes just make my head hurt.) Anyway, the other advantage to trying to shoehorn the EW into the real 1990s was that it just sounded like more fun, and better suited to my own talents and inclinations. There are authors out there who could write a great Clancy-esque, all-out global war novel, but I'm not sure I'm one of them. The whole secret war idea appealed to me more. Of course, this required a ton of research. I drove myself nuts trying to get all the historical and geographical details right. I still have an entire shelf of books on India sitting in my office, not to mention umpteen guides and timelines to the latter part of the twentieth century. At one point, I even called an Indian tourism office to find out what the name of the New Delhi airport was in 1974. (It's the Indira Gandhi Memorial Airport now, but they didn't name it that until after she was assassinated.) All that homework seems to have paid off. To date, I haven't received a single angry letter or review claiming that I got Rajasthan wrong, although I did slip up by having the *X-Files* debut a few months too early in 1993. (I fixed that in the paperback.)"

Greg continued, "I listened to a lot of 1960s spy music while writing these books, by the way. In a sense, Seven and Roberta are the nearest *Trek* equivalents of James Bond or *The Avengers*, so the first book in particular was meant to have the globe-trotting feel of a big Bond epic, right down to Sarina Kaur's secret underground base blowing up at the end. I've flirted with the idea of doing another Seven/Roberta book someday, or maybe even a Roberta/Rain Robinson book, but nothing is in the works at the moment."

THE LAST ROUNDUP
CHRISTIE GOLDEN

JULY 2002 (285PP)

ORIGINALLY PUBLISHED IN HARDCOVER

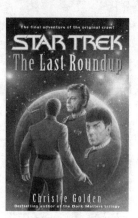

In another "final adventure" of the original crew, Kirk joins his two nephews on a mission to colonize a planet. Dragging Chekov and Scotty along, he promises an exciting opportunity to start a new life. But a hidden agenda lurks and the aliens responsible are willing to destroy the Federation to achieve their goals.

Christie reflected on this novel. "This was quite the milestone for me in many aspects. After several years and a lot of books published, it was my first hardcover."

Christie found herself intimidated: "Kirk and company are legendary. Would I be able to capture their voices and create an interesting story? I was very nervous, but I think I succeeded."

In terms of the story, she said, "my editor at the time had an idea he wanted me to pursue and was very clear that this was to be a Kirk book, but he encouraged me to bring everyone in. So I did my best to have something fun for each character. It was particularly fun having "permission" as it were to go back and watch all the old *Trek* episodes. I have always loved Scotty, and I'll digress a bit here to say my heart broke when I learned of James Doohan's recent battles with Alzheimer's and diabetes, among other things. Very sad, as was losing DeForrest Kelley a few years ago. On a happier note, I *loved* [writing] 'Bones,' especially when he'd go on a rant about Klingons or something. Very fun."

A new character Christie created for the novel is named Skalli, who is a Huanni. She said, "Skalli was a delight to write and she really made people either love or hate her. I liked her so much that I decided to revisit the Huanni in a later book."

In addition to being her first hardcover, *The Last Roundup* was also Christie's first book to be adapted to audio. "I got an e-mail when they were recording the audio book and they asked if the brief opera bit that Uhura performs had a tune. And if so, could I call up the producer and sing it on her voice mail? Um, well, it did have a tune, so there I am on a weeknight, singing Klingon opera into a total stranger's voice mail!"

GEMINI
Mike W. Barr
February 2003   **(297pp)**

Sent to the planet Nador to oversee the election on Federation membership, the *Enterprise* and her crew find more trouble than expected. The rulers of Nador are Abon and Delor, conjoined twins united at the spinal cord. An attempted assassination of the twins by an anti-Federation sect mars the proceedings.

Mike answered, "As I wrote on the bio page of *Gemini*, I became a *Trek* fan at 8:30:01 on September 8, 1966. Something about the show immediately grabbed me—not the least factor of which was that it was being done with a straight face—and I've been a Trekkie (yes, a Trekkie!) ever since. I figure that an even cooler thing than watching or reading your favorite characters is becoming a part of their world by creating an adventure for them. It's almost like living in that universe. (But you don't have to be afraid of wearing a red shirt.)"

He continued, "I had had the idea of Siamese twins conjoined at the spine for some time before I first utilized it as a plot pitched to the producers of *Star Trek: Voyager*, which was rejected. A couple of years later, when looking for ideas for *Trek* novels, I dusted off the idea, retooled it for TOS (always my default position for *Trek*) and, after approval, had at the manuscript. It took about eight months to write (the first draft was completed on July 6, 2000 at 5:40 PM, PST), then it was slotted for publication in March of 2003, almost three years in the future."

GARTH OF IZAR
Pamela Sargent and George Zebrowski

March 2003   **(268pp)**

he maniacal villain from the episode "Whom Gods Destroy" returns. A rehabilitated Garth asks to go to Antos IV, the planet where he developed his shape-changing abilities. Kirk and the *Enterprise* crew are assigned to accompany him on his mission. Has Garth truly been cured, or is he faking for some horrific purpose?

George reflected, "Garth of Izar was a long-standing piece of 'unfinished business.' Garth was 'cured' at the end of the episode, so why not give him back his command and all that he had lost? This gave the story a genuinely important idea at the core, and a dilemma for the characters to resolve. We particularly like *Star Trek*'s utopian ideals about progress, which are often softened, particularly the 'moneyless socialism' of Earth's society. So, given Garth's 'cure,' we decided to hold the entire concept's feet to the fire and see where that led. Answer: to an affecting story, which displays *Star Trek*'s truest ideals, we believe."

Pam continued, "That is really where the idea started. If Garth actually is cured of his mental illness, if we assume that this society, unlike our own, attaches no stigma to people recovering from mental illnesses, then by the logic of that culture, the person who's recovered should be allowed to resume his normal life. In Garth's case, that happens to be commanding a starship again. But of course even in a more utopian culture than ours, things are a lot more complicated than that."

George added, "In addition, we had both admired Steve Ihnat, the great actor who played Garth, and who died much too young. You can see him in a number of films of the '60s. His hometown neighbors wrote us a fan letter when the novel came out, telling us how much members of his family enjoyed seeing the book. I believe (see the afterword to the novel) that if Ihnat had not died, *The Wrath of Khan* might not have been made; Garth might have been Kirk's antagonist instead. As for the problems in Chapter One, we had it right as a Romulan ship, from the teleplay. Someone at Pocket changed it to Klingon. We caught the mistake in page proofs, and the editors swore up and down the galaxy that they would fix it. We gave them a disk file to drop in for Chapter One, and the result was Ta da! An alternating Klingon/Romulan spaceship!? We called this to their attention again. No one answered. The new management says they will fix it if and when the novel is reprinted. To repeat: We had it right, they had it wrong, and fixed it by halves!"

Pam remarked, "It's been my experience that fans of *Star Trek*, of all the series, are very attentive to details. However much I thought I knew about the background and settings, and I know it's not as much as most of the fans know, I always went out of my way to double-check on things. George and I always made sure we had a ton of material—the bibles for the series, books like the *Star Trek Chronology*, engineering diagrams for all the *Enterprises*, and so forth, to consult. We also watched and re-watched episodes and the feature films, since we own a number of them. Because if you make careless mistakes, the fans will jump all over you. So I was very distressed when an error not of our making popped up in the finished book, because you know who the fans will go after—the authors, not the editors."

George remarked, "By the way, it took a year for us to get author's copies."

THE CASE OF THE COLONIST'S CORPSE
TONY ISABELLA AND BOB INGERSOLL

JANUARY 2004   **(273PP)**

Star Trek as a *Perry Mason* novel? The book cover and the red color of the paper create the appearance of it being published in the 1950s—all of the elements are here. Samuel Cogley (the attorney who exonerated Kirk in the episode "Court Martial") has Perry Mason's role; he even has a Della Street like secretary and an investigator in the Paul Drake mode. Areel Shaw still fumes over losing the last time to Cogley, so she is anxious to prosecute this slam-dunk case.

Bob remembered, "I was actually a science fiction fan, before I was a *Star Trek* fan. I discovered science fiction (first through comics and *Tom Swift, Jr.* novels) as an early reader. So, when *Star Trek* came on, I was interested in it from the start. I had already been watching

Lost in Space and *Outer Limits* regularly (although in summer reruns, as I wasn't allowed to watch TV on school nights back then). I watched the first episode aired, 'The Man Trap,' but was a little disappointed in it. It struck me as possibly being more of the same 'monster of the week' we were already getting on regular science fiction TV. And the coming attraction for the next show, 'Charlie X,' also looked a little 'monster of the week' to me, at least in the scenes they showed. As I wasn't allowed to watch on school nights back then, the next episode I saw was part two of 'The Menagerie.' That episode hooked me. Actual cerebral science fiction on TV that dealt with themes and issues. So I was a fan from the start, although a little temerarious. But 'The Menagerie, Part 2' allayed my fears."

When asked about how he got started writing *Trek*, he commented, "Tony and I wrote a few stories for the *Star Trek* comics. So, after our joint *Captain America* novel, we were looking for other novel projects and, as we had some experience writing *Trek*, it seemed a natural. John Ordover, former *Trek* editor at Pocket Books, suggested the idea for *Case*. As I'm a real-life attorney in my day job—a public defender in Cleveland, Ohio—John thought it would be a natural for us to take the Sam Cogley character and write, as John put it, 'A Perry Mason mystery in the *Star Trek* universe.' Once we had the basic idea, Tony and I brainstormed possible plot ideas for the one that we thought best combined the elements of the *Trek* universe and the Erle Stanley Gardner novels. As for the publishing process and retro feel, that was, again, John Ordover. He designed the book's look and retro cover. And he was the one who wanted the red tinting around the outer borders for that real old-time feel."

Tony wrote some *Trek* comics on his own as well as with Bob. He commented on his memories of writing *Case*, "The answer to all of the above is the wonderful John Ordover. He was the editor who asked us to write a Cogley novel and came up with the way cool idea of making it 'Perry Mason in space.' From his inspiration, we went to (hard) work and had a ball doing it."

PRESENT TENSE
(THE JANUS GATE, Book One)
L. A. GRAF

J U N E   2 0 0 2   (2 5 3 P P)

After the events of Psi 2000, when the crew finds themselves with three days to live over again, they decide to rendezvous early with a scientific party on Tlaoli. The crew left behind on the planet has been having a hard time, both with vanishing members and evidence of several crashed vessels. Captain Kirk leads a group into the caves of the planet to find his missing crew. Bad decision.

FUTURE IMPERFECT
(THE JANUS GATE, Book Two)
L. A. GRAF

J U N E   2 0 0 2   (2 5 2 P P)

As a result of events in the previous volume, Captain Kirk has been replaced with himself when he was a teenager, and Sulu has aged twenty years, and has never heard of Captain Kirk. Prior to his arrival, Sulu was fighting a war with the Gorn, and was whisked away seconds before his expected death in an explosion. The Sulu from Captain's Kirk time finds himself twenty years in the future, helping a battle-worn Chekov fight some scary-looking lizard people.

PAST PROLOGUE
(THE JANUS GATE, Book Three)
L. A. GRAF

JULY 2002   (252PP)

Captain Kirk finds himself in the past, when he was part of a delegation with his father. With his shipmates displaced in time, can Spock decipher the alien technology to put everyone back where they belong, and restore the timelines? Rescue and resolution appear to be reached only by a valuable crewmember sacrificing his life to make the technology work.

John Ordover commented, "The idea was to do sort of what hadn't been done before—carefully weave books in and out within the idea of the original series and also do a sort of lower decks feel, from the point of view of the red shirts. The idea came from the *Brother's Keeper* mini series that Mike Friedman did. We're told how close and how good and how agonized Kirk was at the end by Mitchell in 'Where No Man Has Gone Before,' but we've never seen the story of their friendship. We wanted to go in and make it that much more of an impact when you saw the episode again. By the time the random security guard is pushed into the pit at the beginning of 'What Are Little Girls Made Of,' we know who he is and we care."

Julia and Karen Rose recalled, "We had originally been supposed to write a two-book set in honor of the millennium, but the schedules and proposals didn't quite work out for that one. In its place, John Ordover suggested we do a trilogy set in the 'in-between' times between early episodes of the series. We had written so much set in later parts of the timeline that we felt like we had to go 'back in time' mentally to get into the characters as they were at the very beginning of the series. We took that metaphor and used it to spark our time-travel plot, which also let us see different future versions of some characters as well as past versions of Kirk. It was a tremendous challenge writing such a complex plot, but we were very happy with the results and hope that we managed to be true to the characters no matter what 'timeline' they were living in."

When asked about the obvious discrepancies between the story descriptions on the back covers and the content of the books themselves, Julia and Karen Rose explained, "The cover blurb is wrong for the same reason that a lot of our blurbs have been wrong . . . they have to print the cover long before we finish the book, and if we find a plot hole in the middle of writing, we have no compunctions about changing the plot completely around to make the book read better. Fortunately, [John was] very tolerant of this, as long as the final book came out well."

THE EDGE OF THE SWORD
(ERRAND OF VENGEANCE, Book One)
KEVIN RYAN

JULY 2002 (281PP)

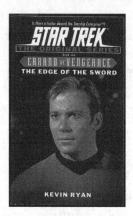

L ieutenant Jon Anderson joins the security team aboard the *Enterprise* shortly before the events with Roger Korby on the planet Exo III. A surgically altered Klingon made to appear human, Anderson's first assignment is to kill Captain Kirk. At Starfleet Command, evidence indicates that the Klingons are ready to launch a war with the Federation.

KILLING BLOW
(ERRAND OF VENGEANCE, Book Two)
KEVIN RYAN

AUGUST 2002 (265PP)

A Klingon officer hunts for his missing brother, not knowing his brother now appears to be human. Anderson finds himself struggling with respect for his captain, plus his growing love of Ensign Parrish, which are both completely against his Klingon heritage. The next mission will tear him apart even more as Klingons and humans fight together to stop the Orions.

RIVER OF BLOOD
(ERRAND OF VENGEANCE, Book Three)
Kevin Ryan

AUGUST 2002 (263PP)

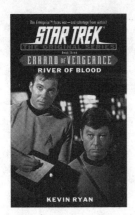

Anderson tries to break up with Ensign Parrish, but he can't stay away from her. To what lengths will he go to complete his mission and keep his true identity from the people aboard the *Enterprise?* Meanwhile, war seems perilously close and the *Enterprise* gets diverted to a remote starbase while an admiral prepares his team for the worst possible scenario.

Kevin Ryan commented, "When I started [as an editor] in the *Star Trek* program, it was just a handful of guys. I was the first full-time employee."

Kevin worked at the company from 1988 to 1996. He continued, "John [Ordover] mentioned that he wanted to focus on lower deck characters [from the original series]. I had been toying with the notion of what it would be like if you were a Klingon on board the *Enterprise.*

The idea of Klingon agents infiltrating the Federation was interesting and had been introduced in the episode, 'The Trouble with Tribbles.' It became more interesting later as we learned more about the Klingon culture, particularly on *The Next Generation.* I wanted to see the Federation through the lens of a Klingon with this great cultural outlook and history. I found a trilogy was the good length to tell my story. In 'Errand of Mercy,' the Organians were able to stop the war. If you know anything about military history, you don't mobilize your forces overnight. There was some sort of lead up to that point. In 'The Trouble with Tribbles,' they mentioned a historical battle twenty-five years before, which was the battle of Donatu 25. It was fought to what essentially was a tie. You take that and the concept of what we know about Klingons and their martial tradition, and a tie would be worse than a defeat. Suddenly, I had a story interesting to me."

EXODUS
(VULCAN'S SOUL, Book One)
JOSEPHA SHERMAN AND SUSAN SHWARTZ

JULY 2004   (265 PP)

ORIGINALLY PUBLISHED IN HARDCOVER

While the Federation deals with the aftermath of the Dominion War, the Romulan Empire finds itself under attack by a mysterious race called the Watraii. Led by Ambassador Spock, Admiral Uhura and Chekov aid the reconnaissance mission to uncover this new threat's motives. The answer lies in Vulcan's tumultuous past, with a figure named Surak.

Susan said, "I'm still surprised that actually came to fruition because it went through many, many stages. First, it was going to be one book, then one huge, HUGE book. Then, it was going to be two books, then a trilogy. Then, we heard that it would have to wait until after *Star Trek: Nemesis* came out, because that film would feature Romulans." That film gave audiences the first canonical look at the Romulans'

secondary world, Remus. "So there we were, left with a radioactive iceball full of vampiric-looking telepaths with far more aggression than is good for anyone and a film that—to say the least—didn't do too well. We really wondered for awhile there if there would be any form of *Vulcan's Soul*. But we kept after it, and John kept after us. I don't know how many more drafts we did."

Elaborating further, Susan said, "Finally, part of it was approved, and we went to contract—delayed—and started writing— even more delayed. About this time, John Ordover left the line, and that was another worry. Orphaned books have, historically, a bad time of things, but Marco Palmieri and Keith DeCandido adopted them. Marco took over the manuscript for *Vulcan's Soul: Exodus*, realized it had come in short, and told us, 'Thirty more pages each, and I want them over the weekend.' I said something intelligent and persuasive that came out as 'eep,' called him, got a very good structural diagnosis out of him for my chapters—and, yes, the ending was a little telegraphed in the interest of time because I had finished two books in six months, in addition to my job as a financial-marketing vice president, and was running on empty. So, I wrote the three chapters that fleshed out the ending of the 'ancient' Vulcan history, producing about forty-five pages, and pleasing my editor (always a good thing). Then, Marco did a superb job of braiding the modern and ancient threads, and created a fabulous cover concept for the trilogy."

EXILES
(VULCAN'S SOUL, Book Two)
JOSEPHA SHERMAN AND SUSAN SHWARTZ

JUNE 2006   **(324PP)**

ORIGINALLY PUBLISHED IN HARDCOVER

oping my own characters and plot material and texture *and* while building up to the climax that begins the retroactive continuity for *Star Trek: Nemesis.* And that's precisely what I did. Meanwhile, Jo was working on the Watraii homeworld, and there was a great deal of overlap between that and the retroactive continuity."

The third book in this trilogy, *Epiphany*, is slated for publication in May 2007.

TO REIGN IN HELL: THE EXILE OF KHAN NOONIEN SINGH
GREG COX

JANUARY 2005   **(326PP)**

ORIGINALLY PUBLISHED IN HARDCOVER

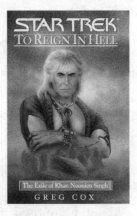

Admiral Uhura has a clandestine mission for Spock. It appears that Chekov survived and is being held prisoner. With the help of Scotty and the exiled Romulan Ruanek, along with Data and Spock's wife, Captain Saavik, the gang tries to covertly rescue their fallen comrade from the Watraii homeworld. To make their mission more difficult, the Romulans have asked to have them find a significant artifact that has deep meaning to their people.

Susan remarked, "*Exiles* follows logically from *Exodus:* If you have the Vulcans leaving the Mother World, you follow them on their journey. I did the ancient history portion of the book, so I'll speak to that. I was asked to follow Diane Duane and Peter Morwood in *The Romulan Way* as closely as I could while devel-

After Kirk regained his ship from Khan, he exiled him and his followers on Ceti Alpha V. What happened to these genetically enhanced beings as they attempted to conquer a new world? What caused Khan's outright hatred of Kirk that sent him on a murderous rampage fifteen years later? About a year after Khan is finally defeated, Captain Kirk heads to the desolate planet to decipher what ultimately drove Khan to seek revenge. He finds a diary written by former Starfleet officer and Khan's lover, Marla McGivers.

Greg commented, "Once we wrapped up *The Eugenics Wars*, the obvious next project was Khan's years on Ceti Alpha V, connecting the dots between 'Space Seed' and *The Wrath of Khan*. The big challenge: Could I get an entire book out of a few dozen people stuck on a barren rock for fifteen or so years? Basically, I had to extrapolate a novel out of a few lines of dialogue in *The Wrath of Khan*. 'The planet was laid waste,' and so on. The trick was to assume that the degradation of Ceti Alpha V's environment took place gradually, over the course of years. The planet didn't go from savage wilderness to lifeless desert overnight, which allowed me to spread the saga of the planet's slow, painful demise over three hundred pages or so. It made sense scientifically, too; global extinction takes time. By necessity, *To Reign In Hell* is very different from the *Eugenics Wars* books: grimmer, more tragic, and less rife with opportunities for cute fannish in-jokes and cameos. I quickly rejected the idea of getting Gary Seven and Roberta involved again; that would have been pushing things. No surprise visits by the Klingons or Romulans either. The movie makes it pretty clear that they were on Khan and his people were on their own the whole time. Think of it as *Survivor: Star Trek*. I also picked up a new major character: Marla McGivers. In some ways, the new book ended up being as much her story as Khan's. In my head, I always thought of her storyline as 'The Reha-

bilitation of Marla McGivers.' Let's face it . . . as depicted in 'Space Seed,' Marla is not exactly the pride of Starfleet and even less of a feminist role model, and yet somehow she became the great love of Khan's life, whose death ultimately drove him off the deep end. My goal was to toughen Marla up some, and give her more of a spine, while still remaining consistent with the character we met in the original episode."

Although not actually involved with the project, editor Marco Palmieri recalls he made a contribution to it. "John had mentioned to me that Greg's final Khan novel was to be called *A World to Win*, echoing a line of Khan's dialogue at the end of 'Space Seed,' in which he said that his exile to Ceti Alpha V was giving him exactly what he wanted. I thought, given the actual outcome of his exile, which Greg's book was meant to illuminate, the prophetic Miltonian reference from the same scene in 'Space Seed' made a stronger, more appropriate title. So I asked John, 'Have you considered *To Reign in Hell*? Next thing I knew, that was the new title of the book.'"

EX MACHINA

CHRISTOPHER L. BENNETT

JANUARY 2005   (366PP)

Shortly after the events chronicled in *Star Trek: The Motion Picture*, our heroes are still reeling from the aftershock. Meanwhile, the colonists of Daran IV—formerly passengers on the Fabrini worldship *Yonada* (from "For the World Is Hollow, And I Have Touched the Sky")—are struggling to hold their society together, and the help they receive from their old friends on the *Enterprise* may do more harm than good.

Christopher was making up *Trek* universe stories before he ever had the idea of writing them professionally. "At age eleven I got a set of Star City building blocks, and imagined that the futuristic cities I built occupied the *Star Trek* universe a century after Kirk's era (an idea ahead of its time, since *The Next Generation* was seven years away). But soon I found that restrictive, and changed the setting to my own original

universe. One day, when I was thirteen, I made up a story about the people inside one of my Star Cities without actually physically playing with the city—just thinking about it. It was a complete tale, with a beginning, middle, and end, with characters and conflict and everything. I realized I was pretty good at coming up with stories, and for the first time I knew what I wanted to do with my life (if you don't count my ambition at age four to be a baseball player). Once I knew I wanted to be a writer, it was just natural that the desire to write *Trek* fiction would come along with that. As I read the *Trek* novels that were starting to come out around that time, I started thinking about how I might write them, what I might have done differently, what stories I might want to tell, and so on. I wrote a couple of fanfics, though I never made any serious effort to get them published or distributed anywhere, and I considered ideas for novels I'd like to write if I ever got the chance. Once there were new *Star Trek* shows on the air, I wanted to write for them, too. In the 90s I wrote spec scripts for *The Next Generation* and *Deep Space Nine*. My DS9 spec script actually got me a pitch invitation. I went out to L.A. and pitched to Robert Hewitt Wolfe; he didn't take any of my pitches, but his comments about them drove home the importance of focusing on character, a lesson that's been very helpful to me. I then pitched to *Voyager* twice (by phone), and got as far as getting one of my ideas brought up in a production meeting, but no farther."

In terms of writing *Ex Machina*, he remarked, "I've always felt that the life-changing epiphany Spock underwent in *Star Trek: The Motion Picture* deserved more exploration than it had ever gotten in the novels. Most novels set after *The Motion Picture* tended to gloss over it, to portray Spock as essentially the same person he'd been in the series. I felt an opportunity was being missed."

Christopher continued, "I felt that stories set between *The Motion Picture* and *The Wrath of Khan* would afford a good opportunity for getting around the limitations that were imposed on *Trek* novels in the 90s, because you could tell stories with real character growth and change without contradicting established continuity. At the time, the prospect of writing *Trek* novels was more a daydream than anything else, but nonetheless I gave some thought to what I'd do if given the opportunity to follow up on Spock's epiphany and the other character threads arising from *The Motion Picture*, or suggested by the later movies. So this was literally my dream *Trek* novel, and once I'd gotten my foot in the door with my previous two entries, I wrote up a proposal and asked Marco if he'd like to see it, and he said yes. The proposal was a bit vague on plot specifics, so I was expecting to be asked for a fuller outline first. But once the proposal was accepted, Marco just told me to go ahead and get the manuscript to him in six and a half months."

Marco clarified, "It wasn't a tough decision. Having already bought a short story from Christopher, I knew I wanted to work with him again. Sometimes an author conveys his ideas with a clarity of thought and a flair for language that you immediately recognize will carry over to the manuscript."

Christopher tied in the original series episode, "For the World is Hollow, and I Have Touched the Sky": "I realized that just exposing the computer behind the curtain wouldn't be the end of the story. People don't abandon their deep-rooted spiritual beliefs easily or all at once. I figured there would be numerous sects arising among the people of post-Oracle Yonada, and that they'd be jockeying for the lead in defining a new direction for their society, and competing with those who embraced a more secular, Federation-type view. This resonated with the things I'd learned in college about the patterns that have been shaping Mideast affairs for the past couple of centuries, and I wanted to tell a story that illustrated those issues—issues that are rarely taken into account when Americans think and talk about current events. Another thing I wanted to do was try to recapture the unique style and atmosphere of *Star Trek: The Motion Picture*. I studied the film and the various references about it in detail, and made a point of describing the sets, uniforms, technology, and so forth, as they'd appeared in the movie. I tried to explore the diverse multispecies crew only glimpsed in the movie, developing several prominent supporting characters belonging to species seen only in *The Motion Picture*. This was an opportunity for the kind of alien-building which I consider one of my greatest strengths as a writer—creating plausible and exotic alien biologies and cultures, and giving alien characters their own unique ways of thinking and perceiving the universe. I also based most of the supporting crew members on bit players and extras that'd actually appeared in the film. After I got the go-ahead, I gave myself a month and a half— until the end of September 2003—to work out a more detailed outline, character backstories, and world-building. I took what the episode gave us about Yonada and expanded it into a coherent history, culture, and technology. There was little enough there that I had a great deal of freedom, but what was there held together surprisingly well. I tried to work out the overall flow of Yonada's history over ten thousand years, giving it enough twists and turns to make the discovery of its history a gradual process, a mystery which would unfold over the course of the novel. . . . What I tried to do was to depict the variety of different ways in which Yonada's history was told and defined by different groups with different agendas—sort of a *Rashomon* approach, I guess. My schedule theoretically left me five months for the writing, and it went along pretty smoothly for the first month. However, the money I got for the novel let me afford to move out of my father's house at long last. The process of apartment-hunting, moving, and recovery took about two months, and I was slow getting back into the swing of writing. So I ended up having to rush toward the end, and to turn in a first draft that wasn't as polished as I would've liked. I was able to fix a lot of the problems in the revision phase—for instance, I caught and corrected a glitch in the timing, trimmed some redundant exposition, and added a bit more nuance to a character who'd come off as yet another Overbearing Federation Official. Still, there are things I wish I could've polished more or developed further. To some extent, I tried to do too much in this book, and some elements got short shrift. Still, Marco was very pleased with the end product, and the changes I was asked for by Marco and by John Van Citters at Paramount licensing were relatively few in proportion to the length of the novel, and I guess I got off relatively easy considering how much I tried to push the envelope with this book."

ENGINES OF DESTINY
Gene DeWeese

MARCH 2005   (338PP)

After finding himself seventy-five years in the future, Scotty contemplates his life and decides to correct a wrong. With the help of a borrowed Klingon vessel, he decides to travel back in time and rescue Captain Kirk before he "dies" on the maiden voyage of the *Enterprise*-B. Thanks to Guinan, Picard catches up to Scotty just as he initiates the time maneuver, and the *Enterprise*-D follows him back into the past. Scotty successfully rescues his former captain, but everything else familiar has been drastically altered. With the Alpha Quadrant completely infested with Borg, and no Federation to ask for help, Scotty and Kirk must team with Picard to restore the timeline.

When asked about this "lost book," Gene said, "I originally wanted to call it *Legacy*, but that title had already been used. It grew out of John Ordover's suggestion that I do something about

Scotty's retirement, but that was way back before lots of other books almost outdated it out of existence. As for why it was considered 'lost' . . . . Apparently it really was literally lost. I turned in a manuscript two or three years ago, did two partial revisions based on Carol Greenburg's comments (which did improve things quite a bit), collected the final part of the advance, and waited. Nothing happened until a few months ago, when Ordover left. My agent inquired for the umpteenth time, but this time his inquiry got to Marco, who wondered what we were talking about.

Marco elaborated, "I did some digging and learned that, sure enough, the book had been paid for years ago but somehow never published. I felt terrible for Gene, and set about correcting the matter as quickly as possible. I asked Keith DeCandido—who, in addition to being one of our authors, also does some freelance editorial work—to see the project through to publication. My only creative contribution to *Engines of Destiny* was the cover concept, the timepiece being shattered by the nexus, which actually turned out exactly as I'd envisioned it."

SEEDS OF RAGE
(ERRAND OF FURY, Book One)
KEVIN RYAN

APRIL 2005 (287PP)

Set immediately after the events chronicled in the *Errand of Vengeance* trilogy. Security Chief Leslie Parrish still mourns the loss of her lover, Jon, when she discovers that she is pregnant with his child. Finding out he was a surgically alerted Klingon complicates matters even further. Meanwhile, retired *Starfleet* officer Michael Fuller reenlists to exact revenge on the Klingons for murdering his son. And a major conflict with the Empire seems certain.

Kevin remarked, "After the events of the first trilogy, we are a little bit closer to war but we are not quite there yet. I wanted to take us to the episode, 'Errand of Mercy.' The last book in these three will end with a partial novelization of the episode. It will follow some of the continuing characters and some of the surviving security people. They got the lowest pay and had the highest mortality in the fleet, so many of the characters in the books don't survive. The primary new character, Sam Fuller, is the commanding officer of the squad that the Klingon infiltrator was part of. He dies at the end of the first trilogy. His dad, Michael Fuller, makes a minor appearance in the Admiral Justman flashback. Michael Fuller reenlists in Starfleet and joins security to get on board the *Enterprise*. His mission: to have a talk with the Klingons who killed his son. He becomes a primary mover as it moves closer to war and 'Errand of Mercy.' "

Book Two of this trilogy, *Demands of Honor*, is slated for publication in February 2007.

BURNING DREAMS
MARGARET WANDER BONANNO

AUGUST 2006   (351 PP)

Ambassador Spock receives a summons from Talos IV and he realizes that over fifty years have passed since he defied orders and the death penalty to give the disfigured, paralyzed cap-

tain a new chance at life. That life is explored fully as we experience the circumstances and events that shaped *Star Trek*'s first captain, and what became of him on Talos IV.

Margaret remarked, "*Burning Dreams* was one of those magical times when an author and an editor bring their respective talents to a happy confluence. I've always wanted to fill in the missing pieces of Christopher Pike's story, and Marco was confident enough in my ability to 'hear' the characters to let me do just that. The suggestion to make Pike a force for change on environmental issues was entirely Marco's idea. It makes sense, of course, since the Talosians nearly destroyed themselves, and they needed Pike to help them rebuild— though not in the way they'd originally intended in 'The Cage.' "

Marco said, "I recall that the idea for *Burning Dreams* started with three questions: Who was Pike, really, as a human being, beyond what we saw in 'The Cage'? . . . How long did he live after his return to Talos? . . . And for what would he be remembered most? To answer those questions, we'd need a story that not only defined the character once and for all, but did it in a way that would give him the closure I'd always felt he was missing. Making that story part of Pocket's fortieth anniversary celebration was a no-brainer."

PROVENANCE OF SHADOWS
(CRUCIBLE: McCOY)
DAVID R. GEORGE III

SEPTEMBER 2006   (627PP)

T he river of time flows in un-expected directions and various eddies and currents force the historian to inquire about what might have been. Doctor McCoy rescues Edith Keeler from a streetcar and his life starts to unravel. He starts to take odd jobs and work alongside Edith at the shelter while waiting for Kirk and Spock to rescue him. McCoy has no idea he altered history when he saved Edith's life, and rescue is impossible. The second story follows McCoy in his parallel life, more familiar, where the rescue from the Guardian was successful and he continues his service on the *Enterprise*. What was and what might have been intertwine.

David remembered, "When I sat down to begin work on this original series trilogy, the first question I asked myself was, 'What do we *not* know about these characters?' In addition to the original three seasons of episodes, these characters appeared in an animated series, seven feature films, and hundreds of published novels and short stories. What fresh story could I possibly tell about them, what new perspective could I bring to the table? In a quandary, I thought and thought and thought about TOS, eventually watching every single episode again. By degrees, I began to notice an aspect of Dr. McCoy's life not generally discussed, less an intentional creation by the writers, I suspected, than simply an unintentional artifact of the collection of stories they'd told. I then also realized that a section of McCoy's life hadn't, to my knowledge, ever been explored, and I saw a way that I could tie that in with my first observation. Not only that, the tale I wanted to tell had a basis in what is widely regarded as one of *Star Trek*'s finest hours in any of its incarnations, 'The City on the Edge of Forever.' This meant that I could hook into a popular episode, and at the same time deeply ground the novel within the series, something I thought important for a novel intended to commemorate the fortieth anniversary of the show. In addition, I saw how 'City' could easily have had a huge impact not simply on McCoy, but also on Kirk and Spock, and I decided that I could use the events of that episode to explore what could have been the single incident—the crucible—that most informed all three lives. That also led me to choosing to pen what would essentially be a Kirk novel, a Spock novel, and a McCoy novel to complete the trilogy, something that seemed apt given the nature of the series itself."

David continued, "Actually writing *Provenance of Shadows* was interesting. For one thing, it really turned out to be two novels in one, with a pair of storylines paralleling each other throughout most of the book. Also, one of these plots developed more as a mainstream piece of writing than as science fiction, which proved a fascinating exercise for me. In all, I enjoyed the process very much, and look forward to reader reaction."

THE FIRE AND THE ROSE
(CRUCIBLE: SPOCK)
DAVID R. GEORGE III

DECEMBER 2006   (390PP)

A look at Spock as he's never been seen before: The untold events—and consequences—of the mission to 1930 Earth play out as Spock reexamines his life's choices, and their cost, both to himself and those closest to him. But as the long years stretch on, his inability to balance the equation of friendship and historical necessity bring his other lifelong struggle into stark relief.

• • •

"As with the McCoy novel, I wanted to find something about the character of Spock that hadn't been explored. Surprisingly, I found myself turning to his dual nature, his logical Vulcan side and his emotional human side. Clearly this two-sided personality has always been a fundamental characteristic of Spock, but I realized that something profound had happened to the character that really hadn't been addressed. I also saw how I could link that with the events of 'City,' and therefore to the McCoy novel."

THE STAR TO EVERY WANDERING
(CRUCIBLE: KIRK)
DAVID R. GEORGE III

MARCH 2007   (320PP)

Forever changed by having to sacrifice the one true love of his life in Earth's past, James Kirk pushes past his pain and returns to the future and the stars. But the hole in his soul never truly heals, and when time and space begin to crumble, Kirk is driven, both by the needs of many—and the one—into an odyssey that tests the limits of his resolve.

David remarked, "The impact on Kirk of what happened in 'The City on the Edge of Forever' seemed pretty clear, and so I wasn't sure what newness I could add to that dialogue—not at first, anyway. Then I saw something that I didn't think had been done, and I ran with it. But in addition to that, I found a different sort of story to tell than those in the first two novels of the trilogy, something more action-oriented than character-oriented, at least in part. Since I wanted variety in the three books, I went forward with that plot, making my way through a complex storyline that weaved in and out of the tales we already know that make up the original series."

THE EMPTY CHAIR
(RIHANNSU, Book Five)
DIANE DUANE

DECEMBER 2006   **(421 PP)**

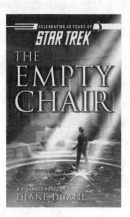

The fifth novel in the *Rihannsu* saga. The *Enterprise* and the Romulans aboard the *Bloodwing* arrive together in the Artaleirh System to prepare for a major battle. A civil war appears imminent and Kirk will do everything in his power to help Ael win. The Praetor demands justice and will do anything to destroy the uprising. Higher ups in the Federation start to believe that Kirk and the crew of the *Enterprise* have gone to the other side and begin to plot their destruction. Meanwhile, a cloaked Romulan ship heads into Federation territory with a dangerous weapon aboard.

Diane remarked, "*The Empty Chair* had always been planned from around the time Peter and I finished *The Romulan Way.* I foresaw that eventually I might be called upon to finish the series out: With the new version of *Star Trek:*

WILLIAM SHATNER AND *STAR TREK* FICTION

William Shatner is, of course, best known for his portrayal of Captain James T. Kirk on TV and in feature films. *Star Trek* readers, however, also know him by his other vocation: coauthor of several novels, together with his collaborators, Judith and Garfield Reeves-Stevens, in which Kirk is alive and well in the twenty-fourth century after the events of *Star Trek Generations*.

How much of the books are actually written by Shatner? Editor Margaret Clark remarked, "They all sit down and do the outline, where they come up with the core of the story together. What is the heart of the story? What is Kirk's motivation? Judy and Gar then go away and write a more detailed outline based on their meeting and their notes. It's a back-and-forth process that extends to the execution of the manuscript. Ninety-five percent of the Kirk material in these books comes from Bill, with gentle tweaks from Gar and Judy. They give the books their excellent continuity."

When asked about why he wanted to write *Star Trek* novels, Shatner responded, "One is acting and one is writing. I'm a writer as well as an actor and it's two different skills."

The writing team came together when then-editor Kevin Ryan, aware of Shatner's *TekWar* fiction, approached his agent and asked if Shatner would be interested in collaborating with the Reeves-Stevens duo on a *Star Trek* novel. Kevin sent the agent a copy of Gar and Judy's *Federation* for Shatner's consideration, and shortly thereafter a partnership was born. "We agreed that we wanted to write together. The way we write is I start things off with an outline. They start work from that outline and then I [go over it], rewrite, and hand it back to them. It's a process of interacting at all phases of the writing. I'm into plot and character more than anything."

The Next Generation just then coming onto the screen, it seemed likely that someone at the Paramount end of things would want to take up the Romulans and start doing something different with them. I therefore began asking myself how it would be possible to 'justify' my image of the Romulans/Rihannsu with the one that was likely to start to solidify soon . . . and how to leave them in a situation which would seem to lead naturally to the new canonical material which was even then starting to be established. I therefore outlined *Swordhunt/Honor Blade* and *Empty Chair*. However, not too long afterwards it became plain that Paramount's priorities regarding the novels were shifting, and there wasn't going to be any interest for the foreseeable future in continuing this particular line of literary inquiry. So I put the outlines aside. However, the future can't always be foreseen . . . I was very surprised, much later, when I got an e-mail from John Ordover suggesting it was time to return to the story. I went back to those outlines again, made some changes, and started work."

When asked about the long delay between *Honor Blade* and *The Empty Chair*, she replied, "I had a series of health problems that started to interfere with my writing, including a fairly severe back injury which fortunately has sorted itself out over time. I've always regretted that long period between books: It took me a while to recover the lost impetus."

THE ASHES OF EDEN
WILLIAM SHATNER,
WITH JUDITH AND GARFIELD REEVES-STEVENS

JUNE 1995   (309PP)

ORIGINALLY PUBLISHED IN HARDCOVER

Six months prior to his disappearance aboard the *Enterprise-B*, Kirk is asked by a young and attractive half-Romulan, half-Klingon woman to help her save her world. Telani offers eternal youth for his help. Of course, Kirk's friends don't take this sitting down. Telani's world of Chal will become the battleground between good guys like Kirk and evil forces within Starfleet that demand the planet's secrets.

Bill replied, "The idea for *Ashes of Eden* came from a screenplay I wrote having to do with the archetypal search for youth."

THE RETURN
WILLIAM SHATNER,
WITH JUDITH AND GARFIELD REEVES-STEVENS

APRIL 1996   (371PP)

ORIGINALLY PUBLISHED IN HARDCOVER

AVENGER
WILLIAM SHATNER,
WITH JUDITH AND GARFIELD REEVES-STEVENS

MAY 1997   (370PP)

ORIGINALLY PUBLISHED IN HARDCOVER

Captain Kirk is resurrected, courtesy of the Borg. His return to life is the center of a Romulan plot to destroy the Federation along with the collective. Our favorite captain becomes a killing machine. His target? Jean Luc-Picard. Picard, with his expansive knowledge of the Borg, is on a secret mission to infiltrate a Cube and stop the invasion.

Bill commented, "The inspiration for *The Return* was Kirk's death in *Generations*. I wanted to come up with a way to bring him back quickly, an idea I went to sell to Paramount. I outlined forty pages around the time we filmed the death of the character."

A virulent plague rampages various Federation outposts, destroying all plant life. Ambassador Spock heads back to Vulcan, investigating the possibility that his father, Sarek, did not die of Bendii's Syndrome naturally. Kirk, still alive, teams up with Spock and Picard to tackle the threat.

Of the three novels collectively called *The Odyssey Trilogy*, Bill remarked, "After *The Return*, I wanted to do a series of books that involved Kirk with a wife and child. I was looking at the question of human continuity and culling from events in my life that I could put down under the guise of science fiction. There were events that happened to me that I tried to shape into some kind of art."

SPECTRE

WILLIAM SHATNER,
WITH JUDITH AND GARFIELD REEVES-STEVENS

MAY 1998 (372PP)

ORIGINALLY PUBLISHED IN HARDCOVER

Captain Kirk has retired and lives peacefully with his beloved Teilani on the planet Chal. The rebuilding process as the results of the plague is slow-going. When Teilani suggests he visit his friends on Earth, Kirk finds himself kidnapped by an aggressive Katherine Janeway. Forced to see the horrifying results of a decision he made years ago, he is also forced to confront the bitter enemy he cannot defeat—himself!

DARK VICTORY

WILLIAM SHATNER,
WITH JUDITH AND GARFIELD REEVES-STEVENS

APRIL 1999 (303PP)

ORIGINALLY PUBLISHED IN HARDCOVER

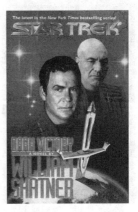

Under Federation orders, Kirk is forced to stay out of the fight because everyone is worried his imposter will take his place. When Teilani is injected with a deadly toxin, Kirk asks his friends for help to confront his mirror self and obtain the antidote. Can he outwit himself to save his beloved and the galaxy?

PRESERVER
WILLIAM SHATNER,
WITH JUDITH AND GARFIELD REEVES-STEVENS

JULY 2000 (374PP)

ORIGINALLY PUBLISHED IN HARDCOVER

James Kirk is able to obtain an antidote for his dying wife in time, but at a horrible price. Investigating a base belonging to the First Federation (from the episode "The Corbomite Maneuver"), the two Kirks uncover a possible larger conspiracy. Discovering an obelisk, the evidence points to a race of beings capable of manipulation on a galaxy scale. Who are the Preservers? The secret will devastate two universes.

When asked about the *Mirror Universe Trilogy*, Bill responded, *"The Mirror Universe* books were of course inspired by 'Mirror, Mirror,' from the TV series as a means to tell a story about the dark side of the human psyche and how we overcome it, or fail to."

CAPTAIN'S PERIL
WILLIAM SHATNER,
WITH JUDITH AND GARFIELD REEVES-STEVENS

OCTOBER 2002 (335PP)

ORIGINALLY PUBLISHED IN HARDCOVER

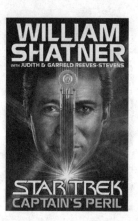

Experiencing a personal crisis, Kirk goes with Picard to an archeological dig on Bajor. When they arrive, the men discover there has been a murder at the camp. Which one of the remaining scientists and workers is the killer? Interspersed with the Bajoran story, Kirk tells a tale to Picard of an early adventure, from when Kirk was six months into his captaincy of the *Enterprise*.

CAPTAIN'S BLOOD

William Shatner,
with Judith and Garfield Reeves-Stevens

December 2003   (335pp)

ORIGINALLY PUBLISHED IN HARDCOVER

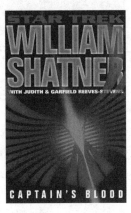

⋀ Spock appears to have been murdered on Romulus while giving a speech. A clandestine mission to uncover the truth leads Kirk and friends to the Romulan homeworld. To the Captain's horror, the plot not only involves Spock, but also Kirk's five-year-old son!

CAPTAIN'S GLORY

William Shatner,
with Judith and Garfield Reeves-Stevens

August 2006   (350pp)

ORIGINALLY PUBLISHED IN HARDCOVER

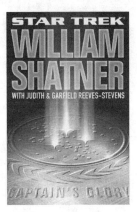

⋀ The *U.S.S. Titan*, commanded by William Riker, attempts to help Kirk and Picard battle the Totality. On a mission to discover what happened to his friend, Kirk's son gets kidnapped. Not knowing whom to trust, he must rely on his instincts if he will save his son and the galaxy.

Commenting on *The Totality Trilogy*, Bill said, "These books are all about love, and the different forms it takes: romance, family, friendship—the essential quality that defines the human experience."

STAR TREK: THE NEXT GENERATION NUMBERED NOVELS

1

GHOST SHIP
Diane Carey

JULY 1988   (258PP)

A creature engulfs a Russian aircraft carrier in the twentieth century, and then the *Enterprise*-D runs across this same creature three hundred years later. Troi hears the voices of the lost crew, and realizes they are still alive!

Diane remembered how difficult it was to write the first original *The Next Generation* novel. She said, "As *Star Trek*'s top-selling author at the time, I was asked to launch the new series by writing the first TNG original fiction book—interesting mostly because it was written without ever having seen the series because TNG hadn't aired yet. We were working strictly from the 'bible,' and many of the characters hadn't been cast yet, so I couldn't even look at photos of the people."

Editor Dave Stern had major difficulties launching the series of TNG novels. He said, "Gene Roddenberry was intimately involved at this point and he had a lot of problems with it, and Richard Arnold had a lot of problems with it."

Richard Arnold remembered, "What I remember about Diane's books is the militarism was really over the top and no matter how many times Gene tried to get across to her that Starfleet was not military and *Star Trek* was not about a militaristic future, she would never accept it."

STAR TREK: MILITARY OR NOT?

The question of *Star Trek*'s militarism, or its lack thereof, has been a source of longstanding debate in fandom. Marco Palmieri, one of the current editors of *Star Trek* fiction, believes this apparent confusion may stem from the source material itself. "The answer actually depends a lot on what episodes you think about when you consider the question. It's certainly true that exploration, scientific discovery, peaceful alien contact, and diplomacy underscored episodes like 'The Cage,' 'Where No Man Has Gone Before,' 'The Corbomite Maneuver,' 'The Devil in the Dark,' and 'For the World Is Hollow, and I Have Touched the Sky.' On the other hand, we also had episodes such as 'Balance of Terror,' 'Errand of Mercy,' 'A Private Little War,' 'The Ultimate Computer,' and 'The *Enterprise* Incident,' all of which appear to support the idea that *Star Trek* had a strong military component from the beginning. Similar comparisons can be made in *The Next Generation* and in each of *Star Trek*'s subsequent incarnations. I think that, in striving to be true to the totality of *Star Trek*, the fiction has, historically, sought to achieve the same balance of thematic and philosophical elements that was in evidence on the various TV series."

2

THE PEACEKEEPERS
GENE DEWEESE

S E P T E M B E R   1 9 8 8   (3 1 0 P P)

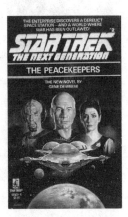

eordi and Data are aboard a deserted space vessel when they mysteriously vanish. While the rest of the crew tries to determine where they disappeared to, the two find themselves on a station orbiting an Earth-like planet. The guardians of the station believe that Data and Geordi are peacekeepers. During their inquiry, they learn the occupants of the planet stumbled onto the station and then used the unknown technology to avert a global war. Now the planet continues to maintain a fragile peace, due to being terrified of the station's destructive potential. An amusing typo on the cover blurb calls Geordi "Georgi."

Gene said, "*Peacekeepers* came out of a *Final Nexus* subplot that never got used. I don't remember any details, but part of the reason was that I had just started writing *The Final Nexus* when Dave Stern asked me if I could drop it temporarily and do a *Next Generation* novel— fast. He sent all the reference material he had, including several scripts, so I wasn't flying completely blind, but I did have trouble making the characters (except for Data) distinctive and probably got it wrong a lot of the time."

3

THE CHILDREN OF HAMLIN
Carmen Carter

November 1988   (252pp)

Fifty years ago, the Choraii destroyed the Hamlin outpost, leaving no adult survivors and abducting the children. They are back, but willing to negotiate this time, exchanging precious metals for the now grown children still living with them. The negotiation leaders are Ambassador Deelor and his mysterious companion, Ruthe, who are traveling on the *Enterprise-D*. With the bizarre alien environment of the Choraii, will the children be able to adjust back to our way of life?

Carmen remarked, "Having gotten one foot in the door at Pocket Books (with *Dreams of the Raven*), I couldn't resist taking advantage of the opportunity to submit a proposal for an-

other novel. This time around I wanted to explore the relationship of humans to other species, but with the tables turned so that humans were the domesticated animal of a more advanced race. The Hamlin legend provided a framework for that comparison and Pocket Books' need for authors willing to write in the new TNG universe again provided me with an entry into the crowded publishing schedule. Since I loved the new show, and was increasingly intrigued by the character of Captain Picard, I was more than willing to switch away from classic *Trek*."

4

SURVIVORS
Jean Lorrah

January 1989   (253pp)

A major uprising on the planet Treva sends Tasha Yar and Data to report on the activities of the warlord in power. While seemingly innocent, the president has something more sinister in mind. She wants weapons that only the Federation can provide. For Tasha, her main adversary, Dare Adin, is a former Starfleet officer who rescued Yar when she was young and became her lover. Accused of a crime he says he didn't commit, he's the Federation's most wanted fugitive. In the meantime, Data sees her relationship with Dare, and begins to show signs of jealousy.

Jean commented, "I was fascinated by the relationship between Data and Tasha Yar, as well as the scraps of Yar's background eked out on the show. I had originally submitted the proposal with a bittersweet rather than tragic ending (obviously Dare and his crew couldn't be added to the cast), but Paramount didn't want continuing characters' backgrounds filled in [by fiction]. But when they wrote Tasha out, Pocket Books called *me* to say 'We want that Tasha book now!'"

5

STRIKE ZONE

PETER DAVID

MARCH 1989 (275PP)

The Kreel have stumbled onto a planet with a storage facility full of extremely powerful weapons that could easily destroy the *Enterprise*-D. They begin using the weapons on the Klingons and now Picard has been asked to facilitate the dispute. Having both races on board the *Enterprise* calls for tact, something the Klingons and the Kreel are severely lacking.

Peter remarked, "*Strike Zone* picked up on story threads and concepts that I had been working in the comic books. I just concluded the story seventy-eight years later. I grafted over several characters from the comic book to *Next Generation*. I did some heavy retooling of the story so it flowed naturally out of *Next Generation* characters because you can't just take Kirk out and drop in Picard and have the story be precisely the same. Obviously that is not going to be the case. So, I had to rethink the story in terms of having it be relevant and organic to the *Next Generation* characters."

POWER HUNGRY
HOWARD WEINSTEIN

MAY 1989   (276PP)

D esperately needed supplies for the planet Thiopa are almost destroyed by marauders. The *Enterprise* crew must decipher the attackers' motives and see if the famine relief will actually be used correctly.

Howard said, *"Power Hungry* came from my appreciation of the work done by the late folksinger-activist Harry Chapin (of 'Cat's in the Cradle' fame) to educate people about the problem of world hunger, and to try to do something about it. The distribution of food can be a potent tool to improve the lot of poor people—or a weapon to degrade and punish people who don't have much to begin with. So this story is quite literally about how rulers exercise—or abuse—power."

MASKS
JOHN VORNHOLT

JULY 1989   (277PP)

T he planet Lorca and its inhabitants never show their real faces to anyone. Instead, they wear masks denoting their status. Various members of the *Enterprise*-D beam down to the surface and promptly lose contact. With their masks on, the crew attempts to find the leader of the planet and re-establish communication with the ship. Since the society resembles a nontechnological feudal state, that will prove to be difficult.

"[*Masks* was] my first published adult novel, my first *Star Trek* book, and a bonafide best seller that was the toast of the beaches in the summer of 1989, when *The Next Generation* was heating up. It was almost an instant book, and the process left me in a daze. Lorca is a primitive culture where everyone wears ornate masks, both for practical purposes and to denote their place in society. I was the first one to get Picard in an intimate relationship, and the story has an unusual high-fantasy feel to it with all the swordplay and masks. Psychiatrists and psychologists love this book and have written me often about it."

8

THE CAPTAIN'S HONOR
DAVID AND DANIEL DVORKIN

SEPTEMBER 1989   (255PP)

The planet Tenara has been attacked by the M'Dok— aliens that look like cats—so now the crew of the *Enterprise*-D and the *Centurion* must protect the planet. The crew of the *Centurion*, including Captain Sejanus, is from the planet Magna Roma, from the original series episode, "Bread and Circuses."

David explained how his son, Daniel, ended up writing the book with him. David said, "We exposed Daniel to endless hours of The Original Series reruns while he was growing up. He became a science fan, a science fiction fan, and a *Star Trek* fan. He and I wanted to write some-

thing together, so a *Star Trek* novel seemed natural. Also, we're both interested in Roman history and both loved the Roman Empire episode of TOS. My wife and I had been addicted to *I, Claudius* and both thought Patrick Stewart's Sejanus was one of the best things in that series. So we put all of that together and came up with the plot of *Captain's Honor*. We couldn't figure out any believable way to make the Roman character an alternate-history version of the original, historical Sejanus, unfortunately. We both really liked the underlying issue of the conflicting views of honor and duty on the part of the two captains. Daniel, who was planning a military career, was especially fascinated by those elements.

According to David, Pocket was a bit leery of having Daniel as a coauthor, since he was only eighteen when they sent in the outline. Daniel wrote the book's first chapter and David wrote the second, and that convinced the publisher that they could do the job. David said, "The writing was complicated by Daniel's going off for basic training at Fort Benning in Georgia before the book was completely finished. We managed, obviously, and after we were done, neither of us were sure which part he had written."

The path to publication this time around surprised David. He said, "The editorial process was [difficult] compared to what I had experienced with the first two books. By this time, the show was back on the air, obviously, and Paramount wanted to protect what was a valuable property for them. They were concerned about remarkably small details in the plot and character depictions. The editor [rewrote] big chunks of the book—something we didn't discover until we saw the published version. Perhaps we were simply experiencing what scriptwriters are used to but novelists aren't. Unfortunately, the cover shows a Roman officer who needs a shave (very un-Roman!) and who doesn't look like Picard even though they're described as practically twins in the book. The cover also has a Japanese sword on it for some reason. That sword will always remain a mystery to me."

With his son, Daniel, David wrote an original SF novel, *Dawn Crescent*.

#9

A CALL TO DARKNESS

Michael Jan Friedman

November 1989   **(274pp)**

A he crew tries to find the whereabouts of the research vessel *Mendel*. Found orbiting a planet and partially hidden behind a strange energy shield, Captain Picard and others beam aboard to determine what actually happened. While on board, they vanish. Riker, desperate

to find them, also has to deal with a mysterious plague that begins to decimate the crew.

Mike remarked, "I wanted to do a *The Next Generation* book. The effect of media on our culture was [on] my mind at the time. I also wanted to place the characters in a milieu where they had to respond to each other, other than along the lines of the chain of command. And by taking their memories away from them and putting them in a competitive, survival sort of situation, I was able to do that and get some interesting give and take that wouldn't have been possible if they knew that they were captains and lieutenants and so on."

#10

A ROCK AND A HARD PLACE

Peter David

January 1990   **(244pp)**

A he terraforming project on the planet Paradise has taken a turn for the worse. Commander Riker receives a temporary transfer to investigate this program. The person in charge of the project happens to be a childhood friend. Riker's replacement on the *Enterprise*-D is Commander Stone, a man with a troubled past whose questionable methods have plagued his every posting.

Peter remembered, "I wrote a proposed teleplay for *The Next Generation* that was a Riker story. The basic storyline centered on Riker being put into a Prime Directive situation where he has to just stand there and watch someone killed. I was watching the original series episode, 'Friday's Child.' When Kirk rescues the Julie Newmar character from death, it is clearly a Prime Directive violation. This woman wasn't turning to Kirk for help; she was prepared to die. Kirk interfered without hesitation and no one mentioned violating the Prime Directive. *Next Generation* was much more obsessive about the Prime Directive than Kirk ever was. My teleplay never got anywhere but it was a similar situation and Riker had to stand there and let someone die instead of violate the Prime Directive. He was devastated by it."

Peter continued, "*A Rock and a Hard Place* stemmed from this idea and I took a Riker-like officer, put him in that situation, and then the guy fell apart. That is where the character Stone came from. The Mel Gibson character from *Lethal Weapon*, Riggs, heavily influenced me. A number of people saw Stone as a dry run for Calhoun. They are not entirely wrong, for no other reason than that I based Calhoun on William Wallace, the title character of *Braveheart*, which is another Mel Gibson movie."

1 1

GULLIVER'S FUGITIVES
Keith Sharee

MAY 1990 (282 PP)

A forgotten Earth colony is discovered during a search for a missing starship. On this planet the people live a sad life. All forms of fiction and use of imagination are crimes punishable by death. The *Enterprise* is invaded and Picard has his memory wiped, creating an automaton that actually believes the "fiction bad" dictum.

Attempts to contact the author for an interview were unsuccessful.

#12

DOOMSDAY WORLD

PETER DAVID, CARMEN CARTER, MICHAEL
JAN FRIEDMAN, AND ROBERT GREENBERGER

JULY 1990   (276 PP)

Geordi, Data, and Worf beam down to an artificial world maintained by the Federation and the K'vin Hegemony. Inspired to do archaeological work, the three *Enterprise* crew members find themselves alone when the ship gets sent on an emergency relief mission. Then to make matters worse, random attacks start occurring and they are accused of being the terrorists!

Bob recalled, "Even in high school, I was writing articles about *Star Trek* for my school newspaper. My first assignment for the college paper was covering a 1976 Labor Day Weekend *Trek* Convention in Manhattan. So, I have been actively writing about the series since 1975. When I graduated SUNY-Binghamton, I was hired at Starlog Press, where I continued to write feature stories about *Star Trek* for *Starlog*

magazine. When I arrived at DC Comics, I began assisting Marv Wolfman who was editing the comic version. I began with issue #9, trafficking the work, taking on the letter columns, and even pitching a story that was bought and used as issue #28. Marv transitioned to full-time freelance writing, so after Mike W. Barr was writer/editor for a bit, I took over full time and had an eight-year history with the comic. Along the way, I made contact with Pocket Books. I wanted close communication between us to avoid contradictions in stories between the novels and comics. The initial editorial crew—David Hartwell, John Douglas, and Mimi Panitch—were kind but they were doing so few novels at the time it wasn't much of an issue. As the line grew and David Stern, Kevin Ryan, and John Ordover each sat in the editor's center seat, we happily coordinated and became friendly. David occasionally would gather the New York-based authors for pizza and invited me as a courtesy. At one of these sessions, we brainstormed *The Lost Years* novel event. David happily let me do some behind-the-scenes coordination and even let me try my hand at pitching a novel outline, entitled *Orion's Belt*. I was clearly not ready to transition to prose at that time. At a subsequent event, though, the notion of collaborating on a novel, similar to the then-popular *Thieves' World* series came up. I teamed up with Peter David, Michael Jan Friedman, and Carmen Carter for the delightful experience in producing *Doomsday World*. It's been growing from there."

How does a story like this get written with four people? Bob commented, "When these collaborations happened, we talked about a general story and then I wrote the outline. It's structured so the crew is divvied up, allowing each other to write independently. In this case, everyone contributed some general notes on the world and characters we were creating. Everyone went to work, writing away. Once we were done, everyone got copies of the completed manuscript and we met over pizza and hammered out the contradictions or where to beef-up subplots. Invariably, Mike Friedman got to do the polish. We all proofed the galleys and cashed the checks."

Carmen remembered working on this novel with the others fondly. "Coauthoring with Peter, Michael, and Bob has to rate as one of the most fun experiences I've had as a *Trek* writer. The brainstorming sessions were almost immediately productive, and so lively that I can't remember where any particular idea came from. The collaboration was much smoother than I expected given how many strong and colorful personalities were brought under one yoke, and the resulting story appears to have been quite popular among readers."

Peter remembered, "Bob came up with the basic concept, if I remember correctly. We all got together and proceeded to totally destroy Bob's concept and totally rebuild it, which is what happens in these kinds of things. It's not like there was anything wrong with what Bob came up with, it's just the routine standing operation procedure that when you get other writers in the room, they stomp on it within an inch of its life, then restructure and redevelop the basic concept, and outline through the course of the meeting. Each of us would write one of the storylines from start to finish, and Mike put the thing together so it read smoothly as one piece instead of a hodgepodge of different writing styles."

1 3

THE EYES OF THE BEHOLDERS

A. C. CRISPIN

SEPTEMBER 1990 (243 PP)

The flagship of the fleet gets called in to investigate several disappearances of vessels along a new trade route. Of course, the *Enterprise* gets sucked into the same fate as the other missing ships. A gigantic artifact lies in the heart of the mystery and its awesome power renders the crew either insane or comatose.

Ann said about this novel, "I first wrote the storyline for what became *The Eyes of the Beholders* as a treatment for a possible *Star Trek* script. But Paramount never responded to my submission. . . . I turned the idea into a book outline instead."

1 4

EXILES

HOWARD WEINSTEIN

NOVEMBER 1990   (271 PP)

For over three hundred years, the Alaj and the Etolos have been bitter enemies. When ecological disaster strikes both worlds, the only hope for salvation lies in a peace settlement. When you need peace, you send in Picard! Some factions don't want peace and would rather watch their worlds perish. Some surprises are in store, however, for everyone when an enormous vessel enters the picture and takes Riker hostage! The back of this novel bears a quote from Gene Roddenberry congratulating Howard on a highly entertaining and socially relevant story.

Howard talked about the genesis of the story. "*Exiles* is an ecology story, symbolically about endangered species, and literally about how *we* become the endangered species if we don't clean up our act and figure out how to get along with the other people (and animals) with whom we share a very limited planet."

When asked about the majority of his novels having an ecological theme, Howard said, "How we humanoids treat the planet we live on and its nonhumanoid inhabitants seems to be linked with how we treat each other. And vice versa. Some people think environmentalism is a luxury we can't afford. Other people think it means preservation of nature to the extreme. I think environmentalism is about balance and responsibility, and about making smart choices that allow us to intelligently exploit natural resources. We've learned through observation and science that nature developed its own system of checks and balances long before humans started changing the face of the planet. So, when I can, I try to have my stories make the point that *we* are part of that system, and when our presence upsets the balance, we have to figure out ways to get what we need and still respect and restore the balance and equilibrium of nature. We already have a pretty good idea of the bad things that are likely to happen if we don't."

When asked about the Roddenberry quote on the back cover, he said, "I'm proud of the fact that when this book was approved by Paramount, the memo from Gene Roddenberry's office included a lovely compliment—at a time when that didn't happen very often, and the novels were often regarded as the unwanted stepchildren of the *Star Trek* universe. I suggested to the editor that we should ask if we could use Gene's comment on the cover. Paramount said OK, so *Exiles* became the only *Star Trek* novel to feature a cover quote from Gene Roddenberry."

1 5

FORTUNE'S LIGHT

Michael Jan Friedman

JANUARY 1991   (278pp)

Many years before, William Riker was part of a delegation that incorporated Imprima into the Federation. Now one of his good friends who remained on the planet has disappeared. Teller Conlon is accused of stealing the precious gem Fortune's Light and it's up to Riker to clear his friend's name and retrieve the stone from the real culprit. A subplot involves Data learning the nuances of baseball.

"*Fortune's Light* was cool. That was actually the second *Next Generation* book I did and it was a Riker adventure, which I really wanted to do. Riker as James Bond is sort of how it started out and I brought in the Ferengi later on as the culprits, but it was really a Riker story and it became very personal to him because it involved his friend. I inserted some flashback scenes that involved Riker and his friend Teller. While

the contemporary story proceeded forward, the flashbacks went backward. I think it worked well doing it that way, but that was taking a chance."

1 6

CONTAMINATION

John Vornholt

MARCH 1991   (273pp)

The famous scientist Lynn Costa, who has been conducting research aboard the *Enterprise*-D, has been murdered. Security Chief Worf is tasked to bring her killer to justice, and helping him in the investigation is Deanna Troi and Wesley Crusher.

"I always liked classic *Trek* for [its] murder mysteries, both in books and original episodes. *The Next Generation* didn't do many mysteries early on, so I wrote one as my second *Trek* novel. I could brag that I was the first to pair Deanna Troi and Worf in a meaningful way, and this book has a lot of real science in the clean-room setting aboard the *Enterprise*. Worf also makes a good plodding police detective, just one step behind the murderer until it really matters."

#17

BOOGEYMEN
Mel Gilden

JULY 1991   (244 PP)

With help from Data and Geordi, Wesley creates a holodeck program that will test his command skills. Unfortunately, the boogeymen of the program escape into the computer core, causing havoc. When a friend of Picard's arrives on board and demands to have his existence wiped out of Starfleet records, the captain will wish he had stayed in bed.

Mel remarked, "Originally, the story that became *Boogeymen* was about Professor Moriarty, the Sherlock Holmes character who was living in the holodeck computer. But Dave Stern told me that I couldn't use Moriarty because the guys writing the TV show might want to use

him again. . . . Perhaps the idea of using Wesley's nightmares to take over the ship ultimately produced a better story. I don't know. I never wrote the other one. I wrote the book before e-mail, and before I even had access to a fax machine, so rewrites were done by regular mail or by my repeating words one at a time to Dave over the phone. Most of Dave's suggestions and Paramount's demands made sense, though a few did seem unnecessarily restrictive."

#18

Q-IN-LAW
Peter David

OCTOBER 1991   (252 PP)

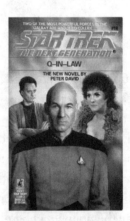

The *Enterprise* is chosen to host a wedding between two rival civilizations. One of the delegates attending the wedding happens to be Deanna's lovely mother, much to the chagrin of everyone else. When she meets Q and everyone warns her about him, that only attracts her to him more. Can Q, the most annoying being in the galaxy, find true love with the most annoying woman in the galaxy?

• • •

Peter commented, "I go to Kevin Ryan and Dave Stern and pitch a story in which Q goes head-to-head with Lwaxana Troi. Neither of them is interested in this story. They approached me about doing a giant novel about the Borg. I told them I would write *Vendetta* for them if they let me do the *Q-In-Law* as well and they agreed. I wrote *Q-In-Law* and it was sent to Paramount. Days and weeks and months go by with no response from the studio. Pocket Books needed notes! No response. I turned it in late 1990 and by February still nothing."

Peter continued, "Majel Barrett was coming to a convention in Long Island. I suggested Pocket give me a copy of the cover proofs and that I'd give it to Majel for her input. This was not unprecedented. I spent a bit of time with Marina Sirtis getting her input for *Strike Zone*. I figured if anyone really knew *Star Trek*, it would be Majel. The folks at Pocket told me that if she hated it, the novel was dead. I was willing to roll the dice since I didn't see another choice. I gave the manuscript to Majel at I-Con. I told her I had written this manuscript that is to be published by Pocket but we were still doing some tweaking. I asked her, 'I would like it if you could give me input into how I handled Lwaxana.' She was a relatively new character and I made some guesses. She looked at the cover and said, 'I'm on the cover.' Of course, since it was Q versus Lwaxana so naturally she would be on the cover. She promised to read the book and get back to me. True to her word, she read the manuscript on the plane ride back home. First day she gets back, she bustles into the Paramount office and proceeds to tell anyone who will listen about the book. Within two to three days after this hap-

pened, Pocket received four pages of comments."

1 9

PERCHANCE TO DREAM

HOWARD WEINSTEIN

DECEMBER 1991 (242PP)

Data and Troi, along with Wesley and a couple of others, head out in a shuttle and investigate a new planet with no evidence of intelligent life. On the way back to the *Enterprise*, their vessel is trapped in a tractor beam of the Tenirans who claim the planet belongs to them. When Picard intervenes to save his officers, he watches in horror as a bright light appears and the shuttle vanishes. Answering the question concerning their disappearance plus the difficulty of negotiating with a new race of beings keeps Picard hopping.

The story for *Perchance to Dream* started as a spec script that Howard submitted to the studio. He said, "They didn't buy it, but Michael Piller thought enough of the script to extend an invitation for me to pitch other stories. However, writers hate to waste good stories, so I rewrote it as a novel."

Elaborating further, Howard said, "All writers who pitched to the TV series were told to focus on interactions between the regular characters, preferably coming up with some interesting combos that hadn't been explored much before. So I had Data and Troi essentially being camp counselors on a training mission involving Wesley and two other kids from the *Enterprise*. When their field trip turns potentially deadly, the kids learn some unique leadership lessons from two very different characters, Data and Troi. There are also underlying themes about the nature of creative expression—we've got some mysterious non-corporeal aliens who rearrange the topography of their planet as a form of art—and about overcoming fear in order to survive (maybe inspired a bit by the encounter with the Horta in *Devil in the Dark*). It's kind of a fun little story, and I still think it would have made a neat TV episode."

#20

SPARTACUS
T. L. MANCOUR

FEBRUARY 1992   **(276 PP)**

Helping a damaged ship brings pain and grief to the crew of the *Enterprise*-D. The inhabitants of the *Freedom* call themselves Vemlans, and claim they are fleeing a war-torn home, looking for a new place to live. A foggy picture gets even more blurry when an entire fleet from the planet arrives and claims that the *Freedom* crew are nothing more than escaped slaves. Picard must use all his cunning to fiddle with the Prime Directive if the *Enterprise* is to survive.

Attempts to contact the author for an interview were unsuccessful.

2 1

CHAINS OF COMMAND

BILL McCAY AND ELOISE FLOOD

APRIL 1992   (278PP)

The *Enterprise* crew discovers a series of Class-M planets that appear to have been destroyed in a major war. While in orbit around a glacial world, they find humans living in slavery. Not knowing there were humans who actually lived as free citizens, the glacial people revolt against their bird-like captors to escape their bonds. Picard must negotiate a peaceful settlement without violating the Prime Directive.

Asked how he came to write a *Next Generation* novel with Eloise, Bill commented, "I'd been working as an editor for a book packager, and Dave Stern, the Pocket Books *Star Trek* editor, had done some writing for me. We got on well, and when I left the job to go back to writing freelance, Dave invited me to play in his sandbox. The problem was he wanted a *Next Generation* book, and I hadn't been following the series. My office-mate, Eloise Flood, had, so I recruited her help."

Eloise elaborated, "We'd both done some writing for paperback series (Bill far more than me). It seemed like a natural. Back in those days in particular, when paperback series were so huge, most people who edited them also wrote them, and we all knew one another. Basically, Bill and I got together and came up with a few story ideas, which we pitched to Dave. He chose one he liked, we did a writing sample, and that was that. The process was pretty smooth. As far as I recall, we submitted an extended plot summary, then a first draft manuscript. At that point we got a new editor, Kevin Ryan, who wrote what I still remember as the most sensible revision letter I ever got. We did a second draft and I think that was it. For the first draft, Bill and I alternated chapters and then edited each other, which worked pretty well overall. The most fun part was working out our aliens' language."

Bill recalled, "We wanted to do a story with a lost human colony, but the storyline was considerably different. Eloise suggested having a planet with a climate like that of, say, Connecticut being deterraformed by an alien race into a chlorine-based atmosphere-a notion that was later used on the show. If I remember, our initial proposal was about a spacefaring agoraphobic race (evolved from mole-like creatures) that used human slaves to pilot an enormous, asteroidal spacecraft. The idea of being out there in the middle of nothingness literally drove the alien masters crazy. After a couple of go-rounds, the alien masters/human slaves story resolved into the storyline for the book. Eloise and I had literally been locked in an editorial office together for several years. I think we knew each other's styles and strong points. It's been a while since I looked at the book, but I suspect unpleasant conflict and fight scenes can be traced to me. When the characters are decent, courageous, or human, that was probably Eloise."

#22

IMBALANCE
V. E. MITCHELL

JUNE 1992   **(280PP)**

The mysterious insectlike race, the Jarada, has asked for Captain Picard specifically to handle negotiations for joining the Federation. When the crew arrives, the landing party is separated, and cut off from communicating with the *Enterprise*. Each person must rely on their own training and skill to survive, plus decipher the Jarada's true motives.

Vicki remembered, "*Next Generation* was in its first season, and they had just started publishing the Next Gen books when [my agent] called and told me to submit some proposals. I

sent in several, most of which I don't remember any more. The one common thread in all of them was that I was *not* going to have anything more to do with the ship than I absolutely had to; if the story was on a planet I made up, [no one could] argue with me about the details. The specific spark for *Imbalance* was the first Dixon Hill episode, 'The Big Good-bye,' where Picard has to flawlessly pronounce a greeting to an extremely xenophobic race of creatures. I started wondering who these creatures were, why were they so xenophobic, what were they like? The story came from trying to come up with a dramatically satisfying answer to those questions.

"Compared to *Enemy Unseen*, writing *Imbalance* was a breeze. The biggest problem with writing the story was when I found out that my book was supposed to be released a year after I sold it. Apparently it had been penciled into the list for the next year's releases when the idea was selected, and no one looked at the time that allowed me. I made the deadline, this time thanks to the trusty Kaypro I bought when I couldn't pry the Osborne away from my husband. Paramount approvals were much easier this time around, too. The biggest problem there was that Kevin and I had thought it would be fun to use Keiko O'Brien as one of the characters, and by the time I was finishing the book, she and Miles were about to be transferred to *Deep Space Nine*. When I had written the first draft, Keiko had just gotten pregnant (in a script that wasn't aired for quiet some time), so we incorporated that element in the book. However, figuring Keiko was a minor enough character that I could create some backstory for her proved to be an unlucky premise, and several pages of material were eliminated from the final book when later scripts introduced her personal history. Her rank also had to be removed when Paramount [revealed] she was a civilian working aboard the *Enterprise*. Still, these were minor problems, and they were easily solved."

#23

WAR DRUMS

JOHN VORNHOLT

OCTOBER 1992   (276PP)

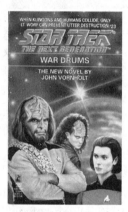

small colony struggles to survive on the planet Selva. On their new home, a band of renegade Klingons fights for survival in the woods beyond the encampment. With aggression escalating between the two parties, the *Enterprise* arrives to render assistance and negotiate peace. Where did the Klingons come from and why did the colonists not notify Starfleet Command sooner regarding their situation? Prejudice and treachery intensifies.

"I really like this one because it features two of my favorite characters, Worf and Ro Laren, in a visit to a weird planet inhabited by feral Klingons. If you think regular Klingons are bad, wait until you meet some who have grown up *Lord of the Flies* style. After the feral youths murder Federation colonists, Worf and Ro have to tame the Klingons while they fight Romulan spies. I was very into drumming at the time, and that's reflected in much of this book."

#24

NIGHTSHADE

LAURELL K. HAMILTON

DECEMBER 1992   (276PP)

aptain Picard, Worf, and Deanna are negotiating for peace. The two factions are living on a dying planet. The *Enterprise* is sent away on another mission. The three of them are left alone to resolve the dispute. A murder occurs, and Picard is accused of the crime. Now he resides in prison. Worf and Troi must discover the identity of the true killer. In the process, Worf learns to be a diplomat.

• • •

Laurell became a fan during the original *Star Trek* reruns. She remarked, "I'd told my then-agent to keep me in mind if an opening came up to write a *Trek* novel. Another writer dropped the deadline and I picked up their slot. Mystery plots are easier for me at short notice. I loved playing with the characters. Some writers complained at the restrictions of writing *Star Trek*, but I found it a pleasant and professional experience. I knew going in, it was their playground and their toys. I knew the world well enough to play by those rules."

Laurell now is a best-selling author of several novels that combine vampires, mystery, and romance.

#25

GROUNDED
DAVID BISCHOFF

MARCH 1993   **(273PP)**

The rescue of scientists in a remote station proves to be the end of the *Enterprise*. Infected with a mysterious substance on the surface of the ship, the stuff begins to gradually disinte-

grate the hull. Forced to evacuate, Picard's crew must watch in horror as Starfleet orders the *Enterprise*'s destruction to prevent the infection of other vessels. Desperate times call for desperate measures, and the situation obviously warrants a bold plan for Picard to defy Starfleet and save his beloved ship.

According to David, "*Grounded* is a novel born of hope, education, and desperation. I have written, by myself and with collaborators, close to a hundred novels. *Grounded* was, is, and will remain an anomaly. I look back at it with awe, wonder, and terror.

"In the early 90s, I went to a signing at Dangerous Visions Bookstore in Sherman Oaks, California. I met an editor from Pocket Books who worked on the *Star Trek* novels. I explained that I was a full-time writer who had published many SF novels. I had come out to LA in 1989 to live (after visiting many times to write TV animation scripts). I had brought with me a speculative script written by Lisa White, Dennis Bailey, and myself based upon a short story that Dennis and I had published in the 70s. After selling 'Tin Man,' Dennis and I had worked on 'First Contact,' [an episode from] the fourth season of the show, and then, having failed to show further promise, got no further script work, despite repeated pitching. I also told the editor from Pocket that because of this I knew *The Next Generation* very well indeed. Would he be interested in working on a *Star Trek* book with me?"

David said he "felt confident that I [could] write a good one. No. I could write many good ones. I knew *The Next Generation* well by then, having watched all the shows, and knowing SF well. I felt that I would be a good choice for a regular Pocket author. The editor signing at Dangerous Visions suggested that I write some outlines based on some of my unaccepted pitches at Paramount . . . then submit them through my agent. I did. After many months the editor asked which one I liked the best. I told him *Grounded.* I wasn't happy with the title, mostly because it was also the title of a Chris Claremont novel. However, I couldn't think of a better one. I'd read a lot of *Star Trek* novels in preparation for writing my outlines. I didn't like any of them. Not one. Not even my friends' novels."

David recalled a conversation he'd had with *The Next Generation* executive producer Michael Piller, when David had mentioned the importance of the *Enterprise* and that it was like one of the characters. "He didn't seem impressed, but I liked the idea. So [for *Grounded*] I concocted a way that the *Enterprise* could get 'contaminated,' have to limp to a Starbase, and eject all crew members, except for Data—who was contaminated as well."

David continued, "*Grounded* did well, although some *Trek* fans didn't like the technical details I'd included and the hard science. They also didn't like that I'd gotten a few details about rank wrong. In any case, be that as it may, [*Grounded* is] a book I am proud of for many reasons."

David remarked, "I have earned more money on *Grounded* than any other novel in my career. It was on the *New York Times* best seller list for three weeks."

26

THE ROMULAN PRIZE

Simon Hawke

MAY 1993 **(279PP)**

On border patrol near the Romulan Neutral Zone, the crew discovers a prototype vessel that dwarfs the *Enterprise* in size. An away team finds all of the Romulans aboard dead due to an engineering accident. The enigmatic vessel carries a deadly surprise and will force Picard to not only face losing his captaincy and his crew, but also visit a world that remains quarantined and forbidden to visit by an edict courtesy of Starfleet Command.

Attempts to contact the author for an interview were unsuccessful.

#27

GUISES OF THE MIND

Rebecca Neason

SEPTEMBER 1993   (277pp)

The *Enterprise* receives an invitation to the coronation of the ruler of Capulon IV. In addition, the planet will sign a charter joining the Federation at the ceremony. Shuttling the religious order of Little Mothers to the event, one of the members, Mother Veronica, has telepathic powers she can't control and begs for Troi's help. On the planet, the future king's evil twin brother kidnaps him and locks him in a dungeon. Can Picard bring the rightful heir to the throne?

Rebecca had written a fair amount of nonfiction and poetry, mostly for religious publications, but never thought of writing fiction. "Then, in autumn of 1985, another friend (a serious Trekkie) found out that I loved the show—but did not know about the books! So one day, she showed up at my door with a box of books—thirty-six of them, I believe. All or most of what were available at the time. For the next six weeks, I did everything with a book in front of my face. Finally, I was on the third to the last book, and lying in the bathtub reading, when I had this plot come into my head. I stopped reading, thought about it for a few minutes, said, 'I could do that,' and went back to my book. A few days later, December 16, 1985, I was at the VA hospital in Seattle, where my mother was having minor day-surgery, and I had taken a notebook and pen to write some letter while I waited. Instead, I started the book. Four months later, I had finished the book and found an agent. This was a classic *Trek* book—all there was at the time—called *The Gift of Silence*."

The next part of the tale she often tells in her workshops for beginning writers as a lesson in the value of patience and perseverance. "I finished the first book and found an agent, to whom I sent the manuscript—fully expecting her to want massive rewrites before she sent it to Pocket Books. Surprise, she sent it as it was! So I waited—and waiting on a first book is unlike any other! Finally, four-to-five weeks later, I hear back from Dave Stern (the *Star Trek* editor at that time) saying, 'We think this is an interesting concept, but it needs some changes. Please change this . . . this . . . this . . . this . . . and get us a new outline.' So I changed this . . . this . . . this . . . and this, and mailed off my first true outline. And waited. Again. But this time, while I waited, I began another fiction project—which makes the waiting *sooo* much easier! Finally, the response came. Dave wrote, and I'll never forget it: 'We still think this is an interesting concept, but it does not have a strong enough action/adventure storyline to fit our needs. Please try us again in the future.' A bit disappointed, I went back to other projects. Then *Star Trek: The Next Generation* started — and *Next Generation* books! I got a letter from Dave Stern saying that he thought the concept in *The Gift of Silence* might work well as a *Next Generation* book — could I get him a new outline? So, again, I stopped what I was doing and wrote an outline, changing *The Gift of Silence* into *Guises of The Mind*. It went off to Dave — and I waited. Eventually, I got a letter saying, 'We like the concept, but it needs some changes. Please change. . . .' I made the called-for changes and this time Dave liked it . . . and it went to Paramount for final approval. Finally I got [comments back, saying,] 'We are trying to stay away from any stories with telepathy or mental powers in them.' Now *Guises* is a Deanna Troi story, and I thought, 'You have a main character who is a telepath/empath, and you don't want to use her!' And I went back to my other projects. Then, January of 1992, my agent was at a party with Dave Stern. She said, 'Do you remember?' And he said, 'As a matter of fact, I do!' So Dave called me a couple of days later, and I told him that I still had the outline that he had liked — and he said to send it along. About two, maybe three weeks later I got a letter saying, 'We like the concept, but it needs some changes. Please change this . . . this . . . this . . . this . . . and get us a new outline.' Once again, I made the changes and sent it in. This time Dave liked it and Paramount okayed it. So, now I had to write the book. I was given eighteen months to finish the manuscript, and I did so in only five months. Pocket Books changed its release date, and it became #27. I think I kept about three sentences of the original book."

The writing path only took a short seven years. Within those seven years, Rebecca wrote a bit more nonfiction, but most of all she used the time to learn the craft of writing fiction — which is very different. "It also taught me that writing was what I was meant to do. You see, all of my life, I've been involved in the arts. I started in small amateur theater when I was ten, and I was a drama major in college. I took several types of dance, from ballet to Scottish country dance. I draw and paint; I do all sorts of needle arts — knitting, crochet, embroidery, needlepoint, cross-stitch, crewel. I'm learning my ninth instrument — and I wrote all the time. I wrote letters by the stack, every week; I wrote poetry, journals, lists — I'm the queen of list making — and I think best on paper. But, throughout all of the other arts I do or have done, I always felt that there was something missing . . . so I'd take another type of dance, or learn another instrument, or another type of craft. I never put the feeling together with the fact that I always had a pen in my hand. It came so naturally to me that I thought everyone did the same thing. And when I started writing fiction, whether the first *The Gift of Silence* or the final *Guises of the Mind*, it was like the floodgates opened, words poured out, and the feeling of place came at last. As I've said, I also spent those years learning my craft. There is an old saying about writing: 'The first million words don't count.' I think I wrote at least half that million during those years."

28

HERE THERE BE DRAGONS

JOHN PEEL

DECEMBER 1993   (275PP)

Investigating massive stellar phenomena, the crew rescues a man claiming to be a Federation Special Agent. He also has a strange story. Inside the cloud where nothing should be able to survive, hides an entire planet. With some advanced technology, the ship arrives to find a world of knights and serfs from Earth's Middle Ages. While investigating, some of the crew are taken as slaves. Unknown to them all, the "gate" that got the ship there safely is starting to close. . . .

He commented, "*Star Trek* for me started as a reading experience, so I guess that helped [me want to write one]. But I never intended to write any *Star Trek* novels. What happened was that Pocket Books had started publishing books based on *Alien Nation*, a series I adored. So I called up to ask if I could write one, but it was canceled before I could. However, the editor,

Kevin Ryan, asked me if I'd ever considered writing a *Star Trek* novel. I hadn't, and told him so. But that night I started thinking, *Well, if I was going to write one, what would I do?* I worked the entire plot out overnight, and called Kevin back the following morning and asked: 'Can I change my answer?' I sent Kevin the outline for *Here There Be Dragons*, and he commissioned it immediately. It was one of the easiest sales I've ever made, and I'm very grateful to Kevin for prompting me.

"[The story was] sparked by my dreadful sense of humor. One of the rules for *Star Trek* is 'no fantasy.' It all has to be science fiction, even if the explanations are in tech-speak. So I wondered how far I could push that rule. In the end, everything in the book is science, even though it looks at first like fantasy. My second thought was that the *Enterprise* bunch always fights these terribly malevolent, implacable foes with incredible high-tech weapons. So I thought it would be fun to give them an underwhelming foe, one they could beat with their eyes closed, and then have Picard make a rare mistake by taking things too easily. When I finished the book and turned it in, I was very nervous. I already knew several of the other writers who'd done *Star Trek* novels, and I'd heard some horror stories about how Paramount [folks] were impossible to deal with, and how they hated everything. In the end, they cut one sequence slightly (Ro as a future sexslave), and their main comment to me was 'Starfleet is one word!' The entire experience was absolutely excellent, even though I had editors change on me midway through the story. Kevin was promoted, and Shawna McCarthy took over his duties to finish the book. And I was absolutely awed by the great cover for the book. Despite the horror stories, *Here There Be Dragons* was a joy from start to finish."

#29

SINS OF COMMISSION
SUSAN WRIGHT

MARCH 1994   (277PP)

A T he *Enterprise* arrives to help the inhabitants of the planet Lessenar whose atmosphere has started to deteriorate. Nearby, a space liner with a captain familiar to Worf explodes and the survivors are evacuated to the *Galaxy*-class vessel. Some of the passengers are strange creatures called the Sli, and they communicate by influencing the emotions of others. Let the murder and mayhem ensue.

Susan has been a *Trek* fan since she was twelve. "[I] obsessively watched original series reruns with my sister and best friend. I made a tricorder and communicator out of electronic gear my dad had in the garage, and one of our favorite games was pretending to be part of the crew. When *The Next Generation* appeared, it

was my favorite show on television. I had published some nonfiction how-to books, and was attempting to write (never completed) science fiction novels. I must have read fifty *Trek* novels by then, so I decided to write a *Star Trek* TNG novel since I understood the characters and premise. I wrote the entire novel and I managed to get an agent to send it to then-editor Kevin Ryan. He liked my writing, but didn't like the story idea. So he suggested that I pitch him other stories. He ended up buying *Sins of Commission* soon after that."

Elaborating on her first *Star Trek* novel, she said, "I wanted to write something that could not be seen in the TNG episodes. Nowadays the Sli could be created using CGI, but in the early 90s, the special effects were much more limited. I wanted to show an intelligent alien species that wasn't humanoid and didn't speak English, so the Sli communicate through emotions rather than words."

Susan remembers her first experience with the licensing department at Paramount. "It was my first experience with the approval process. I never had any problems with adjusting a story to their specifications, though some ideas took more explaining or reworking than others, *Sins of Commission* was accepted without any changes."

#30

DEBTOR'S PLANET

W. R. THOMPSON

MAY 1994   (274 PP)

Before a space probe explodes, it relays data that the planet Megara has turned from a primitive world to a major technological world in an extremely short time. It appears the Ferengi are involved, so Picard takes the *Enterprise* to investigate. Along for the ride is Ambassador Ralph Offenhouse, former twentieth-century businessman who was rescued from cryogenic sleep years earlier. As the investigation progresses, it appears that the Ferengi are merely puppets in a grander scheme.

Bill remarked, "I'm not really a fan. I started watching the show with Grandfather Dubois when it premiered in '67. He'd been a SF fan since the 20s and that rubbed off on me. He liked a lot of what he saw, so for me it was more a matter of 'here's some more good science fiction' rather than anything else."

Bill started writing *Trek* stories because his

then-agent suggested it. "I remembered the Ralph Offenhouse character from a first-season *The Next Generation* episode, especially Mark Richman's performance—I could hear the character talk in his voice, and I thought about how much fun it would be to have Ralph on the loose in the UFP . . . especially because he was the one person uniquely qualified to handle the Ferengi. Sometimes I felt like I was writing a *Flash Gordon* serial, with one problem leading to another, which made it even more fun. I worked on the manuscript for five months, then sent it to my agent, who sent it to the publisher. Then I had to write an outline, because they weren't set up for that. I had to make a few minor changes; the only one that bugged me was changing one character from an Andorian to something else (some local fans are really intrigued by the Andorians, and I'd thought they'd get a kick out of it. Ah, well. . .)."

3 1

FOREIGN FOES

DAVE GALANTER AND GREG BRODEUR

AUGUST 1994   **(276 PP)**

The Hidran people and the Klingons consider each other to be not worthy enough to breathe. Picard is asked to perform the daunting task of mediating a treaty between the two parties. The murder of the Hidran ambassador turns the negotiations into an ugly mess quickly and then Worf stands accused of the heinous act. When Riker and Troi disappear and Data begins to appear paranoid, Picard starts to feel totally alone.

Becoming an author wasn't someing Dave planned, but he started writing at age eight and received his first typewriter when he was thirteen. "The first story I tapped out was a silly little *Star Trek* story. It just seemed natural for me to write one, because I loved *Trek* and loved to write."

When asked how he ended up with Greg as a writing partner, he joked, "Lost a bet. No, just kidding. I met Greg and his wife, Diane Carey, when they were doing a book signing for their first *Trek* book, *Dreadnought!* I was surprised to learn they lived in the same town as I, and we became friends. When I went to college I continued to pursue writing, and one of my professors urged me to show some of my work to Greg and Diane for their opinions since they were professionals. I did, and since Greg was the plot guy for Diane, [he] had extra time to plot with another writer. They took me under their wings—Diane taught me how to write and Greg taught me how to plot. I no longer work with Greg (though would if the project interested us both enough) but it was always a blast to do so."

In terms of this novel, Dave commented, "*Foreign Foes* was actually an idea Greg worked on with Diane and considered pitching to *The Next Generation* in its first season. They decided not to, and Diane was working on some non-*Trek* at the time, so Greg decided to develop the plot with me. It was my first *Trek* book and also my first book ever, so when someone reads the first three chapters they see a significant difference between those three and the rest of the book. I'd written those three and a plot synopsis and gotten that approved by Pocket and Paramount. Almost a year later I began working on the rest of the book. What I'd learned, by working on my style and method in that time, shows and probably makes those first chapters look too choppy in comparison with the rest of the book. It was a learning experience. I remember wondering if I could find the words for an entire book, and then when finished I wondered if there were any words left for a next one. Now I'm hard to shut up. It's been some time, but I remember being grateful that there was Greg to edit what I wrote, then the editors at Pocket, and then even the people at Paramount. It ended up being a much better product for all the people involved. I did balk at some of the rules in place at the time. Someone somewhere didn't want me to have Worf make a joke, as they thought it not in his character. It was early in the series when I was writing it, and he'd not been as well-developed."

#32

REQUIEM

MICHAEL JAN FRIEDMAN AND KEVIN RYAN

OCTOBER 1994   (277PP)

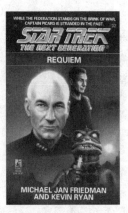

everyone, the captain has traveled back in time to Cestus III, the site of an upcoming battle where the Gorn destroy every living creature on the planet.

Mike reflected, "I think that *Requiem* was pretty much Kevin's idea. He thought it would be cool if we did a story on Cestus III and we decided we'd have Picard there. And Picard of course would be a different personality from Kirk. We got to explore what it was like on Cestus III before the attack. Let's get to know these people, let's get to know how the colony operated, and let's get to know what was lost. I was happy with the job we did and it was fun working with Kevin. He and I were pitching to the show at that time so we were used to working together."

As captain of the *Stargazer*, Jean Luc Picard had negotiated a peaceful settlement with the Gorn. Twenty-five years later, the Gorn have asked for Picard to continue negotiations and celebrate their initial achievement. On the way there, the ship stops to investigate a mysterious artifact, and Picard vanishes. Now Riker must retrieve his captain and make it to the Gorn homeworld in just a few days. Unknown to

3 3

BALANCE OF POWER

DAFYDD AB HUGH

JANUARY 1995   (296PP)

A teacher that Geordi had during his academy days dies and causes havoc throughout the Alpha Quadrant. The dead professor was also a hack scientist, but rumors begin to circulate that he perfected a photon weapon that could easily penetrate a starship's shields. The device will be put up for auction along with other potentially dangerous equipment that the professor worked on throughout his life. The *Enterprise* rushes to the auction to make sure the Cardassians or the Romulans don't succeed in obtaining the weapon.

Dafydd commented, "You have to understand that in the mid-1960s, there *were no* other science fiction television shows where humans were setting out, in a positive fashion, to explore the universe. In fact, there were few SF shows period; those we had—*Twilight Zone* and *Outer Limits*, *The Invaders*, *Voyage to the Bottom of the Sea* (more of a monster series than SF, really)—tended to have the premise that we poor humans are being continually set up by outside forces beyond our control, and we struggle merely to survive. Virtually all SF readers or SF moviegoers became *Trek* fans in the Kirk-McCoy-Spock period, myself included (even as a child). So there really was no point at which I realized I was a *Trek* fan; it was just one of the shows I always watched, like *Zorro* and *The Wild, Wild West*."

Dafydd continued, "I was a writer long before I wrote any *Trek*, having already published two fantasy novels, *Heroing* and *Warriorwards*, plus a novelette, 'The Coon Rolled Down and Ruptured His Larinks, a Squeezed Novel by Mr. Skunk,' that was nominated for both a Hugo and a Nebula before I wrote my first *Trek* novel, *Fallen Heroes*. I enjoyed writing *Trek* books, and it paid more money than I could earn with a midlist SF or F novel, so it just seemed natural."

Regarding his *The Next Generation* story, "Continuing my desire to push the envelope, I started wondering about gold-pressed latinum, the medium of currency introduced either in *Next Generation* or *DS9*, I don't recall which. The first *Star Trek* (now called the original series) basically had no money. I think there were occasional references to 'credits,' but they never went into detail; and there were no stories I can recall that centered on one of the *Enterprise* crew being short of jack when the rent was due, or somesuch. (Having served in the U.S. Navy, I can tell you that monetary concerns loom as large among servicemen as they do among civilians!) A form of money was introduced at some point in the later series, but it didn't really become a central focus until my favorite series, *Deep Space Nine*, when the New Improved Ferengi were introduced as money-obsessed merchants whose only laws are the the Rules of Acquisition. Paramount realized that in a universe that included replicators, money is a real problem: What is the basis of money when anything can simply be replicated in any quantity desired? How valuable would gold be if anyone could make as much gold as he wanted? Its value lies in scarcity. So they came up with something called 'gold-pressed latinum,' whose only property was that you couldn't replicate it. But then they never explored the ramifications of how that would affect society. So I decided to do it for them . . . I asked myself, what would happen if someone *could* replicate gold-pressed latinum? The rest of the novel flows, science fictionally, from this premise. (I also broke another taboo here, making the Federation of planets act as an almost Mafia-like criminal organization. I think I compared them to a galactic squid with its tentacles in everything, grabbing for its cut.)"

3 4

BLAZE OF GLORY
SIMON HAWKE

MARCH 1995   **(277PP)**

Starbase 37 orbits the planet Artemis VI and the Federation presence maintains a fragile peace. The *Enterprise* is ordered to divert to the starbase without an explanation. A dear friend of Picard's runs the station, so the captain feels both apprehension and elation at the upcoming mission. A renegade pirate has obtained an old *Constitution*-class starship and equipped it with a cloaking device. Can Picard and his crew stop the attacks? And how did a pirate obtain a cloak?

Attempts to contact the author for an interview were unsuccessful.

35

THE ROMULAN STRATAGEM
ROBERT GREENBERGER

MAY 1995   (273PP)

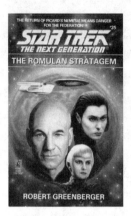

The *Enterprise* warps to the planet Eloh to negotiate a potential Federation membership. Eloh borders the Romulan Neutral Zone, so an ally would be a strategic advantage. When the vessel arrives, they find a delegation of Romulans already there. Led by Sela, their party wants to bring Eloh into the Romulan Empire. Mysterious acts of sabotage begin and both parties are accused. Sela and Data form a temporary alliance to uncover the true saboteurs.

Bob recalls, "Well, after a few collaborations, David Stern thought I might be up for a solo venture. Encouraged, I thought about something that would let me get into the characters. While watching the series, I had always been struck that the Federation always seems to look better to alien races, usually leading to treaties, alliances, or Federation membership. I wondered what if Picard had to secure a planet's loyalty for the Federation in competition with the Romulans? And what if, to make it personal, Sela headed the Romulan delegation? And what if the aliens actually preferred the Romulans? From there, the story developed. The Data/Sela scenes were a great deal of fun to concoct. However, the lengthy banquet scene where we got to know all the players was the part of the book I was most pleased with."

36

INTO THE NEBULA
GENE DeWEESE

JULY 1995   (274PP)

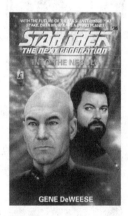

Investigating a strange nebula, the crew discovers a generational ship heavily damaged and in danger of killing everyone on board. The ship originates from a planet in the heart of the phenomenon, and the dust surrounding the planet and the region appears to be the result of rampant polluting of the atmosphere. Generations before, the inhabitants of the planet stopped their polluting ways, but the atmosphere continued to rapidly deteriorate. Now the few scattered and struggling survivors hope that the *Enterprise* can solve their dilemma.

Gene said, "Again, this was an idea that had been in the 'ideas box' for a long time. Originally the nebula in question was a natural one, and the story involved how the world gradually moved out of the nebula and the rest of the universe became visible to the inhabitants. Which, come to think of it, was probably inspired by Asimov's 'Nightfall.' For *Trek*, the nebula became a result of runaway pollution."

---

3 7

THE LAST STAND

BRAD FERGUSON

OCTOBER 1995   (274PP)

Α he *Enterprise* investigates a
T planet on the verge of developing warp technology. When arriving on the planet, the crew is accused of being involved with an alien race intent on destroying their way of life. To Picard's horror, evidence points to a massive fleet of cloaked ships

ready to attack. Can he convince everyone to end hostilities?

Brad remarked, "Kevin Ryan treated me really well with this book. We made edits together and there was zero trouble. I'm really happy with it."

He continued, "I have always thought if you are going to write a *Trek* novel, you should write something they can't film. Put in thousands of things they can't film! I originally proposed *The Last Stand* as a classic *Trek* novel and Kevin mentioned he wouldn't be able to publish it for a couple of years. I thought it would be really good [for *The Next Generation*] because Picard is more of a diplomat and more of the cerebral type. This is going to call not just for negotiation and blind dumb luck but also some brains. I think it would have failed as a Kirk book."

#38

DRAGON'S HONOR

KIJ JOHNSON AND GREG COX

JANUARY 1996   (277PP)

Warring factions in the Dragon Empire have decided to end their hostilities by having the Emperor's eldest son marry the daughter of his rival. After the ceremony, the new government will sign a treaty to join the Federation. Special guests for the blessed event, Picard and crew arrive to discover treachery and hostile lizard-like beings that want to destroy the entire planet. An assassination attempt prompts the captain to use extreme methods to guarantee success in their latest mission.

Greg remarked, "Unlike *Devil in The Sky*, *Dragon's Honor* did not start out as a collaboration. Originally, it was going to be a solo novel by Kij Johnson, who came up with the plot and characters all on her own. Unfortunately, real life intruded when Kij suddenly had to relocate across the country to start a new job, which was going to keep her from finishing the book on time. At that point, I got called in to finish up the book as a favor for a friend. (I'd known Kij for years, ever since she'd served as Managing Editor at Tor Books, back when John Ordover and I were both working there.) Basically, Kij provided me with a partial first draft and a detailed outline of the plot. I fleshed these out into a complete second draft based on her notes. In my head, I still think of *Dragon's Honor* as 'the Kij book' since it was essentially her story; I just finished it for her. (Her name, by the way, rhymes with 'Fridge.')"

Kij commented, "I watched *Star Trek* when it first came out—my parents were SF fans, so we watched it every week, and of course re-watched it all in syndication and read the Blish novelizations when I found them and owned the *Concordance* and the blueprints and all. I loved everything about *Star Trek*—thought Spock was sexy, had a crush on Kirk, wanted to be Uhura when I grew up, couldn't wait for space travel—the works. But I have to admit I lost my heart to *The Next Generation* when that started coming out, and [it] remains my favorite of the series. I started writing fiction in my twenties, and initially wrote a lot of horror and fantasy. Writing a *Star Trek* book always seemed like one of those 'You know you've made it if . . .' things, and I just assumed I'd never do it, because I wasn't even going to be famous enough. I sort of forgot that sometimes you don't have to be famous, you just have to be lucky. I went to work in New York publishing in the very early 90s, and met John Ordover. When he moved to Pocket, he actually asked me to pitch something, and I was thrilled to do so. I pitched a couple of ideas before he gave me the OK on the one I ended up pursuing. One of my favorite [*Star Trek* novels] was *How Much For Just the Planet*, which is (as you already know) a clever Gilbert and Sullivan-style farce by a truly talented literary fantasist, John M. Ford. My initial goal for the book was to write a *How Much For Just the Planet* for *The Next Generation*—something as clever and intricate. My fantasy novel career was just getting started with a book set in eleventh-century Japan—and research into Japan had given me just enough information about China at the time to be really dangerous, so I figured I'd use that as my setting. John Ordover had also been moaning lately about how writers were never taking advantage of the really cheap special effects that come with no visuals—you can blow up a planet on paper, and it doesn't cost any more than having people walking on a bridge—so I added the lizard guys, the G'kkau, and made them scent-based, something you can't ever really explore on TV."

On collaborating with Greg, Kij said, "He's so easy to work with—very smart and funny and efficient. Basically, I sent him all my notes and the manuscript, and he fixed it for me. We always used to joke about the Deanna and Beverly hot-tub scene in the book, which John had inexplicably cut. In fact there never was one, but I loved yanking peoples' chains at panels."

#39

ROGUE SAUCER
JOHN VORNHOLT

MARCH 1996   (271PP)

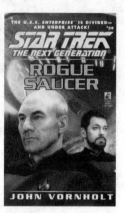

The *Enterprise* limps to a starbase, with its saucer section in desperate need of repairs. Instead of getting shore leave, the command crew is asked to help test an experimental saucer that has extraordinary capabilities. During the test, the saucer vanishes. Unknown to Picard and his crew, the experimental craft has been hijacked. A deadly plot is taking shape, and Picard must gather his scattered crew if they are to save the day.

"Every now and then, I like to write a pure 'bridge' story, where most of the action takes place right on the *Enterprise* bridge, usually in the midst of a space battle. The Maquis, Admiral Necheyev, and several of my favorites are on hand when Maquis agents hijack an experimental saucer section intended for the *Enterprise*. As with *Antimatter*, this story was inspired by cool stuff I read in the *Star Trek: The Next*

Generation Technical Manual. So I dedicated this book to Mike and Denise Okuda, Rick Sternbach, and all the writers and editors responsible for the wonderful *Trek* nonfiction books that have aided me so often."

#40

POSSESSION

J. M. DILLARD AND KATHLEEN O'MALLEY

MAY 1996   (281 PP)

ighty years after the events in the original series novel, *Demons,* scientists on Vulcan are still studying the strange devices. Shortly before the start of a gigantic quadrant-wide science fair, the containers are reopened and the evil is once again unleashed. Now the evil roams the corridors of the *Enterprise* and no one is safe. Who can be trusted?

Jeanne commented, "*Possession* was a *The Next Generation* 'sequel' to my original *Trek* novel, *Demons.* I thought it'd be fun to expose *Next Generation* characters to the same foe fought by Captain Kirk and crew. I chose Kath-

leen O'Malley as my writing partner because I admired her writing and her professionalism. It also helped that she'd been a dear friend for years who had done an amazing job of editing my fiction. I thought it would be enormous fun to work with her, and I was right."

#41

THE SOLDIERS OF FEAR

(INVASION, BOOK TWO; SEE SECTION 12: MINISERIES)

#42

INFILTRATOR

W. R. THOMPSON

SEPTEMBER 1996   (279 PP)

he inhabitants of the planet Hera have genetically engineered themselves to be superior to the rest of beings in the galaxy. A bold plot to eliminate the inferior takes shape in the form of a manufactured plague. And the *Enterprise* will be the testing ground. On board the ship, a new crew member hides her secret heritage and Picard tries to establish a peaceful settlement before war erupts.

"There was that wretched episode about a genetically-engineered bottle society. Aside from the strange opposition to genetic engineering (which must have been thought up by someone who has never dealt with a chronic illness) there was Geordi's inexplicable bad manners toward a genetically-engineered character. Geordi is one of my top two favorite *Trek* characters, and I felt a need to explain why he behaved that way. I think that worked out nicely. Plus, I liked the idea of an alien sneaking aboard the *Enterprise* to observe Worf and his Klingon virtues. Writing the manuscript took about four months, and again, it was fun. Some changes had to be made to keep it in line with the *Trek* background, but I survived."

#43

A FURY SCORNED
PAMELA SARGENT AND GEORGE ZEBROWSKI

NOVEMBER 1996   (275PP)

The people of Epictetus III face total annihilation from their unstable sun. With no way to evacuate even a few of the millions of inhabitants, Picard turns to Data and Geordi to create a solution to stabilize the sun and delay its explosion. Unfortunately, the only solution would destroy the *Enterprise* as well.

George remarked, "A *Fury Scorned* started out as an invitational one-hour script. I wrote the script, the staff all left, and no one knew me from Adam. I showed the script to Pocket's editors, and it was suggested that Pam and I write it as a novel, but with one big change: We couldn't use the transporter in the way we wanted—to save millions of people from the nova. Instead, we moved the whole planet, with Gregory Benford's help in the physics of wormholes, and in the inertial problems of moving a planet without too much harm.

Stephen Baxter wrote to us later, 'I found your/Pam's effort, and couldn't resist it. I thought it was terrific (given the constraints). You gave Picard and pals a genuine dilemma, not to mention something resembling real physics! I thought you brought out Troi well, with a genuine feel for her extra sense.' Writing A *Fury Scorned* went well, right through revision suggestions, which were good, essentially asking for the central viewpoints to be that of the main cast. This was the best experience we had in writing these books."

Pam remembered, "The biggest mistake we made, if you can call it a mistake, was letting our invented characters run away with the story in the earlier drafts. They came close to taking over the story, so we were getting close to a novel where Picard and his people were almost the supporting characters! The solution was actually rather simple, namely to flip the points-of-view in a number of scenes, so that a particular incident is seen from the point of view of Picard, Geordi, Worf, Troi, or another of the regulars instead of from the point of view of one of our own characters. So we were able to keep the story almost exactly as we wanted it to be in the first place. Personally, I also enjoyed giving Troi a demanding and important part to play in this story, showing her courage as well as her sensitivity."

George reflected, "What, if any effect, has writing *Star Trek* novels had on our careers? The money has been good, and we enjoyed doing the work. We often felt that we knew much more about the origins and nature of the series than did the editors, or some of the readers. But then we have both edited major anthologies in the field and written award-winning stories and novels. Writer-editors cre-

ated the SF genre; few major editors have not been writers. Publishers are in the position of having to take authority on faith, so they make mistakes. One Pocket editor said to me, 'Don't worry about the wrong science, or wrong anything. It's only *Star Trek!*' This, we believe, showed a contempt, from the top down, for readers, whose taste can only be degraded by such an attitude, and for which they are later blamed. We wrote with love and attention to *Star Trek* and to science fiction. Critically, in the more ambitious realm of print SF, these books didn't do much for us, but given our reputations prior to these efforts, the *Star Trek* novels did us no harm, with all the mistakes. All the happiness was in writing them."

4 4

THE DEATH OF PRINCES

JOHN PEEL

JANUARY 1997   **(276 PP)**

Two separate and desperate missions split the crew into two teams on distant worlds. A plague threatens the inhabitants of the planet

Buran, and due to social mores and religious beliefs, the inhabitants not only don't want assistance, but also believe the Federation might have infected the populace. On the planet Iomides, a Starfleet officer violates the Prime Directive when she uncovers an assassination attempt. Can Riker repair the damage and save the target from death?

For the concept of this novel, John remarked, "Once again, it was a collision of my love of playing with ideas and my silly sense of humor. It seemed to me that we were always getting stories where the captain had to break the Prime Directive for A Very Good Reason. So I decided I wanted to do a story that would show *why* there was a Prime Directive in the first place. I mean, it had to be a good idea, didn't it, or the Federation would never have adopted it! It was also written while there was a lot of JFK conspiracy material going around, so I thought it would be fun to incorporate that. Then there was Jonathan Frakes hosting the 'Alien Autopsy,' so I couldn't resist having Riker involved in one, too. This book contains more of my silly jokes than any other I've written. The other storyline, with the alien plague, was because I always felt that Beverly was underused, and wanted to give her lots of fun stuff to do for a change."

#45

INTELLIVORE

Diane Duane

April 1997 (239pp)

The *Enterprise*, along with two other Starfleet vessels, investigates the area of space known as the Great Rift. Strange stories of pirates, several ships, and entire colonies vanishing prompt the presence of the three ships. A humanitarian rescue reveals an entire vessel full of catatonic people and leads to a bizarre truth: A renegade planet-like being roams the space and devours the consciousness of its victims.

According to Diane, "There was an image that had been following me around for a while . . . of a rogue planet, sliding in from the dark, and where it passes, nothing is left living afterwards . . . or not *very* living. It first turned up in *The Romulan Way*, but I had little time to do anything with it there. I wanted to follow that idea to its logical (or illogical) conclusion . . . and indulge myself just a little with what was essentially a horror story about a monster that sneaks up on you and sucks out your brains with a straw."

#46

TO STORM HEAVEN
ESTHER FRIESNER

DECEMBER 1997 (278PP)

he planet Orakisa and its inhabitants are dying. The *Enterprise* arrives and takes a delegation to Orakisa's sister planet, Ne'elat. The people of both planets are tied together in more ways than previously thought possible. Can they put aside their differences long enough to save both of their worlds? Meanwhile, Geordi falls in love with a woman who believes he is a "Starlord."

Esther remarked, "I made the leap from watching the show to wanting to write a *Trek* novel because the editor of the *Trek* novel line asked me if I'd like to do so for the new *Deep Space Nine*. I think this invitation came before DS9 began to air, so I didn't have a lot of background to catch up on. The idea for *To Storm Heaven* came orig-

inally from Greek mythology where two giants literally try to storm heaven by piling Mt. Ossa on Mt. Pelion in an attempt to get up to Olympus. Aside from that, additional inspiration came from an ongoing interest in societies and cultures, past and present, that are polarized by elitism of one sort or another—financial, religious, aesthetic, anything that lets one group establish and maintain the old 'We are inherently better than you' rule over another."

#47

Q-SPACE
(THE Q CONTINUUM, Book One)
GREG COX

AUGUST 1998 (271PP)

scientist from the planet Betazed believes he has found a way to safely penetrate the galactic barrier. Picard and his crew are ordered to help him with the tests, and take him to the site responsible for turning Gary Mitchell, among others, into a god. When the *Enterprise* almost reaches the barrier, Q arrives and tries to convince Picard to abandon the test.

| #48 | #49 |

Q-ZONE
(THE Q CONTINUUM, Book Two)
Greg Cox

AUGUST 1998   (270pp)

Q-STRIKE
(THE Q CONTINUUM, Book Three)
Greg Cox

SEPTEMBER 1998   (272pp)

Q takes Picard on a journey, leaving Riker in command. Can he figure out how to protect the ship from the angry Calamarain? Q decides to reveal a major secret from his past, in the hope that Picard will realize that penetrating the barrier would be a very bad idea. Meanwhile, a scientist fumes and plots to run the test regardless of what an omnipotent being wants.

Picard discovers the true horror that waits if the barrier is penetrated. Unfortunately, in order to escape the Calamarain, Riker is forced to take the *Enterprise* into the barrier. The being responsible for turning ordinary persons into gods finds a perfect candidate in Lem Faal, the Betazoid scientist. Can Q help Picard save the galaxy?

Greg remembered, "John Ordover called me up and said, 'Greg, how would you like to do a trilogy about Q?' He thought that *The Q Continuum* would be a great title for a trilogy or miniseries. I was sort of intimidated, thinking, 'Oh my God, I'm not sure I've got nine hundred pages of Q in me.' But I went back and watched all of the Q episodes again. I worked up an outline, got it approved, and I dived into it. Spreading it out over three books was a challenge."

Greg finished, "The trilogy remains my best-selling books, which I think has less to do with me than with the extraordinary popularity of the Q character. One nice moment came a few years later, during a vacation in Italy, when I wandered into a bookstore in downtown Rome to discover the Italian editions on sale! (A "Flora Stagliano" is credited with the translation.) Also, to give credit where credit is due, I should mention that the doggerel poetry recited by the villainous 0 (pronounced *zero*) was written by my girlfriend Karen Palinko, who was much better than me at coming up with that stuff. Karen also served as my first reader on the trilogy, and offered much helpful advice throughout."

#50

DYSON SPHERE

CHARLES PELLEGRINO AND GEORGE ZEBROWSKI

APRIL 1999 (235PP)

About a year after the rescue of Scotty in the episode "Relics," the *Enterprise* heads back to the mysterious Dyson Sphere to investigate its uniqueness. Upon arrival, the crew discovers a neutron star is approaching and will collide with the sphere. With many different life forms living on its enigmatic surface, can the crew divert a cataclysm? An afterword by the authors discusses the possibilities of creating a Dyson Sphere and interstellar travel.

George remarked, "Charles Pellegrino, the multi-faceted scientist and author, and I had written *The Killing Star* together, and one short story, 'Oh, Miranda!' Both were highly praised. We planned the book together as a new *War of the Worlds*, with much new stuff to consider, some of it never before in a novel. Charlie wrote chapters from our outline and I rewrote them, adding material. Avon, unfortunately, published the uncorrected proofs! The same thing happened with my Bantam *New York Times* Notable Book of the Year, *Stranger Suns*. It's a law of nature: Publish the uncorrected proofs, especially if the author gets them in on time. No apologies were ever made. *Dyson Sphere* went about the same in the writing. I wrote a full draft, Charlie rewrote it, and I rewrote that. Pocket and Paramount approved the final text and we were happy. Then, chaos struck: Someone cut the novel by some 20 percent without our knowledge or approval. The first we knew of it was when a box of copies arrived, and we saw that the afterword was nearly a third of the book! Right science was made wrong (harmful to the good name of a working scientist), dialogue cues lost, long sections deleted. This after formal approval had been made. We believe that someone put it up on a screen, forgetting the approved state of the text, and began incompetently 'editing' the text, not realizing how much was being lost. Prior to this, the manuscript and disks had been lost at least twice, forcing us to replace the entire package. The new management of the series has apologized graciously."

#51-56

DOUBLE HELIX

(SEE SECTION 12: MINISERIES)

#57

THE FORGOTTEN WAR

WILLIAM R. FORSTCHEN
(AND ELIZABETH KITSTEINER SALZER)

SEPTEMBER 1999   (270PP)

The *Enterprise* enters Tarn space to negotiate a treaty when the crew makes a startling discovery: the remains of the Starship *Verdun*. Missing since the time of Captain Pike, evidence shows that the ship battled a Tarn vessel and both were destroyed. On the planet below, the descendants of both ships are still fighting a war that technically ended many years earlier. The battle-worn inhabitants don't believe the fighting can cease, so Picard must convince the two hostile parties there is no reason to fight any longer.

Bill remembered, "I'm old enough now that I actually remember the running of the first episode of the original series and was totally hooked."

He continued, "I was contacted by [Pocket] in 1995 to do a *Next Generation* novel. Actually, I first turned it down, since I was no longer current with the series but on the day I took that call I had a remarkable student in my office. I'm a professor of history at Montreat College near Asheville, North Carolina and this student was doing an independent study with me on writing for the commercial marketplace. She heard me turn the offer down and sat there wide-eyed. Then announced she was a major *Star Trek* buff and couldn't believe I had passed on the offer. I had done some contract writing for a couple of other series and the experiences went from OK to miserable. Well, one thing led to another—this student was, without a doubt, the finest I had worked with in years, so I finally called back and said I'd give it a shot if she could be my coauthor.

"I confess: That issue does still bother me today. Her name is Elizabeth Kitsteiner Salzer, a really remarkable talent, and she was a major force behind the story. There was a lot of debate about her name being on the title. I kept insisting it should be, but [Pocket] kept saying they preferred not. There were some other problems as well in terms of author-publisher relationship, but I'll skip most of those. Originally I was given a lot more carte blanche in terms of doing the story 'my way' rather than fit a standard format. That was why I was approached by one of the editors to bring in some new blood to the series and a different perspective. Unfortunately, in the end Elizabeth's name did not appear on the title page where it should have been nor did she even get the acknowledgment she deserved. So I do hope you set the record straight and list *The Forgotten War* with her as my coauthor.

"The idea? It came to me when reading an account of Japanese soldiers who were still being found in the jungles of remote islands as late as the 1980s, never surrendering or giving up, still loyal to the Emperor. The thought hit that with the early days of exploration, the time of Christopher Pike ships would be frequently lost and just 'disappear.' Suppose there had been a battle, with survivors on both sides getting down to a planet's surface and they're continuing their war across hundreds of years. They are cut off, have no idea of the progress made, and in survival, retrofit to a primitive level, our early twentieth century. . . . What would both sides say to discover that we have been at peace for [so long]? The questions it presented were fascinating to me and in discussion with Elizabeth we worked out the story line for *The Forgotten War* and the female character of the historian who gets caught up in this conflict."

#58

GEMWORLD, Book One

John Vornholt

FEBRUARY 2000   (251PP)

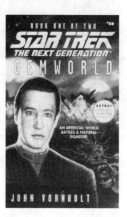

Lieutenant Melora Pazlar, last seen in the DS9 episode, "Melora," finds herself stationed on the *Enterprise*. Experiencing weird dreams, she begs Picard and Barclay to take her home to the planet Gemworld. This artificial world, made entirely of crystal and held together by a force field, might be starting to crumble. Over a half dozen different alien races live on the crystalline planet, and they must all work together to save their world. The planet will disintegrate in less than eight days, and it appears that someone has sabotaged the network holding the force field in place.

#59

GEMWORLD, Book Two

John Vornholt

FEBRUARY 2000 (233pp)

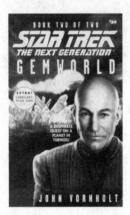

Racing to save the entire world from destruction, Barclay must collect key crystals from each of the six races on the planet to initiate a bold plan. Meanwhile, he finds himself falling in love with Melora. Unfortunately for him, she is keeping a major secret that could doom the *Enterprise* crew and her world.

"In a DS9 episode, Dr. Bashir fell in love with Melora, a humanoid female from a planet that [has almost no] gravity. That intrigued me, and I tried to imagine a low-gravity planet that could support humanoids, along with other weird species. I had just written a war story with the *Dominion War* books, and I wanted to do something more fanciful. I also wanted to feature Lieutenant Barclay, one of my favorite characters. These books went very smoothly, and I really enjoyed all the world-building and

bizarre aliens I got to invent in this 'visit to a weird planet' story."

#60

TOOTH AND CLAW

Doranna Durgin

FEBRUARY 2001 (246pp)

The Tsorans are an alien species that has the technology to help evacuate a group of refugees before their sun explodes. To show the Federation's good faith, Riker offers to escort a young Tsoran prince on his ritual hunt on the planet Fandre, an exclusive hunting preserve. When the shuttle crashes, Riker must not only keep them both alive, but also help his comrade succeed in his rite of passage.

Doranna has always been writing. "At twelve I decided to get serious and actually finish something—also bound and illustrated. My teacher didn't know what to do with me. Shortly after that I went on to write some *Trek*.

Not that anyone will ever see it (I think I actually—wisely—burned it some years ago) but it's an indication of how big a mark the show had made on me. When many years later my agent sent along the guidelines for the books, it didn't take long to come up with some ideas."

Regarding the idea for the story, Doranna remarked, "My old hound was in his last days, and was always on my mind—and he used to love to hunt. He never saw anything quite like the creatures in *Tooth and Claw*, but I think he would have jumped in with all four paws. I enjoyed working with [my editors,] John and Carol. I also enjoyed writing the book and hearing from *Trek* fans."

#61

DIPLOMATIC IMPLAUSIBILITY

KEITH R. A. DeCANDIDO

FEBRUARY 2001   (248pp)

Klingons, but the conquered people are allowed to have their own government as long as they obey the Klingon rules. Some rebels demand the Klingons leave, and force the Federation to send Worf to negotiate for a possible entrance into the Federation. In addition to Worf's first assignment, it also begins the ongoing series of Captain Klag and his crew.

Keith met John Ordover when John was at Tor and Keith worked for *Library Journal*. They remained friends and he eventually starting doing some freelance work for John. "I was the one who picked all the clips for the CD-ROM version of the *Star Trek Encyclopedia*. My big unknown accomplishment in the *Trek* universe."

He continued, "By the time 1999 rolled around I had by then published four novels and a bunch of short stories. All of them were media tie-ins for the most part. After I had pretty much established myself, John said, 'I'd love for you to write a *Star Trek* story.' So I came up with an incredibly brilliant pitch for the original series. Ordover thought it was really cool and it would make a wonderful novel, so of course, he rejected it. Pocket had just gotten the new scripts for 'What You Leave Behind,' the last DS9 episode, and it went with Worf going off to be the Federation ambassador to the Klingon empire. John knew Worf was my favorite character so he suggested I should write Worf's first mission as Federation ambassador. To which I, not being stupid, agreed. And that's how *Diplomatic Implausibility* came about."

Worf is now the Federation Ambassador to the Klingon Empire and his first assignment is a doozy. The planet taD is ruled by the

#62 & #63

DEAD ZONE
(MAXIMUM WARP, Book One)
FOREVER DARK
(MAXIMUM WARP, Book Two)
DAVE GALANTER AND GREG BRODEUR

MARCH 2001	(236 PP)
MARCH 2001	(221 PP)

Strange anomalies are appearing throughout the galaxy. These supposed "dead zones" harm any ship that is unfortunate enough to wander into one. The ship will suddenly lose all power and be forced to run off a dwindling battery supply. When the *Enterprise* discovers this zone, the crew will go to great lengths to solve the mystery. Throw in the Romulans and even Spock to the recipe, and you have a major crisis.

Dave remarked, "The idea for *Maximum Warp* came from a book Greg loaned me about the science behind science fiction. There was a page or two on the oscillating universe theory that suggests the universe might repeat itself over and over again, big bang to expanding, then big crunch into a monobloc of matter and energy, and then another big bang, over and over again. It got me to thinking that if this big-bang/bigcrunch/bigbang repetition of the universe is infinite, and goes on forever—and has gone on forever—then something can be done with that idea. I suggested it to Greg and we played with the notion that there are only a finite number of combinations in which matter and energy can interact with one another to form things which exist. And yet, if the cycle of one universe after another is infinite, there are an everlasting number of chances for which these combinations can come together. That means this universe has existed before—just as it is now—an infinite number of times. And it will exist again in the same way, also an infinite number of times. And every *possible* variation of this universe will have the same number of reoccurrences. The idea fascinated me, and I read what I could about the theory, including a fantastic book by Dr. Michio Kaku called *Hyperspace*, which introduced me to Type I, II, and III civilizations, which we expanded on to theorize about Type IV civilizations. The first idea we proposed was for Picard and crew to actually destroy their own universe and have Riker and Geordi and a few others die in the process. Spock wasn't in the book, and Q was. In the end, Picard took the sphere that we'd made clear was related to the Guardian in 'The City on the Edge of Forever' and made it his mission to travel the multiverse (which the Sphere would allow the *Enterprise* to do) and stop future Picards from making the same mistake. John Ordover asked us to remove Q, so we decided to use Spock. That was a thrill for me. He's one of my favorite characters and I was both excited and a little nervous about putting words in his mouth. Also, John didn't want the whole book to not be our universe's Picard and crew. He felt it was a bit of a cheat to the reader if we revealed at the end that it wasn't *our* Picard, and I understood his point. The ending wasn't my first choice, and I don't know if I did it justice. It was perhaps a bit confusing, and based less on theoretical science and a bit more on *Trek* science than I'd wanted, but I liked many of the characters we used and cre-

ated, and so over all I'm pleased with that. I'd still like to use Folan, Kalor, and Parl again some day. I can tell you this, without Keith De-Candido's tight and helpful editing, both books just wouldn't have been nearly as good as they eventually turned out. It was released, by the way, in two parts because that's what John Ordover asked me for. I didn't want to just stop writing half way and start Book Two, so I made sure that Book One ended on a cliffhanger. For me, it was like a two-part TNG show."

STAR TREK: THE NEXT GENERATION UNNUMBERED NOVELS

METAMORPHOSIS
JEAN LORRAH

MARCH 1990   (371PP)

A The first *Next Generation* "giant" novel and a direct sequel to Lorrah's book *Survivors*. While Data is still contemplating Tasha's death, mysterious gravitational disturbances force the ship to the planet Elysia. Investigating the source, Data ends up on a mystical quest to meet the Elysian gods. If successful, he will receive his fondest wish.

• • •

Jean loved exploring the notion of Data becoming human. When asked about the novel, she commented, "Oh, lord—let's not go into all that. Suffice it to say that the biggest thing readers object to was not put into the book by me."

VENDETTA
PETER DAVID

MAY 1991   (400PP)

S et shortly after "The Best of Both Worlds," the Borg ravages another planet in the Alpha Quadrant. Still weary of his last encounter, Picard must put aside his feelings to answer a distress call from a decimated planet. Upon their arrival, the crew finds the shattered remains of the Borg vessel. Does someone have a weapon powerful enough to defeat the Borg, and how high is the price for possession of this device? The answer lies in Guinan's past.

Peter remarked, "The concept for *Vendetta* came because [my editor] wanted me to do a giant novel about the Borg. I happened to be watching the original series episode 'The Doomsday Machine' and at the end of the episode, we don't really know any more about the machine than when we started. We know it was created by a mysterious alien race and there might be another one floating around. Apparently, it was created to fight a vast enemy. I also came to the realization that there was an inherent problem with what Spock said in terms of where the machine came from. He thought it came from another galaxy but it couldn't because it is a planet eater. There is vast space between galaxies in which there are no planets and soon it's going to run out of gas. By the laws of physics, objects in motion tend to stay in motion until acted upon by another force. Even if the doomsday machine ran out of fuel it would keep moving because there is no friction. So, the concept that it would keep moving is not an invalid one but the problem is that once the thing got to the Milky Way Galaxy it would bounce off the energy barrier that was firmly established in the episode 'Where No Man Has Gone Before.' I came up with the revised notion that it was right nearby our galaxy and that the enemy it was built to stop was the Borg. I wrote the outline and it was approved. I then wrote the novel and it was rejected by the studio

on the basis of one element. The compromise was a disclaimer that is in the front of the book to this day. The wording of the disclaimer is: 'The plot and background details of *Vendetta* are solely the author's interpretation of the universe of STAR TREK, and vary in some respects from the universe as created by Gene Roddenberry.' The plot element that forced the disclaimer was that I had a female Borg. Richard [Arnold] told us that there was no such thing as Borg females. They are completely sexless. They are obviously male. Anyway, he wanted me to take out the character of Rhiannon who was a female Borg. That's why there had to be a disclaimer. This was, of course, before Seven of Nine and the Borg Queen."

REUNION
Michael Jan Friedman

November 1991   **(343 pp)**

ORIGINALLY PUBLISHED IN HARDCOVER

 he first hardcover adventure for the crew of the *Enterprise*-D. Picard's former shipmates aboard the *Stargazer* are arriving to accompany Captain Morgan to Daa'V, where he is resigning from Starfleet to become its new ruler. But someone wants to kill him, and this assassin will take out anyone who interferes. Picard lived with these people for twenty-one years, and now he must find the killer among his friends.

Mike commented, "I love murder mysteries and this was a good chance to meld one with *Star Trek*. It gave me a chance to get into a lot of nooks and crannies, which I love to do. It was the first *The Next Generation* hardcover, so there was some pressure to do well. But it was cool. It gave me a chance to show Picard's old crew interacting with his new crew and that was a wonderful opportunity. I never intended to use these people again, I said, because I didn't think I'd be able to. At that point you couldn't use anybody from anybody else's books. You couldn't use anybody you'd already used in your books. So I figured this was a one-time thing for ben Zoma and the Azmunds, and Simenon and Greyhorse and Pug, and it turned out otherwise."

IMZADI
Peter David

August 1992   **(342 pp)**

Originally published in hardcover

Counselor Troi dies under mysterious circumstances and, forty years later, Admiral William Riker still can't forget. He is called to Betazed to visit her dying mother, Lwaxana. En route, he reflects back on how he met Deanna and became her *imzadi*. Chastised by Lwaxana before she passes, Riker decides on a bold move that will change the fate of the entire galaxy as well as the woman he loves.

Peter replied, "It was the first time that Majel Barrett yelled at me. I got this furious call from Majel saying, 'Peter. I've been told that in your new book, *Imzadi*, you kill off Lwaxana Troi.' She then went off and it was obvious she was tremendously hurt. I asked who told her and she said, 'Marina.' I asked her if she had read the book and she hadn't. I proceeded to explain to her that it happened in the far future and it was an unbelievingly aged Lwaxanna Troi. It was not set in current *Star Trek* continuity and the death of Lwaxana prompts the older Riker to go back in time and set things right so that Deanna lives. The Lwaxana who dies is very old, bitter, and angry over the death of her daughter many years previous. Riker goes back and over the course of the book sets things right so Deanna does not die, and changes his own future. As a result, not only does Lwaxana die in the far future, but that future is changed so by the end of the book it's completely moot. Majel apologized and I can't stay mad at her. Remember, I have her to thank for getting *Q-In-Law* published."

Peter continued, "[My editor] approached me about doing a book about the early days of Deanna and Riker's relationship. I thought if we are going to the beginning, let's go all the way to the future as well. I decided to revisit 'City on the Edge of Forever.' In the original Ellison script, Kirk was ready to sacrifice the universe to save Edith Keeler. That was the depth of his love for her. To me, that was such a powerful concept that I thought if they didn't let Harlan do it, then I was going to do it. I decided to do a story with Riker in the far future where he realizes he doesn't want to live in a universe where Deanna Troi is dead. He has to go back and change history. That was the genesis of *Imzadi*."

Peter continued, "*Imzadi* had the most impact of any *Trek* novel I've ever written. More people cite that as their favorite *Trek* novel of mine than any other book. People tell me that they used Riker's poem to Deanna as their wedding vows. As far as I was concerned it was a wretched poem. But they loved it!"

THE DEVIL'S HEART
CARMEN CARTER

APRIL 1993 (309PP)

ORIGINALLY PUBLISHED IN HARDCOVER

Picard and the crew investigate the slaughter of several Vulcan archaeologists. The head of the party had claimed to find the Devil's Heart before she died. When Picard picks up this historic jewel, he begins to act strangely, making unusual requests. Has the gem possessed him?

Carmen commented, "The editor at Pocket Books had asked me if I was interested in writing a hardcover novel for the *The Next Generation* series, and I'd regretfully passed on the offer because I didn't have any ideas that I felt were suitable for that large a writing canvas. Then the basic premise for *The Devil's Heart* arrived full-blown in my foggy mind during a late-night taxi ride from Manhattan to Brooklyn. By the time I arrived at my apartment, I was scrawling notes on a stray envelope and by the next day I had a proposal sketched out. Unfortunately, the writing of *The Devil's Heart* turned out to be torturous. My personal life was in an upheaval due to a lot of wonderful but very distracting changes that made concentration very difficult. As a result I missed several deadlines, seriously pissed off my editor, and pretty much mined out my enjoyment in writing for the *Star Trek* universe."

Carmen went on, "These days I'm so busy writing computer code that I simply don't have the time to write fiction anymore. Rather late in life I've discovered a love of programming that has overshadowed my interest in writing and provided a secure livelihood as a bonus. Nonetheless, I do hope to return to writing fiction some day, but not *Star Trek* and probably not as a commercial activity either. I write to please myself and that's more easily accomplished without worrying about deadlines and editorial approval."

Carmen still has fond memories of her experiences. "Over the past thirty-five years *Star Trek* has shaped so many aspects of my life that it's difficult to imagine how different my life would be if I had never watched the series. Even though I no longer follow any of the franchise shows, or even give *Star Trek* much conscious thought, it's left an indelible legacy in the form of deep friendships, my partner (who is a fellow *Trek* fan), and my philosophical outlook. Oh, yes, and a basement stuffed full of action figures."

DARK MIRROR
Diane Duane

December 1993   (337pp)

ORIGINALLY PUBLISHED IN HARDCOVER

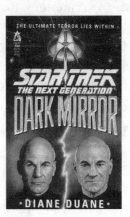

The *Enterprise* finds itself mysteriously transported to an alternate universe, the one from the original series episode "Mirror, Mirror." The inhabitants are extremely violent and brutality is the norm. The crew of the *I.S.S. Enterprise*-D has a plan to invade our *Enterprise*, kill the crew and return to our universe, paving the way for an eventual invasion. Picard, Troi, and LaForge sneak on board the alternate vessel to play their counterparts, but also learn details of the evil invasion plan, plus find a way back to their own universe.

Diane remembered, "I had a fondness for *The Next Generation* . . . possibly understandable, since I was one of the first people to write for it. (Our episode of TNG was the sixth one filmed.) It seemed to me that it was time to do something in prose in that part of the universe. I didn't know what that was going to be, though, until one afternoon when Peter and I were having a late lunch at a place called Gotham Café in Dublin. Gotham has the best thincrust New York-style pizza in town, and we were finishing up a couple of them and discussing costuming in *Star Trek*. Peter was muttering that the uniforms were going downhill, and they ought to do something in black and silver. I was muttering that Peter is always putting his heroes in black and silver, and it was getting old. Somehow or other the topic drifted around to the various changes that the original-series uniforms had undergone, and the coolness of the uniforms of the Mirror Universe characters . . . and there I stopped suddenly and stared at Peter. I said, 'Why hasn't anybody done a Mirror Universe TNG story?' We went around and around all the possible reasons . . . and finally I said, 'The heck with this, let's call Dave Stern and find out.' So we ran outside to the coin phones (this was before cellphones) and I called Dave and said, 'What's the score? Has Paramount told you not to do one of these?' And Dave said, 'No.' And I said, 'Is anyone else doing one?' And Dave said 'No.' And I said, 'Would you *like* one?' And Dave said, 'Yes.' So I went off and outlined it . . . and writing it was a *lot* of fun. I later got a lot of fan mail from young men who wanted me to send them a picture of the Mirror Universe version of Deanna Troi, and her uniform. What there was of it. For a sadistic torturer, she seemed really popular. . . . In any case, a framed copy of the cover of that book hung above that table in Gotham Café for a long time, until our friend David the co-owner co-opted it for his upstairs office."

Q-SQUARED
Peter David

JULY 1994   (434PP)

ORIGINALLY PUBLISHED IN HARDCOVER

Two Q's for the price of one! Trelane, from the original series episode "The Squire of Gothos," returns to cause havoc on the *Enterprise*-D crew. A member of the Q continuum, he's accompanied by another troublemaker, our favorite Q. The author has us question what is reality as several parallel timelines run amok, thanks to Trelane's boyish antics. Trelane has tapped into the ultimate cosmic power source, and now finds himself even more powerful than Q, and boy will he take advantage!

Peter remarked, "*Q-Squared* was the result of the sales of *Q-In-Law*. The concept of whether Trelane was a Q or not came from the TNG episode 'Encounter at Farpoint.' The moment Q showed up I immediately thought he was like Trelane. A number of fans felt the same way. In later episodes, Q became his own character and moved away from being a simple Trelane clone. This stuck in my head, so when I was asked to do another Q book I asked if I could do something that draws a connection between Q and Trelane and was given the go-ahead."

Peter continued, "I don't remember what prompted me to the various dimensions but I can tell you that it was the most insane thing I've ever done. I had to map this thing out and do it beat by beat by beat. *Q-Squared* is almost my challenge to the reader to keep up with me. As I would do each chapter, I checked it off and had to make sure each part ended at the right point so when I had the timelines converge, they converged at the right point. The first point is when Picard is looking in the mirror and sees another version of himself. That was the first time things started to overlap. I got to the point where all three timelines converged and I realized I had just totally f*ed myself because I had three different versions of the characters running around and I had no way to distinguish them in terms of conveying to the reader who was who. They all had the same names! If you were doing a TV show, you could have visual clues. The uniforms could be different colors; the hairstyles could be different. In a book you don't have that option. I couldn't say Track A Picard and Track B Riker in the context of the narrative since that would read weird. I had to find different ways to convey who was who and keep everything straight. I was pounding my head against the wall because I had screwed myself so thoroughly. I had trouble remembering at times! What the hell was I thinking?"

CROSSOVER
Michael Jan Friedman

DECEMBER 1995   (305 PP)

ORIGINALLY PUBLISHED IN HARDCOVER

Security forces on the planet Romulus arrest several sympathizers to the unification cause. These individuals' long-term goal sees their Vulcan brethren and the Romulan people uniting. One of the captured members of the underground movement is Spock. Captain Picard, along with the crew of the *Enterprise*-D and a crotchety Doctor McCoy, are dispatched to rescue Spock before his true identity is discovered and he eats Romulan dust. Don't leave out Scotty!

"*Crossover* was Kevin Ryan's idea. He said, 'What about the Over the Hill Gang rides again? Do you want to do that?' And I said, 'Sure.' And he had all kinds of ideas and they were good ones, as usual. And I ran with it. It was great fun. I mean having McCoy and Picard at odds was wonderful. It just wrote itself.

It gave me a chance to do some funny situations with Data, and juxtapose them with some very serious, grim scenes involving Spock. It was great to do Scotty, it was great to do McCoy, and it was great to do Spock. And to be able to do them all together, even though they weren't meeting, they weren't getting together, they were all pieces moving on the chess board and it was more fun than I've had with almost any other book."

KAHLESS

MICHAEL JAN FRIEDMAN

JULY 1996   (307 PP)

ORIGINALLY PUBLISHED IN HARDCOVER

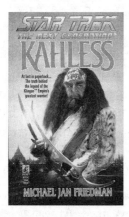

A look into the heart and mind of the greatest warrior in Klingon history. The discovery of an ancient scroll supposedly written by Kahless himself puts the entire belief system of the Klingons into jeopardy. His clone sits as emperor and in order to maintain the status quo, he calls upon Picard and Worf to help. The story tells two distinct tales; one takes place with the *Enterprise* crew trying to save Kahless' reputation and stop a potential overthrow of the government. The other side reveals the secrets of the scroll and a young warrior who takes the destiny of the entire Klingon race into his hands.

Mike commented, "They had already done a book on the early days of Vulcan. Wouldn't it be cool to do a book on Kahless? And wouldn't it be cool if the original Kahless was different from the Kahless we expect him to be? I mean, that's something I like to do a lot. You saw it with Guinan, you see it with *Kahless*, and you see it in *My Brothers Keeper*. I like thwarting expectation and here's a Kahless who is different from the one we saw in the various episodes and references. He's not conscious of his role in history. He's just a guy trying to get along. He's just doing what he thinks is right from time to time and suffering tragedies and failures and doing the best he can. At the end of the book there's a twist when we learn an incredible secret about the Kahless clone that was introduced in 'Rightful Heir.' It just came to me as I wrote the end of the book. I had to call Kevin Ryan and say 'Hey, would it be alright if I . . . do you think I can get away with this?' And he said 'Sure.' So that was an opportunity I might have missed if not for, I don't know, what I had for lunch that day. But it wasn't in the outline."

SHIP OF THE LINE
DIANE CAREY

OCTOBER 1997   (320PP)

ORIGINALLY PUBLISHED IN HARDCOVER

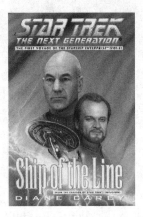

After the events of *Generations*, Picard and the crew anxiously wait news that they will be stationed together on the new *Enterprise*-E. Captain Morgan Bateson and his crew spent ninety years in a temporal loop and are trying to fit in with the future. Winning the sympathy vote, Bateson assumes command of the new vessel and proceeds to the Klingon Empire to launch an attack.

Diane was asked to write the book, which built off the *Next Generation* episode "Cause and Effect." Kelsey Grammer's character of Morgan Bates appears briefly as a ship's captain at the end. She said, "Many people suppose that I fixated on Grammer's character, but in fact I was asked to write this one and was rather dismayed at the idea of creating a whole character based on a cameo. In the history of my writing

for *Star Trek*, I've always scrupulously stuck to the specific actors' versions of their characters, never pushing myself on characters that belonged to someone else. I have a track record for doing excellent Kirk, Spock, McCoy, and Scott, and that's because I watched the old *Trek* episodes over and over, scoping every nuance, every movement, and every method of line delivery, determined to do Shatner's Kirk, Nimoy's Spock, Kelley's McCoy, and Doohan's Scott. The same went with this book and the character played, even for a few seconds, by Kelsey Grammer. The book turned out to be very popular."

Diane had fun writing this book. She said, "*Ship of the Line* is written almost entirely from the points of view of several first officers. This book is a good example of my constant struggle to find new angles from which to look at familiar subjects. Riker's, Bush's, and others' views of their own duties, of their captains, and of command in general, because they're in a position of high command and must make instant decisions, yet constantly wonder what their particular captain would do or should do—there are a hundred prism-effects at work for a command officer who isn't in the highest command. I face a similar situation as a command officer aboard ships. As watch leader, I'm in charge of half or one third of the crew depending upon the captain's preferred watch schedule and how many crew members are available. The crew doesn't go to the captain or mate for questions, problems, and so forth. They come to me. It's up to me to decide when and why to convey information or questions farther up the line. The captain is the last to be bothered. I have to make decisions and use my judgment, anticipating what the captain prefers and just hope I'm right. I have to assess the holes in my own knowledge and decide how to fill them, figure things out, and go to the captain only as a last resort. The first and second mates are often my resources, being more approachable than the captain. This also goes the other way. The captain and mates can't just pluck the nearest crewman when they want something done. They have to come to me, and I choose a crewman to assign to that duty. That's the up-down/down-up function of chain of command."

Diane continued, "This is why, in *Ship of the Line* and the *Challenger* books, I found the point of view of officers caught in the middle to be far more dramatic than that of command officers. Also, First Officer Bush of the Bozeman is named after Mr. Bush, first lieutenant of the *Horatio Hornblower* series, and *Ship of Line* is loosely modeled after the second book in that series, *Lieutenant Hornblower*. It's the only book in the *Hornblower* series that's told from someone else's point of view—Mr. Bush's—and it's my favorite of the series because of that."

One last detail that Diane wanted to convey. "The primary reason for writing the book, [my editor] wished, was to act as a bridge between Captain Picard's loss of the *Enterprise*-D and how he came to really want to be the captain of a new ship. It was a turning point for him, when he had a chance to decide to retire from command and maybe become that archaeologist he should've been in the first place. The book's third purpose was to launch the *Enterprise*-E, another turning point for Starfleet. . . . The primary goal was to arch Picard to his really wanting to command the *Enterprise*-E. The book was also a bridge for me; I had lost my fa-

vorite ship, our beloved Schooner *Alexandria*, and I too was wandering around between ships trying to find a home. I sailed the scruffing 1926 *Baltic Trader*, a three-masted gaff-rigger, for four happy years. The crew was my family. We were all volunteers, always working to keep the old ship going, using our own sweat, tears, and often our money to keep her patched together. In turn, she never failed us. When we hit the bottom off Thimble Shoals in Chesapeake Bay and were taking on 100 gallons of water a minute, she brought us in safely, despite rumors on shore that we had sunk. Same thing off Fort Jefferson—we whacked a Civil War jetty and were taking on 50 gallons a minute but we brought her in. I could train anybody at any position on that ship; she was as forgiving as a good old horse. If one of us made a mistake, she would just wait quietly and keep floating while we corrected it. If ever a ship had a personality, *Alexandria* had one. A self-indulgent lawyer who thought he was Errol Flynn purchased her. Without learning enough about how to work a 1929 sailing ship, he took her away from us and through incompetence and poor command decisions had her sunk within two months. We kept her alive and floating all those years with sweat and pennies, and he lost her barely out of her T-dock. She's down in the waters with the *Monitor* and the first *Pride of Baltimore*, off Cape Hatteras, lost to us forever, for no good reason. Truly sad, and a good example that having a license doesn't make a captain. The slob sank my second home. Having lost my ship, I was primed to write a book about Picard's loss of his ship, because—believe me—it's hard to want another ship when you've lost the one you really thought of as your home. At the end of that book is the first poem I'd written in about twenty-five years, about our *Alexandria*. During the time I wrote this book, I was sailing aboard another ship which I've come to care about, the Revenue Cutter *California*. Next time somebody asks, 'Why is there so much about ships in Diane Carey's books?' you'll have the answer."

PLANET X
MICHAEL JAN FRIEDMAN

MAY 1998   (265PP)

The crew of the *Enterprise*-D meets the X-Men! On the planet Xhaldia, the inhabitants discover a society threatened when many of them begin exhibiting strange mutant powers. Trapped in the future, the X-Men are willing to help resolve the situation on the planet. After all, the mutants are used to dealing with their own kind. But, the threat is much bigger than they realize. Now Picard must not only save the Federation, but also get his friends back to their proper time!

• • •

Mike remembered, "John Ordover came to me—he's a comic fan—and said, 'I think we have a unique opportunity here.' Marvel had the *Star Trek* license for comics. It wasn't quite that simple but basically that was the relationship. Marvel and Paramount were kind of collaborating on something called Paramount Comics. They had already come out with a comic that used Gary Mitchell and kind of crossed over the Original Series cast with the X-Men characters. And now they wanted to do a TNG version. I guess John was talking to them and they decided that they were going to do a combination comic book and novel that would be loosely related. John, knowing I'm a comic fan and knowing I like TNG, asked if I wanted to do this and I said, 'Absolutely!' Worf and Wolverine, and Picard and Professor X. You had Geordi, who as an engineer is related to the transporter, and Nightcrawler who teleports. You had Jean Gray and Deanna Troi— one is a telepath, one is an empath from a telepathic species, so it was a great combination. With comics, you often see these team-ups and its cool because you say, wow, these two characters from different milieus, what would they do if they met?"

Mike continued, "The book sold very, very well. And I did expect some fans to go, *No, No, this can't be! I'm not listening! You can't show it to me, I'm not going to look at it.* I expected that kind of reaction but I was happy with the product and the opportunity. I'd do it again in a second. We kind of knew even before we finished that it would be a one of a kind thing and it would never happen again."

TRIANGLE: IMZADI II

Peter David

OCTOBER 1998   (375PP)

ORIGINALLY PUBLISHED IN HARDCOVER

Worf engaged to Deanna Troi? If you were ever wondering what happened between them from the end of TNG to Worf marrying Dax on *Deep Space Nine*, this book tells all. Sela has hooked up with Thomas Riker, Will's transporter duplicate from the episode "Second Chances." Believing it to be Will, she recruits him into a bold plan against the Federation. To insure his cooperation, she will kidnap his Deanna, not realizing that Deanna and Will are no longer an item. But Tom still has feelings for her.

Peter commented, "What prompted the sequel was being contacted by John Ordover and told that the marketing people wanted another *Imzadi* book. I said, 'What do you mean another one?' John told me the first one sold so

well they want a sequel to it. He then said, 'I have a great idea. This can be about Troi and Worf.' When TNG ended, Worf and Troi were an item. When Worf showed up on DS9 there was no sign of Deanna and she was never mentioned and he looked pissed off. There was a story there. I told John, 'I don't want to call it *Imzadi*.' He said we can call it *Imzadi II* and I hated that. What we were discussing was a completely different book and a different style. If we call it *Imzadi* in any way, shape, or form it is going to make people make comparisons. I can tell you right now that the comparisons will make the sequel suffer. The first book was a romantic story where everything goes right and the second one by definition will be about the total destruction of a romance. It is not going to end happily. The compromise we came up with was the title was going to be *Triangle* and in very small print it would say *Imzadi II*. That is what I was promised and they swore they would do. So what happens is the cover shows *Imazdi II* in gargantuan print and *Triangle* really small which totally pissed me off."

Peter continued, "The other thing that infuriated me was that at the end of the book, I had Riker propose to Troi. Let's have something major happen here. The TV show is off the air, so what the hell? Let them get engaged. The studio would not let us do it because it could step on future story lines. I was left with my head banging against the wall because I had a great scene and I had to trash it and I hated to rewrite it and I hate that chapter and I wish to God we could reprint with the chapter I wanted to do in which he proposes and she accepts. The book is remarkably frustrating to me. The comparisons are odious because the books are so different, it's really apples and oranges and the ending is not even remotely what I wanted to do."

I, Q

John de Lancie and Peter David

SEPTEMBER 1999   (249 pp)

ORIGINALLY PUBLISHED IN HARDCOVER

Coauthored by the actor who portrayed Q on *The Next Generation, Deep Space Nine,* and *Voyager.* The end of existence unites Q with Picard and Data to determine the catalyst and resolve the issue before everything blinks out. Told from Q's perspective, he has a tendency to ramble midway through thoughts, creating a print version of his character.

Peter remarked, "I went out to L.A., and met with John de Lancie for several days. We tossed around various possibilities and together we hammered out the outline for the book. I wrote the first draft then sent that to John. He did a lot of rewrites and changes and sent that back. It went back and forth. John was a 100-percent co-conspirator. You have to listen to the audio version!"

Peter continued, "Some parts of the novel are screamingly mine. The place where John did the most work was on the Q dialogue. He was the one who did wonders with making it sound like Q and the various digressions of the universe."

John de Lancie remembered how he got the role of Q. "I auditioned for the role like everybody else. And I had no expectation that the part would become popular. I did nine shows, which is still disproportionate to the popularity of the character."

John continued, "They asked me to write *I, Q* and I liked Peter. I didn't know enough about *Trek* to write a *Trek* novel. I told them I would write a series of interior monologues because the part I did know was the character. Peter and I sat down and figured out a story. As he would write the story, I would go back on the second pass and fill in all the Q stuff. As a third pass, I tried to condense the story, somewhat successfully and somewhat unsuccessfully. Q works best when the story is of a big and cosmic nature type."

THE VALIANT

MICHAEL JAN FRIEDMAN

APRIL 2000 (279 PP)

ORIGINALLY PUBLISHED IN HARDCOVER

The precursor to the *Stargazer* series. That barrier at the edge of the galaxy that destroyed the *Valiant*, and almost did in the *U.S.S. Enterprise*, comes into play again. Years after Kirk had to kill his best friend, Gary Mitchell, two people arrive at Starbase 209 claiming to be descendants of the original *Valiant* crew. The *Stargazer* is sent to investigate. During a major battle far away from Starfleet, the captain is killed and the first officer becomes comatose, forcing the second officer to take command. He is a young gent named Picard.

Mike recalled, "I've always been fascinated by the story of Gary Mitchell. It was to me the best *Star Trek* episode ever. 'Where No Man Has Gone Before' is such a personal and powerful story, and it was done so well. What could be more horrible than somebody so familiar as your best friend becoming the worst threat the galaxy has ever seen? And of course it had that comic book feel to it. I was a comic book fan so it really impressed the hell out of me when I first saw it and I've been revisiting it from time to time in my books. I threw in some other stuff there with a little bit of an explanation as to why the Klingons in the original series and the Klingons in the TNG era are different. I felt mine was probably as good, frankly, as any that's been offered."

THE GENESIS WAVE, Book One

JOHN VORNHOLT

SEPTEMBER 2000 (308 PP)

ORIGINALLY PUBLISHED IN HARDCOVER

An aging Carol Marcus still has a major security detail accompanying her every move. One day, her supposedly dead son David arrives and takes her away to finish her groundbreaking work. Later, on the planet Pacifica, Leah Brahms successfully tests a new pressure suit as she watches the planet disintegrate around her, killing everyone including her husband. The Genesis wave has returned and its mysterious wave of energy appears unstoppable.

THE GENESIS WAVE, Book Two

JOHN VORNHOLT

APRIL 2001   (282PP)

ORIGINALLY PUBLISHED IN HARDCOVER

Strange alien creatures appear as loved ones to infiltrate the *Enterprise*. Captain Picard works on diverting the wave to an unpopulated region of space and Geordi worries about Leah Brahms and hopes he will have the opportunity to confess his love. Leah, with the help of the aged Klingon Maltz, who was there on the original Genesis planet, hopes to stop the manipulators and Genesis origininator Carol Marcus from causing more damage.

John remembered, "Editor John Ordover came up with the basic idea of a devastating wave sweeping through space, unleashing the technology of the Genesis Device from *Star Trek II* and *III* on an unwitting TNG universe. We were inspired by the DC comic book series *Crisis on Infinite Earths* where various versions of Earth in different dimensions are in peril, and we wanted the same feeling of whole planets falling like dominoes, one after another. This was to be the ultimate disaster story, with the future of the galaxy really at stake.

"I also wanted to explore the romance between Geordi La Forge and Leah Brahms, which had always been doomed because she was married. (I fixed that.) Geordi is a character I've used a lot, especially in my YA novels, because he's a flawed hero. This story needed two characters from the classic *Trek* movies *The Wrath of Khan* and *The Search for Spock*. Carol Marcus, who created the Genesis Device, is kidnapped for her knowledge, and the Genesis secret is let out of the bag. The only living person who has seen the Genesis effect close-up is Maltz, the lone surviving Klingon from *Star Trek III* and he chases it half-way across the galaxy. The wide canvas and diverse characters worked great, and it was fun to have a story that successfully combined classic and TNG *Trek*. Needless to say, I was really excited about the *Genesis Wave* books, because they were my first hardcovers. They started off as a standard duology, except for the longer length, and somehow expanded into a total of four hardcover novels, counting *Genesis Wave Three* and *Genesis Force*. So much was going on in so many different places that I had plenty to tell."

THE GENESIS WAVE, Book Three

JOHN VORNHOLT

JANUARY 2002   (296PP)

ORIGINALLY PUBLISHED IN HARDCOVER

Efforts to clean up the aftermath of the devastation have begun. A Bajoran priest receives a mysterious package and believes the object inside is an Orb. Near the Romulan Empire, the *Enterprise* works closely with a Romulan Commander with a secret agenda. And the fabric of space appears to have been damaged.

John explained, "Since the *Enterprise* and Picard aren't the primary focus in the first two *Genesis Wave* books, I gave them a separate story dealing with the aftermath. This novel is to *Genesis Wave, Book One* and *Book Two* what *The Search for Spock* is to *The Wrath of Kahn* — a sequel dealing with putting the genie back in the bottle. Genesis technology is still floating around and Picard and crew have to keep it from falling into the wrong hands. I also got to

reprise one of my favorite guest characters, Teska, the Vulcan priestess who was but a child when she starred in *Mind Meld* with Spock."

IMMORTAL COIL

JEFFREY LANG

FEBRUARY 2002   (331PP)

Starfleet has been developing a new android, even more advanced than Data. When an "accident" occurs at the laboratory, the *Enterprise* is called to investigate. One of the designers, Commander Maddox, who had unsuccessfully tried to declare Data property in "Measure of a Man," is found comatose in the rubble. Written in blood next to his body is one word: DATA. How is Data connected to the destruction of the lab? As the crew digs deeper for answers, they learn the mystery reaches back into the history of androids and artifical intelligence.

Jeff remarked, "I don't know if I ever *wanted* to write *Trek* stories. I wanted to write *stories* and the opportunity to write *Trek* presented itself.

Long story short: I started writing seriously in my mid-twenties. At the time, I was interested in writing comic books or screenplays, though the first rule of writing is 'Write anything they'll pay you for.' I ended up writing PR for DC Comics, which is where I met Marco Palmieri." At that time, Marco was working in DC's marketing department. "Marco ended up moving on to other things and we lost track of each other. When pitching comic book proposals, the response I got more often than any other was, 'Thanks. Can't use this. But it would make a nice novel.' Sensing the Writing Gods were trying to tell me something, I set about trying to figure out how to contact someone in, y'know, *book* publishing. When I found out Marco was in that particular line, I contacted him and he was decent enough to nurse me through the process. It was one of those weird synchronicity things where he was looking for new writers and knew that I could deliver good material and I wasn't a flake (meaning, I'm reliable). Thus are careers begun."

In terms of the novel, Jeff remembered, "*Immortal Coil* was a monster. It was a bear of a story and I'll state right here that any of the elements in it that don't work (and I freely admit there are many) are my fault. Any that do work are entirely because of Marco.

"This one was really my first book and I worked my butt off on it. Looking back at it, I'm amazed that it came together at all. The original idea came from (ready to be shocked?) Marco. I think I said that I was interested in doing something with Data post-*Generations* because I liked the idea of him having the emotion chip and felt kind of cheated that he turned it off for *First Contact* and *Insurrection*. When Marco suggested the idea of going back

to the beginning with Dr. Soong, I think that's where we started jamming on the idea of Soong getting his ideas from an earlier android maker known in *Trek* history."

Marco added, "The more we discussed it, the more clear it became that *Immortal Coil* offered an opportunity to link together artifical intelligences introduced throughout *Star Trek* history in an interesting way. It became a 'kitchen sink' story—as in, it had everything *but*. One of the things that's always troubled me while watching *Star Trek* is how casually sentience is created—M-5, Rayna, Lore, the Moriarty Hologram, Lal, the EMH—and how often it went wrong. With the possible exception of 'The Offspring,' it seemed as if the power to create a *mind* was pretty much taken for granted. I thought someone needed to step up and point out what was wrong with that—be a voice for AI. From that we came up with the idea of the character of Emil Vaslovik, who has very well-established, personal reasons for taking up that cause." Vaslovik, Marco explained, was named for the immediate predecessor of the android Questor in *The Questor Tapes*, a pilot Gene Roddenberry developed in the 1970s about the latest in a long line of androids set up by ancient aliens to steer humanity toward a positive future. "I loved *The Questor Tapes*. In retrospect it was essentially Data as Gary Seven. Nothing resembling the story plays into *Immortal Coil*, but we both thought it would be neat to have some sort of understated homage to that old TV movie, somewhere in the novel."

Jeff said, "The outline was developed over a very long period; probably the longest time I've ever worked on one and Marco was able to really hold my hand through the process. I doubt if I'll ever have the luxury of that much editorial help again in my life. Somewhere along the line, we got into a discussion about 'Why are there ten thousand androids in the original series and only one or two in TNG?' and that led to us trying to tie together most of the AIs in *Trek* history. Some readers have used the expression 'continuity porn' to describe this (an expression I love, though Marco prefers the term 'fanwank'), and I see their point. If you don't know who or what all the machines are and it interrupts the flow of the story, then it's a problem. On the other hand, I've had other readers tell me this is one of their favorite *Trek* books (despite not getting all the references) because of the love story between Rhea and Data, which is, I think, the real point of the story. I think the moment near the end of the novel where Data actually has a cathartic insight about his state of being is one of the best things I've ever written. Also, I like the idea that the book is a mystery novel. Again, *Immortal Coil* probably had the longest gestation of any novel I've written. Marco gave me a lot of notes and a lot of time to get it right. The fact that it seems to have garnered some amount of notoriety (both positive and negative) is, as I've said on many, many occasions, largely because he gave me the time to figure out what I was doing. Though chronologically the second book to come out with my name on it, I'll always consider it my first novel and I'm damned proud of it."

A HARD RAIN
DEAN WESLEY SMITH

MARCH 2002 (233PP)

The story unfolds entirely in a Dixon Hill mystery, with an occasional captain's log to tell the reader of the horrible danger happening outside the holodeck. The *Enterprise-D* finds itself heading for a region of space known as the Blackness, which emits immense subspace waves that will eventually tear the ship apart. Geordi figures out the mineral Auriferite can block enough of the subspace waves to keep them safe from the anomaly. But the device with the Auriferite disappears; now Dixon Hill must find the "heart of the adjuster."

Dean remarked, "Since I am a fan of the old style of writing, and Dixon Hill is an old hard-boiled detective style of character, I was the logical choice by the editors at Pocket to try that book. I loved doing it, and put every major sub-genre of mystery in there, usually changing from chapter to chapter, all the while trying to solve the crime. Picard never speaks in there except through log entries. Only Dixon Hill."

THE BATTLE OF BETAZED
CHARLOTTE DOUGLAS AND SUSAN KEARNEY

APRIL 2002   (263 PP)

During the Dominion War, the planet Betazed fell to enemy forces. The Cardassians begin to construct the space station Sentok Nor in orbit. With the help of Commander Vaughn from the post-TV *Deep Space Nine* series of books, he and Troi attempt to infiltrate Darona, another habitable planet in the Betazed system. One other person recruited for this dangerous mission is Hent Tevren, a Betazoid serial murderer who kills with his mind.

Susan remarked, "When *Star Trek* first came out on television, it was shown at an hour past my bedtime. While my parents watched the show downstairs in the living room, I'd sneak into their bedroom, turn the volume down low, and watch it every week. The characters and plot captured my imagination, and to this day, I still enjoy *Star Trek*. I've gone on to write science fiction romance for Tor and believe my love of the genre originated with classic *Trek*."

Charlotte commented, "I first became a *Star Trek* fan in the early 70s after the original series had gone into syndication. I would rush home from the school where I was teaching in order to watch an episode before cooking dinner. I'd always loved science fiction and *Star Trek* was the first television program I'd seen that allowed me to suspend my disbelief enough to really enjoy it. I'd never thought of writing for *Star Trek* until I'd actually established a career as a writer, starting in 1990. I began writing Gothics, suspense, and eventually romance for Harlequin. I write very fast and, at the time, Harlequin wasn't buying enough books to keep me as busy as I wanted to be. My critique partner, Susan Kearney, who also wrote for Harlequin, faced the same dilemma. Because we both were avid *Star Trek* fans, we decided in 1995 to put together a proposal to try to sell to Pocket. Our story, centering on Kate Janeway and Q, was rejected, so Sue flew to New York and met with John Ordover to discuss what kinds of plots he was looking for. Over the next several years and through multiple editors, we submitted other proposals. One showed particular promise, but the editor who was interested in it left Pocket. Our orphaned proposal was passed on to Marco Palmieri, who wasn't thrilled with our idea but liked our style. He worked with us to put together the synopsis for *The Battle of Betazed*. Ironically, this was now over six years after Sue and I first submitted to Pocket. By then, we were each writing multiple books a year for Harlequin and had to scramble to clear our writing schedules to find a few months that we could write *The Battle of Betazed* together."

Charlotte continued, "The concept for *The Battle of Betazed* flowed from several directions. First, Sue and I had been writing romance for so long that we decided for this book, we'd rather make war, not love. We picked up on a single sentence in a *Deep Space Nine* episode that revealed that Betazed, Troi's home planet, had fallen to the Dominion. We settled on the theme of the dilemma the Betazoid people faced with the choice between saving their lives or their souls. . . . Sue and I, with ample and admirable assistance from Marco, hammered out the plot. . . . Working with him was a delightful experience. I was blown away by the wonderful cover art and gratified by the positive reactions to our story."

Marco remarked, "It's the kind of story I thought needed to be told: *Deep Space Nine* had established during its sixth season that Betazed had fallen during the Dominion War, but there was no followup. The next time we saw Troi, in *Star Trek: Insurrection*, the war was still on, but she didn't seem preoccupied by thoughts of her homeworld under Dominion control. So the decision was made to set the story of Betazed's liberation during the months prior to the film, and to have Troi and the *Enterprise*-E play major roles in the effort. It also helped to explain what sorts of things the ship and its crew were involved in during the war."

Regarding the inclusion of Commander Vaughn, Marco said, "That was foreshadowed in *Avatar* (May 2001). When the character was introduced, he was a already a man in the twilight of his Starfleet career, looking back on all the bad business he'd been involved in over the course of his life. One of those things was the

liberation of Betazed, just one year prior in story time, but still almost a year away from being published."

GENESIS FORCE
JOHN VORNHOLT

JULY 2003   (320PP)

ORIGINALLY PUBLISHED IN HARDCOVER

The followup to the *Genesis Wave* trilogy takes place entirely on the planet Aluwna. The horrible impending devastation waits, and the people of the planet must figure out how to save everyone. The first third concerns several individuals and how they prepare. The rest of the book looks at the aftermath as some well-known characters enter the picture. Both the survivors and Starfleet struggle to reclaim the planet.

"*The Next Generation* books written in this time period don't have Worf as a crew member, so he's fair game for an alternative story. *Genesis Force* tells us what Worf, his son Alexander, and the Klingon fleet were doing during the Genesis Wave crisis. This book takes place at the same time as the other three books and views one planet going through the entire ordeal, from too-late warnings to mad escape, massive destruction, and reinvention as a Genesis planet. Our Klingon must use brute force to tame the runaway Genesis creatures so that the real inhabitants can return . . . before they die in a decaying system of transporter satellites. John Ordover and I had talked for years about how a few *Trek* species had limited super powers, such as shapeshifting, and they could be assembled into a kind of X-Men or A-Team commando squad. This book is a trial run for that concept, and it allowed me to reprise some guest characters I had created in other books. In these four books, I got to tell the Genesis Wave story from a variety of different angles— from the sweeping 'save the galaxy' story to a small, intense view of one affected planet. It was a real treat to be able to lavish such attention on this saga."

DO COMETS DREAM?
S. P. SOMTOW

JULY 2003   (262PP)

The inhabitants of the planet Thanet believe that their world is destroyed in a worldwide cataclysm every five thousand years, and then the cycle starts over. With a few days to go before the end, the *Enterprise*-D crew discovers a comet heading to the planet. It would be easy to destroy the comet and save the planet, but doing so would destroy the belief system of the Thanet civilization in the process. To make matters worse, Troi senses intelligence inside the comet.

Attempts to reach the author for an interview were unsuccessful.

DEATH IN WINTER

MICHAEL JAN FRIEDMAN

SEPTEMBER 2005　　(328PP)

ORIGINALLY PUBLISHED IN HARDCOVER

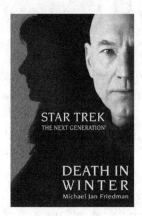

STAR TREK
THE NEXT GENERATION

DEATH IN WINTER
Michael Jan Friedman

While Captain Picard supervises the retrofit and repair of the *Enterprise*-E after Shinzon's attack, he also contemplates the departure of his friends, including Beverly, who is now the head of Starfleet Medical again. Beverly receives orders to conduct a clandestine mission to the planet Kevratas to help stop a plague with similarities to a disease she tackled years ago. Unfortunately, the Romulans control the populace and don't want help. With Beverly captured and possibly dead, Picard realizes his true feelings for her and leads a covert mission of his own to not only stop the plague, but rescue his true love.

Mike remarked, "The idea of resolving the Picard/Beverly relationship came from my editor, Margaret Clark. It was a story she very much wanted to tell once it became clear it wouldn't be told on the screen. The outline went through several permutations as Margaret and I, with ample input from Paula Block at Paramount, hashed out the details of Beverly's abduction and ensuing fate. The first draft of the outline didn't even involve the Romulans, but it became increasingly obvious to me that the first post-*Nemesis* TNG novel simply had to address the Romulan political situation. Originally, *Death in Winter* was supposed to hit the stores before the first book in the *Titan* series, which is why the events in that book postdate the events of *Death in Winter*. Margaret and Marco (*Titan*'s editor) went to great lengths to make sure the *Titan* book didn't give away anything significant about *Death in Winter*, and vice versa."

STAR TREK: DEEP SPACE NINE NUMBERED NOVELS

1

EMISSARY
J. M. DILLARD

(SEE SECTION 10: NOVELIZATIONS)

2

THE SIEGE
PETER DAVID

MAY 1993   (272PP)

An Odo-like shape-shifting being boards the station and starts killing people. Meanwhile, Bashir must question a parent's decision to not have him help their son, and Quark must de- cide if he trusts a potential business deal. The storylines intertwine into a explosive finale.

Peter remarked, "In January 1993, DS9 had just started. The Pocket Books publisher calls Kevin Ryan into his office and says, 'We love this new series. I want to start a *Deep Space Nine* publishing line. Can you get me a DS9 novel out by May?' Kevin, like a chucklehead says, 'Of course I can.' Kevin calls me, who is basically the only human on the face of the Earth that he can think of who could pull this off and says, 'I need a *Deep Space Nine* novel by the end of January.' I'm hearing this the sec- ond week of January. He then added, 'We will throw carloads of money at you. Just one thing. The title of the book is *The Siege*. We need a title for solicitation.' It is the most I've ever been paid for a *Star Trek* paperback. They sent me the scripts and the bible. I read the scripts for the first five episodes and I locked onto Odo. I called up Kevin and told him I under- stand Odo because he is a superhero. I can write a superhero. That's why the book is fairly Odo-centric. His was the easiest character to wrap myself around."

Peter continued, "At the time I was writing this book, I didn't have an office in my house. I was working in the dining room. I moved a small desk upstairs so I wouldn't be disturbed and I sat there pounding out the book in two weeks. I never left the room. My wife brought me meals. Fourteen days is the fastest I have ever written a book. I don't think you can tell. I made sure to pay attention to the conservation of matter so that Odo transforms into a mouse; for example, he is still going to have his mass. Odo turned into a 170-pound mouse. Later episodes of DS9 showed Odo transforming into a bar of latinum or a glass and they could pick it up. Because of this, fans complain that I got Odo wrong in *The Siege*. My response is I got him right, DS9 got him wrong."

(Marco Palmieri adds, "I've heard Peter tell that story many times. I always think, 'This, coming from the guy who writes *The Hulk*.' Then I laugh and I laugh.")

Peter continued, "At one point, the story called for the wormhole to be temporarily impassable. I had to come up with some reason for this that was natural. Having no concept of how to do this, I called up Michael Okuda and told him my problem. Without missing a beat, he tells me subspace compression. *Ha!* What would that be? He told me it was technobabble and it could be whatever I wanted it to be. In the book, I essentially recreated my dialogue with Mike."

3

BLOODLETTER

K. W. JETER

AUGUST 1993   (276 PP)

The Cardassians are constructing a base on the other side of the wormhole, so Major Kira and Doctor Bashir take a shuttle to set up a Starfleet base before the Cardassians succeed. But someone wants to dispose of Kira, blaming her for many deaths during the Occupation.

The author declined to be interviewed for this book.

# 4	# 5

THE BIG GAME
Sandy Schofield

FALLEN HEROES
Dafydd ab Hugh

November 1993 (276pp) | **February 1994 (282pp)**

A poker tournament on Deep Space 9 brings nefarious types from all over the galaxy to participate. When one of the players is murdered, the stakes are raised and with everyone accomplished liars, Odo decides to join the game and watch the suspects, even though he knows nothing about poker. While this is going on, the station finds itself bombarded with subspace waves of unknown origin. As the intensity increases, the power fluctuates from nothing to almost explosive. Sandy Schofield is the pen name of Dean Wesley Smith and Kristine Kathryn Rusch.

Dean remarked, "I think Kris and I thought you couldn't put six names on the cover. Actually, the Sandy Schofield name has published five or six novels now."

A lien warriors storm Deep Space 9 and demand the release of one of their comrades. The crew has no idea about their missing soldier, but that doesn't stop the aliens from killing everyone they stumble upon. Now with security almost wiped out, it appears to be only a matter of time before the entire station falls. Meanwhile, Quark has uncovered a strange device from the Gamma Quadrant. When he activates it in front of Odo, they both find themselves three days in the future on a completely dead station.

"When my agent suggested I write a *Trek* novel, my first thought was how to subvert the universe. Since rule number one was that you could not kill off any of the main characters, I instantly began thinking of a book where I would kill *all* the main characters. In fact, I even suggested to then-*Trek* editor John

Ordover that the back-cover copy should simply read 'Everybody dies.' Alas, Pocket wouldn't go for it!"

6

BETRAYAL

Lois Tilton

MAY 1994   (280PP)

A turnover in the Cardassian government creates havoc for the crew of DS9. A ship arrives at the station, and the Cardassian commander demands the return of the station to its original owners, or there will be hell to pay. One of the vessel's crew escapes and hides in the bowels of the former Terok Nor. These events occur while a very important trade conference is meeting with Sisko as the mediator.

Lois reflected, "I never have been a *Star Trek* fan. I never really watched the show. In fact, I don't as a rule watch television and I think most of the stuff on TV isn't very good. I have for many years been a science fiction reader, and I moved from that point to wanting to write

science fiction—then fantasy and horror fiction. I believe I first became known for my vampire novels. I would say that I'm typical of most *Trek* novelists in this, by the way. Even the authors who would call themselves fans were usually writers first. Fans with no previous publishing experience don't frequently end up publishing *Trek* novels. I wanted to write a *Trek* novel because the opportunity came up, and I erroneously believed this would give me a chance to publish a science fiction novel and perhaps other, original science fiction novels after that."

She continued, "The DS9 series was being developed, and there was a call for experienced SF authors to submit proposals for novels in this new series. All there was to go on at the time was a rather brief outline, most of which was later superseded when the show was actually produced. I liked the ideas in the outline, which held out the promise of something more gritty and realistic than the original *Trek* universe had been. I particularly liked what little I saw of the Cardassians, as I tend to specialize in villains, such as vampires. My idea featured the Cardassian characters, and the proposal was accepted. The publishing schedule required that the book be written before the series aired on TV. Then I had to do an intensive cram session of watching the episodes to make the scenes in the novel consistent with what was shown in the program—some of which had been altered from the outline by that time."

Lois has no plans to write another *Trek* novel. "I did once send in a proposal for a *Voyager* novel, based on the development outline, but I never heard back from the publishers about it, and after I actually saw the first two episodes of the show, I was glad I hadn't. I have concluded that I am not really the right person to be writing media tie-in novels."

WARCHILD
ESTHER FRIESNER

SEPTEMBER 1994   (272PP)

Kai Opaka left a cryptic prophecy behind that compels Sisko to take action. Bajor suffers from a plague that is destroying their agriculture. The commander sends Bashir and Dax to the planet to find, cure, and save the children. Dax has another mission, though, that even Bashir doesn't realize. The prophecy describes one little girl who will save her people. All signs of her whereabouts point to one of the towns ravaged by the plague.

Esther explained, "The idea for *Warchild* simply came from the plight of people dealing with the aftermath of long war, especially those whom the war has rendered as Displaced Persons."

ANTIMATTER
JOHN VORNHOLT

NOVEMBER 1994   (276PP)

The shipyards on Bajor are building an engine for a new starship, which is one of the first steps needed to show their planet will eventually be ready to join the Federation. Terrorists seize a ship full of antimatter and zoom through the wormhole. Sisko, Dax, and Odo follow them to a bizarre planet populated with bugs. Can the DS9 folks stop the thieves from selling the precious cargo?

"I really liked *Deep Space Nine*, plus the Maquis characters from both TNG and DS9. I've used the Maquis in a lot of my books, because they're complex villains with sympathetic motives. This story was inspired by references in the *The Next Generation Technical Manual* to the way antimatter was stored and transported. Considering antimatter is extremely hazardous, rare, and valuable, I thought it would make a great 'hauling nitroglycerine through Apache territory' kind of story."

PROUD HELIOS
Melissa Scott

February 1995 (277pp)

A vessel with cloaking technology starts raiding cargo vessels, killing the crew and taking the goods. The Cardassians are not happy, and demand retribution. Kira and O'Brien are kidnapped and forced to work on the pirate vessel, *Helios*. Can Sisko stop the raiders, rescue his friends, and keep the Cardassians happy?

When asked why she wanted to write a *Star Trek* novel, she commented, "Partly, I think, it's the simple fact that when you encounter a world and characters that you enjoy, you want to be a part of it, too. In a TV series, that temptation is particularly strong, because, after all, it is a *series*. There are people out there who contribute the stories, create the world, and there's always the possibility that you can become one

of them. In my case, because I came to *Trek* from the Blish novelizations, and was acutely conscious of how the written versions compared to the actual episodes, the idea of writing not screenplays but novels was very appealing. Plus, of course, I'm a better novelist than I am a screenwriter!"

Melissa remembers how she got the assignment to write *Proud Helios*. "John Ordover approached me, knowing I was a *Trek* fan as well as an established SF writer in my own right, and asked if I'd be interested in doing a book in the DS9 universe. I really liked the series, particularly the constraints of keeping the show to the single station (this was early in the show's evolution), so I jumped at the chance. I asked if he had any guidelines, any stories he particularly wanted to see, or any he didn't, and he said, no, not really, he'd leave that up to me. So I went home, mulled it over, and came up with the proposal that became *Proud Helios*. I sent it to John, who called me back almost at once, laughing. He'd promised himself that he wouldn't do any stories with space pirates—and here I'd sent him one he wanted to use."

#10

VALHALLA

Nathan Archer

APRIL 1995   (277pp)

Nathan Archer

A vessel emerges from the wormhole and approaches Cardassian territory. With a tractor beam, the ship gets towed into the station. At first, all of the crew appears dead. Soon, reports of a strange giant alien wandering around various sections of the space station sets off an alarm in Sisko's mind. When the Cardassians arrive and demand the vessel be turned over to their government, Sisko must hold off the former inhabitants of the station as well as solve the mystery of the ship and its strange lone survivor.

Nathan Archer is a pseudonym for a writer who does not want to reveal his identity. Nathan commented, "Well, you assume I'm a *Trek* fan. The truth is, I'm not, really. I was when the original series was airing—I was there with the TV tuned to NBC every Friday at ten without fail. My enthusiasm faded, though, after it was canceled. I watched reruns in college sometimes. I liked the show—but I didn't love it, wasn't obsessed with it. I saw all the movies, but *The Next Generation* was at an inconvenient time in the schedule, so I didn't always manage to catch it. I've been to a couple of *Trek* conventions, but it wasn't a big deal for me. I missed the next-to-last season of *Voyager* completely, and most of *Enterprise* after the first season."

When asked about the reason for using a pseudonym, he responded, "I haven't published anything under my real name since August 1975. In a word, it was marketing. It used to be that an author could write all kinds of stuff under the same name, but that's been getting more and more difficult for a long time, and in the early 1990s there was a shift in how books were ordered due to the rise of the big bookstore chains and the use of computers in deciding what to order that made this trend much stronger. The chains took to basing orders entirely on sales of the previous book by that author, regardless of what the two books were, who published them, or anything else— if Author's Last Book sold 50,000 copies, they ordered 50,000 copies of Author's Next Book, and it didn't matter that one was a cookbook and one was a romance novel. All through the 1980s I'd been writing a variety of stuff— fantasy, science fiction, horror, short stories— but that became a serious problem in the 1990s, when computerized ordering came in, because those didn't all sell equally well. My fantasy novels sold much better than anything else did. This meant that every time I published an SF novel, or a horror novel, or a short story collection, it brought down the orders for my next fantasy novel; I was in real danger of wrecking my career because I was writing in multiple genres. 'Nathan Archer' was the name I picked for my science fiction, and the theory was that I would write a few tie-in novels to establish the name, then start writing original SF as Archer. Except that SF sales dropped off across the board, my production dropped off due to health problems, and what with one thing and another I still haven't written any of those SF novels. I did all the prep work—the Archer name's been on half a dozen tie-in novels and a short story or two—but never wrote the novels. At least, not yet."

Why write a *Trek* novel? "For the money, mostly, but also I wanted to write a *Predator* novelization for Dark Horse, but not put my other name on it, and the folks at Dark Horse said that their deal with FOX and Bantam required them to only use established authors. Therefore, I wrote a *Star Trek* novel to get the Nathan Archer name the publishing credit that would convince FOX to let me write a *Predator* novelization as Archer. So I called John Ordover at Pocket and asked how one went about writing a *Trek* novel. My timing was absolutely perfect—he was just assigning the first batch of DS9 novels. He sent me the series bible, I worked up an outline, it got kicked back and forth a few times until we were both happy with it and Paramount had no objections, and I started writing. It was supposed to be either number three or four, not number ten; I'm pretty sure I had about half of it written by the time the show first aired. Unfortunately, I broke my hand, and made the mistake of telling John I'd broken my hand. He assumed that this meant I couldn't type and the manuscript would be late, so he bumped it back on the schedule. I turned it in three weeks before the deadline; I can type quite adequately with one hand. By then it was too late to change the schedule back. That's why a story that clearly ought to be happening early in the first season has references to the *Defiant* clumsily inserted—John added those because the book was coming out a year and a half later than it should have. My original title had been something like *Ghost in the Machine*, by the way; I don't remember when it changed to *Valhalla*, but it was some time in the outlining process, before I'd written the novel. Nathan Archer has written *Star Trek*, *Spider-Man*, *Mars Attacks!* and *Predator*, and to be honest, I was more excited about writing *Mars Attacks!* and *Predator* than about *Star Trek*. *Spider-Man* and *Star Trek* were certainly fun, but it was as much the money and the challenge of fitting a story into an elaborate pre-existing universe as well as the technical challenges to my skill as a writer, that tempted me as a passion for the source material."

#11

DEVIL IN THE SKY
GREG COX AND JOHN GREGORY BETANCOURT

JUNE 1995   (280PP)

To assist in Bajor's mining industry, a mother Horta with her twenty eggs is sent from Janus VI. She can eat solid rock and she anxiously waits, not only to help the Bajorans, but for the birth of her children. A Cardassian kidnaps her for some nefarious purpose, so Major Kira and a security force attempt a rescue. Meanwhile, the twenty eggs sitting in stasis begin to hatch. With nothing to eat but the station itself, the situation soon proves disastrous.

John remarked, "Originally, I had no real interest in writing *Star Trek* stories. A friend of mine became the *Star Trek* editor at Pocket Books about twelve or thirteen years ago, and when I called him to congratulate him, he thought I was trying to solicit work. I told him I didn't want to write *Star Trek* novels. He seemed to take that as a challenge. Every time I talked to him after that, he asked me if I wanted to write

one. I kept saying 'no.' Finally he wore me down. Greg and I were friends long before we collaborated. He worked at Tor Books, and I worked just around the corner at Byron Preiss Visual Publications. A bunch of us editorial minions had lunch every Wednesday, shared news and gossip, and of course talked about writing and publishing. The same friend who got me to write a *Star Trek* novel also wanted Greg to write one . . . but neither of us could come up with a plot. Our editor suggested putting the Hortas on DS9, and voila, instant plot. Greg and I did a detailed outline together, and before we knew it, we had a contract. The outline split the action neatly, so Greg took half the plot and I took the other half. Since our writing styles are very similar, everything integrated seamlessly. Unless you ask, you won't know who wrote which part."

Of the time in which *Devil in the Sky* was developed, Greg said, "John Ordover has moved from Tor to Pocket Books and is now the new *Star Trek* guy. *Deep Space Nine* is starting production, and John suddenly needs a whole bunch of DS9 novels signed up—fast. Fortunately, Ordover had read those *Batman* stories that Betancourt and I had written, so he calls me up with a title and concept already in mind. 'Hortas eating DS9, Greg. Do you and Betancourt want to write that book?' And that's how I got my foot in the *Star Trek* door . . . which was hugely exciting. We had to start working on the book before the first episode of the TV series aired, so we were provided with the script for 'Emissary' and a fairly-detailed technical guide which included a map of the station. I also voraciously gobbled up any advance info of the new series in *TV Guide*, *Starlog*, and so on. Since Betancourt and I had worked together before, the collaboration went very smoothly. Basically, he wrote the chapters involving the Away Team and the rescue of the mother Horta, while I wrote the sequences set back on DS9. Effectively, this meant he got Kira, Bashir, Dax, and the Cardassians, while I got everybody else! Then, after we'd each written our own chapters independently, we got together one snowy afternoon to bring the plotlines together and write the concluding chapters. I recall that I found some characters easier to write than others. I ended up writing a lot of my scenes from the point of views of Miles O'Brien just because his voice came easy to me. He had an everyman quality that appealed to me, plus, of course, I was already familiar with the character from his appearances on *The Next Generation*. Jake and Nog were a lot of fun to write as well. Sisko was more of a challenge, mainly because I hadn't yet figured out how to handle the captains. How do you let a crisis spiral out of control without making the commanding officer look incompetent? And how do you get him (or her) into the thick of the action instead of simply delegating dangerous missions to the crew? The trick, I learned eventually, is to get the captains off the bridge as soon as possible and drop them into a swamp full of alligators, so they're not just standing around issuing orders. But, at the time I was writing *Devil in the Sky*, I hadn't realized that yet, so in retrospect, Sisko ended up a little underutilized. (I had something of the same problem with Janeway in *The Black Shore*.) Still, I like to think the book turned out okay."

#12

THE LAERTIAN GAMBLE

ROBERT SHECKLEY

SEPTEMBER 1995 (273PP)

A smitten by a pretty face, Bashir agrees to gamble for a mysterious woman from the planet Laertes. Promising to gamble until either he runs out of money or Quark goes bankrupt, Bashir finds himself winning against all odds. The more he wins, the more strange things start happening in the quadrant. Quark, almost bankrupt and desperately wanting to win back all of the money, begins to sell off pieces of the station for money and collateral. Can Kira and Dax find an answer to stop Bashir's winning streak?

Robert discussed the book and *Trek* fandom. "I didn't realize I was a *Star Trek* fan until I started writing *The Laertian Gamble*. Before that, I had been critical of *Star Trek*. One always has a dream picture of what the ideal science fiction novel would be. For me, it might have been formed around childhood memories of Edgar

Rice Burroughs novels, especially the *Earth's Core* series around *Pellucidar*. But I soon came to realize that *Star Trek* was a superior concept, one that translated well to novel form, and that gave a lot of room for a writer's ideas. I had never watched the show faithfully, though I did follow it from time to time and was conversant with the characters. It was a pleasure to work on it. I don't remember now how I got the idea, but my *Laertian Gamble* seemed to me original yet also keeping in with the theme of the show, and it gave me a chance to work with several of the characters I liked. I think I did all right by *Star Trek*, since my editor asked me for little in the way of revisions."

---

1 3

STATION RAGE
DIANE CAREY

NOVEMBER 1995   (277PP)

An investigation of the lower depths of the station reveals a tomb filled with several dead Cardassians. Even though the station itself isn't very old, the evidence suggests the bodies have been dead for almost 100 years. Sisko decides to leave the bodies alone to avoid a potential conflict with other Cardassians. A little while later, major malfunctions force a massive evacuation.

Diane said, "I'm always looking for new angles. Greg and I begin every book-development session with, 'Why should anybody read this book?' With *Star Trek*, that question is even more important. What will be examined, revealed, or taught that is worth knowing about? How do we take our characters, which have to essentially be the same at the end of the book as the beginning, and give them some personal arc? After all, we have to provide a dramatic line of change, yet leave the characters intact for the next authors to take over. It's a constant struggle, which I've always taken very seriously. In this book, we decided to examine the past of the actual space station, and force the Starfleet characters to deal with the former owners, who awake from a deathlike sleep and believe their station has been invaded. Both sides are in the right, which is always a better moral struggle than the simple right versus wrong, which is easy. I always avoid right versus wrong, because there's no dramatic question. I always aim for right versus right, the hardest examination of the human (or alien) condition."

Diane was not happy with the back cover blurb. She said, "the only writing in a book that's not done by the author is the cover copy and the teaser on the back cover. I wasn't able to stop the back cover from giving away one of the most important dramatic revelations in the book—the reanimation of the Cardassian mummies. It's always a struggle to keep the cover copy from trumping the author's best surprises. Often once we see the printed cover for the first time, it's already too late."

14

THE LONG NIGHT

DEAN WESLEY SMITH AND KRISTINE KATHRYN RUSCH

FEBRUARY 1996 (274PP)

In order to survive a major coup, the Supreme Ruler of the planet Jibet and his family are placed on a ship and put into suspended animation. Almost 800 years later, the legend of the ship ranks as one of the galaxy's greatest mysteries. Now it appears someone has found it and various factions don't want the ship or what it carries recovered.

Dean remarked, "I wanted to do a ghost ship in *Star Trek* and just pitched this idea. I don't have much memory of anything else about the book."

15

OBJECTIVE: BAJOR

JOHN PEEL

JUNE 1996 (278PP)

Arriving near Cardassian space from another galaxy, the Hive has billions of aliens living on a massive starship. For the inhabitants, they have never even seen the stars. Their bold plan involves converting planets into raw material for fuel for their voyage. The next planet on their list is Bajor and they give the inhabitants three days to leave before its destruction.

John Peel remarked, "John Ordover was in as editor by this point, and I'd sent him a few ideas. When I write novels based on any TV show, I always try to think what I could do in a book that they could never manage on TV. Dragons in *Here There Be Dragons*, for example, which they could never do on TV. I liked *Deep Space Nine* the most of all the *Trek* series, and I really wanted to do a story where they're at war. The most logical thing to me, it seemed, was that the Borg finds DS9, and that's how I pitched the outline to John. John liked the war concept, but pointed out that Paramount might want to use the Borg in DS9 themselves, so he asked me to create another villain instead, okaying the book on that basis. So—creating new villains. Again, I didn't want to simply invent a new nasty species that's after intergalactic conquest, so I started thinking about villains who simply didn't see themselves as villains. The generation starship idea seemed kind of cool, and I wondered about whether people who'd spent their lives—and all those of their ancestors—on a ship would want to leave it. Hey . . . maybe they're claustrophobic! Another nice touch. The final item in the mix came from my own past. I'd spent two years studying Theology at one point, and there you learn about Textual Criticism. It's a method of examining an old manuscript to try and discover if there are older ones that underlie it. So I used that in *Bajor,* too. I think it's probably the only science fiction novel written to use Biblical criticism for a plot basis."

John commented further, "The original draft of the book actually started with Chapter Two. My wife read it and said: 'It's too slow—you need to start with a bang.' After fuming for an evening, I then added the opening. The alien Calderisi are actually named for a TV actor, David Calderisi—I just liked the sound of his name."

#16

TIME'S ENEMY

(INVASION, BOOK THREE; SEE SECTION 12: MINISERIES)

#17

THE HEART OF THE WARRIOR

JOHN GREGORY BETANCOURT

OCTOBER 1996   (274 PP)

A conference on the station has everyone on edge. A Bajoran vedek leads an effort to arrest one of the Cardassian delegates, who the Bajorans believe is the Butcher of Belmast. Meanwhile Kira, Worf, and Odo head on a covert mission into the Gamma Quadrant. Of course, even the best laid plans never run smoothly.

John remarked, "Worf has always been one of my favorite characters, and I wanted to write a book about him but set in the Dominion, where he would find a challenge to his hand-to-hand combat skills. Unfortunately, later seasons of DS9 developed the Founders and Dominion enough that my book is, ah, retroactively contradictory to the official universe in a number of places. Which is too bad because I think it's my best *Trek* novel."

#18

SARATOGA
MICHAEL JAN FRIEDMAN

NOVEMBER 1996 (275PP)

Another vessel will soon be christened the *U.S.S. Saratoga* to commemorate the sacrifices made by the crew of the previous ship during the battle of Wolf 359. The Borg destroyed the vessel and almost destroyed Benjamin Sisko's sanity. Finally able to deal with the pain and loss, he is forced to confront those issues again when surviving crew members visit the station. While on the way to the christening, an act of sabotage aboard the *Defiant* forces Sisko to question who his friends truly are.

Mike commented, "I had so much fun with *Reunion*, I thought it would be fun to do it again. Sisko has a past—his wife died. For God's sakes, what do we know about that? Nothing. He had

a previous command, let's find out about that. It wasn't a murder mystery, really, it was a mystery and it involved his old crew. I see remarks on the Internet sometimes, like 'Friedman just rewrote *Reunion.*' For me, it's a mystery and it worked well before, let's try it again now. I was happy with the job I did but I don't know if I had as much of an affinity for *Deep Space Nine* as I did for *The Next Generation.* In TNG you saved the galaxy from some horrible threat. In DS9 you saved Quark's bar. To me it was a whole different scale and so the motivation in *Saratoga* was more mercenary. It was much more in keeping with DS9, especially DS9 at that point, before you get into the Dominion War. I don't know if it worked as well because of that but I certainly wasn't just recycling stuff."

#19

THE TEMPEST
SUSAN WRIGHT

FEBRUARY 1997 (275PP)

An enormous space storm is heading to Bajor and the space station. As the freak phenomenon intensifies, the crew of DS9 is forced to somehow control the increasing chaos. When Keiko O'Brien uncovers a way to potentially weaken the storm, she and Dax take off in a shuttle, much to the horror of Miles. Will the wormhole have to be permanently closed to stop the destructive storm, or will Keiko's plan work?

Susan said, "*The Tempest* is based on Shakespeare's [play of the same name]. Really. Keiko as Miranda and Worf as Prospero. The storm is a monstrous interstellar plasma phenomenon that causes chaos on DS9."

---

2 0

WRATH OF THE PROPHETS

PETER DAVID, MICHAEL JAN FRIEDMAN,
AND ROBERT GREENBERGER

M A Y 1 9 9 7　　　　　(2 7 4 P P)

A fatal plague has struck Bajor and newly promoted Captain Sisko is forced into a dilemma. It appears the only source of aid he can get is from Ro Laren, a former Starfleet officer who is now allied with the Maquis. Can Sisko rely on her and can she and Kira get along to save the lives of the Bajorans without killing each other?

Bob recalled that, following their collaborations for *Star Trek* and *The Next Generation*, *Deep Space Nine* was another obvious opportunity for Peter, Mike, and him to work together. "I believe Peter had the idea that became the core of the story and I suggested using Varis Sul who was introduced in a first season episode. I got assigned the Dax/Bashir subplot, which didn't thrill me because medical stories aren't my forte and I figured Mike would do that since he wrote so much McCoy material. Nope, he had done enough medical stories at the time and wanted Sisko. So I did my best and grew to enjoy the characters. By this time, we knew each other's styles and strengths well enough that there was very little smoothing over required."

In the finished book, there is a mention of a *Voyager* novel forthcoming. What happened? Robert replied, "Mike and I were keen to tackle *Voyager*, to see if a good story could be done. Peter was less enthused but would go along if John [Ordover] wanted it. John didn't, so it never materialized."

2 1

TRIAL BY ERROR

Mark Garland

N O V E M B E R 1 9 9 7 (2 8 1 P P)

A seemingly innocent business deal with Quark threatens the station. The deal involves
trading trellium crystals from a nonhostile region of the Gamma Quadrant for latinum.
Soon, a couple of ships arrive and demand retribution. Meanwhile in the Gamma Quadrant, a mysterious ship attacks a Klingon vessel.
The shattered ship barely makes it back to the
Alpha Quadrant followed immediately by this
new enemy, who then targets DS9.

Mark remembers the early days of *Trek*. "For
three years I made absolutely certain that nothing would interfere with watching a new
episode of *Star Trek*, as did my brothers and my
best friends at the time. It was like reading *The
Lord of The Rings* trilogy or going to see *2001: A
Space Odyssey* when it came out (or reading
Clarke)—we all did it. There was The Beatles,
and *Star Trek*. The fact that the whole space

race was playing out at the time, and *Trek*'s very
faithful science fiction way of telling a great
story while getting viewers to consider a great
issue from a fresh angle, to consider 'meaning
of life' stuff in a collective manner (my friends
and brothers and I) in an age and at an age
when these things were truly paramount (no
pun intended), made *Trek* incredibly pertinent, of course, and we were caught up in all of
that."

He continued, "I wanted to write fiction
since my early teens, and did years later, starting with short stories and, after selling a bunch
of those, going to novels. I had a number of fantasy novels to my credit when I started writing
for *Star Trek*, but I put it all on hold to write the
Trek novels. . . . I got to use one of the most fan-
tastically imagined and developed worlds and
all its richly drawn characters to tell a couple of
great stories, stories I'd have somehow tried to
tell no matter what, but which, with *Star Trek*
as a vehicle, turned out better than I ever could
have hoped otherwise. *Trek* is as incredible a
canvas on which to 'paint' a story."

When asked about this story, Mark answered, "*Trial by Error* was actually two different ideas that one day came rushing together
quite handily when I considered doing a *Deep
Space Nine* story. It's really a character story, a
very fast-paced one. And the characters on DS9
were terrific. You get to tell a story using characters like this, and kick some butt along the
way, and maybe go out with something profound and meaningful, something worth a lasting thought—before you're done. What's not
to like?"

#22

VENGEANCE

Dafydd ab Hugh

FEBRUARY 1998   (282pp)

Remains of a log entry appear to contain evidence that an alliance between the Dominion and the Klingons has occurred. Sisko takes the *Defiant* into the Gamma Quadrant to discover the truth. Worf, temporarily in charge of the station, has to deal with a hostile force of Klingons taking over. The lead officer of the assault is an honorary blood brother of Worf's, and one of the soldiers used to be Worf's real brother, Kurn, who had his mind wiped of memories from his past life. Meanwhile, a ragtag group including O'Brien and Quark try to gain back control.

When asked about this book, Dafydd had no recollections to share.

#23

THE 34TH RULE

Armin Shimerman and David R. George III

JANUARY 1999   (425pp)

Coauthored by the actor who portrayed Quark on *Deep Space Nine*. Grand Nagus Zek has stumbled across the Orb of Wisdom. Bajor desperately wants it, so Zek organizes an auction. Strangely, the Bajorans are not the highest bidders, and are excluded from further negotiations. When the Ferengi are forbidden to enter Bajoran space, tensions mount further.

When asked how he landed the role of Quark, Armin remarked, "It was an outgrowth of the guest star roles (two Ferengi) that I had enacted on *The Next Generation* In addition, I was put in contention with many other hundreds of actors; my stiffest competition was Max Grodenchek (Rom). For once I was the right stature and had a classical acting background—much needed for the size of the acting needed for *Star Trek*. It was a childhood dream come true."

What led him to wanting to write a *Trek*

novel? "Unlike most series regulars who hanker to get behind the camera and direct, I had since adolescence been interested in writing. In fact, previous to *The 34th Rule*, I had already been commissioned by Pocket Books to do novels of a non-*Star Trek* idea called *The Merchant Prince*. It is a mixture of Shakespeare and Quark."

David remembered, "I'm not aware of any specific moment when I realized that I'd become a *Star Trek* fan, but at this point, I can't really recall *not* being one. I remember quite vividly watching the series for my very first time, at the age of four. Despite that I was so young at the time, the show had an impact on me. The episode was 'The Corbomite Maneuver,' from the original series, and I suppose that I've been hooked ever since. I can tell you the characteristics of the show that *keep* me a *Trek* fan, and those are the themes of tolerance, acceptance, and inclusion that permeate the various series. To me, growing up in New York City in a diverse community, it always seemed outrageous and foolhardy to judge somebody based upon their skin color, or gender, or sexual preference, or age. I had friends of all sorts, and I found the notion of people reveling in their differences a powerful and attractive one. I felt this even as a child. Although there are many things to recommend *Star Trek* and its scions, the most important for me is the optimistic message of humanity evolving beyond its prejudices."

David reflected on how he got started in writing. "For almost all of my life, I've been an avid reader, a gift given to me and my sister, and nurtured in us, by my mother. For nearly as long, I've wanted to be a writer, probably resulting from the combination of my loving to read

and the fact that both my father and grandfather were writers. Perhaps *Star Trek* played a role in that as well, since to this day, reading a good, well-written tale, or watching a good, well-written television show or film, always inspires me and sends me back to my own work with renewed enthusiasm. As for specifically writing *Star Trek*, I suppose it's only natural that I sought to merge my passion for writing with my fondness for the series."

When asked about how he ended up working on a novel with someone else, Armin commented, "David George, partnered with Eric Stilwell, asked if I would join them to pitch episode ideas for *Deep Space Nine*. We worked for several months honing our plot points and eventually had our shot with writer/producer René Echevarria. Unfortunately, No sale. But, that proved the best thing that could have happened. The three of us were despondent after the meeting, so I recommended that we not fritter away our good ideas, but seek to flesh them out in a longer novel form. Eric demurred, but David concurred. Of the three pitch ideas, I gravitated to the one that was most interesting and upsetting. After years of being on *Star Trek* and despite its so-called Prime Directive, I had perceived that the franchise had a strong streak of race prejudice. Throughout the episodes of all the series, there is the unspoken sense that all races are lesser to humanity. Once you get past the 'hew-mons' and possibly the Vulcans, most individual alien characters on first contact are always weighed against racial stereotypes promulgated by the experiences of the series lead characters. It took Worf and other main characters years to break down original Starfleet profilings of entire civilizations in the minds of both the away teams and the minds of the audience. To this day as an example, despite the heroic and noble deeds of Nog and Rom, [the Ferengi] were considered as implicitly imperfect and laughable characters. Pardon the pun, but in many people's eyes they fall short of fans' deserved respect because of their diminutive stature, their 'ugly' faces, and elephantine ears. Instead of being heroically honored for their selfless noble deeds, they are in small part deemed less than serious because of their race's amusing 'otherness.' Though we know them individually pretty well now, their actions are always viewed through the prism of their 'Ferenginess.' A belittling qualification that never happens with human characters—take for example the silliness of Dr. Bashir or the grim austerity of Sisko. My invention of Quark calling humanity 'hewmons' was an attempt to give mankind back a little of what it was dishing out. To Quark's mind, humans as a whole are both savagely brutal and inexplicably confusing. But, if Quark got teed off at Sisko or Kira or Odo, he got teed off at them as individuals and never close-mindedly judged them as manifesting stereotypical traits of their respective races. In contrast, he was never scripted to praise them for being 'better than most hewmons.' This is so because the human writers and their viewers know all people are different. Experiences on the set and at conventions had driven this point home to me. David and I wanted to address this inequality. In addition, like a good Ferengi, I wanted the book's plot to be extremely Byzantine. We spent many weeks working out the intricacies and misdirections. A chess game is what I called it. I so wanted the devoted *Star Trek* fan to be startled by the realization that humans could indeed be successfully out-maneuvered by Ferengi. I may be wrong but Quark and his people (even the wily and successful Nagus) have never succeeded at this on screen against a human—which, after all, is what they are reputedly supposed to be good at. But, more important, it was imperative to remind our audience of the horrors of the fruits that race prejudice can and has borne; the unspeakable atrocities that include Auschwitz, Abu Ghraib, Japanese internment."

David remarked, "Armin and I approached Pocket Books about the idea. We were told that they would be interested in a novel by Armin, but that we would have to go through the approval process as required of every other writer. Armin and I therefore set out to greatly expand the internment tale into something suitable for a novel. Once we had created the complex framework and character arcs for the story, we went back to Pocket, and they contracted us to write the novel. The writing process went considerably smoother than the publishing end of it. Armin and I found that we worked exceedingly well together, and we've since become good friends. Armin is an absolute gentleman, extremely creative and talented, and I feel very fortunate to have gotten to know him. I encountered during the writing of *The 34th Rule* numerous moments of creative joy.

"While the outline Armin and I had put together detailed the plot and character arcs of the tale, I still found a great deal of room for spontaneous creation. For example, I knew that we had to have a scene in which Captain Sisko wonders if he has acted in a prejudiced way, and he talks to his son Jake about it. When I got to that scene, I sat down and wrote, 'Jackie Robinson swung at the first pitch.' Seemingly out of nowhere, I had decided to set the scene in a holosuite re-creation of a Major League Baseball game, which featured a heroic man who contributed enormously to the breaking of racial barriers in America. It felt good, it felt right, and it's an example of how smoothly the process went. The scenes in the prison camp are other examples, showing the continuing horrors of the Cardassian Occupation of Bajor by way of the insanity of a Bajoran acting like a Cardassian, also seemed right. As to the publishing side of things, the project met with several unexplained delays. Worse, my copy edits never made it into the finished product, which was terribly infuriating and the reason that there are so many typographical errors in the book."

Armin remembers the writing process being as smooth as silk. "David was extremely gracious about getting my insights about other characters' foibles and fortes. We bonded almost immediately. He is one of the world's nicest men. The publishing process was made more difficult by my being on DS9. Unlike any other *Star Trek* novel, our novel had to be personally vetted by Rick Berman. David and I weren't quite sure Mr. Berman would continence our work because we drew many of the DS9 major characters as less than perfect. We got our share of notes from Pocket Books, including a directive to cut the concentration camp part of the story. David argued forcefully for it and they saw the wisdom of it. Other than that, they were always thrilled with the novel. Understandably, their admiration of the writing talent has translated itself into a strong use of David as a primary writer. He has continually proved himself to be a master storyteller."

Armin plans to continue writing. Has he read any of the post-DS9 novels? "Regrettably,

I have not. My wife says I only read works that are at least three hundred years old. Antiquity is my passion. David keeps me up-to-date on the new goings-on aboard Terok Nor."

#24

THE CONQUERED
(REBELS, Book One)
DAFYDD AB HUGH

FEBRUARY 1999   **(233PP)**

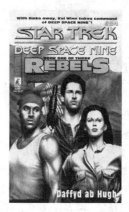

The Federation decides to give Bajor temporary control of DS9. Kira is looking forward to working with Shakaar again. When the shuttle arrives with the new head of the station, she is horrified to discover that Kai Winn will run the show. In the Gamma Quadrant, the *Defiant* discovers a world with primitive people slowly being overrun by the Cardassians.

#25

THE COURAGEOUS
(REBELS, Book Two)
Dafydd ab Hugh

FEBRUARY 1999 (235pp)

#26

THE LIBERATED
(REBELS, Book Three)
Dafydd ab Hugh

MARCH 1999 (238pp)

Space ships from the Gamma Quadrant arrive at the space station and begin a bold attack. Kai Winn reflects on her past and how she lived during the Cardassian occupation. In the Gamma Quadrant, Sisko and crew are stranded. To stay alive, the natives must be taught to fight, which would break the Prime Directive.

The strange aliens from the Gamma Quadrant demand one of the Bajoran Orbs. With Kai Winn refusing any help from the Federation, Kira must trust her new boss to stop the invasion and not give up one of the sacred artifacts of Bajor. In the Gamma Quadrant, Sisko and his crew learn a lot about themselves as they help the technological inhabitants to fend for themselves without the aid of gadgets.

Dafydd commented, "I think the *Rebels* trilogy (my first—and last—multi-part *Trek* book!) was another one suggested by Ordover. Everybody hated Kai Winn (including me), so I decided to make much of the trilogy the story of what she did during the occupation, showing her as a real, bona fide hero . . . but one whose doom was that she had to allow the other Bajorans to imagine that she was a traitor because she was so deep undercover with the resistance that she couldn't let people know what she had done for them, even after the Cardassians were kicked out. I was hoping people would contrast the heroism of her youth with the circumstances of her middle age and decide that, well, maybe she had earned the right to be bitchy and authoritarian."

 # 2 7

A STITCH IN TIME

(SEE SECTION 6: STAR TREK: DEEP SPACE NINE
UNNUMBERED NOVELS—FICTION SET AFTER THE
FINAL EPISODE)

STAR TREK: DEEP SPACE NINE UNNUMBERED NOVELS

WARPED
K. W. JETER

MARCH 1995   (345PP)

ORIGINALLY PUBLISHED IN HARDCOVER

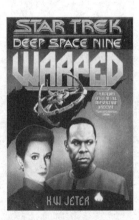

O do discovers a master criminal has arrived on the station and may be responsible for several murders. New holosuites appear and the users of them begin to show strange signs of aggression. The man responsible for the horror on the station appears to be one of the new heads of Bajor, making him untouchable. Meanwhile, Jake discovers one of the holosuites.

• • •

The author declined to be interviewed for this book.

HOLLOW MEN
UNA McCORMACK

MAY 2005   (349PP)

How far to go before a moral line is crossed? Sisko has reached that stage, after the events chronicled in the episode, "In The Pale Moonlight," which forced the Romulans into the war effort. Talks are starting on Earth, and the captain and Garak head to the negotiating table to meet with the Romulans. On the station, a ship has major engine troubles and needs to dock for repairs. And Odo has his hands full with a criminal who has supposedly reformed and who is trying to hold an antique sale in Quark's bar. Even small details will have lasting ramifications as another boundary is trampled in the name of survival.

Una was not really a *Trek* fan as a kid, "Although I was definitely a fan of science fiction TV (mainly *Blake's 7* and *Doctor Who*), and I did like the *Star Trek* films. I got into *Star Trek: The Next Generation* in the late 80s—at the time there was practically no science fiction on television at all, and TNG's arrival was incredibly exciting. . . . I missed *Deep Space Nine* on first transmission in the UK, but a friend of mine kept on telling me that I'd love it if I watched it. I wasn't sure, but just before the series ended this friend forced his tapes of seasons four–six on me. He was, of course, absolutely right—once I started watching I just kept on playing tape after tape. I was completely addicted when I watched 'In the Pale Moonlight' with my jaw hanging open at its brilliance. I started buying the tapes of season seven myself as they started coming out in the UK—in fact, I think I had the last episodes before the friend who had loaned me his tapes did!"

She continued, "I had been reading and writing fanfic in *Blake's 7* fandom for several years, so once I started watching DS9, it was a natural move first to go looking for DS9 fan fiction online, and then to start writing my own. Basically, I wanted more stories about the characters and situations that I'd fallen for, and when I ran out of episodes to watch or fan fic-

tion to read, I had to start writing my own. I really fell for Garak's character, and I loved writing in his voice. Plus writing is my way of processing and responding to something that has had a great effect on me. For example, I was hit really hard by the death of Damar, and what happened to Cardassia at the end of the show, and I wrote a fair amount of fan fiction exploring my reactions to that.

"Basically, *Hollow Men* started out as a short story, then I developed a B-plot to make it novel-length . . . and then there were some fairly radical changes to the original idea. I had already pitched the basic idea as a short story for *Prophecy and Change*. 'In the Pale Moonlight' is my favorite episode of DS9 (it's one of my favorite bits of television), and I really wanted to explore the story further, particularly what would happen if anyone else discovered the details surrounding Vreenak's murder (i.e., that Garak was guilty of it, and that Sisko was an accessory to it). The original story involved Sisko and Garak going back to Earth to explain some of the events of 'In the Pale Moonlight' to Starfleet Intelligence. Once back on Earth, Sisko confesses to being an accessory in Vreenak's murder and, as a result, two Starfleet Intelligence agents use this information to blackmail Garak into carrying out an assassination for them (of an antiwar campaigner). The story culminated in Sisko having to carry out the assassination in order to save Garak's life. Marco [Palmieri, my editor] liked the basic idea, but thought that Sisko's story arc was lacking. He made some suggestions about what to do; for example, having Sisko go visit his old commanding officer Admiral Leyton (from 'Homefront'/'Paradise Lost'), currently languishing in jail. The idea was to have Sisko be looking for someone who would give him absolution for the events of 'In the Pale Moonlight.' Marco also encouraged me to bring in Sisko's father and sister, who he would certainly see while he was on Earth. Once we had decided to develop the idea into a novel, the first thing I had to do was to come up with another plotline, a B-plot to expand the story into book-length. Since the Garak-Sisko story would be taking place on Earth, it was obvious I had to set the B-plot on the station, and I also wanted a story that was lighter in tone and more of a comedy, to act as relief from the pretty dark political thriller going on back on Earth. I started thinking of the 'caper' elements in episodes like 'In the Cards,' or 'Treachery, Faith, and the Great River,' both of which I really enjoy. Eventually, I settled on the idea of having a heist take place on the station, something on the lines of *The Italian Job* (the *proper* 1960s version with Michael Caine and Noel Coward; not the recent remake—good God, no!), in which the mastermind of the robbery would be locked up while it was happening, and there would the space-station equivalent of lots of Minis bringing traffic to a standstill in Turin. . . . Trust me on this! Odo and Bashir don't get much time together in the show, so I thought it would be fun to use these two characters as the main players in the heist storyline. Setting the story after 'In the Pale Moonlight' meant that I had to take into account the events of 'Inquisition,' and this gave me a lead into the story: Odo tries to distract Bashir from the aftermath of those experiences by getting him interested in the events surrounding the heist.

"I had a lot of fun translating the rough idea of the heist into something that could take place on DS9, with all the doors locking and all the turbolifts jamming, so that the station crew weren't able to stop the robbery from happening. I much prefer stories in which all the constituent elements link up, so this meant I had to develop connections between the Garak-Sisko story and the Bashir-Odo story. I decided that the real object of the heist was not the shipment of vials of latinum that everyone thinks is being stolen, but some information contained on the vials which exposes the involvement of Section 31 in infecting the Founders with the disease that is killing them. Someone is trying to get this information out to the Dominion . . . and this is the same person (the antiwar campaigner) that Starfleet Intelligence are busy blackmailing Garak into assassinating. Ultimately, it turns out that the agents who are blackmailing Sisko and Garak are not Starfleet Intelligence but Section 31. I wrote this up as an outline but Paula Block at Paramount had problems with Sisko's plotline as it stood: She wasn't convinced that he would carry out this assassination or that, if he did do the deed, he was unlikely to stay in Starfleet afterwards and would probably resign his commission in disgust. . . . So I got to work on some revisions which basically meant disentangling Garak's and Sisko's plotlines: Garak is still approached by Section 31 and blackmailed into carrying out an assassination on their behalf, but Sisko never finds this out. I also altered the story so that Garak and not Sisko shoots the antiwar campaigner. Paula's instincts were spot on; it's a much more layered story as a result, nowhere near as heavy-handed. Characters don't have important information that other characters have; so Sisko never knows that Garak has been approached by people he would immediately recognize as Section 31; Garak doesn't know about Section 31 and so assumes that the two agents have all the backing of Starfleet and that he can't get out of the situation he's found himself in."

Una went on to say, "*Hollow Men* is the longest thing that I've written, and structurally, too, it's more ambitious than anything I've written before. Both *Face Value* and *The Lotus Flower* have chapters that are pretty much distinct scenes. In *Hollow Men*, I had to keep all the narratives going at once and this meant interweaving stories a lot more than I'd done in the past. I always do fairly detailed timelines and maps and so on, which helped me keep the action in order. The *Deep Space Nine Technical Manual* was a godsend for working out the technicalities of the heist. It was also my first ever purchase on eBay and I spent a happy couple of days distracting myself from writing by engaging in a small bidding war for it! The title of the book is from T. S. Eliot's poem *The Hollow Men*, and there are references and nods here and there to *Heart of Darkness* (amorality beside a river) and to *Julius Caesar* (political assassination). I set the main drama of the book in London partly because I don't know San Francisco at all while I do know London pretty well, but also because it would evoke *The Hollow Men* and the framing sections of *Heart of Darkness*. There are various bits of homage to other things that I love, too: Jedburgh is the name of a character in the 1980s BBC political thriller *Edge of Darkness*, and Enderby is the name of a Le Carré character. I always enjoy spotting these kinds of references in other people's books, so that's why I put them in."

LEGENDS OF THE FERENGI
(SEE SECTION 14: OTHER STAR TREK FICTION)

FICTION SET AFTER THE FINAL EPISODE

THE LIVES OF DAX
(SEE: SECTION 13: ANTHOLOGIES)

THE FALL OF TEROK NOR
(MILLENNIUM, Book One)
JUDITH AND GARFIELD REEVES-STEVENS

MARCH 2000   **(412PP)**

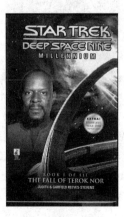

 fter recapturing the station from Dominion forces, Quark stands accused of murdering an Andorian businessman. Supposedly, he had a map that showed where one red orb of Jalbador (out of three) could be located. The Bajoran government believes that the orbs are just legend and don't exist. Supposedly, if the three orbs are brought together, the result would open another wormhole.

THE WAR OF THE PROPHETS
(MILLENNIUM, Book Two)
JUDITH AND GARFIELD REEVES-STEVENS

MARCH 2000   (372PP)

Sisko and the crew of the *Defiant* find themselves in a horrible reality twenty-five years in the future. What exists of the shattered Federation is at war with the Bajoran Ascendancy, led by Kai Wayoun. A bold plan to fix the temporal timeline will soon be implemented, led by a feeble Admiral Picard and Captain Nog, who must betray his best friend to guarantee success. If they fail, the universe will end.

INFERNO
(MILLENNIUM, Book Three)
JUDITH AND GARFIELD REEVES-STEVENS

APRIL 2000   (410PP)

Sisko and his crew find themselves in between time and a chance to restore the proper balance. Each person beams into the station and arrives at different times throughout the six years of the Federation's presence. To succeed, they must not only stop their future selves, but they must also not disrupt the correct timeline.

The authors declined to be interviewed for this book.

A STITCH IN TIME
(STAR TREK: DEEP SPACE NINE #27)
ANDREW J. ROBINSON

M A Y   2 0 0 0   (3 9 6 P P)

From the ruins of postwar Cardassia, Garak writes a letter to his old friend, Julian Bashir, telling the doctor of his people's struggle to rebuild their civilization, interspersed with the story of his life. Of course, every word of the book is true. Especially the lies.

Andy auditioned for the Garak role not long after he was one of the three finalists for the role of Odo. Originally, Garak was booked only for one show, but the producers, in an effort to give the character of Dr. Bashir a more involving storyline, wanted to see if the Garak-Bashir pairing was worth pursuing. Obviously, it was a successful match. Andy remarked, "A *Stitch In Time* came out of a 'journal' that I began to write for Garak shortly after I began the job. Creating a biography for a character is an actor's tool, especially for characters that have no past or precedence. What did I know about Cardassians? What did the writers know? As the journal grew and I became more involved with it, I also began to read excerpts at various *Trek* conventions. I wanted to do something other than answer the usual questions about makeup and stories from the set, and I thought that the fans might enjoy Garak's reflections on being the sole Cardassian on the station. It also gave me an opportunity to fill out his story. I enjoyed the process immensely, and the book just flowed out of the journal after David George, the writer, suggested that I go in that direction. He was the one who introduced me to the folks at Pocket Books. To say the least, I was pleased by the result."

Andy continued, "The idea for the book came out of the idea that Garak, being dislocated and victimized by the disastrous policies of his government (which, in part, he supported), needed to write this journal to make sense of what had happened to him. In the process, he was able to achieve a certain amount of peace and healing."

PLAN 9 FROM OUTER SPACE

"It's not an undertaking for the timid," editor Marco Palmieri said of the decision to continue the saga of *Deep Space Nine* in book form, beyond the final episode of the TV series. "DS9 was a very complex, tightly written, character-driven serial with, I think, a well-deserved reputation for excellence in storytelling. You need to be crazy or arrogant to think you can transition that sort of entertainment experience from television to novels. It's probably fair to say I'm two out of two."

In May 2001 Pocket Books published the two-part *Avatar* by S. D. Perry, which began the publisher's new approach to DS9 fiction and also something not previously attempted in *Star Trek:* the serialized continuation of a television series in novel form. "It was new ground," Marco explained. "When DS9 ended in 1999 with no expectation of it being revisited on screen in any form for the foreseeable future, it represented an amazing opportunity for the fiction to continue where a show had left off—to offer its fans a vision of what happened next. We wanted it to be a true continuation, chronicling events that, like those on the TV series, would be fraught with consequences and free of resets."

Marco went on, "Strictly speaking, *Avatar* wasn't the first post-TV story. It was actually preceded by *The Lives of Dax* (whose framing sequence gave us a glimpse of life aboard the station in the days following 'What You Leave Behind') and by Andrew Robinson's *A Stitch in Time* (which vividly captured the state of affairs on postwar Cardassia). But *Avatar* was conceived as the first installment in the new serial narrative."

The road from TV series to novel series wasn't instantaneous. "It took two years to get from 'What You Leave Behind' to *Avatar*," Marco said. "The first step was to develop a loose narrative framework for the novels, what I like to call the metastory: something that was tight enough to give them all a shared creative direction, but roomy and flexible enough to accommodate sudden inspirations or unplanned twists. The new fiction had to be grounded in how the TV series had unfolded, and the journeys of the established characters, but still dare to imagine where those arcs might lead. We wanted the novels to stay as close as possible to the tone and texture of the TV series while still presenting the audience with something new."

One wrinkle in developing that creative direction was the fact that several starring characters from the TV series were essentially written out in the final episode. "Sisko, Odo, O'Brien, and Worf had moved on, along with a good percentage of the rich supporting cast, including every villain the show had," Marco said. "As a fan, I felt those losses acutely. As an editor developing new DS9 fiction, I was excited by the prospect of the remaining characters dealing with those losses—or failing to—and by the opportunity to introduce prominent new characters into the mix, both of which were hallmarks of the TV series. It would allow the new fiction to demonstrate from the very first page that it would dare to move forward, and do so boldly."

One of the more controversial aspects of the new DS9 fiction was the introduction of new featured characters. "I think DS9 fans generally have an appreciation for that sort of evolution in an ongoing story, since the TV series itself introduced new starring characters through the years (Worf, Ezri), while simultaneously adding and elevating numerous supporting players to a near-equal level of prominence (Nog, Dukat, Garak, Winn, Damar, Kasidy, Martok, Weyoun). Filling the voids created by the characters who had been written out of the story on TV wasn't simply necessary, it was staying true to the spirit of the TV series. And it was a great opportunity to create a new group dynamic where we could explore and learn about the new kids on the block, and explore the old ones in new ways."

Another thing Marco wanted to try was the use of different authors for different stories. "I thought it was important to bring new voices, new ideas, and contrasting sensibilities into the mix. The work is definitely more challenging that way, but ultimately more rewarding, I think. With that in mind, I reached out to authors I thought would get the new novels off to a good start."

Though the new DS9 novels have been a critical and commercial success, it was by no means a sure thing. "It was a gamble," Marco admitted. "Just because DS9 was no longer on the air, that didn't mean that a future *Next Generation* movie, or some upcoming *Voyager* or *Enterprise* episode, wouldn't eventually establish something that would contradict some aspect of the new books. But that's the risk with every *Star Trek* story, and it's been that way since Day One. No author or editor can make creative decisions based on fear. If you really want to do something you think is cool, you need to be willing to seize an opportunity when it presents itself, roll the dice, and take your chances."

"We were fortunate in that the entire endeavor was supported from its inception by the studio; Paula Block in particular, my contact with the licensed publishing office, really got behind the project, and for that I'll always be grateful."

AVATAR, Book One
S. D. PERRY

MAY 2001 (284 PP)

three months after the end of the Dominion War, a surprise Jem'Hadar attack catches the station off guard, sending the Federation, the Klingons, and the Romulans to assume the worst. Meanwhile, a prophecy connected to Kasidy Yates's unborn child has startling implications, while elsewhere, a Starfleet officer at the twilight of his life has a rendezvous with destiny.

AVATAR, Book Two
S. D. PERRY

MAY 2001 (234 PP)

while the crew detains a Jem'Hadar soldier claiming to be sent by Odo on a mission of peace, Kira faces a supreme test of faith that will change her life—just as sabotage forces a station evacuation during a visit from the *Enterprise*-E. And where exactly does Jake think he's going?

Danelle commented, "When I was eleven I would hurry home from grade school to catch the repeats of the original series. I thought Spock and Kirk were really cute. I didn't tell my friends, I just went home and watched it."

She continued, "I didn't want to originally write *Trek* at all. I was working for Marco doing a series of video game novels for *Resident Evil*. When Marco started working on the fiction side of *Trek*, he asked if I would be willing to write a story for *The Lives of Dax*. I said, 'Sure.' "

On landing the job of writing *Avatar*, she said, "I was really lucky. Marco liked what I had done so far with *Star Trek* and asked if I would be interested in trying it."

Marco noted, *"Avatar* set the tone for everything that followed it. Danelle seemed to understand intuitively what I was striving for, how I wanted it to be different from what had been done in the past, and she ran with it. I was asking her to do things that had never before been attempted in *Star Trek* fiction, and the challenge never fazed her."

Regarding the decision to publish *Avatar* in two parts, Marco said, "Hindsight is 20/20, and it's certainly fair to say now that *Avatar* should have been one book, not two. But it was *plotted* as two novels, and I really believed the execution would bear that out. I was thrilled with the outcome, but I can see now that it should have been a single book. There are lessons an editor learns on every new project, and that was definitely one of the ones I learned from *Avatar*. On the bright side, two books meant two breathtaking covers by artist Cliff Nielsen."

ABYSS
(SECTION 31; SEE SECTION 12: MINISERIES)

DEMONS OF AIR AND DARKNESS
(GATEWAYS, BOOK FOUR; SEE SECTION 12: MINISERIES)

"HORN AND IVORY"
(FROM GATEWAYS, BOOK SEVEN; SEE SECTION 12: MINISERIES)

TWILIGHT
(MISSION: GAMMA, Book One)
DAVID R. GEORGE III

SEPTEMBER 2002 (504PP)

Led by Commander Vaughn, the *Defiant* embarks on a new mission to the Gamma Quadrant now that the Dominion threat has diminished. Meanwhile, a major effort to enroll Bajor into the Federation begins on the station.

"Twilight was to be the sixth work continuing the saga of *Deep Space Nine* forward from the

MISSION: GAMMA

Marco Palmieri commented, "*Mission: Gamma* was inspired in large part by my having recently seen a PBS documentary on Lewis & Clark and the Corps of Discovery, which had a great romantic quality to it. This arc of novels was designed to be a revisitation of DS9's original premise, the exploration of the Gamma Quadrant. Of course, this idea has to be taken now within the new context of the postwar era, so the Federation decides to go forward cautiously, letting Vaughn take the *Defiant* on a three-month excursion that will 'test the waters' for a real wave of exploration that will come later, if all goes well. Meanwhile, the sociopolitical storyline involving Bajor and Cardassia moves forward in the Alpha Quadrant, and the buildup toward *Unity* begins. There were specific story points I asked the writers to hit when it came to the AQ arc, but I invited them to go wild imagining what the *Defiant* crew would experience in the GQ."

Marco went on, "The arc was an experiment, structurally. *Mission: Gamma* starts out with a story of 200,000 words, and the novels get progressively shorter and faster-paced as the series progresses toward its action climax. The 'class photo' approach to the cover art was another experiment, not entirely successful because of the uneven photographic reference utilized to create it."

last episode of the series, as well as the first of a four-volume series entitled *Mission: Gamma*. I therefore had several storylines that I needed to continue, and others that I had to begin. Still, for all of that, editor Marco Palmieri provided me a great deal of freedom in determining the sort of story I wanted to tell. In this case, I decided that I wanted to write a love story, but about different types of love. In *Twilight*, I included a tale of romantic love (between Ro Laren and Quark), a tale of what you might call societal love (Kira Nerys's love for her people), and a tale of familial love (between father Elias Vaughn and daughter Prynn Tenmei). The writing of *Twilight* was both arduous and won-

derful. As with *The 34th Rule*, I found myself penning scenes that seemed to work well, and illuminated the themes with which I had started. At the same time, the novel turned out to be exceedingly long (200,000 words), and therefore took a longer time to write. I was fortunate to have Marco Palmieri as my editor, a man who is incredibly creative, extremely easy to work with, and a fine steward of the *Star Trek* fiction line. Marco made the process a great deal easier, and provided me with key input in his editing. The book is immeasurably better thanks to Marco's presence on the project. It even ended up on the *USA Today* best seller list."

THIS GRAY SPIRIT
(MISSION: GAMMA, Book Two)
HEATHER JARMAN

SEPTEMBER 2002 (390PP)

Gul Macet arrives on the station with a surprising passenger. Meanwhile, in the Gamma Quadrant, the *Defiant* stumbles upon the "web weapon" of a nearby stellar empire, effectively crippling the ship. Getting help from the species known as the Yrythny, the crew becomes involved in a potential civil war.

Heather remembered, "I was a fan of *Star Trek* as a young kid. I watched TNG intermittently but never really went crazy over it the way I had with the original series. I rediscovered my *Star Trek* passion in my late twenties when DS9 and *Voyager* were still on the air. At that point, I saturated myself in *Star Trek* watching all of TNG, DS9, and *Voyager* over the course of several months. I've been a hopeless case ever since. *Voyager* frustration prompted me to write my first *Star Trek* story. I felt like they had

missed so many opportunities for both storytelling and character development. I tried my hand at a few fan fiction pieces and wrote editorials for the online fanzine, *The Starfleet Journal*. I contributed a few reviews to the *Voyager* review site Delta Blues as well."

Marco recalls "discovering" Heather. "I was reading *Trek*-related essays on various Web sites when I ran across one Heather had written for *The Starfleet Journal*. I was struck immediately by her eloquence, and started corresponding with her by e-mail. I'd gotten into the habit of recruiting new authors for the fiction, so I invited her to pitch story ideas, and eventually decided she'd make a good contribution to *Mission: Gamma*. The weird thing is that our mutual friend, Jeff Lang, tried to get us talking about a notion she had for an anthology two or three years before I actually contacted her, but I wasn't interested. I didn't realize Heather was Jeff's friend until much later."

On writing the story, Heather said, "Half of *This Gray Spirit* was handed to me—the station outline wasn't negotiable. Unfortunately, Marco gave me a lot of static scenes: negotiations, politics—potentially boring stuff. Coming up with a way to show the themes of the story was the challenge. Ziyal was a character who fascinated me. I was watching the Dominion War arc at the beginning of season six and came up with her art being the 'theme' for the station arc. The Yrythny story was an attempt to tell a big exploration story that couldn't be told on a series because it was too complex and/or expensive in terms of effects and design. I love genetic engineering—I liked the idea of creating a species that had amphibious evolutionary history. From there, the elements fell into place. The writing process was challenging because 9/11 happened the day I was supposed to finalize the Ezri arc with Marco. On a practical level, it shut New York down. On a personal, artistic level, it impacted me emotionally and spiritually in a way that forced me to confront a lot of conflict inside me and to overcome the very real horror playing out daily on my TV. The writing process was more challenging as a consequence. Frankly, *Star Trek* felt irrelevant in comparison to what was happening in the world, so why waste my time? It took some time to overcome that feeling of my work being trivial. Even more difficult was the fact that my writing *This Gray Spirit* paralleled, almost to the day, the last year of my younger brother's life. On a subconscious level, I was telling his story through the Thriss arc. I signed the book contract in June 2001; June 2002, I was sitting on my hotel room floor with the page proofs from *This Gray Spirit* making corrections the night before his funeral. The whole project is bound up in a difficult year of my life. As I re-read it now, I find dozens of areas I could have improved on, but the writing came from my gut, so at least I was being honest."

Heather had some things to say about writing *Trek* stories. "The challenge: Frankly, many readers (and many in the public at large) don't see you as a 'serious' writer. Never mind the hours of research into a multitude of subjects that writing *Star Trek* (and science fiction in general) requires, those of us who do 'work for hire' media tie-in work are often seen as hacks. As someone who studied English literature at the university level (and specialized in British literature), I can usually hold my own in the snotty English major camp when analyzing and dissecting what's deemed 'literature.' It smarts, though, when people are automatically dismissive of *Star Trek* fiction. I don't think it's deserved. Granted, there's a lot of media tie-in that never reaches literary heights but that's a global generalization that IMHO doesn't apply to all of *Star Trek* fiction. The benefit: As a professional writer, I couldn't have a better training ground than having to meet the rigorous deadlines and demands of doing work-for-hire. Unlike other writers—of sometimes literary fiction—I don't have the luxury of spending years writing and rewriting projects. The demands forced me to gain self-discipline that many writers of my acquaintance struggle to learn. Still, I think it is important to tell aspiring writers—and those aspiring *Star Trek* writers need to be especially mindful—to work on their writing skills. Learning how to use the language and how to tell a good story are critical to the development of every writer. I've encountered aspiring ST writers who think that all they need to do is know *Star Trek*. What I tell them when they ask for advice is to seek new experiences, learn about everything, and be interested in everything. Travel. Read. Study. Learn. Have an open mind about life in general—you can learn something from almost every situation and circumstance. Live life—have relationships, friendships, and experiences. One of the best things an aspiring writer can do for his or her writing is to have balance."

CATHEDRAL
(MISSION: GAMMA, Book Three)
MICHAEL A. MARTIN AND ANDY MANGELS

OCTOBER 2002 (404PP)

The *Defiant* encounters an artifact, resulting in life changes for some of the crew. Bashir begins to lose his genetic enhancements, including his surgical skills; Ezri rejects her symbiont, reverting to being an unjoined Trill; and Nog's lost leg regenerates as he starts to again embrace the true Ferengi way. Things aren't going well in the Alpha Quadrant either as the Cardassian-Bajoran rapprochment is stalled, and a schism develops within the Bajoran faith.

According to Mike, "DS9 is my favorite latter-day *Trek* series, so when I heard Marco was putting *Mission: Gamma* together I really went after him to get the gig. Marco allowed Andy and me to participate in some of the planning of the entire four-book arc, including the assembly of a timeline of the Alpha Quadrant/ Bajoran geopolitical arc. This gave all of the *M: G* authors a lot of 'marks' they had to hit. We were lucky enough to get a lot of the really nifty ones assigned to our book. *Flowers for Algernon* by Daniel Keyes inspired the Gamma Quadrant side of the book, which was mostly my work. This is most pronounced in Bashir's arc, in which we see the doctor's genetically engineered intellect gradually, mercilessly unraveling.

Andy remarked, "I, too, liked DS9 a lot, but I had always had a problem with the whole Bajoran religion thing. It bored me to tears on the show. So, once the threads started being laid out that there was a [religious schism developing] on Bajor, at a time of great upheaval, my interest was sparked. I come from a Mormon background, and even though I am not a practicing Mormon now, I still have the awareness of what kind of historical persecution and trials those in the early days of the church went through. I filtered a lot of the theological discussions I had had with others—and in my own mind—over the years, and looked at how the issues of faith, higher powers, acceptance, and tolerance all factored into this *Star Trek* situation. There was one scene I wrote in chapter 16, where I really tried to crystallize what religious beliefs would mean in a *Star Trek* context, wherein different worlds had different beliefs (or non-beliefs), and what the core of the conflict on Bajor was at this point. What does their faith mean when the church and their gods are being tested and questioned and reinterpreted? I had a priest read the section to see if I had managed to put it all in proper context. He told me that not only had I done so eloquently, but also it had made him cry because it expressed how and what faith really meant."

LESSER EVIL
(MISSION: GAMMA, Book Four)
ROBERT SIMPSON

NOVEMBER 2002   (266PP)

I
n the Alpha Quadrant, Kira attempts to understand the event
that occurred at the end of *Cathedral*. In the Gamma Quadrant, the *Defiant*
stumbles upon the remains of both a
Jem'Hadar ship and a Borg-assimilated
Starfleet ship. These events force Vaughn to remember some painful events in his past.

Rob commented, "I've probably been a *Star
Trek* fan my entire life. Growing up I have distinct memories of seeing some of the episodes
of the original series in first-run, even though it
went off the air in 1969 and I was only four at
the time. There have always been people in my
life who were bigger fans of the various incarnations of the show and its characters, so I often
hid how much I really loved the whole world of
Trek, but I'd have to say I was hooked almost
from birth."

He continued, "My pretty short period of
being associated with *Star Trek* publishing
came about because I was doing some freelance editing for Simon & Schuster through
the very kind intervention of two of my oldest
friends, Pocket Books editors Margaret Clark
and Marco Palmieri. The three of us had
worked together in various different jobs over
the years, and my doing work for them came at
a time when I was between staff jobs. Being at
their office handling various editorial duties on
a bunch of books gave me a chance to not only
study the history of the shows but to brainstorm
on some ideas with Marco for pitches to write
some episodes of *Deep Space Nine*. While it
never came to pass that we'd write an episode
of the show together, it was a lot of fun to hash
out some story ideas, a few of which got used in
other ways besides on television."

Robert remarked on *Lesser Evil*. "This came
about through an interesting set of events. Like
I said before, Marco and I were working on
some pitches to present to the DS9 writing
staff; at the time that we were working up our
springboards, the show was entering finishing
plans for its sixth season. We came up with several ideas, one of which was a story reaching
back to the very first episode of *Deep Space
Nine*, theorizing on how Benjamin Sisko's wife
might have been taken by the Borg before the
destruction of their ship at the battle of Wolf
359. But that was just one of the ideas, and we
knew that exploring such a pivotal moment in
Sisko's backstory might be a big reach. While
the producer we spoke with did like a few of
our ideas, by the time we'd finally got around to
our pitch session the writers had already
charted out the final structure of the series.
With a thank you for pitching, that was what I

thought was about it. A few months later, after the show had ended and I'd moved on to another editing job, Marco contacted me and said that Pocket was starting to conceive the next stages of the relaunched *Deep Space Nine* publishing program, and said that he wanted to use some of the story material that he and I had conceived as a launching point for the first wave of books. He asked if I had any problem with it, and of course I said I thought it was fine—when you do this kind of writing you understand that the stories are owned by the company and that other people may wind up working on the concepts. He then offered me writing one of the books in that initial block, which would become *Lesser Evil.* We looked back on the Jennifer-Sisko-Borg idea and knew, taking into account the way the series had ended, that it wouldn't work as it was, so we set to retooling it, all the while interweaving the plot threads from the other books into the novel."

Robert concluded, "I'll always look on my really brief time working in the *Trek* playground as one of the best times of my life. I remain in constant awe over how the many writers and the editors have been able to weave their stories into the greater tapestry of the *Trek* universe, and I thank Margaret Clark and Scott Shannon and Marco for letting me live out a little bit of a childhood dream."

RISING SON
S. D. PERRY

JANUARY 2003   (308PP)

J ake Sisko, lured to the wormhole by a prophecy, believes he is bringing his dad home. Instead, he finds his shuttle adrift until a group of alien "pirates" rescue him and make him one of the crew. Jake finds himself torn between his new friends and the loved ones left behind.

Danelle remarked, "It was hard at first to write a Jake novel. It took me a while to figure out who Jake was exactly. Once I got into the story, it was a lot of fun. Marco does not like to take credit but he had the whole arc planned out."

Marco noted, "*Rising Son* is one of my favorite DS9 novels. Jake's journey is the journey of anyone trying to overcome personal loss and find their way back. His odyssey with the *Even Odds* and its colorful crew of fortune hunters, which Danelle created, presented a rare opportunity to tell a *Star Trek* story entirely outside the usual Starfleet point of view."

THE LEFT HAND OF DESTINY, Book One
J. G. HERTZLER AND JEFFREY LANG
APRIL 2003   (294PP)

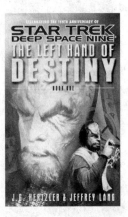

Coauthored by the actor who portrayed Martok on *Deep Space Nine*. Chancellor Martok, leader of the Klingon Empire, returns home following the Allied victory in the Dominion War. With him is Federation Ambassador Worf. But their return is met by a coup d'etat led by the young and charismatic usurper Morjod, who will stop at nothing to remake the Empire in his image, and hunt down Martok and all who follow him.

THE LEFT HAND OF DESTINY, Book Two
J. G. HERTZLER AND JEFFREY LANG
MAY 2003   (330PP)

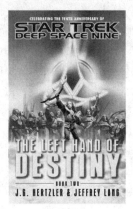

Forced to flee the Klingon homeworld, Martok and his followers unravel the mystery of the upstart Morjod . . . and learn that Martok himself may be responsible for his rise to power. Facing a final, costly battle for the Empire on Boreth, the chancellor meets his fate head-on.

J. G. Hertzler won the role of Martok. "I auditioned as a chair-throwing angry maniac and the part was mine. Oddly, one of my best friends was my only competition for the role at the end, so the victory was bittersweet, although Ron is doing very well in the feature films, so I don't feel all that bad. The travel around the world to conventions and my e-mail correspondence with fans and friends around the globe is a great benefit, totally unexpected."

How did he go from an actor with a role to writing about the character? "Simon & Schuster came to me. I labored for two years getting the story down, about an eighty-page outline, creating the new characters and investing theme in plot. I finally turned in two complete manuscripts that needed revision and polishing and that is when the great Jeffrey Lang came aboard. Working with Jeffrey was a thrill. What a fantastic artist he is."

Editor Marco Palmieri remembers the story's genesis. "I wanted to do a different kind of Klingon story, one with a strong mythic quality like the legends of King Arthur. When Martok became chancellor of the Empire on DS9, that's how I kept seeing him, and I started to draw Arthurian connections to various characters and elements around him. DS9 had already given us the Klingons' Excalibur in 'Sword of Kahless.' Worf was Lancelot, but without the betrayal. Alexander was Percival. Ezri was the Lady of the Lake. The clone of Kahless was Merlin. It all seemed to fit together perfectly. We still needed analogs for Morgan and Mordred, but that required only a little imagination. I knew that J. G. had done some writing, so I approached him with my ideas for an Arthurian Klingon epic focusing on Martok, and he responded very enthusiastically."

Marco went on, "Ultimately, we decided that Martok's arc should take him from being a reluctant leader who was forced into office to a man who finally understood who he was enough to willingly *take* the mantle of leadership."

J. G. continued, "It took forever to get the outline done, and then the writing went actually a lot faster. The manuscripts I turned in needed revisions and polishing and I simply did

not have the time to undertake it alone, so they called to see if Jeffrey was interested and available and he soon was . . . the rest is history."

J. G. has read some of Jeffrey's books, which he calls fabulous. Also, "I read Keith DeCandido Klingon books which I enjoyed very much."

Jeffrey remembered, "Like *Abyss*, I came into *The Left Hand of Destiny* after the outline had been written so I had very little to do with the overall scope of the book. In fact, J. G. had written an entire draft and handed it in, which is when Marco called me. The problem was that though there were lots of really great things in the draft, J. G. isn't really a novelist. His draft read a lot more like a screenplay with blocks of detailed descriptions. Really fun stuff, but y'know, not a novel. Marco asked me if I could 'reshape' it and I said I'd give it a shot. 'And you've got eight months to do it.' OK. 'Both books.' *Gulp*. After a very frustrating month or so, I decided there was no way I could rewrite the thing because the changes just kept accumulating. Also, I realized that the sidekick character Pharh just wasn't working. In the original draft, Pharh was this Ferengi who really, really *wanted* to be a Klingon. He liked Klingons, admired them, and thought they were great. I decided his arc was wrong. His starting point was too close to where he ended (and the ending J. G. had for him was nothing like what we eventually did). So, reluctantly, I decided I had to start from the beginning. And then I wrote two books in about seven months. J. G. read everything as it was produced and sent valuable notes. I also got amazingly valuable editing advice from my friend and collaborator Heather Jarman. She reworked and helped rewrite several scenes, including the amazingly long 'What the heck is going on here?' exposition scene in Book Two. Writing the second half of Book Two is a blur in my memory. There came a point where ideas were coming pretty much as I was writing, with very little planning in advance, but somehow, amazingly, everything fit together in the end. Right up until the end, I wasn't sure what I was going to do with Pharh, but then I got to the chapter when he had to either live or die and I reluctantly concluded that the story only made sense if he was killed. I confess that I got a little teary-eyed when I wrote his last scene. After that, the rest of the book was easy. All in all, *Left Hand of Destiny* was one of the most difficult assignments I ever had, but one of the most satisfying."

UNITY
S. D. PERRY

NOVEMBER 2003   (311PP)

ORIGINALLY PUBLISHED IN HARDCOVER

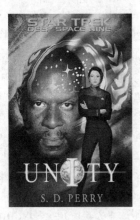

he *Defiant* returns from the Gamma Quadrant to find the station—and indeed, the en-

tire Bajoran system—in lockdown. An insidious alien infestation means that no one can truly be trusted, While Kira and her crew try to contain the threat, Kasidy finally goes into labor, and Commander Vaughn makes an unplanned visit to the Celestial Temple.

Danelle remarked, "It was published in hardcover to celebrate the tenth anniversary of the show. I got a lot of comments that the birth scene—it was very realistic. I wrote that from experience."

Editor Marco Palmieri added, "*Unity* represents the culmination of several short-term goals in the DS9 metastory. Back in 1999, when the studio approved the new creative direction of the fiction, they had only one requirement: no stories bringing back Sisko. The concern was that the novels should not immediately reverse major developments in the DS9 finale. That suited me fine, as I felt similarly that we should be exploring the consequences of the final episode, and not seeking to undermine them."

Marco continued, "The larger truth is that I was also thinking ahead. I did want to spend some time dealing with the fallout of Sisko's absence, but I also knew that DS9's tenth anniversary was just a few years away. My hope for the new novels was that they would be popular enough that I could publish a special tenth anniversary hardcover in which Bajor would join the Federation, Sisko's child would be born, and Sisko himself would return (as the character himself had vowed in the series finale). So I bided my time. When *Avatar* became a big success in 2001, I approached the studio again to ask if they'd consider letting me chronicle Sisko's return in 2003 for the tenth anniversary.

WORLDS OF STAR TREK: DEEP SPACE NINE

Marco Palmieri explained, "Once again, I wanted to do something different. *Unity* wrapped up several major storylines, but also left a few dangling, and started a few new ones as well. I remember thinking I wanted to continue the saga in an unexpected way, and again try something experimental. I'd been a longtime fan of past *Star Trek* novels that had done worldbuilding: *The Final Reflection*, *Spock's World*, *The Romulan Way*, and *A Stitch in Time* are among my favorites. I wanted to bring that sort of thing to the civilizations most closely associated with the characters of DS9: Bajor, Cardassia, Trill, Ferenginar, The Dominion, and Andor (Andor because of the introduction of the Andorian Shar as the station's science officer). The idea was to split the DS9 narrative into six branches, each focusing on different characters, each springing out of the events of *Unity* in some way, and each giving the reader an intimate, in-depth look at one of DS9's worlds."

Framed in that context, the studio didn't hesitate to give its approval."

Marco explained that the road to publication was longer than planned. "Two things happened that delayed *Unity* by ten months. The first was that my wife became preganant with our second child. The second was that Danelle became pregnant with her first child. Under those circumstances, missing deadlines became inevitable. So instead of kicking off the tenth anniversary in January, *Unity* capped off the celebration in November."

WORLDS OF DEEP SPACE NINE, Volume One

JUNE 2004   (361 PP)

CARDASSIA

THE LOTUS FLOWER
UNA McCORMACK

eiko struggles to run a fledgling recovery project in the aftermath of the devastation caused by the Dominion. As the government attempts to restore order, some citizens refuse the Federation's help and will do anything to remove them from their planet.

Una reflected on how she landed the assignment for writing about Cardassia. "I remember seeing a press release online in which the *Worlds of DS9* project was mentioned, and I thought, 'Wow, I really envy the person that gets to write the Cardassia story!' Then I got an e-mail from Marco asking whether I would like to try pitching an idea for it. Again, I think you can imagine my delight! In comparison with 'Face Value,' where I was free to come up with pretty much any story, there was a brief for the *Worlds of DS9* project: The story was going to be set after the events of *Unity*, so it had to be consistent with what had been established in the DS9 Relaunch books and in Andy Robinson's book, *A Stitch in Time*. Marco also asked me to include several specific characters, including the O'Briens, Garak, Gul Macet, and Vedek Yevir from the Relaunch books. Marco sent me a short summary of events of the Relaunch series with an emphasis on what had been happening on Cardassia, and I read the relevant books to get background on Yevir and aspects of the story that related to Cardassia. I also reread *A Stitch in Time* to immerse myself in the details of Cardassian culture that were described in the book, particularly the Oralian Way. My first ideas were to look at how the politicians on Cardassia were keeping up (or not) with the peace initiatives being taken by the religious leaders (Yevir and Ekosha) and I thought that a story about an attempt to destabilize Ghemor's government might be interesting. I also worked from my usual starting place

of thinking which characters would be most interesting to put together; at first I thought I would write about Garak, O'Brien, and Yevir working together to resolve any political plot that was underway. Ultimately, I didn't go with this last idea, but that's what lay behind the scenes between Garak and O'Brien at the start of the book. I thought that the group of people at Andak could provide a microcosm of Cardassian society and the debates that were going on about Cardassia's future, so several of the characters act as mouthpieces for the various points of view on where Cardassia should go next (but not so much that they're ciphers, I hope). Tela Maleren is the voice of the old Cardassia who regrets the need for change, but recognizes that it's inevitable in the situation Cardassia now faces. Marco suggested that I include a character who was a member of the Oralian Way; this was Feric. It's interesting that the voices speaking up in favor of tolerance and moderation in the book are often spiritual ones, like Yevir or Feric. The hardliners are people like Korven or Entor, who don't want anything to change on Cardassia—even though the old way of doing things has brought Cardassia to ruin. Oh, and then there are the shadowy figures that meet at the start and at the end, trying to manipulate events—I think they're very invested in the old Cardassia and the power that they had then. (I call them the Gentlemen, and they're my homage to John Le Carré. Is it obvious that I'm a bit of a fan of John Le Carré . . . ? At the end of *The Lotus Flower*, the Gentlemen hold a meeting at a place very much like Primrose Hill—a spot in north London where all good spies meet up with each other!) The other big theme of the book was how Cardassia would get democracy to work under duress, and when there are powerful elements that want it to fail, and who are prepared to use violence to make it fail. Jartek is someone who has all the appearance of doing things the 'new way,' but is really carrying out business as usual. Garak, more than anyone in the book, understands that Cardassia has to change in order to survive—and, even then, while Garak doesn't do anything illegal to get the results that he wants, he does rely on past, immoral actions (the control he has over Korven as a result of having interrogated him in the past). That's another kind of question that I like exploring in fiction: what effects past choices have on people, and how past choices catch up with them, or how they can't escape the consequences. And, of course, Cardassia's story at this point is all about its changing relationship to the past, and the consequences of its history. It was impossible not to be drawing comparisons with the situation in Iraq but I hope that I wasn't too heavy-handed in that. I tend, actually, to think of post-war Cardassia as being much more like post-war Germany. The story itself took about eight-to-ten weeks to write. In terms of the nitty-gritty, the way I write is to set myself a daily word-count, and stick to that. (And I don't get to leave the computer until I hit that target! Sometimes this means I end up with a free afternoon, sometimes this means I don't get to bed very early!) I broke down the outline into chapters; each chapter ended up as a distinct scene (except for the chapter where the various threads of the narrative draw together); I think this suited the fast pace of the story. Keiko turned out to be the biggest surprise for me while I was writing. I think, in the show, we most often see Keiko through Miles's eyes and,

while Miles loves her a lot, we don't get on with the ones we love *all* the time! Keiko is a smart, dedicated, and hardworking woman, obviously very good at her job, and I think she finds Miles completely exasperating on occasion. I got a great deal out of writing her parts of the book—about her hopes for the project, about her fear for the dangerous situation in which she was putting her children, and about trying to square these domestic responsibilities with her belief that she and the project can do some genuine and far-reaching good on Cardassia. By far the hardest thing about the story was coming up with a good title. I had a working title, 'Regeneration,' but it wasn't great—a bit bland and uninspiring. Not having a title was very unusual for me—the title is usually one of the first things I have when I'm writing, because it sums up the main themes and images of the story, and it's something I can come back to while I'm writing to help me focus if the story starts to get too chaotic in my mind. I didn't have a title until the first draft of the story was written: My other half read the draft, and suggested *The Lotus Flower*. It was perfect: It reflected all the business about agricultural policy that forms the backdrop (and that acts as a metaphor for the changes and regrowth taking place on Cardassia), it put Keiko at the heart of the narrative, and it symbolized the theme of (loss of) innocence that was such a big part of the story."

PARADIGM
HEATHER JARMAN

Ensign Shar ch'Thane is forced to return to his home to confront his family who have practically disowned him. Joined by Prynn, who starts to develop romantic feelings for him, Shar must confront his own attraction to Prynn while setting right the choices he has made. Both stories give tremendous insight into two familiar yet unfamiliar societies.

Heather reflected on her Andor contribution. "*Paradigm* is the most personal story I've written though why that is precisely, I can't say. It is a love story about Shar and Prynn, about Shar and his people, about Shar and his family, and about a proud people who love their history and are willing to go to terrifying lengths to insure their survival. It is the story of someone whose choices have taken him outside the mainstream of his culture, but in a peculiar way—he is more orthodox and faithful to his way of life than many of his peers. It is a story of reconciliation, heartbreak, redemption, and lessons in tolerance, the dangers of being judgmental, and rushing to conclusions. I suppose *Paradigm* is personal because I didn't hold back emotionally in writing it. I poured a lot of my life experiences into the story. I grew up in and still belong to a, for lack of a better word, orthodox, traditional religious community. Trying to define my individuality within the parameters of that community has presented challenges over the years. I've finally made peace with it as I'm pushing forty! So I under-stood Shar's issues—how to belong, yet be self-determined; how to show respect for tradition and history, yet recognize that you can't live in the past. *Paradigm* isn't a simple story, there are a lot of shades of gray in the choices the characters make. I wanted to give *Star Trek* readers a story that challenged their assumptions. I find it amusing when people say the ending was predictable because I had no idea how the book was going to end when I started writing it. About halfway through the writing process, I deviated from the original outline and I didn't look back. I discovered a walk-on character in chapter two that suddenly started talking to Shar, Prynn, and the others. Her cameo appearance allowed me to show the readers how Andorian *zhaveys* feed and care for their young. That was supposed to be all she did. Imagine my shock when her bondmates turned out to be involved in Vretha's kidnapping. I was even more taken back when I realized that she would be Thriss's replacement in Shar's bond. Originally, Shar's new bondmate was going to be an Andorian Starfleet officer who served on Vretha's security detail. I realized, though, that with Shar's evolving relationship with Prynn, how he would bring a new *zhen* into his bond couldn't be as straightforward as *chan* meets *zhen*, *chan* quarrels with *zhen*, like something out of a Hepburn/Tracy movie, *chan* and *zhen* go their separate ways until fate steps in and brings *chan* and *zhen* together. Prynn and Shar needed to develop a legitimate emotional connection. If Shar were courting a new *zhen*, anything he had with Prynn would seem disingenuous and I wanted Shar and Prynn's romance to be genuine young love."

Heather continued, "People who've read

Paradigm need to realize that Shar isn't in love with his new bondmate—Thia is fulfilling a role that her culture has trained her for. For Shar, he's looking for a chance to redeem something from the ashes of the mess he made with Thriss, Anichent, and Dizhei. Unfortunately for Prynn, Shar's timing means that she has to put her relationship with him on the shelf until he's fulfilled his obligation to Andor. I'm glad that Shar was able to fulfill his Andorian destiny on his own terms—I'm sorry, though, that Prynn has to suffer as a result. Developing Prynn was one of the best parts of this project; I hope she's a character that other writers will continue to explore and expand on. I also liked having her interact with Phillipa, a character who is closer to my own age and life experiences. At times, the interactions between the two women were like my younger self having a conversation with my older self."

WORLDS OF DEEP SPACE NINE, Volume Two

FEBRUARY 2005   (380PP)

TRILL

UNJOINED
ANDY MANGELS AND MICHAEL A. MARTIN

On the planet Trill, civil unrest is brewing, and Ezri and Bashir head to Trill to help deal with the unrest. The solution lies in Trill's past. Ezri will risk her life to uncover the answers that not everyone will want to hear.

In terms of "Unjoined," Mike commented, "The idea behind the entire *Worlds of DS9* series is to present these places (Trill, Andor, Cardassia, et al) with a degree of detail and reality never seen before—without delivering a boring Fodor's-style travelogue. That was our guiding principle with the Trill story."

Andy continued, "We had one major assignment from Marco with the Trill story, which was to establish how and what the connection between the parasites and the symbionts were. Beyond that, we got to choose which characters to use, how we would develop things, and what the result would be. We got to play a lot with what exactly Trill's secrecy had already cost them, and what it would in the future, as well as what the elements of Bashir and Ezri Dax's relationship was really founded upon. We also got to revisit the aftermath of events from *Mission: Gamma* and *Unity*, and even reintroduce readers to Ranul Keru, several years after his appearance in *Rogue*."

Andy remarked, "There were a lot of shocking elements we dealt with in the novel, and that kind of upheaval was a lot of fun to write: the resolution of Ezri and Julian's relationship; the truth about how the parasites were really created; the hidden past of Trill; the social upheaval and rioting between the joined and unjoined and its eventual consequences. It was thrilling and scary to write some of these sequences. Trying to make terrorist bombers into sympathetic characters, when the authors and readers are living in the post-9/11 world, was touchy. Figuring out how and why Dax and Bashir both did and didn't work as a couple—and knowing that polarized fans would both love and hate the resolution—presented another challenge. Of all of our books, this one is definitely the most action-packed and grittiest, with lots of danger, violence, consequences, and intrigue."

BAJOR

FRAGMENTS AND OMENS
J. Noah Kym

On the planet Bajor, Ben Sisko is enjoying life with Kassidy and his new child. The leaders of the planet are torn and it appears to be escalating. Joining the Federation shouldn't be so painful. Then Sisko has a horrific vision of the future. . . .

Regarding his Bajor contribution, J. Noah Kym remarked, "I guess I was indoctrinated back in the 70s, when the original series was in syndication. I don't think a day went by while I was growing up when I didn't watch an episode. A lot of my friends who are *Star Trek* fans got hooked the same way. I think some of us who came to know it under those circumstances eventually started craving new adventures. (After all, seventy-nine episodes only goes so far.) I suppose that's a big reason why *Star Trek* books really took off during that time. I think I eventually started to think of them as a natural extension of the TV show. It was the same for me during the 80s, the 90s, and into the new century. So when the opportunity came to write a prose *Star Trek* adventure, it felt completely natural to me."

Noah continued, "My editor, Marco Palmieri, approached me about doing a Bajor story for his *Worlds of Deep Space Nine* miniseries, which was to be part of the novel line he had developed to continue DS9's adventures from the TV show. I had already been enjoying the direction he'd taken with DS9 in the books, and the idea of doing the first story to follow up on Bajor's admission to the Federation (in *Unity*) was too intriguing to resist. We discussed it at length, exchanging ideas, going over the plot points he wanted me to cover in order to move the Big Continuing Story along, and we talked about the themes we thought the Bajor story ought to have. I remember we talked a lot about the story in terms of relationships and destiny, and those became the novel's two through-lines. We had all these different relationships in different stages, and they were all connected to the larger relationship of Bajor and the Federation. We were also exploring the idea of fate, and whether or not there are signs of a larger pattern to be perceived from what's happening around us. These have always been very powerful themes for *Deep Space Nine*, and it's partly from them that *Fragments and Omens* got its title. The writing was challenging at first. The ideas seemed sound enough and were exciting to me, but the execution was proving to be a little daunting. My good friends Heather Jarman and Jeffrey Lang, who had each already worked on some of DS9's continuing adventures, gave me some much-needed perspective. Once I started to see *Fragments and Omens* as a mosaic of little stories that made one big story (which was itself just one small part of an even bigger story), I started to fully appreciate just what I'd become a part of, and I really got into it. As a fan, it was especially fun to be the one who got to marry off Jake, to show Sisko being a dad to his new daughter, to offer a shadowy glimpse of the major new villain who is eventually revealed in David Mack's book *Warpath*, and to be the first author *ever* to have Kira say, 'This is Captain Kira Nerys of the *U.S.S. Defiant*, representing the United Federation of Planets.' That was just too cool."

WORLD OF DEEP SPACE NINE, Volume Three

FEBRUARY 2005   (346PP)

FERENGINAR

SATISFACTION IS NOT GUARANTEED
KEITH R. A. DeCANDIDO

A scandal threatens Rom's tenure as Grand Nagus, and Quark knows it is a setup. Now if he can only prove it. To make it more difficult, Rom's adversaries make Quark a tempting offer.

Keith commented, "I really wanted to do this because I've done a lot of stuff with Klingons. My book in *The Lost Era* had a lot of Klingon stuff in it. I write the Klingon series, *I.K.S. Gorkon*, and I wrote *Diplomatic Implausibility*. So there are many that think of me as the Klingon guy and what better way to fight that stereotype than to do the species that is 180 degrees from the Klingons—the Ferengi. The idea for the story actually came to me while I was writing *Demons of Air and Darkness*. There was a conversation Gaila and Quark had about the troubles Rom would be having as Grand Nagus—somebody who basically is not in the political mainstream of Ferengi society, being asked to enact very major reforms that Zek would have an easy time putting through because he had the weight of his history of Grand Nagus behind him. Rom would have a much harder time of it and I wanted to deal with that. I explored that in a little more depth and get a good look at what life was like on Ferenginar. And it was a lot of fun. A lot of it was building on what was established in 'Ferengi Love Songs' and 'Family Business' and a bunch of other episodes that showed life on Ferenginar all the way up to the 'Dogs of War' and God help us, 'Profit and Lace.' I had to [do this so] that Zek and Brunt and the Nagushood, and Isha's reforms were all a major part of that. The story was naturally titled after one of the Rules of Acquisition, 'Satisfaction is not Guaranteed,' which is rule number nineteen. Each chapter heading also has a rule of acquisition as its title. I think there's quite a few new Rules of Acquisition, and I used ones that other novelists had coined, too. We're trying to keep very close track to make sure we don't duplicate them, but the rules are fun. I also got to deal with Nog who's one of my favorite characters on DS9. I enjoyed writing him immensely in *Demons* and also an *S.C.E.* book that I called *Cold Fusion*. So that was the goal with Ferenginar, to show Ferengi life. Deal with some comparisons. Quark is so much fun to write."

THE DOMINION

OLYMPUS DESCENDING
David R. George III

Odo discovers the true motivation behind the Dominion sending out the hundred infant changelings. As Odo's beliefs are shattered, in the Alpha Quadrant the Jem'Hadar Taran'atar begins to question his place in the universe.

David remarked, "The only guidelines I was given were that the story should include Odo, and perhaps Weyoun. As Marco and I discussed the project, he also suggested that I might consider including Taran'atar and the female changeling, which I thought was a phenomenal idea. Given all of that, I cast about for my theme, which is the point from which I like to begin my writing. I settled on the meaning of God in people's lives, something in step with themes we'd seen in the show, but of course, I wanted to stand those ideas on their heads, and so I applied them not to the Bajorans, but to the Founders. In my outline for *Olympus Descending*, I actually proposed several profound revelations about the Founders, as well as a couple of significant plot twists in the ongoing DS9 tale. I have to give a great deal of credit to Paula Block, of Paramount licensing, whose job it is to vet and approve *Star Trek* literature. Although she and editor Marco Palmieri had some concerns about what I'd proposed, they both agreed to let me run with it, and they ultimately approved the end result. Writing the book, though, was a difficult process, far more difficult than all of my other novels, despite

Olympus being much shorter. One of the primary reasons for this was the nature of the Great Link and how they communicated. According to the show, the link is not about an exchange of ideas, and they didn't really communicate in words. Well, that makes my job kind of tough, since I do communicate in words, as do readers. Wading through the scenes in which Founders communicated was therefore quite cumbersome and slow."

WARPATH
David Mack

APRIL 2006 (338PP)

After the events chronicled in *Olympus Descending,* Taran'atar finds himself on the run and able to trust no one. Stealing a shuttle, he tries to outrun his pursuers in the *Defiant.* In his mind, he has no explanation for his actions and he knows that he has forever lost favor with Odo and the Founders, but he can't stop the compulsion he feels. Meanwhile, a mortally

wounded Kira experiences a vision from the Prophets.

David remarked, "*Warpath* was conceived of as the logical continuation of the events depicted in David R. George III's story *Olympus Descending,* which ends one of its storylines on a shocking cliffhanger: the mortal wounding of Captain Kira Nerys by Taran'atar, who goes on the run. Talk about a tough act to follow! At around the time that Marco Palmieri was preparing that story for press, he contacted me and invited me to write the next novel in the series. So many story threads and character arcs that the series had set in motion were intended to be revealed in this book, and I realized that, while it was going to be a lot of fun, it was also going to be a tremendous responsibility. A lot of other authors have preceded me in this series, all of them of the highest caliber, and it was vital that my work rise to meet the standards that they and Marco had set for the postfinale *Deep Space Nine* novels. So, as I developed the story with Marco, I saw certain long-standing story arcs begin to coalesce, and I saw the opportunity to effect some significant growth in certain relationships and set in motion a whole new set of storylines that could help continue to propel future installments of the *Deep Space Nine* literary saga."

Reflecting on the specific character arcs of *Warpath,* David singled out the Elias Vaughn—Prynn Tenmei dynamic as being central to the story. "Although Vaughn and Tenmei took a significant step toward reconciliation at the end of *Unity,* by S. D. Perry, I felt that it would be too easy to let that one gesture heal all the lingering hurt and resentment of their tortured familial relationship. It's good that Vaughn was ready to set aside his pride and confront her, and it's good that she was able to put aside her anger long enough to consider accepting the olive branch he'd offered her. But in my opinion they still had much more work to do before they could put the past behind them and start again. The heart of their story is about the two of them realizing—and demonstrating—that they are literally willing to die for one another."

The inner struggle of Taran'atar also figured prominently in the larger themes of the novel. "When Marco and I first discussed what had driven Taran'atar to his violent rampage at the end of *Olympus Descending*, Marco had already planted the seeds for the mind-control storyline. 'Think of the *Manchurian Candidate*,' he'd told me when I first started planning the story. At first, I was worried that depriving Taran'atar of free will might undermine his character, but then Marco pointed out that, supposedly, the Jem'Hadar don't have the luxury of free will to begin with. They're slaves of the Founders, bound to their will, genetically designed to accept the Founders' absolute divine authority. It would actually have been a betrayal of character to let him simply defy their will because of stress; instead, by placing him in thrall to a new "god," he gets a new perspective on the life he has lived; he is forced to see that being enslaved by the new god is not all that different from being controlled by the Founders. His breakthrough moment in *Warpath* isn't about him breaking free of the will of others, but rather just being able to admit that he is a slave. That bit of self-knowledge is just the first step on his road to personal growth, though where that road might lead at this point is extremely uncertain."

Another character who goes on a journey of self-discovery is Kira. "Even though Captain Kira spends most of *Warpath* comatose," David explained, "she has one of the key storylines in the book. It's like a *pagh'tem'far*, a vision in which Kira finds herself with the Prophets in the Celestial Temple, trying to unravel their riddles and prophecies. Transposed into another time, another life, Kira endures a medieval-style adventure that serves as a foreshadowing of her future character arc in the post-finale *Deep Space Nine* books, and also for major upcoming storylines. Much of the inspiration for this part of *Warpath* came from my friend Keith DeCandido's story 'Horn and Ivory,' in the book *Gateways: What Lay Beyond*. It was a lot of fun to put aside all the technological gizmos and write action sequences that were so grounded in the rawness of physical violence."

David added, "On many levels, I am very happy with the work that has taken shape in the manuscript of *Warpath*. I feel like I'm starting to achieve a synthesis of the muscular prose I've used for my action-oriented tales—such as *Failsafe* (S.C.E. #40), or the TNG novels *A Time to Kill* and *A Time to Heal*—with the more introspective tones of my first novel, S.C.E. *Wildfire*. Thanks to the consistently astute input I receive from Marco, and from my wife Kara, and from other *Star Trek* authors such as Keith R. A. DeCandido, Dayton Ward, and Kevin Dilmore, I feel like *Warpath* is one of my best works so far."

STAR TREK: VOYAGER NUMBERED NOVELS

1

CARETAKER

L.A. Graf

(SEE SECTION 10: NOVELIZATIONS)

2

THE ESCAPE

Dean Wesley Smith and Kristine Kathryn Rusch

MAY 1995   (244pp)

Investigating a desert planet with a huge graveyard of space-ships, B'Elanna, Harry, and Neelix

vanish while inside one of the vessels. As *Voyager* tries to discover their whereabouts, the three of them find themselves very far from home, with no chance of making it back.

Dean remembers this novel being difficult to write. "I think we got lucky getting even close to right, considering we finished the book months ahead of the first show. Somehow, from the scripts and a thirty-second clip, plus some still photos, we wrote the characters. Just lucky. Guess that's why we also did the first original *Enterprise* book (*By the Book*), because we hit *Voyager* ahead of time."

#3

RAGNAROK

Nathan Archer

JULY 1995 (277 PP)

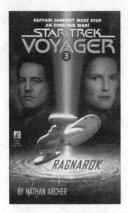

The *Voyager* crew stumbles into the middle of a millennia-long battle between the Hachai and the P'nir. Janeway forces herself on the warring races as a peace negotiator and madness ensues!

Nathan commented, "I liked working with John Ordover, I liked the money—writing *Star Trek* novels was fun and profitable. I wanted to do more. *Voyager* was coming up. I don't remember whether I called Ordover or he called me, but we both liked the idea of me doing one of the first few *Voyager* books and this time he promised not to reschedule it if I broke my hand again. We talked about what sort of story he'd like, and he pointed out that one advantage the books have over the TV show is that the special effects budget is unlimited; with a couple of sentences I could do stuff that would cost a fortune in those pre-CGI days. The idea of continuing the Norse theme for the title was mentioned, I thought of Ragnarok, and hey, there you go—a gigantic, civilization-destroying battle that *Voyager* needs to get through. . . . (Incidentally, I also plotted an original series novel, *Yggdrasil*, and a TNG novel, *Valkyrie*, but those never got written.) The writing and publishing were fairly uneventful. Using the First Federation vessel from 'The Corbomite Maneuver' was John's suggestion, I believe; I know he liked the idea. The writing went very slowly at first; I didn't have a feel for the characters. Whoever wrote the *Voyager* bible was nowhere near as good at character descriptions as whoever wrote the DS9 bible. Then the pilot aired, and everything fell into place once I'd seen the faces and heard the voices. Kes, in particular, was nothing like what I'd imagined from the bible. I finished the novel very quickly once I had that roadblock removed, and everything went smoothly from there."

4

VIOLATIONS
SUSAN WRIGHT

SEPTEMBER 1995   (279PP)

While attempting to discover wormholes, the crew of *Voyager* runs across a consortium of planets called the Cartel. Discovering a ship willing to trade supplies for an anomaly map, the aliens board only to render everyone unconscious. Upon awakening, Janeway and her compatriots discover a missing computer core. The novel takes place before the studio decision to not give the Doctor a name, so "Doc Zimmerman" experiences the computer fritzes.

Susan said, "This was only the fourth *Voyager* book, so I had to write it based on the bible for the television series. I only got to see three episodes before the manuscript was due. That was a challenge. Since the characters were not developed, some interesting contradictions sneaked in. For example, I was told by Para-

mount to call the emergency medical hologram 'Dr. Zimmerman,' but they eventually decided against naming the doctor."

5

INCIDENT AT ARBUK
JOHN GREGORY BETANCOURT

NOVEMBER 1995   (214PP)

The *Voyager* crew stumbles upon a super weapon capable of destroying the vessel like pudding in a blender. Nearby, a shuttle with a mysterious passenger needs rescuing. Soon, the ship from the Alpha Quadrant finds itself surrounded by warships that all want to seize the weapon for themselves. The author's name is misspelled on the front cover.

John commented, "I like traditional 'hard' science fiction, and *Incident at Arbuk* was an attempt to tell such a story within the *Star Trek* universe — in this case, a puzzling large artifact that everyone assumes to be a weapon because its power is discovered. Everyone wants it. And it offers a possible way home for *Voyager*. Basically, it's a problem-solving story. Its one flaw is that it was written before the series aired, based on scripts, so I had little idea of how the characters would interact with one another."

6

THE MURDERED SUN

CHRISTIE GOLDEN

FEBRUARY 1996   **(277PP)**

Neelix gives good sound advice and is promptly ignored by Janeway. The discovery of a wormhole inspires the crew, but to verify where the portal leads, *Voyager* must get involved in a war. Will the wormhole lead to the Alpha Quadrant, or is Janeway going to anger hostile aliens and destroy *Voyager*?

Christie Golden was a fan of the original series since fifth grade. She said, "My best friend Debbie was supposed to get together with me for a play date, but reneged, saying she wanted to stay inside and watch this show called *Star Trek*. I was pretty upset! So I decided I needed to watch this show, to find out what was so great

that Debbie couldn't play with me. Well, I was hooked. I even remember the episode—'Operation: Annihilate!' After that, I became obsessive about it, as I became obsessive about everything I was interested in, and started furtively writing scripts during math class. So while I didn't start doing *Trek* until my fifth novel, when my agent suggested it, I certainly jumped at the chance."

Murdered Sun was Christie's first *Trek* novel. She said, "Astute followers of my work will note that I have always particularly enjoyed working with Paris and Chakotay, and it started here. It was fun having Paris overcome a prejudice against reptiles, and enjoyable creating a culture that Chakotay related to."

Contemplating further, Christie said, "There's a line in there in which Chakotay sums up how I feel about things—I don't remember the exact line, but it's something about how one can understand that the moon is a hunk of rock caught in Earth's orbit and yet it can still be quite beautiful and magical. Science and religion/spirituality don't have to be opposed."

7

GHOST OF A CHANCE

MARK A. GARLAND AND CHARLES G. MCGRAW

APRIL 1996 (276PP)

A *Voyager* is damaged by a surprise encounter with a dwarf star and needs repair. While investigating the planet Drenar Four, another starship enters orbit, its crew promising to help with repairs. At the same time, several members of the crew, including Janeway and Chakotay, begin to experience visions of what seem to be ghosts.

Mark reflected, "This was an idea that had been brewing in the back of my mind for some time, and when the possibility of doing a *Star Trek* novel came along, the two leaped at one another. I took it to Chuck, and the more we talked, the better it got, which is always how it is with a truly good, or workable, or worthwhile idea. It tends to build out nicely. And frankly, there is just so much cool stuff—environment and character stuff—in something like *Voyager* that we sort of had to run to keep up with our-

selves while developing this thing. As for collaborating, when we work together on something, it's usually an idea we develop together, then one or the other of us—in this case, me—roughs in a draft of the story, communicating a great deal along the way and handing off parts that the other can do better. After that, the other one—Chuck, in this case—rewrites, with the same level of communication. Then it goes back and forth another time or two."

Mark commented on the current state of *Star Trek* on the airwaves. "It is my most sincere hope that [the studio] can somehow stop missing so many opportunities and turn this thing around. Maybe saying, '*Trek* is life' is a bit over the top, but they should be thinking that way just the same. The strength of *Trek* has always been a combination of its magnificence and it's consistency—people don't give up on *Trek*, really, it's often more the other way around, I think. There should be, I think, a *Star Trek* feature film every Christmas, reliable as can be. This thing is bigger than *Lord of the Rings*, *Star Wars*, *Harry Potter* and things like *Alien* all put together. Those who breathe life into *Trek*, I think, need to believe that. It's bigger than the UPN network, which probably hurt *Trek* more than it helped; it's bigger than the file budget for next year, and so on. Or at least it can be. Everyone expected spin-offs along the way, but there weren't any. If *Trek*'s creators don't follow that ideal, fans won't either."

8

CYBERSONG

S. N. Lewitt

JUNE 1996   (277PP)

An alien artifact emits an unusual signal that lures *Voyager* into its lair. At first, the vessel seems abandoned, but flickering shadows contradict that hypothesis. Now the computers cannot be trusted, and the crew begins to feel withdrawn and isolated. Will Janeway be able to solve the mystery and possibly use the enigmatic technology to make it home?

During the period when John Ordover was looking at professionally-published science fiction authors for story ideas, he offered Shariann a contract. "The major reason I wanted to write a *Voyager* book was because of a Native American character and a biocomputer. I've written biocomputers a number of times and have even been labeled (inaccurately) a 'cyberpunk' because of that. I particularly enjoy playing with this extremely 'other' life form because it raises so many issues. The idea for the story came from the fact that the computer on *Voyager* was a biocomputer. How sentient is it? How did that open other inquiries? Because *Voyager* hadn't aired at the point I was writing, there were things I wanted to do that I couldn't. The show has to set the parameters and the books have to work within them, so the fact that no one had written any episodes that explored the identity of the computer meant that I couldn't go in and establish those boundaries. That was somewhat frustrating. Likewise, the characters as individuals and their relationships with each other hadn't had a season to develop at that point, so again, what I could do was somewhat limited. Otherwise it was very straightforward."

9

THE FINAL FURY
(INVASION! Book Four)
Dafydd ab Hugh
(SEE SECTION 12: MINISERIES)

1 0

BLESS THE BEASTS

KAREN HABER

DECEMBER 1996   (274PP)

Voyager desperately needs engineering repairs, so the crew heads to the planet Sardalia. The inhabitants seem extra friendly and willing to help. While B'Elanna frustrates herself with the incompetent help from the Sardalians, the rest of the crew enjoys shore leave. Of course, a deadly secret hides in the shadows and just as Janeway starts to suspect something amiss, Paris and Kim vanish.

Karen, wife of Science Fiction author Robert Silverberg, was hooked the day the first episode of *Star Trek* aired. "I was eleven years old, an avid science fiction reader, and I watched *Star Trek*'s debut on a black-and-white television set. Those were primitive times. I think I watched the last season in color after my family upgraded the set. Until then I didn't realize that Mr. Spock was sort of greenish."

She remembers how she came to write a novel set in the *Voyager* universe. "I had been writing and editing science fiction for several years and had several novels under my belt when *Voyager* premiered. I thought the show presented interesting story-telling possibilities. The show revisited the classic *Trek* notion of wandering in the starry wilderness of space while attempting to integrate some more contemporary social notions into the mix. I had high hopes for the show—although I don't feel that it ever realized its potential. An additional motivation for me to write a *Star Trek* book was the fact that my father had just died. He had turned me on to science fiction, and I wanted to do the book for him. It was a good place to channel my grief. I had been playing with a story idea involving sentient animals at risk on their homeworld that are saved by the intervention of intruders/visitors. By adding the *Voyager* framework with its Prime Directive conundrum, I had a nice little puzzle to solve. The *Star Trek* universe was a comfortable place to work in and I especially liked the notion of there being a young untested crew coming together under a female captain and encountering moral ambiguities as they try to cope with the problems of the people—and animals—on this new planet."

Karen encountered difficulty regarding what was and wasn't allowed in the *Star Trek* universe and regarding conflict between characters. "It was frowned upon." Other than that, she enjoyed her solo adventure in the *Trek* universe. "I think *Star Trek* was born in an era of national enthusiasm for both scientific discovery and space exploration. I'm very nostalgic for that kind of energy and interest. I miss the space program. I think it was one of the best things the United States ever did. We should go back to the Moon. And beyond."

1 1

THE GARDEN
MELISSA SCOTT

FEBRUARY 1997   (278PP)

The crew begins to show signs of developing scurvy, a disease resulting from the lack of vitamin C. The food from their last mission appears to take necessary nutrients and block the absorption of them into a human's bloodstream. As everyone on board begins to rapidly deteriorate, the vessel arrives at the home of the Kirse, a reclusive race who appear to have an abundance of supplies that could cure the crew. But at what price?

Melissa remembers writing this novel well. "*The Garden* was much more difficult [than *Proud Helios*], as I started working on it well before the series actually aired. While I had seen some of the actors before, there was a lot I didn't know, so all I really had to work with

were a handful of scripts. Not something I'd like to do again! Plus the concept of the series changed substantially in the period between my turning in the novel and the book's appearing in stores. I'd been warned that it might, and tried to keep the story as self-contained as possible, but it was a tough assignment."

1 2

CHRYSALIS
DAVID NIALL WILSON

MARCH 1997   (279PP)

Neelix knows of a planet that has an abundance of Blort roots, which can supplement the ship's dwindling food supply. When Janeway and her crew land on the planet, they discover ruins of an ancient culture. The current inhabitants consider the area sacred, but are willing to let the crew take what they need. One by one, the crew succumbs to deep comas, and Neelix is not to blame!

When asked about writing his novel, David remarked, "I was in the right place at the right time. When they determined that they were going to start doing the *Voyager* novels, I was on a bulletin board system with John Ordover, both of us in SFWA, and he announced on a private board that they were taking synopses for novels. I wrote back and forth with John, got the bibles and the material, and came up with a few ideas, one of which he liked. The idea for *Chrysalis* is owed in part to my good friend and fellow author John B. Rosenman, who wrote a story titled 'No Dominion.' He allowed me to use his aliens from that story—or a modified version of them—as the basis for my novel, and from that I built *Chrysalis*. The process of writing and publishing was unique. I submitted an idea, it was approved at Pocket, had to be approved by Paramount, then came back. Then the same process was followed with the novel itself, prior to the final revisions. I wrote it on a U.S. Navy ship (the *U.S.S. Bainbridge*—not the *Enterprise*) in spare hours and when on duty late at night. It was a little spooky, really, because by the time I wrote it I'd been watching *Voyager* for some time, and I could almost hear the characters speaking in my head."

1 3

THE BLACK SHORE
GREG COX

MAY 1997   (278PP)

Weary for shore leave, the *Voyager* crew stumbles across a potential paradise in the midst of a supposed desolate area of space. The people of the planet seem gracious and willing to have visitors. With the beautiful beaches, elegant people, and delicious food the crew willingly embraces their new vacation spot. Kes is the first to experience terrifying psychic visions that appear to undermine their hosts' hospitality. Then Chakotay's spirit guide tries to eat him. Something surprising lurks on the planet and the pursuit of the truth threatens all of them.

Greg remarked, "After two collaborations, I was getting itchy to write a solo book. My opportunity arose when *Voyager* started gearing up. Much as with DS9 a year or so earlier, Ordover suddenly needed to get a whole bunch of *Voyager* novels underway, long before the show itself ever aired. 'How soon can you get me an outline, Greg?' So there I was, lying on the beach in Florida, trying to come up with an idea for a *Voyager* novel. Nothing was coming to me, so I started glancing around at my surroundings. Palm trees. Sandy beach. Sun and surf. Hmm. 'Hey, what if the *Voyager* crew visits a tropical beach planet?' As for the plot itself . . . let's not mince words. *The Black Shore* is a vampire novel, even though the V-word is never mentioned. I'm a huge vampire fan, always have been, so it was probably only a matter of time before some space vampires showed up in my *Trek* fiction. (The giveaway is the scene, near the end of the book, where B'Elanna drives a sharpened bone through a bad guy's heart!) Ordover was also encouraging us prospective *Voyager* writers to think in terms of Homer's *Odyssey* when plotting our books, and there was more than a touch of Circe and the Lotus Eaters in the basic idea here. Incidentally, my original, somewhat uninspired title for this book was *Paradise*, but it was felt that this was too close to another upcoming *Voyager* book, *The Garden*, which was going to be published around the same time. Just as well; I think *The Black Shore* is a much more evocative title."

Greg had one final memory about his book. "I read an interview with Roxann Dawson in which she mentioned that she and Jennifer Lien rarely had any scenes together, and that B'Elanna and Kes never really interacted much. This inspired me to throw the two characters together during the latter part of the book, just because it seemed like fresh territory to explore. It also gave me the chance to ask, via B'Elanna, the question we were all wondering: What in the world did Kes see in Neelix anyway?"

1 4

MAROONED
CHRISTIE GOLDEN

DECEMBER 1997   (276PP)

An invitation to a space station proves problematic for the crew. The away team gets attacked, and a space pirate abducts Kes. The ship follows the trail and soon arrives at the pirates' hideout. A rescue attempt proves costly and several crew members are marooned on a hostile world, while Kes contemplates her new life. Meanwhile, Chakotay realizes that a rescue will be impossible.

"John Ordover wanted to do 'an adventure on the planet' type of novel. I wanted to do space pirates. Throw in a damsel in distress in the form of Kes (who's actually rather capable) and voilà, a fun adventure story. Kes's short lifespan always intrigued me—how would she seem to someone who lived for thousands of years? That was at the heart of the story. And this was also the book where I was writing the early scene with Paris in a bar and I stopped writing and thought, 'I'm writing a scene about Tom Paris in an alien bar and *getting paid for it*.' Some days, life really is good!"

1 5

ECHOES

DEAN WESLEY SMITH, KRISTINE KATHRYN RUSCH, AND NINA KIRIKI HOFFMAN

JANUARY 1998 **(278PP)**

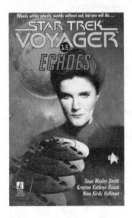

A distress call sends *Voyager* to the scene of absolute horror. At regular intervals, a pulse engulfs a region of space that appears to once have been a planet, and billions of people suddenly appear in the vacuum of space to immediately perish. Like ripples on a pond, it appears in this brief flash that other *Voyagers* and a planet exist. Determining that they are looking at parallel universes, and each pulse sends the people planet-side to the next universe, Captain Janeway must deal with her counterparts to save billions of lives.

Nina was a fan of the original series. "When I was a child (in a family of seven children), we kids were rationed to one hour of television a night. Some nights we had big arguments about which show we would watch, but we always agreed on *Star Trek* (I think it was on Thursday nights, but that was a long time ago, so I'm not sure). 'Plato's Stepchildren,' 'Amok Time,' and 'The Trouble with Tribbles' were some of my favorite episodes. The show made me think; it was topical (though I did think that its depiction of hippies was very silly); and it led me to read and love lots of other science fiction and fantasy. It had a share in shaping me into the writer I am today. It's exciting and strange to think of writing about characters created by other people. Especially entering the *Trek* canon, which is huge and has so many followers. It's almost like a dare: Can I craft a piece of history for someone else's creations, people I've actually seen in action, whose voices I've heard? Can I invent a story where these cultural icons behave in a way that will satisfy all the people who believe in them? Of course, I had the advantage of working with Dean Wesley Smith and Kristine Kathryn Rusch, who had written about *Trek* characters before, so it wasn't exactly boldly going where none of us had gone before. Still, it was an adventure for me. Kris, Dean, and I had been best friends and colleagues for years. It was really a case of them letting me join them in an endeavor they had already embarked on. As for how we came up with the idea, its kernel came from Dean, who can think mathematically in a way I can't (Kris might have this power as well, but in this case, Dean was the originator). Once he came up with the multiple parallel universe idea, we sat around and brainstormed; charts and graphs and calculations were involved. Keeping track of which chapter was taking place in which universe was tricky! We decided to play to our strengths. We did the book in four drafts. Dean was our plotter, and wrote a long plot skeleton. I added in most of the description, and Kris, who has an ear for character voice, layered in the dialogue. Dean did the final draft, melding everything together and adding in parts that were missing, but we all had a say in the finished product. When we got back notes on how to rewrite the book, Dean did the revisions, if my memory serves correctly."

Dean remembered, "Nina Kirki Hoffman is a close friend of ours, and a great writer, and John Ordover thought it would be a cool way to get her into the *Trek* program. She did the strange aliens in the book, mostly. I did all the multi-universe plotting.'

#16

SEVEN OF NINE
Christie Golden

September 1998　　(233 pp)

The crew of *Voyager* seeks passage through a hostile region of space. For a ride, aliens called Skedans offer to provide maps of the area to avoid the more turbulent spots. Shortly after the journey starts, Seven of Nine begins to have visions of large black birds. To make matters worse, her mind begins to relive memories of various individuals she had assimilated over the years when she was Borg.

Christie's memory of the book: "Fun, fun, fun . . . and hard work—a two- month deadline! I wanted to do a follow-up on 'The Raven' episode. I love doing research and especially when it yields cool stuff, such as the fact that the olfactory system is connected to the part of the brain that has memory . . . thought it would be quite torturous for Seven to have to relive the memories of all the people she had assimilated. It was both amusing and distressing to see a *Voyager* episode with almost the exact same plot line air several months after publication of the book. I guess great minds *do* think alike, though I got particularly frustrated with readers who came late to the book saying that I lacked imagination because I clearly 'stole' my idea from the TV episode. Check the dates, guys! The book came first!"

1 7

DEATH OF A NEUTRON STAR

Eric Kotani

MARCH 1999 **(263PP)**

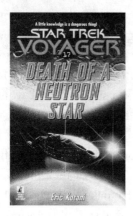

The crew rescues a couple of thieves from a stolen shuttle. Asked by the pursuers of the criminals to turn them over, Janeway refuses until she learns more. The passengers seemed relieved and claim to have been prisoners that escaped their captivity. They also believe that a nearby neutron star will soon perish and the resulting death will decimate their homeworld. Can the captain stop a natural occurrence and save an entire race?

Eric Kotani is the pseudonym for Yoji Kondo. He replied, "I am not sure if I would qualify as a fan, but have enjoyed watching *Star Trek* from time to time. There was no jump from watching the show to wanting to write a *Star Trek* novel. Before writing *Death of a Neutron Star* I had written and published several SF novels. I once gave a talk on 'Science in *Star Trek*' at the AAAS (American Association for the Advancement of Science) symposium on *Star Trek* in San Francisco. [I delivered my talk right next to the speech by Majel.] I also proposed to the IAU (International Astronomical Union) in 1994 to name a Martian Crater after Gene Roddenberry; Carl Sagan and Arthur C. Clarke graciously agreed to cosponsor my proposal. Roddenberry Crater is located at Martian Latitude −49.9 degrees and Longitude 4.5 degrees, in Quad MC26SE on Map I-1682. [Quad defines the name of the map on which it appears and Map is the U.S. Geological Survey number of that map. Its diameter is approximately 140 km, big enough for hosting a large *Star Trek* convention—wouldn't you say?] I was then President of IAU Commission on Astronomy from Space, which might have helped a little in receiving the IAU approval."

The idea for his *Voyager* novel came as follows. "I gave an astrophysical colloquium at Cornell University around 1989–1990 and on that occasion had a lunch with two Cornell astrophysicists. I was at the time completing research for a paper on a neutron star binary system; I was interested in finding out what would happen when a close neutron star binary system reached a terminal stage as the distance between the two stars shrank to a critical distance due to the dwindling of the orbit as the orbital energy is dissipated through gravitational radiation at relativistic velocities. One of the Cornell astrophysicists told me that he just sent in a paper to the *Astrophysical Journal* on the same topic. It appeared that he came to a conclusion similar to the one I was arriving at. He thought, though, I should send in my paper, too—there were aspects in my paper that he did not address in his. However, after the chat I no longer felt like sending it to the

Journal; I thought I might instead write it up as a SF story, possibly in the *Star Trek* universe. Several years later, when I had a dinner with John Ordover, he was interested in seeing this story written. Thus, *Death of a Neutron Star* came to be written. Whatever you might have thought of the story, astrophysics in the story should still be up-to-date."

Why the pseudonym? "Kotani is the name I had been—and still am—using for writing SF novels for various reasons—reasons that are probably too tedious to get into now."

18

BATTLE LINES

DAVE GALANTER AND GREG BRODEUR

MAY 1999 (264 PP)

Exploring a sector while on the way home, the ship finds itself under attack and taken into military service as part of the Edesian Fleet against the Gimlon. The new commander of *Voyager* claims that the Edesian people are fighting only to protect their existence, but Janeway is not too sure. To insure her loyalty,

several "unnecessary" crew members, including Chakotay and Tom Paris, are taken off ship until the war is over.

Dave commented, "The idea for *Battle Lines* came from the somewhat limiting premise of *Voyager*, at least for authors who couldn't make major changes. I mean, *Voyager* when really coming up against a tough situation can high tail it out of the area and run. They have no backup and no support. So I wondered what situation we could craft where the *Voyager had* to stay and work out their situation. I decided to have them drafted into an alien fleet—at the threat of their own deaths, this was as good a way as any. To make that more interesting, we split up the crew so that there was more than one problem (getting away) to deal with. We were pleased with the result. I remember one scene I'd not discussed with Greg that completely surprised him. I leave Chakotay, Paris, and a bunch of crewmen on an alien ship that's about to self-destruct. I wanted to end the chapter on an exciting note, and there was a countdown from the alien computer. Ten, nine, eight, and so on, and the chapter ends with a few seconds left. Greg read it and said, 'Wow! We didn't talk about this! How do they get out of it?' I said, 'You'll see, just wait.' Except I had no idea. I'd not considered that part yet. I had a chapter to write about Janeway and what was going on with her, which gave me some time to come up with a way out of the corner I'd written myself into. In the end, I came up with something just as I sat down to type it up. Also with this book, someone along the way didn't want me to have Chakotay kick a bad guy in his privates. I don't remember exactly why, but I changed it to having him really hurt someone's stomach, and it worked better both logically and story-wise, which is why I'm usually happy to have as many editors as I can get."

#19

CLOAK AND DAGGER
(DARK MATTERS, Book One)
CHRISTIE GOLDEN

NOVEMBER 2000 (251PP)

During the first season of *Voyager*, the crew met a Romulan scientist who promised to relay messages to their families. Unfortunately, he was from their past. Now he is communicating with *Voyager* again. The Tal'Shiar wants *Voyager* and their future technology, so they can use it to take over the Federation in the past. The Romulans have help from a mysterious alien who appears to have the capability to manipulate dark matter. . . .

#20

GHOST DANCE
(DARK MATTERS, Book Two)
CHRISTIE GOLDEN

NOVEMBER 2000 (265PP)

Chakotay and Paris have vanished into another dimension, and a mysterious woman appears in their wake. Harry Kim starts to develop feelings for her, while she copes with her disjointed culture shock. Meanwhile, the dark matter plague seems to be worsening. Can the crew overcome the effects of dark matter long enough to rescue their comrades and stop the Romulans' plans?

#21

SHADOW OF HEAVEN
(DARK MATTERS. Book Three)
CHRISTIE GOLDEN

DECEMBER 2000   (263PP)

Chakotay and Paris are hav-ing difficulty in their new environment. Lots of mistrust and a possible murder escalate hostilities between the former *Voyager* crew and the aliens from the shadow dimension. Meanwhile, Janeway continues to track the source of the dark matter and eliminate the threat of that, plus the Romulan invasion. She better hurry up, because the displaced individuals are slowly dying. . . .

Christie remembered, "John Ordover, my editor at the time, was interested in having me do a trilogy as a way for me to tell a bigger story. It was also my first crack at a trilogy and was a bit intimidating, but I really enjoyed doing it. I am very fond of this trilogy because I did a lot of research into dark matter and the shadow universe theory. I adored Jekri Kaleh, my 'Little Dagger,' and enjoyed her story arc greatly. I hope to use her again in a book one day; I've gotten very good feedback about her from readers and, hey, who doesn't like to play with Romulans? I thought 'Eye of the Needle' was one of *Voyager*'s best episodes, especially so early in the show. To me, it begged for a follow-up and I really enjoyed getting the chance to do exactly that."

STAR TREK: VOYAGER UNNUMBERED NOVELS

MOSAIC
Jeri Taylor

OCTOBER 1996   (312PP)

ORIGINALLY PUBLISHED IN HARDCOVER

Did you ever want to know the childhood of Kathryn Janeway and peer into her life to see how she became the captain of *Voyager?* Trapped in a nebula surrounded by hostile enemy vessels, the captain must use all of her abilities to escape and rescue her crewmen stranded on a hostile planet below. While pondering her moves, she reflects back on her life, from her father's involvement with the Cardassians to her enrolling in the academy under the tutelage of Admiral Paris.

Jeri commented, "I got involved with the creation of *Voyager* at the request of Rick Berman. Paramount had asked for yet another incarnation of *Star Trek*, and Rick knew it was time for a female captain. He felt my sensibilities would serve the project well."

When asked about her first *Voyager* novel, she replied, "John Ordover became editor of the *Star Trek* series, and specially asked me to write *Mosaic*. He felt a book that provided the backstory of Captain Janeway would prove very popular, as it did. I suffered the same lack of sleep (as I did writing the novelization of "Unification") during that process!"

PATHWAYS
JERI TAYLOR

AUGUST 1998 (438PP)

ORIGINALLY PUBLISHED IN HARDCOVER

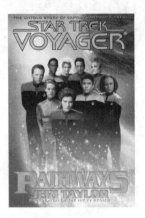

 With the exception of Janeway, the command crew find themselves taken prisoner and thrown in a prison encampment. No hope of rescue seems apparent, so to pass the time, the crew members take turns telling their life stories. As they plan escape, the individual stories reveal their inner souls to everyone, creating new perspectives for all.

"John also asked me to write *Pathways*. In fact, I hadn't finished writing *Mosaic* when he suggested the second book. 'John,' I protested, 'you haven't even seen *Mosaic* yet—what if you don't like it?' He had complete faith in me from the beginning, and with that support, I said yes and consigned myself to another year of sleeplessness!"

She confessed, "In spite of the tribulations of writing three books while holding down a full-time job, I found that I loved writing in the prose form. After the limitations and restrictions of a teleplay, it was fun to be able to let my imagination soar and to write without anyone looking over my shoulder, without worrying about fitting a 42-minute format and creating a universe that had to be built on a sound stage! It was truly liberating."

CAPTAIN PROTON: DEFENDER OF THE EARTH
(SEE SECTION 14: OTHER STAR TREK FICTION)

THE NANOTECH WAR
STEVE PIZIKS

NOVEMBER 2002 (330PP)

The crew of the *Voyager* encounters the Chiar, an alien culture that relies completely on nanotechnology. While investigating the culture, Tom Paris disappears. Trying to find him,

Janeway finds herself thwarted at every turn. Surprise! There is a sinister agenda afoot! Some of the Chiar have learned about the Borg, and believe interfacing with Borg nanoprobes will take their society to the next level of their evolution.

Steve remembered, "I was always aware of *Star Trek*, but I'd only caught a few episodes of the original series—it was canceled before I was old enough to pay attention, and where I grew up, no station ran the reruns. I liked the movies (well, not the awful ones), but didn't really identify myself as a big *Trek* fan. I suppose I became a 'real' fan when *Next Generation* came out, though even that started late for me. I was out of the country the year TNG started and got home after the second season was well underway. Thank heavens for compulsive friends who taped every episode! By the end of TNG's second season, I was a card-carrying Trekker. So becoming a *Trek* fan was a gradual process in my case. I got my start with *Trek* writing interactive fanfic, though the group I was in didn't use the characters from the shows; we created our own characters in the *Star Trek* universe. So trying a novel was a natural step forward. Once I'd sold a couple original SF novels, it suddenly occurred to me that I was 'eligible' to write *Star Trek* books. I sent my agent a proposal, and that was that!"

Regarding his novel, Steve replied, "Our modern dependence on technology rather worries me, and that's where *Nanotech War* started. I started off by creating a society that was completely dependent on nanotechnology—the ultimate tech—and seeing what would happen if I took the nanotech away. I also wanted to see more of Tom and B'Elanna as a married couple, to tell the truth. Married couples don't get much play on the show, and I wanted to explore that some more. Of course, when I brought these two elements together, Tom ended up with amnesia and I was forced to explore what attracted them to each other in the first place. Oh well. Sometimes you just have to let the story run where it will. The story was fun to write (when I wasn't banging my head against the keyboard, that is). In order to sell a *Star Trek* book, you [usually] have to have an agent. The folks over at Pocket don't read non-agented *Trek* material because they'd be avalanched with stuff if they did. I wrote a twenty-page summary of the book, and my agent sent it to the *Star Trek* editor over at Pocket Books. She liked it, and offered a contract. After I stopped doing the Author Happy Dance, I sat down and started writing the actual book. The first chapter was horrible! I didn't feel like I was getting the characters down at all. I ripped out big hunks of text and rewrote them, hated them, went back, and watched some *Voyager* episodes, tried again, banged my head on my keyboard for a while, read some of the teleplays my editor sent me, and tried again. I finally realized that I just needed to run with it and not worry so much during the first draft—just get the thing down and clean it up in the rewrites. The first chapter was awful, but something clicked when I started the second, and everything went much more smoothly. I could hear the characters speaking inside my head, and I just wrote down what they said. Once it was all done, I went back to chapter one and saw how to fix the problems. I also rewrote the ending. Seven was supposed to fix the Chiar's nanotech problem by herself, but I realized that Tom needed to be involved as well—this was *his* story, too. But I couldn't figure out how to make it work. My editor and I brainstormed on the phone—she agreed Tom needed to be there—and together we worked out how to do it. I'm glad we did, since the story came out much stronger. That was actually a little weird—I'd never worked out plot points with an editor that way before. I'd always figured it was *my* job as the writer. Once the book was done, my editor read it, asked for some revisions (which I made), and then sent it to Paramount for approval. They asked for two changes that were so tiny, I don't even remember what they were. I was really glad about that."

COHESION
(STRING THEORY, Book One)
JEFFREY LANG

JULY 2005   (366PP)

The story falls between the fourth and fifth seasons of the show. A discovery of planets in a binary system with one of the stars being a white dwarf proves to be too mysterious to pass up. With all of the lethal radiation flowing in the system, why is there a planet showing signs of life? When the Monorhans ask for help with their vessel, the *Voyager* crew starts a chain reaction of chaos.

"Heather Jarman and Kirsten Beyer wrote the plot outline for the *String Theory* trilogy with very little input from me. We three knew we were going to be cowriting the three books, but when the time for plotting came I was absorbed in another project. This wasn't a problem for me since I knew K&H had a much more in-depth knowledge of *Voyager* and had some definite ideas about what kind of story they wanted to do. I believe that the original plan was that I would do the third book, but because of various scheduling factors, I ended up with the first, which was fine with me because I really enjoy writing Seven and B'Elanna. This is all a protracted way of saying, 'The idea for *Cohesion* wasn't mine.' However, I did have a lot of input into the story details, particularly the creation of the Monorhans. In the original outline, H&K deliberately left their background, history, physiology, culture and so on, pretty vague with the idea that I would fill that in, which turned out to be one of the most satisfying aspects of the project. Also, the time/space mechanics had to be figured out, which ended up being very enjoyable, too (though frustrating at times). I really wanted the science in this book to make sense, which I think it does most of the time (barring the usual *Star Trek* handwaving)."

Jeff continued, "The writing process was much different in this one in that I had to adjust the story and characters to line up with what Kirsten was doing in Book Two (she was working on her rough draft as I was moving into draft two or three) and Heather was planning for Book Three. Most of this worked out very easily since we communicated pretty regularly via phone and e-mail. The biggest problem with my first draft was H&K had problems—very legitimate problems—with my characterization of Janeway. I had trouble getting my mind wrapped around her persona, but H&K steered me in the right direction. All in all, *Cohesion* was a lot of fun."

FUSION
(STRING THEORY, Book Two)
Kirsten Beyer

November 2005   (386pp)

An energy being similar to the Caretaker impersonates Janeway's sister and infiltrates the ship. Altering the memories of the crew, Phoebe searches for the "key" given to the captain as a thank-you gift. Meanwhile, Tuvok answers a "siren song" and travels to an alien space station. When *Voyager* arrives for the rescue, they discover that a parasitic being has infiltrated Tuvok's body and mind. Tuvok demands that he be left to die and even thwarts the doctor's attempts to save him.

When asked about writing *Star Trek*, Kirsten commented, "In the first place, I didn't know I was a writer. I started out as a dancer and realized early on that the part of dancing I loved was telling stories. I was injured at fifteen and moved into acting. I was hooked immediately. From that point on, all I wanted to do was tell stories on stage (and maybe someday on screen). By the time *Voyager* premiered I had completed my Bachelor of Arts in English and Theater and a Master of Fine Arts in acting. I was also really bored. My husband was working on a play, so I had too much time on my hands alone at night and *Voyager* started airing. I have to say . . . I didn't start watching completely out of boredom. A teacher I had just worked with at UCLA was working as a director for DS9 and mentioned she was going to direct a few of the early *Voyager* episodes, so I got to watch her work. But that went by the wayside after a couple of episodes. Then I was just watching to see what happened every week. After the first couple of episodes I had this idea for a show. I thought it was cool so I told my husband about it and he said, 'Sounds good but what are you going to do . . . write it?' Equal parts annoyed and challenged I said yes, and got to work. A few actors I knew had auditioned for the pilot of *Voyager* so they still had their sides and I was able to get my first glimpse of what a script was supposed to look like from that. It took a month or so and I had my first teleplay. What I learned from that process was that whether it was dancing, acting, or writing . . . it was all the same basic thing . . . telling stories. That was the point in my life when I understood that telling stories in any creative form was it for me. It has just sort of played out that I have had more success now as a writer, though I still work as an actor. Anyway, I didn't know about *Trek*'s open submission policy at the time. When I sent my first script to Rick Berman, I was clued in. I did two teleplays and both were rejected. So, I figured that was it, kept watching, but started writing other things. Then, early in season four an episode I will not name aired that just annoyed the crap out of me. It was so bad, it made me angry. So I wrote a letter to Jeri Taylor and told her that I was supposed to be writing for her. Much to my surprise, she wrote back and invited me in to pitch. Once I started pitching for the show (which I did through the first part of season seven) I got really serious about *Trek* and story development. I researched all I could . . . started reading the Pocket novels to make sure I wasn't repeating any developed stories . . . started looking on the Internet for other people who were talking about *Trek* (no shortage there, thank God) and found this girl writing articles for the *Starfleet Journal* Web site named Heather Jarman. I wrote a critique of one of her articles and e-mailed it to her and a friendship and writing partnership that has lasted . . . oh . . . seven years . . . was born. Heather and I collaborated on some of the stories I pitched. Then, Marco discovered her and she started writing DS9 novels for Pocket. I had actually moved on to other writing projects when Heather suggested I might talk to Pocket about writing *Voyager* fiction. I sent a packet to a nice lady named Jessica McGivney and for

several months after that we started working on what I hoped would be my first novel. Then Jessica moved on to other things and finally, at Shore Leave a couple of years ago, Heather invited me to join her and she introduced me to Marco. I told him my story, he asked to see my work and a few months later invited me to start writing for him."

She reflected on the genesis of *Fusion*. "The Tuvok arc of *Fusion* began as a story I pitched to Mike Taylor early in season five. It was called *Siren Song*. The thing was . . . I was kind of fond of the story in my secret heart of hearts and Mike just hated it. I mean, hated it. In fact, he was so adamant in his dislike of the premise and thought the idea so not *Trek* that his reaction ended our meeting. Don't know what got into me. I had certainly never behaved that way at any prior meetings (always with Bryan Fuller who was always generous with both praise and suggestions) but after listening to him rip it apart I basically told him I wasn't going to pitch to him anymore. It was clear to me that he and I weren't interested in telling or seeing the same kind of stories. Much to my surprise, his tone changed immediately. I know for a fact he realized what an ass he was being because he called me at home after the meeting to apologize for his behavior and ask me to please, please keep coming back with more ideas. I'm sure he doesn't remember any of this. I met with him again a year later and he seemed genuinely surprised when I asked him some questions borne of our first meeting. (Meeting two with Mike went much better, by the way . . . but still no sales.) Anyway, on the side, I was trying to get an agent for my screenplay work and met a guy who read the first two teleplays I did for *Voyager* and asked if I had anything more current that was science fiction for a writing sample. When faced with the prospect of doing an entirely new teleplay just for him, I decided to go back to my favorite . . . *Siren Song*. I did it. He loved it. And I was so pleased with the result that I took a chance and asked Bryan Fuller if I could meet with him again to discuss it. I pitched the story to him and he loved it. He even asked if I would have my agent submit the teleplay to Ken Biller as they were looking to fill out the writing staff for season seven. I did, but no reply. So there it sat. Cut to a year and a half ago. After meeting with Marco and submitting my writing samples to him he called and asked me to do the second novel in a *Voyager* anniversary trilogy with Heather and Jeff. I couldn't say yes fast enough. Heather and I started working on the broad scope of the story and once we had established one thing—no Borg—we moved on to trying to figure out who our 'big bad' should be. A part of our mission was clearly to take some of the consistency gaps and missed opportunities that we both saw in the series and try to reconcile them in some coherent fashion; it wasn't hard to start at the beginning. Gee . . . what do we really know about the Nacene? I mean beyond 'Caretaker' and 'Cold Fire' . . . what? Once we had settled on that, we started talking book by book. We knew early on that Book Two would be Janeway heavy, but we were looking for our Tuvok arc and Heather said . . . what about *Siren Song?* With a few tweaks, what had been my secret favorite child for so long became the core story of *Fusion*. The outlines were approved a few months later and I started writing. Getting to write it in prose form was a treat. So much of Tuvok's inner journey that couldn't be told in the teleplay became way too much fun

to play with. So at long last, and no worse for the wear, *Siren Song* became part of *Trek* history over what I am sure would still be Mike Taylor's strenuous objections. Only now it's called *Fusion*."

EVOLUTION
(STRING THEORY, Book Three)
HEATHER JARMAN

MARCH 2006   (398pp)

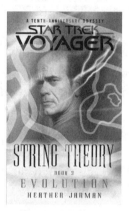

The crew of *Voyager* has to deal with change and inner conflict. Chakotay is captain now that Janeway is incapacitated. The doctor contemplates life on the planet Ocampa's past. Harry and Tom have an unexpected ally help them in their dilemma. With Tuvok as first officer and B'Elanna devastated by Tom's disappearance, can the crew in their new roles get through their latest trials?

Heather remarked, "This really begins back in *Voyager*'s fifth season when I met and became best friends with Kirsten Beyer. Our first discussion was a heated, but polite, discussion of whether or not the Janeway in 'Night' (fifth season premiere) was some kind of Janeway clone or whether she was actually Janeway, since the episode seemed to be so out of character for her. Together, we developed several stories that were pitched to *Voyager*. Our first (and favorite) was a story called *Cohesion* about Seven of Nine and B'Elanna. Once it became apparent that *Voyager* was never going to get over their infatuation with things that go boom, we gave up developing new ideas. Kirsten was busy working on screenplays and having pitch meetings. I was just . . . busy. Shortly after this time, I started swapping e-mails with Marco and was given the opportunity to write for Pocket. I promised Kirsten that I would see if Marco could find room for her on his roster at some point. After the first round of DS9 Relaunch books came out, Jeff Lang and I started working on developing proposals for the next round of DS9 novels. Marco had other ideas so he asked if we would be interested in working on a trilogy to celebrate *Voyager*'s anniversary. My immediate thought was to involve Kirsten. I introduced her to Marco. I also facilitated a writing audition and Marco decided that she passed. I knew she would. She is brilliant. My other reason for wanting to pursue this is that it brought me full circle: My *Trek* writing began with *Voyager* and it seemed appropriate to have my culminating project be for *Voyager*. The time came to develop outlines for the trilogy. Now I adore Jeff. Jeff is my honorary big brother. Jeff, however, was in the middle of some major life issues of his own as well as finishing a writing project that was giving him ten kinds of heartburn. With his blessing, Kirsten and I wrote the outlines for the books—mostly

just to get them approved. Jeff jumped in once his 'to do' list became shorter and worked the finer points of the world building and the technology. We couldn't have done it without him. He filled in all the gaps and really ran with the outline, making it his own."

Heather continued, "We had several goals with the trilogy. First was to give *Voyager* fans something to sink their teeth in. The reality is that *Voyager* is the redheaded stepchild of *Trek* fandom. It is the easiest series to kick around whenever *Trek* fans want to mock something. Being *Voyager* fans ourselves and knowing that we weren't idiots, we decided to respect the fans' intelligence and give them something juicy. Second, we had a long list of continuity bugaboos and complaints about episodes and characters that we felt were never adequately addressed. For example, why is Janeway such a nutcase at the beginning of season five? Where did B'Elanna's self-inflicted pain/suffering come from? How did Tom get into Captain Proton? Why does Seven of Nine act like she runs the ship and can tell people what to do? Don't get me started on the problems with 'Fury' (Kes' return)! As we went through our laundry list of issues, we looked for ways to 'fix' the things that bugged us. Third, we also had a list of things we never saw or never fully dealt with that we wanted to deal with because we thought it would be fun. Tom and B'Elanna's relationship went underground during Roxann Dawson's pregnancy, for example, so we got very little follow-up after episodes like 'Scientific Method.' Getting into B'Elanna's head during this timeframe was wonderful. How did Neelix feel about Kes being gone? And the chance to deal with lesser-used characters like Tuvok was a joy. All three outlines were written at the same time. The first book was loosely based on the pitch Kirsten and I developed for *Voyager, Cohesion.* The second book, Kirsten's, was based on a story and teleplay she wrote called *Siren's Song.* The third book? This is where the migraine starts. There was nothing to base it on. Just all the loose ends from Jeff and Kirsten's book. I wrote a few paragraphs that sounded like I knew what I was doing just so I could get the outline approved, then I waited for Jeff and Kirsten to finish their books. Writing a trilogy is a very get your hands dirty kind of project. If the books were stand-alone, it wouldn't be a big deal. But when you're dealing with heavy continuity and a complex, intricate plot, it becomes a nightmare. I should have known that when we had to submit a backstory outline and a 'definition of terms' as supplements to our outlines that we were being hugely ambitious with what we were tackling. Lucky me, I got the last book. Jeff is a better-known author than I am, so he got to launch the trilogy. Kirsten, being an unknown, is sandwiched in the middle. I get to bring up the rear, which, I must say, is a colossal pain. They get to break all the toys and I have to fix them. Most of the action has to be figured out day to day. I know I have to get from point A to point Z but I don't know what most of the points in between look like. I had almost a thousand pages of Jeff and Kirsten's manuscripts that I carried around in a big bin along with my *Star Trek Encyclopedia,* my *Voyager Companion,* the outlines, the glossaries and histories of this particular region of space, my Ipod and my laptop. There were copious amounts of chocolate involved, too."

Heather noted, "Worldbuilding is something of a specialty of mine, but I've never had to create a theoretical world in subspace before. I also had to create Ocampa pre-'Caretaker' and a part of the Q-Continuum that we've never seen before. One world in a book is a lot of work. Three worlds are like treading water in the ocean with sharks circling around you."

Heather remarked, "I will be forever grateful to Marco Palmieri, Jeffrey Lang, Kirsten Beyer, and Keith DeCandido who opened the doors to this universe and this opportunity to write and edit. For a person who grew up wanting to write books professionally, I've had the chance to realize my dream and that's more than many people can claim in a lifetime."

FICTION SET AFTER THE FINAL EPISODE

HOMECOMING
Christie Golden

JUNE 2003 (262PP)

The first book in the *Voyager* relaunch. The crew is finally home, and everyone assimilates to his or her new lives back on Earth. Unfortunately for them, the Borg have not been vanquished yet, and threaten them still. And why is Starfleet acting strangely toward the crew?

THE FARTHER SHORE
Christie Golden

JULY 2003 (277PP)

Admiral Janeway enlists the help of Data to represent the doctor in his legal fight, and to help the rest of the *Voyager* crew determine the cause behind the seemingly unstoppable Borg plague. Meanwhile, B'Elanna leaves her family behind to go on a quest to find her mother, who might still be alive.

When asked about how she became the author behind the *Voyager* relaunch novels, Christie answered, "It just kind of fell out that way. Once I got my feet wet with *Voyager*, I wanted to stay with *Voyager*. I got to know the characters inside and out. I enjoyed having that depth of familiarity, and my delight with the characters was rewarded with the relaunch. Others are still doing *Voyager* novels, so I'm not the sole voice, but it is wonderful to be the only person charting this territory—no surprises! Except the good kind, of course."

Christie continued, "*Homecoming* was a very controversial book, and that controversy did amazing things to sales. So many people were talking about this book and *The Farther Shore!* It was really 'please all, please none'—people had their own idea about what would happen when the crew returned home and chances are it wasn't what I had in mind (the odds of everyone thinking like me are pretty slim!). So some people could go with that, and others couldn't. The most fun thing about it was planting the seeds for other books that I plan to do later. Some of those come to fruition in the *Spirit Walk* books, others I haven't dealt with yet . . . heh heh heh. . . . Readers will see some characters introduced here that will become 'regulars' in the relaunch. Some of them they might guess, others, maybe not so much."

OLD WOUNDS
(SPIRIT WALK, Book One)
CHRISTIE GOLDEN

NOVEMBER 2004   (273PP)

Captain Chakotay of the *Voyager*, takes his new crew on a maiden voyage to help displaced colonists. An envoy to help with the transition for the settlers is Chakotay's sister, Sekaya. When *Voyager* arrives, the planet is shrouded by a mysterious storm, and the settlement appears deserted. Unfortunately for the new captain, an enemy from his past has been plotting revenge for years, and the time has come to act.

ENEMY OF MY ENEMY
(SPIRIT WALK, Book Two)
CHRISTIE GOLDEN

DECEMBER 2004   (292PP)

 Captain Chakotay and his sister are being held prisoner, and a very much alive Crell Moset plans to utilize their DNA to create a new super species. For the crew of *Voyager*, they believe Sekaya perished on the planet and Chakotay is taking the loss hard. They don't realize that their new captain is an imposter. As suspicions grow, Harry Kim turns to old friends for help.

"I think all of us connected with the *Voyager* relaunch got a very pleasant surprise when we learned how well *Homecoming* and *The Farther Shore* were doing. So the timetable for more *Voyager* relaunch novels got kicked up quite a bit. In these two books we finally have Captain Chakotay and his new crew. Some of these are familiar faces from the show—Harry Kim as chief of security, Vorik as chief engineer, for instance. Another 'familiar' character is one I created—Lyssa Campbell, who has been in every one of my *Voyager* novels. Since we never saw a regular transporter operator, I gave the job to Lyssa. She's a slender, vivacious blond woman with a great sense of humor and loves to pal around with Harry and Tom. You can imagine my pleasure when on the episode 'Eye of the Needle,' which I saw while well into my second *Trek* novel, a slender blond woman was operating the transporter! I wondered if it was pure coincidence or a nice nod from someone in casting! (Probably the former but let me have my fantasy.) Others are new, but people we have met in the previous two Relaunch novels—Dr. Jarem Kaz and Lieutenant Akolo Tare. Some folks are completely new as the Huanni counselor Astall, the first officer 'Priggy' Andrew Ellis, and our perhaps-too-focused science officer Devi Patel. And of course everyone from the show has some part to play in secondary plot lines. There's an arc that carries over from the first two books with B'Elanna and her heritage that I hope to continue in future books, and we see all our old friends in some capacity or another. I'd like this to be the template for future books—having people going their own ways, but still having stories that bring them together. One very great gift that the writers of the show gave me was an episode in the last season where Chakotay threw out the info that he had a sister. No name, no description just . . . a sister. Well. This is the sort of thing that makes novelists rub their hands with glee. I ran with that in *Homecoming*, where Chakotay returns home for a visit, and then I took the bit in my teeth with these books. Sekaya is on the cover of *Enemy of My Enemy* and she is a major player in the story. I really enjoyed her."

STAR TREK: ENTERPRISE NOVELS

BROKEN BOW

(SEE SECTION 10: NOVELIZATIONS)

BY THE BOOK

DEAN WESLEY SMITH AND KRISTINE KATHRYN RUSCH

JANUARY 2002   (252PP)

other continent, a race of spider-like creatures live isolated from the regimented Fazi. Why are the two distinct cultures living so far apart? While off duty, some of the crew take time to engage in a role-playing game created by Ensign Culter. Can the game help in establishing a successful first contact?

Dean remarked, "Kris (my wife) and I were hired to do the first original *Enterprise* novel. All we had was a short trailer and the first three scripts, so we had no idea how the characters were going to act or talk. I think we got amazingly close, considering the book was done months before the first show aired."

The crew of the NX-01 discovers the Fazi, a race that lives under stringent protocols. On an-

WHAT PRICE HONOR?
DAVE STERN

NOVEMBER 2002   (298PP)

A look into the mind of Malcolm Reed. He finds himself falling in love with one of his junior officers, Ensign Alana Hart. Before he can express how he really feels, she dies attempting to sabotage the ship. Malcolm's guilt clashes with his feelings as he attempts to figure out why Alana passed away. The story is told in flashback, with the current mission mysteriously tied into what really transpired.

Dave Stern, former *Star Trek* editor, commented, "I specifically remember not being allowed to stay up and watch the original series, one or two times. What really cemented it for me was that I grew up around New York City, so I watched it on a channel that would run it every night at six."

Dave worked with *Star Trek* prior to his editorial days at Pocket Books. "I got a job with Bantam and after working in marketing and a couple of other places I moved up to editorial and was also a science fiction fan. Bantam had *Trek* books and I was in charge of repackaging those books. Sort of writing new cover copy and helping. I left Bantam and worked freelance. Erwin Athermath, who had been my boss over at Bantam for awhile, got hired over at Pocket and I got asked to work for *Star Trek* in late 1985. I stayed at Pocket until mid-1992."

Dave continued, "I actually had no intention of doing *Star Trek* ever again. I thought I'd had my fill, but when you start writing, and particularly when you're not necessarily hitting it big, you find yourself willing to go back. I'd done some novelization work for Margaret Clark when she asked if I wanted to do an *Enterprise* book. I thought about it for two seconds and said, 'Sure.' My particular feeling about the books is they should be different than the shows, that they should offer something that the shows don't necessarily offer and it would be good to sort of go into the head of one of the supporting characters. I gotta say the show frustrates me tremendously and they have what seems to be a pretty good group of actors and some pretty good ideas for stories, but for some reason it's flat, it just sits there on the screen and nothing happens. I remember this one episode, it was something that takes over the ship, and a security guy takes one look at it and runs away. *That's just not right!*"

He commented on this book. "For someone who is really paying attention, I made the planet and several other parts reference the original series episode, 'Turnabout Intruder.'"

SURAK'S SOUL
J. M. DILLARD
MARCH 2003   **(218PP)**

DAEDALUS
DAVE STERN
DECEMBER 2003   **(326PP)**

While investigating mysterious deaths on a planet, T'Pol shoots someone in self-defense, killing that person, even though her phaser was set on stun. Reflecting on her heritage, T'Pol decides to never use a weapon again, even if it is necessary to save the life of an *Enterprise* crew member. An energy being called the Wanderer comes on board and tries to help the crew determine what killed the people on the planet.

Regarding her first *Enterprise* novel, Jeanne commented, "I wanted to write about T'Pol because I'm fascinated (sorry) by Vulcans. Once I worked out the details of the outline, the writing went fairly quickly. Again, I studied scripts and DVDs in order to get a really strong feel for the characters."

Thirteen years before Trip Tucker became the chief engineer on the warp-five vessel *Enterprise*, he helped design a warp engine with the brilliant scientist Victor Brodesser. On the evening prior to its maiden voyage, Trip discovers a major flaw in the design. Ignoring his warning, the ship launches anyway and explodes. Trip still lives with the memories and he will be forced to confront them again when the *Enterprise* suffers a surprise attack. Only he and Hoshi are able to escape in a cloaked Suliban pod. Their discoveries and how they plan to get *Enterprise* back are going to need to wait, since this is only part one.

DAEDALUS'S CHILDREN
Dave Stern

MAY 2004   (371 pp)

Captain Archer and most of the crew are trapped in a prison, contemplating escape. Trip and Hoshi are attempting to use their influence with their comrades to help find the whereabouts of *Enterprise*, so they can reunite the crew and return to Earth. Due to a spatial anomaly, the parallel universe they find themselves in is slowly killing them. With the clock ticking before their demise, can Archer and crew escape, rendezvous with Trip and Hoshi, stop the bad guys, and make it safely back to their familiar universe?

Dave commented, "That idea started from the character of Trip and the actor playing him, who became my favorite character on the show. Someone commented it was like the original series episode, 'Mirror, Mirror,' in some ways and I thought the idea of not having them real-ize they were in an alternate universe until halfway through was a good hook."

ROSETTA
Dave Stern

DECEMBER 2005   (407 pp)

The crew of the *Enterprise* encounters a vessel that fires weapons near them but doesn't actually hit the ship. Other vessels have not been so lucky. While Hoshi struggles to decipher the alien's strange language, Archer agrees to work with First Governor Maxim Sen of the Thelasian Trading Confederacy. Both Phlox and Mayweather are familiar with Sen and his evil ways and Archer promises to not fully trust the Governor. Unknown to the crew, Sen has big plans for Archer. In addition, Hoshi takes the spotlight and chronicles the beginning of the universal translator.

Dave remarked, "The germ of the idea came from Margaret Clark and I thought it was a really good idea, but the story just didn't want to go in the direction we discussed. One of the things that I decided to keep is the whole business of Hoshi being a translating specialist. The other hook is how the universal translator evolved from the thing we see in *Enterprise* to what we see in the future, and hoping to imply that Hoshi had a large part in the evolution of the device."

LAST FULL MEASURE
MICHAEL A. MARTIN AND ANDY MANGELS

MAY 2006   (334PP)

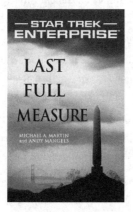

At the beginning of the third season of *Enterprise*, the ship entered Xindi space to save the planet Earth. To help battle this new and insidious threat, the military MACOs joined our Starfleet friends. Immediately, they were forced to share already cramped quarters with each other and make peace. The story takes place between the first and second episode of the season and chronicles how the two groups learn to work together.

• • •

Andy commented, "Mike did the majority of the plotting on *Last Full Measure*, working with editor Margaret Clark. It was plotted more loosely than most of our books, so that once both of us broke it all down into chapters and began writing, there was a lot of room for further character interaction and input. And because the MACOs were mostly ciphers on the show, we got to do a *lot* of character development. From the beginning, this project was intended as a MACO versus *Enterprise* crew book, and we called it 'Squids & Sharks' as a reference to the two branches of the military serving aboard the *Enterprise*. Margaret really wanted us to spotlight the differences in the way the two crews worked and interacted, and the tensions between them. Interestingly, it was the most human cast we had ever written. Even our *Roswell* books had more aliens."

"Since the story was set at a specific point in the third season, we were very structured as to what we could or couldn't do with the novel. But interestingly, since we didn't write the novel until the show itself was off the air, we were able to write a prologue and epilogue that both set the story in context and added a *very* cool surprise for *Enterprise* fans."

Mike commented, "The basic idea behind it is that there has always been tension and rivalry between sailors (squids) and marines (sharks), a phenomenon that continues aboard *Enterprise* during the show's third-season quest for the Xindi and their superweapon. The title, gleaned from Lincoln's Gettysburg Address, refers to the common devotion and sacrifice that links these two branches of the service, despite their many differences."

THE "C" WORD

One of many points of controversy surrounding *Star Trek* fiction is the question of "canon." The reason for this particular controversy, according to editor Marco Palmieri, is that very few people who argue over it really understand what the word means.

"In the context of *Star Trek,* canon refers to the body of information the show and film writers adhere to when crafting new stories. That's *all* it means. Unfortunately, the word is frequently misunderstood and misapplied as a value judgment: 'Such-and-such a story is canon to me.' Or, 'Such-and-such a story isn't part of my personal canon.' This is the wrong way to use the word. It's not subjective.

"It's also frequently and incorrectly used in place of the word 'continuity' or 'consistency.' These terms are not interchangeable.

"As the fiction is not part of the body of information the show and film writers adhere to when crafting new stories, the fiction isn't canon—although it strives to be wholly consistent with what has been presented on screen up to the moment that the text has been finalized. Sometimes, a novel or a short story may end up being contradicted by a subsequent episode or movie. Sometimes it never is. Either way, no work of professionally published *Star Trek* fiction is considered canon. No exceptions. And it shouldn't matter, because a good story is still a good story, regardless of whether or not some future *Star Trek* production eventually contradicts it in some way."

Paula Block, Director of Licensed Publishing for CBS Consumer Products and the studio's primary editorial contact in matters relating to *Star Trek* fiction, illuminated the matter even further: "Frankly, I don't really understand why there's so much confusion or controversy about canon. When I started working at Paramount in 1989, Gene Roddenberry was around to consult with, so you might say I got canon from the Great Bird's mouth. Canon is what is seen on TV and movie screens. Books aren't. End of story. Part of my job in licensing is to hold licensees like Pocket to that standard. Which is not to say that there haven't been times when canon has contradicted itself; those darn producers and scriptwriters don't always keep track of/remember/care about what's come before. So things can get confusing. But books have never been considered part of canon. Producer Jeri Taylor's books were considered quasi-canon for a while because our licensees really wanted some sort of background structure they could utilize for the *Voyager* characters. They found it difficult to accept statements like 'Well, they haven't established that on the show yet. . . .' So we (by this I mean the licensing department and the folks in Rick Berman's office, whom I periodically consulted with) let them consider Jeri's stuff 'quasi-canon' for games and things like that. It didn't seem to hurt anything. And honestly, fans take this subject far too seriously—much more seriously than the-powers-that-be do.

"Take Gene Roddenberry. Gene had a habit of 'de-canonizing' (if there is such a thing) things when he wasn't happy with them. He didn't like the way that much of the animated series turned out, so he proclaimed that it was NOT CANON. He also didn't like a lot of the movies. So he didn't consider all of them canon either. And because he had a less active role in the third season of the original series, he didn't support a lot of things that were established during that timeframe either. He was especially unhappy about the events in 'The *Enterprise* Incident' because he hated the idea that Starfleet personnel would spend their time 'sneaking around' (I heard that expression from him a lot) and carrying out spy-type missions.

"Gene's view of canon was, I think, pretty fluid. After he got TNG going, he seems to have decided some of the first two seasons of the original series wasn't canon either. I had a discussion with him once about some things he didn't like in an original series *Star Trek* manuscript that had been submitted (I have no recollection of which one it was). I couldn't understand his objections, because those elements were very clearly canon in the original series. He smiled, shrugged, and told me that although that was acceptable *back then,* he didn't think that way anymore. In fact, he now thought of TNG as canon wherever there was conflict between the two. He admitted it was revisionist thinking, but so be it.

"That's kind of like God telling you the stuff in that old bible . . . well, he's just not that into it anymore. Anyway, you can see why canon is such a difficult concept (and, from a different perspective, why the approval process for manuscripts was occasionally quite difficult for all parties involved). But I always fall back on the first and original rule (call me a traditionalist)—what you see on the big and small screens is canon and that's what I continue to hold writers to. When you stray too far away from that basic rule, you venture into the land of arbitrary decisions and personal biases—and life just isn't long enough to spend a lot of time dwelling on non-issues like that."

NOVELIZATIONS

STAR TREK: THE MOTION PICTURE
(STAR TREK #1)
GENE RODDENBERRY

DECEMBER 1979   (252PP)

 An adaptation of the first *Star Trek* feature film, by *Star Trek*'s creator.

A persistent rumor about this book is who the real author was. Many different names have been attributed to it. Editor David Hartwell, who launched the Pocket *Star Trek* line and edited the novelization, remarked, "Gene Rod-

denberry wrote the novelization for *Star Trek: The Motion Picture.*"

STAR TREK II:
THE WRATH OF KHAN
(STAR TREK #7)
VONDA N. MCINTYRE

JULY 1982   (223PP)

 An adaptation of the second *Star Trek* feature film.

The author declined to be interviewed for this book.

STAR TREK III: THE SEARCH FOR SPOCK
(STAR TREK #17)
Vonda N. McIntyre

JUNE 1984 (297 PP)

An adaptation of the third *Star Trek* feature film.

The author declined to be interviewed for this book.

STAR TREK IV: THE VOYAGE HOME
Vonda N. McIntyre

DECEMBER 1986 (274 PP)

An adaptation of the fourth *Star Trek* feature film.

The author declined to be interviewed for this book.

STAR TREK V: THE FINAL FRONTIER
J. M. Dillard

JUNE 1989 (311 PP)

 n adaptation of the fifth *Star Trek* feature film.

Jeanne spoke of her experience adapting screenplays. "Let me first give you some insight into how the novelization process of the *Star Trek* movies works. I'm sent a script, which I novelize while the movie is being filmed. So there's no movie for me to watch in order to get it right. At times, I was fortunate enough to go to Paramount Studios and look at stills, so that I could get descriptions of characters, ships, and so forth. Now, I've felt that part of my job as a novelizer—since the script is 120 triple-spaced (or more) pages, and I need to create 400 double-spaced pages—is to create bits of back-story and description that is true to the feel of the film. So sometimes there might be back-story for a character that isn't part of the film; Pocket and Paramount have both been very lenient and receptive to such additions. How-

ever, I do my very best to remain absolutely true to the script and the intent of its writers. By necessity, deadlines are very tight on novelizations; they require a lot of discipline. I've done them in six weeks and three months, sometimes longer. It all depends on when the editor is able to release the script to me."

After she had turned in the manuscript for *Lost Years* to editor Dave Stern, she said, "He called me and said, 'How would you like to do the novelization of the next movie?' I had no idea they were even *looking* for someone. When I picked myself up off the floor, I said, 'Absolutely!'"

STAR TREK VI:
THE UNDISCOVERED COUNTRY
J. M. Dillard

JANUARY 1992 (301 PP)

 n adaptation of the sixth *Star Trek* feature film.

Jeanne commented, "I had the pleasure once of speaking to Leonard Nimoy about the story behind *The Undiscovered Country*. His family came from Russia, and he was very impressed by Gorbachev, who was giving the country its first taste of freedom. He based the Klingon, Gorkon, on Gorbachev. I was able to see a few of the sets, and even caught a glimpse of the actress Kim Catrall in the full Vulcan costume; this was well before her *Sex and the City* days. As for writing the novelization, it has always been easy for me to write about the original *Enterprise* crew, since I know the characters so well. I only needed to do some research on Yosemite and to find out what color the special effects folks were using for Klingon blood."

ENCOUNTER AT FARPOINT
(STAR TREK: THE NEXT GENERATION)
DAVID GERROLD

OCTOBER 1987   (192PP)

 n adaptation of the TNG pilot episode.

The author declined to be interviewed about this book.

UNIFICATION
(STAR TREK: THE NEXT GENERATION)
JERI TAYLOR

NOVEMBER 1991   (245PP)

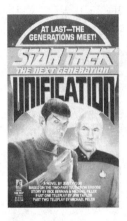

 n adaptation of the two-part episode from TNG's fifth season.

Jeri remembered, "I ended up working on *The Next Generation* by having done a rewrite of the script, 'Suddenly Human.' On the basis of that, I was asked by Rick Berman and Michael Piller to become a member of the staff."

How did she end up writing the novelization for this two-part episode? "I put myself in the running to write the novelization. I contacted Dave Stern, who was then-editor of the *Star Trek* series at Pocket Books, and suggested myself. He asked tactfully if I'd ever written in the prose form, and I replied that I had a half-finished novel I could send him. I did, and he okayed me to write the book. It was obviously crunch time after that—being on staff at *Star Trek* was a seven-day-a-week, ten-hour-a-day job, so there wasn't a lot of time left to do peripheral writing. I didn't sleep much until the book was done!"

RELICS
(STAR TREK: THE NEXT GENERATION)
MICHAEL JAN FRIEDMAN

NOVEMBER 1992   (239PP)

n adaptation of the episode from TNG's sixth season.

Mike remembered, "I had met Jimmy Doohan in Toronto at a convention where he was the media guest of honor and I was the writer guest of honor. So when the opportunity came to do the *Relics* novelization, I was just tickled pink. I read the script and was told that they had left some scenes out that would have partaken of what I thought of then as the Pepsi Cola technology. Pepsi was doing commercials with Fred Astaire and John Wayne. So I called Ron Moore and asked him to tell me what was left out and also if there is anything else he would have put in. He supplied several examples and

I put those scenes in. The other thing I wanted to put in was something about the Dyson Sphere because it was really a McGuffin. There was just nothing about it in there and so I wanted to set up a story that had something to do with the Dyson Sphere. In retrospect, I probably should have done even more with the Dyson Sphere, but you know it's a novelization and these things don't tend to be 400 pages. I had a couple of days fewer than four weeks to write it, which was, little did I know, a luxury." (He had to write the novelization for *All Good Things* in half the time.)

DESCENT
(STAR TREK: THE NEXT GENERATION)
DIANE CAREY

OCTOBER 1993   (278PP)

n adaptation of TNG's two-part season-six cliffhanger and season-seven opener.

ALL GOOD THINGS . . .
(STAR TREK: THE NEXT GENERATION)
MICHAEL JAN FRIEDMAN

JUNE 1994   (248PP)

ORIGINALLY PUBLISHED IN HARDCOVER

The novelization of TNG's final episode.

Mike remembered, "I had two weeks to do it. Dave Stern said, 'You know we've got to get this thing out real quick. Here's the draft of the script that we have; it may change a little bit.' I recall it really didn't, but we needed to do this quickly and I remember it was such a Picard story, and it was written so tightly, that there really wasn't an opportunity to put in interstitial action or even much in the way of set up. It was really a very complete story. So I thought, *I don't want to do this, it's complex enough already.* How could I add material to this that could make it worth buying as a hardcover? And I realized, it's the last episode of the series and there are a lot of little threads hanging, a lot of little things that could be resolved in this book. So I put in a lot of scenes that involved people other than Picard to kind of flesh it out. I had a scene between Lwaxanna and Pulaski. I also had a little scene with Wesley, and I made it less of Picard's personal story, putting it in a larger context by bringing all these scenes in with other characters, and sort of enriched it that way without, I hope, messing with what was really a very good story. I had two weeks. I did it in exactly fourteen days. I don't know if I'll ever be able to do that again! It was ridiculous!"

STAR TREK GENERATIONS
(STAR TREK: THE NEXT GENERATION)
J. M. DILLARD

DECEMBER 1994   (280PP)

ORIGINALLY PUBLISHED IN HARDCOVER

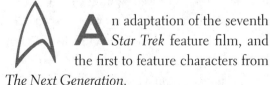

An adaptation of the seventh *Star Trek* feature film, and the first to feature characters from *The Next Generation*.

According to Jeanne, "*Generations* was, for me, a poignant experience. I became addicted to the original series when it first aired, so I felt a great deal of loyalty toward the original characters. It was rather sad to read the script for the first time and realize, 'This really *is* the last movie for Captain Kirk.' "

STAR TREK: FIRST CONTACT
(STAR TREK: THE NEXT GENERATION)
J. M. Dillard

DECEMBER 1996   (276 PP)

ORIGINALLY PUBLISHED IN HARDCOVER

n adaptation of the eighth *Star Trek* feature film, and the second to feature characters from *The Next Generation.*

Jeanne said, "I enjoyed writing *First Contact* immensely because the Borg were such a deliciously evil threat. It was also fun to visit the twenty-first and meet Zefram Cochrane."

This novelization also includes twenty-nine pages of behind-the-scenes material by Judith and Garfield Reeves-Stevens.

STAR TREK: INSURRECTION
(STAR TREK: THE NEXT GENERATION)
J. M. Dillard

DECEMBER 1998   (295 PP)

ORIGINALLY PUBLISHED IN HARDCOVER

An adaptation of the ninth *Star Trek* feature film, and the third to feature characters from *The Next Generation.*

Jeanne remembered, "*Insurrection* was a bit of a challenge to write, because I wasn't able to get my stills (photos) from the film as it was being shot. So I had no idea what the aliens looked like. The draft of the script I received didn't describe them, so all I knew was that they were humanoid."

STAR TREK NEMESIS
(STAR TREK: THE NEXT GENERATION)
J. M. DILLARD

DECEMBER 2002   (227PP)

ORIGINALLY PUBLISHED IN HARDCOVER

n adaptation of the tenth *Star Trek* feature film, and the fourth to feature characters from *The Next Generation*.

Jeanne commented, "*Nemesis* was a pleasure to work on, because I had access to stills from the movie. This allowed me to study the actors in costume, to see the sets, and to see key moments in the story. This helped me to give a lot more detail with confidence."

This novelization includes an introduction by *Nemesis* screenplay writer John Logan.

EMISSARY
(STAR TREK: DEEP SPACE NINE #1)
J. M. DILLARD

FEBRUARY 1993   (274PP)

An adaptation of the DS9 pilot episode.

Jeanne found herself particularly challenged by writing this novelization. "I wrote it without seeing the episode, of course; in fact only a few of the actors had been cast when I first got the script. I saw none of them 'in character,' so I could only imagine what Rene Auberjonois would look like as Odo. It was interesting to watch the actual episode and see how close I was able to come to what wound up on the screen."

THE SEARCH
(STAR TREK: DEEP SPACE NINE)
Diane Carey

OCTOBER 1994 (277PP)

 n adaptation of DS9's two-part third-season opener.

The author declined to comment on this book.

THE WAY OF THE WARRIOR
(STAR TREK: DEEP SPACE NINE)
Diane Carey

OCTOBER 1995 (279PP)

 n adaptation of DS9's two-part fourth-season opener

The author declined to comment on this book.

TRIALS AND TRIBBLE-ATIONS
(STAR TREK: DEEP SPACE NINE)
DIANE CAREY

DECEMBER 1996   (180PP)

n adaptation of the episode from DS9's fifth season.

Diane said, "Of all the novelizations, this one has a warm spot with me because I was able to fulfil a childhood wish—to be the props person hiding in the cargo hold and dropping the last few tribbles on William Shatner. I was able to novelize the popular 'Trouble with Tribbles' episode at the same time as the *Deep Space Nine* spin-off. I scrupulously transferred every movement and sound from the original episode, directly from screen to my keyboard as I watched a tape of 'The Trouble with Tribbles.' I finally got to throw those tribbles onto the captain's head."

FAR BEYOND THE STARS
(STAR TREK: DEEP SPACE NINE)
STEVE BARNES

APRIL 1998   (271PP)

n adaptation of the episode from DS9's sixth season.

Steve Barnes described how he became attracted to *Star Trek*. "Some of my other friends in the neighborhood were watching, and I turned it on and realized that this was the best SF series I'd ever seen on television."

When asked how he got the opportunity to write the novelization for this episode, he said, "I was approached by the editors, who asked me if I'd novelize the *Far Beyond the Stars* script. It had to be done in a month, and I took it as a challenge. I had to create a full wraparound backstory, and do considerable research into New York in the 1950s and 1930s. I had a ball, and the editors were just great."

CALL TO ARMS . . .
THE DOMINION WAR, Book Two
DIANE CAREY

NOVEMBER 1998   (267PP)

An adaptation of the final episode from DS9's fifth season, and the first three episodes from DS9's sixth season.

. . . SACRIFICE OF ANGELS
THE DOMINION WAR, Book Four
DIANE CAREY

DECEMBER 1998   (269PP)

An adaptation of the third, fourth, fifth, and sixth episodes from DS9's sixth season.

Diane commented, "I didn't watch DS9 regularly, so I wasn't as familiar with the characters or the actors' styles as with some of the other shows. However, I do have a pretty good knack at picking up on the subtleties with minimal exposure, and I'm told the novels were well accepted by the fans of the show. The problem with novelizations is that no TV script provides enough scenes for a full novel. That means the writer must contrive what's going on before and after each scene, and other things that are happening to other characters while the scenes are going on. A script is linear. A novel is not. I'm gratified to hear the most consistent comment from fans is that they wait for my novelizations to see 'what else was going on,' and also what the characters were thinking when they said whatever they said in the dialogue. Novelizations provide a unique kind of challenge. I use a whole different set of professional skills than for creating a novel."

WHAT YOU LEAVE BEHIND
Diane Carey

JUNE 1999   (212PP)

he novelization of DS9's final episode.

CARETAKER
(STAR TREK VOYAGER #1)
L. A. Graf

FEBRUARY 1995   (279PP)

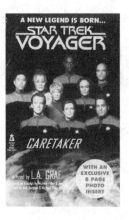

n adaptation of *Voyager*'s pilot episode.

Julia and Karen Rose reflected, "We had written several books by then and usually had only minor rewrites, so perhaps that's why they chose us. Julia did most of the work on this and her only problem was that the script as written didn't quite 'flesh out' to a book-length manuscript. That was why she ended up going into the background of some of the characters in more detail than the script did. She also had to call in some 'fan spy' favors because the manuscript had to be finished before the pilot aired, and no one was allowed to see the ship or the uniforms ahead of time. That made it hard to describe things in a realistic way! Fortunately, some fans on the Internet had pictures of the actors, the uniforms, and the ship, and she was able to make it fairly accurate."

FLASHBACK
(STAR TREK VOYAGER)
DIANE CAREY

OCTOBER 1996   (279PP)

n adaptation of the episode from *Voyager*'s third season.

DAY OF HONOR
(STAR TREK VOYAGER)
MICHAEL JAN FRIEDMAN

NOVEMBER 1997   (247PP)

An adaptation of the episode from *Voyager*'s third season that tied-in with Pocket's book miniseries of the same name.

Mike said, "I think Jeri Taylor, who wrote the episode, did a nice job. I put in more about the species they were trying to help, so we could understand them better. I put in a really fun subplot involving the doctor wanting to learn more about holidays. I had a good time with that. It kind of lightened things up. It was a nice light subplot set off against the kind of life or death threat of Tom and B'Elanna."

EQUINOX
(STAR TREK VOYAGER)
Diane Carey

OCTOBER, 1999   (254PP)

 n adaptation of *Voyager's* two-part season-five cliffhanger and season-six opener.

ENDGAME
(STAR TREK VOYAGER)
Diane Carey, with teaser by Christie Golden

JULY 2001   (231PP)

TRADE PAPERBACK

he novelization of *Voyager's* final episode. Includes a teaser for the post-TV fiction by Christie Golden.

Diane remarked, "The difficulty of novelizations is that the author has no control over the plot, good or bad, the dialogue, good or bad, and must create extra goings-on to fill in several dozens more pages than a script naturally supports. Greg and I tend to add more plot rather than simply extend each scene, which of course also goes on. This means the added plot must pass inspection by the studio as something they also see going on behind the scenes. It's an extremely controlled environment in which to maneuver."

BROKEN BOW
(STAR TREK: ENTERPRISE)
DIANE CAREY

OCTOBER 2001 (232PP)

ORIGINALLY PUBLISHED IN HARDCOVER

n adaptation of *Enterprise*'s pilot episode.

According to Diane, this was, like all *Star Trek* novelizations, "A rush job, to be sure; this was translated from the script, and was written while I was at sea aboard the *Pride of Baltimore II* as ship's cook during the ASTA Great Lakes Challenge. When the ship docked in Detroit, my husband was there with the script and my laptop computer. It was 95 degrees above decks and about 2000 degrees below, [where I was] cooking over a propane stove for a crew of twenty. I managed to deliver the book within two weeks. I'm still recovering."

SHOCKWAVE
(STAR TREK: ENTERPRISE)
PAUL RUDITIS

OCTOBER 2002 (244PP)

ORIGINALLY PUBLISHED IN HARDCOVER

n adaptation of *Enterprise*'s first-season cliffhanger and second-season opener.

Paul reflected on being a *Trek* fan. "It just kind of happened over time. My dad started me watching reruns of the original series when I was so young that all I got out of it were bad dreams. Over time the nightmares stopped and I actually started to enjoy it. I guess it was once TNG premiered that I really got sucked in."

How did he land the assignment to write the novelization of *Shockwave*? He answered, "I wish there was an exciting story about this, but it was simply a case of Margaret Clark calling me up and asking if I was interested in doing it. I had already worked on several projects with her, so I guess she liked my stuff. When I got the assignment, the season finale had already aired so I had the script and the video to work against. If I recall correctly, I didn't have the script for the second episode when I started working on the book. It was weird to start a project not knowing how it was going to end. We were also in a real time crunch. The book was scheduled to come out something like four months from the point I *started* writing." Optimally, manuscripts should be finished and sent to production at least nine months prior to publication. "That was fun because it forced me to really focus on my work and ignore the stupid distractions that can get in the way. It's amazing how much of the day I can fill up just sharpening pencils, especially considering I do all my writing on the computer."

THE EXPANSE
(STAR TREK: ENTERPRISE)
J. M. DILLARD

OCTOBER 2003   (247 PP)

TRADE PAPERBACK

An adaptation of *Enterprise's* second-season cliffhanger, "The Expanse," and its third-season opener, "The Xindi."

According to Jeanne, "Writing about *Enterprise* characters presented the greatest challenge for me, as I hadn't had enough time to get to know them the way I do the other *Star Trek* characters. I re-watched DVDs and studied scripts in order to get the best possible feel for them and the show. I found it interesting to write about the devastation of Florida, especially since I was born and raised there. That gave me the ability to describe it vividly, with accuracy."

KLINGON
(COMPUTER GAME ADAPTATION)
DEAN WESLEY SMITH AND KRISTINE KATHRYN RUSCH

MAY 1996   (217PP)

n adaptation of the CD-ROM game of the same name.

STARFLEET ACADEMY
(COMPUTER GAME ADAPTATION)
DIANE CAREY

JUNE 1997   (223PP)

n adaptation of the CD-ROM game of the same name.

Diane recalls, "I was able to write the book and include some of the most entertaining writing I've ever done—a scene in which Chekov and Sulu pretend to be Spock and Scott (if I remember correctly) and completely confuse the young cadets who don't know what to do with officers who are joking with them and making fun of themselves. That scene was worth the whole project."

ORIGINAL FICTION CONCEPTS

#1	#2

HOUSE OF CARDS
(NEW FRONTIER)
PETER DAVID

JULY 1997 (168PP)

INTO THE VOID
(NEW FRONTIER)
PETER DAVID

JULY 1997 (151PP)

This novel introduces Captain Calhoun and his past on the planet Xenex. Other crew members are introduced as well, including Soleta, the Vulcan who is hiding her true parentage from everyone; and Dr. Selar, the Vulcan, formerly of the *Starship Enterprise*, who has a life-altering occurrence when she experiences *Pon farr*.

Commander Elizabeth Shelby, Borg expert from the episode "The Best of Both Worlds," finds herself in line for first officer aboard the *Excalibur*. Having a "heated" past with the captain, she must bury her feelings for their new relationship to be successful. Si Cwan, the Thallonian Prince, finds himself without an empire to rule. With the help of So-

NEW FRONTIER

John Ordover remembered, "One of the major problems with the novels at the time [the mid-nineties], because you have to remember this was way before the DS9 relaunch and stuff like that, was you couldn't put any inherent continuity into them and you couldn't make any significant changes, so characters couldn't die, they couldn't change, they couldn't leave. The core characters always had to remain the same. After a few years, that gets frustrating for an editor. By the way, I never had any really significant problems with Paula Block at Paramount; there's never anything that I wanted to do that she said absolutely not. Fans tend to demonize [the studio], but the people we worked with at Paramount are intelligent and creative. We don't necessarily see eye to eye on everything all the time, but out of the creative conflict comes usually a better working relationship. She reins me in, I say, I push, she pulls back, it works really well. I call her up and tell her the problem that you have with us is keeping us in continuity. The problem we have with you is keeping us in continuity. What if we had our own ship and crew and we could tell stories that continue from book to book in which characters could live and die and all that sort of stuff that gives complete freedom. It would give a sense of potential for loss, and that would solve all our problems. And she thought it sounded good and had me write it up and send it to her. So I wrote up my core concept. The ship called the *Excalibur,* of Sector 221G that had just collapsed. One of the things I had pitched to *Voyager* was the notion that a Federation-like civilization should have collapsed, fighting the Borg, I mean they fought to exist, but now they've collapsed and they've fallen completely out of contact with each other and each kind has gone off on its own and there's a lot of problems because both tried to specialize in machines without food, another in food but not machines, the machine planet's starving, the food planet is running out of machines. *Voyager* could pick up the job every once in a while helping to re-establish this federation. Another one of those *Voyager* fantasy pictures of mine (that didn't sell). Since I couldn't do it as *Voyager,* let's do it in *New Frontier.* It's amazing how many ideas I got out of frustration with *Voyager* doing what I thought was wrong."

John continued, "Peter David made up MacKenzie Calhoun on his own. I wanted a much more dynamic captain then we've seen lately. Bottom line is, as much as I love DS9, as much as I dislike *Voyager,* the problems, rating wise, with DS9 and *Voyager* is that they changed the concept. It's sort of like saying, *CSI: The Forest Rangers.* You know its not ST because the core of ST is a ship going from place to place having missions. The argument I made was to compare *NYPD Blue* to *Hill Street Blues.* They were essentially the same show. The difference was that *Hill Street Blues* had the tone of the 80s and *NYPD Blue* had the tone of the 90s. So they kept the concept but just changed the tone. *New Frontier* was an attempt to go back to the original concept but change the tone. And the tone was goofy and over the top and I like that. With more humor, with very flawed characters, and a lot more sex."

John added, "At the time the *Green Mile* was setting sales records as chapter books, so we did the first story with chapter books. BANG, all over the *New York Times* list. And then we went on from there.

To be honest the first thought was there's no way in hell we're going to be able to get this thing through. So it was a surprise when all worked out and it's been a good trip."

Peter David remarked, "John Ordover convinced Paramount to let him do an original *Star Trek* book series. It would focus on a new crew. Paramount's belief was that there would be little to no interest from the fans in a *Star Trek* series that did not stem directly from the TV shows. If he wanted to go ahead, he had their blessing, but they did ask for him to include a few familiar faces. This prompted John to add Shelby, Lefler, and Dr. Selar into the mix. There were characters that had a previous history and were popular. John approached me with the basic concept of the downfall of the Soviet Union. The Soviet Union was keeping these smaller countries with a history of hostility towards each other in line but once it collapsed all of the hostilities reared up and all the countries were at war with each other. Let's do the fall of the Soviet Union in space and Starfleet sends in a ship to ride and watch all of this. I'm pretty sure John came up with the *Excalibur.* He told me the characters he wanted to use and I was allowed to run with it. I loved the notion of doing a series where we didn't have to return the characters to square one by the last page. We could do actual change instead of the illusion of change. Calhoun is a shameless riff on William Wallace. The reason that people don't connect him with William Wallace is in the books Calhoun is eighteen when he frees his people. In real life, that was how old William Wallace was. In the movie *Braveheart,* Mel Gibson is in his forties. He was insanely too old to play William Wallace!"

leta, he wishes to stowaway on board the ship. The chief engineer, Burgoyne 172, is a hermat, a being with both sexual organs. And s/he has got hir sights set on Selar.

3

THE TWO-FRONT WAR
(NEW FRONTIER)
PETER DAVID

AUGUST 1997   (152 PP)

W hile the crew of the *Excalibur* helps with humanitarian aid to a stranded vessel, Zak Kebron, the Brikar security chief, and Si Cwan are attempting humanitarian relief of their own. In a shuttlecraft without the *Excalibur* in range to help them, they must decide to trust each other if they are going to survive the trap they've entered. A mysterious vessel shows up to engage *Excalibur*. While the casualties start piling up, the doctor finds herself distracted.

4

END GAME
(NEW FRONTIER)
PETER DAVID

AUGUST 1997   (184 PP)

C aptain Calhoun finds himself having to act against his gut warrior instincts in order to save many lives. First Officer Shelby is torn between her feelings for her superior officer and her duty.

#5

MARTYR
(NEW FRONTIER)
PETER DAVID

MARCH 1998   (282PP)

Arriving at the planet Zondar to stop a potential civil war, Calhoun is greeted as a messiah. Reading the prophecies, it appears Calhoun fits exactly as the man who was foretold would save the planet. But the prophecies also say that the savior will die. When he vanishes, the crew must find him before the prophecies are fulfilled!

#6

FIRE ON HIGH
(NEW FRONTIER)
PETER DAVID

APRIL 1998   (272PP)

A woman sits atop a mountain cradling a superweapon, surrounded by the devastation. Lieutenant Robin Lefler discovers her supposedly dead mother is actually alive and being held prisoner. The majority of the novel focuses on Morgan, Robin's mother.

THE CAPTAIN'S TABLE, BOOK FIVE: ONCE BURNED

(SEE SECTION 12: MINISERIES)

DOUBLE HELIX, BOOK FIVE: DOUBLE OR NOTHING

(SEE SECTION 12: MINISERIES)

#7

THE QUIET PLACE
(NEW FRONTIER)
PETER DAVID

NOVEMBER 1999　　(258PP)

A young woman, Riella, with no memory of her past, discovers her mother is not really her parent. Chased by "the Dogs of War," and attempting to retrieve her memories, she finds herself rescued by Xyon, a space pirate with a hidden agenda. Is Riella really Si Cwan's long lost sister?

#8

DARK ALLIES
(NEW FRONTIER)
PETER DAVID

NOVEMBER 1999　　(256PP)

Calhoun and the gang must engage a seemingly impossible foe. An organism known as "the Black Mass" has consumed several worlds in the Thallonian Empire. Now it heads toward the home planet of the Redeemers. Forced into a temporary truce, Calhoun must put aside his animosity and work with his enemies to stop the creature from destroying their world. Of course, if Calhoun won't help them, the Overlord has plans to blackmail him into complying.

REQUIEM
(NEW FRONTIER: EXCALIBUR, Book One)
PETER DAVID

SEPTEMBER 2000   (267PP)

The crew reunites to reminisce about their memories aboard the *Excalibur*. Afterwards, the crew scatters to various destinations. For Soleta, she decides to confront the Romulan father she has never met. This individual raped her mother, causing her to be conceived. How do you deal with a monster that doesn't know he has a daughter? Ci Swan and Kalinda investigate the murder of a former teacher. Kebron and McHenry are sent on an undercover mission to investigate supposed alien abductions on a backwater planet.

RENAISSANCE
(NEW FRONTIER: EXCALIBUR, Book Two)
PETER DAVID

SEPTEMBER 2000   (270PP)

While the events in *Requiem* transpire, the former chief engineer of the *Excalibur* decides to follow Selar to Vulcan, to claim his proper place as the father of their son. Conflicting with her Vulcan ideals, Burgoyne appeals to the highest level of the Vulcan council, creating a major conflict that neither he nor Selar can truly win. On the planet Risa, Robin and her mother take a vacation to make up for their lost time together. When they arrive, they stumble on a series of strange computer mishaps. Our favorite engineer Scotty shows up, convinced he knows Robin's mother from somewhere.

#11

RESTORATION
(NEW FRONTIER: EXCALIBUR, Book Three)
Peter David

NOVEMBER 2000   (409pp)

ORIGINALLY PUBLISHED IN HARDCOVER

On the planet Yakaba, a mysterious man ends up in a jail cell. Proving his innocence, Calhoun begins to become a major influence in the life of the town residents. Lacking in technology, it appears that he will never be able to contact anyone in Starfleet and he will spend the rest of his life on this planet. Meanwhile, Shelby has decided to take command of the *U.S.S. Exeter*, leaving behind everyone she knew on the *Excalibur*. Her command decisions will prove how important both Calhoun and her former shipmates were in influencing her management style.

COLD WARS
(GATEWAYS, BOOK SIX; SEE SECTON 12: MINISERIES)

#12

BEING HUMAN
(NEW FRONTIER)
Peter David

NOVEMBER 2001   (267pp)

Mark McHenry's past is finally revealed and his secret proves to be a doozy. With his secret past in full view of everyone, will it be the end of both the *Excalibur* as well as the Federation? Is the seemingly only human crew member not human after all? While dealing with the ramifications of McHenry's heritage, Kebron begins to act strangely as well. Seemingly nicer, he starts to lose chunks of his skin.

GODS ABOVE
(NEW FRONTIER)
PETER DAVID

OCTOBER 2003 (330 PP)

The *Excalibur* is decimated and needs to be towed to a starbase for extensive repairs. Captain Shelby is ordered to take the *Trident* back to the planet Danter to negotiate with the beings responsible for the *Excalibur*'s damage. With the fate of the entire Alpha Quadrant at stake, she must tread carefully. Calhoun fumes over the events that occurred. He is determined to send his barely repaired ship and still recovering crew back into the forefront of the battle, primarily for revenge. Having never had his ass kicked so badly before, it's payback time.

STONE AND ANVIL
(NEW FRONTIER)
PETER DAVID

OCTOBER 2003 (296 PP)

ORIGINALLY PUBLISHED IN HARDCOVER

Before starting the novel, make sure to read the dedication. On board the *Trident*, a mangled body leads to the *Excalibur*'s Ensign Janos as the culprit. Calhoun refuses to believe his friend could be a murderer, even though, as they say on *CSI*, the evidence never lies. Half of the novel concerns the mystery and the other showcases Calhoun's life as a Starfleet cadet. Ever wonder how he met Shelby? Curious what he would be like as a roommate? Your answers wait.

NO LIMITS
(NEW FRONTIER)

(SEE SECTION 13: ANTHOLOGIES)

AFTER THE FALL
(NEW FRONTIER)
PETER DAVID

NOVEMBER 2004　　　(329PP)

ORIGINALLY PUBLISHED IN HARDCOVER

Three years after the events in *Stone and Anvil*, the dynamics of the crew have drastically altered. The captain of the *Trident* is no longer Shelby, who has been promoted to admiral and runs Space Station Bravo. Si Cwan is Prime Minister of the New Thallonian Protectorate, and he is constantly butting heads with his wife, Robin Lefler. Burgoyne and his wife, Selar, have separated over their differences in how their son, Xyon, should be raised. Meanwhile, long forgotten foes of the Thallonians are on a collision course with the still tough Captain Calhoun and the crew of the *Excalibur*.

MISSING IN ACTION
(NEW FRONTIER)
PETER DAVID

FEBRUARY 2006　　　(341PP)

ORIGINALLY PUBLISHED IN HARDCOVER

Soleta, on board her Romulan vessel, watches in horror as some sort of multidimensional creature appears to destroy Captain Calhoun and the *Excalibur*. Admiral Shelby believes her husband is still alive but cannot receive permission to launch a rescue effort. Meanwhile, the civil war on Si Cwan's homeworld continues to decimate the population and erode his marriage.

CORPS OF ENGINEERS

Originally titled *Star Trek: S.C.E.*, this original fiction concept began in 2000 as a monthly eBook series. It came about out of a desire by Pocket to create something that would test the possibilities of the eBook format. Keith DeCandido explained, "It was something that had been talked about for a while. And then it was sort of given a kick by Microsoft debuting their new reader and wanting to do something to launch it. That was in the summer of 2000. So it was decided to start with the *Starfleet Corps of Engineers* because if we're going to do something that's eBook-only, what's better than Starfleet tech heads. It would appeal to the type of people who would buy a book electronically and store on their hard drive or their palm pilot instead of on their bookshelf. John Ordover and I sat down and came up with the S.C.E. pretty much over the weekend. He brought me in to help out because of that capacity that I have for useless trivia, which actually has proved to be very useful over the years. And John had the basic concept of the S.C.E. They were problem solvers who would come in and fix things. I was there to call on my trivia to come up with characters. The first person I thought of was Sonya Gomez, the one who spills hot chocolate all over Captain Picard in the second season episode, 'Q Who?' I loved that character and when she came back the following week, I thought she was going to be a recurring character. And then we never saw her again!"

Keith continued, "We basically went through all the engineers who had appeared, who were still active, still in Starfleet, and weren't being used elsewhere. The first thought was Barclay, but *Voyager* was still on the air at the time and his character was tied up in the Pathfinder Project. We did get him to guest star in one eBook but we couldn't use him for the main plot. We did use Duffy who was in the episode Barclay first appeared in. We used Fabian Stevens, who was in the 'Starship Down' episode that John Ordover co-wrote for DS9. The hilarious thing was that I was the one who remembered him, not John. We set up Scotty as the head of S.C.E. He's the one who doles out mission assignments and is the liaison between them and the admiralty. It's the perfect job for him and because it gives us the chance to use the character. And he's a lot of fun and it's good having him there. We needed a chief medical officer, so we brought in Elizabeth Lense who was the valedictorian of Julian Bashir's class. Captain David Gold was a character John and I came up with together, because both of us wanted to have a Jewish captain. Just because the history of the Jewish people is such that it is a valid concern that they might not be around four hundred years hence and we thought it would be different and be nice for a fresh viewpoint. His wife was a rabbi and he's an older man. A lot of S.C.E. is modeled after M*A*S*H in a lot of ways. Because M*A*S*H is a group of specialists who are not regular army and the S.C.E. are a group of specialists who are not regular Starfleet. Whenever writers ask me, as the editor of the series, how should Gold be written, I say, just picture Harry Morgan playing him and you've got it. That's worked very nicely and he's got a different style from the other *Star Trek* captains, which is exactly as it should be. He has his own personality and there are things he would do that the other

(continued)

captains wouldn't. His methods of interacting with his crew are different, so we wanted to give the S.C.E. it's own identity and not have the same structure that the other Trek series have."

Keith continued, "There was nobody working on the staff of Pocket at the time to shepherd a monthly series on top of the rest of the *Star Trek* line, so I was asked to be the editor. It also provided a steady source of income, which as a freelancer is something I value. But it is also a lot of fun to put together. It is a very collaborative process because it's on-going, not an on-going storyline in the vein of a DS9-style story arc, but there are on-going changes. There are sub-plots that run through character developments, that each writer takes and runs with, that we move forward with all the time and the writers are always talking to each other and to me and we're always coming up with new ideas."

1

THE BELLY OF THE BEAST
(S.C.E.)
DEAN WESLEY SMITH

AUGUST 2000

hours until a stroke of luck disables the vessel. The crew of the *da Vinci* and Geordi take charge to investigate the gigantic remains. What at first appears to be an immense cruise ship has a sinister and deadly secret.

Dean remembered, "I have no idea where this idea came from, other than the fact that one day I found myself talking with Keith DeCandido and John Ordover about this cool new idea and that they wanted me to write the first one in the series. Again, a massive amount of fun, but a creepy book."

 giant sphere over fifty times bigger than the *Enterprise-E* battles Picard's ship for several

2

FATAL ERROR
(S.C.E.)
KEITH R.A. DeCANDIDO

SEPTEMBER 2000

Ganitriul, the autorepairing computer located on the Eerlik moon, has malfunctioned. Everyone on the planet relies on the computer fulfilling his or her every need, so the society finds itself on the verge of collapsing due to the breakdown. What starts as a simple repair job turns into a battle for their lives when they discover the computer was sabotaged. Will the S.C.E. succeed, even as the computer starts to crash around them and the *da Vinci* appears destroyed?

Keith remarked, "This grew out of a simple desire to see a reversal of that old *Star Trek* cliché, the world-running computer. Instead of our heroes barging in and dismantling an evil world-running computer, I wanted to turn that on its ear and have the world-running computer break down, thus sending the entire soci-

ety into anarchy and chaos, and our heroes have to fix it."

3

HARD CRASH
(S.C.E.)
CHRISTIE GOLDEN

OCTOBER 2000

The Intarians are renowned throughout the galaxy. A major shock occurs when a ship with a seemingly impervious outer hull crashes into the capital city. Is this a precursor to an invasion or the start of a war? Inside the vessel, the S.C.E. find the remains of a single pilot, who appears to have been impaled to the pilot's seat. Then the ship begins to show signs of restarting. . . .

When I asked Christie about her S.C.E. story, she said, "Boy was this fun! While their individual authors wrote all the stories, there was a great deal of back and forth between all of us. At one point it occurred to me that all the authors should know what the characters looked like, and I mentioned this to John Ordover, the editor. I should have known better—John promptly said, 'Great idea! Why don't you work that up for us, Christie?' Ulp! So I did, and for good or ill, I am responsible for how the crew looks."

She continues, "I also got to give 'Em' (how EMH sounds if you pronounce it like a word) his very gentle bedside manner in contrast with our grouchy holodoc on *Voyager*. I realized, too, from the others' outlines that we had several stories that featured dangerous aliens, and I wanted to do a story in the noble *Trek* tradition of the Horta—the misunderstood but ultimately benign alien. So I invented Friend and Jaldark and, let me tell you, I cried a little myself writing certain passages."

#4 – #5

INTERPHASE,
Book One and Book Two
(S.C.E.)
DAYTON WARD AND KEVIN DILMORE

MARCH 2001; APRIL 2001

The crew of the *da Vinci* receives the assignment of recovering the *Constitution*-class *U.S.S. Defiant* from interdimensional space. Aboard the ancient starship, the engineers find themselves fired upon by a Tholian vessel and now appear to be trapped forever in the spatial rift. In the meantime, Kieran Duffy, in reluctant command of the *da Vinci*, must decipher how to prevent a war and rescue his crewmates.

Kevin remembers how he became a *Star Trek* fan. "My conscious entry into *Star Trek* fandom occurred when I was nine and a big watcher of Saturday morning cartoons. That was back in the fall of 1973, so any fellow fan worth his or her salt can guess the confluence of events from that point. I found myself completely swept into the Filmation Studios' *Star Trek* cartoons (OK, OK, *animated series*, like that lends it more credibility). I really dug them, and thought this was major-league science-fiction storytelling . . . until my best friend who lived across the street tipped me to the live-action *Star Trek* series that was on TV every day after school! We watched a lot of them together, then played many games of 'Landing Party' in the wilds beyond our dead-end street. I moved into building the model kits and reading the Alan Dean Foster *Star Trek Log* books and the James Blish write-ups of the original series, then the Fotonovels . . . and on from there."

Kevin always wanted to write *Trek* stories. He said, "What fan doesn't want to put words into their heroes' mouths? Frankly, I never imagined back in the day that I would have the opportunities to romp in the worlds of *Star Trek* in the manner to which I've grown accustomed. I wrote a little (very little) in my grade-school and high-school days beyond school assignments. I went to college to study film-making, then detoured to write about movies rather than make them and entered journalism school. Two degrees later, I took a job at a small-town newspaper and put away thoughts of writing for anything connected to the entertainment world, let alone *Star Trek*, for a number of years."

In recent years, Kevin was a writer for *Star Trek Communicator* magazine. It was on assignment for *Communicator* that he met his future writing partner, Dayton Ward. "In March 1998, I was assigned to write a piece on the contributors to Pocket Books' first *Strange New Worlds* anthology. The great majority of the piece depended on telephone interviews with more than a dozen writers across the country.

But one guy lived within an hour's drive from my house, so I gambled that he might want to meet for a cold one and a chance to talk in person. He did, and before long, Dayton and I had set aside the interview to share all sorts of common fanboy interests. We decided to link up to go to a con a few weeks down the road, and that led to our hanging out quite a bit. Leading us to the fall of 2000, by which time Dayton had racked up two more *SNW* credits and was starting a *Star Trek* novel of his own and I still was plugging away for *Communicator*."

The assignment that changed his life was from John Ordover. Kevin said, "John gave me the exclusive to write up (for the magazine as well as StarTrek.com) the announcement for the new electronic-book series *Star Trek: S.C.E.* He was detailing the concept of the series to me, saying that the stories would center on engineering challenges faced by the crew of a twenty-fourth-century ship of troubleshooters. And I said, 'Oh so you could do something like, um, rescue the old *Defiant* out of the interspatial rift from "The Tholian Web." ' There was a pause, then John said, 'Yeah, we could do something *exactly* like that.' Then it was my turn to pause, then I said, 'Um, can I pitch that to you as a story idea?' And, with my once again being the beneficiary of grace from friends, John encouraged me to do so. As soon as I hung up from John, I called Dayton and said, 'I just got myself into serious trouble and I need you to bail me out.' So Dayton agreed to work with me on the pitch and the story."

Dayton remembers the phone call from Kevin. Dayton said, "The next thing I know, Kevin's on the phone calling me and saying, 'I think I'm in trouble, dude.' So, armed with the general idea and a few suggestions from John,

Kevin and I spent one Saturday afternoon at a local bar (this is a recurring theme, by the way), hammering out the proposal."

Kevin continues with the narrative. "We pitched it as a one-shot 20,000-word story titled 'Defiant' (we even toyed with 'The Defiant Ones,' I think). I got the call that the project was approved on Oct. 31st, 2000 and (if memory serves) we got a deadline of Dec. 15th for Book One and Feb. 1st for Book Two. Book One was on time and Book Two was two weeks early. Those were very exciting times for us, but especially for me given that I never had made a professional sale of any fiction, period. I'm convinced that John's trust in Dayton to make this happen was equal to my trust in him to make this happen, or there would have been no contract. I didn't have any business running in this league of writing by myself. For 'Interphase,' we holed up in a tavern for a couple of hours and just started throwing stuff around. This was fanboy blabbing along the lines of, 'Wouldn't it be cool if someone fell through the *entire ship* during interphase?' or 'Hey, let's have her crawl past a dead guy in a Jefferies' tube!' and so on. From that mishmash came the proposal."

In terms of how they write together, Kevin said, "we approach it a bit differently each time. We always break the story together, working out the large-scale as well as the minor plot points and scenes for our written proposals. Details such as points-of-view come on our own as we write. We agree together that we must get from Point A to Point B in a given chapter, but how we get there is up to us independently. Dayton and I work well together in that we can check our egos at the door and do what it takes to make our stories the best they can be. Each of us tackles the parts of a given story that speak

to us. We don't keep track of whose final draft of something made the cut and whose didn't. We do our best to keep the word counts split evenly. The bottom line we set is that we enjoy the process and we stay proud of the end result. We've stayed true to those goals each time."

Dayton agreed, saying, "We've always taken the stance with our collaborations that it's equal work, equal credit, and equal blame, and it started right here. (Okay, in reality I shuffle most of the blame to him, but don't tell him I said that.)"

#6

COLD FUSION
(S.C.E.)
Keith R.A. DeCandido

July 2001

Deep Space 9 needs a new fusion core and Nog asks for the help of the S.C.E. A fully working device is on the sister station Empok Nor, so they travel to the abandoned station for what should be a routine mission. But the Androssi has other ideas. . . .

Keith remembered, "I get a call one afternoon from both John Ordover and Marco Palmieri, and they say it would be really cool to cross over S.C.E. with the new DS9 novels that were continuing the story beyond the finale. The three of us brainstormed the notion of filling a small gap between *Avatar Book Two* and *Abyss*, involving Nog's salvage of Empok Nor, established at the beginning of the latter novel."

---

7 & # 8

INVINCIBLE,
Part One and Part Two
(S.C.E.)

DAVID MACK AND KEITH R.A. DECANDIDO

AUGUST 2001;
SEPTEMBER 2001

Commander Sonya Gomez gets sent to the planet Sarindar. Equipment problems are an everyday occurrence and with the entire

surface completely scan- and transporter-proof, she has her work cut out for her. Add scientists who don't believe a woman can be capable of anything and a gigantic monster killing off the party, and you have a far from routine mission.

According to David, the story was "inspired by the nineteenth-century true story of the Tsavo Lions, a pair of giant cats that killed dozens of native workers who, under the supervision of an Irish engineer named John Patterson, were trying to build a bridge over the River Tsavo. As a tale about a solitary engineer suddenly thrust into a hostile foreign culture and pitted in a life-or-death struggle against a brutal predatory animal, it seemed ideally suited for an S.C.E. story."

David remembered the series had only just begun when he pitched the idea to John Ordover and Keith DeCandido. David said, "at this point, I had written *The Starfleet Survival Guide* trade paperback, so I didn't yet feel ready to write a narrative-prose story on my own. So, I asked Keith to co-author it with me. I drafted a detailed outline, and he wrote the manuscript, on which I offered him some notes."

The themes of the story had some personal associations for David. He said, "the story sprung from events that had at that time just transpired in my life. A few months prior to pitching the story to John and Keith, I had nearly died of an accidental internal hemorrhage. Only good luck and good friends helped me cheat death in February 2000. I emerged from that experience determined to take a proactive approach to life and happiness, to live in the now, to go after the things that I wanted. I changed my job, my relationship, the whole shebang, in the few months that followed. That idea is reflected in Sonya Gomez's desire to change her own life and romantic situation after narrowly surviving her battle against the monster Shii on Sarindar."

THE RIDDLED POST
(S.C.E.)
AARON ROSENBERG

A station on the planet Bor-Situ Minor has major holes in the structure and almost everyone is dead. Oddly, their shields are undamaged. Is there some new weapon that can penetrate a shield without leaving evidence of its existence? The two survivors have no clue to what transpired, so the S.C.E. must solve the mystery.

Aaron remarked, "I wasn't really a *Trek* fan until TNG started. I watched that right from the pilot and at college we used to eat dinner quickly and then run upstairs to gather in the TV lobby and watch the new episode each week. I liked the novelization of the first movie even more than the movie itself, because it revealed a lot of character details that you couldn't get just from the films. I've always loved writing, so it was a natural progression to want to write for *Trek*. A friend mentioned the S.C.E. series to me when it was just starting out. The way he described it, I immediately thought of one of my favorite shows, which is *CSI*. I love mysteries, and the idea of doing mysteries in the *Trek* universe was really exciting. That got me thinking about how some of the classic mystery tropes would fit in that universe, and how they might change. And one of the great classics is the 'locked room.' So I started tinkering with that idea. I pitched it to John Ordover, who was still on S.C.E. at the time, and he liked the notion. Keith took over the series soon after that, and also liked the idea. So did Paramount. That was *The Riddled Post*. Of all my S.C.E. stories it's the one that's had the most corrections from Paramount, because it was my first *Trek* story and so I had a few errors in the tech, but they were easy to fix and otherwise it was a very smooth process."

#10	#11

HERE THERE BE MONSTERS
(S.C.E.; GATEWAYS Epilogue)
KEITH R.A. DECANDIDO

NOVEMBER 2001

AMBUSH
(S.C.E.)
DAVE GALANTER AND GREG BRODEUR

DECEMBER 2001

Immediately after the seven books in the *Gateways* series, some big "monsters" start decimating the planet of Maeglin. Having helped the planet's inhabitants before, the S.C.E. come in to try to contain the creatures. How can they send the beings back to their proper existence, now that the Gateways are closed?

Keith commented, "John Ordover and I are both comics fans, and we were talking about the idea of doing an S.C.E. story that was like the old monster comics from the late 1950s/early 1960s. Only, of course, with a twist. . . ."

The Starship *da Vinci* is attacked, leaving them on the verge of destruction. Meanwhile, a station waiting for replacement parts from the *da Vinci* is on a countdown to total structural failure. Can the S.C.E. escape from their attackers, fix their ship, and rescue the fifteen people from the station in time?

Dave noted, "*Ambush* was sparked when we considered that all these Starfleet engineers on a ship were akin to having a group of Mac-Gyvers around. They could probably handle anything one might throw their way, and so that is what I wanted to do. They're not a warship, but they had to do battle with the Munqu, and they couldn't just run and get help because they needed to save these miners. It was my attempt to put a little action into their lives and see how they handled it. I think they did quite well."

Dave continued, "The Munqu, by the way, were virtually monkeys. In the plotting stage I was having a bit of fun, calling the bad guys— who I'd not defined yet—'evil monkeys' who do this or that. I decided to describe them as a bit monkey-like and call them the Munqu. The book was a pretty quick write and I don't remember a lot of things we needed to change. Greg's time was limited at this point and he gave an idea here or there and read the final manuscript after I'd sent it in, but this was really my first solo work."

#12

SOME ASSEMBLY REQUIRED
(S.C.E.)
SCOTT CIENCIN AND DAN JOLLEY

JANUARY 2002

On the planet Keorga, a computer system is wreaking havoc on the planet's ecosystem, destroying structures and causing massive earthquakes. The S.C.E. have no idea what they are in for when they arrive, and they are running out of time to save the planet.

Scott felt the pull of the characters on the various incarnations of *Star Trek*. "When I heard about S.C.E., I realized that an opportunity was before me to help, in some small way, to define some new and cool characters in the mythos, so I wasn't about to turn that down."

He had, "A desire to write a fun 1950s-style humorous Science Fiction story, and with the S.C.E. it was natural to have it revolve around misunderstandings about alien cultures and technology." Scott had just written an "Angel" novel with Dan and wanted to work with him again. "Dan and I collaborated on the basic ideas, I wrote an outline, we divided it into chapters, then passed the work back and forth until we were done. Pocket has done a sensational job of getting these stories out there both in 'E' and book form."

#13

NO SURRENDER
(S.C.E.)
JEFF MARIOTTE

FEBRUARY 2002

A prison station orbiting the planet Kursican Primus begins to malfunction. With the possibility of the station burning up in the atmosphere and destroying anything on the planet unfortunate enough to get in its way, the crew of the *da Vinci* speeds to assist. For Captain Gold, the assignment becomes extremely personal.

Jeff said, "when Keith was getting the S.C.E. line up and running, he approached me for a contribution. I was honored to be asked, and playing around in the *Star Trek* sandbox seemed like a lot of fun. There hadn't been a whole lot done with Captain Gold at the time, so I decided to make him the focal character, and expand on his past a little. I also was very interested in the idea of a single horrific location in space, which became The Plat—an or-

bital prison knocked askew so that if the prisoners didn't kill you, physics would. I put those two ideas together and the rest of it just worked itself out. I had a great time writing it."

#14

CAVEAT EMPTOR
(S.C.E.)
IAN EDGINTON AND MIKE COLLINS

MARCH 2002

The *da Vinci* stumbles into a Ferengi life pod, apparently ejected from its vessel after a disaster struck. The Ferengi inside surprisingly demands to be left alone.

Mike was a *Trek* fan from the first day he saw it. "Ironically, the version of *Star Trek* I saw first was the UK comic strip, which—due to some bizarre scheduling—ran *before* the TV show aired over here. I've done much *Star Trek* comic strip work, which to me is actually its 'home.' Kirk and Spock became instant heroes, Roddenberry's 'hope for mankind' message thrilled me even if the occasional story seemed off kilter . . . even to a pre-teen, there was something oddly wrong about 'Spock's Brain. . . .' As a kid I wrote and drew my own adventures of the crew of the *U.S.S. Enterprise.* I'd always wanted to do comics and *Trek* was foremost in my interests. I'm one of those mutant beings, the writer/artist . . . happy in doing either, or both."

In terms of the concept for *Caveat Emptor,* "The idea was all by co-writer Ian Edington. He ran into scheduling difficulties and—as we'd worked together on comics properties and I'd written some *Doctor Who* short stories as well as scripts for DC's run of *Star Trek*—he figured my off-kilter mindset would suit in helping him finish the story. I contributed much of the strangeness of the scenes on the Ferengi ship, and the Rom as Grand Nagus scene. Keith had to pull us up on one character who—for reasons that still escape me—we'd accidentally given a sex change to."

Mike still has his hand in the *Star Trek* universe. "I continue to do the covers for the S.C.E. eBooks ('cover' sounds odd when describing a non-physical thing!) and I recently turned in my 50th consecutive illustration. Ian and I have ideas for other stories—we'd hoped to get something done for the *Angel* book franchise but I'm not sure of the status of the novels with the cancellation of the show. We've other ideas for *Trek* stories—whether singly or together."

Mike had this to say for final thoughts: "*Star Trek* has endured because it's an ultimately hopeful view of mankind's future, it's a fantastic concept, beyond the obvious rocket ships and monsters of traditional space-opera. I still get a giddy thrill from the shows when they really 'click' as to its message. There's so much

more we can be. It's a genuine pleasure to be part of that astonishing universe in whatever way I can be."

1 5

PAST LIFE
(S.C.E.)
ROBERT GREENBERGER

APRIL 2002

The natives of the planet Evora have only recently discovered they are not alone in the universe. The Federation protected their world during the Dominion War. In the aftermath, an archaeological dig uncovers a high-tech device over one hundred thousand years old.

"Keith was nice enough to invite me to pitch to this series. Having read the first few, I began considering a situation where the engineering team had to figure out what a high-tech artifact was doing that its very presence threatened to undermine a society's belief system. It wasn't a bad story but could have been weightier and played with the themes a lot better. On the other hand, I got to quickly grow fond of the characters and even got Gold off the bridge for a bit, which was nice."

#16

OATHS
(S.C.E.)
GLENN HAUMAN

MAY 2002

Captain Gold is concerned about Dr. Lense. She has been neglecting her duties, relying more on her EMH program and spending her time playing solitaire on her computer. The transcripts of Gold's attempts to uncover her issues highlights the majority of the narrative.

Glenn was raised, like so many others of his generation, on daily reruns at 6 PM on WPIX, channel eleven in New York. "Oddly enough, I back-doored my way into writing *Star Trek*. I was doing editorial consulting on the *Star Trek* CD-ROMs for Simon & Schuster Interactive—the *Star Trek Omnipedia*, the *Borg* and *Klingon* CD-ROMs, the *Interactive Technical*

Manual, *Captain's Chair*, and *Starship Creator*. On the last two, additional content was needed—what the buttons on Captain Kirk's chair actually did, for example; and what were the names of Dr. Pulaski's three previous husbands? So that would be my first contributions to *Trek* lore, aside from errors I put into the Encyclopedias to keep the fans on their toes."

When asked how he received the assignment to write this S.C.E. story, he commented, "*Oaths* was part of a series of story pitches that came about when I first heard about the S.C.E. line. The impetus was the debate on stem cell research—specifically, how a bunch of people who had no real clue about the science and medicine entailed involved themselves into whether or not we should do so. Many individuals had already decided that we weren't going to find anything, so we weren't even going to look. This, to me, is antithetical to open thinking. It occurred to me that this sort of situation was going to happen on an S.C.E. ship, sooner or later. Captain Gold isn't a scientist; he's more of an administrator. There are going to be a multitude of issues where he is not going to have the know-how to fully understand the problem in the time allotted. What does he do? His people are telling him one thing, the law is telling him another—which way does he jump? This is a problem that seems to pop up more in medical situations, by the way. Tell someone that there's a problem with a nuclear reactor, they default to an expert. Heck, for a lot of people, indicate that you need to assemble furniture and they get 'a friend who's handy with that sort of thing' to do it for them. But let there be a medical problem, and everybody seems entitled to an opinion, informed or not. I also wanted to deal with some of the unspoken assumptions about Dr. Lense, how she ended up where she did after the Dominion War. She struck me as a bit more damaged than most, and I really wanted to explore why. And if she was going to be in bad shape, I wanted to see the deterioration—and I thank Bob, Mike, Ian for putting the hooks in their preceding stories. Lense is also unique in that she has the capacity to relieve the captain of command. I wanted to see what would happen in a case where the reasons to remove command were somewhat ambiguous, where the doctor had her own reasons for doing so. And then September 11 happened. Everybody has his or her September 11 stories. I have mine, you probably have yours. I saw the towers collapse from my street. Spent the afternoon buying supplies and cooking food, and brought it down to the staging area in Jersey City that night. *Oaths* was started before and finished after 9/11 (And if you think it's fun writing a story about a deadly plague while the building across the street from where your wife and friends work has anthrax mailed to it . . . on the only bright side, I didn't have to go far for preliminary research, it was in the papers every flipping day.) If I didn't address 9/11 in some way, I wouldn't have been able to write at all; as it was, the bit about the axe ended up being so powerful that it made me write the rest of the story so that the piece could make it into print."

#17, #18 & #19

FOUNDATIONS, Book One, Book Two, Book Three
(S.C.E.)
DAYTON WARD AND KEVIN DILMORE

JUNE 2002; JULY 2002; AUGUST 2002

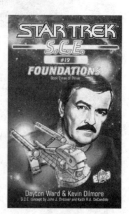

The *da Vinci* attempts to rescue inhabitants of a space ship traveling at warp speeds and hopelessly out of control. While investigating solutions, Captain Montgomery Scott recalls three early missions of the S.C.E. that he participated in, during his time aboard Captain

Kirk's *Enterprise*. The missions take him from the edge of the Romulan Neutral Zone to the planet where everyone enjoys the Festival. (Are you of the body?)

Dayton said, "This project came about after John Ordover, who at the time was still overseeing much of the S.C.E. series, asked if Kevin and I would be interested in writing the 'origin story' of the S.C.E. The three of us thought it would be fun to take a story with the current crew and tell a set of stories set in past time frames that could be used to explain how the group evolved from a 'dirty, thankless job' type of unit to the multifaceted organization they are in the twenty-fourth century." Kevin said, "It's no secret that Dayton and I have our fanboy hearts deep in the twenty-third century. So here's John, giving us an excuse to write a twenty-third century story with a legitimate purpose in the S.C.E. framework. We jumped on it."

Dayton said, "The original idea we had was much more political in tone, set almost entirely on Beta III (Landru's planet, from 'The Return of the Archons'). It had planetary revolts, terrorist actions, and an overall darker theme. I admit that I wasn't too keen on the overall idea even then, but Kevin and I kept with it until we found an approach we liked." Kevin said, "That story was interwoven with flashback tales for only two of the three parts (the first flashback being pretty much what happened in Book Two and the second flashback involving the out-of-control warp ship in Book Three) but the bad guys were not our homegrown Lutralians but the Legarans—our idea was to depict a botched first contact at the hands of the S.C.E. that led to the Legarans

being so mad that it took Sarek eighty years to sort it out," Kevin laughed.

With the events of September 11th, the story took a turn. Dayton said, "The notion of writing such a story lost all its appeal to us. Honestly, I just couldn't get myself energized to write something that in many instances would be very much an unhappy ending for several of the characters. Not that we were killing anyone off or anything like that, but that they'd be losers in some respects, and Kevin and I decided we wanted to write something more positive. I wholeheartedly understand that many people, including several friends of mine who live in New York, were compelled to express their feelings about that tragic event through the written word. I support them in that regard and much of what they've written in response to how 9/11 affected them is some of the most compelling stuff I've ever read. But, typical me, I went in the opposite direction. I wanted to write a story where our guys are heroes, damn it. Thinking back on it, I probably just wasn't ready to try and tackle anything that might be construed as my feelings on September 11 and its aftermath. So we started over from the beginning with our proposal for the trilogy, coming up with a completely different framing story and jettisoning 95 percent of what we'd devised for the three 'flashback' tales. About the only thing which survived was that one flashback story was set on Landru's planet." Kevin said, "We hit on a new tack for the S.C.E.'s development over a much longer period of time, we created the *Lovell* and her crew, and a revised pitch was approved in November 2001. Book One was finished on January 15, 2002 with Book Two done on March 5th and Book Three on April 9th."

Dayton said, "For the paperback reprint, we had a chance to take the three parts—which had been written as separate installments and released monthly as S.C.E. #17, 18, and 19—and restructure them a bit so that they would read better as a single novel-length story. We removed the 'cliffhanger recap' narratives that originally started the second and third installments, reordered the chapter numbers, just little things like that. John and Keith worked with artist Sonia Hillios to come up with the cover for the paperback, with its old-style fonts and original series *Trek* logo, and the whole package just came out fantastic. I'm particularly proud of the way the book turned out."

2 0

ENIGMA SHIP
(S.C.E.)
J. STEVEN YORK AND CHRISTINA F. YORK

SEPTEMBER, 2002

The *U.S.S. Lincoln* mysteriously vanishes without any evidence to theorize what happened to the vessel. The *da Vinci* is called in to investigate and they discover the ship is trapped by a gigantic holographic craft. With the help of Scotty and some old technology, the S.C.E. race to save countless lives, including their own.

Christina remarked, "Where do ideas come from? With exceptions, like 'Life Lessons,' that question becomes difficult to answer. As a writer married to another writer, we are always finding ideas. If one of us doesn't see something, likely the other does. After a while, we really don't know where a specific idea originated. As for working with J. Steven, well, it was a matter of the whole being greater than the sum of the parts. Steve had worked with Keith DeCandido previously, in another tie-in universe. They worked well together, and when we heard Keith was doing S.C.E. it seemed like the right time for Steve to get into *Trek*. I freely admit that he is the tech-head in this relationship, and I often rely on him for the nuts and bolts, even in my solo work. With my SNW credentials, and his experience with Keith, we were a good combination when there was a spot open.

"Collaborating was another new process, however. We had never actually done any collaborative work when we pitched *Enigma Ship*. We did sell a short story ("Technomancer's Apprentice," *Mage Knight Collector's Guide, Volume 1*) in the meantime, and practiced our collaboration skills. (Keep in mind that we had close to twenty years of marriage before we tried this. Don't try this at home, kids. We're professionals!) The writing process was a matter of drafts passing back and forth from his machine to mine, and each of us trying to integrate our contributions smoothly into the whole. We made our deadline, and each of us went back to our own work. The publishing process was a dream. I can't say enough good things about Keith as an editor. First, he knows *Trek*, as Dr. Seuss would say, 'Inside, outside, upside down.' He catches technical and continuity snags better than anyone I have ever worked with. He knows his stuff. Second, he is a pro, and he treats his writers as pros. He's on time, he tells you what's going on, and he will follow up on business issues if you need him to. Third, he's a genuinely likeable guy, who treats writers as people, too. And, fourth, he knows where that body. . . . Wait, never mind. Move along. Nothing to see here."

#21–#22

WAR STORIES,
Book One and Book Two
(S.C.E.)
KEITH R.A. DECANDIDO

OCTOBER 2002;
NOVEMBER 2002

The Androssi Overseer is hacked. The crew of the S.C.E. has beaten him twice and he can't figure out why. Purchasing personal logs of the various *da Vinci* crew members during the Dominion War, Brion hopes to decipher their minds and figure out how to defeat them once and for all.

When asked about these two novellas, Keith answered, "Simply a desire to look back at the war and see what the *da Vinci* crew were doing. We'd been told in various stories about Gomez's trick behind enemy lines and Lense's nightmares on the *Lexington*, so I dramatized those, and also told a story about Faulwell doing cryptography work. I wanted to show the *da Vinci* in action, and introduce the readers to Gomez's predecessor, Salek. It also gave me a chance to write 110 and 111 together."

#23 & #24

WILDFIRE,
Book One and Book Two
(S.C.E.)
DAVID MACK

DECEMBER 2002;
JANUARY 2003.

The *Starship Orion* finds itself in trouble while navigating in the atmosphere of a gas giant. Everyone on board is presumed dead, but that doesn't stop the *da Vinci* from rushing to the scene for a rescue attempt. To make matters more harried, the *Orion* was testing a new prototype stellar-ignition warhead, code-named *Wildfire*. This device's purpose is to aid in terraforming by making gas giants become small dwarf stars. The result would be an extra energy source for a remote planet. Unfortunately, this device could also be used as a devastating

weapon. Can the crew recover the device before it's too late?

David said, "Ever since I first watched Wolfgang Peterson's seminal U-Boat film *Das Boot*, I had wanted to sink a starship. My first attempt, with John Ordover, was the *Star Trek: Deep Space Nine* episode 'Starship Down,' which, though I enjoyed it, was limited by the constraints of a television budget. Basically, I still had an itch to tell a *Star Trek*-based disaster story of a type no one had tried before. Something that would be too expensive to put on TV."

David submitted the story outline to John Ordover and Keith DeCandido. They both liked the story, but suggested dropping the happy ending. David said, "He and Keith agreed that if we were going to tell this kind of story, it had to have teeth. Now, when I first pitched *Wildfire*, I had expected to co-write it with Keith, as I had done on *Invincible*. After the September 11, 2001, attack on New York City, however, I felt a deep need to write *Wildfire* myself, in my own words. I asked Keith if he would mind if I took on that project solo; he said, Go for it. He gave me tons of great advice, made sure I was on the right track, then set me loose to learn for myself how to write a story from start to finish."

David was happy to write in a universe with no on-screen counterparts. With this in mind, he said, "we were in a position to alter the status quo and not have to hit the reset button at the end of the story; this was going to be a story whose consequences would alter the direction of this series and shape its characters' lives for years to come. As a result, the story is far more powerful than if we had taken the easy way out;

it challenged me more as a writer, and it made this into a work of which I expect I will always be proud."

#25

HOME FIRES
(S.C.E.)
DAYTON WARD AND KEVIN DILMORE

FEBRUARY 2003

After the tragic events aboard the *da Vinci*, Corsi and Stevens head to the planet Svoboda II, for rest and relaxation. Corsi's parents live on the planet and she hasn't seen them in some time. Joining her father on a cargo run, she finally has the opportunity to talk to her father and discover why he has such a hatred for the uniform she wears.

Kevin has strong memories of this story. "This project came to us by request. John and Keith DeCandido knew Dave Mack's *Wildfire* was coming, and they very much wanted a set of four stories to follow that one with a specific aim. If *Wildfire* was to S.C.E. what 'Best of

Both Worlds' was to TNG, then these four stories would be S.C.E.'s 'Family.' They thought Dayton and I were well suited to take one of those slots, which we found very flattering. I said I'd be interested if we could do a story with Corsi and Stevens. So we set to work on *Home Fires*, or, as Dayton and I wanted to title it, *Inner Corsi*. Tee hee hee."

Kevin continued, "On this one, our work was the most delineated of any of our projects. I wrote the first draft of the present-day wraparound story and Dayton wrote the first draft of the flashback. This one was as personal of a *Star Trek* story as I have written, as I was writing it while my best friend was in the last weeks of his six-year fight against brain cancer. I felt like I had a handle on the issues of loss and healing that the story tries to address and it proved to be very helpful to me as I sorted things out myself. According to my computer file, we submitted *Home Fires* the day after my friend died."

Dayton reflected back on the story. "The story didn't get as much attention early on as *Interphase* and *Foundations* received, but I'm still proud of it. The framing sequence in particular was a change of pace for us, and the scenes that Kevin wrote with Corsi and her father are just terrific stuff."

#26

AGE OF UNREASON
(S.C.E.)
SCOTT CIENCIN

MARCH 2003

A Carol, Bart, and Soloman are sent to introduce new technology on a world driven by emotion. When a murder occurs, and a rival of Carol's seems responsible, can she overcome her hatred to solve the mystery? And what kind of mysterious technology has the government hidden from its people? When the three of them uncover the truth, will it cost them their lives?

Scott remembers, "My editor, the fantastic Keith DeCandido, really liked that we put focus on the character of Carol in *Some Assembly Required* and suggested doing more with her. I'm also a big fan of Alfred Bester's work and wanted to work with some of the themes running through his work, so the story came together quickly, though it was very different from the first one. Dan had just sold an original comic book series to DC and been hired to launch a new version of *Firestorm* with them (along with previous commitments on two other titles). Comics are his first love and he couldn't clear the room in his schedule. I love comics as well, and even had a chance to do a TNG miniseries for WildStorm called *The Killing Shadows*."

Overall, Scott had a wonderful experience with his two S.C.E. stories. "Keith had terrific ideas and insights, as always. The *Star Trek* experience has been very rewarding to me and I'm very grateful for my chance to be a part of this rich and exciting universe."

#27

BALANCE OF NATURE
(S.C.E.)
HEATHER JARMAN

APRIL 2003

A P8 blue heads home to potential anarchy. Visiting old friends, an earthquake shatters her happiness. Disappearances soon follow, and then evidence arrives that an old truce has evaporated. Can she overcome society hierarchy and help save her homeworld?

"The challenge of *BoN* was how to make the story of a Nasat (an oversized pillbug) compelling. Falling back on the basic rule of storytelling, I looked for a conflict. I found one in my home. The biggest inspiration for *BoN* came from my twin daughters who were diagnosed with dyslexia early in elementary school. They're both brilliantly creative (Rachel draws, paints, and excels in computer graphics; Allyson writes, cooks, and designs/sews clothing) and have exceptional abilities in understanding storytelling and literature. Yet, written language has been a challenge for them. They literally had to relearn how to read and understand words starting at phenomes. I watched them struggle and saw how they were treated in the classroom by those who only saw the disability and not their creative genius. I deeply believe that many individuals who are labeled as being disabled or having a 'disorder' simply have brains that are differently-wired and that somewhere in the scheme of things, we need those differently-wired brains to complete our human family. I transferred some of the same issues that confronted my daughters to Pattie. For me, I loved the opportunity for world building. I think the S.C.E. format is a terrific training ground for writers starting their first major media tie-in projects. I believe this is one of my tightest projects, writing-wise."

#28

BREAKDOWNS
(S.C.E.)
KEITH R.A. DeCANDIDO

MAY 2003

Captain Gold is cleared of any wrongdoing at Galvan VI. To recuperate, he heads home to visit his family. Sonya Gomez heads home as well, still struggling with her indecision with Kieran. Captain Gold contemplates retirement, and Sonya mulls over various issues, including blaming Gold for the events of the disaster. Is their extended family destined to no longer be together?

Keith remarked, "What has always been of more interest to me than the crisis is the aftermath of the crisis. I always want to know what happens next. That's probably why the (*Next Generation*) episode 'Family' is of more interest to me than (the TNG episode) 'The Best of Both Worlds.' With *Breakdowns*—and with the other three post-*Wildfire* stories—I wanted to show the trauma of the deaths on the *da Vinci*, and how they affected everyone, particularly Gold and Gomez. It was also an opportunity to show people's families, especially those of our two lead characters, which did a great deal to enlighten us as to why David and Sonya are the way they are."

#29

AFTERMATH
(S.C.E.)
CHRISTOPHER L. BENNETT

JUNE 2003

San Francisco and Starfleet Academy still have major rebuilding projects ahead, courtesy of the Breen attack during the Dominion War. A major explosion rocks and shocks the inhabitants of the area, so the S.C.E., along with Miles O'Brien, investigate this potential new threat. Can they decipher the mystery and get along with their brand new teammates?

Christopher commented, "The assignment for *Aftermath* actually came before the idea. Keith DeCandido, who'd become acquainted with

me through my posts on the TrekBBS, invited me to pitch an idea for the *S.C.E.* series. Since I wasn't familiar with the series, I thought I'd make it easier on myself by focusing on more familiar characters. I chose to set the story on Earth so I could use Scotty and O'Brien. An Earth-based story about the Corps of Engineers suggested something involving the rebuilding of San Francisco after the Breen attack in 'The Changing Face of Evil.' Since Keith had told me about the tragic events planned for *Wildfire,* I had the idea to set my story just after it, allowing me to tie in the physical rebuilding with the characters' efforts to rebuild their lives. This actually ended up delaying the story's publication substantially, since I didn't realize how far in advance the series was being planned. Also Keith decided to add the four spotlight stories between *Wildfire* and *Aftermath,* delaying it still further. I also thought that a story about engineers should have a significant hard science fiction component, and would be a good place to present some of my thoughts on how to reconcile *Trek* physics with real physics. *Trek* physics has always been of variable credibility, but there are some ideas on the cutting edge of modern theory that seem to mesh together pretty well with *Trek* physics. I started with Chris van der Broeck's proposal of a micro-warp bubble, considered the ramifications of such a technology, and devised a plotline that let me explore *Trek* physics in real-physics terms—while also giving the aliens their own form of 'aftermath' to deal with. Not long after I submitted the proposal, September 11th, 2001 happened, and it changed the way I thought about certain aspects of the story. So I amended my outline to incorporate those ideas."

He continued, "The other major addition to the outline came from Keith. Because of when I chose to set my story, I got the honor of introducing the new second officer, Tev. Keith gave me the basic character brief—essentially 'Charles Emerson Winchester the Tellarite,' brilliant, arrogant, rude and hard to get along with—but gave me a lot of freedom in filling in details. I decided his arrogance and rudeness came from a cultural difference—his people abhorred dishonesty and saw courtesy, tact, and modesty as forms of deceit. (As it happens, there was a species mentioned in TNG's 'Coming of Age' that had the same cultural idiosyncrasy, but I'd totally forgotten it.) I also coined the 'Mor glasch' part of his name. Additionally, I got some advance word about the O'Briens' arc from *Unity*, so I could keep *Aftermath* consistent with those plans. *Unity* was supposed to come out first, giving me a chance to see it and tweak the details to fit. Unfortunately, the pregnancies of S. D. Perry and Marco Palmieri's wife delayed the process and made things very hectic, and fitting the details of *Aftermath* and *Unity* together kind of got lost in the shuffle. So there are some slight inconsistencies between the two. I also came up with three new characters of my own, but only had room for two: Rennan Konya, a Betazoid security guard, whom I created because I wanted to play against the usual 'tough guy' type with a character who saw security in a gentler, nonviolent way (since I'm something of a pacifist myself); and Ellec Krotine, a Boslic woman with cherry-red hair, who was a Tuckerization of a girl I knew in my first year of college. (She was human, but did dye her hair cherry red.)

"The writing was fairly straightforward, but I rushed the ending, adding an epilogue that I soon decided wasn't working at all. I kept hoping to fix it, but I kept assuming I'd have time to get to that later, and by the time Keith got around to editing it, there wasn't enough time to spare. So we just cut the epilogue altogether, leaving a story that ends a bit abruptly and has one small detail left dangling. The Vulcan worker in the opening scene was originally written as a Suliban. I figured that, since the Suliban were nomads and most of them weren't in the Cabal, logically some groups of them would be unaffected by whatever fate eventually befell the Suliban on *Enterprise*. So I didn't think including one would step on any continuity toes. Apparently others saw it differently, though. I guess following up on twenty-fourth-century Suliban will have to wait for a later work."

#30 & #31

ISHTAR RISING,
Book One and Book Two
(S.C.E.)

MICHAEL A. MARTIN & ANDY MANGELS

JULY 2003; AUGUST 2003

Dr. Pascal Saadya has a reputation for succeeding under impossible conditions. With his crack team, he has spent the last six years of his life trying to terraform the planet Venus. With the help of his good friend, Captain Gold, plus the S.C.E. team, the doctor believes nothing can go wrong. The mission will bring painful reminders of Galvan VI, plus Soloman will face other Bynars for the first time since the separation, forcing him to deal with prejudice.

When asked about the story, Mike said, "I was reading a book about Venus and I thought it would be really cool to show an *Analog* magazine-type effort to terraform the place, but in the context of *Star Trek*, where Venusian terraforming had already been established to some degree. Since the S.C.E. series involves engineering problem-solver types, it seemed like a natural place for a story like this. I think Keith suggested focusing on Soloman for the intimate human(oid) portion of the story. Then it sort of wrote itself."

Andy expressed his thoughts. "Once we got an idea for the terraforming problem, we had to figure out the S.C.E. solution. The funny thing is, science and math are my two worst subjects, and I largely came up with the solution. I had Mike explain to me the problem in non-heavy-science terms (I jokingly told him to put it into grade school science), and asked questions, and then applied *Star Trek* science logic to it. Could this work? How about this? Eventually, the solution was arrived at. We incorporated that search for a solution into the book. *Ishtar Rising* also gave us a fun opportunity to write some unusual characters. I really enjoyed writing the lonely Soloman, and had a ball doing the rescue scenes with the giant pillbug, P8 Blue (Pattie)."

#32

BUYING TIME
(S.C.E.)
ROBERT GREENBERGER

SEPTEMBER 2003

The new and old crew members of the *da Vinci* are still trying to get used to each other when they receive news that an area of space is showing evidence of chroniton particles. A Ferengi has discovered a time travel device, and he will use it to achieve ultimate wealth. Tev, along with Gomez, Corsi, and Abramowitz, will travel into Ferenginar's past to stop him.

"In *Doors into Chaos*, I had a scene where Troi arrives on Ferenginar and, following custom, disrobes to properly appear before Grand Nagus Rom. It was to be played for some humor since, under Rom, women can wear clothing. Paramount had some concerns with the scene so it got truncated. John Ordover and Keith wanted me to write a story where three members of the S.C.E. team have to conduct a mission on Ferenginar, in the buff, to prove it

can be done. With that as a starting point, I knew it meant time travel and what Ferengi can't resist using a time machine to his advantage? It was a fun process. For a throwaway, I had Songmin Wong talk about playing the Ferengi market and owning a yacht. Other subsequent authors ran with that and it's become a part of the S.C.E. mythos and, to me, that's one of the best parts of the series."

#33 & #34

COLLECTIVE HINDSIGHT,
Book One and Book Two
(S.C.E.)
AARON ROSENBERG

OCTOBER 2003;
NOVEMBER 2003

When the Vulcan Salek was the first officer, the crew of the *da Vinci* encountered a strange vessel that appeared to run entirely on solar energy. A threat to the sector, the destruction of the vessel results in Salek's death. One year later, the *Dancing Star* mysteriously reappears.

How did the ship survive and can they destroy it for good this time?

"I'd been thinking of what I wanted to do for a second S.C.E. story, and had the idea of a case that the S.C.E. had already completed but wound up having to go back and redo. It was based upon that old line about hindsight being 20/20, but I thought it'd be even more interesting if it was an entire group trying to recreate what they'd done wrong before. And, since the S.C.E. team has changed a little since it started, and since Duffy had just died, it gave me the chance to do the original team for the first half and the current team for the second, with only Solomon, P8, and Duffy around for both. Keith liked the idea, and gave me permission to do Salek's death, which was great."

#35 & #36

THE DEMON,
Book One and Book Two
(S.C.E.)

LOREN L. COLEMAN AND RANDALL N. BILLS

DECEMBER 2003;
JANUARY 2004

When attempting to pinpoint a distress call, the crew is horrified to discover the message originates from the edge of a black hole. Using their collective knowledge, a rescue attempt appears possible. But things can never go smoothly. The aliens resemble snakes, and when a ship arrives and confronts the *da Vinci*, can Captain Gold keep his cool? And, why do the aliens not want anyone rescued? Is this Galvan VI all over again?

Loren realized he was a *Trek* fan "About 1978 or so. I was nine or ten, and I already had most of the classic episodes memorized. It was a contest to see who could name the episode from the first few minutes, and a really big deal to me if I hadn't seen the episode before."

Loren considers himself a writer even before he discovered *Trek*. "When I decided to do it professionally and make a career of it, I started to keep an eye out for how to write for *Trek*. When the opening came up, I jumped for it. Before then, I'd already published about a dozen or more SF novels. Being able to write *Trek* was like icing. *The Demon* was an idea I had rolling around in my head for awhile. Sparked off a title of the old sci-fi news show *Prisoners of Gravity*. I had this idea about throwing a prison station full of convicts into a black hole to forget about them. When Randall and I listed some pitches to Keith DeCandido, it was one I threw onto the table as a possible S.C.E. story. Keith liked it. Randall and I had been talking about doing a collaboration. Paramount approved it. It just sort of all fell together nicely. And writing it was a blast! Randall and I have been friends for awhile, and we tried collaborating as an experiment. And enjoyed it. We've gotten lots of positive feedback from the fans regarding *The Demon*."

3 7

RING AROUND THE SKY
(S.C.E.)
ALLYN GIBSON

FEBRUARY 2004

Welcome to the planet Kharzh'ulla, where centuries before, the Furies from the *Invasion!* series lived. Home to the most complex artificial structure in the Alpha Quadrant, the planet has a giant ring encompassing the entire planet. The inhabitants use the ring as a space station and elevator to move payload around their world. An attacking Jem'Hadar ship damages a major portion of the structure and the S.C.E. must repair the damage before the elevator shaft falls to the surface and potentially kills millions.

Allyn commented, "I can't remember not being a *Star Trek* fan, though my affection for the series waxes and wanes over time. My first real memory of *Star Trek* is of the animated series, circa 1977 or 1978. What I remember most is 'The Slaver Weapon.' I couldn't say for certain what the first 'real' episode I saw was—it may have been 'Where No Man Has Gone Before' in 1981 or 1982. I started reading the *Star Trek* comics in 1983, when DC Comics launched their first series. I can honestly say that were it not for those comics I might not be a *Star Trek* fan today. I loved the characters. I loved the artwork. To this day Konom remains my favorite *Star Trek* character and, given the chance, I'd love to write a story about Konom. The first *Star Trek* book I read would have been one of the James Blish collections in junior high school. The first *Star Trek* book I bought was Vonda McIntyre's novelization of *Star Trek III: The Search for Spock*. The first original *Trek* novel I bought was Margaret Wander Bonanno's *Strangers from the Sky*. To me the novels and the comics were always part of the 'real' *Star Trek*. Those stories, more than the classic reruns, were what kept me coming back to *Star Trek*."

Allyn continued, "I don't think anyone sets out to write *Star Trek* fiction. I think people set out to be writers. Writing *Trek* just happens to be what some writers do. I started writing early. The earliest story I can recall writing was a Sherlock Holmes story. I started writing *Star Trek* fan fiction at most two years later, inspired in large part by an essay in *The Best of Trek, Volume 9* entitled 'The Three-Foot Pit and Other Stories.' The essay described the experience of writing fan fiction and getting it published, and that would have been the moment when I realized that I, too, had *Star Trek* stories inside me to tell, waiting to get out. I may have written a dozen stories in those years until I graduated from high school. Very few stand out in memory today."

Allyn continued, "Somewhere along the way I learned something important. I learned how to plot. I learned how to structure a story. I needed a roadmap, an outline, to keep me on point, to keep me from straying, to bring me back around. There's a reason I sometimes refer to myself as 'Allyn Gibson, perennial *Strange New Worlds* loser.' The essential characteristic of being a writer is writing and submitting what has been written, and in that regard 'losing' has been an education. I've 'lost,' but I've learned something valuable in the losing and that's how to be a better writer. When the winners for the *Strange New Worlds* contests are announced each January on the various bulletin boards there are the inevitable congratulations to the winners from past winners, fans, and other writers, and I've posted the last few years that even those who 'lost' are still winners because they had the courage to put their stories into an envelope and mail them off, something so many people who call themselves writers never accomplish. I have always wanted to write. *Star Trek* just happens to be an outlet for the urge."

Eventually, Keith DeCandido invited Allyn to pitch for S.C.E. "I put together three pitches. One was a steampunk story—the Moriarty hologram escaped and turned a planet into a tech-heavy Victoriana culture and Duffy had to remove the program from the planet's computer network. Another was an Abramowitz story about a derelict spaceship buried miles beneath a medieval-level coastal city and an observation post with some unusual problems. Being unfamiliar with the format, these weren't pitches so much as they were short outlines of about a page. The third pitch was what became *Ring Around the Sky*. It ran four or five sentences at most and it didn't even mention a character focus. It took about a month for Keith to reply. He wanted the one with the space elevators. In the pitch I had mentioned it was a colony world, so could I make it a Tellarite colony? Duffy was being killed out, so could I do some character stuff with the new guy on the block, Tev? It took about a month to write the outline that ran to twelve pages. A month after that, Keith came back with some suggestions and asked that it be rewritten to half the length, so I made revisions and sent it back. The outline went to Paramount, and in November he told me the story had been approved. *Ring* went through three different phases in its storytelling. The first was a kind of flashback—Pattie visits Kharzh'ulla in the twenty-sixth-century for the dedication of the newly-built elevator to replace the one that the *da Vinci* removed for stability reasons, and she gives her reminiscences of the repair mission in the twenty-fourth-century as a kind of living history. All told I spent a month writing the story from Pattie's perspective, but I realized by early February this wasn't working and decided to take a more straightforward approach. The second phase lasted from February to April, and half of the published book comes from this period. The Furies from *Invasion!* entered the picture about midway through, and it came as quite a surprise to me. In my initial outline I wrote that the elevator system was an ancient artifact, tens of thousands of years old, and its builders had died out far in the past. It occurred to me, why not the Furies? They date from the right period, they would have had the engineering know-how, and they provided a good explanation for building the Ring in the first place—it would make for a *huge* drydock facility which they

would have—needed for their war against the Unclean. The Furies fit so well that the idea actually frightened me. What was different about the second phase and the published book? The location of Prelv, the capital city. Prelv had been built on the equator, at the base of one of the elevator shafts, coincidentally the elevator damaged by the Jem'Hadar during the war. In late April Keith e-mailed me Mike Collins' cover art for *Ring Around the Sky* and I realized I had a problem. The cover was absolutely fantastic. I've been a fan of Collins' work for a long time, and his work for *Ring* may be the best I've ever seen. Unfortunately, the cover art depicted a scene I didn't have in the story, and it depicted Tev looking at the elevator shaft from what I presumed to be Prelv. That couldn't be—it would be like trying to see the top of the Empire State Building while you're standing flush against its surface and looking down the street because that would have been the same vantage Tev would have had of the elevator from Prelv. I loved the cover. I had to have that cover. I had to make it fit with my story. Hence, phase three—move Prelv a few thousand miles off the equator. It may not seem like a major change, but several scenes and two entire chapters needed alteration. I essentially treated this as a new draft and wrote from scratch. Tev's nested dreams entered the picture here, though they were never intended to open the book that they do now. Also, Fabian's restaurant tour of Prelv emerged in this phase, inspired in large part by the *Doctor Who* story, 'The Two Doctors.' Editing the three phases into something coherent took the story into June, and then it became a matter of Keith suggesting and requesting changes and Paramount to give their approvals. Nothing stands out in my mind as not passing Paramount muster except for some punctuation or spelling issues."

#38

ORPHANS
(S.C.E.)
KEVIN KILLIANY

MARCH 2004

aptain Gold and the crew of the *da Vinci* must work with a Klingon version of the S.C.E. to solve a puzzle on a colony vessel. The mysterious ship careens out of control between Federation and Klingon space, and appears to have been traveling for at least a thousand years. The two S.C.E. teams join forces and sneak aboard to repair the obvious damage. Unfortunately, they are captured and the aliens don't take kindly to strangers.

Around the time of *Strange New Worlds V* and placing "Monkey Puzzle Box" in the anthology, Kevin said, "I met Keith DeCandido on line. S.C.E. was just getting underway then and, after he told me he'd liked [my other SNW story,] 'Personal Log,' I asked if I could write for him. He explained the pitching process and I started sending him ideas. A version of *Orphans* was the fourth story I pitched. Keith liked the originality of the ship and its culture, the nature and resolution of the engineering problem, and the Klingon S.C.E. That's all of the original pitch that made it into the final ebook. I think the story went through three versions before I found a balance Keith thought would work."

Reflecting further, he said, "Writing it was very much a labor of love. The exploration of space with colony ships is one of my favorite subgenres in science fiction. In fact, the title of the story is a homage to Robert Heinlein's *Orphans in the Sky*. The operation of the ship and the make-up and society of the People were worked out in far greater detail than ever made it into the story. I also had a blast working with the Klingon S.C.E."

#39

GRAND DESIGNS
(S.C.E.)
DAYTON WARD & KEVIN DILMORE

APRIL 2004

The colony world of another planet has asked for Federation membership. When a threat of "weapons of mass destruction" suggests an attack, the *da Vinci* arrives to mediate, plus look for these weapons. An investigation proves there were never weapons. (Sound familiar?) With the Federation not wanted and hostilities continuing to escalate, it's only a matter of time before tensions explode.

Kevin talked about where the idea for the story originated. "This was one of two proposals we submitted in November 2002. This one was spurred by an idea from John, who thought it would be interesting to see the S.C.E. as weapons inspectors (not unlike the UN weapons inspectors in Iraq at the time). We decided to make it into a brisk action piece, one in which the *da Vinci* crew would continue to become accustomed to Tev, the new second-in-command. We didn't set out for this story to parallel any realities or stir up any political overtones, but events between our writing the book and its release seemed to, well, make it so."

Dayton wanted to clarify something with the story. He said, "We did not set out to mirror what at the time were current events (the ongoing issue of weapons inspections in Iraq before the war), and in fact took great pains to avoid having our story painted as a 'ripped from the headlines' kind of thing. Naturally, all that effort proved to be quite the waste as we watched current events turn and dodge until our story ended up resonating rather well with what was going on in the world, at least to a certain degree. We also tried something different with this story, in that we started it by throwing the reader headfirst into an action sequence in the first chapter, which leads into a cliffhanger, and then backing up a couple of weeks in the next chapter to lay out how the story gets to that point. I'd always wanted to do something like that in a story and this project just seemed perfect for that approach. We had a lot of fun putting this one together."

#40

FAILSAFE
(S.C.E.)
DAVID MACK

MAY 2004

The S.C.E. meets modern warfare. A warp-driven probe crashes on the planet of Teneb, and all of its self-destruct mechanisms fail. With a danger of the advanced technology either exploding or having the inhabitants use it for destructive purposes, four of the *da Vinci* crew beam down right into the middle of a battlefield to secure the probe. With limited technology to assist them, the engineers have little chance of success or survival.

David remembered his proposal for the story. He said, "I pitched it as S.C.E. meets *Black Hawk Down*. What it became is an unflinching look at the brutality of modern warfare, as well as a fast-paced action-adventure. It's gritty, violent, dark, hard-hitting, but also in parts funny or poignant. I know that something this bellicose might not be every reader's cup of tea, but

so far this ranks among my favorites of all the *Star Trek* stories I've written."

#41

BITTER MEDICINE
(S.C.E.)
DAVE GALANTER

JUNE 2004

Allurian society has been wiped out by a plague and the S.C.E. find a vessel that appears to have no life aboard. Evidence shows that the virus might have originated from the derelict ship. Further investigation finds a little boy who is the sole survivor, and has been alone for a very long time. Dr. Lense conducts tests and discovers the boy is a prime carrier of the disease. Can she keep a promise and cure him?

Dave said, "*Bitter Medicine* was my attempt to shift *Trek* gears. It's really my first non-action piece, and I wanted to prove to myself that I could carry a story that didn't rely on a battle or a punch. It's a story high on pathos and regret and hope as well, and it wasn't at all any more or less difficult than an action/adventure story. I enjoyed it a lot. I can't for the life of me remember why I decided to do that particular story. I just wanted to do something that focused on Dr. Lense. Keith helped a lot, as per usual."

#42

SARGASSO SECTOR
(S.C.E.)
PAUL KUPPERBERG

JULY 2004

Assigned to an area of space with millions of derelict ships, the crew must carve a path through this "Sargasso Sea" of space to insure safe passage for other vessels. Minor computer glitches soon escalate into full breakdowns on the *da Vinci*, causing Captain Gold to question reality. Are the failures just random acts or is a sinister force involved?

How did he end up writing a S.C.E. story? "Well, the opportunity just kind of presented it-

self. I was talking to Keith DeCandido and he mentioned that he was looking at ideas for S.C.E. stories. At first I wasn't interested—I figured *Trek* was one of those properties that required a heavy-duty knowledge of the deep background, but after reading a few S.C.E. stories, I thought this was a spin-off I could get into. I guess after thirty years of writing comic books, I've gotten used to stepping into long-running series and picking up on the characters and situations with a little bit of reading and study. Plus, I knew that for any real background info, I had an ace in the hole: my friend and colleague from DC Comics, *Star Trek* expert and author Bob Greenberger. If all else failed, I knew I could write a story and have Bob help me fill in *Star Trek* backstory later. I had just finished reading a book on the California Gold Rush of 1849 and, for whatever reason, a factoid about the amount of trash the wagon trains travelling across the country to California left in their wake stuck in my mind. Everything from dead livestock to pot belly stoves to grand pianos were dumped on the side of the trails and I thought it would be interesting to transplant that concept to a 'wagon train' that had passed through some newly discovered sector of space, only with high-tech trash. Keith actually suggested the change to a Sargasso Sea concept, a dumping ground for millions of years and hundreds of thousands of abandoned ships, which I thought was way cooler. The rest of the story was sparked by a *New York Times Magazine* article I'd read earlier that year about chance and odds, which got me thinking about probability as a fifty-fifty proposition. It really read to me as if it were saying that reduced to its basics any conceivable event either will or will not happen: crossing

5th Avenue, I'll either be hit by a taxi cab or I'll make it safely across. My chances for survival every time I cross 5th Avenue are fifty-fifty. Specious as that concept may be in reality, and being a big Douglas Adams fan, I concocted the alien Uncertainty Drive as the agent to implement the concept and had my story. The writing of *Sargasso Sector* was surprisingly easy. I'd read a lot of the S.C.E. stories that came before and thought I had a fairly good grasp of the characters and I found that I really liked writing most of these people, particularly Captain Gold and Soloman, who kind of worked their ways to the lead of the story as I went along. I also really liked Pattie and enjoyed playing with Tev . . . my natural tendency is to poke sticks at stuffed shirts, so Tev was the perfect foil for that. I was gratified to see that in the end, when I handed the finished story to Bob Greenberger to review before sending it off to Keith, he had only three or four minor fixes on characters and continuity, including adding a few of the aforementioned backstory elements. All in all, I was pleased with the way it came out and with the reaction it's received."

#43
PARADISE INTERRUPTED
(S.C.E.)
JOHN S. DREW
AUGUST 2004

A trip to Risa proves to be anything but restful for the crew. Major malfunctions threaten the guests and appear to be sabotage. The maintenance crew assigned to Risa doesn't appreciate the help of the S.C.E. and a kind of turf war results. Meanwhile, a little boy explores the caves of the planet and discovers an unusual inhabitant.

John got into writing *Trek* stories because "I wanted to beat Howard Weinstein (TAS: *Pirates of Orion*) as the youngest *Trek* writer when I submitted *Trek* stories to DC Comics when they had the license in the 80s at the age of seventeen. I never sold anything, but then-editor at DC Bob Greenberger was always kind enough to send me critiques that helped me to shape a better story. He also helped me develop a thicker skin. Afterwards, I made pitches to both TNG and DS9, but didn't have any success there. It's a great format to tell tales of the future, a hopeful one, but one where we can still struggle to do the right thing. Honestly, I'm always the guy that looks for the hook on how to sell it. Most *Trek* shows have done a Risa episode, so when I saw somewhere how the S.C.E. was referred to as almost like a television series, I thought, why not a visit to Risa then?"

John continued, "I've been friends with Keith R.A. DeCandido since high school. I had a few short stories published, so Keith offered me the opportunity to pitch him a story. *Paradise Interrupted* was the first one that Paramount and he both liked. I have to say I learned one great lesson in writing this story. It's one thing to have a great idea, it's another thing to be able to put it to paper. I made a great many mistakes and I'm fortunate that Keith is a patient person, but I would have to say that the most important thing about writing a *Trek* novel, in whatever venue, is to know your characters. I thought I did, but in the editing process it was clear I didn't get it."

#44

WHERE TIME STANDS STILL
(S.C.E.)
DAYTON WARD & KEVIN DILMORE

SEPTEMBER 2004

A couple of years after Kirk's experiences in the Delta Triangle, the S.C.E. arrives to not only try out a method for safe passage, but also catalog the various vessels that were originally lost to the strange anomaly. In the future, the S.C.E. must travel into the Triangle to deliver a most unusual package.

Dayton was stunned that the proposal for the story received approval. "This was an idea Kevin and I pitched on a lark to Keith. We'd had this idea for doing a sequel to the animated episode 'The Time Trap' and using the twenty-third century S.C.E. characters we'd created for the *Foundations* trilogy. After kicking around the basic idea, we wrote up a proposal and sent it along with the outline we'd written up for *Grand Designs*. Given that the animated series wasn't looked on as 'canonical' or part of the 'official' *Star Trek* universe, we figured this idea would be rejected, if not by Pocket Books then by Paramount's licensing folks, who approve all of the fiction at the proposal and manuscript stage. Imagine our surprise when Keith came back and gave us a big thumbs-up."

Kevin was stunned as well. He said, "It all started when we picked up a copy of the then-new (and brilliant) book *Star Charts* by Geoffrey Mandel. On one map, we noticed Mandel had depicted the Delta Triangle, which we immediately recognized from the animated episode, 'The Time Trap.' Turning in the proposal, we thought we'd get a polite 'Nice try, buttheads.' But what we actually got was, 'Get to work!' "

Kevin and Dayton are huge fans of the cartoons. Dayton said, "We were so completely juiced when we got the go-ahead to write that story, I can't tell you. It was fanboy heaven, for crying out loud. We contacted a couple of people on the Internet who had extensive websites devoted to the animated series in order to get some facts checked, and naturally they came back with suggestions of things that we could address during our story (attempting to reconcile some prickly continuity issues between the animated show and, for example, *Trek* history as later depicted on *Enterprise* or in *Star Trek: First Contact*). We even tried to get the S.C.E. cover artist to render the cover in a style reminiscent of the animated series, but cooler heads prevailed on that item. Oh well, a guy can dream, can't he?"

Kevin said, "Another thing we worked into that story was an homage to the old Sega vector-graphics *Star Trek* video game, the *Star Trek Operations Simulator*, I think it was called. The Gorn mine generator is based on the 'Nomad'

minelayer in that game. No one may catch the reference, but we loved working it in."

#45

THE ART OF THE DEAL
(S.C.E.)
GLENN GREENBERG

OCTOBER 2004

A successful entrepreneur named Portlyn seeks the help of the S.C.E. to transform a devastated agricultural planet into a major industrial complex. While the crew works with the inhabitants of the planet, random terrorist attacks on other worlds owned by Portlyn force the *da Vinci* to leave some of the crew behind to investigate.

"I remember that the original *Star Trek* series was on every night at 6 o'clock—this was back in the mid-1970s. My older brother and sister were first-generation *Star Trek* viewers and they loved watching the reruns on Channel 11 here in New York City. I was just a little kid and I used to fight with them all the time over what to watch. I wanted to watch *The Brady Bunch*, but they were the older ones so they won out more often than not so I used to watch *Star Trek* with them. It was actually the first movie that made me a fan; my sister took me to see it and that's when I really fell in love with it. I was already familiar with the characters, but after seeing them on the big screen, that's when I really became a fan. I always liked writing. I grew up reading comic books, and as a kid, I wrote and drew my own comic books. Some of them were *Star Trek* comic books, so you could say I was in training from a fairly young age! I found that I loved writing stories featuring the original crew. And after reading *Star Trek* novels like *Yesterday's Son*, by A. C. Crispin—which I read in its entirely over the course of twenty-four hours because I was enjoying it so much— it became a dream of mine to one day write those characters 'for real,' on a professional basis. So you can imagine what a thrill it was for me when I got to write a five-issue *Star Trek* comic-book limited series, featuring the original crew, for Marvel Comics! It was called *Star Trek: Untold Voyages*, and it featured the adventures of Captain Kirk and his crew after *Star Trek: The Motion Picture* and before *Star Trek II: The Wrath of Khan*, so I was able to explore the characters and the choices they made and the directions they went in between those two films."

Glenn continued, "*The Art of the Deal* was originally conceived as a novel featuring the original crew, and the story very much centered on Captain Kirk. It was really about him and a tragedy from his past that had been established in one of the original TV episodes. But when the opportunity to write for the S.C.E. series came along, I was able to extensively re-work the story so that it fit into the S.C.E. mold. I didn't just go in and erase Captain Kirk's name and put in Captain Gold's. It really was a total rewrite, completely overhauled to suit the S.C.E. concept, so a lot of changes were made. It was a fabulous experience, a whole lot of fun, even though the finished product is pretty different from what I originally proposed. I remember that when I first proposed the S.C.E. version of the story, the focus was on Commander Sonya Gomez. I sent it off to Keith R.A. De Candido (the editor of the S.C.E. series) and when I got his comments back he said, 'The way this is written, everything that Gomez needs to accomplish in this story would really be more appropriate for Security Chief Corsi.' So I went back and reworked the whole thing again so that now Corsi was fulfilling the role I had originally intended for Gomez. I remember writing to Keith, 'If this was a TV show, and I was the actor playing Gomez, I'd be really, really angry right now!' I ended up turning in two drafts of the finished manuscript, but the second draft was mostly to add things that would better connect my story to other books in the series and to set up some character stuff for future books."

#46

SPIN
(S.C.E.)
J. STEVEN YORK AND CHRISTINA F. YORK

NOVEMBER 2004

A planet abused by the Breen during the Dominion War now seeks Federation membership. When a derelict ship appears to be on a collision course with the planet, the *da Vinci* crew arrives for what they assume will be a routine mission. Why did the crew of this strange vessel abandon ship? Or, is the ship harboring a bizarre secret that could destroy the peace process?

Christina reflected, "*Spin* was a lot like *Enigma Ship*, with an added complication. Steve was on deadline for another project, so I ended up doing a lot more of the final draft work. But once again, the editing and publishing process were smooth, thanks to Keith. (Sorry I don't have any real dirt to spice things up, but we actually like working with him.)"

#47 & 48

CREATIVE COUPLINGS,
Book One and Book Two
(S.C.E.)
GLENN HAUMAN AND AARON ROSENBERG

DECEMBER 2004;
JANUARY 2005

Captain Gold attends the wedding of his granddaughter to a Klingon. With everyone involved demanding the ceremony utilizes the different cultures, the whole affair threatens to explode into a diplomatic incident. Meanwhile, Fabian helps out a friend who has designed a new class of starship. Offering to train cadets on a holodeck programmed with the ship's schematics, he thinks that the class will be routine. Unknown to Fabian, someone has tampered with the program and everyone's lives are in jeopardy.

Glenn remembered, "I wanted to write something funny and light. The original inspiration thrilled my editor but not Paramount, who disagreed on certain points required to establish the story. (No, I'm not telling you what, I still plan to resubmit it one day.) They said we'd have to make changes, maybe have it take place back on Earth. I couldn't see how, complained about it to Aaron, and he said, 'Oh, that's easy. Do this and this and this, and you're done.' Seemed only fair to offer him half the book at that point. I came up with the other half—why would the *da Vinci* be back on Earth so soon after the events of *Wildfire*, etc.—and came up with the wedding between Esther and Khor which Gold had to officiate. Originally, the idea was going to be that we each take a thread in the first book, end it on a cliffhanger, and then switch plots and see how we wrote our way out of each other's mess in the second book. Aaron wimped out."

Aaron remarked, "Glenn and I have been friends for years—he's actually the one who first mentioned the S.C.E. series to me. He'd pitched an idea for it, but Paramount didn't like it because it went against some of their notions of how Starfleet members behave while on missions. Glenn mentioned it to me, and I suggested a way to keep the intent but not violate those notions by modifying the pitch a bit. He liked the suggestion, and asked me if I wanted to co-write it with him, and I agreed. The process was interesting. We bounced the ideas back and forth, developing two intertwined storylines. They wound up being too big to fit in one book, so we set it up as a two-parter. Once we were both happy with the pitch, we submitted it. It was approved easily, and we decided to each take one of the two storylines to start. We thought we'd trade off with the second book, but both wound up so entrenched in our storylines that we simply kept

to them, so really Glenn wrote one full story and I wrote another, and we twined them together. But we read over each other's sections repeatedly, critiqued them, and tweaked them as we went. Then Keith tweaked a little more. Paramount approved the first one without a single correction, and had only minor tweaks for the second book, so I guess the collaboration worked."

Aaron had some final thoughts. "If you asked me what my favorite *Trek* series (TV or print) is and why, the answer would be S.C.E., hands down. It's great to write for, and great to read, because the characters are clearly part of the *Trek* universe but, because they're all new (or at least had only appeared briefly before), there's a lot more room to play with them and to develop them. And the stories have a lot of variety to them as well. Of the TV series I'd have to go with *Deep Space Nine* as the most interesting, because of its complexity, but *Next Generation* still has a special place in my heart because it was the first *Trek* series I really followed. I also think *Trek* still has legs. I do, because of things like S.C.E. and the *Forgotten Years* books. There's a lot of space to play within the established series, and around their edges, and even off to the side. People know and like the universe, they're comfortable with it, and so they like reading or seeing stories set there, as long as those stories and the characters are engaging in their own right."

#49

SMALL WORLD
(S.C.E.)
DAVID MACK

FEBRUARY 2005

A spider-like being begs the crew for help before it collapses. While Dr. Lense tries to resuscitate the creature, the artifact that it was carrying appears to be a small planet encased in a pyramid. Somehow the entire planet has been shrunk and placed in this device. Can the crew find a new home for the refugees and restore the planet to its proper size? To make matters worse, a hostile force appears and demands the artifact.

The original concept for the story was a pitch for *Star Trek Voyager* that he developed with John Ordover. David said, "John graciously allowed me to sell and write it solo for S.C.E. Basically, I was looking for something tech-oriented that would work well with the S.C.E. series concept. I tried in this story to combine what worked so well for me in my previous sto-

ries, but especially 'Waiting for G'Doh. . . .' My goal with *Small World* was to craft something fast-paced but lighthearted; I wanted it to feel like our heroes were at risk, but I didn't want it to come off as doom-and-gloom. Basically, I wanted to broaden my narrative palette with a few brighter tones than I've used lately."

#50

MALEFICTORUM
(S.C.E.)
TERRI OSBORNE

MARCH 2005

Security chief Corsi receives part of a transmission and when she investigates, she discovers a dead body. It appears to be murder, but she has a difficult time proving it, let alone finding a motive. When another crew member dies under the same mysterious circumstances, she has to utilize the talents of her fellow crew to solve the mystery and bring the killer to justice.

Terri can't remember a time when she hasn't been writing something. "My mother gave me the first story I ever wrote, which she says I wrote at the age of six. While *Wrath Of Khan* was what got me hooked on *Trek*, the idea of actually writing *Trek* stories didn't really occur to me until I saw the first season of DS9. I don't know exactly why it took that long. I've still got some fan fiction for the other franchises floating around at home that was written before that, and I even tried—goddess help me—writing a Garfield comic book once. (It sucked, but I was only twelve.) A story I wrote that was steeped heavily in Greek mythology won a local writing contest in high school. *Trek* was about the only universe I didn't stick my nose into to write about in some manner, until DS9. What got me was Julian Bashir. There was something I could finally identify with in Julian. I'd been in gifted student programs all through school, graduated top ten percent of my class in high school, the works. I knew too many kids that basically were Wesley Crusher. I didn't identify with Wesley, but I could relate to him. Beverly Crusher even reminds me of my own mother a little bit. I also graduated from college a little less than two years before DS9 premiered, and that newness in the real world was still fresh in my mind. When that character finally came along that I could identify with and relate to, story ideas for him started popping into my head. That was pretty much what got me going on writing *Trek* stories."

Terri has tried to break into the *Strange New Worlds* anthologies, but none of her stories made the final cut. The first question that everyone seems to ask about her first S.C.E. story is where does the title come from? "It's a homage to those who were killed in the Salem Witch Trials. (Yes, I know the book involved in

the Witch Trials was really called the *Malleus Maleficarum*, but it's occassionally been mistakenly referred to as the *Malleus Maleficto-rum*. I wanted to use the less-obvious reference for reasons that should be evident when people read the story.)"

She continued, "Landing the story for me was not easy. I had a hurdle to climb on S.C.E. that I don't think anybody has had in a long time with *Trek* fiction, if ever. When I began submitting stories to *Strange New Worlds* in 2001, Keith and I agreed that we wanted to do everything possible to avoid the stigma of nepotism, without cutting the *Trek* market off to me completely, since that would stop me from entering SNW, too, and he thought I had some interesting *Trek* stories I wanted to tell. So, we came to a compromise. We agreed that the S.C.E. market specifically would be cut off to me until I'd met Keith's criteria for it opening. I wasn't allowed to even ask to pitch a story until then. When first Marco Palmieri, and then Peter David, bought stories from me, the door for S.C.E. opened. What sparked the idea for *Malefictorum* was the first time I'd watched the movie *The Ring*. The 'What if?' hit me, and I threw the basic idea at Keith one day. It appealed to his sense of the perverse. Keith was fairly confident I'd be able to write a good Corsi, and encouraged me to develop it as an S.C.E. story, especially since we all know Corsi hates mysteries. The thought of developing this idea as a *Star Trek* cop story appealed to me. It was a writer/editor friend in my writer's group that, upon reading the first draft, said, 'Too much *Star Trek*, not enough *CSI*.' That one comment put the story in laser-focus for me. *Malefictorum* is very much a "*Trek*-meets-*CSI* kind of story."

#51

LOST TIME
(S.C.E.)
ILSA J. BICK

APRIL 2005

Distortion waves begin to erupt from Empok Nor. An investigation by the S.C.E. leads to a bizarre theory that the waves are coming from a parallel universe. When Soloman starts to investigate the data stream to end the fluctuations, he discovers to his horror that in the other universe, his dead partner in this universe is very much alive and is working with his own counterpart to stop him. This leads to Gomez theorizing that her dead lover might be alive in that universe as well.

Ilsa commented, "You know, I have to say that this one just kind of wrote itself. I'm not sure where I got the idea except I'd been thinking in terms of regrets, and I'd already come up with another S.C.E. story that will, I believe, see the light of day next year and deal with something similar only differently. Anyway, I felt that

Soloman's encounters with those other Bynars must have sparked something that would lead him to wish to revisit the kind of intimacy he'd had before. So I decided to do the DS9 mirror universe thing but make it a totally different place than we'd seen before. Then, too, I've seen a fair amount of death, being a doctor. I've had patients die, but also friends and relatives, and I know that it takes a long time before you can think of them without wanting to cry. So I really felt that as much as, say, Sonya would be moving on with her life, she would still be stuck in emotional time, that little hiccup in the stream of her life to which she'd always return. Moving on is a bad way to phrase it, too, because that implies that one ought to and can just push past things. Sure, you can; but I think that traumatic deaths in particular—and deaths where there's unfinished business— those don't heal over so well. Your psyche kind of snags on them. Anyway, I'd also wanted to give the crew a lot more latitude: some space, for example, or a situation where Gold could really shine. Let some real nastiness come out; people are too darned polite sometimes. He's a great captain in his own right, but I wanted to turn him not into his opposite but an exaggeration of what I think he is. For one thing, he's not a quitter. For another, he is kind of a patron saint of lost causes; he and his crew go and pull off the impossible. Then, too, I wanted to look at the willingness of a military or government to use religion for its own ends. We have a lot of that going around these days, both here and abroad. I wanted to be able to use this kind of exploitation to reveal the cynicism and also that, sometimes, there really are elements of spirituality that come out of people when they least expect it. For Gold, his life was somehow snagged around Rachel's death; she'd become his religion in the same way that one hundred eleven is Soloman's. And, really? At the risk of sounding corny? I wanted to try and say something about the immutability of love."

#52

IDENTITY CRISIS
(S.C.E.)
JOHN J. ORDOVER

MAY 2005

G omez is almost over with shore leave on the station Hidalgo. Investigating a central control room malfunction, she finds a discarded message that is nothing more than a scam artist trying to get money quickly. When she deletes the message, the control room locks down and she watches in disbelief as an image of her threatens to kill the inhabitants of the station unless her bizarre demands are met. Will Captain Gold figure out it is not really her? Can Gomez stop the program in time before people die?

• • •

John commented, "The story for this started with my wanting to do a *Trek* variation on the movie *Phone Booth.*"

#53

FABLES OF THE PRIME DIRECTIVE
(S.C.E.)
CORY RUSHTON

JUNE 2005

T he survivors of Coroticus III are picking up the pieces after the Dominion War. During the crisis, the Federation pulled out, stranding a man, and hasn't been able to come back until the conflict resolved itself. The people of the planet seem to worship a god who looks like a Vorta, shattering the Prime Directive. When a mass-murderer shows his ugliness and attacks the S.C.E. crew on the planet, can they survive long enough to stop the killing? And, is the killer the Starfleet officer who was left behind?

Cory commented, "Reading the novels, and having ambitions as a writer anyway, made it natural to want to write *Trek*. *Fables* was my third professional sale, which makes it part of making a living as well as a dream fulfilled. *Fables* started as a SNW story starring Chekov, which was to be a sequel to 'Who Mourns for Adonais?' Once Peter David essentially wrote the sequel to this episode as part of the *New Frontier* series, I abandoned the story entirely: However, the initial scene with Chekov and a retiring station commander eventually became the scene in which Stevens and Johal reflect on the Dominion War. More generally, I'd always been both fascinated and (at times) annoyed by the Prime Directive, especially in the latter stages of TNG's run: Abramowitz's own log entry, which among others she reads during *Fables*, reflects what I see as the inconsistencies. (Strangely, I think *Voyager* often handled the Prime Directive better than TNG did.) Add to this the reality of *Trek*'s dangerous universe, and the story wrote itself: S.C.E.'s use of a cultural specialist was an essential element in pitching the story for that series in particular, and now I can't imagine the story as anything other than S.C.E. Makk, too, was a bit of a gift: I had already planned a Sigma Iotian character, and felt Keith wasn't going to let me get away with it. So imagine my delight . . . I think the story also reflects my adherence to *Trek*'s skepticism concerning religion and its relationship with cultural progress, which is a little out-of-sync with modern *Trek*'s low-key return to faith."

#54

SECURITY
(S.C.E.)
KEITH R.A. DeCANDIDO

JULY 2005

A new officer from the planet Izar joins the security team on the *da Vinci* and Corsi uncharacteristically treats him like dirt. Ten years before, Corsi and Christine Vale tracked down a serial killer on the planet and Corsi has never been the same. Meanwhile, the crew starts investigating the disappearance of Doctors Bashir and Lense, who never showed up at a medical conference.

"In *The Belly of the Beast*, we hinted at a strange past relationship between Corsi and Vale—disdain of the latter for the former, but near-hero-worship of the former by the latter. In *Cold Fusion*, Corsi seduced Stevens on the anniversary of something that happened with someone named Dar. We kept dropping hints about it, but never went anywhere with it, and finally I decided to stop stringing folks along and tell the damn story. I wanted to keep the characters moving forward, and Stevens and Corsi had stalled, so I thought this would be a good way to jump-start their relationship and also answer a long-standing question. The subplot with Tev grew out of a similar desire—Tev needed to make some progress or be drummed off the ship, which meant he needed to get a serious ass-chewing from Gomez."

---

5 5 & # 5 6

WOUNDS,
Book One and Book Two
(S.C.E.)

ILSA J. BICK

**AUGUST 2005;
SEPTEMBER 2005**

⋀ This is the story of what happened to Bashir and Lense on the way to the medical conference. The shuttle crashes into a subspace anomaly and the vessel crash lands on a planet. Bashir and Lense are separated and both think the other one is dead. While Bashir tries to con-

vince a doctor that he is not an enemy, Lense ends up with freedom fighters and finds she is falling in love with one of the leaders of the group. Cold and brutal, the chances of either one of them surviving are slim.

Ilsa remarked, "This is actually something I've been tossing around for a long, long, long, long time. Way, way back—like 10 years ago—I wrote a book featuring the original *Enterprise* crew in which I'd speculated about the origins of the Borg. The Borg have always fascinated me; they still fascinate me. At the end of the book, I implied that Kirk and company were somehow responsible for the Borg's development in somewhat of the same way that I imply that Bashir and Lense have unwittingly supplied the Kornaks with the technology they'll need to get off the planet. I also remember what John Ordover said about the book (and this was right after I won in *Strange New Worlds* II), so that must mean I'd had the chutzpah to just send in the manuscript and synopsis: that the good guys couldn't be responsible, in any way, for the bad guys. So the book died, and I was crushed. . . . Then S.C.E. came along, and by then, Bashir and Lense had some history together, and I wanted to revisit the idea from a different angle. Specifically, Lense is such a bitter, narcissistic, self-absorbed depressive! My goodness, I find myself wanting to write a prescription. Bashir, I've never really bought as a doctor. Sure, I know a lot of self-aggrandizing physicians; I've hung around with a lot of cowboy surgeons, and those guys are really narcissistic. But they have to be; anyone would have to be to do the kind of things they do. But Bashir is always so polite, so nice and all that . . . I just want to slap him silly. I never saw him as fitting the persona of any doctor I hung with who'd have to do all the things he did. And I sure didn't buy that any person would handle the break-up of a love relationship so . . . nicely. So decently. Where were the screams? Where were the tantrums? Why wasn't something broken? So . . . then I got to thinking about how arrogant these two are. I mean, no matter what, they just suck it up and everything works most of the time. Even when the *Lexington* was getting creamed, Lense still had her instruments and her EMH, things were bloody, but she had all this great equipment. I mean what I say when I write that I doubt she's ever really listened to someone's heart; you got machines for that. So I wanted to put her in a position where she would have nothing remotely like what she was used to. I wanted Julian Bashir to be recognized, again, as being very different and I never, ever bought that all these people crash in these shuttles, and not once does anyone ever suspect they aren't whom they say. So I wanted to, literally, box the two docs into no-win situations and see what they did. Which, of course, begs the question of Kahayn and Arin and their crazy world: These people were desperate, and I think that ethics get bent a lot when you're desperate. All you have to do is look at the doctors who worked for the Nazis, or even the doctors who treat soldiers on the front lines. In another universe, I wrote a story called 'Damage Control,' and the title really is the term military psychiatrists (and I was one) use to describe the work they do on the front lines. You want to limit the damage; you want to get soldiers out to fight again. So, as a doctor, what you're really doing is taking a normal fear response, treating it, and then sending some person off to fight and,

maybe, die. As a military doctor in that situation, the mission comes first. Same thing for Kahayn who, of course, had another agenda, too—that maybe something good would come out of all this death. And that's why I let Lense get pregnant."

5 7

OUT OF THE COCOON
(S.C.E.)

WILLIAM LEISNER

OCTOBER 2005

The ramifications of a decision made by Captain Picard years earlier cause problems for the S.C.E. crew. Two races forced to live together begin to show signs of civil war. When the *da Vinci* is asked to come and help purge some older technology, Captain Gold agrees. When the ship arrives, a new person runs the government and orders them to leave.

William said, "After my third SNW sale, I talked with Dayton Ward about his transition from SNW to novels, and he suggested approaching John Ordover. John, in turn, pointed me to Keith DeCandido, suggesting that I should try writing for S.C.E. first. I pitched three short ideas to Keith, and he asked me to send them back with more details. On this second pass, Keith decided he liked the idea for *Out of the Cocoon*, and after Paramount had approved it, gave me the assignment." When asked what was the idea behind the story, he said, *"Out of the Cocoon* is a sequel to the second-season TNG episode 'Up the Long Ladder,' the one where the colony of back-to-nature utopians are rescued from their doomed planet, and relocated to another colony populated by clones. It was, I believe, the third of three ideas I came up with, and I basically just started flipping through the *TNG Companion*, looking for episodes that might present problems requiring the S.C.E. to follow up. 'Up the Long Ladder' presented me with the question, well, what happens when you put these two peoples together, the one forced to become *more* dependent on technology, the other *less* dependent on it?"

5 8

HONOR
(S.C.E.)
KEVIN KILLIANY

NOVEMBER 2005

Corsi wakes up and finds she is no longer on board the *da Vinci*. Her entire body hurts and she is being worked on by creatures she considers half chipmunk and half centaur. Meanwhile, Pattie crashes her vessel on a planet surface and ends up in sort of a zoo. Without her combadge, how can she communicate with her captors?

Kevin reflected, "The S.C.E. story featuring Corsi began as a pitch for a Meuller story to the *New Frontier: No Limits* anthology. It never got past Keith DeCandido, who was first reader on that project. He said he thought it would be a great Corsi story and asked me to repitch it for S.C.E. In *Honor* Corsi, stranded alone on a pre-industrial planet, is the only thing between the ardently nonviolent natives and invaders who think they should be exterminated as ver-min. To protect their nesting grounds, they stand shoulder-to-shoulder testifying to their belief all life is sacred as invaders physically hack their way through them. Corsi can both honor the Prime Directive and stay out of the situation or honor her own beliefs and take a hand. Keith suggested I add another member of the S.C.E., perhaps captured by the invaders to give the story a wider perspective. He also wondered what the *da Vinci* was doing while all this was going on. So I threw in Pattie, always a delight to write, once again mistaken for a bug without her technology, and an engineering project that was in fact the basis of another S.C.E. pitch I'd planned on making. Unlike *Orphans*, wherein much of the story was told through the perspective of aliens witnessing the S.C.E. in action, *Honor* is seen entirely through the eyes of Corsi, Pattie, and Bart Faulwell. Paula Block passed on *Honor* the first time she saw the pitch. The ending was too pat and the philosophy of the natives sounded suspiciously Christian. I gave the story a less happy ending, put a Zen/Hindi spin on the native faith, and resubmitted. Got the go-ahead to write the story on the second try."

59

BLACKOUT
(S.C.E.)
PHAEDRA M. WELDON

DECEMBER 2005

Bart starts to question his life and his relationship with Anthony when the S.C.E. gets the call to help archaeologists. The unusual culture on this world has the inhabitants changing sex. Once this transformation occurs, the person must abandon their previous job and interests for their change. New identity equals new life. Bart starts flirting with one Jewlan, one of the archaeologists who is getting ready for her transformation.

Phaedra commented, "I'd always been interested in races that could shift sexes. So I was excited when the episode 'The Outcast' premiered on *The Next Generation*, and fans were introduced to the J'naii. I loved it. Thought it was one of the best directed, best acted, and best thought-provoking episode I'd seen in *Trek*. But I wanted to create a race that physically changed sexes. But I promptly tucked the idea into the subconscious. There was never any chance of me using such a thing in *Star Trek*, so I figured I'd use them in my own writing. Until I met Keith DeCandido at a workshop, and was given an opportunity to pitch for S.C.E. Sitting in my room, I thought, 'Hm . . . it'd be crazy to have the *da Vinci* visit such a race and fix something for them. Would be even crazier if their contact was female one minute, and then was physically male the next. And what if Bart abruptly had feelings for . . . !' Bingo! No one up to that point had really messed with Bartholomew Faulwell. He'd always played a supporting role. Mostly. And Bart—being my favorite character—just needed to be messed with. With the help of Paula Block and Keith, we hammered out a plausible synopsis and the story bloomed."

Phaedra continued, "I turned it in and three days later, I received files on upcoming eBooks in the series and notes from Keith as to specific characters and changes. One huge change sort of messed me up (brilliant though it is!) but didn't change my use of that character much. I rewrote some things and resubmitted."

#60

THE CLEANUP
(S.C.E.)
ROBERT T. JESCHONEK

JANUARY 2006

The Miradorn are a society consisting primarily of telepathically linked twins. Allied with the Dominion during the war, the government wants to make amends with the Federation. The S.C.E. receives the call to the planet to help deactivate several nasty devices left behind by their former allies and all of them have the potential to explode and destroy the entire planet.

Robert remarked, "I came up with the idea for *The Cleanup* while wondering what might have happened to all the ordnance left behind in the Alpha Quadrant after the Dominion War. Abandoned munitions would pose a threat, just as minefields do in today's former war zones. I thought that cleaning up high-risk sites after the war would be a job that naturally would fall on the shoulders of the Starfleet Corps of Engineers. I built on the central idea by bringing in the Miradorn, a race introduced in the *Deep Space Nine* episode, 'The Vortex.' The introductory episode hinted at various aspects of the Miradorn species, such as the existence of 'twinned Miradorn' who function as two halves of a single being, and the Miradorn's reputation as 'a quarrelsome people.' Later, another DS9 episode revealed that the Miradorn had signed a nonaggression pact with the Dominion during the war. This made them the ideal focus for the story: They had a shady past, and we knew just enough about them to want to know more. I had plenty of opportunities to do some world building, and I tried to make the most of them by exploring as many Miradorn people and places as possible. While the central species was in place from the beginning, I changed the focus characters of *The Cleanup* significantly from the early planning stages of the story. Originally, Soloman was the heart of *The Cleanup*, bonding with Em-Lin, a Miradorn woman who lost a twin in a tragic accident. As the story developed, however, Assistant Security Chief Vance Hawkins pushed his way onto center stage. I brought in Vance to show that there were some lingering hard feelings in Starfleet because the Miradorn had sided with the enemy in the Dominion War. Before long, Vance took over Soloman's role altogether, at first feeling resentment when he was forced to work with Em-Lin and eventually developing a real respect and friendly affection for her. Carol Abramowitz also forced her way into *The Cleanup* after being left out of the original outline. With her cultural expertise, Carol was the perfect person through whom I could explore the many facets of the Miradorn homeworld, Mirada. Like Vance, she was also a lot of fun to write. I enjoyed putting Carol

through one comical predicament after another, then shifting gears and immersing her in apocalyptic chaos as a Dominion secret weapon wreaks havoc on Mirada. Just as Vance confronted dark corners of his own soul in *The Cleanup*, Carol endured a crucible that tested her inner strength and resilience when she was faced with overwhelming circumstances."

#61

PROGRESS
(S.C.E.)
TERRI OSBORNE

FEBRUARY 2006

Set during the time Gold was captain of the *Progress*, he contemplates his next command while on a mission to Drema IV. Dr. Katherine Pulaski wants to check up on Sarjenka, a little girl who Data corresponded with during the *Next Generation* episode, 'Pen Pals.' Pulaski wiped her mind of the incident but wonders if the memories might return. A mining accident throws them all together and they have to work together in order to survive.

• • •

Terri commented, "I honestly admit that revisiting Sarjenka and Drema IV was something I've wanted to do for a very long time. One of my rejected SNW stories covered it, as well as a novel proposal that Marco Palmieri rejected (and, on rereading, rightly so, it wasn't my best work). So, the idea went back into the file, waiting on the right time and place for it. While I was writing *Malefictorum*, I had an idea for a prequel story with Gold where we'd see what his assignment prior to the *da Vinci* was like. I'd just seen something about the Springhill Mine Disaster, and it occurred to me that we hadn't really done that kind of natural disaster story yet. (At least, not that I'd seen, and not that Keith could remember when I asked him about it.) So, the backdrop of a mine disaster was laid for *Progress* and I just had to figure out where to put it and when. Several changes that came about with the Dominion War, *Insurrection* and *Nemesis* gave me that opportunity. It also, in a small way, helps explain the rather quick resolution to the Warp Speed Limitations that we saw in the *Next Generation* episode 'Force of Nature.' The idea occurred to me that it was possible that during the buildup before the Dominion War, especially with the biggest natural dilithium source ever found, Drema IV would be just the kind of resource the Federation would want to make sure was on their side. I had a dilithium mine on Drema IV, and a story about a mine disaster that needed a location. The rest, as they say, is history."

Terri continued, "However, it wasn't that simple. While I was writing *Progress*, Ilsa Bick turned in *Wounds, Book Two*, which ends with the revelation that Elizabeth Lense is pregnant. *Progress* establishes that Sarjenka ended up

studying medicine, and shortly after Keith saw the end of *Wounds Two*, he asked me what I thought about bringing Sarjenka on to the *da Vinci* as an assistant medical officer, to take over when Lense goes on maternity leave. So, halfway through writing it, the story turned from a Gold-centric flashback piece to the introduction of a new character to the team. Thankfully, I was able to talk a lot with Keith and we figured out what kind of personality she should have as a doctor going forward, and how she's going to fit into the dynamic of the *da Vinci* crew. I hope I was successful in pulling back that personality to a younger version, and one that will work well with the Sarjenka we knew in the *Next Generation* episode 'Pen Pals.' "

 # 6 2

THE FUTURE BEGINS
(S.C.E.)
Steve Mollmann and Michael Schuster

MARCH 2006

 cotty tells Geordi the story of why he resigned from running the S.C.E. the first time. A secret mission that involved a theft from a non-Federation world made him mad enough to quit. Admiral Ross pesters him to reconsider but he will not come back because of Admiral Nechayev. Finding odd jobs, Scotty can't escape the call of Starfleet. . . . Includes a timeline of "Scotty's post-Relics journey."

Steve commented, "I've been a *Star Trek* fan almost as long as I can remember. My mother was a fan from when she was a child, watching the show in syndication in the 1970s, and my earliest memory is when she taped *Star Trek II* off the TV for me to watch. I saw all those movies out of sequence and without a lot of information: When I watched *Star Trek IV*, I thought the bird-of-prey was called a 'cling-on ship' because it could cling on to the *Enterprise*. When I was in fourth grade, my family got AOL, and I joined their kids' *Star Trek* club, which included a weekly chat-based 'sim' about the adventures of the *U.S.S. Explorer*, an academy training ship. I would write up loose adaptations of these adventures in my English notebook at school, which were the first *Trek* stories I ever wrote. Ever since then, I've been writing *Trek* stuff of some sort, and I've always had a desire to write my own *Trek* stories."

Michael remarked, "In retrospect, I guess I've always been a writer. Even when it was a simple writing assignment for school, I enjoyed it immensely, and coming up with new stories to tell was a sort of hobby for me. My early *Trek* stories never got finished, mainly because I never plotted them out all the way through to the end. Then, when I started my university education, I wrote two or three longer stories—in German, of course, since my English wasn't good enough at the time—and actually fin-

ished them. My first *Trek* story written entirely in English was intended to be my contribution to the fanrun *Star Trek: Excelsior* fiction series, but for various reasons that never came to anything. Still, I finished two parts of the three-part story, and as it turned out later, I was able to recycle my ideas for an original alien species in my cooperation with Steve, when I used not only the name but also the unusual anatomy I came up with."

Steve continued, "I've known Michael on-line for some time now. He'd submitted a couple proposals for S.C.E. novellas to Keith. Would I be interested in collaborating with him on this? As he said, 'Not only would we be able to have twice the creative input, but there's a good chance that you'll spot my mistakes.' Of course I jumped at the opportunity, and hence was born a beautiful collaboration. First I helped him spruce up one of the ideas he'd already submitted to Keith, a flashback story about Captain Gold's days as an ensign, and then we explored one of my ideas, about an ancient space station in a nebula. When we first started exchanging e-mails, one of the earliest ideas Michael had was investigating the Scotty backstory. Why did Scotty take over the S.C.E.? How do we account for his time spent on Risa as a still-retired civilian in the *New Frontier: Excalibur* trilogy? Those books occur after the Dominion War, but according to S.C.E. Scotty joined the S.C.E. during it. The problem we had: What was the story? It needed to be about something. We had the idea of uniting all of Scotty's twenty-fourth-century adventures into some sort of coherent form, but that's not a story. I kept on coming back to the idea of using the 'discrepancy' of the *New Frontier* books as a plot point. Why would Scotty quit Starfleet, and then join right back up a few months later? It sounded like a story. We went through a few ideas: a friend of Scotty's dying. Some sort of problems adapting to the twenty-fourth century (but that wasn't a road we were eager to retread). One of the sources we'd been trying to reconcile was [Shatner/Reeves-Stevens] books, since they provided the useful datapoint that after Scotty served on the *Enterprise*-E (as per *Ship of the Line*), he'd gone on to the *Sovereign*—which, according to [some books], was Nechayev's flagship. Could one of Nechayev's black ops (established in *New Frontier*) have turned him sour on Starfleet? Michael said we'd need a mission only Scotty could perform, to establish why Nechayev would tap him, of all people. A technology only Scotty had experience with seemed a good idea, hence the use of multitronic computer technology. What if there was an alien race (called the Kepzyrs in the first outline) that had some sort of advanced warp drive Starfleet wanted to get its hands on? And Scotty was the only person to do it, because of his knowledge of the M-5 computer. We back-and-forthed the outline a bit, working through the basics. I outlined the first flashback, detailing why Scotty left the Fleet, and Michael outlined the second, explaining why he came back. A few tweaks, and we sent it off to Keith in May 2004. Not long later, we heard back: He hadn't liked our first two ideas, but he did like this one, and he was sending it out to Paramount. In February 2005, we finally heard back. Paramount like it well enough, except for the advanced warp drive, which they didn't see as a strong enough motivation for the whole operation. Could we come up with something more compelling? This is where we hit upon the idea of the Breen

energy-dampening weapon, since the first flashback had to be set after the Breen entry into the war, as 'Safe Harbors' in *Tales of the Dominion War* had established Scotty to still be in Starfleet as of 'The Changing Face of Evil.' From there, we wrote the actual story, dividing up the work in much the same way we'd split the outline: I wrote the first flashback and the frame; Michael wrote the second flashback. We finished that up right on time to submit to Keith."

Michael continued, "There are some things in the outline that were changed in the final version, but those were minor. The writing process was rather enjoyable, since we could concentrate on our respective parts and didn't have to send stuff back and forth the entire time. I discovered that I tend to overwrite, which isn't such a good idea when you're writing a novella that shouldn't really be much longer than thirty-thousand words. However, I also discovered (as did Steve) that seeing things from Scotty's POV is rather a lot of fun. I acquired a remarkable knowledge of Scottish curses and phrases in the process, which I feel adds to Scotty's character and maybe even provides the reader with a few nice moments. Nechayev also is a lot of fun to write for, but for completely different reasons. She simply doesn't buy that 'living legend' myth that's sort of surrounding Scotty wherever he goes and instead treats him like she would every other Starfleet officer. She has a job that needs doing, and she needs Scotty to do it, regardless of whether he likes it or not. I can honestly say I thoroughly enjoyed writing this story, and I believe the same is true for Steve."

#63

ECHOES OF CONVENTRY
(S.C.E.)

RICHARD C. WHITE

APRIL, 2006

Before Bart Faulwell was the linguist aboard the *da Vinci*, he was chosen to be on an elite team during the Dominion War. Hidden on a secret base, it falls to him and his fellow teammates to decrypt and translate transmissions from deep inside enemy territory. The secret they uncover could turn the tide of the war.

Richard commented, "I've been a writer for a while (doing other licensed stuff and independent comics), as well as a fan of earlier *Trek* novels. I'd met Keith years ago when we were both doing work on Marvel Comics stuff and when I heard he was doing some work on *Star Trek*, I figured it was a good time to approach him about an idea I had. He suggested I take a shot at doing an S.C.E. story before trying to pitch a *Trek* novel, and he made a couple of

suggestions about something he'd be interested in. I shot him two proposals, and he declined on one but liked the other idea. We expanded on it and Paramount liked it also, which is what led to me doing S.C.E. #63. Keith wanted me to do a story centered around Bart Faulwell since he is the S.C.E. cryptologist/linguist. You see, I was an analyst/cryptanalyst/linguist in the Army for fifteen and a half years, so I have an idea of what Bart's skills are. Since this was going to be set in the Dominion War era, I thought taking a scenario from World War II and transposing it into the future might be a fun approach."

Richard continued, "Writing it took a lot of research. I read every S.C.E. book that was available at first to try to capture the feel for the characters and ensure my ideas meshed fairly closely with what had been seen before. I also used a number of sources (*Star Trek Encyclopedia*, *Star Charts*, StarTrek.com's library function, etc.) to help refresh my memories. Unlike Keith, I don't have every episode memorized. Once I had the final proposal ready, I sent it into Keith who made some suggestions and then Paramount made some suggestions and I got to work. I try to write a couple hours each night, so it took me about two months to finish the first draft. Keith did some line edits that really improved the story. It was fun to start to flesh out a portion of the *Trek* universe that hasn't been visited too much (Starfleet Intelligence). There's a lot more to Intel than 'Section 31' and I hope to get an opportunity to tell some more stories about the men and women who work in the shadows trying to keep the Federation safe."

6 4

DISTANT EARLY WARNING
(S.C.E.)

DAYTON WARD AND KEVIN DILMORE

MAY 2006

The crew of the *Lovell* arrives at the newly built Vanguard station and find themselves engulfed in a mystery. Major malfunctions frequently occur and when the problems are fixed, more crop up as if it was an act of sabotage. When a murdered crewman is found in one of the Jeffries tubes, the S.C.E. crew and the Vanguard personnel must stop a murderer and keep the station from self-destructing.

Dayton remarked, "When we first heard about the concept for the *Vanguard* series, and even before our involvement with the series, Kevin and I hit on the idea of crossover potential with that group and the crew of twenty-third century S.C.E. characters we'd created for *Foundations* and *Where Time Stands Still*. Both Marco and Keith were open to the idea, but we didn't do much with it at first. Then we read the bible for

Vanguard and the high-concept storylines that would drive the series, we saw that Marco and David Mack had taken our original idea of having the S.C.E. crew work with the *Vanguard* team and expanded upon it, actually incorporating it into the ongoing Vanguard storyline by having their ship, the *U.S.S. Lovell,* assigned the station for a time. When we started talking with Marco and fleshing out the story for the second *Vanguard* book, *Summon the Thunder,* we knew we'd be bringing the *Lovell* into the story and so had to create a plot point or two to showcase them to a certain extent."

He continued, "Then Keith told us about the *What's Past* series of stories for the S.C.E. line, and told us to work out a story with our original crossover idea as an installment for that series. Since we were already well into plotting *Summon the Thunder,* we were able to quickly develop a story that would serve multiple purposes: 1) Give Keith what he wanted for the S.C.E. series, as well as allow Kevin and I to write a story that would in effect plant a few seeds not just for *Summon the Thunder,* but actually the whole *Vanguard* storyline. That became *Distant Early Warning.*"

Dayton commented on the challenges of the story. "First and foremost, writing it as an S.C.E. story, rather than a *Vanguard* story. To that end, we made sure that no scenes in the novella are told from the point of view of a Vanguard character. The reader is introduced to the station just as our characters experience it: for the first time. Additionally, we wanted to be sure that S.C.E. readers who might not have read the first *Vanguard* book didn't get anything spoiled for them, and *Vanguard* readers who were sampling S.C.E. via our story wouldn't be confused, either. It was a tough balancing act, but I think we pulled it off well enough."

6 5

10 IS BETTER THAN 01
(S.C.E.)
HEATHER JARMAN

JUNE 2006

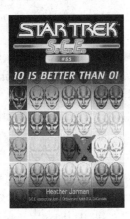

Thanks to the Dominion War, Lieutenant Temperance Brewster receives a daunting assignment: recruit Bynars for Starfleet. She has a tough time convincing any of them that Starfleet is worthwhile. When a Bynar is murdered, the lieutenant is the primary suspect, since there is no crime on the planet. Then her guilt seems assured when she escapes from her cell. A study of the Bynar culture and how 110/111 joined the S.C.E.

"Because this was a *What's Past* episode for S.C.E., Keith felt like it was important we tell a story that might provide deep background on why Soloman decided to remain solo instead of taking a new mate. For whatever reason, I decided that I wanted to follow a 'procedural' format—think *Law & Order*, so I knew we'd have to have a criminal component. The only scenario that would lend itself to exploring Soloman's singular state would be a Bynar losing a mate, perhaps to murder. My original intent was to have a 'noir' feel to the story, though I believe that tonal element didn't really define the story as much as I'd envisioned. Writing this story presented one fundamental challenge: How do you write in the point-of-view of characters who think/talk/function in binary/computer language. I'm not a math person—never have been—and that extreme level of logic proved problematic in terms of mapping out actions, motives, perspectives. Everything is black and white to a Bynar that operates on an either/or paradigm. The nuances and complexities that make for an interesting story nearly don't exist in this world. This is an alien race that sees the word 'I' as taboo! As I began, I realized that I would have to employ a tactic I've used before in world building and that was to bring in outsiders to offer their perspectives. Still, it wasn't fair to tell a story about Bynars and not allow the Bynars themselves to share their point-of-view. In re-reading early S.C.E. books, I came across a few projects that utilized an unconventional format. I decided to take a risk and use a combination of personal logs, recordings, reports, and transcripts to tell the story. Everyone could have their say. This also allowed me to show the same events from different perspectives, reinforcing the similarities and differences between the various cultures. The format is risky—I concede that. I chose an unconventional path, but this story demanded an unconventional approach. Ultimately, I think it works."

Heather continued, "The writing process for this project was similar to other world-building projects: Start with the end (in this case, the Bynars) and work backwards, trying to figure out a plausible anthropological, evolutionary back story. Their world needed to be an outgrowth of their culture and evolutionary needs and so on. Keith and I brainstormed a lot about how the Bynars could be computer dependent/interconnected from an evolutionary perspective since computers don't spontaneously

rise out of the mud. This is where the AI evolutionary story came from. That . . . and I happened to be rewatching *The Matrix Trilogy* at the time I was outlining and found the interdependence of machines and organics to be fascinating. There are elements of my personal life, as always, that color my writing. This project was no exception. This time, this project helped me express my observations about how the anxious expectations of a rigid society can impact those who don't quite assimilate into the mainstream. For whatever reason, this is a theme throughout most of my *Trek* work . . ."

STARGAZER

Mike remarked, "It's a soap opera. This is one of those experiments. Fans can get lots of great stuff from all the great writers who are writing now and rather than do more of what I'd already been doing, I figured let me give them a different flavor. Especially in the beginning, the adventures they were having were secondary to the relationships that were developing and in the first book I was halfway through it before I even embarked on an adventure. I wanted to show all these interpersonal relationships. I didn't want to do what I'd already done thirty times and I wanted to do something different. You know what's going to happen to many of these characters, which is why I put in a few additional ones. You know the Federation is going to survive, you know Picard's going to survive, you know all these things so a sense of jeopardy is not available to you. So this intensely interpersonal soap opera kind of story is the way I chose to go. Is it successful? Well, it was certainly commercially successful. Is it successful artistically? You know, I don't know."

REUNION

(SEE SECTION 4: STAR TREK: THE NEXT GENERATION
UNNUMBERED NOVELS)

THE VALIANT

(SEE SECTION 4: STAR TREK: THE NEXT GENERATION
UNNUMBERED NOVELS)

THE FIRST VIRTUE

(DOUBLE HELIX, BOOK SIX; SEE SECTION 12: MINISERIES)

GAUNTLET
(STARGAZER)
MICHAEL JAN FRIEDMAN

MAY 2002   (266PP)

he first book of the *Stargazer* series investigates Picard's first mission as the new captain.

The White Wolf, a space pirate who has been pillaging several sectors, has been extremely elusive. It is up to Picard and his new crew to stop him. The mission is designed to fail, disgracing Captain Picard before he even gets his space legs gravity-free!

PROGENITOR
(STARGAZER)
MICHAEL JAN FRIEDMAN

MAY 2002   (263PP)

Captain Picard and members of the crew accompany Chief Engineer Simenon to the planet Gnala, where he is ready to spawn. A major ritual is part of the process, and the crew of the *Stargazer* is reluctantly allowed to join Simenon on his journey. But someone is sabotaging their efforts, and they not only have to complete the grueling ritual, but also must survive to figure out who is the guilty party.

THREE
(STARGAZER)
MICHAEL JAN FRIEDMAN

AUGUST 2003   (247 PP)

While investigating an anomaly, the transporter picks up a passenger who looks exactly like identical twins Gerda and Idun Asmund. Having no idea how she arrived, it appears she is from a parallel universe. Meanwhile, Vigo heads to a conference to witness a new phaser weapon demonstration. Of course, bad things happen and he ends up having to fight for his and the fellow attendees' lives.

OBLIVION
(STARGAZER)
MICHAEL JAN FRIEDMAN

SEPTEMBER 2003   (259 PP)

Picard meets Guinan for the first time, though Guinan has met him before in the past. Huh? Before a clandestine meeting with someone having vital intelligence for the Federation, a bomb goes off and Picard is blamed. He escapes from his cell by the help of Guinan, and the two proceed to prove his innocence and obtain the information.

ENIGMA
(STARGAZER)
Michael Jan Friedman

August 2004   (259pp)

Admiral McAteer informs Captain Picard that he will soon be facing a board of inquiry to investigate his supposed incompetence. Meanwhile, Starfleet ships are being attacked by mysterious vessels that decimate the ships, but don't steal or kill anyone. The attacks are so specific, that it appears that the mysterious aggressors have inside knowledge of Starfleet vessels. Throw into the mix a saboteur aboard the *Stargazer*, and chaos ensues.

MAKER
(STARGAZER)
Michael Jan Friedman

September 2004   (275pp)

Ensign Nikolas finds himself on a freighter, trying to forget the events that changed his life forever on the *Stargazer*. An alien with godlike powers kills the crew, leaving Nikolas alive for nefarious purposes. On the *Stargazer*, Picard awaits the hearing to decide the future of his captaincy. When a woman from his past appears, the fate of the galaxy depends on him trusting an untrustworthy adversary.

I.K.S. GORKON

Keith remarked, "The response from the readers (regarding *Diplomatic Implausibility*) was fantastic, partly because of the gorgeous cover, partly because everybody really thinks the Gorkon is a really cool thing. In light of that and Pocket Books recent expansion into different corners of the ST universe, they were willing to take a chance and see if there would be readership interested in the Klingon series. I'd already set it up in *Diplomatic Implausibility* and *The Brave and The Bold*. So I took it forward with the two *I.K.S. Gorkon* books, which came out in 2002. The third book came out in 2005 and hopefully will go beyond that."

Regarding why he used Klag as the captain, Keith commented, "It was the second-season *Next Generation* episode 'A Matter of Honor' that made me want to use him. I really liked the character. I liked the friendship he and Riker developed over the course of the episode and I liked the whole back story with his father. I thought it was ripe with story possibilities. In doing the Klag story, I love the personality. In most cases, all of the Klingons, particularly the ones with small roles, the actors did not put any thought into it or any depth to it. They just snarl a lot and shout a lot and hit things really hard. The characters I wound up choosing for the Gorkon one, when I was cherry-picking from the various TNG or DS9 episodes, were ones I thought were beyond that. Brian Thompson as Klag was one. He had more depth to him then somebody who babbled about honor and hit things real hard. Leskit was another one. Leskit was in fact my first choice. As soon as I started creating the Klingon crew, the absolute first person I wanted in there was Leskit because he was a snide, obnoxious Klingon, which is never simple. That really appealed to me, somebody who was that much of a wise ass and who was very much a Klingon. He walked around with Cardassian neck bones around his neck. So this was not exactly a friendly, happy wise-ass Klingon. I put Rodek in there because he was the new identity that was given to Kurn. I wanted to explore the new identity he was forced to accept at the end of the DS9 episode, 'Sons of Mogh,' after his memories were wiped. Tok I put in because I just liked the enthusiasm of the character in TNG's 'Birthright' and I just wanted to see where he went, once he was brought back into Klingon society by Worf at the end of that episode. He is just the eager young guy that gets on everyone's nerves. After that, I made up characters because I did get several complaints that every Klingon we ever saw on TV ended up on the damn ship! One character I ended up falling in love with is Wol. The leader of the squad I introduced. I want to show the grunts, the ground troops, the Klingon version of the lower decks characters and what life was like for them as opposed to the officers. All we've really ever seen on the TV shows are the officers and the elite warriors. The episode 'Once More Unto the Breach' established something that I always thought was implied anyway, which was that there was a very rigid class system in the Klingon Empire and the warriors are at the top of it. An actual warrior culture would never survive to build spaceships, if nothing else, and create a large empire. But

(continued)

warriors are a bit of the upper classes and they're the ones who run things. And then there are the people lower down who do all the work. I wanted to show that, and Wol just wound up completely running away with every scene she was in. And she plays a very large role in *Enemy Territory* which wasn't entirely planned but did surprise me when it happened as I was sitting down to write the book."

DIPLOMATIC IMPLAUSIBILITY
(STAR TREK: THE NEXT GENERATION #61)
(SEE SECTION 3: STAR TREK: THE NEXT
GENERATION NUMBERED NOVELS)

THE FINAL ARTIFACT
(FROM THE BRAVE AND THE BOLD,
BOOK TWO; SEE SECTION 12: MINISERIES)

1
A GOOD DAY TO DIE
(I.K.S. GORKON)
Keith R.A. DeCandido
NOVEMBER 2003 (258 PP)

In the vein of the *Enterprise* seeking out new life and civilizations comes the *Gorkon*, a vessel and its group of officers whose sole purpose is to seek out civilizations for conquering. Sent by Martok to the Kavrot sector, the crew finds a race with a deeply ingrained warrior culture that rivals their own Klingon heritage. The followers of Kahless are offered a contest to determine who should rule the planet and the challenges are too good for Captain Klag to pass. Will the Klingons win, forcing the planet to cede them to the Empire, or will they lose like bitter dogs, and become an embarrassment to the entire Klingon race?

2

HONOR BOUND
(I.K.S. GORKON)
KEITH R.A. DeCANDIDO

DECEMBER 2003 (258PP)

Captain Klag has made a vow to the Children of San-Tarah that the Klingons will leave them alone. When he makes his report, General Talak orders him to conquer the planet anyway. Refusing, Talak gathers a force and heads to the disputed region. Now Klag must fight against his own people to keep his honor. To help in the upcoming battle and stand alongside the honorable inhabitants of the planet, Klag decides to call in the Order of the Bat'leth.

3

ENEMY TERRITORY
(I.K.S. GORKON)
KEITH R.A. DeCANDIDO

MARCH 2005 (336PP)

The Elabrej hegemony believes that they are the only beings in the universe and to think otherwise constitutes heresy. When a Klingon vessel enters space near their planet, the explosive result has several ships destroyed and several Klingon prisoners that the inhabitants begin to experiment on. Captain Klag receives orders to find out what happened and initiate a rescue. While the *Gorkon* warps to the site, several conspirators plot a mutiny.

TITAN

Wherever one stands on the movie *Star Trek: Nemesis,* there's no denying it provided the fiction with no shortage of extraordinary storytelling opportunities. Some of the most compelling were William T. Riker's captaincy, his marriage to Deanna Troi, and his taking command of a mysterious starship named *Titan.*

"Developing a new *Star Trek* series concept for the fiction is never something we undertake lightly," editor Marco Palmieri explains. "It's done with a lot of careful thought, a lot of discussion and debate, and a lot of aspirin. There was never any question that fiction about *Titan* would be published; *Nemesis* had handed us that opportunity on a silver platter. The real question was what it would be about, and what would set it apart from every other *Star Trek* concept on screen and in print and allow it to claim its own unique identity."

Ultimately, *Titan* fiction would be defined by its creative approach, which was developed by taking into consideration the character of its captain and his wife, their unique personal histories, and the moment in history when *Titan*'s mission would begin. Marco explained, "*Nemesis* was set roughly four years after the end of the Dominion War. Prior and even during that conflict, *Star Trek*'s audience witnessed hostilities with the Klingons, attacks by the Borg, trouble with the Cardassians and the Maquis. Somewhere along the way, the *Star Trek* universe had become less about experiencing wonder than it was about the next threat we'd meet. I wanted to restore the balance—to reassert Starfleet's mission of peaceful exploration, diplomacy, and the expansion of knowledge. The essence of the *Titan* concept came to be about getting 'back to basics' at a turning point in Federation history, about getting *beyond* the strife of recent years, in part because the fiction has, during the same period, been oversaturated with such strife. The postwar, post-*Nemesis* era offered the opportunity to do exactly that, with *Titan.*"

One of the things that would set *Titan* apart from other *Trek* fiction sagas (something it would have in common with Pocket's other new fiction concept, *Vanguard,* launched the same year) was its large palette of principal characters. "The idea there was to allow different authors to focus on as many of them, or as few, as they wanted, according to the needs of the story and the leanings of the authors." As an added twist, part of *Titan*'s conceit was that it had the most biologically varied and culturally diverse crew in Starfleet history, with humans only taking up 15% of the 350-member crew. "*Titan* doesn't show a perfectly integrated crew, not at first. What it portrays, rather, is something *Star Trek* has never shown us before: that for a shipload of people this different from one another—and at the start of their mission—to get along isn't necessarily something that comes naturally, or immediately. They need to make an effort in order to live and work together, to learn about and celebrate their differences."

The fact that *Nemesis* never gave audiences a look at *Titan* also allowed the novels to decide what the ship would look like, and Pocket Books elected to open the design of the ship to fans by holding a contest. "It was an interesting experience. I'd never done a contest before. I'm quite happy with the outcome, a design by Sean Tourangeau of Colorado Springs, CO, that currently appears on our web site, www.startrekbooks.com, but the contest was abominably costly and took up more of my time than I thought it would." One thing that surprised a number of fans was *Titan*'s size, landing somewhere between *Voyager* and the *Enterprise*-D. "Yeah, there was a lot of fan speculation that the name 'Titan' must imply great size. That's precisely why we took our inspiration from a different Titan . . . one that was a better fit for the spirit of exploration we had in mind for the novels: We decided it was named for Saturn's largest moon, part of the new *Luna*-class fleet."

TAKING WING
(TITAN)
MICHAEL A. MARTIN AND ANDY MANGELS

APRIL 2005 (359PP)

Captain Riker takes command of the *Titan*, and along with his new responsibilities comes a new crew. With the most diverse crew in the fleet, humans are actually in the minority. When Admiral Akaar arrives with a new first mission, Riker must utilize the talents of his new crew for a much different purpose than he expected. Sent to Romulus to negotiate the peace after Shinzon decimated the Romulan Senate, can the newly commissioned captain create trust between the Remans, Romulans, Tal Shiar, and the Klingons? Meanwhile, in an isolated Romulan prison, a battered and beaten Tuvok loses all hope of a rescue.

Mike explained that how *Titan* would begin "was dictated by the events of *Star Trek Nemesis*, specifically the assassination of the Romulan Senate (talk about your 'nuclear option!') and Riker's line at the film's end indicating that his first assignment was the Romulan Neutral Zone ('it seems they want to talk'). Much of the rest came out of the new crew settling in and getting used to one another, Riker taking on his first permanent command and encountering difficulties he hadn't anticipated (such as integrating his wife into his command staff and getting used to a radically nonhuman CMO). We also were careful to take into account the *A Time To . . .* novels." Those novels chronicle the year leading up to *Nemesis*, with the conceit of explaining the changes shown in the lives of the various TNG characters, such as why Riker and Troi finally decided to marry, and what led Riker finally to accept a captaincy.

Mike continued, "The writing went quickly. Because of some other concurrent commitments, we had a fairly short, frantic writing schedule. Marco's perspicacious input kept us from committing various plotting and pacing blunders, and his insights shaped a lot of the alien characters, as did the comments and world-building talents of Christopher Bennett (author of *Orion's Hounds*, the third *Titan* novel)."

Andy answered, "When Marco discussed *Titan* with us, he wanted the ship to go further into scientific exploration, getting back to the tenets of the original *Trek*. I think it was a confluence of ideas between Marco, Mike, and I that led to the ship having the most alien of crews—only a small fraction of the crew members are human. As we began constructing the cast list, we were able to 'cherry pick' a bit from previous *Trek* characters, so we chose some that had previously been seen on-screen in live-action or the animated series, or in comic books or novels. Christine Vale was a decision early on, as well as Alyssa Ogawa, and we wanted Ranul Keru to come onboard from the start as well. I had wanted to use Melora Pazlar in *Trek* stories even going back to our Marvel Comics run, and we finally got a chance to use her. Tuvok was another choice that we thought would be good; we both liked him on *Voyager*, and had used him in *The Sundered*. Other characters were elements of taking an alien race we wanted to use, and figuring out where an interesting assignment for them would be, and what kind of personality they had. Our Ferengi, Bralik, was chosen to be a woman to take advantage of the changes to Ferengi society that had been happening since DS9 was on TV. I think of her as 'Bette Midler as a Ferengi,' and what I mean by that is she's brassy and loud and will say or do whatever is on her mind. Very little sense of propriety, but a big heart. Dr. Ree was an absolute kick to write, as we like the irony of having the most terrifying creature on the ship be the doctor, because everyone would have to see him. But it still is fun to have this big velociraptor/kimodo dragon with claws and teeth and a carnivorous appetite be gentle and funny. We also tried to mix things up a bit. A major crew member not making it through the first book alive. A horndog old engineer with a tragic past. A gay crewmember who was *not* going to become Keru's boyfriend. A pregnant crew member giving birth. A past sexual liaison of Riker's serving under him. Alien crew members who didn't quite believe that the captain was walking the walk as much as talking the talk as relates to the crew's diversity."

Andy continued, "Mike handled much of the Romulan intrigue, while I handled a lot of the character stuff on the ship and the Romulan prison sequences with Tuvok. If you detect a touch of HBO's *Oz* series in the prison sequences, it's purely unintentional," he said with a grin. "It was unusual to be writing sequences in the book wherein Riker was unhappy that *Titan*'s first assignment was not what their mission statement was. But part of what Mike and I both like about Riker is his willingness to do things his way, sometimes coloring outside the lines. His brokering of the resolution at the book's end is a perfect example of that."

THE RED KING
(TITAN)
ANDY MANGELS AND MICHAEL A. MARTIN

OCTOBER 2005   (364PP)

The *Titan* crew find themselves over 200,000 light years away from Romulan space. The Neyel, originally from Earth, live in this region and have a religious belief that an energy being called the Red King, when awakened, will engulf their planet. When a strange anomaly that fits the description of the Red King arrives in the area, Riker must evacuate the remaining Neyel if the race is going to survive. And Riker must ask the help of his new crew and the Romulans in order for everything to work smoothly.

Mike remarked, "*The Red King* is actually a minor character from Lewis Carroll's *Through the Looking Glass*, and became a metaphor that is used as a touchstone throughout the story."

Andy said, "Once we were mostly through with writing *The Sundered*, it became clear to Marco, Mike, and I that there was going to eventually need to be a return to the Neyel. When we talked about the concepts for *The Red King*, the most obvious choice all around was to make the return of the Neyel a major part of the plot point. Since we had the 'Great Bloom' left over from the film, and radioactive explosions almost always lead to some kind of spatial anomalies in *Star Trek*, we had an easy way to get to Neyel space. Mike had brilliantly set up the disappearance of the Romulan war fleet in *Taking Wing*, so we could follow that up. I think Marco was the one who came up with the genesis of the Red King entity, and then we developed it further, trying to figure out the scientific logistics to it. Really, in writing *Trek* fiction, there are multiple sets of logistics to work through: plot logistics—does the story make sense plotwise; science logistics—even with Treknobabble, does the science hold true; and character logistics—do the characters act and interact as appropriate. We also had several character-related plot threads to continue on from *Taking Wing*. The resolution of Keru's coma. Akaar and Tuvok's backstory. Whether the Reman would remain on the ship. Just how trustworthy Donatra truly was. One interesting element was figuring out how the *Titan* crew would respond to a full-scale ecological/spatial disaster, instead of just some threatening military force or intrigue."

ORION'S HOUNDS
(TITAN)
CHRISTOPHER BENNETT

JANUARY 2006   (379PP)

The multi-species crew battles their prejudices and Riker and Troi work hard to make everyone function as a cohesive unit. While exploring the Gum Nebula, the bridge crew watches as the space jellies from the *Next Generation* pilot, "Encounter at Farpoint," are attacked. The aliens responsible for the slaughter use the translucent dead bodies as their ships. Riker realizes he must convince the aliens to stop their hunting. Part of their culture for centuries, the hunters refuse. Unknown to the *Titan* crew, the halting of the hunt will have extreme consequences.

"This project also started at Marco's invitation. After *Ex Machina*, he felt I'd be a good fit for the approach he had in mind for *Titan*, featuring a multispecies crew even more diverse than the one in *The Motion Picture* [and my post-TMP novel,] *Ex Machina*. The plot for this started out as an unsold *Strange New Worlds* submission called 'Spirit of the Hunt,' which was a VGR story. Ever since "Encounter at Farpoint," I'd wanted to see the 'space jellyfish' creatures again. In thinking about spacegoing life forms in general, I figured they might originate near the center of the galaxy, where the conditions would be dynamic and turbulent enough to drive the formation of life and the stars close enough together to provide ready energy sources. Since *Voyager* would've passed near the galaxy's central bulge starting after about 'Dark Frontier,' I had the idea to do a VGR story about the 'star-jellies,' as I called them. Since they were so shiplike, I came up with a plot about a race that hunted them and used them as ships, and the conflict between the two species' needs. However, the concept was too big for the short-story format. In retrospect I realize it was too rushed, too superficial, and too inconclusive. I still liked the idea, though, and I tried pitching it for *Distant Shores*, again without success. When the *Titan* offer came up, I decided I could rework and expand it, with Deanna Troi filling a role similar to Tuvok's in the original. When I learned Tuvok would be part of *Titan*'s crew, I was able to recycle his arc from the story largely intact. Janeway became Riker, and Chakotay's material was split between Christine Vale and Dr. Ree. Zones of active star formation within our galactic arm replaced the role of the center of the galaxy. (I always try to ground my science fiction, including *Trek* fiction, in hard science and astronomy.) The need to expand the story to novel length allowed me to make it much grander in scope, to explore not just one spacegoing life form but the entire galactic ecosystem. I made a list of all the spacegoing life forms ever seen in *Trek* and thought about ways to work them into a larger context. I didn't include them all in OH, but all the basic types are represented, plus a number of new critters of my own. I've given some thought to writing original fiction about spacegoing life forms, and some of those ideas ended up here. The greater length also let me tell a story that was far more epic. The events of 'Spirit of the Hunt' became pretty much the first half of the novel, after which new revelations came and the stakes were revealed to be far greater than the crew had suspected. Even in that first half, though, I was able to go into far more depth, exploring both the star-jellies and their hunters more thoroughly. OH let me make up for my two main regrets about *Ex Machina*. One is that *Ex Machina* was too much of a sequel, too dependent on what came before. OH is loosely a sequel to 'Farpoint' and one or two other TNG episodes, but is mostly about exploring new worlds and civilizations rather than revisiting old ones. My other regret was that *Ex Machina* didn't capture the epic scope and sense of wonder that TMP achieved. With OH I wanted to tell a really vast, cosmic story full of extraordinary vistas. Particularly since this would be the novel where *Titan* began its official mission of exploration. I wanted to tell a story that was really *about* exploration, and that showed the audience something new and different, rather than a routine 'starship goes to planet and gets involved in local politics' story."

Christopher continued, "One of the first things I did, even before I had an outline, was to propose several nonhumanoid aliens for the crew: Orilly Malar, Torvig and K'chak'!'op. These were actually based on aliens I created for my original SF universe years ago, for a planned starship-exploration series that would've had similar themes to *Titan*. So the characters were a good match. Orilly's cultural background was originally part of K'chak'!'op's species, but I figured that was too much for one supporting player so I split it between two. I had a rather tight deadline on this novel, only 100 days from approval to due date, and that was of some concern to me. I also chose to write the novel fully on my new laptop, so as to be free of the distractions I associated with my desktop computer. Still, it was slow going for the first few weeks. With 100 days to do 100,000 words, I was trying for a minimum of 1,000 words a day, and was behind that goal for most of the first month. But after that I managed to pull ahead and build plenty of momentum. I finished the first draft with over a month to spare. I actually finished it before Andy Mangels and Mike Martin finished their first draft of *The Red King*. But I still had to wait a few weeks for their manuscript so I'd know what changes I had to make. There were a few significant alterations I had to make in several character arcs, but they mostly served to improve the novel, I felt."

VANGUARD

In 2005, Pocket broke new ground again with the launch of *Vanguard*, a new *Star Trek* fiction concept set during the time of the original TV series. As Marco explained, "We'd done a lot of work in the novels over the years exploring the *Star Trek* universe during the era of *The Next Generation, Deep Space Nine*, and *Voyager*. I'd been itching for some time to take a look back, and delve deeper into the time of Kirk's original five-year mission. I had a concept in mind: a starbase whose ships and crew were caught up unraveling an ancient mystery, and I invited author David Mack to help develop it into what became *Vanguard*. Dave was also the author of the first *Vanguard* novel, *Harbinger*."

Marco added, "As I've said, developing a new *Star Trek* series concept for the fiction isn't something to be undertaken casually. With *Titan, Nemesis* had given us a starting point—a few core characters and ideas from which we could extrapolate, and around which we could create a series of books. *Vanguard*, by contrast, was built from the ground up."

Marco went on, "What we imagined was a continuing story that would run parallel to Kirk's original five-year mission, and offer a new perspective on the era. We wanted to show how various events that unfolded on screen impacted other parts of the *Star Trek* universe, and how some of those events might have been influenced by what was happening in the Taurus Reach, the region of space where *Vanguard* is set."

One of the ways *Vanguard* stands apart from other incarnations of *Star Trek* is its focus on nontraditional main characters. While *Star Trek* has repeatedly presented, with slight variations, the same group model (captain, first officer, science officer, engineer, security officer, pilot, etc.), *Vanguard* focuses instead on characters with roles different from the ones fans were used to seeing on a regular basis. "The idea there," Marco said, "was to open the way for stories that fell outside the usual *Star Trek* paradigms, requiring authors to develop new ideas for characterization and interpersonal relationships. *Vanguard*'s main cast includes an intelligence officer, a JAG officer, a civilian reporter, a soldier of fortune in the tradition of Harry Mudd or Cyrano Jones, a Federation ambassador, a Klingon spy, and several other notables designed to give the milieu the feel of something familiar yet refreshing. There's also an extended cast of richly drawn characters both on the station and aboard the three Starfleet ships assigned to the base."

The added twist, Marco said, is that not all the protagonists are immediately likeable. "That was risky, but quite deliberate. We wanted *Vanguard*'s story to be not only the puzzle they are all trying to solve, but also the story of how the characters evolve from that endeavour and for the reader to gain new insights into who they really are as people."

For the design of Vanguard station—also known as Starbase 47—Marco turned to fan artist Masao Okazaki. "I'm a longtime admirer of Masao's work, which is strongly influenced by the design sensibilities of the original *Star Trek*. He did a fantastic job with the station, and the *Harbinger* includes a color foldout of his designs."

HARBINGER
(VANGUARD)
David Mack

August 2005   (386pp)

Captain Kirk has just finished with the incident involving Gary Mitchell when the ship receives orders to make haste to Vanguard, a state of the art space station situated perilously close to Klingon and Tholian space. Why was the station rushed into service? The story focuses on the diverse population of this new outpost and its hidden purpose.

According to David, "The concept of *Star Trek Vanguard* began with Pocket Books editor Marco Palmieri. After the publication of my novel *A Time to Heal,* he contacted me and asked if I would be interested in working with him to develop a new *Star Trek* book series set during the time of the original series. By the fall of 2004, we had hammered out a fairly epic series concept. It was designed from the outset to have a continuing story arc that would play out over the run of the series, but also to be flexible enough to support any number of stand-alone stories unconnected (or only tangentially connected) to the continuing meta-story. Writing the first book in a series packed with all-new characters and situations required me to treat this, in many respects, like the pilot episode of a new series: I needed a core storyline that would involve all my characters, either directly or indirectly, and provoke conflicts that would enable me to illuminate some facets of their personalities and perhaps hint at others. The destruction of the *U.S.S. Bombay,* and its impact on everyone, from the civilians to the upper echelon of Starbase forty-seven's senior officers, provided me with a very dramatic basis for the story. Once I realized that practically every other event in the story either led up to that incident or resulted from it, I knew I had found the foundation upon which to construct my tale."

Summing up his thoughts, "This book is unlike anything else I've ever written; I hope people who have come to expect a certain type of story from me won't be disappointed to see me exploring new narrative ground in *Harbinger.* Also, Cervantes Quinn was one of my all-time favorite creations. I found his scenes a pleasure to write."

SUMMON THE THUNDER
(VANGUARD)
DAYTON WARD AND KEVIN DILMORE

APRIL 2006   (416PP)

Following the events of *Harbinger*, the cost of secrecy continues to rise. As the Klingons and Tholians prepare for war, another interested power player secretly enter the picture. Meanwhile, the Starship *Endeavour* makes a find that could shed light on the mysterious meta-genome . . . if its crew survives the discovery.

Dayton commented, "Marco approached us about doing the second *Vanguard* novel in late 2004/early 2005. We had the series bible, plus Dave's outline and first draft of the manuscript for *Harbinger* to work from. The bible has an overview of the basic 'big picture' for the series." In developing the story for *Summon the Thunder*, Dayton and Kevin introduced several new ideas that have helped that original meta-story to evolve.

On writing for the new characters, Dayton said, "I'm naturally drawn to whoever's in charge, in this case Commodore Reyes. I'm enjoying the Quinn/Pennington dynamic we've set up. T'Prynn and Sandesjo are proving to be both interesting and tricky for me. We're trying very hard to avoid the usual cliché that would be easy to employ with these characters, not only as individuals but also with respect to their relationship. Also, even though I said I liked Reyes, that doesn't mean he's an easy character to write. He's a complicated man, not only professionally but personally as well. The same can be said for all of the *Vanguard* main characters. When handled properly, as Dave Mack did with *Harbinger*, that can translate to some fantastic storytelling, and I hope we're living up not only to that challenge but also to the standard Dave set with the first book. I don't mind saying this book may well be the most demanding work I've done in my brief writing career."

Kevin added, "I'm right with Dayton on his assessment as a whole. On one hand, we don't have the luxury we enjoyed when writing the *Next Generation* crew in A *Time to Sow* and *Harvest* as we don't have the wealth of screen hours to watch for nuances of performance, mannerisms, character interplay and so forth. On the other hand, we don't have a completely free rein to create characters from the ground up as we did with the *Lovell* crew in our twenty-third-century S.C.E. stories. This is more like the experience we had coming to the *da Vinci* crew early in the game with *Interphase*—but even *that* set-up was reasonably close to a meat-and-potatoes *Star Trek* adventure with a standard crew complement. *Vanguard*'s playing field is more like a very rich dessert, as it is filled with all sorts of colorful characters and is hardly limited to a bridge crew and lower-deck officers. Hmm . . . anyone else hungry? But I also found it to be my most challenging work as a fiction writer, but it was made *much* easier thanks to Dave." Kevin noted that he's grown attached to the crew of the *Endeavour*, which figures prominently in *Summon the Thunder*. "I really have taken a shine to the characters on that ship. I'm also identifying a lot with Lietenant Xiong, whom I see as the moral center of *Vanguard*, as well as Ambassador Jetanien and Dr. Fisher (but that's no shocker, as I always enjoy writing the medical folks)."

Dayton remarked, "Despite what I said about the challenge of writing this book, let me be clear—there should be a law against having this much fun while you work. Writing *Summon the Thunder* has re-energized my enthusiasm for the original series, which is saying something considering I'm a diehard fan of the show. I've been watching and re-watching key episodes on DVD as well as combing my library of 'ancient' and old-school *Trek* reference works. I've also been reviewing a few other *Trek* novels looking for ways to tie into those, and I even have music from the series playing when I work on certain scenes to help keep me in that mindset. The only thing missing was an old AMT model of the *Enterprise* hanging over my desk, so I went and found one at a con, and I'm building it right now! More than all of that, though, *Vanguard* represents a way to expand upon many of the things I love about the original series—events seen or perhaps only mentioned and later referenced in the spin-off shows, for example—and the way they fit into the larger tapestry of the *Star Trek* universe. We're getting the opportunity to tie into events that, at first glance, might not seem to have log-ical connections to what's taking place in the Taurus Reach, but when viewed as a part of the larger history make perfect sense."

On how their most recent twenty-third-century *Corps of Engineers* story, *Distant Early Warning*, fits into the *Vanguard* saga, Dayton explained. "The crew of the *Lovell* has only been seen in a few stories to date, so in reality there's still quite a bit about those characters that hasn't yet been revealed. *Distant Early Warning* is set before the events of the first *Harbinger*, but after the events of the S.C.E. series' *Foundations Book 1*, in which the crew of the *USS Lovell* first appeared. Further, this story will not feature a 'wraparound' story with the S.C.E. series' regular characters from the *USS da Vinci*. Our aim is to make the story fun and accessible both to those who follow the S.C.E. series but might not have read *Harbinger* as well as *Vanguard* readers who plan to seek out this story even though they don't normally read the S.C.E. tales."

Kevin agrees, noting that *Distant Early Warning* was designed to serve both sagas while still being novice-friendly. "The true barometer with a *Lovell* story, we always think, is whether it rings true not just with a reader's expectations of an S.C.E. story but also with his or her expectations of a original series-era story. If a reader has some familiarity with those conventions, then we hope there are no other hurdles to clear before starting *Distant Early Warning*."

OTHER ORIGINAL CONCEPTS

THE BEST AND THE BRIGHTEST
(STAR TREK: THE NEXT GENERATION)
SUSAN WRIGHT

FEBRUARY 1998   **(277PP)**

The story of six cadets attending Starfleet Academy and their trials and tribulations during their four-year term. Set during the time period just after the events at Wolf 359, the characters include a newly joined Trill; a human who finds herself hopelessly in love with the Trill; a cat-like alien raised by humans, and a Bajoran Vedek who wishes to distance himself from his native planet.

This novel was groundbreaking, not only in terms of having brand new characters. Susan said, "I always wanted to create a gay relationship in a *Trek* novel because I felt that the promise of a future without discrimination and bigotry had not been fulfilled. So when John Ordover asked me to create a whole new cast of characters who were attending Starfleet Academy, I wanted to include gay characters. *The Best and the Brightest* was the first *Star Trek* novel with main characters who were gay. Paramount agreed to my story proposal, but they insisted that the word "gay" should not be included. They said that in the *Trek* universe sexual orientation was not even noticed. I've always wanted to bring these characters back in a DS9 novel, because Moll Enor and Jayme Miranda were posted there at the end of *The Best and the Brightest*. It was fun because at times I used all six of the characters like Forest Gump, placing them in key *Trek* moments such as the crash of the *Enterprise*-D."

CHALLENGER
(SEE NEW EARTH; SECTION 12: MINISERIES)

FICTION WITHOUT CLOSETS

On screen, sexual orientation within the *Star Trek* universe is generally treated as a non-issue. And yet, despite the egalitarian philosophy *Star Trek* strives to project, the idea of depicting gay characters or same-sex relationships with greater frequency and prominence has yet to take hold in any *Trek* TV series or movie. However, in keeping with *Star Trek*'s longstanding tradition of acknowledging and celebrating human diversity, the fiction has, particularly in the last decade, seized the opportunity to introduce gay and bisexual characters. And while these efforts have been greeted enthusiastically by the majority of readers, editor Marco Palmieri readily concedes that the positive response has not been universal.

"I always find the controversy that erupts over the inclusion of gay characters in the fiction puzzling, as the arguments inevitably make a bigger deal of them than the books do. Detractors throw out words like 'gay agenda' pretty liberally, but that just isn't what the stories are about. The truth is that *Star Trek* fiction treats such elements the same way it treats any other relationship or personal characteristic . . . as part of the background color of the *Star Trek* universe, one tile in the *Trek* mosaic among many—something that's no more or less relevant than skin color, sex, ancestry or species. And that's the point, really: that sexual orientation in *Star Trek* isn't especially noteworthy.

"The irony of all this is that numerous alien species have been depicted or referenced, on screen and in print, with cultural and sexual norms different from those of heterosexual humans. *Star Trek* is a mythos in which interspecies sexual relations, intermarriage, and interbreeding are all taken for granted, and have been since the creation of Spock. It's a universe that has always celebrated the coming together of hearts and minds, regardless of the shells they wear. The fiction strives to be true to that ideal."

STARFLEET: YEAR ONE

MICHAEL JAN FRIEDMAN

MARCH 2002   **(287PP)**

The story was originally published as a once-a-month serial novel at the back of various *Trek* novels, starting with *The First Virtue* in August 1999. Running a year, the twelve parts are here compiled into one book. Set during the inaugural year of Starfleet's existence, Friedman introduces several people who are destined to be the first captains of the space vessels. Of all of the captains, the one who proves the most worthy will receive a commission aboard the state of the art starship, the *Daedalus*.

Mike remarked, "Peter David had come up with the *New Frontier* series and that was doing pretty well and John Ordover said, 'So, do you want to do one?' And I said, 'Absolutely!' I'd just researched this book *A Star to Steer Her By*, which was part of a kind of a package with an action figure, which was being produced.

There was a limited number and this book came as part of the package and I did that for Margaret Clark. And while I was writing about it, I started out by talking about the earliest captains and how exciting this was that they were out there on their own so far from Star Fleet command to take all their marching orders from them. How they had to make their own decisions off the cuff and I said, gee, this would be a great era to explore. So when John asked me that question I said, 'I want to do *Starfleet: Year One*.' That appealed to him because he was also a comic fan and they were doing year ones in the comic book world so he said, 'And then you can do year two and year three.' I said, 'That's what I want to do, year one through seven.' And then I did that in serial form but as it was coming out we were starting to get rumors about the fifth ST series about how it would be set a hundred years before Kirk. More and more it sounded like it would be at odds with *Starfleet: Year One*. So even though I loved doing *Starfleet: Year One* and the conflict between the military types and what I call the butterfly catchers, it became obvious that with *Enterprise* coming out it would be a bad political move to try to come out with a series that completely conflicts with *Enterprise*. So we did *Starfleet: Year One*, it got published as it's own book but we put the rest of the Starfleets on the back burner, which is where they are now. And that was a disappointment to me because that is the series I wanted to do. So when I couldn't do that one anymore, John said, 'So what do you want to do now?' And I said, 'I don't know.' We came to the conclusion that it would be a good idea to work on the *Stargazer* series, using the characters I started with in *Reunion* and who had since come up in a couple of other books.

By then *Valiant* was already in the works and it was somewhere in the process that we decided that would be the first *Stargazer* book."

ARTICLES OF THE FEDERATION
KEITH R.A. DECANDIDO

JUNE 2005 (402PP)

A followup to *A Time For War*, *A Time For Peace*, chronicling the first year in office of Federation President Nan Bacco. With her trusted aides, she dives into the politics of the job while trying to maintain her fairness and moral values. From a potential war with the Romulans to a first contact situation, Nan's job never relents. Meanwhile, a reporter starts investigating the mysterious resignation of the previous Federation president, threatening a scandal that could lead the quadrant into war.

"The idea first came several years ago, when John Ordover came to me with the idea of doing a *Star Trek* version of *The West Wing*. He thought my dialogue skills were compatible with the show's unique (at the time) voice, and thought it might be a good match. I even did a sample scene (an early draft of the scene in Chapter 4 when Z4 is chewing out the guy from the travel office about the non-working transporters). Time passed, nothing much happened, and then the *A Time To . . .* series started being developed, including David Mack dealing with the end of a Federation presidency in *A Time To Kill* and *A Time To Heal*. Several of the concepts originally intended for the *West Wing* pastiche wound up in the original conception for the two-book finale, *A Time For War* and *A Time For Peace*. Then it was decided to cut what had originally been planned as a twelve-book miniseries to nine books, I carved out the political stuff and added a lot more, and that became *Articles of the Federation*."

Keith continues, "The notion was to show in detail the Federation government. After forty years, we know more about the Klingon government, the Bajoran government, the Cardassian government, and the Romulan government than we do the Federation government. We thought it was past time to address that, extrapolating from what little we did get on screen. After John left Pocket, Marco Palmieri took over the project, and he was the one who suggested it be a more ambitious book. John's and my original notion was to do a month in the life of the Federation president; Marco thought, wisely, that it should be an entire year, which made for a much more in-depth and (dare I say) epic book."

MINISERIES

INVASION!

Invasion! was the brainchild of John Ordover and Diane Carey. When John was first hired to the Pocket editorial staff, they were producing six original series and six *Next Generation* novels a year. *Deep Space Nine* came along, adding another six novels a year into the mix. *Voyager* created another six per year two years later. *Invasion!* came about when John came to the conclusion that publishing *Trek* books on a regular monthly schedule was similar to comic books. Realizing that stories in the graphic world did crossover story lines on a regular basis, he applied this idea to the *Trek* line. While the *Lost Years* saga was an attempt to do a series within the line, *Invasion!* was the first to be written and published in a short timeframe.

John remembered, "I called Diane Carey and I said, 'Here's what I can give you. A menace attacks in the original series era. A hundred years later it comes back worse. DS9 deals with a different aspect of it and then finally *Voyager* encounters the source of the invasion.' She came up with the rest." He took the idea to the writers and they began putting their own spin on the concept. "It was only after this process was ongoing that I began to understand the complexity of having all the writers write a continuing series simultaneously in novel form."

INVASION!

BOOK ONE

FIRST STRIKE
(STAR TREK)
DIANE CAREY

JULY 1996 (289PP)

A Klingon general finds himself living a nightmare. Aboard a mysterious vessel, the inhabitants of it seem to represent stories of Klingon culture that are used to terrify children into submission, like the boogeyman of our childhood. The general escapes, and realizes that to defeat this enemy, he will have to gain the trust of another enemy, Captain Kirk.

Diane and John Ordover came up with the concept for the first series to cross into the four *Trek* shows at the time. She said about *First Strike*, "A supremely popular bestseller, selling in the multiple hundreds of thousands. The plot involves ancient Graeco-Roman and Celtic mythology, because with every book we write we try to have something unique or to explore a new angle. I

had just come off *First Frontier*, which was a huge book of hard science. I wanted to go away from hard science, so I moved to mythology as the basis for this book. Many of the recognizable personae from Earth mythology were represented in the alien collection James Kirk had to deal with in this book. The book culminates in an ancient Celtic ritual, the burning of the straw man, with human sacrifices trapped inside—namely, McCoy, who had violated a cultural taboo by doing an autopsy on a 'poppet,' a type of voodoo representation of a living individual. The clash of cultures is an excellent example of what science fiction exists to examine: the coming together of our future selves with our past selves, in an uncontrollable environment."

BOOK TWO

THE SOLDIERS OF FEAR
(STAR TREK: THE NEXT GENERATION)
DEAN WESLEY SMITH AND KRISTINE KATHRYN RUSCH

JULY 1996 (234PP)

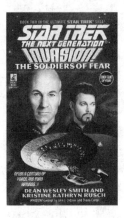

he Furies have returned, and the *Enterprise* finds itself at the gate of the invading force.

Using a powerful mind-control weapon that incapacitates most of the crew, the invasion seems certain to succeed. To beat these foes, the crew must conquer their fears and make the battle a level playing field. When the opportunity to stop the Furies for good is presented, Picard must choose which crew member and friend to send on a suicide mission.

Dean reflected, "First cross-over series that was done, and our best-selling *Trek* novel. I have no memory as to how we got into it, but I do remember that the authors worked a lot on keeping the details straight from book-to-book."

BOOK THREE

TIME'S ENEMY
(STAR TREK: DEEP SPACE NINE)
L.A. GRAF

AUGUST 1996   (338PP)

aptain Sisko, Dax, and Bashir are called to a secret meeting just outside the Earth's solar system. A startling discovery has been unearthed and only the three of them can hope-

fully provide an explanation. Found encased in ice for the last five thousand years is the Starship *Defiant*. Inside a chamber is the still living symbiont, Dax. How did the *Defiant* find itself five thousand years in the past, and can they avoid making the same mistakes twice, saving themselves from an icy grave?

Karen and Julia remarked, "Most of the credit for *Invasion!* has to go to John. All we did was try to fit the *Deep Space Nine* crew into the mix. We wanted to make use of the wormhole and we also wanted to add a new element, another and (if possible) even scarier alien into the series so it wasn't just four repetitions of the good guys beating up on the same bad guys in the same way. This was our first DS9 book, so it took us a little while to 'get into' character. Julia had no problem writing Kira, but Bashir was her other point-of-view character and he wasn't quite as 'action-adventure' oriented. Similarly, Karen Rose got to write for scientist Dax which was fun and easy, but also had to do Sisko which was more of a stretch. In the end, though, we were so happy with the plot twists that we came up with that in many ways we feel this was our best book."

BOOK FOUR

THE FINAL FURY
(STAR TREK: VOYAGER)
DAFYDD AB HUGH

AUGUST 1996 **(308PP)**

The crew of the *Voyager* uncovers a Starfleet distress call, which leads them to a planet of horrifying beings straight from their various homeworld's mythologies. Realizing these beings are the Furies, who attempted to invade during Kirk's era, Janeway confronts a dilemma. Commit mass murder and destroy billions of lives, or let the Furies create a wormhole that will engulf their entire planet, possibly leading to another invasion of the Alpha Quadrant.

Dafydd recalled, "This was the first *Trek* book where Ordover came to me and asked me to author one of the parts, batting cleanup (he also told me which *Trek* universe it would involve, *Voyager*, in this case). Since we knew that no *Trek* crew would ever be mass murderers, I decided to set up a situation where the crew of *Voyager* would be forced to—in essence—commit genocide, while the readers (I hope) would be forced into complicity. In other words, I tried, yet again, in my tiresome and increasingly annoying way, to violate another important canon of *Trekhood*."

DAY OF HONOR

BOOK ONE

ANCIENT BLOOD
(STAR TREK: THE NEXT GENERATION)
DIANE CAREY

SEPTEMBER 1997 **(280PP)**

To the Klingons, honor is more important than life. A sacred holiday to celebrate their lifestyle is called the Day of Honor. Worf must spend this holiday away from Alexander, because he is on an undercover mission to infiltrate a criminal cartel that uses rogue Klingons as their muscle. Alexander searches for honor among his human heritage, so Picard shows him life during the Revolutionary War.

• • •

DAY OF HONOR

John Ordover reflected, "Nothing gets you in bigger trouble then having a successful concept, because now everybody wants you to top that. So I wanted it to be a crossover but I didn't want it to be yet another contrived enemy that happens to fight across all the centuries. It's not like all the ST novels were contemporary. At that time they were taking place in different times and in different places in the galaxy and stuff like that. So what made sense to me was to come up with something that links people down the ages." John, who collaborated on the concept with Paula Block, concluded that a holiday commemorating a historic event fit the bill nicely. "The fun thing about that though is that it actually led to a *Voyager* episode." As the books were being developed, John contacted *Voyager* executive producer Jeri Taylor, who had worked on her *Voyager* novels *Mosaic* and *Pathways* around this time—and told her about the *Day of Honor* miniseries, on the off chance that she might wish to tie-in an episode with the project. He told her, "There's this Klingon holiday called the Day of Honor which is kind of like the Jewish Yom Kippur, where you take the measure of your honor for the past year. It seemed like a perfect storyline for B'Elanna so I just called you up to say this is what we're doing.' And they tied into it." It was the first time a *Star Trek* episode had been created around a *Trek* book concept."

Diane said, "Ancient Blood was another 're-quest' [by my editor. He] wanted to examine the Klingon concept of 'honor.' I never take anything at face value, including concepts. Just as I examined the young James Kirk through the prism of his being a juvenile delinquent instead of the straight line of a 'perfect' young officer, I didn't like the idea that Klingons think 'honor' is how hard and bad a person can fight and that being a warrior is the be-all of life. Somebody had to build their ships and clean the hallways. Everybody can't be a warrior, and they can't hold those who aren't warriors in contempt, or their society would collapse. I don't like one-dimensional characters and I certainly don't like one-dimensional cultures, a too-common element in science fiction."

Pocket Books asked Diane to usher Worf's son Alexander through the Klingon rite of passage called the "Day of Honor." She said, "I decided to show Alexander what honor means through his human heritage rather than his Klingon heritage. Picard, chosen by Worf as Alexander's mentor for this rite, decides to take him back to his Revolutionary War ancestor, and figure out what's honorable while also learning something about his American heritage. The writing challenge was to make the story interesting and dangerous even though it happened on the holodeck, where nobody could really be hurt. In the end, Alexander discovers that honor is not, in fact, how well, how hard, nor how much a person fights. It's why we fight. Real honor is in the human idea of honor, not the Klingon idea."

B O O K T W O	**B O O K T H R E E**

ARMAGEDDON SKY
(STAR TREK: DEEP SPACE NINE)
L.A. GRAF

HER KLINGON SOUL
(STAR TREK: VOYAGER)
MICHAEL JAN FRIEDMAN

SEPTEMBER 1997   (279PP)

OCTOBER 1997   (275PP)

The *Defiant* crew races to rescue a ship of scientists that were near a planet bombarded with comets. Upon arrival, the crew discovers that the devastated planet has Klingons living on the decimated surface. To rescue this group of exiles would bring them dishonor. To make matters worse, Commander Kor arrives and threatens to destroy the *Defiant* if they interfere. Can Sisko rescue the scientists and give these Klingons the honor they are lacking?

Julia and Karen remarked, "Karen Rose wanted to play with a new geological disaster in the background, so we did the meteorite impact theme. We're not huge Klingon fans, so our main problem was trying to really 'get' the attraction those characters had for readers. We hope we managed to portray them in a way that was true to the series and their various personalities."

B'Elanna Torres despises the Klingon holiday and doesn't want anyone to remind her of it. She was on a mission with Harry Kim, and the Kazon captures both of them. When another ship arrives and fires on the Kazon, they think their luck has changed, but these aliens are even worse and force B'Elanna and Harry to mine a deadly radioactive substance. Can *Voyager* find them both before they die of radiation exposure?

Mike remarked, "This was fun as well but to tell you the truth I don't know if I really did my best work on it. It's part of a contrived event. Jeri Taylor was great. She actually took the concept and ran with it and it became a bigger event, both for TV and for the books."

BOOK FOUR

TREATY'S LAW
(STAR TREK)

DEAN WESLEY SMITH AND KRISTINE KATHRYN RUSCH

OCTOBER 1997 (277PP)

A Klingon farming community sends out a distress call and both Captain Kirk and Commander Kor arrive to help the colonists. An unknown alien fleet attacks the vessels above and small ships open fire on the crops and colonists below. The two adversaries must put aside their differences to stop the aggressors. As a result of their truce, the Klingons and humans learn about honor from each other, and the eventual holiday is created. The crew of the *Farragut*, from the novel *Rings of Tautee*, makes another appearance.

Dean remarked, "Since I had done the Klingon CD-Rom, I was considered an expert, thus they hired me to do the final and most important book in the cross-over series. Another fun book to write."

DAY OF HONOR
(EPISODE ADAPTATION: SEE SECTION 10: NOVELIZATIONS)

THE CAPTAIN'S TABLE

BOOK ONE

WAR DRAGONS
(STAR TREK)
L.A. GRAF

JUNE 1998 (261PP)

Captain Kirk takes Captain Sulu to the mysterious bar. Kirk tells the patrons a tale involving strange lizards and the difficulties with talking to them, because the translator device had difficulty with their strange language. Many years later, when Sulu is in command of the *Excelsior*, he runs into the same creatures. Unfortunately, Starfleet has classified any information about the strange beings.

Karen Rose and Julia remarked, "This was another series idea from John, and the spark was

THE CAPTAIN'S TABLE

John Ordover remarked, "*Captain's Table* is probably my favorite because it told the most different stories. It brought the bar concept which is a standard in [literature and] science fiction going back to Chaucer. Spider Robinson's *Callahan's Crosstime Saloon* is a bad comparison. [The real inspiration] is a combination of Arthur C. Clarke's *Tales from the White Heart* and A.E. Van Vogt's *The Weapons Shops of Isar*."

"Once again, I was faced with the problem of needing to do another crossover series. What do we do that gets everybody into a similar mode, and I only wanted it to be officers first in, but what is the excuse, what's the schtick? It occurred to me, in Van Vogt's book, people would be down-trodden and depressed and suddenly the door to a shop and a sign would appear that said 'Weapon Shop' or 'The Weapon Shop,' I forget exactly what it is, or you would open the door and walk in and no matter where you were walking in from, you wound up in the same place and the doors could appear anywhere they were needed. And you open the door and you walk in and you find yourself in the weapons shop, the weapon shop is inter-dimensional. So that's where I get that. So, I thought about what should be on the other side of the damn door. And what occurred to me were things that ST hadn't done but that science fiction had done, which was a bar! And it just happens that one of our regular writers, Dean Wesley Smith, was a bartender for seventeen years. So I knew he could set up a good setting for us."

"The reasons Spider Robinson's stories are not a good comparison is because in *Callahan's*, someone comes into the bar with the problems, relates the problem, and then the problem is resolved in the bar. At the *Captain's Table*, people come in, tell a story, other people listen to the story, and the story gets complete in the telling of it. The people in the bar do not contribute to the solution of the problem."

Captain's Table has the distinction of having the main narrative of each tale told in the first person. "The approach gave the books a fresh appeal at the time because we hadn't been doing it."

John and the authors may be seen as background characters on the cover art of all six books. "All the authors are in the background, and I think Mike Friedman is actually on two books, since we had a crowd scene anyway. It was just fun."

asking writers to abandon their usual third-person writing styles and write from the first-person point of view. At first, Julia and I thought we couldn't possibly co-write this way, given that we usually attached our different writing styles to different characters. But when John gave us permission to use both Kirk and Sulu as point-of-view captains, our dilemma was solved and we had a lot of fun with the book. The aliens we made up are based on our pet leopard geckos, by the way, and if you look on the cover mural you can see a leopard gecko in there somewhere."

him. Does he hold the key to finding a technological treasure that could shift the power in the quadrant?

Mike commented, "Ordover had this idea that we would do these sort of sea shanty kind of books. It was that kind of tale and in retrospect I think there are probably other or equally more interesting things I could have done with that set up, had I taken the assignment less literally. But I did have fun with it and it gave me a chance to highlight Picard and make him kind of a romantic action figure. And Worf had some good stuff in there, too."

BOOK TWO

DUJONIAN'S HOARD
(STAR TREK: THE NEXT GENERATION)
MICHAEL JAN FRIEDMAN

JUNE 1998   (272 PP)

BOOK THREE

THE MIST
(STAR TREK: DEEP SPACE NINE)
DEAN WESLEY SMITH AND KRISTINE KATHRYN RUSCH

JULY 1998   (271 PP)

At the bar, Captain Picard tells a tale of going undercover with Worf to track down the *Dujonian's Hoard* treasure. A former Starfleet officer has disappeared, and everyone from the Romulans to the Cardassians is looking for

Captain Sisko's tale in the enigmatic bar. Answering a distress call that appears to come from nowhere, the *Defiant* finds itself in an alternate dimension. A civil war is brewing in the "mist," and Deep Space 9 may turn the tide in the wrong direction. As Sisko watches, the station is engulfed. As the clock ticks, can he bring both the station and the *Defiant* back home?

Dean remembered, "John Ordover and I worked to developed the *Captain's Table*, and since I was a bartender and have a degree in Architecture, I actually made floor plans for the bar. I also developed the cast of characters that were regulars used in every book."

BOOK FOUR

FIRE SHIP
(STAR TREK: VOYAGER)

DIANE CAREY

JULY 1998   (274 PP)

Captain Janeway tells her tale of the events that transpired when she watched *Voyager* explode, killing everyone aboard. She finds herself rescued by aliens that don't believe she could be the captain of her own ship. Forced to swab the decks, she has to convince the chain of command she is worthy if she wants to uncover what happened with her former ship and help her new crewmates win a major war.

Of the story, Diane said, "Captain Janeway was separated from her ship with absolutely no proof of her authority, her experience, or her rank. She tries to convince the poverty-stricken crew of a salvage vessel that she's really the captain of a huge wealthy ship and if they'll just risk everything they have to take her back, she can help them. They say, 'That's nice, honey, here's a broom.' Captain Janeway, daughter of an admiral, who has never had a really hard moment in her life, is now forced to come up through the ranks from the lowest position on a ship—something she never experienced. For the first time in her life, she has no credentials and no one has a reason to do what she says. She's always been able to just snap orders before, so this is a new experience for her. She has to use her wits and cleverness to force this stressed captain and crew to listen to her when they have no reason to do so. In order to have power, she has to trick and cajole those around her into doing what she needs to happen. Janeway basically goes to the place where she has never been: a lowly deckhand. She's starting where I started on my ships—swabbing, scraping, sanding, varnishing, hauling and mending. I confess to enjoying the chance to watch her actually do the work of the lower decks for a change. I always had the idea that James Kirk had scrubbed decks, but I never had that feeling from Janeway. Admiral's daughters don't usually have to actually get dirty, so I wrecked her hairdo in this one. It's interesting writing female heroines in these situations, because I always try to let them go ahead and be girls. A woman working on a ship had better realize she's a woman and sometimes will need help with physical things, while still maintaining the authority she deserves, if she deserves any. As watch leader on sailing ships, I've had to live this reality."

B O O K   F I V E

ONCE BURNED
(STAR TREK: NEW FRONTIER)
Peter David

O c t o b e r   1 9 9 8   (2 6 2 p p)

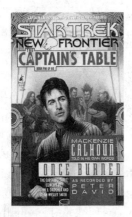

Before Calhoun took command of the *Excalibur*, he was first officer aboard the *U.S.S. Grissom*. The tragedy that occurred on his watch resulted in a court martial. Even though he was exonerated, Calhoun resigned from Starfleet in disgust. The events have been hinted in previous books, but now the captain finds himself in the bar forced to tell a tale, so he decides to finally reveal the true events that transpired.

Peter remarked, "I had a lot of fun with this one. It didn't tie in with a major storyline. In-stead it was, 'Here is the starting point. Go for it.' I had an absolute field day with that. I had dropped hints about Calhoun's earlier experiences and this gave me the opportunity to actually write a whole book that focused on it and it allowed me to introduce an entirely new crew. Kat Mueller first showed up in this book. I introduced her and others in this book and then when I introduced the night crew on the *Excalibur*, I just simply had it be those characters."

B O O K   S I X

WHERE SEA MEETS SKY
(STAR TREK)
Jerry Oltion

O c t o b e r   1 9 9 8   (2 6 7 p p)

Captain Pike tells the aliens at his table of an assignment to the Aronnia System. Upon arrival, the crew of the *Enterprise* finds giant whale-like creatures in space called Titans. Pike must make a horrific decision, since the creatures are vital to the survival of one culture, but are destroying another.

• • •

Jerry remembered how the background for the story came into his mind. He said, "I was guest of honor at a convention in Missoula, Montana back in the mid-80s, and one of the panel discussions was on brainstorming. We decided to brainstorm an alien species that lived in space, and we came up with these cool space whales that scooped hydrogen from the atmospheres of gas giants for food and laid their eggs on terrestrial planets. Phil Foglio was the artist guest of honor at that convention, and he drew sketches of the creature and displayed them on an overhead projector while we talked, so we actually got to see our creature evolve as we zeroed in on its characteristics. George Takei was the media guest at that same convention, so there was a lot of talk about what would happen if the *Enterprise* encountered one of these space whales. We had fun speculating, but after the convention I forgot about the space whales until John Ordover asked me if I wanted to write a Captain Pike novel for the *Captain's Table* series. I cast about for the kind of story that would fit the rough-edged feel of the *Enterprise* and crew as we saw them in 'The Cage,' and finally realized that a Jules Verne kind of story would be perfect. The space whales immediately came to mind. Sadly, Sulu wasn't in the crew during Pike's first mission, so I couldn't write him into the story. I hope George Takei has forgiven me for that!"

After the novel was published, Jerry found himself furious about an editorial move. He said, "There was one editorial move that really messed up this book: *Where Sea Meets Sky* was the final novel in the *Captain's Table* series, but John Ordover decided at the last moment that he wanted the books to make an endless loop, so he tacked the first few pages of book number one onto the end of my book, with only a blank line to indicate the break. I've had many people come up to me and say, 'Dude, your book was booming along great, and it reached this cool point where everything was tied up perfectly, and then it just got bizarre. What happened?' What happened is that everything after the break on page two hundred forty-one was part of somebody else's book!"

NEW EARTH

BOOK ONE

WAGON TRAIN TO THE STARS
(STAR TREK #89)
DIANE CAREY

JUNE 2000   (352PP)

Earth has been saved again by the crew of the *Enterprise*, this time from the threat of V'Ger. Soon after, Kirk receives an invitation to lead several thousand colonists in a massive caravan to their new home six months distant. Along the route, mysterious occurrences including

NEW EARTH

John Ordover remarked, "I wanted to do a big original series arc because we hadn't done much recently and it occurred to me, *Star Trek* had originally been pitched as 'Wagon Train to the Stars,' but we had never actually done that story. There were too many books with evacuating the planet stories [in *New Earth*], but I thought the covers really kicked ass and overall I thought it was a very good concept."

John explained the "origin of the concept was a personal reaction to *Voyager*. My problem with *Voyager* is they don't really have any turf to protect. They don't have any real stake in anything that they do. Optimally they could wrap themselves in an impenetrable cocoon, go into suspended animation, and point the ship toward earth. They don't have an emotional tie. What if you went outside the known galaxy or outside the common area to find a new colony and you were assigned to stay there and protect them for a while? This planet is now a member of the Federation and it's our new home base and from now on we'll be expanding from this new region, trying to get planets to join the Federation; and they're trying to set up their own new Federation. In essence, they'd set up a colony and would then have to defend it. So I took that idea and turned it into *New Earth*."

an illness and possible sabotage threaten everyone involved. Meanwhile, at the colony's destination, an alien race waits to destroy this new enemy.

Diane remembered her editor wanted to use *New Earth* as a springboard to a new continuing book series that she would write, as Peter David was doing with *New Frontier*: "New captain, new ship, new crew, and new situation, bringing *Star Trek* back to the original concept of 'being out there' with limited contact, essentially in a wild west town and having to fake it, hacking our way to civilization the hard way. Greg and I developed the situation for *New Earth*, then wrote the bracketing support books, with other authors writing the middle books of the series."

Looking back at the story, Diane said, "One of the interesting parts of that book is that the ships' manifests and organizational work Kirk had to do was essentially what a real commodore in a mismatched fleet would have to do. Each of the *Star Trek* officers had to take on new assignments to make sure they could usher this regatta of vessels, pioneers, and supplies all the way out to their destination, in good order. I put my knowledge of boson's work and ship organization to good use, basically figuring out what Kirk would have to do to make such a project happen. Ship's business and organization has always been an underlying element of *Star Trek*, and it gave us a chance to see our favorite characters actually doing the nitty gritty of their real jobs. 'It's not all phasers and pretty girls, y'know.'"

BOOK TWO

BELLE TERRE
(STAR TREK #90)
DEAN WESLEY SMITH WITH DIANE CAREY

JUNE 2000   (237PP)

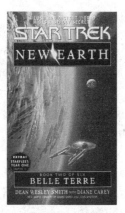

The colonists have just settled on their new home world when Spock discovers that one of the planet's moons will explode in approximately eight days. A temporary evacuation will not save the colonists, since the resulting explosion will make the planet inhospitable for human life for over a hundred years. Can Spock use his computer brain to save the colonists and their world?

Dean reflected, "Kris and I wrote book five in that series as well, but Diane was supposed to write one, two, and six. The first book turned out to be harder than she expected, so John and her called me in to write book two from her outline, and then we worked on it together some, I think. Memory fades."

BOOK THREE

ROUGH TRAILS
(STAR TREK #91)
L.A. GRAF

JULY 2000   (360PP)

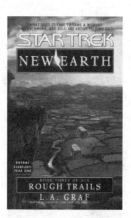

While Captain Kirk takes the *Enterprise* away to patrol the region, Sulu, Uhura, and Chekov stay behind on Belle Terre to help the colonists adjust. As a result of the moon's explosion, the planet suffers from extreme hostile conditions and radioactive areas. Isolated areas on the planet have their own set of laws and ruthless murder for supplies doesn't cause the inhabitants to blink an eye. Then Chekov's shuttle crashes, and he must fight to survive the harsh conditions and the nasty inhabitants of the region.

"This was fun for us, because we got to recreate a local western Pennsylvania natural disaster: the Johnstown Flood! (If you check the names of several towns on the planet, you'll find they're from the Johnstown area.) By this time, Julia was also doing a lot of herding with her border collies, so we wrote border collies into the plot and used the names of many of our dog-owning friends (with their permission) as characters. And Karen Rose got to use another generation of geoscience students as the scientific crew!"

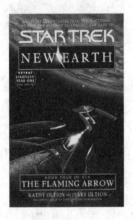

BOOK FOUR

THE FLAMING ARROW
(STAR TREK #92)
KATHY OLTION AND JERRY OLTION

JULY 2000   (283PP)

The Kauld, who wants to rid the planet of its new inhabitants, has developed a super laser. By firing from a considerable distance, the beam will not only reach full power when it hits the planet, but will also be impossible to stop once launched. Once Kirk hears about the diabolical plan, he tries to stop the weapon from activating. Unfortunately, he is already too late.

Jerry and Kathy talked about the idea behind the story. "We had to work within the con-

straints of the overarching six-book plot, but we had pretty much free rein to tell whatever story we wanted within that framework. We wanted something that fit the frontier motif, but still had the techie aspects of a *Star Trek* story. Since our book was number four out of six, we figured any parallel with North American history would put us at about the 'attack on the fort' phase, which led to the idea of flaming arrows, and from there it was a simple jump to laser beams, and from there to one great BIG laser beam. And since the *Enterprise* can travel faster than light, we had the ultimate ticking clock, and the rest of the story fell into place from there."

Kathy and Jerry's first collaboration was a wonderful experience for both of them. They said, "Writing together was a dream! Our styles matched so well that we hardly had to rewrite anything. We could (and did, many times) trade the sections we were writing in mid-scene, and the other person could carry on without pause. The results were so seamless, we can't tell which parts each of us wrote. There's an old saying that each writer in a collaboration puts in eighty percent of the work, but we felt like this one was about twenty percent each, and the rest happened by magic."

Looking at the result after a few years, they said, "It was . . . interesting trying to write a book in a multi-author series. Everybody was writing their books at the same time, and we kept getting frantic notes from John Ordover saying things like, 'So and so just sent Chekov away on another mission, so you can't use him in your book.' Oookay. It felt like we were building a bridge between two shores that were both shrouded in fog, while trolls were busy knocking out the supports from under us. The last-minute changes kept rolling in, so we did the only prudent thing we could do: We finished our book first so everybody else would have to follow our lead from then on."

BOOK FIVE

THIN AIR
(STAR TREK #93)

DEAN WESLEY SMITH AND KRISTINE KATHRYN RUSCH

AUGUST 2000 (219PP)

he aggressive Kauld just won't stop trying to eliminate all of the settlers. An attack ship is destroyed in the upper atmosphere, releasing a deadly biological agent into the ecosystem. While the planet slowly becomes inhospitable to human life, Kirk takes the *Enterprise* to fight the Kauld in a final showdown. Can Spock find an answer to the plague and the aggressiveness of the Kauld be curtailed?

Dean remarked, "A fun idea in that one, foam covering a planet as a way to attack it. I had a blast."

BOOK SIX

CHALLENGER
(STAR TREK #94)
DIANE CAREY

AUGUST 2000 (396PP)

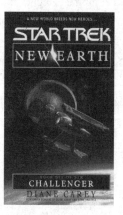

he starship *Peleliu* heads to Belle Terre to relieve the *Enterprise* crew from their duties. During a fight with the Kauld, the captain shows signs of losing his mind. Officer Nick Keller must choose to disobey his captain and report his suspicions to Captain Kirk, or ignore them and hope nobody dies as a result. When the *Peleliu* is attacked, Keller must take control to save not only his ship but the *Enterprise* as well.

With the last book in the series, Diane left the ending open to possibly start a new series. She said, "The new 'sheriff' in these parts was Nick Keller, a first officer plagued with an unstable captain who was forced to take over a ship and dispossess his captain in order to save his ship and mission. The idea was for Kirk to leave Keller in the wilderness to be the Starfleet law

DOUBLE HELIX

John Ordover remembered how *Double Helix* came about, "That was in the context of there being a lot of movies like *Outbreak* and the *Hot Zone* and stuff like that. So I agreed it was time for a *Star Trek* medical thing. But we wanted it to be a recurring threat over years rather than one directly connected story. We set up the bad guy, who was recurring and hidden and then revealed in the last book. It was fun to do things like Chakotay when he was still in the Maquis. Personally, I didn't think that one came together as well as the others."

When asked why they were sold under the TNG moniker, John responded, "At the time the sales force said TNG is our best seller. If you are going to do this, do it as TNG miniseries. And we tried to put at least some TNG element into each one."

Regarding the covers, John felt, "The covers were lousy! They were what I would call color forms; bad likenesses of the characters pasted down on the covers."

enforcement force in the unstable Belle Terre system. Nick Keller's ship was destroyed, and he comes up with the idea of cobbling together a ship from old parts, then cobbling together a crew from the immediate reservoir. The ship *Challenger* was named after the space shuttle *Challenger*, a suggestion from John Ordover."

DOUBLE HELIX

BOOK ONE

INFECTION
(STAR TREK: THE NEXT GENERATION #51)
JOHN GREGORY BETANCOURT

JUNE 1999 (226PP)

Shortly after Jean-Luc Picard takes command of the NCC-1701-D, the ship is sent to respond to a virulent epidemic on the planet Archaria III. The peculiar bug is nasty and appears to be genetically created to jump species. According to the doctors on the planet, the disease can infect the host, even under strict isolation and sterile conditions. The sheer design of it reveals its manipulation by human hands. When Dr. Crusher brings someone on board for testing, the plague begins to infect the *Enterprise*. Ultimately, the release of the disease is only the first stage of a bigger threat.

John remarked, "John Ordover, the *Star Trek* editor who came up with the idea for *Infection* with Michael Jan Friedman, asked me to write the first book as a kind of apology. He had held a couple of outlines for several years, promising to buy them and never did. (He also misspelled my name on the cover of the first edition of *Incident at Arbuk*.)"

BOOK TWO

VECTORS
(STAR TREK: THE NEXT GENERATION #52)
DEAN WESLEY SMITH AND KRISTINE KATHRYN RUSCH

JUNE 1999   (260PP)

When Dr. Pulaski transfers off the *Enterprise* to let Dr. Crusher resume her position as chief medical officer, Pulaski's ex-husband calls in a favor. On Terok Nor, the mysterious disease has somehow taken hold, and both the Cardassians and Bajorans are ravaged by its effects. With the help of a rebel spy named Kira, can Pulaski save the day?

Dean commented, "A summer cross-over book. I have no idea why I was picked to do it, but it was fun."

BOOK THREE

RED SECTOR
(STAR TREK: THE NEXT GENERATION #53)
Diane Carey

JULY 1999 (293PP)

An ensign named Stiles leads a group to rescue Spock. As a result of the mission, he is captured and held prisoner for several years. His only friend during that time is a Romulan named Zevon. After his release, Stiles finds himself working with Spock again, when the members of the ruling family on Romulus are stricken with the mysterious disease seen in the previous two books. The only hope appears to be Stiles' Romulan friend he was forced to leave behind.

"Red Sector is one of my favorite books," Diane said. "Another chance to explore the *Star Trek* universe from a new point of view, and a chance to see Spock at his best, with humor, compassion, and humility. I've always held that Vulcans, as portrayed so well by Nimoy, had all kinds of emotions, but simply controlled them.

The interest of the characters is that they control what they feel and are always straining to hold reactions in. That's what made them interesting and dramatic. In this book, Spock combines forces with a young man with a serious case of hero worship for him. I like Stiles and his character growth; it's why (Greg) and I write."

Another reason this novel is one of her favorites is "It also gave me the chance to showcase one of the workhorses of the military fleet, a tender vessel called Combat Support Tender, a 'moveable starbase' that is derived of real 'floating shipyards' in the US Navy. I've always looked for ways to show that the queens of seagoing vessels, the carriers and high-profile vessels, are supported by dozens of other kinds of ships. Interestingly, in the early days of my *Star Trek* writing, I tried to have destroyers and tenders, but I wasn't allowed to show any other kind of ship than a starship, as if all ships were starships. Remember the line, 'He commands not just a space ship, but a starship.' If there are no other kinds of ships than the big starships, then what makes the starships special? It took a long time to convince the powers at Paramount that there's no way to have a fleet without other types of vessels with other duties. While writing this book I served briefly aboard the Schooner *True North*; I really enjoyed my service aboard and trowled all my shipmates into the book. Almost all the characters aboard Eric Stiles' ship were named after shipmates of mine on that voyage."

BOOK FOUR

QUARANTINE
(STAR TREK: THE NEXT GENERATION #54)
JOHN VORNHOLT

JULY 1999 (259PP)

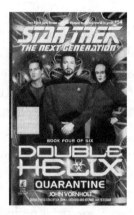

▲ Tom Riker, Will's transporter duplicate, works for Starfleet Medical. The enigmatic plague has stricken a planet in the Demilitarized Zone, bringing the Maquis into the mix. Captain Chakotay uses Riker to obtain the medical supplies desperately needed to save the inhabitants. The Cardassians, however, have other plans. The story showcases what turned Tom Riker toward the Maquis philosophy.

"This has to be the grimmest *Trek* novel I've ever written, because it's about a planet dying from a horrible plague. Readers of the *Double Helix* series know that the plot wove through six novels, but number four was a tough one in the series to do. In the overall plot, it was the low ebb, with the bad guys winning. I couldn't advance the plot much, and I couldn't reveal any secrets or conclude anything either. So I

went with angst and atmosphere—imagine *Trek* meets Kafka. I really enjoyed using the Maquis members—of the *Voyager* crew, before their contact with *Voyager*. Captain Chakotay, Tuvok, etc. were a fine crew to work with, and the futility and grimness of this story left them prepared for the big change that was coming in their lives."

DOUBLE OR NOTHING
(STAR TREK: THE NEXT GENERATION #55)
PETER DAVID

AUGUST 1999 (277PP)

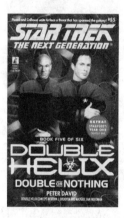

▲ The cast of *New Frontier* joins forces with the *Next Generation* crew to stop the scourge responsible for the plague in the previous books. Captain Calhoun goes undercover as a rogue Federation operative and discovers the key to the puzzle is buried in his past. For Captain Picard, the villain has an even more personal vendetta. The end result will have huge ramifications for everyone, especially the crew of the *Excalibur*.

• • •

Peter remarked, "I have no recollection of this book at all."

BOOK SIX

THE FIRST VIRTUE
(STAR TREK: THE NEXT GENERATION #56)
MICHAEL JAN FRIEDMAN AND CHRISTIE GOLDEN

AUGUST 1999   (271PP)

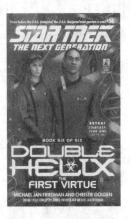

A plot for revenge carried out in the previous volumes had its origins when Picard was the captain of the *Stargazer*. While Jean-Luc tries to establish peaceful ties between some very stubborn people, Jack Crusher and Tuvok work undercover to investigate a series of terrorist attacks. The results of their actions will create dire circumstances in the future.

Christie recalled, "So out of the blue, Michael Jan Friedman calls me up and wants to know if I'd 'help him out' by collaborating with him on this final book in the *Double Helix* series. Um . . . YEAH, duh! He had a very clear idea of what I would develop and what he would work

on. He started it off, I took over at a certain point, and he wrapped things up. One area in which I think I really contributed was the development of Grace, the Orion slave girl. In the outline, she was mentioned merely as part of the scene. I decided that she would be the one to help free our heroes and die heroically as a free woman. The whole Orion thing has always been fascinating to me, which was why I had fun dealing with it in *The Last Roundup*. Also a hoot is a Vulcan getting naked in a steam bath-type of environment. Go Tuvok! Tight deadline, lots of dead brain cells, but an honor to work with Mike. I'm flattered he asked me."

Mike remarked, "John Ordover and I came up with the *Double Helix* idea which wasn't spectacularly original but we hadn't done a disease yet in these contrived multi-book series, and it allowed us to come up with some very cool team-ups. The idea was that I was going to do the prequel and it turned out I had too much on my plate at the time so I asked Christie to lend a hand. It was a little strange because I hadn't read any of the other books even though they kind of sprung from the concept that John and I originated. So I really didn't know too much about what I was pulling off. It was good that Christie was available to help."

THE DOMINION WAR

BOOK ONE

BEHIND ENEMY LINES
(STAR TREK: THE NEXT GENERATION)
JOHN VORNHOLT

NOVEMBER 1998   **(269PP)**

R o Laren has a message for her former captain. Deep inside Cardassian territory, the Dominion is attempting to create an artificial wormhole. If successful, the Dominion will be able to bring reinforcements and bypass the Bajoran wormhole entirely. Can Picard trust Ro, though she is now a Maquis? He decides to make a bold move.

BOOK TWO

CALL TO ARMS
(STAR TREK: DEEP SPACE NINE;
SEE SECTION 10: NOVELIZATIONS)

BOOK THREE

TUNNEL THROUGH THE STARS
(STAR TREK: THE NEXT GENERATION)
JOHN VORNHOLT

DECEMBER 1998   **(269PP)**

P icard decides to go undercover as a Bajoran and lead a group of Maquis into the Badlands to stop the deadly construction. The hopeless task appears even more so when acts of sabotage start plaguing their efforts. Can Picard find the traitor and destroy the Dominion's efforts?

John remarked, "This was my attempt to explain what the *Enterprise* was doing during the Dominion War, and I wanted to pull out all the stops and write an exciting war story. It was also my first duology, even though it came out as books one and three of the *Dominion War* series. These books are a favorite of mine, because they started me writing a string of duologies, and they were very popular. This was also yet another time I employed two of my favorite semi-regular characters, Ro Laren and Admiral Necheyev. The DS9 TV show also developed a story line about the Dominion building an artificial wormhole, which had to be destroyed by a dangerous commando raid. I didn't know about their story until later, but we beat them to the approval step. They chose to abandon their story line, which I felt badly about. There was room for both of us!"

BOOK FOUR: SACRIFICE OF ANGELS

(STAR TREK: DEEP SPACE NINE;
SEE SECTION 10: NOVELIZATIONS)

SECTION 31

ROGUE
(STAR TREK: THE NEXT GENERATION)
MICHAEL A. MARTIN AND ANDY MANGELS

JUNE 2001   (362 PP)

Six months prior to the events chronicled in *First Contact*, a mission will force Captain Picard to face the true horror of the organization known for subterfuge. His friends from academy days are on board, and they both have secret agendas. And a young lieutenant named Hawk will be asked to join the secret organization.

Mike became aware of *Star Trek* during its syndication renaissance in the early 1970s. "There were no VCRs in those antediluvian days, but by 1975 James Blish's paperback adaptations were available. In a way, it was those very early Bantam Books *Trek* tie-ins (including Blish's

SECTION 31

Editor Marco Palmieri remembered, "From the moment the concept was introduced in the *Deep Space Nine* episode 'Inquisition,' I knew I wanted to do *Section 31* stories. Here was a secret, autonomous black ops agency, willing to take whatever action was needed for the safety and security of the Federation, and the elimination of all threats to it. The controversy that erupted in fandom over *Section 31* didn't surprise me; in fact, it only fueled my desire. Some fans argue that it goes against the fundamental ideology and the basic philosophical assumptions that *Star Trek* is built upon. Others say it adds texture and greater complexity to the *Star Trek* universe by retroactively introducing the idea of a necessary evil. What I realized is that this very argument is what's so compelling about the concept in terms of storytelling. These were the kinds of questions the familiar heroes of *Star Trek* would wrestle with in the novels, because *Section 31* is an enemy their training *doesn't* prepare them for."

Marco continued, "The reason I wanted to do *Section 31* as four novels was in part to explore the organization's effects upon different crews beyond the DS9 milieu, and in part because I thought too many of our miniseries in those days were multipart stories, where the reader would have to sometimes read four, six, or more volumes in order to get a complete story. By contrast, *Section 31* is four standalone novels. No connecting story, no numbers on the books to denote a reading order, just the unifying theme. The idea was to give the reader the option to read as many or as few of the *Section 31* novels as he or she wanted, in any order. I think readers appreciated that approach; the *Section 31* novels ended up being the top-selling mass-market *Star Trek* titles that year."

On his approach to the unifying cover design, Marco said, "I was really pleased with how the covers turned out. They were simple, elegant, conveyed just the right mood, and were completely unlike anything we'd done up to that point."

Marco recalled, "My boss at that time, associate publisher Scott Shannon, urged me to follow up with more *Section 31* books right away. I resisted the idea for several reasons. I hated the thought of beating a story concept into the ground—I hated it then, and I hate it now. I also think *Section 31*, like the Borg, works best when used *sparingly*, and only when the right story presents itself. Lastly, I wanted to develop other *Star Trek* story concepts. I'm glad the miniseries was popular, but I'd much rather go on to the next cool idea than repeat myself so soon. I think that's one of the key ways to keep the *Star Trek* fiction line fresh and interesting."

1970 original novel *Spock Must Die!*) that made me a confirmed fan."

For Andy, "I watched reruns of the original series on our black-and-white TV. Living in a small Montana town, I could only get them on a snowy UHF channel from the next state over. It wasn't until I was in college that I saw *Star Trek* in color, on laserdisc! I read the Blish books and the various comic book series: a few Gold Key, and most of Marvel and DC's output. I followed the other TV series as they came out. I don't consider myself a hardcore Trekkie, but I'm definitely a fan."

When asked why they wanted to write *Trek* stories, Andy remarked, "It was serendipity, each time. The first time was in the 1980s, when Kimberly Yale was editing *Star Trek* comics at DC. She offered me a fill-in job on the TNG comic, and I plotted a sequel to 'Wolf in the Fold' that would have loosed RedJac on the *Enterprise-D* through a holodeck scenario. It was quite a good horror story that involved mainly Data, Riker, and Geordi, plus Moriarty. But as I began scripting the comic, the TV episode 'Ship in a Bottle' came out, and a major portion of my plot had to be reconfigured. A succession of changing editors meant that my story was never finished; thankfully, I was paid for it. The second time, I was writing articles for editor Tim Tuohy on a Marvel Comics newsmagazine. He offered me a fill-in job on the DS9 comic, and I asked Mike to pitch along with me as a co-writer. While I'm a *Trek* fan, Mike is a walking encyclopedia of *Trek* lore. Our first story got the fastest approval Paramount had ever given, and we were immediately made the regular writers for the series. We worked on a large number of *Trek* comics for Marvel, many of which didn't come out due

to Marvel's cancellation of the line. Interestingly enough, one of the new series we were doing had some very Section 31-like elements, prior to that agency's actual first appearance on DS9. Once Marvel ended their line, Paramount kept sending us to various licensees, where we wrote lots of licensed *Trek* products. Eventually, we landed in the capable hands of super-editor Marco Palmieri, and our novel career had begun (though I had written many non-fiction books prior)."

Mike added, "Because many *Star Trek* characters have always spoken to me (though not in a 'I hear voices in my head' sort of way, so don't worry), writing *Trek* stories always felt natural and right. *Star Trek* always seemed to tower above everything else on the tube, at least back in those early days (of course that's not difficult to do when your alternatives are *Green Acres* and *Gomer Pyle*). So even as a wee bairn I dreamed of participating in the show's creation in some small way."

When asked about the inspiration for *Rogue*, Mike said, "After Andy and I finished our tenure on Marvel's monthly DS9 comic, I discovered that Marco Palmieri was the very same Marco Palmieri I already knew from my previous life in the comics industry. I started an e-mail correspondence with him and set up a meeting between him and Andy at the 1999 San Diego Comicon. That meeting got us an invitation to pitch for the TNG slot in Marco's four-part *Section 31* series. So we batted out story treatments, and our third one seemed to work. Marco supplied the title, which guided the story development process, and over a period of a couple months we turned our pitch into a detailed outline and got it approved."

Andy added, "One of the things Marco has always pushed us (and all of his writers) toward is to think outside the TV box. We don't have a budget to concern ourselves with, so the aliens and the concepts can be much larger than life. But in the process of that, we also wanted to make the human element a core to each story. Allegory has always been a large part of *Star Trek* storytelling, so the political and personal conflicts in *Rogue* carried more weight when they were relatable for readers. Due to our story preferences, Mike tends to take more of the heavy science chapter and the *Trek*-continuity chapters. I prefer to write a lot of the 'character' material, and both political and theological debates. But because the chapters don't break down so simply, we end up writing both elements. And once we do the refining of our material, where we go over each other's work, we really work out any rough patches. Thankfully, our writing styles and 'voices' are very similar."

Mike continued, "Andy and I worked out our prose collaboration process for the first time with this one. That is, we work out the plot details more or less together until the story makes us happy, and satisfies both Marco and the studio. Once everyone has signed off on it, Andy and I decide where to put the chapter breaks and agree which of us is to write which chapters. Then we write, trade our chapters, and make editorial suggestions, and struggle to make all the 'joins' between chapters dovetail (think carpentry). Then we turn it in, wait for revision notes from Marco and Paramount, and make whatever changes they ask for (which usually aren't extensive or difficult)."

One element of the story that caused some controversy was the portrayal of Lieutenant Hawk, who was first seen in the movie *First Contact*, as being involved in a same-sex relationship. Andy remarked, "A basic tenet of *Star Trek* is 'Infinite Diversity in Infinite Combinations,' and I found it frustrating and disappointing—not just as an openly gay writer but also as a lifelong fan—that gays and lesbians had almost no representation in the future world of *Star Trek*. Just as *Trek* has over the decades been a beacon of hope for millions of minority racial, ethnic, and philosophical groups who have had reason to worry about their future, it seemed only fitting that *Trek* fans of varying sexual orientations got to share that optimism of a better and more inclusive world."

It's worth noting that for all the controversy over that aspect of the novel, *Rogue* was not the first work of *Star Trek* fiction to include a gay character, nor the last. Andy concluded, "Like a lot of *Trek* authors, Mike and I infuse our projects with characters of different sexual orientations, biologies, religions, politics, and personal lives, in the true spirit of *Star Trek*."

Rogue was the single bestselling mass-market *Star Trek* title of 2001, going back to press multiple times.

SHADOW
(STAR TREK: VOYAGER)
DEAN WESLEY SMITH & KRISTINE KATHRYN RUSCH

JUNE 2001 (250PP)

Deadly "accidents" seem to be following Seven of Nine. Is someone or something trying to eliminate the babe Borg? Meanwhile, the Starship *Voyager* stumbles upon a giant vessel of refugees attempting to flee their solar system. Two suns are about to collide, and unless the crew can do something quickly, the resulting explosion will destroy the ship of millions of people.

Dean remembered, "Taking Section 31 into *Voyager* was a real challenge. I'm not sure how it came about, but I do remember enjoying working with Marco on it."

Marco explained, "The challenge was in coming up with a plausible Section 31 scenario for *Voyager*, given its distance from the Federation. We hit upon the idea that an agent had been imbedded on the ship specifically for *Voyager*'s mission to the Badands, because of the escalating threat to Federation security posed by the Maquis. The twist was establishing that she was already deceased by the time *Shadow* takes place (the nameless blond officer in 'Scientific Method' who dropped dead on the bridge), but that action she'd taken prior to her demise had just begun wreaking havoc on *Voyager*."

CLOAK
(STAR TREK)
S.D. PERRY

JULY 2001 (211PP)

The *Enterprise* answers the distress call of the *U.S.S. Sphinx*, and discovers everyone on board dead. Higher up in the Starfleet chain was Captain Casden, a pacifist who planned on passing vital information to the Romulans. Told to not investigate it any further, Captain Kirk's warning lights go off in his head. A group of scientists are about to unravel a seemingly impossible concept that could potentially become the ultimate weapon for Federation superiority. Can the crew stop these mad scientists before the unthinkable happens?

Danelle commented, "Marco was talking to me about one of his pet projects and I pretty much begged for the original series. I was lucky again."

ABYSS
(STAR TREK: DEEP SPACE NINE)
DAVID WEDDLE AND JEFFREY LANG

JULY 2001 (292 PP)

One of the core titles in the post-TV DS9 fiction. Planning a vacation with Ezri, Bashir is approached by an operative from Section 31. Cole wants him to stop another operative who was also genetically enhanced. Dr. Ethan Locken envisions a new empire modeled after Khan, and fiddles with Jem'Hadar soldiers to achieve his goals. Bashir assumes the mission is straightforward, but appearances are deceiving.

• • •

The plot for *Abyss* was originally developed by David and Marco, shortly after the *Deep Space Nine* television series had ended. Marco recalled, "One of the great things about David's involvement in the project was that *Abyss* was the story that followed up on *Avatar*. It was extraordinarily cool to have one of DS9's TV writers developing a story for the post-TV fiction, with its mix of old and new characters."

David was to have written the book himself, but had to bow out when he got a new TV-writing gig. Marco then turned to Jeff and offered the project to him. Jeff remarked, "My contributions to the story were plot details and the character bits. In particular, I'm pleased with the characterization of Taran'atar. He was pretty much a tabula rasa when I got him and it was fun to try to figure out what made him tick. Also, I tried to make Locken the Pseudo-Khan less of a 'Bwah-ha-ha' villain and more of a tortured soul. The writing and publishing process was pretty straightforward: Marco said, 'Here's the outline; can you have the book back to me on Thursday?' Okay, maybe not that short, but we were working on a tight deadline. Since then, I've learned that we're always working on a tight deadline. An interesting side note is that *Abyss* was not the first book I was contracted to write. My first contract was for *Immortal Coil*, but since the book didn't have a firm publication date when I started it and since *Abyss* had to come out when it came out, Marco asked me to set *Immortal Coil* aside and write *Abyss*, which, in the end I think made *Immortal Coil* a better book.

"Beyond that, *Abyss* was a pretty straightforward assignment. I wrote it, then rewrote it, then handed it over to Marco, who, as I recall, did a minimal amount of editing. One of the few changes we made was to add the little scene at the end where it turned out that the aliens were transported off their planet with the holoship from *Star Trek: Insurrection*. This was one of the many examples that can be found in the Marco-edited books that we authors collectively call 'Marco-isms.' They usually start with Marco calling and saying, 'Hey, you know what would be neat?' When you get one of those calls, you get your pen and take notes because, inevitably, he's right: It's something neat."

GATEWAYS

BOOK ONE

ONE SMALL STEP
(STAR TREK)
Susan Wright

AUGUST 2001   (237pp)

I mmediately after the events chronicled in the original series episode, "That Which Survives," Kirk and his crew investigate the remains of the Kalandan station. When a ship arrives with the beings aboard claiming to be the lost Kalandans, they demand

their outpost back. To make matters more disconcerting, the gateway that hurled the *Enterprise* almost one thousand light years away has been reactivated. Can the "Kalandans" be trusted?

Susan was thrilled to be writing the first book in a series, plus an original series book. She said, "Bob Greenberger came up with this story for *Gateways*, the cross-over series of books he was editing. I had always wanted to do a *TOS* book, but hadn't found the right story. This book had to take place right after *TOS: That Which Survives* and use elements from that episode. It was constraining, but I liked the challenge. I also got to develop the Petraw aliens for the other books in the cross-over series."

BOOK TWO

CHAINMAIL
(STAR TREK: CHALLENGER)
Diane Carey

AUGUST 2001   (334pp)

T he crew of the *Challenger* encounters a bizarre planet made entirely of metal. As a result

GATEWAYS

When asked why the *Gateways* books were published in paperback and the final book published in hardcover, John Ordover remarked, "To make money. Basically, the deal we worked out with the authors was that we'd publish the paperbacks and they'd essentially save the conclusion of everything that happened after our characters went through the gateway. The rest of that book would go into the hardcover for all the authors. And that would make up the hardcover and we wouldn't pay the authors extra for the hardcover. But in return the royalties for the hardcover were split among the authors and would not be held against their advance. So basically they get royalties from the sale of the first book, split between them, and we get an extra hardcover and it worked out well for everybody. And some of the fans found it very annoying and cheesy marketing and I am the first to admit I may have gone too far. But they keep saying more, more, more, and you try to give it to them."

John remembered, "*Gateways* actually came more from the *Hitchhikers Guide to the Galaxy*'s concept of the Babel Fish than the second-season TNG episode. The Babel Fish is something you stick in your ears that instantly allows you to understand all intergalactic languages. Well, the line in the radio drama, which I think is the pure form of *Hitchhikers*, says, 'And the Babel Fish, by effectively removing all barriers to interstellar communication, was responsible for more and bloodier wars than anything else in history.' So what I wanted to do was remove all barriers to interstellar communication and travel. The general idea was what if old enemies suddenly found themselves in effect de-facto next to each other? In other words, what if you took the Israelies and moved them to Australia and the Palestinians and moved them to Siberia. That would be one way to solve the problem. But then what if the Gate suddenly opened that let you walk from Siberia to Australia? What would the old enemies be then?"

of the events on the surface, Bonifay defies a direct order from Shucorion to save his life. While Shucorion appears grateful, Kauld law stipulates that disobeying a direct order is punishable by death. In addition, descendants of an expedition near Belle Terre return with knowledge of a Gateway.

Diane said, "The continuation of Nick Keller's adventures as the wild west/deep space law enforcement sheriff. This was a true science fiction story, with completely new science. I got the inspiration while watching a TV commercial in which a car was driving across a liquid metal backdrop (or something). It's an excellent example of teamwork between my husband Greg Brodeur, the plot machine, and I. I challenged him: 'What if there was a planet where everything was made of metal?' He said what he always says, 'Impossible.' I said, 'So come up with it anyway.' That's when the creative juices start boiling and we get supreme sci-fi by making the impossible somehow survivable."

Looking back at the creation of the characters, Diane said, "Nick Keller is named after my grandfather, Nicodemus Jacob, and my childhood heroine, Helen Keller. If I were casting the role of Shucorion, it would be Adrian Paul, and John Stamos would've been the gypsy boson Zane Bonifay—just one of those little inspirations that help a writer get a grip on a character."

BOOK THREE

DOORS INTO CHAOS
(STAR TREK: THE NEXT GENERATION)
ROBERT GREENBERGER

SEPTEMBER 2001   (300PP)

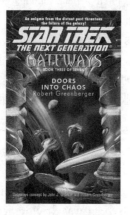

Aliens claiming to be the ancient Iconians arrive in the Alpha Quadrant and offer their gateways to the highest bidder. An emergency meeting splits the *Enterprise* crew so they can contact various races in the quadrant and join a force to confront the Iconians on a level playing field. Can Picard hold a thinly disjointed alliance together long enough to uncover the truth behind the aliens and the activated gateways?

Robert reflected, "John had grown fond of stealing comic book marketing gimmicks to help juice the *Star Trek* novel sales. One of those ideas was the crossover. Starting with *Invasion!*, he was doing annual events. One year he was casting about for new ideas and I pitched him three or four. He didn't love those but in the course of an online conversation, we brainstormed what became *Gateways*. As I understand it, John thought a good idea would be to have six books end with cliffhangers, all of which would be resolved in a seventh ... which would be a hardcover. In retrospect, this was not a good idea and people have come to resent the series because of the caper costing twenty-four dollars after investing in six five dollars and ninety-nine cents books. Since I got co-creator credit, I also got a book and he decided I'd do TNG since it would be the lynchpin to the event. Given the outline we created, there were certain things I needed to complete but the actual story for my book was inspired by *The Magnificent Seven* as Picard had sought out allies from around space. I had a tremendous amount of fun with the *Marco Polo* scenes since it showed Troi in command, something we hadn't really seen before. The lengthy conclusion in *What Lay Beyond* was again dictated by the outline. The fun there was showing Picard things that weren't what they seemed and then the finale when I cut to fifteen different locations letting a variety of characters from other *Trek* book series cameo."

BOOK FOUR

DEMONS OF AIR AND DARKNESS
(STAR TREK: DEEP SPACE NINE)
Keith R.A. DeCandido

SEPTEMBER 2001   (292PP)

One of the core titles in the post-TV DS9 fiction. Why are there no activated gateways near the Bajoran Wormhole? In the Delta Quadrant, the Malon dispose a huge amount of toxic waste into a newly activated gateway, which opens on a populated world in the Alpha Quadrant. Kira leads the rescue effort and tries to stop the threat at the source. Meanwhile, Nog looks for a way to shut the portals down and Quark negotiates with the Iconians for the right to possess the amazing technology.

Keith remembered, "John Ordover had used me as a continuity editor for several of the miniseries, *New Earth*, *Double Helix*, and *Gateways*, so I was already going to be involved in them, just to make sure that all the books were consistent with each other. I have a ridiculous capacity for useless trivia, particularly as it re-

lates to the ST universe and because I am good at juggling several things happening at once, so I was perfect for the role. Marco thought I would be a good choice for *Demons* because we'd already been talking about his direction for the new DS9 novels, and because I was already plugged into the mini-series. This also meant I got to write 'Horn and Ivory,' which was the follow up to the way *Gateways* worked with each book ending in a cliffhangar that was resolved in the final book, *What Lay Beyond*. And that was a huge treat, much more than I realized it would be when it started out, because if Worf was my favorite character, Kira is my second favorite character. But sometimes they switched places. 'Horn and Ivory' was great fun to write because it was such an important story for Kira and I was thrilled by the great response to it. After that thing, once you start the snowball going down the hill it just turns into one really big, really fast snowball and that's pretty much what happened to me."

Marco said, "My involvement with *Gateways* was limited to the DS9 portions. The post-TV novels were just getting underway. John wanted *Gateways* to span the entire *Star Trek* mythos as it existed at that time, so I faced a choice: relinquish control of the tightly-plotted DS9 serial for the duration of *Gateways*, or step up and make the most of the storytelling opportunities the miniseries presented. I ended up opting for the latter. And while I wish *Gateways* had been handled differently, *Demons of Air and Darkness* and 'Horn and Ivory' both served the continuing DS9 narrative superbly, advancing the storyline and the character arcs, setting up new plot threads, and introducing new supporting characters."

NO MAN'S LAND
(STAR TREK: VOYAGER)
Christie Golden

OCTOBER 2001   (232PP)

As the crew of *Voyager* prepares to enter a hostile region of space, the mysterious gateways appear and alien vessels from all over the galaxy arrive. Janeway uses her head and creates an armada to not only solve the mystery of how the gates operate, but to have tremendous firepower for the trip into "No Man's Land." Of course, murder and treachery, along with a cute dog, all add to the adventure.

Christie remembered, "This was a real challenge—I had to make sure my store jived with the basic theme. I enjoyed creating my scaredy-cat little teddy bear aliens, though. The inspiration for them is a real live creature called the Tennessee Fainting Goat. It's been bred so that it has an extreme reaction to fear—it collapses. It's put in with a herd of other animals, such as sheep, so that if predators appear, they go right for the poor fainting goat and leave the sheep alone. I thought my poor little adventurers were very brave to do what they did!"

BOOK SIX

COLD WARS
(STAR TREK: NEW FRONTIER)
Peter David

OCTOBER 2001   (364PP)

In the region of space formerly the Thallonian Empire, Captain Calhoun operates the *Excalibur* and Shelby commands the *Trident*. Almost a century ago, the Thallonians separated two feuding factions by moving them to different planets. Lacking space travel, the two alien races still fumed at each other over the long distances. Now with the discovery of the Iconian Gateways, the aliens have an opportunity to attack each other and start the war again. The crew of both ships must find the gateways and deactivate them before the two races annihilate each other. Two major new characters are introduced into the *New Fron-*

tier universe. Both M'Ress and Arex served under Captain Kirk when he was more animated than his usual self, and now are literally out of time.

Peter commented, "It was different to do because the impetus came from outside of my own stuff. It was essentially the same as doing a comic book crossover. I have as much fun with it as I can but it's not going to be as near and dear to my heart as some of the others. John Ordover suggested I bring in the animated characters and I loved it. I worked with them when I worked on the *Trek* comics so the chance to bring them back was exciting to me."

BOOK SEVEN
WHAT LAY BEYOND
VARIOUS

NOVEMBER 2001   (373PP)

ORIGINALLY PUBLISHED IN HARDCOVER

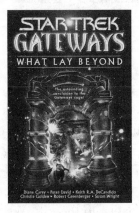

T he conclusion to each of the preceding six novels. Includes "One Giant Leap" by Susan Wright; "Exodus" by Diane Carey; "Horn and

Ivory" by Keith DeCandido; "In the Queue" by Christie Golden; "Death After Life" by Peter David; and the conclusion of the series, "The Other Side" by Robert Greenberger.

HERE THERE BE MONSTERS
(GATEWAYS EPILOGUE; S.C.E. #10; SEE SECTION 11: ORIGINAL STAR TREK CONCEPTS)

BOOK ONE
THE BADLANDS
(STAR TREK and STAR TREK: THE NEXT GENERATION)
SUSAN WRIGHT

DECEMBER 1999   (271PP)

T he region of space responsible for the hurling of *Voyager* into the Delta Quadrant receives recognition across all four television series. In the first book, Captain Kirk confronts the Romulans and an unexpected illness among the crew. Picard faces the same perilous region

years later when Riker and Data are held captive by the Cardassians.

THE BADLANDS
(STAR TREK: DEEP SPACE NINE and STAR TREK: VOYAGER)
SUSAN WRIGHT

DECEMBER 1999   (256PP)

The second book covers *Voyager*'s journey prior to its encounter with the Caretaker. The last part concludes the storyline with Benjamin Sisko and the gang finally solving the dilemma.

Susan reflected on writing two books that incorporated all four *Trek* incarnations. She said, "I was able to pick certain points in each series when tensions were high, yet each section is united by the common thread of a dangerous phenomenon the crews discover in the Badlands. They build on each other's work, until the DS9 *Defiant* crew solves the problem. My favorite section was the *Voyager* one because I was able to show the crews of both the Starfleet and Maquis ships in the Alpha Quadrant, going about their usual business just prior to being sucked away to the Delta Quadrant."

DARK PASSIONS
SUSAN WRIGHT

JANUARY 2001   (232PP)
JANUARY 2001   (200PP)

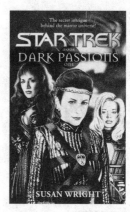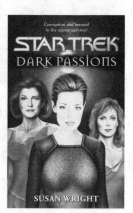

Before Kira and Bashir stumbled upon the mirror universe, there was plenty of intrigue going on. Agent Annika Hansen of the Obsidian Order has been ordered to eliminate the new Overseer of the Alliance, Kira. Even assassins don't appear immune to her considerable wiles, however. Familiar characters play evil and manipulative to the hilt. When Kira obtains an Iconian transportal device, no one is safe from her wrath.

Susan said, "I'm fascinated with parallel universes. 'Mirror, Mirror' was my favorite TOS episode, and I enjoyed the DS9 mirror universe episodes. So when my editor at Pocket Books, John Ordover, said he wanted me to write a 'bad girls' of *Trek*, I was up for it. I created the story for one book, and afterwards it was expanded to two books. I made Seven of Nine and Intendent Kira the two main characters, and put them in a relationship. I thought it was great that Paramount allowed the interaction. I loved writing characters that were familiar yet fundamentally different. For example, Seven was trained to be a Cardassian assassin since there is no Borg in the mirror universe."

boxes of Malkus. With four deadly machines scattered around the galaxy, Archer creates a General Order for ships in the future to be warned if a box is discovered. Captain Kirk, along with Commodore Decker, help the colony of Alpha Proxima II battle a deadly plague. The plague is a result of a Malkus device. Can they stop the plague and recover the box? Commander Ben Sisko, along with Captain Declan Keogh of the *Odyssey*, are helping Bajoran farmers relocate. One of the farmers is a former Bajoran terrorist, and when he discovers a device, there will be hell to pay!

BOOK ONE

THE BRAVE AND THE BOLD
(STAR TREK: ENTERPRISE; STAR TREK; and STAR TREK: DEEP SPACE NINE)
KEITH R.A. DeCANDIDO

DECEMBER 2002   (266PP)

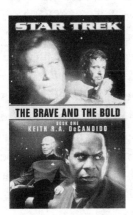

 n epic story that spans the five *Trek* series. Captain Archer and his crew discover the

BOOK TWO

THE BRAVE AND THE BOLD
(STAR TREK: VOYAGER and STAR TREK: THE NEXT GENERATION)
KEITH R.A. DeCANDIDO

DECEMBER 2002   (300PP)

 ieutenant Tuvok infiltrates the Maquis and has his hands full when the third artifact shows up. Will the rebels use this new weapon against the Cardassians and possibly the Federation? When the final artifact is found, several people who have dealt with the other devices mysteriously disappear. Can Picard and Captain Klag prevail against impossible odds and mind-controlled foes that are also their friends?

"Originally I was going to pitch it as one big six-book crossover event. John Ordover looked at it and said this would work better if you pared it down a little. So we wound up having it be a two-book series in the same format as Susan Wright's *Badlands*, which came out in 1998. We just cut it down to four team ups instead of the six I'd come up with. The story was much better for it in that way and I got to write two books instead of one book out of six. And then he also let me use the *I.K.S. Gorkon* crew I'd created for *Diplomatic Implausibility*. In the back of my head I thought it would be cool to do an ongoing series on a Klingon ship, but I didn't think it would actually happen. But I liked the opportunity to actually create the crew and use the characters I did in *Diplomatic Implausibility*. This did lead to the *Gorkon* series."

THE LOST ERA

2298

THE SUNDERED

MICHAEL A. MARTIN AND ANDY MANGELS

AUGUST 2003   (387PP)

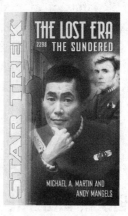

The first book of a series of six set in the timeframe between the *Star Trek Generations* prologue and the start of the *Next Generation* television series. Five years after Captain Kirk's supposed death on the *Enterprise*-B, Captain Sulu and the crew of the *Excelsior* are negotiating for peace with the Tholians. As a result of the negotiations, the ship finds itself uninvited in Tholian space, fighting an enemy called the Neyel. This new adversary has unknown ties to Earth, which will have deadly ramifications for peace. Readers will recognize most of Sulu's crew.

Mike remarked, "The central idea of *The Sundered*—that there's an alien race out there that is to humans what Romulans are to Vulcans—came out of a phone conversation between Marco and me. Andy and I ran with it, and all sorts of continuity Easter eggs just presented themselves. This book was also written very quickly, which, again, I hope doesn't show. The book was also greatly influenced by the works of Robert A. Heinlein, which are among my early favorites."

Andy said, "Marco had asked us again to come up with some really 'out there' science fiction concepts, so between the true nature of the Tholians and the history of the Neyel, we hope we accomplished that. I was pleased that we actually got to create and write some very strange history and world building for the two races. Mike handled much of the Neyel material, and I got to do a lot of the hive-minded Tholian material. I was also pleased with what we got to do with Ambassador Burgess. She was such an unlikable character, and yet at her heart, you couldn't really argue with her motives. Writing her backstory was very touching, and the coda ending brought many sniffles."

Mike remembered, "It was very satisfying providing the Tholians with a little worldbuilding, and it was great fun presenting Sulu and his latter-day crew, particularly the longtime friendship between Sulu and Chekov. I also enjoyed drawing the contrast between Akaar (a warrior from Capella) and Lojur (a pacifistic Halkan patterned after Sgt. York)."

Andy concluded, "Funny story about Captain Sulu. We were still unsigned for the writing job, and we thought we might give an extra nudge to Marco. We happened to interview George Takei live at a convention, for the British *Star Trek* magazine. We knew that he really wanted more Captain Sulu adventures.

So we had a pitch for him to read into the tape recorder that said something like 'Marco, I think you should hire these two to write more adventures for me, Captain Sulu.' George read it aloud once, and then decided he didn't want to commit to that without reading our plot. I had the tape recorder on, so actually got him reading the part the first time, but we never played it for Marco. We relied on the strength of our pitch to win the day!"

Upon learning about this anecdote, Marco's only response was a baritone "Oh, my."

2311

SERPENTS AMONG THE RUINS
David R. George III

September 2003 (371pp)

Captain Harriman of the *Enterprise*-B, played by Alan Ruck in *Star Trek Generations*, has a backbone after all. During a test of a prototype starship with hyperwarp drive, the ship explodes. A peace conference between the

THE LOST ERA

Editor Marco Palmieri explained, "Like the *Section 31* miniseries two years earlier, *The Lost Era* was designed to give readers options. Although it was conceived as spanning a specific block of time, published in chronological order, with each book dated accordingly on the covers, they were still stand-alone novels. The connections among them were all thematic, not narrative. So again, one could read as many or as few as desired, in any order. Taken collectively, however, the idea was to convey a sense of moving through this largely undeveloped period of *Star Trek* history.

"The era is framed by two key historical moments: Kirk's presumed death aboard the *Enterprise*-B in *Star Trek Generation* (the latest filmed moment of the twenty-third century) and the beginning of TNG's 'Encounter at Farpoint' (the first filmed moment of the twenty-fourth century). In between those moments were seventy years of unchronicled *Star Trek* time. We knew some things that fell within the period—the Tomed Incident and the destruction of the *Enterprise*-C, to name a couple—but most of that time was blank slate. It was the time of the latter day careers of many original series characters, and the early careers of the twenty-fourth century characters. The storytelling possibilities were immense. I thought the time was right for us to explore them.

"If I have any regrets about *The Lost Era*, it's that there was less thematic variety among the stories than I was hoping for. In putting together notes about the period to help the authors get started, I realized that most of the things that had been established about those years were military in nature—wars, battles, etc. We knew far less about discoveries, first contacts, scientific breakthroughs, etc. I'd already committed to doing two stories that were specifically military in nature, the Tomed Incident and the Betreka Nebula Incident. But I'm a guy who likes variety, so when I sent out my notes to the authors, I told them, 'Okay, looking at the timeline of established events, its easy to get the impression that there was nothing but conflict going on, so I'm hoping to see proposals that show more than that.' Wouldn't you know it—every proposal had some element of political discord, military conflict, covert ops, etc. In retrospect, it's arguable that I should have been more of a hardass and insisted on some thematic changes in some of the stories, but in the end I decided to stick with the direction the authors clearly wanted to go in. That said, I still feel it's a strong set of novels with some really outstanding storytelling."

Klingons, Romulans, and Federation proves to be at risk when the explosion appears to be the Federation testing a superweapon. To solve the crisis, Captain Harriman decides on a bold move. This solution will live in infamy as the Tomed Incident.

David remarked, "While I was finishing up *Twilight*, editor Marco Palmieri came to me and offered me the *Lost Era* novel that would detail the Tomed Incident, an event mentioned once in *Trek* (in the first-season *Next Generation* episode 'The Neutral Zone'). We talked briefly about it, I accepted, and then at the eleventh hour, seeded a scene from it into *Twilight* (at Marco's suggestion). I tried to write something relatively generic, so that I wouldn't hamstring myself when I actually got to plot out *Serpents*, but I ended up including some details that would later make my life difficult. *Serpents* was an interesting writing experience for me, in no small part because I had more freedom with it than on my previous *Trek* projects. This was because the book was set in a little-explored era of the *Trek* universe, and because it would only include three characters that we'd seen on screen: John Harriman, Demora Sulu, and Azetbur. The only thing editor Marco Palmieri wanted me to do was to reveal what exactly the Tomed Incident was. All we knew about it from televised *Trek* was that it resulted in the deaths of thousands of Federation citizens, and caused the Romulans to retreat into isolation. Well, I think the general fan thought that a war or battle had taken place, causing the Federation deaths and the Romulan retreat. That seemed too easy. I wanted to turn the thing on its ear, give readers the unexpected. To that end, I devised a complicated

and Machiavellian plot that had a lot of gray in it, as opposed to the frequent black and white we see in the show (the Federation is good, the Romulans are bad). In the novel, Harriman enacts a bold plan to avert a war, but along the way, takes some actions that might easily be considered immoral. In the end, he saves billions of lives, but did that justify his actions? I wanted to leave that up to the readers to decide, and some (according to reviews on Amazon) decided that I was despicable for having developed such a plot. I'm sorry that some readers feel that way, as I intended the story as a means of raising what I thought were interesting and even important questions, given the United States current 'war on terror.' Another interesting aspect of *Serpents* for me was the character of Captain John Harriman. He was introduced in the film *Generations* as something less than the cool, capable captain we saw in Kirk. The question I felt I therefore had to answer was how such a man could have risen to a starship captaincy. Did he deserve it? Would he become a good captain? In preparing to write *Serpents*, I read the only other works in which Harriman had appeared, Peter David's novel *The Captain's Daughter*, and his short story 'Shakedown.' Although not strictly required to do so, I wanted to remain consistent with those works. In *The Captain's Daughter*, Peter David introduced Captain Harriman's father, a difficult man who was also an admiral in Starfleet. That gave me some of the ammunition I needed to explain Harriman the younger. A career officer, the elder Harriman had pushed his son through the ranks of Starfleet, perhaps getting him into a captaincy before he was quite ready. I then had to make Captain Harriman into his own man, growing out of that and becoming completely worthy of the position to which he'd been assigned. And in the end, I wanted to take him to a place we had never before seen a Starfleet captain. As for the publishing part of it, Marco Palmieri did his consistently fine work as editor, and the book actually ended up on the *New York Times* bestseller list."

2328-2346

THE ART OF THE IMPOSSIBLE
KEITH R.A. DeCANDIDO

OCTOBER 2003   (356PP)

Star *Trek* as a political thriller? The discovery of a Klingon battlecruiser wreckage on a planet becomes an interstellar cold war between the Klingons and the Cardassians. Curzon Dax negotiates a controversial peace plan and for a period of time it seems that peace will prevail. Behind the scenes, spies on all sides are manipulating events to gain the upper hand. Beginning thirty-five years after Kirk's "death" aboard *Enterprise-B*, the eighteen-year span of the story showcases the powerful events that could have redrawn the political map of the galaxy.

Keith commented, "A thirty-second conversation between Bashir and Garak in (the *Deep Space Nine* episode) *The Way of the Warrior* established 'the Betreka Nebula Incident.' All we know is that it was between the Klingon Empire and the Cardassian Union, it was 'ages ago,' and, peculiarly for an incident, it lasted eighteen years. Marco Palmieri was putting together *The Lost Era*, and we talked about doing Betreka. I realized that the time between when Bajor was annexed and the Khitomer Massacre was eighteen years, and we were off to the races. It's my most ambitious novel to date, and one I'm still very proud of."

2336

WELL OF SOULS

ILSA J. BICK

NOVEMBER 2003   (468PP)

Rachel Garrett, Captain of the *Enterprise-C*, as never revealed before. Ruins of an ancient Cardassian civilization attract nefarious types to uncover its secrets. With her family in danger, Garrett must work some magic to save everyone. Speaking of secrets, the new first officer has a whopper. Could he have ties to the Orion Syndicate?

Ilsa got her start in the *Trek* universe by writing stories that won the Grand Prize in SNW II and Second Prize in SNW IV. Ilsa became a fan of the original series when she saw *TOS* on reruns. She said, "I was too young to catch it first time around (though I remember seeing the earliest episodes on a black-and-white television and being totally wowed when I saw my first episode—'Arena'—in color). The first glimpse I even had of the show was at my piano teacher's house; her kids were upstairs watch-

ing it while I was banging away in the basement. The piano got jettisoned; my interest in *Star Trek* remained. I'd already been reading science fiction, and I remember not wanting to miss an episode of *Lost in Space*. My parents didn't allow me to stay up long enough to catch that particular show, and so I used to sneak into their bedroom where the television was and turn down the sound so I was standing there, with my ear glued to the speaker. Needless to say, this wasn't the greatest viewing experience. But space travel was very cool. Bottom line: I was pubescent and Captain Kirk was hot."

Ilsa's mind turned to writing when she was young. Ilsa said, "One of the very dreary things I did as a kid was cut the grass: mow the lawn and then clip around every damn fence post and tree. Every . . . damn . . . one. Every week. On a half acre of land. That's a lot of fence. Lot of trees. So I used to daydream: make up stories in my head about adventures with the crew (I always had a prominent role and usually saved the day). Basic early adolescent, geekoid stuff. I remember that I read a couple of novels when I got older. But I was reading a whole bunch more 'mainstream' Science Fiction, too. And I thought: I can do that. So, eventually, I did— but only a really long, long, long time after. I wrote reams of heartfelt poetry when I was a late adolescent. I double-majored in English and biology in college and wrote a lot of thoughtful critiques of 'real' literature, but I did manage to sneak in a whole winter semester of reading nothing but science fiction. Got approval to read x-number of books and write a great big paper. I read a lot of books—easily fifty or so in four weeks. I wrote a great big paper, and I think I got a good grade. After college, though, I was pretty busy in medical school and residency and then a fellowship. Started out in surgery, ended up in child psychiatry: another long and tortuous story. Along the way, though, I got bored and went to Wesleyan University at night and got my masters in film and literature. Then I started writing a bunch of psychoanalytically based critiques of science fiction literature and film. Went to a bunch of meetings, presented gobs of papers, published quite a bit. Did three years of analytic training then decided that if I was publishing stuff, I didn't really want to waste time with a non-viable treatment, however mentally challenging. Gave the opening lecture at the 1991 Smithsonian exhibition on *Star Trek*; met William Shatner and the rest, except for Nimoy who wasn't there. Published that particular paper in a couple different places, and I just heard from an old academic film buddy that it's still being taught in film classes. But it was around about 1994 or so that my husband told me to stop writing analytic papers and start writing-writing. I dithered for a little bit; continued writing my analytic-academic stuff and then started writing stories. Just a couple. Sent them out, got rejections. And then I bit the bullet and wrote a *Trek* book. Wrote three *Trek* novels, in fact, all mercifully unpublished. But I had a blast writing them."

This novel went through a couple of permutations. She said, "I pitched about three ideas to Marco, and he liked the first and third and told me to combine them, make up the crew, etc. So I did. Then we went back and forth about two, three times, tweaking the outline, Marco guiding me every step of the way and being just an all-around pleasure to work with and learn from. I mean, he's the editor; he's been doing this a long time; and I'm a newbie,

so I was pretty much of a mind to do what Marco thought might work. As it happened, he pretty much approved everything, though he was incredibly helpful about names. I'm horrible at picking names; things with apostrophes and such, they turn me into a blithering idiot. I mean, my most original name is something like Bob. Frank. I'm fond of John and Jack. You know, name-names. Marco helped the most when he pointed out that there's got to be a second act—no straight lines necessarily—something I knew about from short stories but hadn't really considered in terms of the longer form. Anyway, I made it a point to be early with everything: proposal, outline, and finished product. Got approval from Paula Block on October 16th while I was away and so started writing the next week. Dean Smith, who I met from *Strange New Worlds*, was, again, absolutely wonderful in terms of helping me work up a schedule: so many pages a day, so many days a week. Doing it that way, I was able to churn out much more once I got going, and finished the book on January 11th."

Ilsa continued with the story. She said, "I sent it to Marco. Waited a couple of months to hear back (Marco's always swamped). When he did come back, he was very positive; thanked me for sticking to the outline (which was humongous: fifty-single-spaced pages; something like thirty-five thousand words right there. I think the only thing I didn't put down was when someone went to the john). But the book was too long, and he'd handed it to Keith DeCandido to go through. Keith got to me within two weeks. Liked what he'd read and had some suggestions. He'd gone through the thing with a fine-toothed comb, and with his help and Marco's, I trimmed about one hundred pages in about two, three weeks, I guess. Keith liked it; I liked it; Marco liked it. Production folks had a cow, still worrying that it was too long. Marco saved the day, though; I think he really believed the story had to be told the way it was. So he did a thing where he ran the chapters together; instead of starting a chapter on a new page, you'll see that each chapter follows the end of the last. You'd be amazed how many pages you save that way (another great thing I learned through this experience). After that, it was just doing the galleys (very cool), having headaches about what editing convention the copy editor was using when it came to colons, and then it was gone. The first time I saw it as a book was when I visited Marco in New York that September. Very cool."

Summing up the experience of her first novel, she said, "I said it in my acknowledgements, and I'll say it again here: I couldn't have done this without Marco, who I absolutely adore and is just the best editor for someone like me; he's very attentive to detail, and I tend to be a nitpicker when all is said and done though I start out hazy: like a Boeing 747 in the clouds. I know where the runway is, just not how I'm going to get there. I couldn't have accomplished it without Keith doing a superb job of going through this and making very constructive and supportive suggestions. And I couldn't have done it without Dean Wesley Smith who supported me through this and stuff afterward and has been the finest colleague, critic, and mentor I could possibly wish for."

2 3 5 5 - 2 3 5 7

DENY THY FATHER

JEFF MARIOTTE

DECEMBER 2003   (351 PP)

William Riker attends Starfleet Academy. Estranged from his father, Kyle, Will tends to keep to himself, concentrating solely on achieving the best grades he can. Kyle was the sole survivor of a Tholian attack on a starbase. Now someone wants him dead and it appears that his death is only the tip of the iceberg in a larger Starfleet conspiracy. The chapters alternate between the two Rikers.

Jeff became a fan when he saw *Star Trek* for the first time. Prior to that, his exposure to science fiction had been limited to books like Robert Heinlein and Andre Norton juvies, and kids' stuff like Tom Corbett. He said, "*Star Trek* was something different—something that was obviously geared toward adults, who previously I had thought couldn't possibly be interested in such stuff. I was still a kid myself, but I was drawn to the adventures of the *Enterprise* crew then, never knowing it would become such a long-lived part of pop culture."

Jeff had never read much of the *Star Trek* fiction, though he knew a lot of the authors through his parallel careers as a science fiction bookseller (with Books, Inc., Hunter's Books, and finally Mysterious Galaxy, the store of which he continues to be one of the three owners), author, and comic book editor. Jeff said, "when WildStorm Productions, the comic book company for which I worked, got the *Star Trek* license, I was made the editor of the line because I did know so many Science Fiction and *Trek* authors. I pulled a bunch of the *Trek* writers over from prose to comics, and added other Science Fiction luminaries who loved *Trek* but had never written it, and/or never written comics. We ended up publishing work by David Brin, Janine Ellen Young, K. W. Jeter, Kevin J. Anderson and Rebecca Moesta, Keith R. A. DeCandido, Andy Mangels, John Ordover and David Mack, and many, many others. I still think it was one of the best runs of *Trek* comics out there. While working on that line, though, I became friendly with Marco and John over at Pocket's *Trek* office. I had already known Marco from other projects—our careers have kind of overlapped for a long time now. And Keith I've known for years, since he edited my first novel, *Gen13: Netherwar*, written with Christopher Golden."

Reflecting on writing *Deny Thy Father*, Jeff said, "I was approached by the *Trek* office. Marco was putting together the lineup for the *Lost Era* project. Once again, the idea of writing a story that filled in some of the history we've seen so little of seemed like a lot of fun. I've always been intrigued by the relationship between Will and Kyle Riker, which was only explored in one episode, so decided to center on that, to see why two men who hadn't spoken in fifteen years could turn out to be so similar. It's a story about the Rikers, but also about fathers and sons. Having lost my father shortly before, I guess it was also working out some issues of my own."

Regarding the title, Marco noted, "Originally, I had hoped the book would be entitled *Daedalus*, a title I thought was befitting of a prequel to 'The Icarus Factor,' the episode in which Kyle and Will's bad blood was revealed. That lasted about five minutes, when I learned that Dave Stern, now an author writing for editor Margaret Clark, was using *Daedalus* as the title of his new *Enterprise* novel. Thwarted of poetic ambitions in ancient Greece, we turned next to Shakespeare, took inspiration from *Romeo and Juliet*, and decided to call the book *Deny Thy Father*, which I think works well for the story."

2 3 6 0

CATALYST OF SORROWS

MARGARET WANDER BONANNO

J A N U A R Y 2 0 0 4   (3 3 4 P P)

Admiral Uhura is the head of Starfleet Intelligence and one day Zetha walks into her office. She has vital information that has the potential to destroy life across two quadrants. A virulent plague showcasing different symptoms in different species threatens all living beings. Uhura orders Lieutenant Benjamin Sisko, Lieutenant Tuvok, and Dr. Selar to accompany Zetha across the Neutral Zone to determine the source of the virus and find an antidote.

When asked about using Uhura as the primary character, Margaret said, "I chose Uhura as my focal point because I'd worked with Nichelle Nichols on *Saturn's Child*, and wanted to show aspects of Uhura's character we never got to see onscreen."

Margaret enjoyed being back in the *Trek* universe after a ten-year absence. Thinking she was blacklisted from ever writing a *Trek* novel again after events surrounding *Probe*, she was urged by fans to contact Marco Palmieri, one of the *Star Trek* editors who had signed on during the years after *Probe* was published.

Marco remarked, "I remember thinking 'Blacklist? We have a blacklist? And nobody told me?' I thought the idea was absurd, but just to be absolutely sure about it, I asked around. People around the office kept laughing at the idea. I asked Paula at Paramount. She laughed, too. I asked these same people if there was any reason I couldn't hire Margaret, and was told, 'No, hire whomever you want.' Obviously there were people on all sides of the *Probe* issue that felt burned in some way, but none of them were on staff at Pocket or at the studio anymore, so I told Margaret she was welcome to pitch for *The Lost Era*, which I'd started developing around that time."

A TIME TO . . .

John Ordover commented, "One of the major complaints the fans had about *Nemesis* was how did we get there from here? So, let's do a series about that. I originally envisioned it as a twelve-book series, cut back to nine because we also felt that it was stretching it to be twelve books. Also we'd been a little starved for *Next Generation* for a while and one of the approaches I attempted, that worked to some extent, and didn't to another extent is essentially and intentionally to starve the fans from a particular series for a while and then blast out. Riker and Deanna are getting married. We never saw the proposal; we never saw what made them decide. Riker's finally taking his own captaincy and Wesley is back. My reaction to *Nemesis* was, it's like somebody looked at it and decided to roll everything back to the fifth season without any explanation."

John continued, "I have to tell you one of the things that amused me most was the people who asked how we got the rights to name this, using the lyrics from a song by the Byrds for the books. Hello!! The Bible!"

A TIME TO BE BORN
John Vornholt

FEBRUARY 2004   (284PP)

The first of nine books set during the year prior to the events in *Star Trek: Nemesis*. The Rashanar Sector was the site of a major battle against the Dominion and now is nothing more than a ship graveyard. The *Enterprise* patrols outside the perimeter while others enter the area and retrieve bodies and/or vessels. Sinister forces are at work, however, and it's not just Wesley. (Yes, he's back and a Traveler.) During the course of a retrieval mission, Data makes a discovery that will change the very nature of their mission and jeopardize their entire future in Starfleet.

A TIME TO DIE
John Vornholt

MARCH 2004   (296PP)

For the events that occured in the previous book, Picard finds himself committed in an asylum and being prepared for his court martial. The crew readies themselves for dispersion, but they don't know that Wesley is back in the picture and willing to use his Traveler abilities to make things right. Riker leads a covert operation back to the Rashanar Sector to prove Picard's innocence, but will he find the evidence in time?

"Although I've written a lot of *Trek* books, I haven't been included in the multi-author series very often, so I was pleased when John Ordover included me in this one. It sounded very ambitious, and it was. Since I had written several TNG duologies, I guess I was a natural choice to start the series, which attempted to bridge the gap between the movies *Insurrection* and *Nemesis*. For years, I had wanted to write a

Wesley Crusher story, exploring what happened to him when he went with the Traveler, but Ordover kept telling me the time wasn't right. For one thing, we didn't know whether Wesley Crusher was alive or dead, and a chance reference to him in a TV episode might mess up the whole book. Then he popped up at Troi and Riker's wedding, so he was alive. They cut most of Wesley's lines from the movie, meaning he was alive and wasn't burdened with any backstory, so the way was clear. As a Traveler, Wesley made a great reluctant super-hero. As far as the overall arc of the series, I wanted to leave the *Enterprise* crew with a dark cloud hanging over their heads that would carry throughout the other books."

that slowly travels the cosmos. Many generations later, Captain Picard and his crew are sent to investigate what happened to their race. Even at warp speed, it takes weeks to arrive. When they do, they discover the remains of the Dokaalan homeworld and the survivors of the devastation living a minimal existence among the asteroids of the area. With offers of Federation assistance, the Dokaalans seem willing, but an evil agenda lurks under the surface.

A TIME TO HARVEST
DAYTON WARD & KEVIN DILMORE

MAY 2004   (332PP)

A TIME TO SOW
DAYTON WARD & KEVIN DILMORE

APRIL 2004   (316PP)

The Dokaalan world experienced planet-wide disasters that destroyed their planet. A last ditch effort to seek help, they launch a probe

Asked to assist in the terraforming of a planet, the crew is only happy to oblige. Violent acts of sabotage threaten not only the colonists, but also everyone aboard the *Enterprise*. Picard is already torn with issues resulting in the need to prove to his superiors that he still deserves to be captain. Can Picard save the colonists and his career? The terrorist agenda is truly surprising and frightening as one of the agitators is running interference in Geordi's engine room. He has already taken Data out of the equation and has his sights set on tampering with the warp core. Make sure to check out the amusing acknowledgments.

Dayton said, "Our involvement in this project came about sort of late in the planning game, as I understand how events unfolded. John Ordover had conceived of a twelve-book miniseries that would showcase the TNG crew during the period between *Insurrection* and *Nemesis*, with the overall goal of showing how the characters came to be at the point in their lives that we find them at the beginning of the latter film. According to his idea, six writers would each take two books and tell stand-alone stories with the larger arc of the twelve-book series, with different books concentrating on different characters and so on. One of the writers who had initially been involved in the project had to step out of it, (Dave Galanter), so John came to me and asked if I (or Kevin and I) would be interested in tackling two of the books. How do you say no to something like that? Work with established writers like John Vornholt, Bob Greenberger, and Keith De-Candido, as well as promising newer talent like David Mack? What's to think about?"

Kevin continued, "As far as the creative process goes, chalk this one up to an afternoon brainstorming session fueled by Coca-Cola and buffalo wings at a suburban bar and grill. Our starting point was this suggestion by John in an IM volley he had with Dayton: 'I can tell you that the two books before yours are space adventures, and the books after yours are a planetary adventure, so try to come up with something that's neither of those.' Sure thing,

John, no sweat. Thus was born the asteroid-based civilization of the Dokaalan. I was pleased to take the third and fourth slots of the series as we got to show the crew's innermost thoughts during what was likely the low points of their careers, then take them to success once again. The character arcs in our books were the most fun for me."

A TIME TO LOVE
ROBERT GREENBERGER

JUNE 2004 (263 PP)

For one hundred years, the Bader and the Dorset races have lived in harmony on the planet Delta Sigma IV. When a murder occurs and the accused man runs, the *Enterprise* arrives to handle the investigation. For Commander Riker, the mission will force him to question his life, because the accused happens to be his father, Kyle.

A TIME TO HATE
Robert Greenberger

JULY 2004   (282 PP)

detail how they win back respect and make the decisions as seen in *Nemesis*. To me, one of the niggling questions from *Nemesis* was why we didn't see Kyle Riker at the wedding of Riker and Troi. Answer: He couldn't be there because he was dead. How did he die? Doing the Federation's work. From there, I crafted a story about a civil war, and Riker caught up in politics. John didn't like the outline at all. Over lunch, and this has to be late summer 2002 now, John, Keith, and I had lunch where John effectively dictated the premise that became the novels. John likes working in this style, more or less brainstorming the full story from one of his notions. It certainly was a stronger story than what I had and I eventually went to work on turning it into *A Time To Love* and *A Time To Hate*."

The *Enterprise* discovers that the reason behind the peaceful existence between the Bader and the Dorset is a naturally occuring gas in the atmosphere. Unfortunately, the gas is slowly killing the population. To neutralize the effects will mean massive outbreaks of violence. To do nothing will mean extinction for its inhabitants. Meanwhile, an angry William Riker confronts his father.

Bob recalls, "On January 11th, 2002, Marvel Comics fired me as their Director-Publishing Operations. Once word got out that morning, John immediately called and invited me to lunch the following week to discuss a series of books. His idea was to bridge the gap between *Star Trek: Insurrection* and *Star Trek: Nemesis* with a year-long series. The notion he was using was one of redemption; something tore down the prestige of Picard and crew and the year will

A TIME TO KILL
David Mack

AUGUST 2004   (344 PP)

uring the Dominion War, the Federation secretly armed the planet Tezwa with

weapons of mass destruction as part of a contingency plan. The Prime Minister of the planet has gone mad with power and demands restitution, even if shatters the fragile peace between the Klingons and the Federation. Captain Picard forces Ambassador Worf to make a terrible choice, and certain people in the government will do anything to keep the truth a secret forever.

A TIME TO HEAL
DAVID MACK

SEPTEMBER 2004 (346 PP)

With the new government of Tezwa firmly in power, the *Enterprise-E* crew helps in relief efforts to start the rebuilding of the planet. But rebels loyal to the previous regime have kidnapped Commander Riker, and Troi fears the worst. It also appears that someone is going to painstaking efforts to eliminate evidence of the planet's secret, a secret that could topple the Federation itself, even at the cost of innocent lives.

• • •

David wanted a chance to shape the series and franchise, which is why he started writing *Trek* stories. He said, "Unlike many *Star Trek* authors, I earned my first credits writing for the TV series (*Star Trek* editor John Ordover and I sold two story outlines to *Star Trek: Voyager* and *Star Trek: Deep Space Nine* in 1995, and soon afterward got the script assignment at DS9.) That opened a lot of doors with regard to writing for the *Star Trek* books, and it was an opportunity I eagerly embraced." A mutual friend, Glenn Hauman, another current *Trek* author, introduced Dave and John.

Regarding his first novels, David said, "I'm sure that some readers will be shocked—shocked!—to learn that *A Time to Kill* and *A Time to Heal* were motivated by my opposition to the U.S. invasion of Iraq and my dismay at how the subsequent occupation has unfolded. Of course, the outlines for both of these books were heavily revised and polished to make certain that the story didn't degenerate into a simple rehash of current real-world events. The principal goal, at all times, was to make certain that the focus stayed firmly on our characters, and on the effects that these events have on their lives and points of view."

Contemplating further, he said, "By my standards, the writing of *A Time to Kill* and *A Time to Heal* were very quick—much more so than I would have liked. In addition, I wrote both books while coping with the planning of my wedding, the death of a beloved pet, the holidays, and the chaos of having just moved out of an apartment I had lived in for twelve years. The editing of both novels happened insanely fast, and it is a testament to the skills of Keith R.A. DeCandido and Edward Schlesinger that they are as tightly woven into the overall continuity of the *A Time to . . .* series as they are."

A TIME FOR WAR, A TIME FOR PEACE
KEITH R.A. DECANDIDO

OCTOBER 2004   (341 PP)

 he Federation readies itself for an election for the next president. Ambassador Worf must

rescue people, including his own son, from the Federation Embassy on Qo'noS, which has been taken over by terrorists. The *Enterprise* crew prepares for major changes in personnel and an unnecessary inspection. If everyone can ride through the turbulent storm unscathed, they have a Reman named Shinzon waiting for them.

Keith commented, "John Ordover wanted to do a big miniseries that would chronicle the year leading up to *Nemesis*. I made it abundantly clear that I would commit massive acts of homicide if I wasn't the one to chronicle the story of how Worf wound up back in Starfleet. Since the dialogue in the script indicated that Worf's return to Starfleet was recent (a line that was later cut), it made sense for that to be in the closing part of the series. So I wound up with the concluding storyline, which also tied the entire series together and set it up for the movie, and what would come after."

ANTHOLOGIES

STRANGE NEW WORLDS

Dean Wesley Smith remarked, "John Ordover and I had been talking about a way to help new writers break into *Star Trek* fiction for years. When he finally got the contest through the legal departments, and since I was not only a professional fiction writer, but had been a short story editor for three different magazines, I was the logical choice. And ever since it has been a blast to help out new writers and read their stories."

How does the process of submitting the stories for consideration work? Dean answered, "The fans send their stories to New York. Someone there boxes them up without opening the envelopes and sends them to me. I have piles and piles of them that I read after the deadline. I give every story the exact same chance, ending up with what I call my second read pile of about three hundred plus manuscripts. I read those a second time, carving that down to the top forty-plus, then I try to decide which are the best twenty-three out of that to go into the book each year."

When asked about particular favorites, Dean responded, "Oh, sure, I remember an amazing number of them, considering I sometimes can't remember my own stories. 'Ribbon for Rosie' by Ilsa Bick just tore my heart out when I read it and I still consider it one of my favorites. 'The Million Year Mission' by Robert Jeschonek is I think the best pure *Star Trek* and science fiction story I have gotten."

VOLUME ONE

STRANGE NEW WORLDS

DEAN WESLEY SMITH, WITH JOHN J. ORDOVER
AND PAULA M. BLOCK, EDITORS

JULY 1998   (371 PP)

ORIGINALLY PUBLISHED
IN TRADE PAPERBACK

"A Private Anecdote"
(GRAND PRIZE)
(STAR TREK)
LANDON CARY DALTON

The vegetating body of Captain Pike is on Starbase 11, but his mind is still active.

Landon remarked, "I first began to consider writing my own works of *Trek* fiction after I read about David Gerrold's experiences in his book, *The World of Star Trek*. Many years later I read an article in *Starlog* magazine about how to submit a spec script to the producers of *Star Trek*. I sent in a *Voyager* script called *Yesterday's*

Son and waited. In late 1996 I received a phone call informing me that the script had received a favorable response, and that in 1997 I would receive a phone call from one of the producers, at which time I would receive the opportunity to pitch three story ideas. The week before the scheduled phone call I picked up an issue of *Cinescape* magazine and read a brief article about the *Strange New Worlds* contest. I thought about it for a few days, then wrote the story 'A Private Anecdote.' I dropped it in the mail the day I received my phone call from producer Joe Menosky. The story 'A Private Anecdote' was based on the original series episode 'The Menagerie.' I thought it might be interesting to tell a story in which Pike possessed some crucial piece of information vital to the survival of the Federation, but was unable to express it to anyone. I played with this idea for a while, but it wasn't working. Then I came up with a refinement on the idea. What if the idea was not vital to the Federation, but just personally important to Pike himself? What if he had a joke he wanted to tell, but he had no way to tell it? This became the acorn from which my story grew."

Landon told the results of the Joe Menosky phone call. "It did not go well. He listened well and did seem to give my story ideas reasonable and fair consideration, but he did not elect to purchase any of my pitches. I returned to my ordinary life and put my dreams aside for the time being. Months passed. I had heard nothing from Pocket Books about my short story and I assumed it had been lost in the mail. One Sunday afternoon I came down with a bad cold. I took some cold medication and went to bed. I was awakened a few hours later by the ringing of the telephone. I finally picked up the receiver. It was some guy called John Ordover, and he claimed to be calling live from some Internet radio broadcast. I didn't know who he was, but I wasn't really interested in buying whatever he was selling. I was groggy and grouchy and just wanted to go back to bed. I got rid of the guy on the phone and returned blissfully to sleep. The next day I was not entirely certain whether the call had been real or the product of a drug-enhanced dream. Fortunately I received a letter from John a few days later, explaining that I had won the Grand Prize, and that I was going to see professional publication for the first time. When the book came out in June of 1998, I got to participate in a book signing, was interviewed for a magazine and a couple of newspapers, and even appeared on the very same local television station which had aired *Star Trek* reruns during my youth."

"The Last Tribble"
(STAR TREK)
KEITH L. DAVIS

For the last seventeen years, Cyrano Jones has been picking up tribbles on Space Station K-7, and the end is in sight.

Attempts to reach the author for an interview were unsuccessful.

"The Lights in the Sky" (THIRD PRIZE)
(STAR TREK)
PHAEDRA M. WELDON

Federation Ambassador Shanna, from the episode "Gamesters of Triskelion," looks for her rescuer, Captain Kirk.

Phaedra remembers playing *Star Trek* as a child during the summer months, and answering her parents with the word, "Illogical," even though she had no idea what it meant. While playing *Trek*, she and her friends made landing party adventures, and would then create her own adventures on lined notebook paper and dream of a way to get the actors to film her scenes. She didn't know the show had been cancelled years earlier.

She heard about *Strange New Worlds* at a South Western Writers Conference, since she sat next to Dean Wesley Smith. She remembers, "I was shy, bashful, and all out terrified when I learned he wrote *Trek*. I don't think I breathed. I listened while he explained the idea of *Strange New Worlds* to one of the other people seated at the table. My heart dropped when I found out there was less than a month left before the deadline." Even with the tight deadline, she was able to turn in two stories to the contest, with the other one being a DS9 story.

The idea for the story actually came from Dean. According to Phaedra, "I remember Dean answering the question 'So what would you write a story about?' His response was 'Anything. For instance, wasn't there a show in one of the series that you thought wasn't finished? That you thought should have a part two? Write that.' I don't think the person he was talking to got it, but I did. First thing I thought of was Shahna. And how Kirk had promised to come back to her. Did he ever do that? And if he did, what happened? We know they never got together, so did he just forget her? It went from there."

She remembers the writing of the story being easy and fun. She watched the movie *Generations* and the episode "Gamesters of Triskelion" over and over until she felt she could blend them together. She also spent hours online at various *Trek* sites looking up Romulan history.

"Reflections"
(STAR TREK)
DAYTON WARD

In the last moment before Kirk dies on Veridian III, the Organians show him his life if he had resigned his commission upon returning from the Guardian of Forever and Edith Keeler's death.

When John Ordover announced the first SNW contest in the spring of 1997, he posted the notice on AOL, where Dayton was volunteering in the *Star Trek* Club, where he helped with the message boards, trivia games, and moderated the *Trek* books site. Dayton remembered,

"Once the contest was announced, Deb Simpson, a good friend of mine who had read some of my *Trek* writing, urged me to submit a story. I submitted 'Reflections' and one other story, the name of which I can't even remember now."

For the genesis of the story, Dayton said, 'Reflections' actually started as the fifth part of a five-part story I'd written earlier. After *Star Trek VI*, when the original crew has supposedly retired, I wrote this story where Kirk is called out of retirement to deal with a Romulan threat. I originally wrote it as four parts, and Kirk gets killed in the last scene. Later, I came up with an idea for an addendum chapter, which I originally titled 'Crossroads.' When *Generations* came out, the idea behind my story pretty much got shot out of the water, but for some reason I decided to rewrite 'Crossroads' to fit with the film's continuity, and that became 'Reflections.' Deb Simpson and I, along with a few friends, were publishing this little fanzine at the time and she even decided to post the story to it, allowing a grand total of about twelve people to read it, as I recall. When the SNW contest came along, I really wanted that story to be a submission, so I essentially rewrote the whole thing from top to bottom, fixing a lot of rookie mistakes and such that I'd made the first couple of times through. I ran it past some test readers who helped me smooth it out some more, and let it fly. And lo and behold, Dean Wesley Smith liked it."

Dayton talked about being selected and the drama in waiting for his name. "Dean and John held a live announcement online on AOL, and Dean read off each winner one at a time, with these dramatic pauses between each name. Even though my story was a TOS entry and was among the first listed, it still seemed to take forever. When they made the announcement, the chat room went nuts, since maybe two-thirds of the people in there knew me from my AOL hosting gig. It was one heck of an ego-boost, I have to say. I think I might even still have the chat transcript stored somewhere!"

"What Went Through Data's Mind 0.68 Seconds Before the Satellite Hit"
(STAR TREK: THE NEXT GENERATION)
DYLAN OTTO KRIDER

hat happens during a span of time that to Data, feels like an eternity,

Dylan has been a *Star Trek* fan since he watched the original series reruns on TV. He became a huge fan when TNG came out. "It was the only science fiction on TV back then, and I was a huge science fiction fan."

When asked about his story, he remarked, "I wrote the story because I had decided that I wanted to be a writer, and the contest offered a great opportunity for me to merge my interest in writing and my interest in *Trek*. I can't remember how I found out about the contest. I believe it was posted on an on-line forum some place. My idea for 'What Went Through Data's Mind . . .' came from a fascinating quote from *First Contact*, where Data . . . said, '0.68 seconds for an android is an eternity.' I began to think about what it would be like to have a

positronic brain that worked so much faster than human brains, and thought it would be interesting to have a situation where Data would have only 0.68 seconds to save the ship."

He found he had won the contest by mail. "My wife cried. It was extremely exciting for me and did wonderful things for my career. I have the same agent as Alex Garland *(28 Days Later, The Beach)* and am writing the English scripts for several anime titles for ADV Films. I'm a full-time writer working on my second novel and who knows? I'd love to do another *Trek* story again."

"The Naked Truth"
(STAR TREK: THE NEXT GENERATION)
JERRY M. WOLFE

arclay is terrified assuming his first command.

Attempts to reach the author for an interview were unsuccessful.

"The First"
(STAR TREK: THE NEXT GENERATION)
PEG ROBINSON

Stumbling upon a small ship, the crew finds Werta, the first person from her planet to venture out into deep space.

Peg reflected on how she started writing. "Honestly, it's one of those demented life-trips that look like insanity, and years later you're still not sure it wasn't. When my child turned two I finally decided that if I didn't start working—really working—to become a writer I never, ever would become a writer. While tootling around looking for forums to practice my typing I oozed on over to online fanfic: It combined my interest in *Trek* and my curiosity as to how *Star Trek: Voyager* was being received, and it was a forum in which amateurs were able to write and be read. Since I'd never had any continuing desire to write fanfic I didn't really intend to do my practice work there. But I found a friend, and a story, and a theme, and the next thing I knew I was writing *Star Trek* stories. It was all very unexpected, but by the time I was done at least I knew I could do the research, put together the plots, and for heaven's sake type. Not well—and my spelling and punctuation were still atrocious. But at least I could get a story I liked in type without spending all my time muttering 'Oh, drat, where is the comma key again?' My friend and I had finished our big project. Neither of us were planning on doing more fanfic. But just as I was figuring out

how to make the shift the contest was begun. My writing buddy and a number of other friends all seemed to think I had to enter. I know it sounds coy and way too sweet and 'little old me never thought she might win,' but I didn't think I'd get in. I entered because I mainly run honest: With my friends bugging me to enter I knew I'd feel better if I entered something, rather than just lying and pretending I'd sent something in. I could tell my friends that I'd submitted and when I lost I'd just say, 'Hey, come on, hundreds of people entered, someone had to be the loser.' So I sent in two stories, expecting neither to be accepted. Instead Dean Wesley Smith took 'The First.' Which left me with no prepared comment when people started congratulating me, but it's hard to complain. It was a shock, but a really nice shock."

She continued, " 'The First' came out of my sense that there was more and more conflict between the ideal of respect for other cultures (good old Prime Directive stuff) and the Federation acting like a paternalistic super-power, often more in its own self-interest than in the interest of the cultures it encountered. I was brought up by a serious history teacher, so I understand the inevitability of some of the practical paternalism, and the neo-colonialism, but also the ideal of wanting to respect other cultures. I went dinking around trying to find some place in the canon, and some character within the canon that would give me a chance to present the dilemma: the need to protect the interests of the Federation, and the need to respect and keep your hands off the new cultures coming in. Picard stepped into some mental spotlight and offered to star—I think because he's an ethical worrier and a natural for that sort of fretfulness. Beyond that it was one of those stories that puts itself together. Once I knew who I was writing about I found myself knowing a bit about 'when' in the canon. Once I knew when, I started knowing the how and the why—history presents us with too many innocent cultures trapped in the traffic lanes of military karma. The Dominion War had plenty of 'victims of circumstance' already. One more seemed quite appropriate. 'The First' wasn't the only submission I sent in—I know I sent in one satirical piece starring Data. I'm less sure if I sent in a third piece. I don't think so, though there were a few false starts. Winning came as a surprise to me. I learned online the morning after—my phone must have been tied up that night, as my first clue was e-mails congratulating me. After that I remember John Ordover contacted me out of the blue and I just sat at my desk staring and trying to figure out if it was for real or if someone from fandom had come up with a fake screenname just to jerk my chain. How it all played out? Actually it was a bit peculiar, and the currents of people's reactions were all over the place. I got some of the paranoia backlash from folks thinking I'd 'sold out' to Pocket Books. Also the hooplah of *Star Trek* publishing and fandom is larger than life. I can't claim to be modest or humble, but when you've been assuming your first actual sale will come, oh, three or four more years down the line and will probably be in a minor publication and go unheralded and unsung, and maybe even unread, it's a bit startling to find oneself in the midst of an internet stampede of reacting fans, editors, online publicity events, and so forth. I had real life friends who had wanted to write professionally themselves, and there was a predictable blend of delight

and envy from them. That would be hard enough to surf through with warning. Having had every expectation of accomplishing a diplomatic loss, I wasn't ready for success in the least little bit. I'm very happy it happened. But, oh, it took some getting used to."

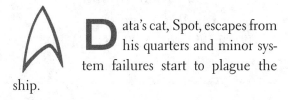

"See Spot Run"
(STAR TREK: THE NEXT GENERATION)
KATHY OLTION

Data's cat, Spot, escapes from his quarters and minor system failures start to plague the ship.

Kathy remembers how she became a Trekker. She said, "I was hooked on *Star Trek* when the original series aired in the '60s. The characters and situations captured my kid's imagination. When I went off to college in the late '70s, the original series was in perpetual reruns. By then, Jerry (Oltion) and I were already dating, and we'd gather every afternoon in a friend's room and watch an episode before dinner. We all knew the shows so well that we'd recite the lines with the actors."

Kathy knew Dean Wesley Smith through the writing community in Eugene, Oregon and when he got the editorship for the contest, "every science-fiction writer in Eugene heard about it." She had lofty ambitions of writing a story for each series at the time—four—and submitting them to increase her chances of placing a story in the anthology. She said, "In the end, 'See Spot Run' was the only one I finished in time. I'm a cat person, and I thought it was so cool that Data had a pet cat on board the *Enterprise*. I wanted to center a story around how an android would take to having to deal with a seemingly misbehaving feline. The image of Spot shoulder-deep in Picard's fish tank struck me as visually humorous and the rest of the story just fell into place. And, of course, in the end, Spot saves the day."

"Together Again, for the First Time"
(STAR TREK: THE NEXT GENERATION)
BOBBIE BENTON HULL

A story of Picard's first meeting with Guinan, who helps the *Stargazer* crew try to locate their kidnapped captain.

Bobbie never thought about writing a *Trek* story at all. "About five years before SNW, I started a science fiction novel, but never finished it. It stank. The idea was good, but I didn't know how to write a novel. I had no desire to write *Trek* until I heard about SNW. . . . An online friend of mine knew I was working on a science fiction novel, so when she heard about *Strange New Worlds*, she forwarded the information to me. I hadn't written any short fiction since high school, some twenty years before."

She remembers the exact day and time she got the call. "On Monday, December 8th, 1997, at 1:15 pm Pacific time, John J. Ordover woke me from a nap to inform me that I had won Honorable Mention in the first SNW contest. It was the only submission I made for the contest that year. The idea for 'Together Again' came from the episode 'Times Arrow, Part Two' in which Picard and company go back in time to 1890 San Francisco and Picard meets Guinan there. Of course, he knows her, but she doesn't know him. In the closing scenes, Guinan is hurt and Picard is taking care of her until he can return to his own time. Before he leaves, Guinan says, 'I'll see you in about five hundred years,' to which Picard replies, 'I'll see you in about five minutes.' The look Picard gives Guinan when he returns to his own time says, 'You little stinker. You knew. You knew everything.' That got me thinking. Guinan had to wait over four hundred years for Picard to even be born! And the things that she knew that she couldn't tell anyone. She knew all along that Picard would come back from being Locutus in 'Best of Both Worlds.' She knew so much but couldn't say anything. She knew she would meet Picard, but when? Where? Picard didn't tell her. He knew her when he was in 1890 San Francisco, but she knew nothing about him. So, my story was about not only when she met Picard again, but what happened to make it so that he would trust her with not only his life, but the lives of the crew of his ship, as well."

Bobbie submitted stories to SNW two, three, and four. She didn't win. "Dean Wesley Smith, the editor, told me that the stories were good, but they just missed out. He said that if I was serious about having a writing career, to write in my own universe—it would be easier to sell and I would make more money. He was right." She has signed a major book deal with

Windstorm Creative publishing and has started a *Missionary Kids on Mars* series. She also writes books under the pen name of Roberta Layne. "If not for SNW, I would not now be a professional writer. It was a dream I had as a child, but never thought I could ever obtain. You see, I am the child of migrant farm workers. My dad is illiterate and my mom an 8th grade drop-out, married at fourteen to a twenty-four-year old man in order to escape working in the fields. I am a college graduate (Soil Science) and now have a writing career. I worked hard to get to where I am and SNW was what put me over the top. Thank you S&S, Paramount, and Gene Roddenberry, for making it all possible. And Dean Wesley Smith, too. He has taken me by the hand and guided me in my career to be a professional writer."

"Civil Disobedience"
(STAR TREK: THE NEXT GENERATION)
ALARA ROGERS

In a Borg-assimilated Earth, Q wanders through the devastation and ponders what might have happened if he didn't introduce the *Enterprise* to the Borg.

When asked about the idea behind her story, Alara remarked, "I had been writing stories for some time which took the premise that, rather than being the general irresponsible ass he appears as in most of the *Star Trek* episodes, Q has his own conflicts with his society, and that he is often put in an untenable position by internal

politics. My picture of the Continuum in these stories was a fairly ruthless one. I began to wonder why, when Q had introduced humanity to the Borg, he never appeared during *Best of Both Worlds* or even mentioned Picard's assimilation. If my interpretation of his character—that he was actually sincere when he said Picard was the closest thing he had to a friend—was correct, then Q theoretically should have intervened to help Picard during that incident, but obviously did not. Arguably, Picard's assimilation was his fault, but he did nothing. And then I thought, what if he did do something? What if things would have been much worse without Q's intervention? So 'Civil Disobedience' was born."

"Of Cabbages & Kings"
(Second Prize)
(STAR TREK: THE NEXT GENERATION)
FRANKLIN THATCHER

The crewless *Enterprise* stumbles upon another empty vessel, the *Carpenter*.

Bruce remembers exactly when he became a *Trek* fan. "In the fall of 1966, at the ripe old age of twelve, I walked into our living room where my sister (a teenager) was watching television. On the TV, I saw a ship unlike any I had ever before seen whoosh past stars and a planet. 'What're you watching?' I asked eagerly. 'Nothing,' she snapped. 'You wouldn't understand it.

Go away.' And the rest is history. I've made a point over the last four decades of not letting her live those comments down."

Aside from his enjoyment of the characters and setting established on television and in the movies, "Trek lends itself to a variety of literary approaches and topics. I found that versatility appealing, and it was a comfortable genre to write in. I wrote my first fan-story back in the mid-70s. I even got serious and wrote an 110,000-word novel in the early 90s; a cross-series techno-thriller set in the TNG environment. While that novel won me fans among those few who've read the manuscript, it will never be published due to broad violation of Paramount and Pocket Book submission guidelines."

Regarding the story, "There were two ideas, really. The first stemmed from a paper I wrote while working on my computer science degree. The topic was computers in combat, and part of my research showed that Nimitz-class aircraft carriers of today have a certain amount of self-direction in answering threats if the crew does not respond. Extrapolating that to TNG-level technology provided the main direction of the story. The trick then was to figure out how to believably isolate the ship from its crew in hostile territory. The second idea came from Lewis Carroll's poem about the walrus and the carpenter in 'Through the Looking Glass.' Careful readers will find many parallels to that poem, not the least of which is the 'talk of many things' between the Picard simulation and the main computer."

"Life's Lessons"
(STAR TREK: DEEP SPACE NINE)
CHRISTINA F. YORK

Nog, just back from the academy, offers to pilot Keiko O'Brien to Bajor.

Christina commented, " 'Life's Lessons' was the only story I wrote for the first SNW. Frankly, at the time it did not occur to me that I could submit more than a single story. It was a subject that I cared deeply about, and I think that showed in the way I wrote it. The idea for the story came directly from an episode of the show. Keiko's baby had been transplanted to Kira, there was a growing closeness between Kira and Miles, and the episode had a strong B story about the Kira/Miles relationship. I felt (and still do) that if Miles was growing closer to Kira, Keiko would have been aware of it, and she was an important part of that dynamic. My feminist sensibilities were offended that the male writers chose to ignore the wife in this triangle, so I wrote her story. (I don't remember now if the writers actually were male, and I understand the restrictions of time, budget, and guest stars—but why ruin a good case of indignation with the facts?)

I was also delighted to write Cadet Nog. I have always regarded this incarnation of Ferengi as adolescent males, and to write an adolescent Ferengi was great fun. It allowed me to go way 'over the top' because it fit the character."

"Where I Fell Before My Enemy"
(STAR TREK: DEEP SPACE NINE)
VINCE BONASSO

⋀nswering a distress call, the *Defiant* finds the *Amhurst* minutes before the warp core is going to blow.

Attempts to reach the author for an interview were unsuccessful.

"Good Night, Voyager"
(STAR TREK: VOYAGER)
PATRICK CUMBY

⋀he ship experiences a massive system failure in the bio-neural network, creating a race to enable repairs before life support ceases.

Patrick remembered, "There was a big void in the 70s when there was no new *Star Trek* being produced, other than the occasional Bantam novel. I realized then that if I wanted to experience new *Trek* adventures, I'd have to write them myself. I wrote several really bad *Trek* stories (and even a couple of novels). I saw the information about *Strange New Worlds* on the startrek.com website. My wife encouraged me to enter the contest."

Patrick actually submitted two stories. "My first story was a carefully crafted tale about Scotty and McCoy stranded on a shuttlecraft that was slowly being pulled into a black hole. I labored over the story for weeks, making it perfect in every way. The characters were true to life; there was great drama and sacrifice, excitement and adventure. The science was carefully researched. It had good pacing, and eloquent use of metaphor. The tone and setting were meticulously constructed to make the reader feel like he was in the claustrophobic confines of the doomed shuttle. It was a great, terrific story—perfect in every way, a sure-fire winner. I also wrote a second submission, almost as a throwaway, in just three days. I didn't have time to review it and had to FedEx it to get it in by the deadline. That second story was 'Good Night, Voyager,' and of course, it won. *Voyager* was then in its early years, and I assumed that there would be fewer *Voyager* submissions than others. I was less than thrilled about much of the writing on the show, so I set out to write an episode that I would like to see, that featured the characters as I thought they should be. I wrote 'Good Night, Voyager' to be a shipboard story without a bad guy. (I always hated the planet-of-the-week and villain-of-the-week stories). I featured Harry Kim and the Doctor, two interesting characters that had yet to be fleshed out on the show. The protagonist was the ship herself. I had a blast writing it, but never assumed it would win. It was just for fun (which, in hindsight, is why it was a better story than my first effort). I knew when they were going to announce the winners on the website, but I was too busy with my work to check the site. I really had no expectation that my stories would win, so it was quite a shock when my wife called to tell me that my story had been selected, and an even bigger shock when she told me which story had been selected. Pocket Books editor John Ordover, who informed me that the story had been selected out of a field of over three thousand entries, then contacted me. I was quite flattered. There was a brief editorial process where the editor changed a couple of words, then a long wait before I actually saw the book on the shelves. What a feeling that was, to know you could walk into Barnes & Noble and buy a book that contained your words you'd written! Of course I bought a dozen copies and gave them to my friends and family. Barnes & Noble invited me to do a book signing along with Dru Blair, the amazingly talented airbrush artist that created many of the *Trek* book covers. That was a real treat, getting the star treatment from the bookstore. It was a great experience (I still have the notification letter from John Ordover framed above my desk). I would like to encourage any budding young writers to take a shot at writing *Star Trek* 'the way it should be.' It's fun and quite satisfying to put words into the mouths of the beloved characters, to explore neglected regions of the *Trek* universe that intrigue you."

"Ambassador At Large"
(STAR TREK: VOYAGER)
J.A. ROSALES

Answering a distress call, the *Voyager* attempts to rescue the inhabitant of a small vessel when Mondasian fighters suddenly surround both ships.

Attempts to reach the author for an interview were unsuccessful.

"Fiction"
(STAR TREK: VOYAGER)
JaQ ANDREWS

A woman named Ranaii is looking at the stars and trying to encourage her husband, Chakotay, to join her in stargazing.

Attempts to reach the author for an interview were unsuccessful.

"I, Voyager"
(STAR TREK: VOYAGER)
JACKEE C.

A being able to change its shape and appearance at will finds the crew of *Voyager* a fascinating species to study.

Attempts to reach the author for an interview were unsuccessful.

"Monthuglu"
(STAR TREK: VOYAGER)
CRAIG D.B. PATTON

Told entirely in log entries, the crew discovers a new type of nebula.

Craig realized he was a fan "In the late 70s when I was eight or ten years old. Like so many others, I was drawn in by the syndication run of the original series. I remember my mother being a bit anxious given the skimpy costumes the female crew members and aliens wore and Kirk's romantic exploits. I had actually shut down my writing and other creative work for a number of years after college. Eventually, my artistic side rebelled. I just had to start writing stories again. My problem was I had no idea what to write and felt incredibly rusty. I stumbled across the *Strange New Worlds* contest and realized it offered two things that would help me get started again: 1) a deadline to work against and 2) the chance to write a story without having to create absolutely everything from scratch. So, for me, it wasn't specifically about wanting to write a *Trek* story. It was more about fortuitous timing between my own creative life and the start of the *Strange New Worlds* contest."

Craig continued, "I had been reading a lot of dark fantasy and horror in the year or so prior to writing 'Monthuglu.' In particular, I found myself drawn to ghost stories, so I decided I wanted to try writing a ghost story set in one of the *Trek* shows. I chose *Voyager* because I felt it had the most potential for what I wanted to do. A lot of classic supernatural tales take place in remote settings—backwoods cabins, remote villas, crumbling towers, etc.—so a small Starfleet vessel alone in an uncharted part of the galaxy seemed like a good fit. The next big choice was to write an epistolary style, using only the recorded first-person accounts to tell the tale. It's a writing style not used very often today, but I had been really impressed with how it made Bram Stoker's *Dracula* work and wanted to experiment with it. The various ship logs, officer logs, personal logs, etc. that are so familiar to *Trek* fans made this approach an easy one to develop, though getting the voices right became critical or the story just wasn't going to work at all. I watched a lot of *Voyager* episodes over and over to try and get as much of the characters' inflections, vocabulary, and perspectives in there as I could. The basic plot came easily. Captain Janeway had an established tendency to take risky short cuts trying to get them home sooner. So, putting the ghosts inside a huge, forbidding nebula that they can't scan the inside of felt like a plausible set up. I worked on it off and on for months, doing a lot of revision work to get the pacing, the mounting sense of tension and (I hoped) dread right as well as the voices and the technobabble. Finished it with a bit of time to spare, sent it off, and patted myself on the back for doing what I had set out to do: I'd written a story. Didn't give it another thought. Several months later, while I was away on business, John Ordover from Pocket Books called my home and gave my wife the good news. She tried to put him in touch with me but he graciously deferred and let her call me instead. I was in my office and just started screaming in joy and surprise when she told me. My coworkers were a little startled, but excited for me once I got off the phone and explained myself."

Craig has fond memories of his experience. "Having 'Monthuglu' published was, quite literally, a life-changing event for me. In high school and college I had pursued writing, television, and film as possible careers and had, for various reasons, abandoned them. Seven years went by without me writing so much as a paragraph of fiction. Then, out of the blue, I wrote a story that wound up in a pro-rate anthology edited by Dean Wesley Smith and published by Pocket Books. . . . It made my head spin. I took it as a real wake-up call, that I had talent and wasn't using it, that I had given up too easily, that maybe if I worked hard at it, I could eventually be a full-time writer. I've been pursuing that dream ever since, writing more and more. I had a story published on Horrorfind.com in 2003 and have made it to the final round of several anthologies. I also have something like one hundred rejection letters, but I'm not letting them deter me. I'm work-

ing steadily, reading lots, participating in workshops, and generally doing everything I can to 'make it' as a writer. I owe a huge debt of gratitude to Dean Wesley Smith and John Ordover for starting me out on this path."

"The Man Who Sold the Sky"
JOHN J. ORDOVER

A tribute to The Great Bird of the Galaxy.

John remembered, "I wrote it the week of Gene Roddenberry's death (Gene is, of course, the unnamed man in the bed who is the point-of-view of the story). I hadn't started working at Pocket yet, and in fact might not have even been working at Tor Books yet, although I was freelancing for the *Trek* office. Anyway, if you want the date the story was written, it was written the week Gene died. I didn't try to sell it anywhere, I wrote it just 'cause Gene's death sparked something in me. The title, and some of the feel, is a homage to Heinlein's novella *The Man Who Sold The Moon* and its short story sequel, 'Requiem.' In 'Requiem,' Harrisson, the man whose action led to us actually going to the moon, has been enjoined, due to ill health, from ever going there. He manages to hire a couple of guys who don't recognize him to take him there anyway, but dies of a heart attack on landing, and is buried on the moon. So I wanted to do a different twist on that concept—in a way, I thought Gene dying was unfair, that he wasn't going to live to see the future he always wrote about."

John continued, "The story just sat there in my files for years until I decided to stick it into SNW I, along with a story by Paula Block that she had written even more years earlier. As you can see, we labelled that section *Because We Can* and made it clear that no one else's story was bumped to make room for ours. If there was an ulterior motive to it, it was to show the fans that, yes, we in the *Trek* office and at Paramount were fans, too."

"The Girl Who Controlled Gene Kelly's Feet"
PAULA M. BLOCK

 A psychological profile of yeoman third class Minnie Moskowitz of the *U.S.S. Enterprise*.

Paula, who for years has worked as part of the licensing and approvals department of Paramount Pictures and, as of 2006, CBS, has been a fan since the beginning. She loved the show in first run and was very happy when she could see the reruns in syndication during the early 70s. She commented, "By that time I was in college (at Michigan State), and I remember watching it before going down to dinner in the dorm. It was kind of a closet fixation of mine until I saw an ad in the school newspaper announcing the formation of a *Star Trek* club on campus. I went to their first meeting and was shocked, shocked I tell you, to discover that there were other people who loved the show.

We'd all read Stephen Whitfield's book, *The Making of Star Trek*, so we all knew the names of the episodes and all the background info on the show. It was kind of like going home and finding the family you never knew you had. Before I knew it, I'd been sucked into the world of fandom and conventions. It was a lot of fun. After I got out of college (with my BA and MA in English) I began working in the publishing industry, in Chicago and New York. I worked for McGraw-Hill for ten years, writing and editing articles for the publications in their trade magazine division. Then I moved to Los Angeles, where I discovered there are a lot fewer publishing opportunities. I freelanced for various local magazines for about a year, hoping I'd find something full time, and then one day, a miracle happened. A friend of mine had worked on one of the *Star Trek* films and someone in Paramount's licensing department asked him if he knew anyone who had a publishing background—and who knew a lot about *Star Trek*. He immediately called me—I immediately called Paramount—and I became the luckiest gal in town."

Paula had the opportunity to include a short story she had written in the first *Strange New Worlds* anthology. "I wrote 'The Girl Who Controlled Gene Kelly's Feet' in 1976, while I was working on my doctorate in English. I'd loved college up to that point—as I mentioned above, I already had a BA and an MA—but suddenly college no longer seemed like the place I was supposed to be. Even though I was very comfortable in an academic setting, I knew that it was time to get out into the real world. A lot of those feelings went into the tale of Minnie Moskowitz, yeoman third class aboard the *U.S.S. Enterprise*. Minnie had gone through the academy and been placed on the *Enterprise* . . . only to discover that she didn't want to be there. She came up with a unique solution to her problem—one that was influenced by the fact that I was spending a lot of my spare time watching those *Star Trek* reruns . . . and old movies like *Singin' in the Rain* and *The Wizard of Oz*. It was kind of an odd story—for some reason I didn't put any of the *Star Trek* regulars in it—but it was published in a fanzine (*Menagerie*) and people seemed to like it. As for how it wound up in the first SNW anthology. . . . During my days in fandom, I read a lot of wonderful amateur *Star Trek* stories. I remembered how excited I was when Bantam published *Star Trek: The New Voyages* in the 70s. Fanzine stories in real books! It was wonderful validation for those fan writers, graduating to pro status. But alas, there were only two *New Voyages* books published. After I started working at Paramount, I talked to Pocket Books about doing something similar to *New Voyages*, but nothing gelled. Finally, John Ordover came up with the idea of running a contest for new amateur fiction—not previously published fanzine stories—and that's how the *Strange New Worlds* books came about. I was very pleased when John asked me to be one of the judges, along with him and Dean Smith. As it turns out, John had written a fan story, long ago. And he knew that I had, too. (Dean declined to submit one, so I don't know if he had one locked away in a closet or not.) We decided to include them—not to show off (they weren't nearly as good as those submitted by the winners of the contest!)—but to kind of let the readers know that we were just like them. The only problem was, our stories broke the rules established for the contest. Both of them

would have been eliminated if they'd been submitted in the appropriate manner. But since we weren't competing for prizes and weren't getting paid, we included them in a separate section that we called *Because We Can*—because, well, we could!"

VOLUME TWO

STRANGE NEW WORLDS

DEAN WESLEY SMITH, WITH JOHN J. ORDOVER AND PAULA M. BLOCK, EDITORS

MAY 1999   (341 PP)

ORIGINALLY PUBLISHED
IN TRADE PAPERBACK

"Triptych"
(SECOND PRIZE)
(STAR TREK)
MELISSA DICKINSON

 What if Captain Kirk failed in stopping McCoy from saving Edith Keeler?

Attempts to reach the author for an interview were unsuccessful.

"The Quick & the Dead"
(STAR TREK)
KATHY OLTION

 Kirk is dying and McCoy struggles to save him on a bizarre planet.

Kathy said, "I find chaos theory fascinating, and even though I don't have a deep understanding of the theory, I grasp enough to play with it a little. In this instance, I came up with a planet ruled by chaotic weather patterns. Dr. McCoy was always one of my favorite characters on *TOS*: a little cranky and irascible, a very human counterpoint to Spock's logical bearing. So making him the hero of a story that had some really nitty gritty world-building in it was a lot of fun."

"The First Law of Metaphysics"
(STAR TREK)
MICHAEL S. POTEET

Captain Spock must help a little orphaned Vulcan girl through the ritual known as the First Meld.

Michael remembered, "I wrote *Trek* stories as soon as I became a fan. I had a big, three-ring binder full of loose-leaf, handwritten efforts, including a *Star Trek* 'Choose-Your-Own-Adventure'-style story; a story in which Kirk left Starfleet to become a space pirate (and, a variation on the theme, a collaboration with my aforementioned best friend in which Spock left Starfleet to become a stand-up comedian—the title was 'Day of the Rubber Chicken'); and even a cliffhanger titled—I kid you not—'Who Shot Mr. Spock?' Thankfully, this juvenilia is no longer extant! But it does show that I had the urge, common to so many fans, to hear more stories about the crew. If I had to write them myself, so be it! When I learned of the *Strange New Worlds* contest years later, I was thrilled to think that I could actually contribute something to the *Trek* universe. To leave your fingerprints on a world you've enjoyed for so long, to move from spectator to participant . . . who could turn down a chance like that? I learned about *Strange New Worlds* through a magazine blurb (I forget which title) at a local bookstore. I worked on a story for the first contest, but did not finish in time to meet the deadline."

• • •

Michael discussed the origin of his winning story. "'The First Law of Metaphysics' arose from the ambiguous scene in *Star Trek III* in which Saavik helps the rapidly-developing Spock through pon farr. I knew that the writers of *Star Trek IV* had originally planned for Saavik to be pregnant with Spock's child, but abandoned that idea. I wondered, however, 'How far could I push up against that limit?' So I decided to create a story that would introduce a half-Vulcan child of the right age in a daughter-like relationship to Saavik, and that would keep the readers guessing until the end, 'Well, is she or isn't she?' Judging from feedback I received, the story worked."

"The Hero of My Own Life"
(STAR TREK)
Peg Robinson

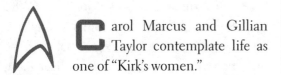

Carol Marcus and Gillian Taylor contemplate life as one of "Kirk's women."

Peg recalled, "'Hero' grew out of decades of friends and fans muttering about Kirk and his women. Whether you think he's a serious, sensitive stud-muffin or just an intergalactic playboy with problems committing to a relationship, he's got a fair number of ladies in his past. Thanks to the obvious requirements of storytelling, the primary traits those ladies share in common are their relationships with J.T. Kirk, and the fact that every single one of them is interesting enough in her own right to rate at least a portion of a story line. I came of age with the perennial question of Kirk's women dogging me: were they bimbos? Heroines? Suckers? Mere cardboard cutouts for the Real Hero to chase, argue with, adore, defend, and later mourn? I'm female and I never wanted the entire point of my life to be subordinate to some XY individual's own story line: It's one thing to be the spear carrier some of the time, but who wants the job all the time from birth to the grave and all the moments in between? I'd rather get at least the occasional starring role. And I'd just been rereading *David Copperfield* with that lovely question as to whether the reader will decide that Copperfield was the hero of his own life. . . . So somehow out of that came the idea of what those women were worth — what they might have in common that made them heroes in their own rights, and whether you could get two or more together in one place, and what they'd have to say to each other when they shared so little in common but Kirk. The practical issues of canon dictated some of the result, and my feelings about the three main characters dictated some more, and then I got caught up in real delight thinking about what George and Gracie Humpback's beautiful baby boy might turn out like."

"Doctors Three"
(STAR TREK)
CHARLES SKAGGS

 dmiral McCoy visits Dr. Zimmerman as he works on perfecting the EMH program.

Charles reflected, "As a newly married man in the process of changing jobs, I had little time to explore the internet, so I didn't learn about the contest until I saw the rules for *Strange New Worlds II* in the back of the first volume. I really wish I had known about the first volume earlier, because as a *Star Trek* fan, I obviously like the idea of going where no one has gone before. If I recall correctly, 'Doctors Three' was originally inspired by the classic *Doctor Who* episodes 'The Three Doctors' and 'The Five Doctors,' which featured multiple incarnations of the doctor that often bickered with one another. I originally envisioned a story that featured Admiral McCoy, Doctor Bashir, and Doctor Zimmerman because all three characters have such strong, confrontational personalities. As I began to plot out the mechanics of the story, I started focusing on Bones and Zimmerman and then the fanboy in me screamed, 'Bones could help Zimmerman create the Emergency Medical Hologram!' Once I realized that Bones would be pissed as hell about a holographic doctor treating human beings, I knew I had my story.

"Finally breaking through after years of frustration as an aspiring writer was an incredible feeling, and I am immensely grateful to Dean Wesley Smith, John Ordover, and Paula Block for creating *Strange New Worlds* and for selecting 'Doctors Three.' One side benefit was being able to have a small book signing at my local Barnes & Noble, which was great to have for my family and friends, but also somewhat sad because the signing took place the day after DeForest Kelley passed away."

"I Am Klingon"
(THIRD PRIZE)
(STAR TREK: THE NEXT GENERATION)
KEN RAND

A bioengineered Klingon from the past wants to die an honorable death and asks for Worf's help.

Ken remembered, "I watched the Original Series when I was in high school. I had been a science fiction fan since Sputnik, or maybe slightly before, and *Star Trek* was so far out I couldn't wait for each episode. I've always been a writer, have been since I was four. (I put out a little crayon picture newspaper in my neighborhood. My distribution was scant because I wasn't allowed to cross the street. I retired after the first issue because there was this little red-haired girl. Or maybe it was naptime; I forget which. But I've always written.) I started writing radio news and ad copy in 1968, so I've been a paid writer for more than thirty-five years."

Ken continued, "I don't recall exactly how I heard about SNW. I read the trades routinely, but I was also acquainted with Dean Wesley

Smith and with the Eugene Profession Writers Workshop (WORDOS) of Eugene, Oregon. I jumped right on it, wrote for the first volume. Wrote three stories, in fact. I wanted in."

Ken recalled how he originated the idea for his story. "I'm walking through the living room on my way to the refrigerator from my office, when I see this *Deep Space Nine* episode my wife is watching. It's where the crew goes back to TOS 'Trouble With Tribbles' episode to save Kirk from the bomb. I saw the scene where Bashir asks Worf about the difference between TOS Klingon physiology (the bad make-up) and DSN Klingon (the walnut forehead). 'We don't talk about it,' Worf said, or something like that. 'Oh, yeah?' says I, and I abandoned the fridge expedition to see what Paramount would do about the question. Well, they never answered it! 'Aha!' says I, and back to the office I go to write the story. My goal was to explain the physiology difference in a story that might make a cool filmed episode, and that wouldn't interfere with anybody's fixed timeline or canon."

"Reciprocity"
(STAR TREK: THE NEXT GENERATION)
BRAD CURRY

 Strange gravity waves rock the ship and lead to a remarkable discovery.

Brad remembered, " 'Reciprocity' was my only submission to SNW II. The idea for it was sparked by *The Next Generation* episode 'The Chase.' The notion that an ancient race had deliberately placed a message in our genes struck me as a very clever concept, and it made me curious as to whom those people might have been and what might have motivated them. Discovering the SNW II contest only a few weeks before the submission deadline was actually a plus for me, I think. With so tight a deadline, I really had to focus my energy into getting the story down on paper. With my talent for procrastination, if I'd come across the contest anytime sooner, I probably would have dawdled around and never got anything written. And finding out I was one of the contest winners was truly a surprise—to be honest, when I submitted the story I was less concerned with winning and more concerned with not embarrassing myself by sending out a really awful story. 'Reciprocity' was the first science fiction short story I've actually completed—not to mention submitted for publication—so it was definitely a thrill to see it in print."

Brad continued, "Being published in *Strange New Worlds II* was a really satisfying experience—and an educational one. The energy and effort I put into writing the story gave me a new appreciation for the professional writers who do this kind of thing day in and day out. And, I also discovered, it's not such a bad thing to be paid for one's creative efforts (although I would be very appreciative if one day someone would explain to me the royalty statements I've continued to receive over the years. . . .)."

"Calculated Risk"
(STAR TREK: THE NEXT GENERATION)
Christina F. York

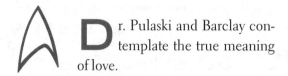

Dr. Pulaski and Barclay contemplate the true meaning of love.

Christina recalled, 'I guess I was a slow learner, because by the time SNW II came along, I still hadn't figured out that I could send more than one story. I'm not sure exactly where I got the idea, but I knew I wanted to write about the women characters, and Pulaski seemed the perfect candidate. From a purely practical standpoint, there was less canon where she was concerned, which made staying inside the lines a lot easier. The writing process was similar, though I did worry about using Barclay. He's quite popular among some writers I know, because he's different, and fun to write. Actually, that's one reason I love about writing *Trek*, some of the characters are just fun to play with. The announcement on SNW II was really a thrill. The date was our regular Tuesday night workshop, and once again the announcement was live on a Web chat, though without the audio. One of the group brought his computer to the bookstore where we held the workshop, and it was a magical night. Three more winners from our group—Kathy Oltion (again), Dustan Moon, and I—and watching the names come across the screen and hearing the cheers from our fellow members was a huge thrill."

Christina actually came extremely close to landing a story in SNW III. "If you have read the introduction to the third volume of *Strange New Worlds*, you know that my story was the last one cut from the book. It made it all the way through, but was pulled due to a continuity problem that I still can't exactly identify. But without that error, I would have been eliminated from SNW by selling three-in-a-row. It says a lot about the dedication and caring of Dean Wesley Smith that he took the time to call me on the day of the announcements. He wanted to let me know just how close I had come, and why I didn't make it in. That phone call is indicative of the kind of guy Dean is, and the way he encourages new writers. Having someone like him, or Keith, to help writers through the pitfalls of this business is one of the greatest things about working in the *Trek* universe. It amazes me to look back at the writers in the first couple volumes, and realize the number of people I have met because of my association with *Strange New Worlds*, and with *Trek*. People that I consider good friends, who I didn't even know when we shared that first table of contents. People everyone knows, or will know, for their ability and imagination—and I get to play in the same sandbox. That's pretty great!"

"Gods, Fate, and Fractals"
(STAR TREK: THE NEXT GENERATION)
WILLIAM LEISNER

 gents' Lucsly and Dulmer from the Department of Temporal Investigations are on the case.

Bill can't "recall a time when I wasn't a fan, to at least some degree. I remember watching the original series in syndication as a kid, every Saturday night at 7:00. I rediscovered the show during my freshman year at college, when the local PBS station played mini-marathons late Saturday nights/Sunday mornings, while we were getting drunk in our dorm rooms. Then *The Next Generation* premiered my junior year in college, and I made sure to have a front seat in one of the big screen TV rooms in the student union that night. I was a regular weekly viewer from that point."

He wrote a DS9 spec script in 1993 and, according to William, "I sent it to Paramount under their open-door policy at the time, which earned me an invitation to pitch stories to the producers of that show, and then later to *Voyager*. Unfortunately, little ultimately came of these efforts, and I started to redirect my creative energies toward fan fiction and internet round-robin storytelling. While I was honing my writing skills this way, I saw the announcement on AOL's *Trek* boards of the first *Strange New Worlds* competition, and decided to give that a try."

• • •

William submitted two stories to *Strange New Worlds One* and, "I knew at least one of them was sure to make the cut. Neither did, and I made the very stupid error of airing my frustration on the very same BBS where Dean Smith and John Ordover posted. They kindly but firmly told me that I should vent privately, get it out of my system, then just try that much harder with my next story. The next year I wrote and sold 'Gods, Fate and Fractals.' "

Remembering how the story came into existence, he said, "the first inspiration for 'Gods, Fate and Fractals,' of course, were the temporal investigators Dulmer and Lucsly, from 'Trials and Tribble-ations,' who I thought were terrific characters in a terrific episode. Also, I'm a big fan of Harry Turtledove and alternate history in general, so I wanted to try to do an alternate history story in the *Trek* universe. And I chose the creation of the Maquis as my point of divergence, largely as a reaction to the way the *Voyager* producers had abandoned all they had set up about that group in TNG and DS9, and wondering what would have happened if they had never come into being?"

"I Am Become Death"
(STAR TREK: THE NEXT GENERATION)
FRANKLIN THATCHER

 future Data reels in horror as he realizes what his life has become.

Bruce commented, "I wanted to throw one of the characters into a situation where he must make a rational choice to do 'evil' deeds to prevent a greater evil. Data, by virtue of his reliance on logic, and his extraordinary life span, was the best choice. It also allowed me to begin with a very strong first line (important to editors), and permitted him to live out two lifetimes made parallel by the convenient literary device of time travel. Deciding to do the story from a first person viewpoint and in present tense was a tough choice, but I felt it would suit the sense of immediacy I wanted in the story. After the first draft, the only way I was able to accurately distinguish between present tense, flashback (past tense), first person viewpoint, or interior monologue was to color-code the text for the editing process. That helped me identify and fix several problems, but it still wasn't until I received the galley proofs from Pocket Books that I found Data using both of his hands just after he had lost one of them in combat."

Bruce had some final thoughts. "For all of those new writers out there, the SNW competition may be stiff, but it's well worth submitting for. And it's great fun besides. For all those 'serious' science fiction writers out there that turn their noses up at the contest, it's a mistake to dismiss it so lightly. In spite of the 'written by fans for fans' slogan, SNW is a professional publication credit, and if you make it to publication (whether you win or not), you're the cream of the crop, and it gets your name out there. Lastly, a plea to all *Trek* fans and readers: if you're a woman, get a regular mammogram; if you're a man with women in your life (and who of us doesn't have a mother or sister or female friend), persuade them to get regular mammograms. Cancer doesn't just happen to those over fifty, and ignoring it or pretending

symptoms aren't there can cost you, or someone you love, their life."

"Research"
(STAR TREK: DEEP SPACE NINE)
J.R. RASMUSSEN

A writer reveals the "real" way he gets ideas for the series.

Jeannie became a fan of the original series when the syndication airings started. She commented, "I've been a newspaper reporter, columnist, and editor for many years and done a lot of fact-writing; I wanted to try my hand at science fiction and *Star Trek* was where I felt at home. Now, I'm working on my own universe science fiction novel and non-science fiction screenplays; *Star Trek* is wonderful but I'm just a tourist."

She continued, "I submitted a truly awful (I know now) story for SNW I. For year two, I wanted to climb out of the box. While I was hunting for ideas, the next generation episode, 'A Matter of Time,' ran in syndication and I got the usual weren't-funny-the-first-time jokes about my name being Rasmussen and the bad guy being Berlinghoff Rasmussen. I decided— what the heck—maybe we are related. Research is more of a goof than an actual story; it came together in a couple of weeks. When John Ordover called to tell me it was picked, he said that Dean Smith fought hard for it because it tickled his sense of humor. Dean's a great writer and poker player, but you have to wonder about that sense of humor."

"Change of Heart"
(STAR TREK: DEEP SPACE NINE)
STEVEN SCOTT RIPLEY

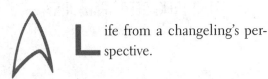 Life from a changeling's perspective.

Steven worked in the theater for a long time acting, writing plays, and stage-managing. In the mid-90s, he decided to start writing science fiction and fantasy. So when *Strange New Worlds* came along, a year or so later, it was a natural progression. "What was enormously appealing, along with the happy fact that it was *Star Trek*, was the richness of history, legacy, details and characters that exist in the *Star Trek* world."

He heard about *Strange New Worlds* from his friends Eve Gordon and Harold Gross, who wrote 'An Errant Breeze' under the name Gordon Gross in SNW III. 'Change of Heart' is a story of intrigue on a planet under the control of the Dominion. The two main characters are a changeling, one of Odo's people, who's investigating a mysterious murder on the planet, and a Dominion slave, a Vulcan woman who assists the changeling in their investigation. They actually find [things in common] and gain a certain respect for one another over the course of the story. What intrigued me from the start was writing a story about a *Star Trek* 'villain,' particularly a changeling. While Odo was well developed and arc'ed over the years in DS9, the other changelings were one of the villain sets who had the fewest points of recognizable reference with humanity. My goal was to present a changeling so that by the end of the story, though we may not exactly empathize with the character, we could at least understand more clearly the changeling's point of view."

As for writing the story, Steven remarked, "I'm not a 'write it all in one draft, polish it up and good to go' kind of writer. My stories go through multiple drafts as I work through them in passes. At a certain point I say 'done' and send it out. This story had an extra challenge as I wrote it in first person present from the changeling's pov. I'd say it took me a few months to write, working steadily with four to five hours on a weekend workday and one to two hours on a day job work night. I'm aware this process is pretty time-consuming and I've worked to 'write slower' which, ironically, speeds things up in the long run as I end up getting to the done point from fewer passes. I also do a lot of research beforehand, filling up note pads with details for characters or setting or plot. I love doing research for stories—it's my favorite part of the process! And of course there is so much material to use for *Star Trek*."

"A Ribbon for Rosie"
(GRAND PRIZE)
(STAR TREK: VOYAGER)
ILSA J. BICK

 A little girl has visions of a grown woman trying to convince her not to leave on a planned trip.

Ilsa submitted only the one story to the contest. She said, "I don't believe in multiple subs for me, personally. You shoot your wad on one; you can only embarrass yourself with something else that might not be as good. Or maybe that's me rationalizing about my lack of ideas . . . I have no idea what sparked the story. Really. I think I had some degree of healthy indignation where Seven's parents were concerned. Such selfish people! Being a military kid— my dad was Air Force and then Public Health Service—I could relate to getting yanked around, having to make new friends, and having no friends. Not a great life, believe me. And, being a child psychiatrist, I was seeing a lot of kids who were just getting torn apart by their parents' narcissism and self-absorption. You'd be amazed how blinded parents get by their own ambitions—or what they want their kids to accomplish for them. I used to call it the 'North Virginian Overachiever Syndrome.' I think that just about every single one of the kids I saw was involved in multiple things, being driven here and there . . . no wonder the kids

were having problems. No one ever gave them a chance to be kids."

In terms of how she wrote the story, Ilsa said, "I sat my butt down in a Borders, drank gallons of coffee, wrote it in longhand in a week, then typed it up, edited it and sent it. Didn't spend more than ten days on it, I think. I would always be in tears by the end of the story myself, and I was worried I'd just ruin it if I kept tinkering. Besides, I'd said what I needed to say."

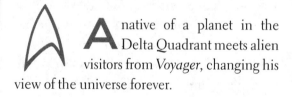

"Touched"
(STAR TREK: VOYAGER)
KIM SHEARD

A native of a planet in the Delta Quadrant meets alien visitors from *Voyager*, changing his view of the universe forever.

When asked about the idea behind the story, she commented, "I thought it would be neat to view the *Voyager* crew from an outside perspective, plus first contact stories always fascinate me. I sat down with only the premise of 'Chakotay crashes another shuttle and meets a young alien on a planet that hasn't met offworlders yet' and wrote 'Touched' in a very short period of time. At the beginning of the story, I had no idea how it would end and was just happy it all worked out! I found out I won at a chat John Ordover had on AOL during which he announced the winners. My name and story title were the first he typed out for *Voyager*, and I called for my husband and started jumping up and down. (Later) I signed the contract, had it notarized, read through the galley proof (found no mistakes and very little changed from the original), and returned my bio information and voila! I was in a book!"

"Almost . . . But Not Quite"
(STAR TREK: VOYAGER)
DAYTON WARD

Lucsly and Dulmer again, as they try to stop a temporal shift from occurring in 1996 Los Angeles.

Dayton said, " 'Almost . . . But Not Quite' was the only story I submitted for SNW II. The inspiration for it came from watching the three *Back to the Future* movies one snowy weekend, particularly the second film where we see Marty working in and around the events from the first film. *Trek* has their version of this, of course, with 'Trials and Tribble-ations,' so there's an obvious riff from that, too. Along with that, I really get a kick out of *Trek* stories where they come back in time to past or present day Earth, so the story practically wrote itself."

"The Healing Arts"
(STAR TREK: VOYAGER)
E. CRISTY RUTESHOUSER &
LYNDA MARTINEZ FOLEY

The *Voyager* crew encounters a world where medical science is unknown, thanks to a race of people called "Healers."

Lynda remembered, "I saw the very first *Star Trek* episode on September 20, 1968. I was home babysitting my one-year-old sister because my parents had taken my five-year-old sister to the hospital. When they got home I didn't even ask about my sister's condition. I ran to the door and told them, 'Tonight I saw the best TV show ever!' And I've been watching it and its various offshoots ever since. Like so many other fans, *Star Trek* had an impact on my life when I was in my formative years. The show taught me to take risks, be tolerant, and avoid wearing red shirts. I used to write fan fiction as a teenager, but I didn't pursue writing because I thought it didn't pay. Then, when I decided to quit my risk management job to be a stay-at-home mom, I suddenly had the time and inclination to write. I began by writing scripts, and I was accepted into the screen writing internship program at *Star Trek: Voyager*. I worked for Jeri Taylor during *Voyager's* second season, but I was not a fan of the script writing process. Very little of the author's original work seemed to reach the finished product, although the pay was excellent. I decided to go freelance and write short stories and novels instead. My first professional sale was to *Strange New Worlds*."

She continued, " 'The Healing Arts' was basically Cristy's idea. She had spoken to Bob Picardo (the Holographic Doctor on *Voyager*) and he had expressed disappointment that he and his character never had the chance to work with DeForest Kelley (Bones McCoy). So she decided to write a story involving the Holographic Doctor and the doctor from the original series. And she asked for my assistance. I mostly helped her find the focus of the story, edit the story, and polish the story. We were thrilled to find out that our story had been chosen. I have collaborated on scripts, short stories, and pitch ideas with a number of friends, but my favorite collaborative experience was with Cristy. She writes fast, she writes great dialogue, and she's not afraid to edit."

"Seventh Heaven"
(STAR TREK: VOYAGER)
DUSTAN MOON

 Seven of Nine receives a unique offer from some rather unorthodox Borg.

Dustan doesn't consider himself a *Trek* fan. "Fans propel a lot of air around. Couldn't say I'm a *Trek* fan. More like a *Trek* sail. As a kid in the early 70s, I watched every episode of the original series, letting it fill the sails of my imagination. I loved being taken to other worlds, and they played true to their promise. I'd be playing outside and I'd hear the *Trek* theme song, and it would be drop the ball and race for the door. *Star Trek* was on. You guys can play without me."

Dustan continued, "I submitted two stories to SNW II. I made some major modifications to the first *Trek* story I wrote, but it was the new story that won (and that's a word to the wise . . . your best story isn't the one you've already written, it's the story you're about to write). The idea I had sparked off *Voyager's* Seven of Nine. Let me begin by saying what is the most difficult thing about writing for this contest. The most basic rule of a story is that a character starts as one person, and through the experiences he or she encounters in the story, ends as another. A protagonist must change by the end of the story. And this is the most difficult challenge in writing for *Trek*. You can't [actually] change these characters. Paramount owns the characters, and they are very specific that they remain exactly as portrayed in the series. So [an SNW] writer must accomplish a change in the protagonist without anyone crying foul! How do you change someone without changing them? Change their world without changing their world? Try it sometime. It's the most difficult parameter you can put on a story. And every single one of these *Trek* writers did it. How does one tackle such a task? Answer: be a sneaky weasel. Accomplish something grand through a very simple act. Make one look, one act, one thought so monumental, their internal world changes. I began by thinking, 'Who'd be the toughest person to change?' Easy. Seven of Nine. At that time in the series Seven was fresh off the Collective, ordering nuts and bolts from the replicator while Janeway ordered java. How would I change her? Why, make a stone cold cyborg fall in love, of course. What would it take to get someone as frigid as Seven of Nine to fall in love? Okay, okay, if she's too removed from humanity to fall in love, how could I at least resurrect romantic feelings in her? Without changing her character as portrayed by the series. I had to find some small act at the end of the story that would show her internal world had been turned upside down. And then it hit me. A shell. What if she could hold a shell to her ear and hear something besides whirling air molecules? Bang! Now who gave her the shell? Who in all the *Star Trek* universe could possibly have the know-how to reach her emotions? Only another Borg freed from the Collective. Hm. Small palette to work with there. Bang! Cyborg Hugh could do it, and he'd still be out there somewhere, and I bet he's busy freeing other Borg since Picard set him loose. And so the story was born. Now I just had to figure out how I could get Hugh and Seven together, and they'd do the rest, bringing her to that inevitable conclusion I had already written. 'She lifted a hand to her ear. In her palm was a shell. She could almost hear a whisper.' "

Dustan fondly remembers hearing how he won. "Several of us in the Eugene Professional Writers Workshop (WORDOS) had set a goal to submit to SNW II that year. Some may be aware there is an online forum for the contest on AOL, and that year, John Ordover and Dean Wesley Smith announced the winners live in a chat room. So, on the night of announcements, Jerry Oltion tied our workshop in via the internet. We brought treats to make it festive, and I brought party poppers and handed them to everyone to set off in the event any of us won. John announced the extra prize money winners, then went down the list. Kathy Oltion was announced first from our group,

and amidst cheers we fired off some party poppers. I had never used the things before and was a little suprised to discover they had gunpowder inside them. The descending smoking bits made me a bit nervous, since gunpowder, firebrands, and bookstores do not mix. But we set nothing aflame, had streamers and confetti flying everywhere, and amidst the blue haze of smoke had high hopes for more winners. Sure enough, Christina York was announced, and another twenty-one-gun salute went off in the bookstore. That's when the real tension for me began. We were approaching the end of winners, and I was looking down the barrel of another empty year. John announced the remaining *Voyager* winners: 'Touched' . . . I certainly felt that in the brain pan . . . 'Almost . . . But Not Quite' . . . darn it, that title sounded ominous . . . 'The Healing Arts' . . . I'd need more than a healer's powers to save me from this emotional crash, because now there was only one slot left. 'And last but not least, 'Seventh Heaven' by *BANG BANG BANG* (and the crowd roared) Dustan Moon.' The fireworks went up, everyone cheered, and through the settling smoky haze I remember the best vision a man could have: my wife looking at me from across the table with fierce pride, the only person that truly knew how much a win in this contest meant to me. It was a great moment, made all the better because I didn't have to explain to the owners how we had set their bookstore ablaze."

VOLUME THREE

STRANGE NEW WORLDS

Dean Wesley Smith, with John J. Ordover
and Paula M. Block, editors

MAY 2000   (305 PP)

TRADE PAPERBACK

"If I Lose Thee . . ."
(FIRST PRIZE)
(STAR TREK)
Sarah A. Hoyt & Rebecca Lickiss

hura travels back in time, courtesy of the Guardian of Forever.

Sarah remarked, "I used to watch *Trek* when I was about twelve. This was in Portugal and the only competition to *Star Trek* in Portugal were *Space 1999* and some strange Hungarian (?) series about a magical pebble. *Star Trek* won hands down. Then when I got married, I found my newly acquired husband came with a *Star Trek* rerun watching habit. One of those unpredictable things. Since there was no twelve-step program for *Star Trek*, I was—you understand how these things happen—forced to watch *Star Trek* reruns every night. However, the whole concept of fandom still remains a mystery to me, in many ways. So I don't know I could say I ever realized I was a 'fan.' "

Rebecca reflected, "I didn't realize I was a fan until in college, when someone pointed out to me that I arranged to arrive at dinner very early every day, so that I'd be finished in time to go watch *Star Trek* re-runs in the lounge. Seemed like perfectly normal behavior to me."

Sarah continued, "Around 1998, I'd been writing in the hopes of publication . . . forever. Or at least it seemed like it. I should say I'd been writing in the vague direction of publication. However, all I had to show for it were a couple of one-fourth-cent-a-word sales. And I thought since the whole point of it was to be read by other people, I should just write *Star Trek* fanfic for the fan boards. They seemed to have plenty of readers. I never did it, though. Somewhere between the thought and writing a story I sold more of my original fiction and there was hope for more. So it never happened. I was in a weekly writers' group (with Rebecca and Alan Lickiss) so I'd heard about the contest. Every year a few people entered. Somehow—lack of confidence or bad organization?—I never thought I had a strong enough idea to warrant writing a story. And then by that time there were several *Star Trek* series out and we had—for various reasons—spent almost ten years without a TV. Which meant, all I knew was original *Star Trek*. It seemed . . . limiting. Well, I'd just finished my—later—first published novel, *Ill Met*

By Moonlight, which is a magical reconstruction of a Shakespearean biography. I sold this novel on proposal and had been asked to write it in six months. So, I spent three months reading all the Shakespearean biography I could find, then another three months writing. A day after I finished the book, at our meeting—what was it, Becky? Four days before the contest deadline?—I was a walking-dead-writer, a walking-dead writer who could only think in terms of Shakespeare. So, while everyone around the table was discussing their SNW submissions, I said something stupid like 'Hey, how come no one has ever done a Uhura as the dark lady story?' The usual snide remarks were made by all, and I was left alone to kinda sleep through the meeting. I thought it was the end of it, till Rebecca Lickiss called me at 9 PM on Sunday. She told me the story wouldn't leave her alone and we had to write it. Did I mention my brain was fried? I thought we had a snowball's chance in Hades and the deadline was on . . . Wednesday, I think. But I certainly was in no state to resist a determined writer with an idea that wouldn't leave her alone. The next couple of days are a blur. I remember at one point our husbands got rather testy because we were talking on the phone and using the additional line to edit live over the Internet. Which left each house virtually inaccessible to communication by anyone not working on the story. At the end, the story surprised us, taking on a life of its own and a voice quite unlike our separate voices. There was Becky's irrepressible humor, of course, but it somehow got blended with my tendency for character introspection, and meanwhile she kept my characters from going so deep into their own minds that they couldn't find their ways out with a pocket full of bread-crumbs and a ball of yarn. And the whole was just . . . sexier, more interesting, more sparkling, than our individual writing. Besides, of course, there was that *Star Trek* magic. We found out we'd won on my birthday—which was a nice touch—and these many years later, I still can't believe we won. In a way, it wasn't us—it was Uhura and the story, taking off all on their own."

Rebecca remarked, "I'd had ideas for *Trek* stories for years, but never wrote them down, since I knew you had to be a professional before you could write *Trek* for publication. Also, I was afraid that I couldn't do justice to the characters I loved so much. My husband, Alan, and I heard about it from Dean Wesley Smith at a writer's workshop we attended. I was too scared of fouling up to write any stories on my own, but Alan and I collaborated on a TNG story for SNW II. The story Alan and I collaborated on was modified and re-sent for SNW III. So that year I had half of two stories in the contest. It was truly amazing how the voice ended up. Except for two or three sentences neither Sarah nor I can remember who wrote what, though she gets credit for the details of life in Elizabethan England. There were times when I felt certain we were doomed to failure. I used MS Word and Sarah used Word Perfect, at the time, translating from one to the other caused all kinds of problems, from formatting to dropped passages to plain gibberish appearing in place of our story. And we did this multiple times in the forty-eight hours we were writing. We were doing it all at a distance, via computer and over the phone. Worst of all, the story kept growing and growing, until it was too big to meet the word length requirements. Cutting was then very difficult for both of us. After

SNW III neither Sarah nor I qualified, since we both sold novels and were now professional writers. I'm still too nervous about playing in the *Star Trek* universe to try writing anything more there on my own."

"The Aliens Are Coming"
(STAR TREK)
Dayton Ward

What happened to Captain John Christopher after his experiences aboard the *Enterprise?*

Dayton said, "This was one of three stories I submitted for SNW III, and was another story that almost did all the work by itself. I had recently re-watched the first *Men In Black* movie, and 'Tomorrow is Yesterday' had been shown on the Sci-Fi channel a few days before. Also, the whole 'Did Roswell really happen?' thing had always interested me, not so much in the 'do I believe in aliens' aspect as the 'what is the government covering up?' angle. I get a kick out of conspiracy theories, the wackier the better. In fact, friend and fellow SNW alum Bill Leisner once wrote a story that had the X-*Files* agents investigating Captain Christopher from 'Tomorrow is Yesterday' that I really liked, so I'd have to say he provided a bit of inspiration as well. All of that seemed to gel during that weekend, and then I pulled the tape of 'Little Green Men' off the shelf, and the idea for 'The Aliens Are Coming' just clicked. I think I wrote the first draft of that story during a Saturday night/ Sunday morning cram session. It was just too

much fun to set aside. Looking back on it, I wish I'd done more with that story. It's my favorite of my SNW entries, and the one I think offers quite a few follow-up storytelling opportunities (that's a hint, readers)."

"Family Matters"
(STAR TREK)
Susan Ross Moore

Spock visits his human aunt and she is not too fond of Vulcans.

Susan commented, "I've been involved in fanzines off and on for years, so I had written some *Star Trek* stories even before SNW came along. I had heard it was going to come out, but I thought 'Oh, yeah, Paramount is going to support newbies playing around,' so I didn't try to prepare anything. Then, Volume One hit the stands, and I started writing. 'Family Matters' was turned down for Volume Two, but I revised it for Volume Three and was successful. I will probably remain an original series fan. It's what I grew up with. Even though I'm a devout McCoy fan, I decided to probe Spock's family and see what his family was like and to what extremes he would go to help a family member in distress. The writing process was pretty straightforward. The only thing I did differently was to try to adhere completely to canon, unlike what most people do with fan stories."

"Whatever You Do, Don't Read This Story" (THIRD PRIZE)
(STAR TREK: THE NEXT GENERATION)
ROBERT T. JESCHONEK

Data recalls a story to his crewmates and causes much turmoil.

Robert remarked, "I would say that my introduction to the world of *Star Trek* was the reverse of the usual route. My love of *Trek* started with the printed page instead of the TV screen. As a child, I was hooked on the adaptations of the original series episodes by James Blish and the animated episodes by Alan Dean Foster. After getting into the books, I watched syndicated episodes of the original series, which truly blew my mind and hooked me for good. Having become addicted to *Trek* through the print novelizations, I flipped when Bantam began issuing original novels and anthologies based on the series. Though these novels and anthologies were few and far between, I eagerly snatched up and devoured every one of them. Because of those books, starting with *Spock Must Die* and *Star Trek: The New Voyages*, I first got the idea that I might someday be able to write my own original stories about *Trek*. I remember fantasizing often about walking into Waldenbooks and seeing my name on the spine of a *Star Trek* book on the shelf. From a very young age, I had a great interest in writing fiction. This, combined with my dream of becoming a published *Trek* writer, led me to generate *Trek* fan fiction. When I found out about SNW, I realized that I finally had an opportunity to make my dream come true beyond the fan fiction realm. After reading about the first volume of SNW in an issue of *Star Trek Communicator*, I cranked out a Harry Mudd/Nagus Zek piece titled 'When Harry Met Zekky' and submitted it to the editors. This submission did not make the cut, and neither did my Ilia piece for SNW II . . . but editor Dean Wesley Smith's encouraging note on my SNW II rejection pushed me to reach higher for my next try. I was wracking my brain, striving to come up with a truly innovative idea for an SNW III entry, when the idea for 'Whatever You Do, Don't Read This Story' came to me. It literally burst out of my subconscious fully formed, and I could not wait to get it down on paper. Though I was not sure if it was something that had not been done before, I knew that it was something that I personally had never seen. 'In Whatever You Do, Don't Read This Story,' I decided to make the story itself a character, interacting directly with the reader. I also decided to give it multiple levels, both by layering a story within a story within a story and by making it a metaphor for the way that all stories have power and a life of their own. Real-world stories might not possess malevolent sentience, but they certainly have the potential to inspire us to take action for good or ill. The story's snarky self-narrative was a blast to write. Appropriately enough, the text rushed out of me as if indeed it possessed a mind of its own."

"A Private Victory"
(STAR TREK: THE NEXT GENERATION)
TONYA D. PRICE

What went through Lieutenant Hawk's mind as he was assimilated?

Tonya recalled where the idea originated. "In the movie *First Contact*, Lieutenant Hawk is captured by the Borg. He is taken away, but returns within a short time. He is still wearing his space helmet. Borgs don't need space helmets. You can see the veins in his face, which is not totally grey. He doesn't have all the tubes assimilated Borg wear. There is a moment when he hesitates while battling Picard and I believed I could see the struggle he was going through trying to resist the Borg and protect his captain. A struggle that would be possible only if his assimilation was not yet complete. While the movie played in the theater I was already wondering: Why did Hawk return to fight Captain Picard and Worf by himself? What happened to the other Borg with him? Why did the Borg send him back to fight Picard when he was not yet fully assimilated? At the end of the scene Hawk spirals into space after losing the battle with Picard. Was Hawk dead at that moment? What if he wasn't dead yet? What was he thinking? I was looking for a good plot for a *Strange New World* story and while my family was on a driving vacation we spent long hours speculating about these questions. This was a plot hole, the kind that I, as a *Star Trek* fan, love to find. Filling in the blanks seemed like a per-

fect story idea and by the end of the vacation I had the story written in my head. The story was rejected the first year it was sent in for SNW II because I had Hawk kill himself with his phaser as a final gesture of self determination, the theme of the story. The story came back with a note stating in *Star Trek*, characters cannot commit suicide, and requesting that I rewrite the ending and resubmit. I did so gladly, rewriting only the last few sentences. I had Hawk seize an opportunity to kick himself off the *Enterprise* as his gesture of self will. Not as dramatic an ending but one that side stepped the no suicide directive. Despite the encouraging note of the previous year, I never assumed the story would be accepted. The competition was intense. I sent in eight other stories. My entire family kept checking the voice mail every day during the timeframe when we knew the winners would be notified. One day I came home from work and my two daughters and husband were in the kitchen. They told me I had a voice mail I might want to check. When I heard John Ordover say that 'Private Victory' was an Honorable Mention winner in the *Strange New World* contest I shouted and danced and screamed for a good ten minutes with my family joining in. We celebrated that evening and talked and talked about the story for days."

"The Fourth Toast"
(STAR TREK: THE NEXT GENERATION)
KELLY CAIRO

Captain Richard Castillo remembers the one true love in his life, Tasha Yar.

Kelly remembered, "When I was about three, the original series was on around dinner time. My dad would lean back in his chair to try and watch it on the living room (the only) TV. Mom was not pleased about this activity, and I knew it must be something very exciting. Plus, I was hooked on the music and sound effects long before I remember actually seeing the show."

She read the novels growing up and enjoyed them as much as the shows. It seemed to her like a fun world to write in. After seeing a copy of SNW in a bookstore one day, she thought she should give it a try. "I sat down and analyzed the stories appearing in SNW. Fortunately, as the SNW deadline approached, there was a Labor Day TNG marathon on TV. When I found myself wondering about what might have happened following the events of yesterday's *Enterprise* and how Richard Castillo would be affected—especially knowing what we do now about Tasha Yar and Sela—I started writing. It was my first short story."

"One of Forty-Seven"
(STAR TREK: THE NEXT GENERATION)
E. CATHERINE TOBLER

Life in the Nexus snatched away.

"I became a fan of *Star Trek* when *Next Generation* debuted. Granted, I had always known about the original series, but didn't get into it until *Next Generation* caught my interest. I have always written, so wanting to write *Star Trek* stories seemed like a natural thing. Good characters, a fun universe. I heard about *Strange New Worlds* because I frequented the *Trek* message boards on AOL. The moment the SNW board opened up, I was there, eager to hear what the editors had planned. I submitted stories to the first four SNW anthologies. 'One of Forty-Seven' was published in Volume Three, and 'Flash Point' in Volume Four. By the time Volume Five came around, I was ineligible thanks to other fiction sales."

"Again, 'One of Forty-seven' simply went back to me choosing a character I liked and a moment that I found interesting for her. Guinan being taken out of the Nexus clearly bothered her, so I wanted to explore what that environment had been like for her, and what it was like to suddenly leave."

"A Q to Swear By"
(STAR TREK: THE NEXT GENERATION)
SHANE ZERANSKI

 Q influenced the Riker family even in Earth's past.

Shane became a *Trek* fan when he was in sixth grade, when his family finally got a TV and *The Next Generation* was all he got to watch. Shortly thereafter, he started reading the books. Shane said, "I've always been a writer and always will be. It was only natural to begin writing about the already established world and characters I loved. There's a sort of control in writing, and making the characters I'd watched for years do whatever I wanted them to do was supremely pleasing."

Shane found a copy of *Strange New Worlds II* in Barnes & Noble, so he read the winning entry from the contest, went home and began writing. He said, " 'A Q to Swear By' was my first and only attempt. I had just watched that *Voyager* episode where Q2 wants to commit suicide and thought we definitely needed to know more about this character. And since TNG is a much more interesting series to me, I placed it there. Wrote the piece in two days, mentally shelved it, got the call from John O. a few months later, and was very excited."

"The Change of Seasons"
(STAR TREK: THE NEXT GENERATION)
LOGAN PAGE

 Picard asks for a miracle from Geordi.

Attempts to contact the author for an interview were unsuccessful.

"Out of the Box, Thinking"
(STAR TREK: THE NEXT GENERATION)
JERRY M. WOLFE

 Moriarty saves the day.

Attempts to contact the author for an interview were unsuccessful.

"Ninety-Three Hours" (SECOND PRIZE)
(STAR TREK: DEEP SPACE NINE)
KIM SHEARD

 A look as Ezri Tigan as she becomes joined with the Dax symbiont.

"I thought the world deserved to know more about the Dax symbiont taking a turn for the worse and ending up merged with Ezri Tigan. This story was more difficult to write, though, requiring watching several key Dax episodes and working and reworking the story line. I found out it won second prize when John Ordover called me one morning at work and told me so. I did not get much work done the rest of that day!"

"Dorian's Diary"
(STAR TREK: DEEP SPACE NINE)
G. WOOD

 An ensign from Red Squad tries to adjust after a life-changing incident.

Guy remembers hows his personal life affected his SNW submission. "My marriage was going through a very shaky time. . . . My marriage counselor asked me to describe my feelings and I was so inarticulate, I couldn't figure out

how to explain stuff. My pastor told me to get a journal and write down whatever [I was] feeling, what things come to mind, and whatever happened to [me] in a day, and show it to him the next week. My wife quit the counseling after nine months and I stayed for nearly three years. I kept the journal for six months and each week we would go over it."

Guy recalls what inspired his story. "I was watching *DS9* and I got to thinking about the episode featuring the Red Squad. What would it be like if everybody I worked around for the last eight months were dead? I then thought, a counselor would suggest she write a journal. I wrote the story in a two-week stretch, each day writing it just like as though I were writing a journal. After it was finished, I gave myself a thirty percent chance of getting in. I told somebody that, and they thought I was dreaming. Yes, I dream big."

"The Bottom Line"
(STAR TREK: DEEP SPACE NINE)
ANDREW (DREW) MORBY

 Nog tries his hand at the Kobiyashi Maru scenario.

Attempts to contact the author for an interview were unsuccessful.

"The Best Defense . . ."
(STAR TREK: DEEP SPACE NINE)
JOHN TAKIS

 Bashir and O'Brien play in the battle at the Alamo.

John noticed he was a *Trek* fan "When I realized that other people weren't *Star Trek* fans! Basically, as soon as I was old enough, I began watching *Star Trek* with my mother . . . the first five movies and TNG. *Star Trek VI* was the first *Trek* film I saw in theaters, and I remember highly anticipating the premier of DS9. I have been a voracious reader all my life. Sci-Fi/ Fantasy was my favorite genre growing up, and I had a huge stack of *Trek* novels. I had always wanted to be an author, and had been making up stories since I was a young child. At one point, fantasizing about writing a *Star Wars* book, I actually started to write a letter to Lucasfilm to the effect of 'I know I'm only fourteen and unpublished, but. . . .' Years later, when I found out about the SNW story contest, entering seemed like the natural thing to do. At the time, I was working at Waldenbooks. I was stocking the first two SNW books, and noticed 'enter the contest' on the cover."

John did not submit any stories to the first two contests and his winning entry was the only one he sent for SNW III. "It got mailed-out at the last possible second! I was ecstatic when I got in. I don't remember what exactly sparked the idea . . . I think it was the potential of the show itself. At the time, Bashir was my favorite character, and I loved his friendship with O'Brien. I always wanted to see one of their Alamo adventures. So I sat down with a few encyclopedias and wrote the story over the course of a few days."

"An Errant Breeze"
(STAR TREK: DEEP SPACE NINE)
GORDON GROSS

 Damar's son, Sakal, realizes the true sacrifice of his father.

Gordon Gross is the pseudonym of husband-and-wife team Harold Gross and Eve Gordon. Harold commented, "Both Eve and I grew up watching *Trek*, and have followed it through every incarnation (even the painful ones). Recently we even got to meet Nichelle Nichols and George Takei at lunch for the new Science Fiction Museum and got to thank them for all the enjoyment they've brought us over the years. We've both been writing for most of our lives and began publishing in magazines, such as *F&SF* and *Analog*, about ten years ago. The joy of writing in the *Trek* universe is that we know these people and their voices. They're friends, or feel that way. In some ways, the stories almost write themselves because the characters are so well defined."

When asked about SNW, Harold remarked, "We submitted the same story to the first two contests at the behest of Dean Wesley Smith. While we kept getting close, the story we wrote about Odo achieving sentience, the forever-lost 'A Sense of Order,' never made the final cut. However, after reading the first two anthologies, we got a better sense of what we thought would make the grade. Also, as several friends of ours had made those anthologies, it was quickly becoming a matter of honor! 'An Errant Breeze' was sparked by the DS9 episode 'Tacking into the Wind.' It drove us nuts that Damar, in a throwaway line, receives the news that his wife and child are dead. It is a major turning point in his life, and we didn't get to experience it. While this was the beginning seed of the story, it didn't really gel until the bombing of Kosovo. We were returning from Westercon in Spokane and the image of a child looking up at the sky while bombs ordered by his General father fell crystallized while listening to the news on the long drive back to Seattle. The story took only a few hours to write after that. In this particular collaboration, I wrote the first draft and left the research to Eve. Getting all the Cardassian and Bajoran information accurate was essential, as the story has to be ready-to-go when it is judged. There is no chance for an edit. I handed off a first draft and, in the morning sitting in front of my coffee in the fridge, a second draft was waiting for me. It wasn't elves, but Eve who had stayed up working that night on the story and the voice of Damar's son. The story was pretty much complete within the two drafts."

"The Ones Left Behind"
(STAR TREK: VOYAGER)
MARY WIECEK

ieutenant Carey's wife left behind on Earth as she waits to hear word about *Voyager*'s fate.

Mary started writing fanfic. "I started writing my own story as a teenager in the 70s. It was going to be a friendship story involving Spock and Chapel, but I never did finish it. I wish I could read it now. I'm sure it was perfectly awful! I didn't write again until *Star Trek Voyager*, when I got involved with internet on-line mailing lists. I wrote many, many *Voyager* fanfics and found that I enjoyed the writing process. In college, and when I was working in the environmental consulting field, I wrote a lot of technical stuff, which came easily to me. But this was the first time I'd really tried fiction. I loved using words to draw out emotional reactions in myself and in my readers. I was excited when *Strange New Worlds* came out, because I remembered the two *New Voyages* books from the 70s, which I'd really enjoyed. I bought both *Strange New Worlds* volumes, but it never occurred to me to submit a story.

"Then I realized that some of my friends in the *Voyager* fanfic community were submitting stories, and I thought, 'What the heck, I'll give it a try. . . .' 'The Ones Left Behind' was the first thing I ever submitted. I think I sent one other story in, on a whim, just days before the deadline, but I was never even sure if it got there on time. The idea for the story came about because I couldn't believe *Voyager* hadn't done an episode about the loved ones that the *Voyager* crew had left behind in the Alpha Quadrant. It seemed like we were missing half the story, and it frustrated me. So I decided to write one myself. I chose Joe Carey's family, because he was a minor character and I'm always fascinated by the 'between the lines' aspects of *Star Trek*. There's something about the show that makes us want to fill in the gaps, either in our own minds, or by writing stories. It's a rich universe, and I always find I want to know more than what I'm shown on the screen. The writing process was far more difficult than I anticipated. I enjoyed it, but in the end, I think I tried to cram too much detail into the story. If I had it to do over again, I would write it differently. Finding out that I'd won was a problem, because—and this is painful for me to admit—I forgot to include my telephone number with my submission! I have an unlisted number, so they couldn't call me! Doh! Ah, well. At least they could be certain I was an amateur! I found out when I logged onto the computer that night. The list of winners had been posted all over the net, and my mailing list friends had seen it. When I checked my e-mail, there were about two dozen messages with subject headers like 'Woooo-EEEEE!' and 'Congratulations!' Actually, in retrospect, it was a pretty cool way to find out after all."

"The Second Star"
(STAR TREK: VOYAGER)
DIANA KORNFELD

 An alien walks in the woods and stumbles into an injured Chakotay.

Diane remarked, "I have always loved the written word. I majored in literature in college and now teach high school English. I had always wanted to write but hadn't attempted anything for years. It just seemed the perfect opportunity to try something new. I did submit a story to the first contest, but didn't make that one. I was a total beginner in terms of publishing and didn't even include a self-addressed envelope. I was just thrilled to get a rejection letter. It meant I'd accomplished something—I'd actually put pen to paper. When the first book came out, I was eager to read it and learn. I started with a very episode-like piece, but it was evident from the first book that these were true genre stories—very well written, character or theme driven, revolving around a central conflict. I submitted 'Second Star' to SNW II, and this time I got some feedback from Dean. I remember him inviting me to submit the same story to SNW III. I followed his advice, and 'Second Star' was chosen for SNW III. I remember being intrigued with the idea of how a first contact with an alien race would affect that race if only one person made the contact. I also wanted to focus on a time of cultural change, in particular, a change in the status of women. Having lived through the feminist movement, and witnessed a phenomenal degree of change myself, I wanted to play with how those two threads would interact. I chose a first name for the character based on an early female Italian astronomer that I had read about."

"The Monster Hunters"
(STAR TREK: VOYAGER)
ANN NAGY

 Paris and Kim try to rescue Naomi from a monster.

Ann doesn't remember exactly how she heard about the *Strange New Worlds* contest, but she might have seen it mentioned in one of the *Trek* books, since she heads out every month and looks for the newest *Trek* books at the bookstore. Upon hearing about the contest, she submitted several stories to the first two contests. "The first year, one story came back with a rejection letter on which Dean Wesley Smith had written, 'Ann—This one got close. Dean.' The second year he wrote, 'Really fine writing in this one but the story didn't make my first cut. Two years in a row you've been close. Maybe three will be the charm? Keep writing.' Dean was right. The third year, I got chosen. I framed all three letters and hung them in my hall. I'm proud of all of them."

When asked about the idea for "Monster Hunters," "Fiction writers spend a lot of time with their characters, so when I start a story, I choose main characters whose company I'll enjoy. I like Tom and Harry, so when I started

on a story for *Strange New Worlds Three*, I thought about what they do on *Voyager* in their spare time and what exciting things the ship would find. Eventually I came up with 'The Monster Hunters.' I wanted to publish a *Star Trek* story for years. I took writing classes, bought about one hundred books on writing, and almost quit reading fiction because I was so busy studying. I used to work on the line in a brewery, and on breaks, I'd sit in the cafeteria reading grammar books. When I finally got published, I was thrilled. I remember when the *Communicator* issue with the author pictures and interviews came out. At a bookstore, I bought a stack to send to my family, and at the checkout I used my debit card to pay. The cashier asked for ID so I flipped open *Communicator* and showed her my picture. I'm still proud of my story."

"Gift of the Mourners"
(STAR TREK: VOYAGER)
JACKEE CROWELL

 The *Voyager* crew rescues someone unusual from an exploding vessel.

Attempts to contact the author for an interview were unsuccessful.

VOLUME FOUR

STRANGE NEW WORLDS

Dean Wesley Smith, with John J. Ordover
and Paula M. Block, editors

MAY 2001 (312PP)

TRADE PAPERBACK

"A Little More Action"
(STAR TREK)
TG Theodore

omeone from the planet Sigma Iotia is after Kirk.

TG pitched to the various *Trek* shows for ten years. "I write mostly for stage, TV, and screen. Never had the patience to write prose. Sold one story to DS9, but they changed their minds before any contracts were signed. Part of the biz. . . ."

TG learned about *Strange New Worlds* in an interesting way. "Lynda Martinez Foley, an on-line friend whom I encouraged to apply for a *Voyager* internship. She got it, worked on the show for a year, and befriended most of the staff and cast. She was about to be published in Volume III and told me about SNW. Since I wasn't a pro yet, I decided to take a crack at Volume IV. We both ended up in the book, which was great! Many of my stories pitched to the TV shows revolved around loose ends. And since I like humor in *Trek*, 'A Piece of the Action' was always one of my favorites. I was looking for a unique POV for the story, so I focused on just how Kirk was going to get his 'cut' every year. Once I devised the line 'I'm an Iotian dick,' I knew I had the tone and style I wanted."

"Prodigal Father"
(STAR TREK)
Robert J. Mendenhall

avid Marcus has a revelation about his father.

Robert reflected on writing. "I was writing science fiction and comic book stories longhand since my early teens. I entered the Army at twenty-two as a broadcast journalist for the American Forces Network Europe, and my writing began to improve. I wrote a dozen or so radio plays and news features and, after I left active duty, began submitting my short fiction to paying markets. I began writing a *Trek* novel as a hobby, without a thought to it seeing print. But the hobby became an obsession and after a few years and about five drafts, I completed *Patterns of Deception*, a 127,000 word 'epic.' (Aren't they all?) I submitted it to John Ordover at Pocket Books and received a very short rejection from an associate to an assistant of the assistant to a secondary editor of some sort who, although in kinder, gentler words, said the thing sucked. I began work on a second novel, but laid it aside after a rough outline and a couple of chapters. This was a few years before *Strange New Worlds I*. I heard about SNW I from an online writers group I was in. It made a short reference to the contest and listed the rules. I thought this was an outstanding opportunity and went to work. By the time I found the contest, however, there was only about two months remaining before the deadline. I took a couple of subplots from *Patterns of Deception* and reworked them into stand-alone short stories and sent them off. I had enough time left to take the essence of that second novel and fashion it into a short entitled 'David, David.' None placed and none even made the alternate list. I submitted three more for SNW II, including 'David, David' from SNW I. None placed, although I later learned from editor Dean Wesley Smith, that he had, in fact, selected 'David, David' to be included. Paramount had the last say and cut it plus several others from the final content. I submitted six for SNW III and Dean mentioned on the rejection notice for 'Pike's Peek' that it had also made the final contents list before it was cut."

Robert continued, "*The Wrath of Khan* was one of the better *Star Trek* motion pictures, possibly the best of the bunch. But a glaring inconsistency was David Marcus's abrupt change of heart from hatred of Kirk, his father, to respect and pride. There was literally no explanation for it and no indication it was occurring other than a few facial expressions. 'Prodigal Father' was my offer of an explanation for it. I had submitted another six stories to SNW IV,

and once I had submitted them, I put them out of my mind and began working on my submissions for SNW V. John Ordover left a message on my answering machine telling me that 'Prodigal Father' had been accepted and I was so stunned I had to replay the message over and over, annoying my son to no end! It was the single-most feeling of accomplishment I've experienced since I began submitting to any market and a feeling not even my next two sales to SNW would match."

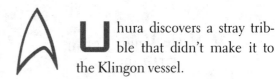

"Missed"
(STAR TREK)
Pat Detmer

Uhura discovers a stray tribble that didn't make it to the Klingon vessel.

Pat can't remember how she heard about the contest, "But I think five or six years ago I was poking around AOL looking for *Trek* stuff, and stumbled onto the Strange New Writers message board, where the contest was the topic of conversation." She sent in about five stories to SNW III with no SASE, a rookie mistake. For SNW IV, she sent in ten stories, a personal record. For her winning entry, she commented, "I figured that there was no damned way they could have found every single tribble on a ship that size. (We must, of course, suspend the knowledge that they would probably show up as life forms on a scan, but we'll chalk that up to creative license. . . .)"

"Tears for Eternity"
(STAR TREK)
LYNDA MARTINEZ FOLEY

Tetusa, the honored last, waits to meet with Spock.

Lynda remarked, "I always loved the 'Devil in the Dark' episode of the original *Star Trek*. My first AOL address was Hortal1701, in honor of the rock creature who was the ultimate mother in that episode. So I submitted a Horta-centered short story for *Strange New Worlds III*, which reached the second read pile, but wasn't a final selection. I kept only the setting, then created an entirely new plot, with new characters. When I learned that my submission had been accepted, I was ecstatic, especially because I had just learned that another of my stories, a folktale, had been accepted for publication in a textbook anthology."

She concluded, "I'm glad *Star Trek* is taking a break. Eventually I hope the next series or movie will once again embrace Gene Roddenberry's original vision of the future. Although I doubt I will write in the *Trek* universe again, I am grateful that *Star Trek* was my stepping stone toward becoming a professional writer."

"Countdown"
(STAR TREK)
MARY SWEENEY

The thoughts of the *Enterprise* as it explodes above the planet Genesis.

Mary said, "I've been a fan since the first episode aired. I was ten years old at the time, a very studious kid, interested in science and the space program, and I immediately identified with Spock. I also appreciated the fact that women were a part of the crew of the *Enterprise*. At that time if you saw a woman in a science fiction show chances were she was there to provide a love interest for the male protagonist. While it's true that most of the women in the original series were in traditional female occupations, at least they had real jobs and were treated with respect. My experience with science fiction wasn't limited to what I saw on TV—I loved to read, too. So after the original *Star Trek* series was cancelled, I read every *Star Trek* book that came out. If I really liked a book I read it two or three times; if I didn't like it, I started thinking about how it could be changed to make it better. From there it wasn't much of a leap to start thinking about my own stories, and finally, to start writing them down."

Mary heard about the contest from another *Trek* fan. "I submitted stories to the first three contests—one each year. The first one came back with a standard rejection letter, but the second and third rejections included some encouraging comments from Dean Wesley Smith that inspired me to keep trying. 'Countdown' was my only submission to SNW IV. There were two driving forces behind the story. The first was a desire to explore a theme that I think about a lot: the idea that humans might one day find themselves face-to-face with a non-human intelligence and, for one reason or another, not recognize that intelligence for what it is. The second was a desire to find a way to break free of the rules and limitations of the SNW contest. The writers are not allowed to 'establish major facts about or make major changes in the life of a major character.' So I asked myself where I could find a major character that had already undergone some very dramatic change that had not been fully explored. It turned out that the answer was to alter the definition of 'major character'—a twist that also allowed me to explore the alien intelligence theme. While I was working on 'Countdown,' I got out my tape of *Star Trek III: The Search for Spock* and watched the destruction of the *Enterprise* over and over and over again. At first I was watching just to come up with a plausible description of the technical details of each step in the process, but somewhere along the line I became very emotionally involved in what was happening—a result, perhaps, of thinking about how each step would 'feel' to the ship. I was a little surprised by the strength of my reaction: *Star Trek* means different things to different people, and there have always been fans who loved the show partly because of the ship, but I had always been more interested in the interactions between the characters. Now I can't watch the destruction sequence without cringing. I'm glad that watching the destruction of the ship af-

fected me as strongly as it did, because I know it improved my writing."

"First Star I See Tonight"
(STAR TREK)
Victoria Grant

 Kirk returns to Earth to visit his dying mother.

Victoria remarked, "You can only watch reruns so many times, and then you're hungry to take the characters on more adventures. I started writing stories at age thirteen. Really schlocky stuff, but at least it was New *Trek*. I wrote other things as well. I knew then I wanted to be a writer, and I wrote about what I loved. *Trek* is the American fable of Camelot, in a way. It's a purely American invention, and very optimistic, the way our country used to be. By the way, tinfoil bikinis notwithstanding, the original series is still the best version of *Star Trek*."

Victoria heard about *Strange New Worlds* by accident. She had just enough time to submit a story for SNW III, but her submission was entirely too long because she didn't read the rules thoroughly. Realizing rejection is part of the process, she didn't let it stop her. When asked where the idea for her winning story originated, she commented, "My story starts out with a house fire. Another irony is that it's not even a science fiction story. Dean remarked on the Strange New Writer's message board that it was a 'different' setting and a problem not seen before. Plus, I was interested in exploring Kirk's past, particularly his mother. She raised him, and did a remarkable job, and she's never even mentioned. As a mother myself, I felt she deserved praise and Kirk's undivided attention for a while. The story was not my only submission. It was my third. I didn't expect it to win, because I knew it was too far outside the sci-fi world. Plus, it only took two days to write, and I polished the other two over the course of months. I just put it in the envelope as an afterthought. Goes to show you: let the judges judge. And don't question your good fortune!"

"Scotty's Song"
(STAR TREK)
MICHAEL J. JASPER

 Scotty's unique abilities help George and Gracie.

Michael reflected, "I never even considered writing a *Trek* story, even though I'd read four to five of the tie-in novels and quite liked them (one was a Vonda McIntyre Spock novel that was awesome, and another was a Tasha Yar one that I also enjoyed). Then I ran into Dean Wesley Smith in 2000. I heard about *Strange New Worlds* from him at the Writers of the Future workshop and awards ceremony in Los Angeles, where I'd been invited for selling my first professional story, 'Mud and Salt.' We had a weeklong writer's workshop, and Dean was one of the guest writers. Along with most of the other writers, we chatted with Dean after class,

and he said the deadline for this anthology he was editing was coming up, in two weeks. I took that as a challenge, and on the flight home from L.A., I started thinking up the story. I knew I'd have to do something from either *Next Generation* or the classic show, probably one of the movies, because I hadn't kept up with the shows that followed like *Deep Space Nine* or *Voyager*. And I wanted to do something that didn't require an encyclopedic knowledge of a show. So that led me to believe that I'd need to do a character-based story, and so I rented *Star Trek IV: The Voyage Home*, as that's one of the best character-based movies of any of the series. And the whales were cool. So I continued the storyline about the whales once they were brought to the future, but ultimately the story was about Scotty. And I had fun getting him and Uhura to flirt! As I had precious little time before the deadline hit, I wrote fast, getting up early before work and spending most of a weekend working on the story. I watched the fourth movie a couple times, taking lots of notes, because I wanted to write about what happened to the whales after they made it to the future. I also had to research whales a lot, and that was fun, though time consuming. I got the story in the mail a day before the deadline and overnighted it to Dean. I found out I'd won about two months later, as John Ordover called me up and told me I'd won. I was flabbergasted. But in a good way. Getting my story accepted and published at that point in my career was a huge boost to my confidence, and I've gone on to sell over three dozen more stories to places like *Asimov's*, *Strange Horizons*, and *Interzone*. The writing bug has bitten me in a big way, and I have no complaints! I owe huge, huge thanks to Dean Smith for getting me motivated to write more and work harder than I knew I could."

"The Name of the Cat" (FIRST PRIZE) (STAR TREK)
STEVEN SCOTT RIPLEY

McCoy and Lieutenant Mears crash their shuttle on a trip exploring Mars.

Steven submitted a story involving Deanna Troi to SNW III, but it didn't make the cut. For this story, "I went through the same period of research as the previous story and spent two to three months writing it. DeForest Kelley had just passed away and honoring his legacy and his brilliant work as Dr. McCoy was my main reason for writing the story. I was really proud to win for the story. I put a lot of heart and effort into it. One of the great things about writing for *Star Trek* is the work of the many actors (and writers and directors and producers and designers and technicians) who have lived the characters. I find I can hear their voices very clearly the deeper I work into *Star Trek* stories, and I think in 'The Name of the Cat' I heard Kelley as strongly as any character I've written. And I really put him through the paces in the story. Writing the scene where he makes his tortuous way from his downed shuttlecraft to the cave where the alien is staying, through a ripping sandstorm, was just a heap of fun to write, and challenging. I also enjoyed creating a bizarre

time-shifting alien. An interesting side-note about writing stories for *Strange New Worlds* is that, while you know that if you win and are published, the end result is not considered canonical as far as the *Star Trek* timeline goes, still, you have to write it as if it is going to be anyway. There are goofs and spoofs and other types of story-tropes you can do, that is something else, but for me, I always enjoy writing for *Star Trek* as if the stories are part of the 'real' *Star Trek* universe—and even though they aren't, for me, frankly, they are."

"Flight 19" (STAR TREK: THE NEXT GENERATION)
ALAN JAMES GARBERS

An archaeology team makes an amazing discovery.

Alan realized he was a *Trek* fan in 1966. "My big sister had a crush on Kirk, so I had to watch. It didn't take long before I was also a fan. (Spock was cool!)"

Writing was a hobby and he enjoyed *Star Trek*, so he felt it was inevitable. "Besides, the compelling, lovable characters have already been developed and that's half the battle."

Alan heard about SNW from a friend who is an avid *Star Trek* reader. "He has every *Star Trek* book that has ever been printed. He knew about my hobby and suggested I give it a try."

He submitted two stories for SNW IV. The inspiration for 'Flight 19' came from just asking the question "What if?" regarding the real Flight 19. "I was very excited when I got the call from John Ordover. I never figured I would win the first time out. Only after I found out that I had been selected out of 4,500 stories did it sink in. Then I was ecstatic."

"The Promise"
(STAR TREK: THE NEXT GENERATION)
SHANE ZERANSKI

 Kamin makes a promise to his sick daughter.

This story was the only one Shane submitted to the contest. He said, "Knowing Picard had lived an entire lifetime in 'Inner Light,' of which we only got to see 48 minutes, left much to the imagination. I mean, Picard had kids for heaven's sake. That's some serious emotional baggage the guy's carrying around; I thought we needed to know more about that. Wrote this one in two days, as well. Liked it so much I kind of expected to get the call. Got it, and was pleased (although now I like the story much less . . . or at least the writing)."

"Flash Point"
(STAR TREK: THE NEXT GENERATION)
E. CATHERINE TOBLER

 A seven-year-old Ro Laren witnesses horror during the occupation.

"My idea for 'Flash Point' was fairly simple. I liked the character of Ro. I always had. I wanted to do something with her and the thing that interested me most at that moment was the story she had told about her father's death. 'Flash Point' was my only submission to SNW IV; in fact, I hadn't planned on submitting anything, but a week before the deadline, I got the idea, wrote the story literally in the middle of the night (about 2 AM, I was furiously scribbling by longhand while in bed), typed, proofread, and sent it off the next day."

"Prodigal Son"
(STAR TREK: THE NEXT GENERATION)
TONYA D. PRICE

 The being from the second-season episode "The Child" returns.

Tonya remarked, " 'Prodigal Son' was the result of deliberately throwing two plots at each other and seeing what might result. I am a huge *Next Generation* fan and a devoted *Imzadi* fan, so I was looking for a story idea that would allow me to include Riker and Troi. I always loved the story 'The Child' and wondered what happened to the non-corporeal alien. He loved Troi enough to sacrifice his physical existence to save her. Did he ever think of her after he left? Did his experience isolate him from his companions? Did he ever look for her? Would he be willing to sacrifice his life to save her if given the opportunity? He was intensely curious. He must have wondered how she was and if he came in contact with the *Enterprise* would he be able to resist checking on her? Another of my favorite episodes was 'The Loss'—the show where after a long time period we once again hear the term Imzadi and see Will and Deanna's relationship explored. The conflict of the two-dimensional life forms provided a good backdrop to explore Ian's devotion to his mother, and I felt fit in well with the family theme of the series. I'm a mother myself and I had fun exploring the bond between Troi and Ian as well as Ian's insight into the bond between Troi and Riker. Once the basic plot for 'Prodigal Son' was formed, the story came together quickly."

Tonya continued, "By now, SNW IV, I had started to take advantage of the unlimited submission rule. I had read Dean Wesley Smith's advice that writers should write and do so on a regular basis. I began to write in my own universes for a minimum of two hours every day, but I set myself a goal of writing a SNW submission story every month and sent in ten stories for SNW IV. By this time I could write a SNW story in a week. These stories were all different. Some were based on original plot ideas, some simply tried to plug plot holes and 'Prodigal Son' was an exercise in integrating two plot

ideas: an attempt to examine an episode from a different, alien, angle. The second sale was as exciting as the first. Again I got the voice mail message inviting me to call John Ordover. I tried but got his voice mail. The next morning I was online and he IM'ed me and we had a great conversation. What a wonderful treat to be able to 'talk' to him in person."

"Seeing Forever"
(STAR TREK: THE NEXT GENERATION)
JEFF SUESS

Lieutenant Hawk visits his father before shipping out on the *Enterprise*-E.

Jeff remarked, "I've been a fan of *Star Trek* since I was a little kid. Reruns of the original series ran about dinnertime and I have memories of colorful aliens and neat spaceships while eating. I can't really remember a time when I didn't know *Star Trek*. Then my tastes and personality really blossomed around 1987. I started reading comics, got into the Beatles and *Doctor Who*, and *Next Generation* started. Watching *Star Trek: The Next Generation* became a ritual. I've always wanted to be a writer. Writing *Star Trek* just became a natural extension. When *Next Generation* came out, I started a story about the *Enterprise*-B with a whole new crew and Admiral Sulu. I was in the seventh grade. Then I became a big fan of the novels, especially Peter David's. *Imzadi* is just incredible. My personal reading was mostly *Star Trek*. So in high school, I started seriously writing my own *Next Generation* stories. Today I guess that would be labeled fanfic, but I had aspirations of publishing them. I wrote on little yellow legal pads in this itty-bitty writing. In college, I started a *Star Wars/Star Trek* crossover and e-mailed chapters to my friends. They really liked them, which encouraged me as a writer."

Jeff continued, "I was a regular reader of *Star Trek* books and worked at a bookstore at the time of the first contest. But I never got a story I liked well enough to submit until 'Seeing Forever,' which I submitted to *Strange New Worlds III*. But it didn't work out. I sent it in right at the wire. I was a little naïve and didn't realize I could get feedback, so when the contest started up again, I sent it in to *IV*. I thought it was a solid story and had what I wanted to say. It turns out there was another Lt. Hawk story in *III*. If I had read that before mailing in my story again, I probably wouldn't have sent it. My goals were to write a literary story that worked in the *Star Trek* universe. I wanted to flesh out one of those red shirt security guys who die every episode without even a name, but I was more familiar with *Next Generation*, so I set it there. I chose Lt. Hawk from *Generations* because his story was finished—no one was going to write about him again. Of course, now he's in two short stories and a novel. Oh well. I set out to see what people did outside of Starfleet. So I went the other way: Hawk and Starfleet look to the future; his father is an archaeologist and looks to the past. Their divergent worldviews set up their conflict. I wanted to make the story accessible to anyone, whether a *Star Trek* fan or not. If you're familiar with *Generations*, the story has an added poignancy, but you don't miss out if you aren't. Research was essential

for making the story work. I tried to make the Mayan temple as interesting and detailed as the alien worlds they always visit in *Star Trek*. I was pleased that the relationships worked so well, especially Hawk's and Abram's, because I didn't really have a model for that. For Joli, I channeled my wife. And the metaphors actually worked. I understand what my English professors were talking about now. I'm proud of that story. I think I accomplished what I set out to do. When I got the call from John Ordover that my story was chosen for *SNW IV*, I had actually forgotten that I'd sent it in—which is usually the way for me. If I forget about it and don't obsess over it, something good may come of it. It's been a real kick having my story in print. And having 'Seeing Forever' in the timeline in the back of the *Gateways* hardcover gave me chills. I had actually contributed to *Star Trek*. Neat!"

Jeff had a final thought: "*Strange New Worlds* is a terrific idea. It has been one of the most vibrant aspects of *Star Trek* publishing the last few years. It's an experiment that I'd like to see other fandoms explore."

"Captain Proton and the Orb of Bajor"
(STAR TREK: DEEP SPACE NINE)
JONATHAN BRIDGE

 The transcription of a radio show that guarantees certain doom for our hero!

Jonathan was extremely excited to discuss his story. "I grew up in the sci-fi renaissance of the late 70s (*Star Wars*, *Battlestar Galactica*, and, of course, *Star Trek—The Motion Picture*). The more I was exposed to these franchises, the more I had to know what was out there in space even if it was only imagined. Reruns of the original *Trek* series gave me a steady diet of that. I wanted to put my mark on the *Trek* apocrypha if not its canon any way I could do it. The year *Strange New Worlds* started I saw an article about it in the *Communicator* magazine. During the fourth year I submitted three stories. When I heard *Voyager* was featuring a Captain Proton holodeck program I was very excited about it as old-time movie serials is one of my hobbies. I also knew I could do something with Captain Proton for SNW. The first thing I thought of was a lost script for a movie serial that had *Voyager* characters as Flash Gordon types (B'Elanna Torres as a Dale Arden type, Seven of Nine as a Princess Aura type, et al). But the more I thought about it, the more I thought about radio and how important a medium it was back then and that Captain Proton should have been on the radio as well.

Later I bought and read the Captain Proton mock pulp magazine where I read a letter 'written' by Benny Russell. That was what clinched it for me. I would take Captain Proton characters and *Deep Space Nine* the way Russell had first thought of it and put them together to make a radio play Russell himself would have written had he been on the writing staff. I took the format used by the *Superman* radio program in the 40s and used that as my pattern, which included a fifteen-minute script with a single sponsor, and commercials that pandered to children. I knew my idea was both different and ridiculous. And I was not sure that if any of my three submissions were selected, it would be this one. But I was both surprised and elated when it was."

"Isolation Ward 4"
(THIRD PRIZE)
(STAR TREK: DEEP SPACE NINE)
KEVIN G. SUMMERS

 The journal of Dr. James Wykoff, who has an unusual new patient, named Benny Russell.

Kevin reflected on being a *Trek* fan. "I've been a fan of *Star Trek* since I was seven or eight, which is also the same age when I realized I wanted to be a writer. My mom had watched TOS in its original run, and when I was growing up we watched the reruns religiously. My favorite character as a kid was Dr. McCoy. I think I liked his mixtures of southern gentle-man and cynical humanist."

Since "Isolation Ward 4" is set in the DS9 milieu, Kevin said, "I liked DS9 fairly well, but the episodes that clenched it for me were 'Past Tense Part I and II.' I thought they told an exceptional story, a socially conscious story, and after that, I never missed an episode. The pinnacle of the series, for me, was the episode 'Far Beyond The Stars,' which was, of course, the inspiration for 'Isolation Ward 4.' "

Kevin watched the episode and wanted more. "After I saw Benny Russell carted away in the ambulance, I wanted desperately to know what happened to him. He appeared again in 'Shadows and Symbols' (I believe that's the one) in one of the most enigmatic scenes in ST history, but still, I wanted more. Honestly, when Sisko was chasing after Dukat during the series finale, I kept expecting to see Benny Russell one last time! Only that never happened."

Kevin gets passionate about things he likes, and after DS9 ended its seven-year run, he went through withdrawal. He said, "I kept watching tapes of the show, and that was when I started reading ST books. It was during this time of withdrawal that I picked up a copy of *Strange New Worlds III*. After I finished the book, I knew I wanted to give SNW a shot."

Kevin tried starting several stories, but nothing seemed to work. He remembers, "Someone, I have no idea who, said that all good stories are about change. I kept thinking of that, and looking at the Benny Russell story and wondering whom on earth I could change. I knew I wanted to write about Benny, he intrigued me, especially one line in his dialogue: 'You cannot destroy an idea.' The more I thought about Benny, the more I thought

about that scene where he was writing on the wall, and his doctor, who seemed to think he was a joke. I realized the doctor was the key, he was the character that I could change."

Kevin decided to write the story in first person, so he came up with the idea of writing a journal. "The story came out in two or three manic bursts . . . I think the first draft was done in a week. The ending, however, was weak. Benny left the hospital, and all was well, but the doctor's change was not BIG enough. I sent it to several trusted readers, and it was my friend Andi Apple (who is now Andi Johnson, wife of Jim Johnson, who wrote 'Solemn Duty') who suggested I show Dr. Wycoff during the civil rights era. Her suggestion was exactly what the story needed."

When he found out he had won, Kevin said, "I was at work several months later when I got the call from John Ordover. I was stunned. I'd been working at my own original fiction for years, waiting for this moment, and here it was . . . I was going to be published. I can tell you, nothing short of the birth of my daughter has compared to seeing my name in print that first time. My friends and family know me as a pretty sentimental person, and I have to admit, I shed tears."

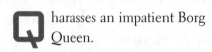

"Iridium-7-Tetrahydroxate Crystals Are a Girl's Best Friend"
(STAR TREK: VOYAGER)
BILL STUART

 Q harasses an impatient Borg Queen.

Bill commented, "I had never thought of writing for *Star Trek* until I saw the *Strange New Worlds* contest. It looked like fun and I liked the shows, so I thought I would give it a try. The idea for my story came from an ad campaign I was dreaming up. I had an idea that I wanted to work for an ad agency so I designed a mock commercial with the Borg Queen and Q, with Q offering her flowers and chocolates and the like and failing until he gave her chocolate. When I got a phone call from John Ordover telling me I had won, it was really kind of shocking. I was very nervous and did lots of stupid things."

"Uninvited Admirals"
(STAR TREK: VOYAGER)
PENNY A. PROCTOR

 Owen Paris and Gretchen Janeway deal with the unknown concerning their siblings.

Penny remembered when she became a fan. "The first time I saw the show—which happened to be the very first time it aired—I was eleven years old and surprised by how quickly I was hooked by the characters, who were believable (especially compared to another science fiction series of the time) and accessible. Also, like most Americans of the time, I was enthralled by the space program and our efforts to get a man to the moon. *Star Trek* made that goal seem possible. It also steered me to reading science fiction, which was really eye-opening. I had a tendency to write stories about all my favorite shows. After all, I knew those characters as well as anyone, and had lots of ideas for them. Back then, my sister made fun of me for it. Now people are posting fan fiction for everything from TV shows to other people's novels. Fast-forward to the moment when middle age is on the horizon and you make that list of things you want to accomplish before you die. Writing a novel was at the top of my list, but I had never really tried to write fiction before. They say, write what you know. I knew *Star Trek*, so that seemed like the best place to start. Then, I discovered *Star Trek* fan fiction on the Internet and it seemed there was a place to experiment and get feedback."

Penny stumbled onto the announcement of the winners of SNW III. "I was astonished: *Trek* short story anthology? For amateurs? Getting a story published in some future edition became a burning goal immediately. I submitted two stories for SNW IV—'Uninvited Admirals' and one called 'Confrontation,' which was a *Voyager* action story. The original idea for 'Admirals' began with the *Voyager* episode 'Hunters,' in which the crew received letters from home. One of the elements that *Voyager* never explored adequately, I thought, was the impact of the ship's disappearance on the families back home. It takes a special kind of strength to be a military (or Starfleet) wife or parent. Before the story was in final form, though, the episode 'Pathfinder' aired and that dictated a different ending for my story. My husband got home from work before I did one day, and called me to play a message on the answering machine. It was John Ordover, telling me that 'Admirals' had been selected. I started to gasp so deeply I hyperventilated. We kept that message until the answering machine died."

"Return"
(STAR TREK: VOYAGER)
CHUCK ANDERSON

revis and Flotter realize Naomi is growing up.

Chuck remembered, "I realized I was a *Star Trek* fan when I was a kid, and I kept watching TOS over and over. It was on every afternoon when I was in first grade, and I didn't know about syndicated television shows at the time. Yet I kept watching and hoping for new episodes. But I don't think I knew I was a *Star Trek* fan until TNG came out when I was in college, and I knew I couldn't miss any of them."

When asked about writing *Trek*, he commented, "It seemed like the perfect thing for a beginning writer to do and a challenge that I knew I wanted to try. We had always been big readers in my house with my daughter, and ours was always full of picture books for her. Anyone who reads to a small child knows they have to read the same story over and over again, but every child grows up and moves on to more complex books and my daughter was no different. So that was how I got the idea to write a story about Naomi Wildman getting tired of the Trevis and Flotter stories holo-deck and wanting to do other things. It took me three times to get a story published (I think my first attempt was a horrible story about Tom Paris and Harry Kim surfing on the holo-deck. Thank God, they passed on it), and when this one was accepted, I was blown away. I still think it might be the shortest SNW story. While I have gone on to sell other fiction, 'Return' in SNW is the one that still brings me the most recognition."

"Black Hats"
(STAR TREK: VOYAGER)
WILLIAM LEISNER

 arry alters the Chaotica program.

According to William, "The story came from asking myself the question: Why would Tom Paris, the pilot of a 'real' interstellar spaceship, have such an affection for Captain Proton, a very unrealistic anachronistic fictional space hero? That led me into questions about his self image and subjective views of good and evil."

"Personal Log"
(STAR TREK: VOYAGER)
KEVIN KILLIANY

 sequel to the fourth-season episode, "Living Witness."

Kevin said, "I wrote some fanfic which other Trekkies and I exchanged [the stories] through the mail and swap meets. I stumbled across a community of *Trek* fanfic writers online in the mid-90s. I didn't have the energy for complete stories—I was an exceptional-children's teacher at the time—but I joined a couple of round-robin groups, adding pieces to stories already in progress."

When asked about *Strange New Worlds*, he said, "I first heard about SNW when the group I belonged to posted [an erroneous] warning that Pocket was planning on suing all fanfic writers for copyright infringement. To this end they were staging a fake contest—fanfic writers who entered would be added to a database for future lawsuits. This was about two weeks before the deadline on SNW I, so I didn't get a story in. However, I quit writing fanfic at that moment because now that I knew there was a potential paying market I wasn't content to give stories away for free."

A version of "Personal Log" was among the stories Kevin sent in to *Strange New Worlds II*, and the only one that made the second read pile. Kevin says, "Dean wrote a note on the title page asking me to send it back for SNW III. I sent it in, along with a few others, and again it came back with the note: 'Rough spots lose reader.' Looking it over with this in mind, I saw that I was a bit fond of 'dramatic' transitions and had gone over the top a bit in my impression of Robert Picardo's verbal stylings. I smoothed out my transitions, trimmed about 800 words of showing off, and added the opening line about the Borg cube. It made it into SNW IV."

"Welcome Home"
(STAR TREK: VOYAGER)
DIANA KORNFELD

Janeway falls asleep in the Delta Quadrant and wakes up next to Mark on Earth.

After placing in SNW III, Diana remembered, "I submitted both 'Witness' and 'Welcome Home' for the next competition. I was amazed to find that 'Welcome Home' made it and 'Witness' made the alternate list that year. 'Welcome Home' was just fun to write. I wanted to do something light, something I could play around with. I also wanted to try third person as opposed to first person writing. This story gave me both opportunities. I started with the idea of what it would be like for the *Voyager* crew to be back home—and then what if that change happened suddenly; what if they just woke up one day back in their own homes? I knew I would use Janeway for the focus character—I liked her character and wanted to explore the effect of such a crazy situation on her. I also thought it would be fun to use some of the details of her backstory that we'd been made aware of through the show and other fiction. Getting in SNW IV was just as exciting as III. I was so pleased—just jumping around again like some middle-aged child."

"Shadows, In the Dark"
(SECOND PRIZE)
(STAR TREK: VOYAGER)
ILSA J. BICK

Chakotay is badly hurt and *Voyager* can't rescue him.

Ilsa had submitted a story to SNW III, but it didn't make the final cut. "DeForest Kelley had just died, and I'd always had a soft spot for him, probably because being a doctor, I could relate. So I wrote this really atrocious story about McCoy getting old and Spock happening by to keep the old duffer happy and play a game of chess. I cringe when I look at it. I'm amazed Dean still talks to me. That story eventually morphed, after about three years, into 'Beyond Antares'—same title, by the way, just a totally different take—and was picked up by *Talebones* and published in the Winter 2003 issue. No Bones at all, and a better story all the way around."

Ilsa had met Dean and said, "I was still worried about embarrassing myself (and yes, so what was I thinking, sending in my first incarnation of 'Beyond Antares?'), but I was writing a bunch more: a story a week. When SNW IV came around, I'd done a kind of streak thing: won SNW II, then got second place for Writers of the Future the next year, and I think I'd gotten another story accepted by a very minor literary magazine without the kind of circulation that would disqualify me. I think I must have picked up on something subliminal between

Seven and Chakotay because the very next season, they became an item. Shocked the socks off of me. Again, I employed a Dean Wesley Smith rule: Write as fast as you can, turn the thing around in a week, get rid of it, and don't look back. When I won, I was floored. I mean, I was running this great string: two SNW wins and a WOTF. It was enough to get me to start believing that maybe, if I worked really hard, I could kind of do this."

VOLUME FIVE

STRANGE NEW WORLDS

DEAN WESLEY SMITH, WITH JOHN J. ORDOVER
AND PAULA M. BLOCK, EDITORS

MAY 2002 (371 PP)

TRADE PAPERBACK

"Disappearance on 21st Street" (GRAND PRIZE) (STAR TREK)
MARY SCOTT-WIECEK

The story of the first person to run into the maniac McCoy in the 1930s.

After placing a story in SNW III, Mary sent two stories in to SNW IV. "One was way too technical, and I'm not surprised it wasn't chosen. The other submission, in my own opinion, was one of the best things I've ever written. I was a bit surprised it wasn't chosen, because I thought it was much better than 'The Ones Left Behind.' It didn't even make the alternate list, though, so it just goes to show you, you never know what they're going to like, or not like!"

Mary continued, "I submitted both 'Disappearance' and 'Widow's Walk' for SNW V. 'Widow's Walk' ended up getting into the next volume. The process of writing 'Disappearance' was much different than anything I'd experienced before, either in fanfic, or in other SNW submissions. Writing that story was almost an act of love—I knew I had to write it whether I ended up submitting it or not, or whether anyone else ever even read it or not. From way back in the 70s, when I became a *Trek* fan, I always wondered about that poor bum that vaporized himself with McCoy's phaser by mistake in 'City on the Edge of Forever.' How incredibly sad! Edith Keeler made a huge difference in the timeline, one way or another, yet this poor guy was wiped off the face of the earth without even a blip. Didn't he matter at all? Are there people who just don't matter at *all?* I couldn't believe that—it was too depressing. And now that I was accustomed to writing stories that 'filled in the gaps' of my beloved *Star Trek,* I knew I had to write about this guy. A little research revealed that he actually had a name in the script, although we never heard it spoken in the episode. His name was Rodent. And I thought, 'that's perfect.' I just started writing it. It practically wrote itself. It was a joy to write, even though the subject matter was dark, because I kept finding places to put things in that I knew were so significant to a *Trek* fan. At one point, Rodent tells the lost child, 'Let me help,' the very words that Kirk tells Edith will be recommended by an Orion poet over 'I love you.' That's the sort of thing that left me sitting over my keyboard rubbing my hands and cackling. To be able to get that line into that story was very satisfying to me! Finding out about that win was also interesting. I'd been in a car all day, driving back from Christmas vacation with my husband and three young children. An all-day drive with kids in the car is enough to make anyone delirious, and on top of that, I had a horrible cold. When I heard the message from John Ordover on my answering machine, I refused to even believe it. Did he say I'd won the grand prize, or was I hallucinating the whole thing? I had to go online and find the actual list before I would believe it!"

"The Trouble With Borg Tribbles" (THIRD PRIZE) (STAR TREK)
WILLIAM LEISNER

 Can the Borg resist the cute tribbles, though it's futile?

Bill remembers the basis for the idea. "On the AOL *Trek* boards, where Dean Smith regularly answered questions about the contest and writing in general, someone asked the question: Could a story about Borg tribbles get into SNW? I laughed at this exchange, thinking there was no way to create a believable story around assimilated tribbles. However, my brain latched onto the questions of how the Borg could possibly run across tribbles in the first place, why they would bother assimilating them, and so on. After about a week, my subconscious had come up with the answers, and a week later, I had the story written and in the mail. And no one was as surprised as I was when the story not only made the book, but was a top prize winner to boot."

"Legal Action"
(STAR TREK)
ALAN L. LICKISS

Kirk gets sued for not supplying enough of the action.

Alan remarked, "At the time *Strange New Worlds* started I was unpublished, but regularly writing and submitting science fiction and fantasy stories to various magazines. When I heard about SNW I was almost giddy. I could spend time writing *Star Trek* stories and submit them to a professional market. I had not written any *Star Trek* stories before because I wanted to write what I could sell. I heard about SNW from Dean at a writer's workshop (Southwest Writers Workshop) about a month before the deadline for SNW I. That was a Saturday. When I saw him the next morning I had already been to the Web site for the guidelines and had a story churning in my head. I submitted one or more stories to each of the first five contests. Dean is great about letting people know if they got close, and I did get close a couple of times before SNW V."

The idea for the story came from watching a SCI-FI channel marathon. 'A Piece of the Action' came on. This has always been a favorite of mine, so I was very focused on the show. At the end of the show I turned to my wife and said something like, 'He cheated the kid.' During the show Kirk had promised the street urchin a piece of the action, but at the end of the show nothing was given to him. Those are the kinds of springboards I love. I submitted the original version of 'Legal Action' to SNW III. While disappointed it didn't make it, there was much joy in my house as that was the year my wife Rebecca cowrote the grand prize-winning story. When I got the submission back, Dean had made a note that he liked it, but it was too slow in the middle. I reread the story and agreed with him. I added the subplot about the assassin trying to kill Kirk, putting more action into the middle of the story, as well as allowing me to show how Kirk figured out the solution. I submitted the revised version to SNW IV. That year it made Dean's alternate list and his note was to send it back again. I submitted it, without changing so much as a comma, to SNW V. I got a phone call from John Ordover at Pocket and was to say the least 'overly excited.' I think John was worried I'd pass out from hyperventilating. One of the reasons for the overexcitement was this was my last year to get into the anthology. Over the years I had sold a couple of stories to *Analog,* and had recently sold a third story. The third story would be published the next summer, so I would be ineligible for SNW VI. I had to get in volume five, or never at all."

Alan had some final thoughts: "Some people don't want to try for a contest like SNW because if they don't get into the anthology they can't market the story elsewhere. But what they can do is use aspects of their non-winning stories for non-*Trek* stories. I had a lighthearted *Next Generation* story that didn't make the cut one year. I liked the application of technology I used in the story, and it became a springboard for the first novel I wrote. That was how I learned I could write a full novel. Thank you SNW."

"Yeoman Figgs"
(STAR TREK)
MARK MURATA

 yeoman had a "red-shirt" day on a planetary excursion.

Attempts to contact the author for an interview were unsuccessful.

"The Shoulders of Giants"
(STAR TREK)
ROBERT T. JESCHONEK

 he history of a planet courtesy of observations provided by the society.

Robert remarked, " 'Shoulders' evolved from my impulse to see how much I could pack into one story falling within SNW's 7,500-word limit. My original idea was to show the varying effects made on a single civilization by every known *Enterprise* captain. I revised this plan, limiting the captains to four: Archer (largely unknown then, as the *Enterprise* series had yet to premiere), Kirk, Garrett, and Picard. Once I'd made up my mind to follow this framework, I decided to vary the kinds of stories told within the overall story as much as possible, including variations on a religious text, a quest fantasy, a war story, and a murder mystery. I also decided to tell each story from an alien point of view using a wide range of narrators, including the alien equivalents of an adult male, a twelve-year-old boy, and an old woman. I then added plenty of references to *Trek* lore, from 'Vegan choriomeningitis' to Narendra III to Armus. In the end, I was pleased that I managed to fit so much pertinent content into 'The Shoulders of Giants,' including personal stakes and character arcs for each narrator and captain. My favorite part of this story, however, might just be the story of the old woman, Nyda, who had the chutzpah to refer to Picard, Riker, and La Forge as Snooty, the Bearded Weirdo, and the Wallflower, respectively."

"Bluff"
(SECOND PRIZE)
(STAR TREK: THE NEXT GENERATION)
STEVEN SCOTT RIPLEY

 ajo gets his day in court.

Steven said, " 'Bluff' was all about Data and poker. The villain of the piece was Fajo, who kidnapped Data and wanted to keep him as a unique toy for his collection. I had noted in the episode 'The Most Toys' that there was a bit of a moral character hole at one point, where Data lied in what seemed most out of character for him. And yet he did lie, and he had a justification for doing it given the dire circumstances, and I wanted to explore how he learned to lie. And then it occurred to me that poker IS lying, bluffing is the heart of the game, and Data loves poker, so I built up a story that, by inference, shows the connection between Data's participation in poker bluffs and his ability to lie. I chose not to make an arrow-pointing neon sign connection; just wanted to lay out the fabric and hope people saw the connecting lines in the tapestry. I hope it worked—I think it did."

Steven's friend and coworker, Dana Rice, helped inspire the story. He commented, "My happiest moment about this story involves poker. I knew absolutely nothing about it when I began writing. So I got my research on and began soaking myself in the subject, especially learning the language of the game while it is played, how players talk and act and bluff. So when editor Dean Wesley Smith, who is a poker player, expressed extreme disbelief that I'd never played poker in my life, after reading it, I thought—done and done, Ripley. I was pleased. The only down moment about winning was the bummer knowledge that I'd won my third and final time for *Strange New Worlds*, but it was a great run and a grand experience. My spot in the *Star Trek* legacy is not large, but it is mine and I'm proud of it. I'm grateful to John and Dean and Paula for keeping me in the mix. They've created a fantastic opportunity for early career writers, and it is just *so* much fun to write *Star Trek* stories. If you are a writer and love *Star Trek*, it is a dream come true."

"The Peacemakers"
(STAR TREK: THE NEXT GENERATION)
ALAN JAMES GARBERS

 An Arizona Ranger in the 1880s discovers something extraordinary.

Alan submitted two stories to this contest. "I have always loved the American West. I lived in Arizona and Colorado for nine years. I also worked in Mesa Verde for six months in 1987 (that's where the story starts and ends). I have lusted after a vintage Colt Peacemaker, but could never afford one. (They cost thousands of $$$.) Knowing Picard's love of archaeology, I started having him delve into the mystery of the Anasazi. The rest fell into place."

"Efflorescence"
(STAR TREK: THE NEXT GENERATION)
JULIE A. HYZY

 Boothby reflects on his life as he faces retirement.

Julie commented, "I wish I'd been a fan from childhood, but the fact is, I came in around the fourth season of *The Next Generation*. I became quite a *Next Generation* fan. I couldn't believe how good television could be and I started to read more about the characters, more about the actors, and so on. Online, I visited a few *Trek* sites but none of them fit my personality. A few were positively strange. The AOL *Trek* board piqued my interest, and I clicked on *Star Trek, The Written Word*. I'd always wanted to be a writer—ever since I was a kid, and I'd even written a bunch of mystery novels (à la Nancy Drew). As an adult, I'd let my dreams die out for a while as life got busy and family took precedence. Here were two things I cared about—writing and *Star Trek*—in one place. So I stepped in to take a look. I found the *Strange New Worlds* contest and a sense of community among its participants. I think the second-year contest had just ended, or maybe the third was about to begin. Not sure. All I know is that I started to read the message boards, and I became interested in what people were saying about the contest and about writing in general. Dean's comments and suggestions and writing lessons were invaluable, and I started to feel the urge to write again."

Julie submitted one story to SNW III and made every mistake in the book. "I didn't format it correctly, I didn't include a cover letter, I sent it return receipt—so somebody had to sign for it (shudder)—and I didn't include a SASE. And that's not including all the problems with the story itself. Yikes! The following year, I revised the story a bit and decided to resend it, this time with a SASE. Even if it didn't win (and I didn't expect it to since it hadn't the year before), I reasoned that maybe I'd get some feedback on it to help me in the future. That final week before the deadline, I reassessed my motives. . . . Why was I mailing a story with the expectation of it being rejected? I didn't like the way that felt, so in those last couple of days, I decided to write a new story and I decided that, even if it wasn't a traditional approach, I

was going to write it from my heart. I did. Cost me bunches to overnight it, but it turned out to be money well spent. Guess what? It didn't win. But, something (almost) better happened. Dean called me at home about the story. I flipped out when he identified himself. The winners had been announced, so I knew he wasn't calling for that. I was absolutely taken aback when he told me that he really liked the story, but that, because it dealt with a pre-teen committing suicide in order to join Starfleet (hard to explain), it couldn't be in the book. Let me tell you, that phone call made all the difference. I always wanted to write, but I never knew if I had any talent. Here was Dean Wesley Smith, the online mentor whose every comment on 'how to write' I'd printed out and saved, and reread, calling me to congratulate me on writing a good story. It sealed it. From that point on, I was in for the long haul. One of the things that Dean suggests on the board is to write outside the *Star Trek* universe, so I spent that next year doing mostly that. I wrote only one submission, 'Efflorescence,' for SNW V, but I wrote more in future years."

When asked about the idea behind her winning entry, she remarked, "Boothby captured me from the moment he came onscreen. I'd loved *My Favorite Martian* as a kid, and I thought it was fabulous to have Ray Walston on *Trek*. I loved the hints they dropped about Picard being in trouble as a student at the academy, and even though I knew I couldn't invent the actual incident (canon issues), I could allude to it. I had a lot of fun with this one. We all know the timeframe that John Ordover usually makes his very-welcome phone calls, but I know I was going nuts, hoping I'd make it in the book, wishing I'd written ten stories instead of one, jumping every time the phone rang. I also hung online, waiting for the announcement. Once the announcement comes, if you haven't been called, you know you haven't made it. So part of me listened for the phone, part of me dreaded checking online. When the phone rang, it was a snow day for the kids, so they were home. My youngest, interestingly enough, said, 'Do you want to answer this one, Mom?' and I did. And it was John with the good news. I think I might've squeaked in excitement."

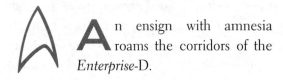

"Kristin's Conundrum"
(STAR TREK: THE NEXT GENERATION)
JEFF D. JACQUES AND MICHELLE A. BOTTRALL

An ensign with amnesia roams the corridors of the *Enterprise*-D.

Jeff has always loved writing. "As far back as grade school and the journals we used to keep, I liked to write. Actually, my first foray into real *Trek* writing started with tackling teleplays for both TNG and VGR when they had their open submission policy. I think I sent a couple in for TNG and one for VGR. Nothing came of those, of course, but it was fun to do and the notion that there was a possibility (however slim) that an episode I wrote could be produced kept me trying. Hey, if it worked for Ron Moore, it could work for me, right? But the idea of writing in the *Trek* universe continued to appeal to me and SNW came along, it seemed like the perfect venue to try my hand at creating adventures for the characters I had come to love and enjoy watching week to week on the various series."

When asked if "Kristin's Conundrum" was his first story attempt for the contest, he remarked, "Definitely not my first attempt. I started submitting the first year of the contest and submitted twenty-two stories before SNW V started, ranging from my comparatively awful first two DS9 submissions to a couple of stories I liked so much I re-sent more than once over the years. During the first four years of the contest, my output ranged from just those two for SNW I, to eight submissions for SNW III. One thing all those submissions gave me was practice. It's interesting to look back now at those first two submissions and see how truly bad they were! I'd never written stories for a professional venue before SNW and it definitely showed. But the more I wrote, the better I became and that was clear in the quality of work I achieved, even if I still hadn't gotten into the book at that point. For the SNW V contest, I had my name on a total of three submissions, my second-lowest yearly output to this day. My other stories that year were a TNG short-short about the painstaking moment just before Riker gave the order to open fire on the Borg vessel in 'The Best of Both Worlds,' and a romantic TOS story about Khan and Marla Mc-Givers leading up to the destruction of Ceti Alpha VI."

Jeff continued, "The 'Kristin's Conundrum' saga is an interesting one, I think. First, we must go back in time to the fallout of SNW I. A group of us who hung out on the SNW board started a writing group whose express purpose was to help improve our writing and get published in SNW. Our group, 'The Queue Continuum,' has had tremendous success on that front, in fact. In SNW V alone, there were six past or present writers from the Queue who had stories printed, which was a thrill in itself. Anyway, at one point during the run of the SNW V contest, the group of us decided to do a round robin project based on the TNG episode 'Conundrum,' where each of us would write from the perspective of one of the characters in the episode. At one point we considered actually submitting it for the contest, but decided to do it just for fun, to see how it would work. For one reason or another the project died before it got off the ground, but the idea did have some merit. It was at this point that Michelle approached me and asked if I would like to work with her on the 'Conundrum' project. I had only sent in two stories that year, so I was itching to work on something else before the deadline. It was decided that we would use Kristin as our main character. She was the young woman in the bathing suit that Dr. Crusher examined at the beginning of the episode, and I think she had been my character choice in the aborted group project. Basically, we looked at the jarring situation in the episode 'Conundrum' through the eyes of that minor character Kristin, hence the title 'Kristin's Conundrum.' Clever, huh? The actual writing of the story was done in kind of a relay fashion via e-mail, since Michelle lives in Michigan and I'm up in Canada. Michelle came up with a rough outline indicating the key points of the story, then she wrote the first few pages and sent me what she'd done. I then went over those pages, adding detail here, expanding the narrative there, then continued the story for a few more pages. Then I sent what I'd done back to her and the process continued like this, back and forth, until the story was complete. This whole process took about two weeks in September, and with a little more than a week left before the deadline, Michelle mailed the final copy to New York. We were both very pleased with our collaboration, but I don't think either of us really expected it to get picked for publication. So you can imagine our surprise when the winners were announced! As it happened, though, this moment was not without its harried moments either. Neither of us received the traditional victory phone call from John prior to the winners being announced, so we figured that was that. And then John posted the list of winners on AOL's SNW board and there, to our astonishment, was 'Kristin's Conundrum,' but without either of our names attached to the title! Was this a mistake? Some evil typo that slipped in to raise our hopes before sending them crashing into oblivion? Thankfully, no, and John assured us that we did get in and the omission of our names was quickly remedied. The following year was full of excitement as well, what with checking over our own copies of the galley proofs (and making some minor changes), signing contracts, and ultimately being able to go into a book store and see an actual book on the shelves with our names printed on the cover and our story printed within. During all this, of course, the SNW VI contest was in full swing. . . ."

"The Monkey Puzzle Box"
(STAR TREK: THE NEXT GENERATION)
KEVIN KILLIANY

D ixon Hill has a unique mystery to solve.

Looking back at the genesis of the story idea, Kevin said, "It started as a noir detective story. I'd always wondered about Dixon Hill, a character whom we've never seen, and thought of him as a Sam Spade/Philip Marlowe sort. It took me a couple of weeks to work out the story, setting up a situation wherein a holoprogram character could save the ship without ever realizing what was going on, then filling the plot with all the tropes of the noir genre. It was grim and it was gritty and I didn't like it."

Putting the story on hold for a while, Kevin worked on another hobby, refinishing old furniture. Kevin said, "I was in my garage sanding orange varnish off an ancient secretary (that's a bookcase with a built-in desk, not a clerk/typist) without a dust mask, when the image 'mouth full of used armpits' came to me. I mean, really, have you ever had a mouth full of varnish dust? Suddenly, I realized I had the opening line of my Dixon Hill story. I went into the kitchen, where the family computer is, and got sweaty orange varnish dust all over the keyboard. Referring to a hard copy of the story I'd written to be sure I got the elements in order, I rewrote the story from the ground up, trading in the Spade/Marlowe toughness and grit for some Travis McGee/Archie Goodwin flare and wit. Did it in about four hours. After showering

so I wouldn't get varnish dust on it, I printed the story out and mailed it that night."

"The Farewell Gift"
(STAR TREK: THE NEXT GENERATION)
TONYA D. PRICE

A n alien remembers a memorable visit from our favorite Starfleet officers.

Tonya remembered, "I submitted ten stories for SNW V and resubmitted two stories that had been considered for SNW IV, but had not been chosen because each winner can only have one story selected. Again, I sent in a variety of stories. I was part of a group of fans who loved to write *Star Trek* fan fiction and were determined to get into the anthology. The group called themselves 'The Queue Continuum' and many sales came out of that group even though no professional writers or editors were members. We got together once a week to give each other feedback on stories we had written and to support each other in our desire to get into SNW.

"During one of our chat meetings, someone pointed out if I sold a third story I would no longer be eligible to enter the SNW contest. I had been writing SNW stories for five years. If I wasn't writing a story during that time I was thinking about a story idea. It would be hard not to be a part of SNW anymore if I made that third sale. I had been part of an Imzadi fan fiction e-mail group for a long time and I knew this might be my last chance to try and get a bit of Imzadi in for them. In a fit of nostalgia, I began to think about how much I would miss writing *Star Trek* short stories. I thought of all the wonderful e-mails I had gotten from fans regarding 'Private Victory' and 'Prodigal Son.' *The Next Generation* was no longer on the air and my local TV station had quit carrying the reruns. I missed the anticipation of new episodes and the adventures of the characters. I had wanted to write a fantasy-based TNG story rather than a science-based story and had been struggling on and off for over a year on a story idea that speculated what would happen if a *da Vinci* arose on a primitive world. Would the Federation assume someone had violated the Prime Directive? Would they send someone to check out the person? *Insurrection* provided details on how the Federation monitored a planet's developmental process. The break-through for me came with this story when I realized a *da Vinci* in the future might well become the focus of a plot to manipulate an emerging planet's future. The dog, based on my beloved Karla, my first doberman who had passed away, grew in importance and became a central figure. The further I got into the story the more the girl's character resonated with my own farewells. When I got the voice mail message that 'The Farewell Gift' had been selected for SNW V, I was even happier than I had been in previous years. I feel it was the perfect story to end my SNW adventures."

Tonya continued, "I take every chance I get to express my gratitude to John Ordover, Pocket Books, and Dean Wesley Smith for providing a venue for *Star Trek* fans to write and publish *Star Trek* stories. Many people become science fiction writers without ever watching *Star Trek*, but *Strange New Worlds* has given those of us who took a different path, who started out *Star Trek* fans, to also learn what it takes to become a writer. I have finished my first novel and am halfway through my second—both in my own worlds. I continue to write short stories in a variety of genres. I would never have learned how to pursue a writing career if it hadn't been for the hours John Ordover and Dean Wesley Smith provided freely to *Star Trek* fans who had never published before. Their willingness to answer our questions and to destroy the writing myths that held us back allowed many of us to pursue our dreams. I will always be grateful to them and to Pocket Books for providing the anthology contest and to Gene Roddenberry for creating such a wonderful universe in which to play."

"Dementia in D Minor"
(STAR TREK: THE NEXT GENERATION)
Mary Sweeney

 Sarek's thoughts as he experiences further signs of losing control of his emotions.

Mary commented, "Getting a story published in SNW IV boosted my confidence, and I think that affected my writing for SNW V—I was more relaxed with SNW V and had a great time getting into it. 'Dementia in D Minor' was inspired by *The Next Generation* episodes 'Sarek' and 'Unification,' in which we saw Sarek suffering from Bendii Syndrome—a disease that was robbing him of his ability to control his emotions. Until I watched these episodes, I'd thought of Sarek mostly in terms of his relationship with Spock, but watching him struggle with Bendii Syndrome made me think of him more as a character in his own right. Sarek has always been portrayed as an extremely skilled diplomat, highly respected not only on his own planet, but also throughout the Federation. Yet despite all of the triumphs of his long career, in his last days he was haunted by difficult memories from his past. In the aired episodes we saw only the barest hints of what those memories might be: I wanted to explore what, exactly, might be going on in Sarek's mind and I decided to use music as the framework for that exploration. This was a natural choice for me since I love music myself and almost always have music playing while I write. In 'Sarek' we saw how deeply the ambassador could be affected by music and we also learned that he has a particular fondness for Mozart. Because of this, and because I think there is a certain parallel between the Spock/Sarek relationship and the relationship Mozart had with his father, I decided to pick a piece by Mozart (Piano Concerto No. 20) and let it drive Sarek's thoughts. I played a recording of the concerto over and over again as I wrote the story, and I tried very hard to match Sarek's moods to those of the music. The second time John Ordover called to tell me one of my stories would be published, I was a little calmer. Just a little."

"Fear, Itself"
(STAR TREK: DEEP SPACE NINE)
ROBERT J. MENDENHALL

ake must conquer his fear to save his friends.

" 'Fear, Itself' is my least favorite of anything I've done so far. But, as Dean Wesley Smith preaches, writers are their own worst critics. 'Fear' had no plot to start with, no theme, nothing but a vague idea about some DS9 characters being marooned on a planet of junk and derelict spacecraft, having to build a space ship out of spare parts, and naming the ship the *U.S.S. Frankenstein.* That was the whole idea. The working title was 'Ahoy, Frankenstein!' But as the writing progressed and things like 'plot' began to rear their heads, the story actually developed. They were still marooned, but the focus shifted from the cool Frankenstein angle to an examination of fear and how one deals with it. I was blown away when John called again (another message on my machine), and was amazed that 'Fear, Itself' was the one selected. I had submitted a piece I really cared for, called 'Random Acts of Destiny,' which chronicled Ezri Dax's journey to the symbiont. When I received the rejection notice back on that piece, Dean wrote he liked it, but Paramount had said no."

"Final Entry"
(STAR TREK: VOYAGER)
CYNTHIA K. DEATHERAGE

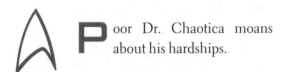

The journal entries of a woman mourning the loss of her family, not knowing the surprise that awaits.

Attempts to contact the author for an interview were unsuccessful.

"The Difficulties of Being Evil"
(STAR TREK: VOYAGER)
CRAIG GIBB

Poor Dr. Chaotica moans about his hardships.

"I've always been an avid *Star Trek* reader, even back when I was fifteen, when the first volume of SNW came out. I saw it in the bookstore and immediately bought it, spending an entire month's worth of allowance on it (allowance was $20 a month and the book with my book club discount and sales tax was just under $20—I'm in Canada, that's where the price difference comes from). I took it home and read through it in a matter of days. That's basically how I found out about the contest—by having the first book in my hands. As I read through it, a few plot possibilities formed in my head, but being too young to enter, I didn't bother writing the stories out. *Strange New Worlds V* was the first volume I was legally old enough to enter. I sent in two stories, got a little lucky, and was published the following year. 'The Difficulties of Being Evil' was one of two stories I submitted to SNW V, the other was also a *Voyager* story. To tell the truth, I personally thought my other story was a little stronger and didn't expect 'Difficulties' to win. But, I guess the editors' tastes were a little different. The idea for this story simply came from watching an episode of *Voyager* that featured Dr. Chaotica—I believe it was the one where Janeway goes undercover as Queen Arachnia. I felt that more could be done with the character of Dr. Chaotica—I wanted to try and get the readers to almost root for him. I tried to flesh out his character a little bit and add that dimension that would hopefully make him more than a stereotypical sci-fi villain, hopefully also encouraging a little sympathy for him. Writing the story was surprisingly easy compared to some of the other things I've tried to do. If I remember correctly, I wrote the whole thing in two or three hours, edited it the next day, then sent it off the day after that. And with my writing, once I put something in a mailbox, I put it out of my mind. By the time early January had rolled around, I had actually forgotten I submitted a story to SNW. I got the call from John Ordover on the first day back to university after the New Year. I came home around 12:30 since I only had morning classes and just as I got in the door, my sister hands me the phone. At first I couldn't quite hear what Mr. Ordover was saying—I'm hard of hearing, and due to feedback with my hearing aids, I have to actually turn them off when using the phone, so they acted like earplugs, and since I just got home, my yappy little dog was so excited to see me that she was barking and whining beside me. I actually had to have Mr. Ordover repeat himself. I acted calm as I got the news, then hung up and ran up and down the hall a few times. I jumped up and down and then called a bunch of family members to let them know. I was in a very good mood for at least a week. And, if I remember correctly, my sister, who is not impressed by all things literary, kept rolling her eyes at me."

"Restoration"
(STAR TREK: VOYAGER)
PENNY A. PROCTOR

 very weary Kes returns to Ocampa.

" 'Restoration' was my only entry that year. I'd written the basic draft some time earlier, almost immediately after the *Voyager* episode 'Fury' aired. It's hard to exaggerate how much I hated that episode for the way it treated the Kes character, for no good reason. I set the story aside, hoping there might be another Kes episode before the series ended that would set things right. (Never happened.) Then, my father became ill over the summer and died in August. Working on the story was grief therapy for me; the story began to seem very personal, and I almost didn't submit it because of that. I mailed it on September 10, 2001. Events of that week made the contest seem less of a priority. Once again, the notification came through

the answering machine. John Ordover called while I was at work. Saved that message, too."

"On the Rocks"
(STAR TREK: VOYAGER)
TG THEODORE

 followup to the episode "Threshold."

TG submitted two stories to the contest. "One made the alternate and would have been included if two stories by the same author were allowed. Again, this story was based on a loose end. We only saw Janeway and Paris' kids for about ten seconds, and then they were just left behind! I wanted to explore what life was like from their point of view. And I wanted to do it through humor."

"Witness"
(STAR TREK: VOYAGER)
DIANA KORNFELD

 female hologram in love with Harry Kim.

Diana commented, "I submitted 'Witness' again for SNW V along with two other stories. This time 'Witness' made the book and, surprisingly enough, the other two made the alternate list. Since this was my third story, the other two stories didn't have a future, but I was thrilled that 'Witness' made it. The idea for 'Witness' came from another aspect of *Trek* I've always been fascinated with—the idea of the holograms and just how much intelligence such a creation would possess. I love the TNG episode where Picard argues for Data's humanity—such an interesting question. At what point does intelligence become sentience? What would happen if a hologram possessed such intelligence? What would such a creature think about the humans on the ship? What kind of life would this being have?"

Diana continued, "I just want to express my appreciation for this incredible opportunity. I'm proud to be a part of it, and I'm always amazed at the quality of the SNW stories—I eagerly await each new installment of this book that allows us ever fresh insights into these characters and this world that we all so much enjoy."

"Fragment"
(STAR TREK: VOYAGER)
CATHERINE E. PIKE

After making it to the Alpha Quadrant, Seven of Nine fears her trip to Terra firma.

Catherine had been fiction writing since junior high. "Oddly enough, I had never considered writing *Trek* stuff until just a few years ago, when a friend at work told me about *Strange New Worlds* and how they were soliciting writers. She wanted to write a Janeway story with me. I started the story (really having no idea

what the contest was about because at that point I hadn't even seen a copy of one of the anthologies), but she never helped me with it, and I left it for lack of direction. She changed jobs a short time later, but she's the one that introduced me to *Trek* fiction as a writer . . . although I had been reading *Trek* fiction for years. For *Strange New Worlds IV* I submitted two *Voyager* stories: a Christmas story called 'Merry Christmas, Captain' and a story called 'A Voice in the Night.' Dean sent back this latter story with some wonderful comments on it. I rewrote it, changed the point of view from Seven of Nine to Naomi Wildman, sent it back in, and it was accepted as 'The Little Captain' in SNW VII!"

When asked about the idea for 'Fragment,' Cathy commented, "*Voyager* was ending, and I wasn't entirely satisfied with 'Endgame' (I don't know that anyone was). I was really curious about what would happen to Seven on Earth. She really had no desire to be on Earth, with family she never remembered, and she was Borg. Surely there would be a lot of prejudice against the Borg on Earth and, thus, against her, perhaps the only drone most people would ever see. I wanted to explore how she was feeling as her friends were going their own ways and she was finding herself truly directionless. It's actually branched out since then to become a potential book. Once I had this premise the story was written very quickly, with few changes. I originally had Naomi leaving a teddy bear behind, but that wasn't right, I knew it wasn't right, and out of the blue the Flotter doll came to me and that put the icing on the story. I found out I won when I got home from grocery shopping one day and there was a message from John Ordover on my machine. As I live just with pets, they didn't quite understand why I was screaming and yelling! I proceeded to call my three best friends (and best critics) and they all screamed, too."

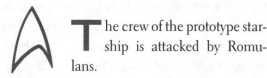

"Who Cries for Prometheus"
(STAR TREK: VOYAGER)
PHAEDRA M. WELDON

The crew of the prototype starship is attacked by Romulans.

Phaedra submitted a story to SNW II, and got cut in the final layout. She received a copy of the table of contents prior to the cut and framed it beside the first anthology. She submitted several stories to SNW III, but none to SNW IV. Winning eluded her until this story. She ended up submitting three stories to SNW V.

Phaedra remarked, "I thought 'Message in a Bottle' was one of the most poignant episodes of the *Voyager* series. What happened to those crew members bothered me for several nights after I watched it. When something bothers me that much, I usually find it's important. I wrote the story not long after I saw the episode. I gave it to my first reader and he insisted I send it back into SNW. So I waited till the contest opened again. John called all the winners by phone, and since I was working late, my husband listened to the message. He called me. 'Hey . . . you need to hear this,' and he played it out for me. I think I did the scream thing again then, too."

"Remnant"
(ENTERPRISE)
JAMES J. AND LOUISA M. SWANN

The *Enterprise* responds to a distress call.

Louisa remarked, "Not only was 'Remnant' the first *Trek* I'd written, it was my first collaboration. My husband Jim shaped the bones of the story; I put on the skin and clothes. Surprisingly enough our marriage survived," she said with a grin. "Jim often thinks about stuff like faster-than-light travel and space ships—what would happen if a colony ship failed in its mission and had to try to get back to earth? And what would happen if *Enterprise* rescued this vessel? The answer to those questions gave birth to 'Remnant'."

Louisa continued, "The writing process was different in that I wasn't sure how to get a feel for the characters before the show premiered, so I went online and found everything I could, including interviews to get a feel for the different voices, every picture I could get my hands on, and so on. Then I turned back to the story we'd started and fleshed it out with the new info. After that, we just had to sit tight until premiere night—which we had to go to my parent's house to watch and tape. I ran over the tape the next day, compared the feel I got for the characters with the story, made a few tweaks, and sent it off to New York. It really wasn't all that difficult, just a little nerve-wracking because it was my first real deadline pressure. Finding out that 'Remnant' was an

SNW V finalist was a whole new ball game. My husband and I take Friday mornings off during the winter and go skiing and I just knew that if a call came, it would come while we were out playing in the snow. Sure enough, we got in that Friday morning and found a message on our answering machine (my husband is a civil engineer with his own business). I screeched and went through the roof—Jim couldn't tell what was going on. Needless to say, we did a bit of celebrating and not much work for the rest of the day."

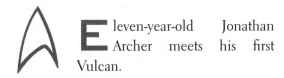

"A Girl for Every Star"
(ENTERPRISE)
JOHN TAKIS

Eleven-year-old Jonathan Archer meets his first Vulcan.

John remarked, "I did not submit any stories to SNW IV. I made an effort to complete one in time, but I couldn't get it to work. I wound up rewriting that one and submitting it to SNW VI two years later. It didn't make the cut. I'm not really surprised, since it was very experimental in tone and touched on sensitive canonical ground. 'A Girl for Every Star' was my only SNW V submission. I managed another submission for SNW VII, but again, it was very experimental and 'out there,' and not terribly polished. It didn't make the cut. I had read a lot about *Enterprise,* and was excited about the show's potential. I knew I would only have the opportunity of viewing one episode, which

wasn't such an obstacle, since I was very interested in a story that would help to bridge the gap between *First Contact* and *Enterprise*. I was actually thinking that submitting an *Enterprise* story would work to my advantage, since there would be so few of them to choose from. Turns out there were more than I expected, but I still got in. It's funny how I found out . . . the call went to my dorm room while I was home for Christmas break. I had forgotten to check the Internet for the winners, so I found out while listening to my voice mail. It was a pleasant surprise."

He concluded, "After my second story got published, my local *Star Trek* club contacted me. I hadn't been aware of their existence, but they offered to take me out and treat me to dinner and a movie. Dinner was good—a nice, juicy steak. The movie was significantly less so—*Battlefield Earth*. My boss and coworkers at Waldenbooks also insisted on me doing a 'book signing.' It was a little embarrassing doing a book signing with only two short stories to offer, but my family thought it was hilarious, so . . . I also got invited to an advance screening of a *Voyager* season premier when the 'Trek club was asked to make comments for the city newspaper. That was a neat experience."

"Hoshi's Gift"
(ENTERPRISE)
KELLE VOZKA

A family heirloom causes problems for Hoshi.

Kelle remembered, "Everyone in my writer's group who was eligible was entering and we were all excited about the new upcoming *Star Trek* series. It was a challenge to write and submit an *Enterprise* story to this anthology. I was very afraid to write a *Trek* story because if you make a mistake with continuity, *Trek* fans tend to notice. It's ironic that I wrote an *Enterprise* story, which I thought was safe because it was new, and still got a character mixed up. I'm not sure what sparked the idea for 'Hoshi's Gift.' My best ideas come on the relaxing, quiet drive home after getting all jazzed up at the workshop I attend and that's where the idea came to me. We had decided as a group to each submit an *Enterprise* story for the anthology. However, the show aired on a Wednesday and the following Monday was the deadline for submissions. So we got together and recorded the show. We had a nice dinner, watched the premiere, and then threw a bunch of story ideas around. When I left the house I still had no concrete ideas for a story. The advice I got was 'just write a good science fiction story and tailor it to *Trek*.' So on the way home I thought up what I felt was a good story, *Trek* or not. I took the next two days off from work. On Thursday I wrote the story and then we had a workshop that night to go over our submission stories. I had originally written the story with two point-of-view characters and it wasn't working well. Friday I rewrote the story from scratch with one point-of-view character and stuck it in an envelope."

Kelle continued, " 'Hoshi's Gift' was the first story I ever submitted anywhere. For my first published story it was extra special because there is so much support, community, and excitement with the winners. Our group, for the fifth anthology, mailed a box of books all around the country so that everyone could sign the books and we all have a copy now of the anthology signed by each writer, one of my most-prized possessions."

Kelle also wanted to mention, "I have to say that I owe any success I have at this point to Loren L. Coleman. It's funny how life works. I was on the phone talking to my sister's son's baby-sitter because I was going to start buying some nutritional products from her and we got to talking. I told her that I was writing science fiction and she got really excited and called Loren, her sister's husband, and conferenced him in to the call. We talked and Loren was in the process of starting a new writing group and invited me in. My first week there he ripped the story I submitted to shreds and I remember just smiling and smiling through the whole thing. He was worried that maybe I was taking it badly. The truth is I was very happy to finally be in a group where I was going to get good, honest, worthwhile critiques. I was finally going to learn how to do this right! The best advice Loren ever gave me was 'Dare to be bad!' and 'Put it in the mail.' It was because of Loren that I submitted to *Strange New Worlds* and learned that yes it is possible to make it as a writer if you just keep it in the mail and keep on writing."

VOLUME SIX

STRANGE NEW WORLDS

DEAN WESLEY SMITH, WITH JOHN J. ORDOVER
AND PAULA M. BLOCK, EDITORS

JUNE, 2003   (357PP)

TRADE PAPERBACK

"Whales Weep Not"
(THIRD PRIZE)
(STAR TREK)
JUANITA NOLTE

 detective investigates the disappearance of a prominent whale biologist.

Juanita had submitted a mystery novel for the Malice Domestic contest. She didn't win, but she had so much fun writing it, she next set her sights on penning a science fiction mystery story. When asked about how she discovered *Strange New Worlds*, Juanita commented, "My daughter Samantha is a second generation Trekkie. Her favorites are *Star Trek: The Next*

Generation and *Voyager*. She not only watches all of the shows, but also reads most of the novels. She had just discovered *Strange New Worlds* IV and V. She was home from college, handed me the book, and said, 'Mom, you should enter this contest.' The deadline was in three weeks, so I wrote the story and submitted it. I know the characters from the original series and the movie *Star Trek IV: The Voyage Home* was my favorite. The missing person angle seemed like a mystery line I could tug at. I sent it in and really forgot about it. When they called, it took me a minute to realize what they were talking about; of course I was ecstatic upon learning that I'd placed third. I had to go back and reread my own story. I couldn't even remember what I had written. Being published was a great morale booster. It gave me a much-needed motivational jolt knowing that someone actually liked my writing besides my family. Seeing your name in print is a writer's high. I thank them for that."

"One Last Adventure"
(STAR TREK)
MARK ALLEN AND CHARITY ZEGERS

 renegade Romulan buys the opportunity to destroy Captain Kirk.

Attempts to contact the authors for an interview were unsuccessful.

"Marking Time"
(STAR TREK)
PAT DETMER

 McCoy confronts a despondent Kirk after the events with the Guardian.

Pat submitted eight stories to SNW V without success. "I turned in maybe six or seven this time, and three or four were ones I'd written earlier and sent back in at the request of Dean, who liked them, but didn't have the spot for them before. My mother was dying of cancer, and as I wrote the story, I thought that's why it was so dark. Only after I'd won and read it months later in the pages of the book did I realize that the whole thing was about *me* and my high-stress upper-management work situation where I eventually and deliberately martyred myself for what I believe was the common good. The message for me personally: Martyrdom is overrated. . . .

"It was a real revelation to me when I realized that I wrote the whole goddamned thing and didn't even know it was about me until much, much later. Didn't know I could do that!"

"Ancient History"
(STAR TREK)
ROBERT J. MENDENHALL

 Scotty and Captain Bateson have something in common besides being displaced in time.

" 'Ancient History' had been a SNW V submission which had made Dean's alternate list for that year. I resubmitted it to SNW VI with some minor tweaking of the opening scene. Of the three that have seen print, this is my favorite. I love the Scotty of the later years and wondered what might have happened to him after he found himself alone in the twenty-fourth century. The same thought occurred for Morgan Bateson, and although Kelsey Grammer said less than a paragraph of lines in *The Next Generation* episode in which he appeared, I was taken with the potential of the character. Bateson was another character ripped from his own time. And although their disappearance from their own time was many years apart, their reemergence in the twenty-fourth century was relatively close. I wanted these two to have history together, but I didn't want them to be friends. I wanted them to be enemies. Rivals. What could fuel that? A woman, of course. And Scotty's only real on screen love was Mira Romaine, who we never saw nor heard about again. There it was. The rest was easy. I put Scotty in a natural setting, a saloon, and let nature take its course. Of course, when he called John got my machine again. This time there was a twinge of regret swirled in the elation. With this sale, I knew that I was no longer eligible to enter SNW. But, what a ride."

"Bum Radish: Five Spins on a Turquoise Reindeer"
(STAR TREK)
TG THEODORE

 Scotty was a miracle worker even in his youth.

"About the title: It came from an online competition in the AOL Strange New Writers forum. A new writer asked Dean if titles made a difference, and of course Dean said he doesn't look at titles before reading the story. The same person asked if a really *wild* title would attract attention. So I started a little game about the nuttiest title we could come up with. I won with 'Bum Radish.' Dean said if I could write a story that would match the tone of that title, that I'd win awards. Oddly enough, it turned out to be a rather sweet little Christmas story. I worked my way backward from the title.

Reindeer = Christmas.
Bum Radish = Sick = McCoy (or his dad)
Turquoise Reindeer = Ride
Broken Reindeer = Scotty
Christmas = Children

Scotty and McCoy meet as children at Christmastime. Scotty's mom was named for my Junior Prom date in 1972. She LOVED it! I only submitted 'Radish' and my previous alternate for VI. (The title of my alternate was 'Wake Me When the Planet Gets Back'—A humorous DS9 story which again made the alternate list.)"

TG wanted to add: "SNW is a GREAT opportunity. Many thanks to Dean, John Ordover, and Paula Block! It's much like the open submission policy that TV *Trek* had for such a long time. I've made many great friends (and contacts). Hopefully the friendships will continue and the contacts will prove fruitful!"

"A Piece of the Pie"
(STAR TREK)
G. WOOD

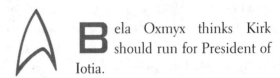 **B**ela Oxmyx thinks Kirk should run for President of Iotia.

Guy remarked, "I came up with the idea for the story in the year 2000. Both Canada and the U.S. were having elections. I started thinking about Bela Oxmyx and wondering what would happen if his term was limited. What is he going to do and who should succeed him in office?"

"The Soft Room" (SECOND PRIZE) (STAR TREK: THE NEXT GENERATION)
Geoffrey Thorne

 A Vulcan woman helps a man restore the damaged parts of his mind.

Geoffrey remarked, "I've been a *Star Trek* fan since I first watched the TOS reruns with my dad as a kid. Although it sometimes drifts away from true science fiction, the multiethnic themes, the triumph of wisdom and inquiry over bigotry and fear, the simple notion that we *can* all get along—these were like manna to me and still are. In *Star Trek* we are at our best when we most fully embrace our diversities. Violence only as a last resort. Knowledge as the ultimate panacea for what ails. I know some people like to knock Trekkers but, really, they do so at their own ethical peril. You can't beat *Trek* values and I defy anyone to try. I stuck with the show and even read the first round of novelizations—I still have Blish's *Star Trek* and Bear's *Corona* around. I also have the amazing novelization of *The Wrath of Khan* by Vonda McIntyre. I stopped reading *Trek* lit after that for some reason. Not sure why. It certainly had nothing to do with the quality. Maybe it was the influx of girls and dance clubs devouring my spare time. Anyway, when TNG came on I was out of control. Klingons allied with the Federation? New aliens? An android? Come on! How can you beat that? I'm not rabid. There are a

few episodes I could have done without (and which I'll never mention) but, you know, *Trek* was back! Real *Star Trek*. So I stuck with it all the way through *Voyager*, though, for some reason I had trouble synching up with DS9 for a while. Not sure why, but I'm over it now. I became minorly disillusioned with *Voyager*. I felt they had this *amazing* gutsy premise ('Palestinians' and 'Israelis' forced to coexist and accept each other in order to survive) that they immediately allowed to become diluted. I watched the show through this filter for the first two seasons and was so upset that I started asking my friends who still read *Trek* lit, if any of it was any good. There was something about *Voyager* that made me think the powers that be had forgotten what 'real' *Star Trek* was and I needed a booster shot. I was pointed directly to Peter David's *New Frontier* series and was immediately sucked back in. There were a host of authors whose names I didn't know and I started to dig in. The Reeves-Stevenses, DeCandido, Mangels, and Martin (these are just the first ones that come to mind). These folks were doing wicked cool, innovative *Trek* stories in ways I hadn't thought people would ever be allowed."

Geoffrey continued, "It was during this time that I came across *Strange New Worlds*—number III, I think. I submitted one story to SNW V, something about Tasha Yar before she got off her brutal home planet. It was rejected, but with a note at the bottom from Dean Smith saying I was a good writer and to send more the following year. So I did. I sent in five stories to SNW VI and 'The Soft Room,' amazingly, took silver. I hesitate to talk too much about how I thought of that story because I don't want to kill it for anyone who hasn't read it. Let's just say that I saw a loose end in TOS and wanted to tie it up. People who've read it seem to like it."

"Protecting Data's Friends"
(STAR TREK: THE NEXT GENERATION)
Scott William Carter

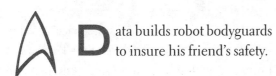

ata builds robot bodyguards to insure his friend's safety.

Scott commented, "I was aware of the original series from an early age, but I became a 'fan' in high school when *The Next Generation* premiered. I've been a writer since an early age, but I decided to get serious about it right before my first child was born. *Strange New Worlds* was a great market for new writers, and since I was also a fan, it seemed like a good thing to try."

Scott continued, "Well, my original idea was to do a riff on 'The Trouble with Tribbles' (hence the self-replicating robots), but the eventual story ended up quite a bit different. I had a lot of fun writing it, which, if you're a fiction writer, is always a good sign.

"John Ordover left a message on my answering machine telling me I'd made it into the anthology, which was a pretty nifty way to find out! 'Protecting Data's Friends' was my first sale, and I'm pretty appreciative of Dean Wesley Smith for that. In the last few years, I've gone on to sell over twenty other short stories, to *Analog, Asimov's, Weird Tales*, and lots of other places, but none of those sales had quite the same feeling as that first one."

"The Human Factor"
(STAR TREK: THE NEXT GENERATION)
Russ Crossley

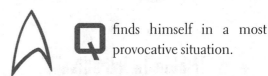

finds himself in a most provocative situation.

Russ said, "I've a large collection of *Star Trek* fiction dating back to the 70s. I've read a lot of other SF as well. I'd always understood that the publisher would not accept works by unknown authors, so when I started writing seriously I decided to get known first then submit ideas to Pocket Books. Thankfully, two very bright men named John Ordover and Dean Wesley Smith made it easier to get into the world of *Star Trek* fiction by starting *Strange New Worlds*. The simpler answer is if you love something why not take a shot at trying to write it, and use your imagination to take the characters where Hollywood budgets can't?"

With *Strange New Worlds*, "In the first year I met Dean Wesley Smith at a writers convention and sent in my first story. As I recall the deadline was very short. And the good thing is Dean always gives feedback if you include a SASE. I submitted three stories to SNW VI. The idea for 'The Human Factor' came from a discussion with Dean about three characters in *Trek* he doesn't care too much for. I said I'd write a story with all three as a challenge. He said go for it and I did. My writing process is always the same: I write the best story I can. I have my wife, who's also a writer, read it and give me feedback, and then I mail it. I absolutely do not try to fix stories that don't work.

I throw them out and start again. I usually spend no more than a week on a short story, but I can write one in a day. If I write it that fast, then I put it aside and look at it later in the week. My best stories are usually written fast when my internal editor is shut off."

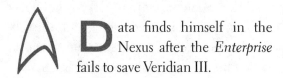

"Tribble In Paradise"
(STAR TREK: THE NEXT GENERATION)
LOUISA M. SWANN

Data finds himself in the Nexus after the *Enterprise* fails to save Veridian III.

Louisa remarked, "Getting into SNW V really started the ball rolling. I figured we'd made it once, it wouldn't hurt to keep trying. When SNW VI was announced, however, Jim's business was really swamped, so I was on my own for this one. I sent in two stories and 'Tribble' . . . made it! I got to talk to John Ordover this time in person—what a thrill! To top it off, several of my writing friends from all over the country and Canada—including Annie—made it into SNW VI as well. Fun stuff! 'Tribble in Paradise' was almost born in one sitting. I love Data and I love tribbles. All I had to do was figure out how to put them together. One of the things I'd always pondered about was what happened to everyone else while Picard was in the Nexus. Here was my chance to explore that scenario. Bingo—story done. Wish they were all that easy," she said with a grin.

"Fabrications"
(STAR TREK: DEEP SPACE NINE)
BRETT HUDGINS

Another example of why one should never mess with Garak.

What led Brett to writing *Trek* stories? "At my school library I discovered that *Star Trek* wasn't limited to television or movies—there were books! Not as many then as now, but perfect brain candy for a voracious reader with a pre-existing interest in the subject matter. I started with the James Blish adaptations and quickly moved on to the Pocket originals. It was also around this time that my interest in writing ignited. Teachers praised my talent and I realized that I liked telling stories, and that maybe I could entertain readers the way so many authors had entertained me. With *Star Trek* so new and fresh to me at the time, it was only natural that I'd want to write stories about some of my favorite characters. In a way, my eventual publications were seventeen years in the making. How did I hear about SNW? In a panic, that's how—right after the deadline for the first contest passed and I realized I might have missed my best opportunity to be a *Star Trek* author. Oh man, was I choked. Fortunately, the contest became an annual event. For volumes II through V, I submitted a total of seventeen stories, with my best result being a single story on Dean Wesley Smith's SNW V, alternate list, 'Phasers, Blood and Babes'—I think he just liked the title."

Brett continued, " 'Fabrications' was one of ten stories I entered in SNW VI, seven new and three from the previous year that Dean invited me to resubmit. Interestingly, 'Fabrications' was one of the resubmissions. Obviously it made a better impression on him the second time around. The idea, very simply, came from form, not plot. I'd been having virtually no success writing from the traditional third-person perspective and I wanted to try a story in a more intimate, personal voice. The best voice of that sort is Garak's. With the double-edged title already in mind—'Fabrications,' about a tailor telling lies (or is he?)—I began what is essentially a monologue, letting Garak play his charming and ominous wiles against a nameless Bajoran would-be terrorist. Of every SNW story I wrote, this was the easiest, taking only a couple of hours on a Saturday afternoon and surviving virtually unchanged from the first draft. Finding out I'd won was, to trot out the old cliché, a dream come true. The culmination of seventeen years of ambition, if not constant practice (I didn't write much *Trek* before SNW). The feelings of triumph were particularly acute because I'd invested so much effort and hope in previous years of the contest and took each failure very hard indeed. But I never stopped trying."

"Urgent Matter"
(STAR TREK: DEEP SPACE NINE)
ROBERT J. LABAFF

 A changeling from the Great Link arrives on the station for a priority mission.

Why did Robert start writing *Trek* stories? "To tell you the truth, I would start to think of what happened at the end of a really good episode and if the show (TNG, DS9, or VOY) ever went to the big screen, how the producers could roll the ending into the opening of a movie. I discovered the first (SNW) while shopping for books with my Christmas cash. The second one was already set to be published by then. I did write up a couple of pages of various story ideas, but never really focused on them to enter in Book Four or Five. I was reading Book Five at lunch at work one day and my associate asked which series it was from, and I explained how and when the books had started. She was a college student majoring in English lit. I made a joke about my past dreams of writing and she offered to read them for me. She really motivated me to see what I could do. She helped and encouraged me to pull it all together."

The idea for 'Urgent Matter' arrived as follows. "As I watched Odo say good-bye and join the Great Link, I started thinking of how he and Kira could be together again. I knew that it couldn't be a quick and easy reunion, and I remembered how Barclay recreated the crew of *Enterprise* to spend time with them, I decided why not? I had other stories that I was working on as well, but of them all I decided to put all my time into just this one. I was a fifty-plus-hours-a-week retail manager who also drove one hour and ten minutes to and from work everyday. At one point I really did not think I would have time for my associate to reread it and then correct any new issues before sending it out. The process wasn't time consuming, but finding the time was. I would try to rewrite what I could while on lunch and then stay up late retyping corrections and adding on to it as I went. When I would get three or four new pages done I would let my associate take it home to proofread it and find any new issues. I would have to say that finding out I won was a life-changing experience. *No joke.* Truth be told, my 13-year-old son played the answering machine the day the call came in. He forgot to tell me about it. A couple of days went by, I was at an all-time low with my career and was looking to find a new job. We were having car problems and a leaking roof on our house. All in all I was off for New Year's Day. I had been cleaning off the roof of our house for hours and had come in to eat lunch. The answering machine light was blinking, but I hit all messages button instead of new messages. I have no clue who it was that actually called that day because as soon as I heard the message from publishers notifying me that I won and how to contact them, I was on the phone to my wife to let her know. I then was on the computer e-mailing Mr. Ordover all the info he needed. A week or so after I decided if I could be lucky enough to be published, I decided to try interviewing for a new job. Sure enough after only one interview, I had a new place to work making more per hour and better benefits for my family."

"Best Tools Available"
(STAR TREK: DEEP SPACE NINE)
SHAWN MICHAEL SCOTT

 N og takes the Kobayashi Maru test.

Shawn remembered, "I had to be about five or six years old. My brother, Joe, who's seven years older than me, was a kid during the original series' first run. He would watch the shows in syndication every chance he got. I remember seeing 'Arena,' and the Gorn scared the stuffing out of me. I was hooked. My brother and I, because of the difference in our ages, didn't have much in common, but we did have *Star Trek.* Even today, we still have *Trek.* When I was in school, all I ever wanted to be was an artist. I wanted to draw comic books. Due to my college-prep curriculum, my classes always conflicted with the available art classes, so I had to drop art. In my junior year, my English teacher encouraged me to write. She saw a creative spark in my essays and writing assignments. I tapped a creative vein that I didn't know I had. For years, I would come up with my own little storylines and plots, but never really thought about doing anything with it until a very good friend of mine gave me *The Making of Star Trek: Deep Space Nine*, by Judith and Garfield Reeves-Stevens. There was a chapter in the book called 'How to Write for *Deep Space Nine.*' It gave an address to write to in order to receive an information packet on submitting screenplays. I sent for it and found it informative and discouraging at the same time. Informative because it provided a behind-the-scenes look at the *Trek* franchise and discouraging because I didn't have the foggiest idea of how to write a screenplay. I had what I thought to be a great story idea, one that I even hope to recycle someday, but I didn't know how to voice it. There was also another little side note in the packet, almost an afterthought. A summation called 'Rules for Submitting Novels' (or something to that effect . . . it's been a long time and the details are fuzzy). I thought 'why not?' From that day on, I worked at sculpting my story ideas. I honed my craft by working with a comic book-themed amateur press association called *Teams N' Titans*. The feedback I received from the association's other members was invaluable and helped me mold my stories even more. When I first heard of *Strange New Worlds*, I felt my ship had finally arrived. I saw the first volume in a bookstore and thought 'HOT DAMN!' "

Shawn procrastinated and didn't submit any stories until SNW VI. "Why? Probably fear of rejection. Writing little superhero stories for a small clique of fans was one thing, but putting myself out there for criticism from an honest-to-God editor. . . . I just didn't know if I could do it. I didn't know if I had the raw talent to hold a real editor's attention. Now, as corny as it may sound, something sparked in me after my wife and I had to put our dog, Sara, to sleep. She had been suffering from a brain tumor for months. Something about facing that mortality up close, even though it was only a pet, made me realize that I wasn't getting any younger and opportunity only knocks so often—this and that my wife, Laura, got tired of listening to my inane ramblings about stories that I had in my head but not on paper. I was always a huge fan of Ray Walston and thrilled to see him play Boothby, Starfleet Academy's curmudgeon groundskeeper. I also knew that I would love to see more of him. Since Nog was officially in *Trek* lore as going to the academy, I figured the two must cross paths sometime. So the story started out as Nog encountering Boothby and benefiting from his sage advice. I then went on to write about just how Nog followed his advice. What resulted turned into a nice little coming-of-age story with a side note on racism and tolerance."

Was it Shawn's only submission to SNW VI? "Not only was it my only submission to SNW VI, it was my first submission anywhere. I never thought it would be selected. I didn't have the first damn clue about what an editor looks for, so I just wrote it as I would like to read it. Not too flowery, not too descriptive, but just sparse enough to let the readers fill in their own blanks. My wife proofread it about nine times to make sure my spelling and grammar were correct. The story was also written in a marathon six-hour session after realizing that the deadline was less than two weeks away. I wasn't thrilled with the ending, but I knew that if I went back to it, I'd never send it in. I promised myself that something, anything, would be submitted. Finding out was pretty amusing. It was December 30. My wife had stayed home sick that day. She didn't answer the phone all day, leaving the voice mail to take messages. Around 4:30 in the afternoon, she got up to let our dogs out and decided to check the messages. When she heard the message from John Ordover stating that 'Best Tools Available' had made the book, she wasn't sure she understood the message, so she played it back. When she realized what it was, she threw the phone down and screamed. Needless to say, the dogs rushed to her side. She tried to call me at work, but I had left early to run some errands. I neglected to turn my cell phone on, so she couldn't reach me. She tried calling all the places she thought I might go, only to find I had just left. So, around 5:30, I pulled into the garage and began to get out of the car. The garage door swung open, and there's my wife, standing in the door, with a very distressed look on her face. 'What did I do now?' I thought. 'Did you check the messages?' she demanded. My mind raced . . . did I do something wrong? 'Uh . . . no,' came the uncertain reply. She proceeded to break down in tears as she told me that 'Best Tools Available' was going to be published. I was stunned. The house could have lifted up off the foundation and dropped on me and I wouldn't have been as shocked as I was at that moment. I'll never forget it. Shawn . . . welcome to the wonderful world of *Star Trek*."

Shawn concluded, "The whole experience has been surreal for me. As a lifelong *Trek* fan, to see my name attached to a *Star Trek* book and appear on Startrek.com and to have a profile and my picture in *Communicator*, the *Trek* magazine, is just about as insane as it can get. To have friends and family ask me to sign their copies of SNW VI is just too much. I'm not a movie star or a celebrity. My autograph? Are you kidding me? I give it to the Mortgage Company every month and they're not impressed. I'm like a kid in a candy store when it comes to talking about 'Best Tools.' "

"Homemade"
(STAR TREK: VOYAGER)
Elizabeth A. Dunham

 ooking a surprise for a soon to be arriving guest.

Elizabeth commented, "When did I realize I was a *Star Trek* fan? Oddly enough, my introduction to *Trek* was not via the TV, but via James Blish's novelizations of the episodes. They came in big omnibuses in my local library, and I started reading them in early high school in preparation for the release of *Star Trek: The Motion Picture* so I could enjoy it with my geek boyfriend (who is still now one of my best friends). (Yeah, I was a geek, too.) And while I steadfastly refused to watch *Next Generation* for about a year after it began, once I watched, I was hooked—and would watch any form of *Trek*. Funny thing: My love of ST has moved on to my son, Wesley, now almost thirteen (and no, he wasn't named after 'the boy'). When he was a baby, *The Next Generation* music could stop his crying."

She continued, "I'd read *Star Trek* first, so it was a natural. *And* . . . what fan doesn't like to explore more of the wonderful universe that's already been created? I submitted a story for SNW IV. It didn't win. I'm a mom. I had always wondered (after, in part, reading Jeri Taylor's 'Mosaic') how Gretchen Janeway had coped with the loss of her daughter. I had actually written the beginning and end of 'Homemade' years before I finished it. They just came to me (sounds like a cliché, but it's really true). Then, just before the SNW VI deadline, I took a day off from work and finished it. I got some feedback from a writing buddy that I should set it more clearly in the *Trek* universe, and that's where the italicized flashbacks grew out of. I submitted it, and figured, eh, nothing lost, nothing gained. Oddly enough, on December 31, 2002, I looked at the file on my computer and thought, well, I didn't win again. Came home and almost erased John Ordover's message because it started out almost like a telemarketing voice mail . . . 'Hi, this is John Ordover,' in radio-type voice . . . and then my brain processed his next phrase, 'from *Star Trek* Pocket Books . . .' and I literally started screaming. I called everyone I knew. A buddy of mine, a local folksinger, actually recorded the voice mail for me and set it to music. I still have the tape. It's entitled 'Beth Gets Published, Disco Mix.' "

"Seven and Seven"
(STAR TREK: VOYAGER)
KEVIN HOSEY

 Seven of Nine meets Gary Seven.

What inspired Kevin? "Seven of Nine and Gary Seven are two of my favorite characters. I realized one day that they are *very* similar. Both are human beings who have been drastically altered by an alien race. So I thought it would be fun to team them up and play them off each other. Basically I develop a main idea and just start writing. My brain takes over and it pretty

much writes itself from there. In fact, the only frustrating thing about it is I can't type as fast as my brain writes. Then I go back and begin editing. Once I am happy with it, I go back again and edit to fit the 7,500-word limit. That's pretty tough because I sometimes have to delete scenes I really like."

"The End of Night"
(STAR TREK: VOYAGER)
PAUL J. KAPLAN

 Voyager is responsible for destroying the entire universe and only Captain Kirk can stop them.

Paul commented, "I'd always been aware of *Star Trek*—there was a kid in my kindergarten class who had a gold uniform shirt that I thought was really cool—but I probably didn't become a true fan until 1980 or so. I was ten or twelve or something, and my mom let me browse in a used bookstore while she shopped next door. I discovered the Blish and Foster adaptations, and I was hooked. I tracked down all the old Bantam novels and bought every one of the Pocket Books when they came out. My favorite novels are still from those early Pocket days—Vonda McIntyre's *The Entropy Effect*, John M. Ford's *The Final Reflection*, Diane Carey's *Dreadnought!* and *Battlestations!*, and Ann Crispin's *Yesterday's Son* to name a few. Back then, before *The Next Generation*, the Internet, or DVDs, the books were the only 'new' *Trek* there was. And I bought every one they printed for years, until there were just too many to keep up with. Plus, I grew up; college, law school, starting a family and a career all ate into my hobby time. But I never lost my love for it. I've seen every episode of every series, and I still pick up a novel when I can. The Internet makes it a lot easier to know what's out there, even if I can't read them all. I started writing *Trek* for two reasons, really. First, it was a way to connect with characters and ideas I really enjoyed. And second, it was the hubris of youth. I'd read the novels and think, 'Hell, I could do that.' It's one of those things that's so easy to say when you're a goofy kid and don't really know how awful your stuff really is. I wrote a bunch of stuff in high school, just for my friends and me—a bunch of parodies and some 'serious' stuff, but all starring us on a ship of our own. Real kid stuff. I started a *Trek* novel in college but never went anywhere with it, and then I didn't write a word of fiction for about ten years. Then came *Strange New Worlds*."

Paul continued, "I just stumbled across volume one in a store. I hadn't heard anything about it, and I was amazed that they were opening *Trek* up to the fans like this. Getting amateurs published in a real live book—it was amazing. Those same thoughts came flooding back—'Hell, I could do that'—but, like so many would-be 'writers,' I didn't do anything about it. Volumes two, three, and four all came and went, and I never carved out the time to sit down and write. Finally, in 2001, I got serious, and I submitted one story to SNW V. It took me about two months to write, in little bursts here and there, and I loved it. Thought it was great—I *knew* it would win. And, of course, I didn't get in the book at all. That story was 'The

End of Night.' I had no idea why it hadn't worked—I was too much of a newbie to even enclose a SASE when I submitted it. I figured I didn't need the story back, and it never occurred to me that Dean would actually take the time to give feedback—which he does, much to his credit. So I lost. But I believed in that story. I just really liked it. So I submitted it the next year to SNW VI, without changing a word. And this time—hey presto!—I became a published author. I found out online. I gave them my home number, but of course I was at work during the day, so I missed John Ordover's call. I just came across the list online, on either PsiPhi.org or TrekBBS.com. John's message was on my machine when I got home that night, so I knew it wasn't a typo. The idea for the story started with that first line—the end of everything. I wanted to tell a 'big' story, and that just seemed like a good place to start. I do most of my thinking in the shower—much to my wife's chagrin—and the story just kind of took shape from there, over the course of many mornings and a lot of hot water."

"Hidden"
(STAR TREK: VOYAGER)
JAN STEVENS

 Janeway's nightmare becomes a horrifying reality.

Jan remarked, "I'm not sure what caused my writing epiphany. I just started dreaming up *Voyager* stories and writing them down one day about seven years ago. Several yellow pads, stubby pencils, and aching hands later, I had a couple of stories to show for it. Writing suddenly became a passion, so I bought a computer (the heck with yellow pads!) and started taking a few classes in novel and short story writing at a local vo-tech school for fun. I was very fortunate to have two excellent teachers because, in retrospect, my early writing really was lousy. Continued practice and reading other author's work shows me how much I've learned and how much I still have to learn. That is why being chosen for the anthologies is so amazing to me."

Jan heard about the SNW contest on the AOL *Trek* boards. "I already had a few story ideas, so I began submitting one or two stories at a time beginning with SNW III. I kept my hopes high, but success eluded me. One rejected story was a comedy that I thought was pretty good. Every one of my fellow Trekkers who read it thought it was hilarious, but I guess comedy is a hard sell. Even though those early stories weren't chosen, I got several nice comments and greatly appreciated suggestions from Dean Wesley Smith about my stories. Those thoughtful comments helped me improve my writing, and eventually I learned what it took to write a winning story. [The idea behind 'Hidden' came] when my friend Lee, my comrade-in-arms and fellow Trekker, had a crazy dream about being aboard a starship surrounded by eerie orange lights. She thought it would make a good suspense story, so I expanded the premise and submitted it to SNW V. Dean sent it back with the comment that my open ending didn't work, but he would reconsider it for SNW VI if I changed the ending. His suggestion led to a simple one-page change that made all the difference. In late 2002, I got a wonderful after-Christmas present in the form of a phone message from John Ordover that 'Hidden' had been chosen to appear in SNW VI. I still have trouble believing that I was chosen to be published along with so many talented writers. That experience humbled me. It still does."

"Widow's Walk"
(STAR TREK: VOYAGER)
MARY SCOTT-WIECEK

 he journal entries of Anne Carey, Joe's wife.

"Because Dean had asked me to resubmit 'Widow's Walk,' I knew it had a good shot, unless dozens of people submitted something better. Since it's always possible that dozens of people will submit something better, I did send in two other stories, hoping my 'something better' would trump theirs. But they didn't even trump my own 'Widow's Walk.' I really liked one of the other submissions, but I liked 'Widow's Walk,' too, so I wasn't disappointed. 'Widow's Walk' was a follow-up to 'The Ones Left Behind.' When they killed off Joe Carey in *Voyager*'s seventh season, my thoughts immediately went to the fictional family I'd created for him in the earlier story. I also thought it would be a good hook—to open a story with someone *not* being pleased to see *Voyager* come home. The story's focus changed a bit as I wrote it, though, and ended up being a 'father and son' type of story. That's a powerful bond, the sort a wife/mother can appreciate, even if it means she might lose them both to this thing that they love—space exploration. I found out about the win via a message from John Ordover on my machine, again, and again after the same post-holiday drive with the husband and kids. It was still wonderful, of course, but I'll admit that it wasn't as exciting as the first two times. Isn't that awful? Look how fast you can take these things for granted!"

"Savior"
(ENTERPRISE)
JULIE HYZY

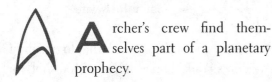 rcher's crew find themselves part of a planetary prophecy.

"I sent four stories in for SNW VI. As a matter of fact, I never thought 'Savior' would win because I thought it might be too controversial . . . a bit Jesus-y. But, Dean's right. We should never assume we know what an editor wants. And so, after a number of false starts on that story, I wrote it. The idea came during Easter Mass, to be honest. I was sitting there, letting my mind wander, and I thought, 'What if a time-traveler had stopped the crucifixion?' And then I kind of wondered how Picard would have stopped the time-traveler . . . but then the more I thought about it, the more I wanted it to be an Archer story. Once I made that shift, the story worked itself out."

Julie continued, "I missed John's call this time. But I kept it alive on my answering machine for a long time afterward. It was a huge

thrill to make it into a second volume of SNW and when I found out that another of my submissions had made it onto the alternate list, I was absolutely ecstatic. That felt really good."

"Preconceptions"
(ENTERPRISE)
PENNY A. PROCTOR

 teenage Trip participates in a unique summer program.

Penny remembered, "Oh, I went all out for SNW VI, in part because of encouragement from other authors in SNW V (a great group!), and in part because my ego wanted to make it three in a row. I submitted four stories—two for *Enterprise*, one for *Deep Space Nine*, and one that crossed between *Next Generation*, DS9, and *Voyager*. Not surprisingly, 'Preconceptions' was inspired by an episode of the series. Early on, *Enterprise* aired an episode called *Strange New World*. I thought the behavior of Trip in that episode was inconsistent. On the one hand, he becomes absolutely paranoid about Vulcans; convinced they cannot be trusted. On the other hand, it is the memory of a Vulcan teacher he had in high school that finally convinces him to lay down his weapon. I began to wonder about that teacher. How could Trip mistrust Vulcans so much as a race and yet still have so much respect for one individual Vulcan? It was an interesting puzzle. And yes, John Ordover's message was waiting for me on the answering machine one day after work. I kept all three messages until a five-day power failure in 2003 wiped them out (along with everything in my refrigerator and freezer).”

"Cabin E-14"
(ENTERPRISE)
SHANE ZERANSKI

P hlox visits Daniel's room.

Shane submitted one story to SNW V. He said, "The story was called 'Payback'—a DS9 comedy piece that takes place backwards, starting at the end and touching every major character. That backward *Seinfeld* episode sparked the idea. This is still my favorite story; why it wasn't accepted, I'm not sure, but it's definitely the story I think is the best. It took much longer, a lot of plotting and attention to detail since it was written backward. It took a few weeks. By this time, I'd made the anthologies w/ only one story apiece, and I fully expected to make the cut for V . . . but never got the call. So goes it. I sent in 'Payback' again for SNW VI and then wrote 'Cabin E-14' for insurance. 'Cabin E-14' was accepted. I like that one a lot, but not as much as my DS9 story. I don't quite remember where that story came from, other than the temporal cold war plotline during the first season of *Enterprise*. Wrote that one in about three days."

"Our Million-Year Mission" (GRAND PRIZE)
(SPECULATIONS)
ROBERT T. JESCHONEK

T he continuing adventures of the *UberEnterprise* and its crew.

Robert commented, "I wanted to shake things up by stretching the characters, technology, and concepts of *Star Trek* as far as I could. By setting the story a million years after the original series, I was able to let my imagination run wild. Even as I ventured into new territory, I tried to make the story a tribute to the spirit of *Star Trek*, with its sense of infinite wonder and possibilities. From the start, I had a good feeling about 'Our Million-Year Mission' . . . but completing the story had its rocky moments. When my wife and first reader, Wendy, finished reading the first draft, she said that half of the story was strong, and half was in need of drastic revision. According to Wendy, the lacking half was the original sequence featuring Data and Geordi. In the first draft, Data was deactivated from the start, and Geordi and Reg Barclay spent half the story working to return him to consciousness. Wendy, whose editorial instincts are excellent, said that she felt strongly that the deactivated Data sequence dragged. With just a few days until deadline, I decided to take my wife's advice and rewrite half of the story. Wendy was right. In the rewrite, I kept Data conscious—and seemingly insane—from

the start. Making Data a more active participant from the start injected needed energy into
the story. As the deadline raced closer, I
wrapped the rewrite, handed off the new draft
to Wendy, and held my breath. She loved the
new draft. I made a final pass through the manuscript, giving it a quick polish, and mailed it.
As 'Our Million-Year Mission' headed for
Pocket Books, I felt tremendous relief and optimism. At least until I saw the film *Star Trek
Nemesis*. In my story, set one million years after
the original series, Data was a featured character. In *Nemesis*, however, Data was destroyed. I
had not foreseen this possibility while writing
the story; I now thought for sure that my story's
chances of making it into SNW VI were nonex-
istent. I completely gave up hope that 'Our
Million-Year Mission' would see print. As dis-
mal as things seemed, the story not only made
the cut but also won the grand prize. The editors used it as the basis of a new category, 'Speculations,' which would feature stories that bend
or break continuity to expand *Trek* in new directions.

"Funny story: After I had submitted 'Our
Million-Year Mission' but before the SNW VI
winners were announced, my wife, Wendy,
and I visited SNW editor John Ordover at the
Pocket Books offices in New York City. On a
bulletin board in John's office, I glimpsed a list
of winners for SNW VI, but I could not bear to
read it and immediately looked away after spotting the title. If I had kept reading, I no doubt
would have seen my own name. Later, after
Wendy and I returned home, John Ordover
and Dean Smith called and told me that I had
won the grand prize."

"The Beginning"
(SPECULATIONS)
ANNIE REED

 dying child tries a radical
new treatment.

Annie remarked, "The year after the first
Strange New Worlds anthology was published,
I attended The Kris and Dean Show sponsored
by my local writers group. The K&D Show was
a two-day seminar on both the craft and busi-
ness of writing presented by Dean Wesley
Smith and Kristine Kathryn Rusch. During the
seminar, Dean talked about the *Strange New
Worlds* contest and how to submit stories for
SNW II. I went out and bought SNW, read the
stories in it, and submitted a story to the SNW
II contest."

She submitted stories to each of the contests
until she struck gold with her submission in
SNW VI. "There's actually an interesting story
behind 'The Beginning.' I submitted an earlier
(and much rougher) draft of 'The Beginning'
to SNW II. It didn't make the initial cut, but I
received a nice note from Dean. Then I started
hanging around the SNW *Trek* board on AOL
and learned that I could resubmit a story if I
rewrote it. Well, my husband always liked the
basic story of 'The Beginning,' and after a couple of years of writing and studying the craft, I
realized that it was the manuscript that didn't
work, not the story. I rewrote 'The Beginning'
and submitted it to SNW IV. It made the alternate list that year, only I didn't know it because
the manuscript was lost somewhere in New

York and was never returned to me. So I didn't know I should have resubmitted to SNW V. When I did find out it was an alternate, I resubmitted it to SNW VI and it made it in the anthology that year. I guess that's a lesson in never giving up. So essentially four years after I wrote the first draft, the story made it. As for what inspired the story, that's easy: the Borg Queen in the movie *Star Trek: First Contact*. I wondered who she might have been before she became Borg. Why was she different from all other Borg? If she was the starting point for the Borg, what circumstances led to her becoming the first Borg? Answering these questions gave me the story."

VOLUME SEVEN

STRANGE NEW WORLDS

DEAN WESLEY SMITH, WITH JOHN J. ORDOVER, ELISA J. KASSIN, AND PAULA M. BLOCK, EDITORS

JUNE, 2004   (293PP)

TRADE PAPERBACK

"A Test of Character"
(STAR TREK)
KEVIN LAUDERDALE

The story of Kirk taking the Kobayashi Maru test is revealed.

Kevin remarked, "I grew up in Los Angeles, watching TOS reruns. It was on every night at 6 PM on KTLA, channel 5. My mother was a big fan as well, and I discovered the novels when she brought home Jean Lorrah's *The Vulcan Academy Murders*. I've always wanted to write (I have published nonfiction: some freelance work for the Los Angeles Times, some magazines and encyclopedias. I'm even a 'real poet,' having appeared in Andre Codrescue's *Exquisite Corpse*), and especially science fiction. And, since I love the *Trek* universe, of course I'd love to write novels. But I never dabbled in fan fiction. I was aware that it existed, but since it wasn't official there didn't seem to be any point. And, of course, the publishers (then) wouldn't look at any manuscripts unless you had an agent. In fact, John Ordover (who created SNW) said constantly in Bulletin Boards and newsgroups that the thing to do was write your own material, publish, get an agent, and then ask to submit to Pocket Books. So, for years, I had all these *Trek*-related ideas and thoughts, and no outlet for them."

Kevin continued, "Then Ordover announced SNW! At last! I submitted one story to SNW I, and I didn't get in. Undaunted, I continued. I submitted from one to three stories to

II, III, and IV. No luck. I was getting better. Dean started including checklists in our SASEs. I started making it to the second read pile, which meant that of, say, 4,000 stories submitted, mine was one of the 200 or so good enough for a second look. I first submitted 'A Test of Character' to SNW V. It made the second read pile, and I thought, 'Oh well . . .' and went back to new stories. Over the years, the Internet had blossomed, and I started reading and posting at psiphi.org and trekbbs.com. It was around this time that Kevin Killiany sold 'Monkey Puzzle Box.' At psiphi he mentioned that he had received a little note from Dean at the bottom of the rejection form for 'MPB.' Based on the five or six words of commentary, he had rewritten the story, and resubmitted it. And it had made it. *Resubmitted it!?* Well, I didn't have a note from Dean, but it had never occurred to me to try to fix the thing. One of the great things about using a computer is that it's easy to just fire up the ol' word processor, open that file from a couple of years ago, and do SAVE AS 'Character v. 2.' I didn't try to rewrite all my stories, just 'A Test of Character' because it contains what I feel is the single best *Trek* idea I've had to date: how a good guy like Kirk could cheat without really cheating. I tweaked it and sent it in (along with other things) to SNW VI. This time it not only made the second read pile, but I got a few coveted words from Dean. In fact that's just one of the best things about SNW. You occasionally get comments (brief as they may be) from the editor. That's unheard of if you submit a story to a SF magazine. You get the form letter and that's *it*. Dean's words: 'Ending just trails off.' "

Kevin knew that Dean was right. "I thought about the story and its lack of an ending for a month before I came up with something. The version I submitted to SNW VII is basically the SNW VI version but with a few more pages (and a real ending) at the end. I guess I've finally learned how to write because 'Character' made it, and the other story I submitted made the alternates list."

"Indomitable"
(STAR TREK)
KEVIN KILLIANY

A young ensign Chekov questions his career choice.

Kevin remembers how "Indomitable" came about. "When my grandmother and I saw Ensign Chekov step onto the bridge for the first time in 'Catspaw,' she said, 'He looks awfully pleased with himself.' He did, grinning from ear to ear; that was the first piece, though I didn't know it then. Many years later, I heard Walter Koenig's infamous explanation of why Khan recognized him in *The Wrath of Khan*; that was the second piece. In his autobiography, *Warped Factors*, Koenig wrote about the Rosenberg conviction and how that made him feel as a Jew in America and also about the frustration of his early years trying to break into Hollywood; those were parts three and four. The fifth and final piece came from an article in a back issue of *Discover* magazine on theories about the behavior of particles near the event horizon of a black hole in July 2003. Call it thirty-seven years from beginning to end. Of course, once the idea had fully gestated, I wrote the story in less than a week."

"Project Blue Book"
(STAR TREK)
CHRISTIAN GRAINGER

ieutenant Colonel Carver discovers some old files that lead him to a former captain named John Christopher.

Christian learned about *Strange New Worlds* and thought the stories were fantastic. He commented, "Believe it or not, 'Project Blue Book' was the first story I ever sent in to anyone. I have been writing for eight years, though, and I just wanted to get something of mine in front of professional editors. I couldn't believe it when they bought my story. I got the idea for 'Project Blue Book' from an episode of *X-Files*. I have always loved detective fiction and to use the format of the supernatural and UFOs was very intriguing to me. When I got the call from John Ordover I thought it was for a different job. I was unemployed at the time. And then I realized who it was and began screaming in my apartment. I then went over to my friend's and hyperventilated. She gave me some soup and I calmed down. It was very wonderful."

"The Trouble with Tribals"
(STAR TREK)
PAUL J. KAPLAN

ow do tribbles perceive humans?

Paul remembered, "I actually submitted two stories to SNW VI—'The End of Night' and 'The Trouble with Tribals.' With 'Tribals,' I was looking for a good twist, a way to turn something on its head. The idea of using tribbles came to me, again, in the shower, and I wrote the story that afternoon. You'd be surprised, though, how long it can take to write something that short. At right about 400 words, it's probably the shortest SNW ever, but it was fun. Dean had some kind things to say about it in his note, so I resubmitted it the next year, and it wound up in SNW VII."

"All Fall Down"
(STAR TREK)
MURI McCAGE

McCoy and Kirk adjust to their lives after the events on Rura Penthe.

Mary, who writes under the name Muri, commented, "[Using the pseudonym is] my way of carrying on my family name. Also, a little mystique enhances the whole writing experience."

When asked how she became a *Trek* fan, she commented, "It wasn't until I picked up a TNG novel on a whim that I became a serious fan, around fifteen years ago. I had seen a couple of the movies and watched TNG casually, and one day I was in a bookstore and noticed the *Trek* novels. I thought, 'Hmm, I wonder if I'd like these?' I not only liked the one I got for a test read, I loved it, and was soon devouring as many as I could find. Once I got started on the TOS books, there was no looking back. Those characters drew me in so completely that I tracked the series down and started watching it . . . and the movies. Somewhere in the early stages of reading the TOS novels was when it hit me how much I loved the *Trek* universe. It was sort of like coming in through a side door."

She had always known on some level that she needed to write fiction, "But it took falling totally in love with written *Trek* for me to act on that knowledge. So, I did it backwards, watching after wanting to write *Trek*. Somewhere along the way, as I read and got to know the characters . . . simply put, they inspired me. I've read more than 200 *Trek* novels, yet there are always more stories I want to tell about those characters."

Mary learned about *Strange New Worlds* and started submitting one story a year with SNW III. When asked about her inspiration for her winning entry, Mary commented, "There was such a dark tone to 'The Undiscovered Country.' From the ominous weightless blobs of Klingon blood, to Kirk and McCoy in the docket at their trial, to their Rura Penthe experience, there was a visceral sense of unrelenting fear and danger and the kind of stress that can't be easily shaken. That combined with the camaraderie and sense of family those three men shared, made me want to explore what happened after the fear and danger was over. How do heroes of such legendary stature react to almost unbearable experiences? When they all fall down together, do they get back up together to fight another day? Do they emerge changed, yet still the same? And wouldn't Spock, who claims the least humanity among them, act with innate compassion and empathy when his dearest friends are struggling? I was also intrigued by the idea that McCoy carrying Spock's *katra* even briefly would have lingering effects on them both, and decided to tie that into this critical point in their later lives. I tend to have several projects going at once; so I paused other stuff long enough to write 'All Fall Down,' proofread it, and send it out. After that I got to work on an original SF novel and tried not to think too much about the odds of winning. When I got the call, I was thrilled of course. I was also stunned because entering any writing contest is a leap of faith that someone else will love what you've written as much as you do."

"A Sucker Born"
(STAR TREK)
PAT DETMER

 pock offers to help with repairs for HFM *Enterprises*.

Pat sent in five stories for this contest, "Four of them old ones at the behest of Dean Smith. The winner was the only new one that I wrote that year. A killer-whale-watching trip off of

Vancouver Island about three years ago sparked the story."

Pat continued, "I adored writing these stories, and have missed the process this year—now that I'm ineligible—immensely. For me, the joy is in the journey, the joy is in the act itself, and not in the winning. Don't get me wrong. Winning is a kick in the pants, a real validation. But for me, the process, the act itself is the joy, since it's all about learning. This answer goes for all three, because I can't remember one win from another. One time I got John Ordover live, once he left a message on the home machine, and once he e-mailed me because he couldn't get me by phone. A great feeling to get those calls and messages, but for me, it's about the doing, not the winning. Once I'd won and let a few people know, the winning quickly became ancient history to me, a warm memory but nothing more. I don't look back much."

"Obligations Discharged"
(STAR TREK)
GERRI LEEN

Elaan looks back on her life and contemplates seeing Kirk again.

Gerri commented, "I've been a *Star Trek* fan since I was a kid. Technically, I'm old enough to have seen the original series when it first aired, but I was pretty young then. So I guess that I really started to get into it when it was in reruns in the early 70s. I like most of the other

series, and I love *Deep Space Nine* as much if not more than the original series, but I detest *Enterprise*. (Can I say that?)"

Gerri used to write poetry that was not *Trek*-related, but quit after her mom passed away. "So I guess I needed an outlet to express myself. *Star Trek* was safe and fun, and there is a robust online community that can help you become a better writer. It was a great way to hone my skills. Some others who were online were talking about it and/or got into the book, so I was curious and bought one of the volumes to see what it was like. When I decided to give it a try, I read all the volumes, and one of my friends on AOL collected Dean's preferences/advice/general wisdom on writing from his postings on the *Strange New Worlds* AOL board. I did a lot of homework for this before I ever submitted."

While not submitting stories to the first six contests, she sent ten stories for SNW VII. " 'Obligations Discharged' got in, and two others made it to the alternate list. Ironically, 'Obligations Discharged' was the first story I wrote of the ten. I was planning on writing a Miramanee story. But when I watched 'The Paradise Syndrome' on DVD, it just didn't spark any ideas. So since I had the disk (insert plug for Netflix here), I watched the other episode, which was 'Elaan of Troyius.' Never a favorite of mine, this time around it just hit me and sparked some heavy emotions about what this woman's life must have been like. I wrote the story in a couple of hours. My writing process is a bit different than a lot of my compatriots. Dean is on record as saying, 'Don't edit your work,' but I can't work that way. I'm lucky to have two trusted friends who edit my stuff, and this story had another person who read it for errors—then I let my stories sit for a while so they become fresh again, and I can go over them with a new eye. In the case of this story, I also spent a good deal of time trying to add in texture—sensory details and such—because at the time I wrote 'Obligations Discharged,' I hadn't gotten to the point where I could get that stuff in as much as I needed to while I was writing. I'm doing better at that now.

"I didn't find out that I got in the book the way most did. I don't know if my phone machine ate the message during one of our frequent storms or what, but I never was formally notified. I found out from one of my friends when she saw the list go up online and forwarded it to me. It's exciting no matter how you find out."

"Life's Work"
(GRAND PRIZE)
(STAR TREK: THE NEXT GENERATION)
JULIE A. HYZY

 The life of Dr. Soong and how his obsessions disrupt family life.

"I again sent in four stories this year, and I think two of them made it to the alternate list, which just thrills me to no end. I'd only seen the episode 'Inheritance' once, but I'd been moved by the idea that Dr. Soong had created Juliana to replace his dead wife and that the android he loved had chosen to leave him. He was perfectly capable of changing her—of ad-

justing her so that she wouldn't want to leave—and yet he'd let her go. I knew that had to be a heart-wrenching decision on his part and I wanted to see it. So, I wrote it. I started this one a couple of times, trying to find the right moment to open the story. I actually put it away for a while, but it tugged at me. A friend of mine (my trusted first reader) challenged me to write it over a long weekend. So I did. And I was pretty happy with how it turned out."

"Adventures in Jazz and Time"
(THIRD PRIZE)
(STAR TREK: THE NEXT GENERATION)
KELLY CAIRO

 Wesley gives Riker a birthday present.

Kelly commented, "When my story made it in SNW III, I found out that it didn't matter if 'they' had heard of you. And in SNW IV, V, and VI, I learned that it didn't matter if they had heard of you, or if you'd previously appeared in SNW."

For the story that won third prize, "I have always been interested in mysterious characters, and when Wesley seemed to have something in common with the mysterious Traveler, I started working on a novel. I stole the idea for the short story from that novel-in-progress. Just before hearing the news (that I'd won), I bought a couple of the *Trek* pro-anthologies and saw [several] familiar previous SNW authors in the pages. I was concerned that it had been a while since I was published in SNW III, and I didn't know how these other people were moving forward. So when I got the news that I not only made it in the anthology, but also was a third-prize winner, I jumped on the opportunity to get out there and see what I could make happen. I e-mailed anyone that seemed approachable for advice. I subscribed to writing magazines, joined a writers group, and began lurking about the *Trek* Internet sites. I went to Shore Leave and listened to other authors, shook some hands, and took Ann Crispin's writing workshop. I went to a weeklong Oregon Coast writing workshop on Work for Hire. I am working hard on pursuing fiction writing."

"Future Shock"
(STAR TREK: THE NEXT GENERATION)
John Coffren

Journal entries written by a displaced Captain Bateson.

John read a blurb about *Strange New Worlds* in *Cinescape* magazine, and thought, "Like everyone else who enters, I can do that. As a journalist, I'd written hundreds of articles for newspapers like the *Washington Post* and the *Baltimore Sun*, but I really wanted to take a stab at writing fiction. My early attempts at horror were unsuccessful. Horror stories are supposed to be scary. I don't get scary. Science fiction is weird. I get (understand) weird. A *Star Trek*-themed short story collection provided the ideal writing opportunity because I felt comfortable with the subject matter from years

of TV viewing. The fact that this was the closest I'd get to a level playing field (amateurs only and after three sales you get kicked out) made it irresistible. I wouldn't have to compete against the heavyweights (pros with multiple short stories and novels) because they were ineligible."

John has written close to twenty short stories, and the first time he submitted "Future Shock," for SNW VI, it didn't make the cut. John said, "In a hand-written note, Dean told me that the story made the alternate list and to 'please try me again with this.' I did after making a few small changes and it made it in SNW VII."

The idea behind the story was conceived when he started thinking about Dylan Hunt, from another Roddenberry creation, *Andromeda*. John said, "I realized that he was an archtype character. A man from the past who gets stranded in the future (Hunt, Khan, and Morgan Bateson). I like the fact that nobody hit the reset button on these characters and sent them back to their original time but left them stuck in their respective futures. When I zeroed in on Bateson, I thought how did he go from being clueless at the end of *The Next Generation* episode, 'Cause and Effect,' to battling the Borg in the motion picture, *First Contact?* There had to be an adjustment period and learning curve. Once I settled on a framing device, epistolary, I would sit down every night and make a journal entry as Captain Bateson dealing with life in the twenty-fourth century."

"Full Circle"
(STAR TREK: THE NEXT GENERATION)
Scott Pearson

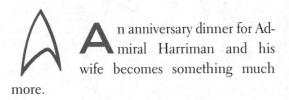

An anniversary dinner for Admiral Harriman and his wife becomes something much more.

Scott wanted to be a writer for almost as long as he had been a *Trek* fan. "So it was only natural that the two things would intersect at some point. I started writing a *Trek* novel in 1987, the same year I had my first professional fiction sale. I quit work on that novel when the *Trek* comic book at the time ran a series remarkably close to my mirror universe story. The mirror universe stories that eventually turned up on *Deep Space Nine* rendered my idea obsolete. Shortly before *Strange New Worlds* came along, I finally did write a *Trek* novel, which is ready and waiting to be pitched. If it never gets published, I'll just consider it practice for the next one. I learned about SNW when the first one hit the bookstores. I couldn't believe that I hadn't heard about it before, and started submitting with SNW II. I sent in one story each year. For SNW VI, I submitted a revised version of the story I had sent in for SNW V. Later, I found out that the original version had made Dean's alternate list—basically the stories that were runners-up. Word in the SNW community is that if you make the alternate list, you send that story back in without changes, since it was good enough the first time, but just missed the final cut. The revised one didn't make the alternate list. Whoops!"

When asked about his inspiration for "Full Circle," Scott remarked, "After McCoy appeared on *Next Generation*, you couldn't help but wonder if any other original series characters were still alive in that timeframe. So one day it just hit me—what if Harriman was still alive when Kirk came out of the Nexus? How would he react to the news? It was the only story I sent in for VII. I actually got the idea a few years earlier, but didn't start writing it until SNW VI. I didn't have time to finish it that year, and finally got it done for SNW VII. I had the first draft from the previous year along with all the ideas I had been thinking about for a few years. I knew that the major scene would be Scotty and Harriman. It was coming together nicely, but then I read David R. George III's *Serpents Among the Ruins* and loved it. I went back and rewrote 'Full Circle' to maintain the *Lost Era* continuity. I had to have my wife FedEx the story just a couple days before the deadline. Then one day I was at my new day job when my wife called and told me there was a message on our answering machine and that my story had been chosen. 'It was John somebody,' she said. 'John Ordover?' I said. 'Yeah.' It was hard to work the rest of the day. I transferred that message to my computer and listen to it from time to time."

Scott wanted to give a big tip of the hat to: "All the people who worked on Harriman before me: Rick Berman, Ronald D. Moore, Brannon Braga, Peter David, David R. George III, and, of course, the great Alan Ruck."

"Beginnings"
(STAR TREK: THE NEXT GENERATION)
JEFF D. JACQUES

Data tries to play match-maker for Chief O'Brien.

Jeff sent six stories in for SNW VI, two TOS stories and four TNG stories, one of which made it to Dean's alternate list and would subsequently become his winning story in SNW VII. For SNW VII, he sent in a total of nine stories, four TOS, two each for DS9 and TNG, and one ENT.

Regarding 'Beginnings,' he remarked, "Ever since the O'Briens married in TNG's fourth season, we've seen them as a representation of a genuine family, experiencing real-life ups and downs against the backdrop of the galaxy, both on TNG and more prominently on DS9. In the TNG episode 'Data's Day' (in which the pair got married), it was revealed that it was Data who introduced Keiko to Miles, and I thought this would be a fun jumping off point for the story. I wanted to show in an amusing way that these two were not the smooth fit that they appeared to be later on and that initially they weren't particularly fond of each other at all! And it's always entertaining to see Miles all flustered, so it was quite enjoyable to write him that way for most of the story. I think I was pretty successful in channeling Colm Meaney for O'Brien's dialogue."

Jeff continued, "The writing of the story was pretty much standard for me. For short stories, I tend not to use an outline. I generally just get the idea in my head and start writing, hoping that the story takes me through to the end in a satisfying manner. Winning again was still a thrill. The resubmission of a previous year's alternate list does not necessarily guarantee placement in the book, but as has happened in the past with other writers, this was indeed the case for me. And this time I did actually get the congratulatory phone call from John, though I wasn't present to answer, so I ended up with a message on my answering machine. This was a good thing, actually, because I was able to play it back numerous times over the following week as a reminder that I really did win and it wasn't a dream. I did speak live with John on the phone a day or two later, so I did get that honor in the end, too. And the perks of getting into the book over the next few months were all great, too, with the galleys, contract, the check, and the realization that I'd once again made a contribution to *Trek* literature and that, as a result, I am a *Star Trek* writer."

What happened to Michelle, his writing partner for 'Kristin's Conundrum'? "To be honest, the idea of a follow-up collaboration never came up. After SNW V, we left the door open to pair up for a future story, but it never happened. It wasn't that we didn't enjoy our team effort on 'Kristin's Conundrum,' but we were both busy with our own solo projects and that ubiquitous bother called real life. In the meantime, I will, in the words of Dean Wesley Smith, continue to 'write, send, repeat.' "

"Solemn Duty"
(STAR TREK: THE NEXT GENERATION)
JIM JOHNSON

Picard returns from Veridian III to inform Admiral McCoy and Captain Scott about the events that transpired there.

Jim watched reruns of the original series, but realized he was a life-long fan when he started watching TNG. His friend, Kevin Summers, won third prize in *Strange New Worlds* IV, and introduced him to the contest. Jim said, "From there, I bought the previous volumes and hunted down all the SNW information I could find online. Other than the *Trek* AOL board, there wasn't much, so I started a Yahoo! Group for SNW writers and had a huge response."

Jim sent two stories to SNW VI, which were both rejected. "Solemn Duty" was one of three stories he submitted for SNW VII. The idea behind the story came from watching *Deep Space Nine*. "At some point in the DS9 marathon, it struck me that both McCoy and Scotty are alive and well in the TNG era, and wouldn't it be interesting if Picard came back from his events in *Generations* and told these two shipmates of Kirk the news of Kirk's death. That was it really, just a little spark—Picard tells Scotty and McCoy about Kirk's death. The story came together really quickly, and it wasn't hard to write."

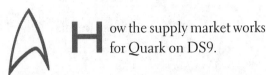

"Infinite Bureaucracy"
(STAR TREK: DEEP SPACE NINE)
ANNE E. CLEMENTS

How the supply market works for Quark on DS9.

Anne sent in one story for SNW III, two for SNW IV, three for SNW V, two for SNW VI, and three for SNW VII, including the winning story, "Infinite Bureaucracy." "The title came first, and the story was built on that. We had a bit of a regime change at my day job, and the new management team brought in a host of new procedures and controls—all well-intentioned and ultimately productive, but there was a certain period of, shall we say, *adjustment* required. At that time I found myself wandering the halls muttering 'Infinite Bureaucracy in Infinite Combinations!'—unfortunately, very few people there got the reference, but it occurred to me that it would make a wonderful SNW story title. After all, in a Federation composed of thousands of technologically advanced civilizations, let's face it, despite Mr. Roddenberry's utopian biases, that is *exactly what* you'd get! So, how to demonstrate that, in an interesting enough fashion to snag the editors' attention? Again, my day job involves writing and maintaining software for, among other things, order processing, and I knew how the information on a set of order records, from initial order through invoice, can tell the story of the shipment. Obviously, in the future that would be supplemented by video recordings of the actual negotiations involved, which gives us description and dialogue to supplement the dry lists of facts—which are themselves, if you look closely, very informative (despite a few typos that made it through the proofing process). I also managed to get in quite a few 'in-jokes,' which were irresistible after so many years of hanging out on the SNW message boards. I'm not sure whether anybody actually caught them, but they were certainly fun to put in (carefully, without detracting from the story for the general public!)."

"Barclay Program Nine"
(STAR TREK: DEEP SPACE NINE)
RUSS CROSSLEY

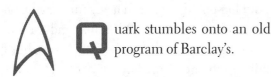 uark stumbles onto an old program of Barclay's.

"I submitted three stories for SNW VII. The idea came from the end of *The Next Generation* episode where Barclay saves one program (nine) and we never found out which one number nine is. I thought it might be fun if when the *Enterprise*-D is destroyed someone sells what's left for scrap. Of course, who would buy scrap and try to make a profit from it? A Ferengi naturally!"

"Redux"
(STAR TREK: VOYAGER)
SUSAN S. McCRACKIN

 'Elanna finds herself alive, thanks to the heroics of Seven of Nine.

Susan fell into creating new *Trek* stories in an unusual way. "Writing *Trek* stories was both an accident and an act of desperation. I was during a heavy period of traveling and there was no *Voyager* on any television in any hotel I stayed in. I turned to the Internet and stumbled on a couple of fan fiction sites. I started reading and was pretty impressed with the stories I read. I read all of the good ones I could find. Some were not as good as others and some were downright bad. I remember reading one and thinking I could do better than that. Then I wondered if I really could. I had always had stories in my head and had even tried to write a time or two, but I could never finish. A couple of failures had made me gun-shy about trying any more. I don't know what made the difference this time, except I had an idea, and I had a laptop. I could type much faster than I could write with a pen. I sat down and started a story. I remember finishing that story and typing 'The End' and crying when I did. I couldn't believe I had actually done it! I sent the story to one of the better Web sites and the webmaster posted it. I was thrilled to get e-mails from people who took the time to write and tell me they enjoyed my stories. I started writing more. I think I finally knew I had something in me when I wrote a story and it led to another, which led to another and another and so on. By the time I finished, I had a twelve-part saga that lasted over seven hundred pages! And I had friends who wrote me and supported me from the beginning to the end. I read that story now and just groan over how bad the writing was in those first stories, but I could also see how I improved and grew. I still think that that story might just be one of the best ideas I ever had."

Discovering *Strange New Worlds* was another accident. "I was browsing at the local Barnes and Noble and pulled SNW II off the shelf. I leafed through the book until I got to the *Voyager* section and read the first line of a story that caught my interest. It made me decide to buy the book. It was a Saturday afternoon. I came home and sat down to read the story that had interested me. I can still remember sitting in my chair after reading that story, just crying. I went to bed and that story was the first thing I thought of when I woke up. I sat down and read the story again and cried just as hard. The story was 'A Ribbon for Rosie' by Ilsa Bick. I knew I wanted to write like her when I grew up! That story made me read others, and it made me very curious about the contest, and I wondered if I would ever be able to write anything that would be good enough to be published. So, I wrote a story and mailed it off for SNW IV. I was disappointed when it didn't make it (but not surprised). But what was so exciting was getting the note on the cover letter from Dean encouraging me to submit something for the next contest! I was hooked!"

Susan submitted a story for SNW V. Furthermore, she said, "For VI, I submitted four stories, one of which was 'Redux'—it made the second read pile. That was the first time I had gotten that far. Once again, I have to thank Ilsa Bick. I read her story 'Shadows in the Dark.' Actually, I probably read it five times and it set a mood in me and something started in the deep shadows of my mind that just wouldn't let me go. Finally, the first sentence of 'Redux' popped into my head. It kept at me until I finally sat down and started to write. I had no idea when I started where it was going to take me. I just started typing and the story took off. It was probably one of the most visual stories I had ever written. I could see everything that was happening and all I did was describe it. One of the things I loved about that story was being inside B'Elanna Torres' head. I've always liked her character, but she came alive for me in that story. When the chips are down, I'd want her on my side. And it was fun playing off the tension between B'Elanna and Seven. There is no love lost between those two, but I think each one ultimately has a respect for the other. I found out that I was a winner with a phone call at work. It was John Ordover on the other end of the phone, but when he told me his name, it sounded a lot like the name of someone's file I was working and I couldn't figure out why this girl's father was calling me. It took a moment or two for it to connect. I've never been as surprised or as excited in my life. I probably sounded like an idiot. The publishing process was fun. Elisa Kassin did a great job, so it was pretty painless. The hardest part was waiting to get the books in my hands. That moment was totally surreal. The best part, though, was all of the friends I've made. There are a number of SNW VII writers in the Northern Virginia area and we've gotten together a couple of times."

"The Little Captain"
(STAR TREK: VOYAGER)
Catherine E. Pike

 Naomi must take charge on an away mission gone awry.

Cathy submitted two stories to SNW VI, but neither made the final book. For her contribution in this anthology, she reworked a story she submitted to SNW IV. Another story called 'Maturation,' made Dean's alternate list. "I can't remember how the idea for the story actually took form, except I knew that I wanted to write a Seven/Naomi story and that I battled forever before the shape took form. I wanted to do a peril kind of story, and had all sorts of stupid scenarios, before hitting on the one I went with. Once I realized the true point of view of the story was Naomi (when I began rewriting it) the story flowed and became much better than the original. Again, I found out I had won via a phone message! I was working the graveyard shift then, and kept my phone turned off during the day while I slept. So I literally slept through the good news."

"I Have Broken the Prime Directive"
(STAR TREK: VOYAGER)
G. Wood

 What happened to the doctor when he visited the world in the sixth-season episode, "Blink of an Eye."

According to Guy, he wanted to explore what happened to the doctor in the years he spent on the planet.

"Don't Cry"
(STAR TREK: VOYAGER)
Annie Reed

Miral's childhood memories and experiences living aboard *Voyager*.

" 'Don't Cry' was my only submission for SNW VII. I usually only submit one or two stories a year, and that year 'Don't Cry' was the only one. The idea was sparked by the last episode of *Voyager* and Miral's eagerness to help Janeway. Although Miral was a minor character in that episode, to me she was incredibly brave and selfless. By agreeing to help Janeway, she was agreeing to basically wipe out her entire life to that point. All of her experiences, good and bad, would be changed if Janeway were successful. Why would Miral do that? Answering that question was the spark for the story. When I sat down to actually write it, the focus became Miral's close relationship to her father, and it was that relationship that the story actually explored."

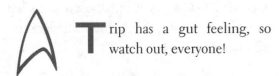

"Earthquake Weather"
(STAR TREK: ENTERPRISE)
LOUISA M. SWANN

Trip has a gut feeling, so watch out, everyone!

The nerves hit for Louisa when SNW VII was announced. She was wondering if she could pull a hat trick. "It seemed like I'd never find the 'right' storyline. I worried over stories like a dog worries a bone, until I became seriously sleep-deprived at a workshop. That's when the idea for 'Earthquake Weather' shimmied into my head. I was totally stunned to get John's message on our answering machine this time—after another morning of skiing. Three times in a row! Yippee!"

She had some final thoughts about her three appearances. "Not only has it been great being a part of the *Strange New Worlds* family—the finalists in each issue chat online and often get together at different cons—I've been fortunate to meet Dean Wesley Smith, Kristine Katherine Rusch, and Keith DeCandido, talk on the phone to John Ordover, and have been in e-mail contact with other venerable *Trek* authors. What a thrill!"

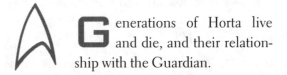

"Guardians"
(SECOND PRIZE)
(SPECULATIONS)
BRETT HUDGINS

Generations of Horta live and die, and their relationship with the Guardian.

" 'Guardians' was one of ten entries for SNW VII, six new and four resubmissions, two of which were rewrites that Dean didn't specifically ask to see again. 'Guardians' was one of the new ones. That was a great year for me. In addition to selling the one story and winning a prize, I placed four of the others on Dean's alternate list, meaning he thought five of my ten entries were good enough to be published. That's a thrilling achievement after so much rejection, and proof of how SNW helped me become a better writer. I owe a lot to this contest. As for the idea, if you look at the story you'll see it's actually a number of ideas tied together by a framing device. I wanted to enter in every category I could. The creation of the Speculations section the previous year inspired me to think on an epic scale. I wondered what would happen if someone rigged the Bajoran Orb of Time to blow up the Guardian of Forever, or if Borg cubes could evolve, or if Q was more than he seemed. Or, most pointedly, if the Horta colonized the Guardian's seemingly lifeless world to protect the ancient time portal. Everything snapped together as soon as I had my theme: guardians.

"The writing was challenging, largely because I had the *Star Trek Encyclopedia* propped open on my lap the whole time. Also, there was the not-so-insignificant matter of creating fifty thousand years of future history, getting all the characters and references right, and not losing sight of my through-line. It couldn't just be a series of vignettes. It had to tell a complete story from beginning to end. Learning I'd won, and snagged a prize to boot, was just as exciting as the previous year. Whenever I put that much work and heart into something, I sweat the results. There's no better validation than success. Impressively, 'Guardians' has gone on to be quite well reviewed, which is a satisfying conclusion to that particular odyssey."

"The Law of Averages"
(SPECULATIONS)
AMY SISSON

ax confronts the possibility of death if a new host can't be found quickly.

Amy decided in college that she wanted to be a writer and settled on science fiction. "It was sci-fi first (although I didn't manage to write much) and *Trek* later. SNW gave me a reason to write something specific. And it's an easy way to start—the settings are there, the characters are there—I just had to supply a plot. And I found it easy to write in the characters' voices. I think I saw SNW I on the bookshelf and immediately bought it, but the deadline for SNW II had already passed. I anxiously awaited publi-

cation of II so I could make sure there would be a III. Then I started submitting to SNW III. I submitted one story each year to SNW III, IV, V, and VII. (Missed VI—couldn't make my story work, let it sit for a year, then it became my entry that made it into SNW VII.) I would also note that every year I have had to overnight my submission to get it there by October 1. I definitely find deadlines inspiring. One tip I learned from fellow SNW VII writers is that they have resubmitted previous entries that made Dean's second read pile. I always assumed that was a big no-no. I am going to rewrite my SNW IV entry, and hopefully finish one or two new stories. This is just my gut feeling, but I have the impression Dean likes to see people repeat."

"Forgotten Light"
(SPECULATIONS)
FREDERICK KIM

he homeworld of the Borg is discovered.

Frederick found his desire to write after reading *Star Trek: The New Voyages* edited by Sondra Marshak and Myrna Culbreath. "It was a revelation to read those stories, real *Star Trek* stories, and know that they hadn't been written by glamorous, magical Hollywood types, but by fans not too unlike myself. Those two volumes of *The New Voyages* stirred me to believe I could write a story for *Star Trek* one day. I'd already come up with the idea for 'Forgotten Light' as a possible teleplay (this was back when Paramount still took unsolicited submissions), but ultimately decided that it would make a better short story than an episode. I remember wishing to myself that they still published *Trek* stories written by fans, like they did with *The New Voyages*. And then one day, while shopping in a drugstore, I just happened to come across the mass market paperback edition of the first volume of *Strange New Worlds*—there was an invitation, right there on the cover, for me to submit my story for next year's contest! Even after I learned about *Strange New Worlds* it took me several years to get around to writing 'Forgotten Light.' I kept telling myself that someday I'd have a block of free time in which I could sit down and write the story, but finally had to face up to the fact that that was never going to happen. So I started writing any spare moment I could snatch from the day. The first time I submitted was for SNW VI, but didn't get in. Once I got over my disappointment, I was able to go back over the piece and work on areas that I thought could be improved upon, and then resubmitted the story for SNW VII."

When asked about the inspiration for the story, Frederick remembered, "Back when *The Next Generation* was in its seventh season, I was thinking about how the Borg were the perfect villains for *Star Trek*, because they're the antithesis of everything for which Picard and the Federation stand. And around this time there was that whole media hype about cyberspace and how the Internet was going to solve all our problems, which I personally found nauseating, because I don't believe technology by itself will save us from the worst aspects of ourselves—only a dedicated effort to grow and evolve can do that. So from that came the idea

that maybe the Borg had started out in a civilization like ours, even had a society with a lot of admirable qualities, but it was their infatuation with technology that led to their downfall. Writing the story was difficult at first, since I was such a novice, but as I got further into the process it became a lot more fun and much less of a struggle. After the story was rejected for SNW VI it was hard to go back and make revisions, but ultimately very worthwhile, and I think I learned a lot about writing because I made that effort. Winning was a great thrill, obviously. The day I found out I'd won I came home from work and noticed that the message light on my answering machine was blinking, but instead of checking it I went to the computer and read my e-mail. Afterwards I went to the SimonSays Web site, and read some posts about how the winners for SNW VII had been announced. Instead of checking the list of winners online, I rushed back over to the answering machine, crossed my fingers, and played the message. Hearing John Ordover's voice tell me that I'd made it into the book is an experience I'll always cherish."

VOLUME EIGHT

STRANGE NEW WORLDS

Dean Wesley Smith, with Elisa J. Kassin
and Paula M. Block, editors

July 2005   (358pp)

TRADE PAPERBACK

"Shanghaied"
(STAR TREK)
Alan James Garbers

The *Enterprise* is called to Earth to investigate something unusual discovered on a sunken Confederate vessel.

Alan talked about the origins of his entry in this anthology. "I was reading an article in *National Geographic* about the discovery of a Civil War ship. As I was studying the pictures of artifacts, I thought, what if? Over the next hour the rest of the story grew in my mind to the point I was about to go crazy. (This was two weeks before the deadline to have the stories in.) The writing process was very frustrating as I knew what I wanted to do and where the story needed to go, but I am a hunt-and-peck typist, so it went slooowwwlyyy, and I knew I had to get it done, proofread, redone, and make it in before the deadline. I was hoping to be in the anthology one last time, but I didn't expect 'the call' before January 1, so when my wife told me I had gotten 'the call' I thought she was pulling my leg!"

"Assignment: One"
(STAR TREK)
Kevin Lauderdale

Gary Seven must deal with one of the most horrifying moments in U.S. history.

" 'Assignment: One' is the story of Gary Seven on 9/11, and how (and why) his job is to save only one person that day. It's the most meaningful story I've ever written, and it has the most complex history. To begin with, the story as published will be three pages shorter than originally written. This is a function of the way I like to write. I like to start with a real knockout first sentence. So one day I was thinking, 'What would be an opening that would get a reader's attention?' September 11 had happened about six months before, and it just came to me: 'Gary Seven stood on the corner of Liberty and West, looking up at the Twin Towers of the World Trade Center. He knew that tomorrow they would be gone.' And then I went on to talk about how Seven loves New York, and how he would miss this and that. Then he gets a beep from his computer and he goes back to his office: start of scene two. Well, after I read the whole story through, I asked myself (as anyone who wants to write for SNW should do): 'Does this violate any of the advice that Dean Wesley Smith has given us?' Immediately the answer was 'Yes.' The first three pages of the story were what Dean calls 'Walking to the problem.' Sure, my opening grabbed your attention, but nothing really happened. Also, on reflection, there wasn't anything that moved the plot forward or that wasn't said differently later on in the story. So . . . I cut the entire first scene. This required me to tweak the new page one and two a little (the new first sentence still isn't really a knockout, but it will do), but from then on, the rest of the story remained unchanged. And I found that by *not* telling the reader what the story was all about in the first sentence, I actually created a bit of dramatic tension and mystery. It's not too much mystery; people will get that what Seven is concerned about is actually 9/11 pretty early on. But it's better than hitting them over the head with it in the first sentence. The whole question of how early to make it plain that this is a 9/11 story was something I gave a lot of thought to. In writing about a real event—and one which was very fresh in people's minds and which is filled with emotions—it just seemed too coy to try to 'hide' the fact that this is a 9/11 story until the very end (or even the middle). It's the central event of the story (though it takes place 'off stage'), and therefore the proverbial 800-pound gorilla. You can't ignore it, but it's not the first thing you should say. In the end, I have Seven thinking about 'attacks' and then planes . . . people catch on pretty fast.

Kevin continued, "This is the first story I've written where I had things I wanted to *say*. In 'A Test of Character,' I just told a fun tale with my take on certain aspects of Kirk's character. I don't think there's all that much about the human condition in that story. But in 'A: O' I found the perfect venue for things I had been thinking about for years. In the story, Seven muses about how fashionable it is to call Earth a 'small world,' but how to him, it really is *huge*. This was an epiphany I had when I was nineteen and went to England for the first time. Here I was standing in another country, and I looked down the street and saw hundreds of people going to work. And it occurred to me that each of them had a job and life, and people they loved. 'The world is *huge*,' I thought. That made it into 'A: O.' Also, of course, the story is one way of exploring and explaining 9/11. 'How could God let this happen?' was a question a lot of folks asked. I'm not particularly religious, but I got to explore that. Seven knows what's going to happen, and he could possibly stop it, but that's not his job. His job is, however, to save one particular person. The sentence that crystallized my feelings about it, and the sentence that's the crux of the story, is one I'm quite proud of: 'Seven thought of the people who would die or whose lives would be changed the next day as characters in a story that they were unaware was even being told.' That's us. We are all just characters in something. . . ."

Kevin thinks that his story is the only one ever to make the jump from the alternates list one year to the anthology the next. "Of course, that's largely because people who make the alternates list, even if they resubmit the same story (which is what you are supposed to do), also submit even better stories the next time. I didn't. I submitted four stories; 'A: O' made it into SNW 8, and none of the others made it to the alternates list. I guess I was lucky. Winning was a bittersweet experience for me because I became friends with a few of the SNW VII authors who live near me. When I made it in, and a couple of them didn't, I realized that at least part of making it into SNW isn't about pure talent (because I'm not any better a writer than they are), but about how well a particular story might fit into the overall mix of stories for that year. It's like college admissions. We might all be 4.0 students with great extracurricular activities, but the school only needs one more hockey player this year, so it's going to be the other guy not you."

learn at the end that the entire event never happened. It was merely a psychological test, similar to the Kobayashi Maru test, given to Captain Kirk without his knowledge by Section 31, the covert division of Starfleet Intelligence. They wanted to determine if he was mentally fit to join them. He, of course, refuses to join because he abhors their tactics. I learned that I would be a part of SNW 8 when one of the editors, Elisa Kassin, called me just before Christmas. I was VERY excited."

"Demon"
(STAR TREK)
KEVIN ANDREW HOSEY

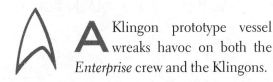 Klingon prototype vessel wreaks havoc on both the *Enterprise* crew and the Klingons.

"I came up with the idea for 'Demon' many years ago and actually submitted it three times. Third time was a charm, it seems, since it was accepted. Some of my favorite *Trek* stories have always been the ones where you think a major crew member had died, but of course they didn't really. So I wrote one along that line. (The story) deals with the *Enterprise* being destroyed and the crew killed by a Klingon battlecruiser controlled by an alien entity. We then

"Don't Call Me Tiny"
(STAR TREK)
PAUL C. TSENG

 hat was Sulu like as a sixth-grader?

Paul got into writing *Trek* in an unusual way. "You can imagine the excitement that *Star Trek: Nemesis* generated when it first appeared. But at the end, I was quite disappointed with the very weak send-off they gave Data. Then everyone kept going on about how this would be the last movie for the TNG crew. I was disappointed and feared the demise of the *Trek* franchise so I decided that I must come up with some ideas and find out how to send them to Berman and Braga. I came up with this huge epic where TNG would pass the torch to a new crew/ship. That is now my trilogy (I'm halfway finished with Book Two). Long story short (too late), someone on the psiphi.org TrekBBS recommended I try to enter SNW. After reading up on the guidelines I decided to enter SNW

VII. Initially, it was so difficult fitting my stories into the 7,500-word limit. But having that limit really forced me to learn about being direct and concise (HAHA, you'd never guess that, reading my posts and e-mails, would you?). So my first venture was six stories for SNW VII. I was not totally surprised that none of them got in, considering it was my very first try. But I was encouraged that four of the six stories got to the second read pile with some nice comments from Dean. So, as some of you know, Dean posted on AOL that anyone who sent in ten or more stories for SNW8 would be given a really good look. So I decided to task myself with sending in not ten but twenty stories. By the end of September, I had fifteen stories and my friends who were reading my trilogy were bugging me to stop writing for SNW and finish the trilogy. I was tired and decided that fifteen were enough. It took hours to print and mail those stories, but when they went out, I let out a big sigh of relief. Then someone on the AOL board challenged us to send in one more story in the last week before the deadline. That's when I decided to take that challenge and send in three more stories (two of which are among my four that made the SNW 8 alternate list). So I still fell short of my twenty-story goal, but aiming for it was really a great thing to do."

The spark for the story came as follows. "That scene from *Star Trek III: The Search for Spock*, where Sulu decks and flips a security guard twice his size always intrigued me. We all cheered in the movie theater when he did that, and when he said 'Don't Call Me Tiny' we all cheered. That line always intrigued me and after all these years I decided I had to tell a story about why Sulu gets really fired up if someone calls him 'Tiny.' My mother passed

away just before the deadline for SNW VII. I was determined not to get so depressed that I would stop writing (I already had four stories ready to send at that point). The thought that kept me going that year was that she would have wanted me to continue excelling in my life and not to slow down on her account. By the time SNW VII was over, I already had ideas mapped out for SNW 8. I set myself a goal to send in twenty stories and then forced myself to write. It was the sheer flow of writing and ideas that sustained my momentum for SNW 8. Honestly, after I sent in the stories, I had to take a short breather and not think about them. By the time I got the call that I had made it into the anthology, I had long since stopped thinking about SNW 8. It was a nice surprise when I got the call because it was the last thing on my mind at the moment."

"Morning Bells Are Ringing"
(STAR TREK: THE NEXT GENERATION)
KEVIN SUMMERS

Marissa Flores, the young girl trapped in the turbolift with Captain Picard in the episode 'Disaster,' begs for the captain's help.

"Here's the scoop on 'Morning Bells Are Ringing,'" commented Kevin. "My wife, Rachel, is a huge fan of that show *Dr. Quinn, Medicine Woman*. I've been buying her the DVDs and watching them with her. As we were watching them, I discovered that Erika Flores, one of the leads on the show, did an episode of TNG. I went back and watched the episode 'Disaster,' and remembered loving it the first time around. This is, of course, the episode where Worf delivers Keiko's baby, which I thought was hysterical. Anyway, Picard was trapped in a turbolift in this episode, with these children, one of whom was Erika Flores's character, Marissa. She was painfully shy in the first part of the episode, and there was never really an explanation of why. I saw in Marissa an opportunity to fill in her backstory, and to flesh out a character that we spend some time getting to know and then never see again. When I started writing the story, I knew I wanted to use Picard. He and Marissa had fantastic chemistry, and the way he had to play against his normal disdain for children made him seem much warmer than we usually get to see him (at least during the run of the show).

"The device of the story (the temporal hole) was something I've been holding onto for a while, looking for the right characters. The ship that Marissa is on, by the way, is named after General Lawrence Chamberlain, the Union officer that ordered his men to salute the Confederate troops when they surrendered at Appomattox Courthouse. I wrote the story in about a week, sent it in, and hoped for the best. I was thrilled when Elisa called; it was about a week before Christmas. It wasn't the same feeling as my first sale (euphoria) or my second sale (relief). I've changed my writing patterns dramatically since 'Isolation Ward 4.' Back then, I used to write in bursts of mania. Now I'm very structured, I write six days a week, and I shoot for 1,000 words a day. When I got the call from Elisa, I felt like my hard work and dedication had paid off, so in many ways this sale felt like

the sweetest because I worked for this one the hardest."

"Passages of Deceit"
(STAR TREK: THE NEXT GENERATION)
SARAH SEABORNE

aptain Picard goes on an archaeological survey that goes awry.

"I grew up in rural Oregon watching *Star Trek* reruns. I was an adult and hooked on *Next Generation* when I started calling myself a fan. Of course, other people called me obsessed. I've been writing short stories since I was twelve years old. *Next Generation*, even more than the original series, gave me a vast universe to write about. It also gave me characters that believed in the importance of doing the right thing, even if it wasn't necessarily the best thing for the individual. I know I submitted a story to the first *Strange New Worlds* competition, but I don't remember how I learned about it. I submitted two other stories during the years."

In terms of 'Passages of Deceit,' Sarah commented, "The concept that Picard had a genetic defect that might cause him to become senile came out of *Next Generation*'s final episode. Section 31 is a DS9 creation, but it started me thinking about a darker side of the Federation. If a species petitions for membership, and there is some question about their true intentions, how far will Starfleet go to uncover the truth? And if the species is one of the most advanced telepathic species the Federation has ever encountered, how do you go about getting the truth? That's where Data comes in. Much of this story is about the relationships these people have developed over the years. That is what has always attracted me to *Star Trek,* from the original series on through *Enterprise.* I can't say *Star Trek* has taught me everything I needed to know about life, but it has taught me much of what I needed to know to be true to the people around me."

"Final Flight"
(THIRD PLACE)
(STAR TREK: THE NEXT GENERATION)
JOHN TAKIS

 The captain tries something radical that might bring back his dead friend, Data.

John said, "Believe it or not, 'Final Flight' was born because I hated *Star Trek Nemesis.* In my mind, *Nemesis* was a great big turkey on just about every level—and this coming from someone with a huge affection for *Star Trek V!* I certainly never intended to write a story set in or around the events of *Nemesis*—why dignify a movie I would rather pretend never existed? But due to my passion for all things *Trek,* I spent a great deal of time picking apart the film, analyzing what I felt were its various flaws and shortcomings. Then, unbidden, this story came.

"The writing came easily, and I was pleased and a little surprised by how it played out (the

'Order of Sybok' just kind of introduced itself, for example). It was the earliest SNW story relative to the deadline I ever produced; but for several months I sat on it, unsure and a little embarrassed to have written it. Finally, I wrote two other stories, neither of which came so easily, and neither of which felt ultimately comfortable. I submitted all three just under the deadline, genuinely torn over which story I was 'rooting for'—a new experience, since this was my first year submitting multiple stories. Subconsciously, though, I think I wanted 'Final Flight' to win. It was the first TNG story I had ever written. It had McCoy, one of my all-time favorite characters, very fun to write for. It was written in multiple tenses, which I know is risky, but which I love doing. It had a tip-of-the-hat to *Star Trek V,* my guilty pleasure. So looking back, I'm glad 'Final Flight' is the one that made it in—my third and last appearance in *Strange New Worlds.*"

"Trek"
(STAR TREK: DEEP SPACE NINE)
DAN C. DUVAL

 A Klingon discovers a crashed shuttle with an injured Trill aboard.

Dan had been writing stories for a long time, but also worked in the high-tech industry, which left him little time or energy to write much. As he said, "Who wanted to sit in front

of a computer screen all night, after doing it all day?"

He continued, "I did not submit to any previous contests, SNW 8 was my first. My friends have been encouraging me to write for it but I could just never get a story finished in time. At least, not one I thought was worth seeing the light of day. I submitted two stories, one selected for publication and the other in the alternates list. This story, 'Trek,' allowed me to put my ideas forward on why the Klingons of TOS differed from the later Klingons (putting a political spin on it.) I was also intrigued by the *Lives of Dax* anthology, which gave me the idea of using Torias' shuttle accident as Dax's introduction to Klingons, as an inciting incident to drive the Klingon story forward, and to try to explain how Joran Dax might have come about. This is my first professional sale, so I could say that I am still dancing from hearing about it."

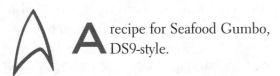

"Gumbo"
(STAR TREK: DEEP SPACE NINE)
Amy Vincent

A recipe for Seafood Gumbo, DS9-style.

Amy discovered *Star Trek* through the novels first. "When I was about thirteen, I picked up *The Entropy Effect* by Vonda McIntyre just while browsing in a bookstore. The back copy said that Captain Kirk was killed—and even as little as I knew about *Trek* (I hadn't seen an episode), I knew that was a big deal. So I

bought the book and was enthralled. That's how I became interested, though I don't guess I was really hooked until TNG began to air."

When asked about writing *Trek* stories, she commented, "It seems like two sides of the same coin: 'I love this, and therefore I want more.' So I wrote more. I heard about SNW when they first announced it, and I thought it was interesting. I never entered, though; I don't think I ever really gave it serious thought before this year. I'm not sure why!"

Her inspiration for the story was a friend. "Seema just wanted a *Deep Space Nine* story, and I know that she likes stories with unusual structure or story-telling devices. I hit upon the idea of doing a story as a recipe; after that, Jake Sisko was the obvious narrator, given the Sisko family tradition of fine cooking. It fell together fairly quickly after that. After I showed it to her, she said that I should send it in to SNW; my friend Rocky, who edited it for me, seconded the idea. It was about two weeks before the contest deadline, and I had a slow day at the office, so I figured, 'Why not?' I sent the story off and promptly forgot all about it. Then, about three days before Christmas, I got the call. I was so excited—and it was a lot of fun that way, because it really did come as a surprise! This story wasn't written as an SNW entry; it was written as fanfic, pure and simple. I know a lot of people like to say there's some sort of conceptual divide between fanfic and the kind of story SNW publishes, but I'm here to tell you that's not necessarily true."

"Promises Made"
(STAR TREK: DEEP SPACE NINE)
David DeLee

Kira rescues Tom Riker from a Cardassian prison camp.

David commented, "I first heard about *Strange New Worlds* while cruising the Internet one night and happened on the contest announcement on AOL. It was for the very first one. I was traveling a lot for work back then (two to three trips a month with overnight stays of up to three nights) and thought it would be a kick to write a story and submit it. It was awful. I'd never written a piece of fiction in my life before that, except maybe for a five-page story I did when I was around thirteen. After that, it just started to be something to pass the time while I was away on business trips—in hotels, on planes, that sort of thing. About two, two and a half years ago I decided to get more serious about my writing. In addition to SNW, I started writing and submitting stories to other contests, to a lot of the magazines. I'm writing about twenty to twenty-five short stories a year now, and as I said, seven of them were for SNW. Finding out was kind of funny. I got the call from Elisa on the Tuesday before Christmas. It was a great feeling to be told I won."

The germ for the story came from the episode of DS9 called 'Defiant.' David's story is a sequel of sorts. "In the episode Tom Riker steals the *Defiant* and kidnaps Major Kira. By the end of the episode he's turned over to the Cardassians and sentenced to life in prison.

Kira promises to get him out. In the series, they never returned to that, never told what happened to Riker. 'Promises Made' is about Kira trying to rescue him."

David had some final remarks. "I'd just like to thank Dean, Eliza, and Paula for buying my story, and Pocket Books and Paramount for making this all possible. I'm really grateful to think, at least in some small way, I'm now a part of the *Star Trek* universe."

"Always a Price"
(STAR TREK: DEEP SPACE NINE)
Muri McCage

Vic tells Kira she must visit a part of Bajor.

Mary Lee, who writes as Muri, commented, "From the beginning I was drawn to Odo; his personality and his progression from gruff constable to noble romantic. I'd had a vague idea for a long time, where he uses his shapeshifting ability to surprise Kira . . . a sort of gift. The rest was built around that. [DS9 is] a fascinating series, with so many characters intertwined in major and subtle ways and then such growth for so many. Several cool characters worked their way into this story, and I really enjoyed writing it. 'Always a Price' was the first time I'd written DS9, so I was a bit surprised, and pleased, when I found out that it had won."

"Transfiguration"
(STAR TREK: VOYAGER)
Susan S. McCrackin

 A little girl loses her engineer mom in a fire, and ends up badly burned also.

"The week before the contest ended, Dean encouraged everyone to write, print, and mail. There was a lot of chatter about people taking up the challenge and getting stories in the mail. I privately thought that would never work for me because my writing process did not work like that. Then, the Sunday morning before the contest deadline, I woke up with the first line of the story in my head and a concept whirling around in the back of my mind. I sat down and started writing Sunday afternoon and came home from work early Monday afternoon to finish the story. I quickly got it into the hands of a couple of friends saying 'read it quick!' and 'what would you name it?' Tuesday night all of the editing and naming work was done and one of my friends ran it to the post office on Wednesday morning to overnight it. Well, it made it—pun intended! This story worked from beginning to end, and it basically flowed without me really knowing what was coming next. And everything about it was new for me. The story is told in first person and from the point of view of an eight year old. The call from Elisa came while I was driving down I-95 to go home to family for Christmas, so I wasn't home to get *that* call. I didn't find out until I arrived in South Carolina and called back to my Northern Virginia home. Suffice it to say that I was thrilled with my 'present from Santa Elisa!' I was really surprised that 'Transfiguration' made it into SNW 8. And I did not have the story with me so I couldn't read it! It wasn't until I got home after the Christmas holidays that I could sit down and read it. It was good—better than I remembered. (And let me say that Dean is a very smart man.)"

"This Drone"
(STAR TREK: VOYAGER)
M. C. DeMarco

 The Borg loses one of their own.

When asked about writing, M. C. commented, "I always thought of fiction as something only the professionals wrote, until I stumbled across fan fiction online. Then it seemed like something that crazy people wrote, but when I had an idea for a story the natural thing was to type it up and post it on the Internet like the other crazy people were doing. I heard about [SNW] from the crazy people, but I didn't submit any stories until SNW VI. I figured the professionals got money for their stories, and we crazy people just posted them online for free. But I was enjoying writing so much that I decided to try to become one of the pros—though not necessarily a *Trek* pro because I was too accustomed to writing about what I wanted to start playing by the rules. Nevertheless, I submitted one story to SNW VI and three to VII."

SNW 8 marks her first time making the anthology. " 'This Drone' started out as a more ambitious project to psychoanalyze Seven of Nine. Her sensitivity to light and sound in the story came from research into autism, which was my Theory of Seven at the time. I was looking into her behavior after she was first separated from the Collective for material I could work into my theory, but then her shifting pronoun usage took the story in an entirely new direction. I wrote it with the intention of submitting it to SNW VII, but at that point I still had just an idea without a plot so it stayed home when the other stories went out. In the summer of 2004, I attended the Odyssey Fantasy Writing Workshop and learned how to spot (and sometimes fix) problems in my stories. I tried fixing 'This Drone,' and apparently it worked. I also reworked two of my three submissions to SNW VII, one of which made the alternates list for SNW 8. When I got the message that I'd won, it took a while to sink in. I wondered why someone from Pocket Books would leave me a message, and then I wondered why [they'd] taken 'This Drone' over the story I'd thought had more of a shot."

"Once Upon a Tribble"
(STAR TREK: VOYAGER)
ANNIE REED

Tom and B'Elanna's daughter, Miral, is terrified that there might be a tribble hiding under her bed.

When asked about the story, Annie commented, "I had this idea about Tom Paris telling his young daughter a story to help her get over a nightmare about monsters under her bed. I always wanted to write a tribble story, and for Klingons, tribbles are monsters. Once I had the main character in Tom's fairytale—Fluffytail Fuzzypants—the story just came together. The writing process on this one was fairly easy. Sleep deprivation tends to shut down my internal editor and just let me write. I let myself have fun with this story, even with the more serious elements that come into play eventually, and it only took me about five hours to write. Finding out I won—I got a call on my cell phone from Elisa Kassin. I've been putting my cell number on manuscripts lately, and it was much better talking to Elisa in person than listening to a message on my answering machine. I was sitting in my car after I just got off work from my day job when Elisa called, and let me tell you, that call was the best part of my entire day. The competition for SNW just gets harder and harder every year, so I was really surprised and happy that 'Once Upon a Tribble' made it."

"You May Kiss the Bride"
(STAR TREK: VOYAGER)
AMY SISSON

 The rocky relationship of Tom and B'Elanna does not lead to a smooth wedding.

"I don't recall *exactly* what sparked the idea for 'You May Kiss the Bride.' In a general way, however, it was partly because I thought the *Voyager* series handled Tom and B'Elanna's 'wedding' just right—they didn't show it. Instead, we have Tom and B'Elanna experiencing their usual tumultuous relationship, deciding to get married practically without realizing what they were doing—and then cut to the shuttle with 'just married' on the back of it. At some point, months or years after that episode aired, it occurred to me their wedding would likely be as chaotic as their relationship. It seemed a fun opportunity to try and nail several *Voyager* characters' personalities and voices, especially Neelix, the Doctor, and Seven of Nine, all of whose quirks play a part in the wedding I imagined for Tom and B'Elanna. This is all a little ironic, considering that *Voyager* is my least favorite *Trek* show. (I'm not counting classic *Trek* anywhere in my 'ranking' because I didn't grow up with that show and have never seen the whole thing—I came to the *Trek* universe already familiar with *Next Gen* special effects and sensibilities, and couldn't successfully transition to classic *Trek*.) Part of the reason *Voyager* is my least favorite *Trek* show is that in my mind, there are actually few truly memorable episodes—I have to think hard to remember specific ones that I really enjoyed, unlike *Next Gen* or DS9. Even the controversial *Enterprise* seems more on top of things than *Voyager* did. But Tom and B'Elanna's relationship was one of the things I liked. I like the female characters to have strong personalities, and there's no denying that B'Elanna has a personality! And, really, I thought that the way the show handled the 'wedding' (or lack thereof) was perfect, especially considering we'd already seen a 'wedding' of who we thought was Tom and B'Elanna, but who turned out to be alien entities that believed they actually *were* the *Voyager* crew. Anyhow, this is a story I had submitted to an earlier SNW volume which had made the second read pile. This was the first time I'd ever tried resubbing; I'd always assumed it was verboten, but then saw on the boards that everyone else was resubbing, many of them successfully. And my reaction to having this one accepted: happiness, of course, but also surprise that it was this story over my other sub for SNW 8—even a little disappointment, because that other story is DS9 and Dax—my all-time favorite *Trek* show character—and instead my light and fluffy *Voyager* story got in."

"Coffee With a Friend"
(STAR TREK: VOYAGER)
J. B. STEVENS

A guilt-ridden Janeway bares all to the owner of a coffee shop.

Jan remarked, "I confess to being an undisciplined and often lazy writer, so I sat out SNW VII due to apathy."

For her winning story in SNW 8, she commented, "I'd been working on this story off and on for about three years. It started out as a way for me to vent my feelings after a very personal heartbreak, a time when I desperately needed a guardian angel of my own. When I lost my father two years ago (I was reviewing the galleys for 'Hidden' the day before his funeral), the story took a very different tack. I thought, what would happen if Janeway's father sent her an angel to help her cope with the shock of returning home, and the story evolved from there. Writing dialogue between Janeway and the angel that didn't sound stilted or like a psychology textbook was quite a challenge. I had to utilize a few resources on self-forgiveness before it sounded right, but I was happy with the final outcome. Obviously the editors were pleased as well. I got my 2004 Christmas present early when Elisa Kassin from Pocket Books called me at work with the good news. I'm not sure if there was any divine intervention involved in my good fortune, but I'd like to think that if I were in need, my father would send me an angel. In fact, there is no doubt in my mind

that he would. This story is dedicated to his memory."

"Egg Drop Soup"
(STAR TREK: ENTERPRISE)
ROBERT BURKE RICHARDSON

Phlox has an unforgettable lunch.

When asked about writing *Trek* stories, Robert commented, "I got into *Trek* literature through *Trek* literature. David R. George III in particular inspired me to turn my pen Trekward through a series of e-mail conversations as well as the personal nature of his own *Trek* work. *Star Trek* is a living mythology and the chance to have a small hand in shaping it is too tempting to pass up."

Robert has a history of submitting stories to the SNW contests. "I submitted five stories to SNW IV (none of which made the cut), and then decided to focus exclusively on original fiction. Shortly after the deadline for SNW VI, however, the idea that would become 'Egg Drop Soup' formed in my mind and demanded to be explored. I submitted the story to SNW VII—it was rejected, but with notes on how it could be made to work, and eventually found a home in SNW 8. The ingredients for 'Egg Drop Soup' are all there in the first episode of *Enterprise*, 'Broken Bow,' as background details for Dr. Phlox. I wrote the last paragraph of 'Egg Drop Soup' an hour or so after my grandfather passed away, still in that serene but twilit headspace some people will be familiar with, and the story is particularly precious to me because of that connection. The story is very sparse—the first draft came in at exactly 1,701 words—and it's almost as if I didn't write it, but rather that it was somehow written through me. There is a wonderful tradition in SNW where an editor (in the case of SNW 8, Elisa Kassin) calls each of the winners. I had all but forgotten about the story and thought at first that Elisa was calling about my student loan. I remained a step behind her for the duration of our conversation and vaguely recall stuttering foolishly. The news didn't actually sink in until about five minutes after I hung up; at which point I zipped gleefully around the room on one of those office chairs with wheels. I may or may not have spilled my tea."

"Hero"
(STAR TREK: ENTERPRISE)
LORRAINE ANDERSON

The ship's janitor and new barber saves the ship.

Lorraine remarked, "I can't remember how I heard about *Strange New Worlds*. I do remember that I was at the World Science Fiction convention—LoneStarCon—in 1997 where Dean Wesley Smith was a panelist and I asked him a couple of questions about it. (I believe his wife was a Hugo Nominee; I was at the Hugo loser party with a friend who was a Fan Artist nominee and he brushed by me.) I think I may have heard about it through the Kalama-

zoo *Star Trek* club I was in at the time. I submitted stories to all but one contest."

In terms of the idea for her story, she commented "I guess I've always wondered how the ships stayed looking so clean, so I invented a janitor. I placed him on Archer's *Enterprise*, because that *Enterprise* was still in the experimental stage, mechanical- and personnel-wise. If the ships have barbers, they must have some kind of maintenance system, apart from the engineers. Where there are people, there's dust! And the janitor doesn't necessarily have to be the smartest guy on the ship. It was my only submission this year, not that I've had a chance to submit multiple submissions in previous years. I had a major car accident in May; while I managed to (more or less) walk away with a concussion and major bruises, it took most of the summer for the double vision to fade. The deadline was coming up, so I thought that I just couldn't let this year go by without at least an attempt. I was angling for a nice rejection slip like I've had in previous years, because I was sure I didn't have a chance this year. This is part of the reason why the story is only 900 words. My writing has been hit-and-miss in the past eight years, since my parent's health started going downhill. (My dad died in 1998, my mom was in a wheelchair from 1998 until her stroke in 2000.) Since finding out I've won—which was a major shock, by the way—I finished one fan story that I promised a fanzine."

"Insanity"
(STAR TREK: ENTERPRISE)
A. RHEA KING

An alien hides a strange device on board, causing havoc.

Annette doesn't consider herself a *Trek* fan. "I took an interest in *Enterprise* because something in the characters, something that I can't quite put my finger on, sparked my interest. (Or maybe it was just Keating and Trineer's accents.) Actually, I want to write for *Enterprise* or a show in the same genre, but I write my scripts way weird. I write out a short story or novelette, and then format the short story into a script. Then I pack rat every story I write, so I now have a mess of *Enterprise* short stories living on my hard drive."

She heard about SNW at a convention in 2004 and submitted ten stories for the eighth contest. The idea for her story? "That's a story in itself. I have a nephew, just turned three. I love the little bug to death, but there are days that if the Goblin King were to step out of the *Labyrinth* movie, I'd hand him over! One day he was being a stink and I put him in the time out chair. I didn't know he had marbles in his pocket when I put him there. Being angry with me, he chucked one of the marbles at me. It was a perfect comedy scene! The dang marble boinked me in the head, took out my sister's favorite figurine, and nailed the cat! But it gave me an idea: a device that looks innocent and causes complete chaos. Originally the story

was going to focus on Reed's aquaphobia, but by the time the idea was finished, I had written this version of 'Insanity' instead. And for the better.

"This quote from the book *The Lord of the Rings and Philosophy* sums up why I like the idea so much: 'Even things that seem to be evil in themselves are not completely evil. . . . They are composed of parts that are not in themselves bad things. . . .' (p. 101). I was actually on the phone with a friend when I got the call, and what's odd is I don't normally answer calls from numbers I don't recognize. I'm glad I did."

"A & Ω" ("Alpha and Omega")
(FIRST PLACE)
(SPECULATIONS)
DEREK TYLER ATTICO

A Borg supercube appears in orbit above Earth and appears motionless.

Derek remembers watching certain TOS episodes as a kid and thinking how cool it was that Kirk would always think his way out of stuff and get the girl. "I loved the TOS movies but I think I really became a fan when I started to watch TNG and DS9. At the heart of every single story was the human condition and issues that made me consider the possibilities; I was in love. To me, the most powerful thing about *Star Trek* isn't the special effects or the cool ships, but that it gives inspiration. *Star Trek* flourishes and continues because while it entertains it shows us we can be better, be more than just the sum of our parts. The opportunity to add to that in some small way and be associated with people who think like that was irresistible."

Derek had no idea that the *Strange New World* contest existed until one day in a bookstore he stumbled upon SNW VI and bought it on the spot. "I really enjoyed all the stories by such talented fans and was totally blown away by the possibilities of the 'Speculations' section, like a kid being given his first box of crayons."

Regarding the grand prize-winning story, "I wanted to do a story that had all the elements I liked about *Star Trek*: great peril, personal conflict, and drama with a message that reached you no matter who you were. So I started looking at all the protagonists and antagonists in the *Star Trek* universe and the pieces started to fall into place for me. I have a background in Film; when I was thirteen I worked with Independent filmmaker Alonzo Speight, shooting, editing, everything. So as a writer I've adopted a film style to my writing, I do preproduction, production, and postproduction for all stories I do. For 'Alpha and Omega' preproduction consisted of reading all the encyclopedias and companion books (they were invaluable) as well as every official behind the scenes/production *Star Trek* book I could get my hands on. I'm very interested in the genesis to everything in the *Trek* universe. I spoke via e-mail with Astronomers and ex-NASA scientists on what would happen if a body half the size of the moon would take a geosynchronous orbit over Earth. I watched hours of *Trek* with the sound off to get the body language and demeanor of

the talented actors down, then I'd listen to other episodes and not watch the picture to get the cadence, rhythm, and tone of the voices; I find it all helps when I'm writing. For production I created a shooting script/plot outline—turning the story into scenes, assigning a rough word count for each scene. I'd go to the Writers-Room, a loft here in New York and stay till 2–3 AM working on the story. In post I wound up taking out the entire first chapter/scene that I'd written for the story; there was just no way to keep it and adhere to the 7,500-word limit. [When] I got the call from Elisa, all I remember is her telling me that my story got into SNW and that there was more . . . it had made first place. I was stunned."

"Concurrence"
(SECOND PRIZE)
(SPECULATIONS)
Geoffrey Thorne

 he crew of the Starship *Fenton* answers a distress call.

"When 'The Soft Room' won second place (in SNW VI), Dean was still doing his AOL master class for SNW hopefuls (or anyone who just wanted the nuts 'n' bolts of fiction construction). After the winners were announced he was asked to give a detailed analysis of why/how he chose a given story and how it got its particular place in the sequence. He was REALLY complimentary about 'The Soft Room' (I still have the original AOL post somewhere) and he ended by saying there was 'a novel's worth' of story left untold. Which was sort of the intent (not for a novel, exactly, but just to leave the question hanging creepily at the end). I submitted a bunch of stuff to SNW VII and didn't get the nod, so I went back to the drawing board. One of the great things about SNW is that it's the only time a *Trek* writer can just *write* the story without having to adhere to editorial guidelines of any sort beyond the contest rules. I knew that, with 'Chiaroscuro' being in *Prophecy and Change*, and that I was already in preliminary talks about a *Voyager* novel (back-burnered since then, unfortunately), that SNW 8 might be the last chance I had to really just flex without any constraints in the *Trek* universe. So I wrote one story for each series (I was really fond of one that had Worf visiting a Klingon monastery after Jadzia's death. Oh well) and I also wrote what I thought would be the next 'appropriate' chapter in the life of M5/Risak, and brought in the androids from 'I, Mudd.' The big hurdle was to continue what began in 'The Soft Room' without giving away what I was doing and to maintain the level of increasing creepiness that I tried to put into the first one. It never tracked for me that Mudd's androids would have been so passive after Kirk's defeat and subsequent reprogramming of their society. It occurred to me that a machine that sophisticated would have all sorts of back-ups and contingency plans. If their first attempt to 'take care of the Federation' hadn't worked, it made sense that they'd take what they'd learned from their failure and have another go. So I came up with the idea of Simulants—androids of such sophistication that they would pass for organic even under intense medical scanning. After I worked out how they

might accomplish that, the rest was pretty easy. As for getting another silver SNW medal, that was totally unexpected. The quality of the writing increases with every book, IMO, so I was frankly just happy to get in. When Elisa told me I got the silver again I was floored. Ask her. I acted like a complete monkey."

"Dawn"
(SPECULATIONS)
PAUL J. KAPLAN

 The crew of the *Enterprise*-D beam aboard a strange passenger.

"Figuring I was on a roll, I took the one other story I'd submitted to SNW VII and resubmitted *it* the next year, to SNW 8. But this time I broke the streak: My rerun was rejected again, but my new story (unlike some, who are wildly prolific, I seem to submit no more than one new story a year) made it in. That story, 'Dawn,' almost didn't happen. The idea came from the use of Ceti Alpha V in the *Enterprise* episode, 'Twilight'—it's probably the best episode of that series so far, and it's one of my favorite episodes of any series. The basic premise came to me pretty quickly—what if that timeline had continued and those last survivors had found Khan, instead of Kirk—and from there I quickly found my setup: A mystery guest appears, gasps 'Thank Khan,' and drops. But I had a heck of a time figuring out what to do with it. It took me several months and a lot of hot water to work out the plot. When I finally had it settled in my head, I couldn't find time to write. So with the submission deadline just a few days away, I had only about five pages written and figured I'd never get it done. But then I got inspired by some last-minute e-mails among fellow SNW alums and decided to push through. The day before the story had to be mailed, I stayed up into the wee hours writing and then took it to work with me the next day. I took care of my most pressing business, closed my door, and wrote for the rest of the day in my office. I finished it just in time for one final read and then overnighted it to New York. Even though the idea took several months to come together, I'd never committed something to paper that fast. But I was really pleased with the result, and I hope readers enjoy it. With three sales under my belt, I'm allegedly a 'professional' now and can no longer submit to SNW. I'd love to keep writing, though, and we'll see what happens. But whatever comes next, I'll always be grateful to editor Dean Wesley Smith, Pocket Books' John Ordover and Elisa Kassin, and Paramount's Paula Block for embracing the fans and giving us such a great way to add to the tapestry of *Trek*."

VOLUME NINE

STRANGE NEW WORLDS

DEAN WESLEY SMITH, WITH ELISA J. KASSIN AND PAULA M. BLOCK, EDITORS

AUGUST 2006   **(365PP)**

TRADE PAPERBACK

"Gone Native"
(STAR TREK)
JOHN COFFREN

What happened to the Kelvans from the Andromeda Galaxy after they settled here?

John wanted to tell an old school, science fiction story of a human being interacting with a non-bipedal, otherworldly alien and his story that won was his eighth and final submission. He said, " 'Gone Native' was one of the first stories I worked on for the contest but I abandoned it about halfway through. Seven stories later and with the deadline looming, I really felt compelled to get one more story in. I rediscovered it on a floppy disk, worked out the rest of the narrative, and mailed it in three days before the contest closed. I was asleep when the call came. (I'd put in a late night at the newspaper.) I walked to the kitchen and saw the message button flashing. When I hit play and heard Elisa's voice, I said to my wife and kids, 'I won!' A lot of the credit for this story has to go to the Paneranormals, Jim Johnson's writing group that I joined last spring. Eight stories are the highest output I've ever had for a contest. Funny thing, I didn't have time to show the group 'Gone Native,' so the story that won is the story they didn't critique. I have since quit that group. (Jim, I'm only joking.)"

"A Bad Day for Koloth"
(STAR TREK)
DAVID DELEE

 Koloth's ship after they left space station K-7.

The story is essentially a sequel to the classic "Trouble with Tribbles" episode and tells the tale of what happened on Koloth's ship after Scotty transported all the tribbles over to it at the end of the show. David said, "I think it's a question many, many fans have wondered about since that episode aired nearly forty years ago. I hope I did it justice. 'A Bad Day for Koloth' was one of seven stories I submitted this year, coincidentally the same number of stories as I submitted last year for SNW 8. If I were superstitious I'd say seven is my lucky number."

He continued, "I started writing new stories early last year, right around the beginning of the year. When SNW 8 was released several reviewers commented on how dark the stories were, overall, compared to previous years. This was not a knock of the book, but more a general comment. I remember looking at some of the stories I'd finished for SNW 9 and thinking they too were rather dark in tone, so I set out to write something lighter. Of course when you're dealing with the Klingons, the humor ran more to black comedy than was my original intent. As for waiting on the call, that is of course always a nerve-wracking experience. This year the calls went out later than last year so in between I continually vacillated between hopefulness and convincing myself I hadn't been selected. I guess that made getting the call that much more exciting in the end."

"Book of Fulfillment"
(STAR TREK)
STEVEN COSTA

 The Klingon subjugation of a world.

Steven heard about *Strange New Worlds* when he was browsing in a bookstore one day and his brother pointed it out to him. The second anthology had just been published, and he was immediately fascinated by the concept of fans writing stories for the *Star Trek* universe. Steven said, "Several years ago, I submitted a story called 'Depth Charge,' but unfortunately, I didn't have a thorough grasp of the rules at the time. I placed my story in the *New Frontier* setting, thinking I'd garner some attention by doing something unusual. Last year I also submitted a story, 'Fairest of Them All,' a *Voyager* story set in the Mirror Universe. It made the alternate list, which really encouraged me to enter again this year."

When asked about his story, he commented, "I'm one of Jehovah's Witnesses, and I was attending a Bible convention in early September. I started to wonder what the sacred texts of alien cultures might look like. That's what gave me the idea of structuring a story in the Chapter/Verse format you see in the Bible. Also, I'm a big fan of the 'shared universe' concept called the 'Wold-Newton Family.' It's a sort of literary game in which you try to find or infer interactions between famous fictional characters. I wanted to do something similar, but in a *Trek*-related way. That's why, in my story, I had Captain Picard's archaeology mentor discover an ancient scroll that features Captain Kirk and refers to Captain Archer."

Steven sent in five stories for SNW 9. He commented, "Unfortunately, I'm still learning the self-discipline I need to be a successful writer. In addition to the stories I sent in, I had seven more in various stages of completion that I just couldn't get myself to finish on time. The stories I did send were all mailed at the very last minute. In fact, 'Hell's Heart' very nearly didn't make it at all. When the date listed in the rules for the notification of the winners was approaching, I was naturally becoming more and more nervous, haunting Dean's forum and the SNW Writers Group on Yahoo!. When the twenty-third came and went, I started to get very downhearted. I was pretty depressed I have to admit. I had high hopes for this year's batch

of stories. When I came home and found the message on my answering machine that I'd actually won . . . well, I confess: I danced around my apartment, pumping my fists and hissing 'Yessss!' over and over. Not my proudest moment . . . actually, on second thought, I think it was!"

"The Smallest Choices"
(STAR TREK)
JEREMY YODER

 T'Pring's life after her decision to marry Stonn.

Jeremy was thrilled after learning about SNW because he couldn't believe there was an outlet for upstart writers to write *Star Trek* fiction that didn't require an agent. He immediately started writing. He entered a story the year after he discovered the contest but it was rejected. However, after several edits, it made the alternate list this year. He sent in a total of nine stories and two made the alternate list. He said, "As any fan of TOS knows, the story of Spock and T'Pring in 'Amok Time' is brilliant, and in the back of my mind, I've always wondered how life played out for T'Pring. Did she ever regret her rejection of Spock? As a Vulcan, could she even allow herself to think about it? My story, set far into the future, attempts to answer those questions from her perspective as she and Spock come together for the first time since that episode."

Writing the story almost didn't happen. " 'Amok Time' is a classic, and I felt somewhat arrogant to even consider touching such a wonderful story and characters. Yet I always questioned why T'Pring selected Stonn. She gives a reason for rejecting Spock, but not a reason for choosing Stonn—and as a true Vulcan, it shouldn't be 'love.' However, as I started writing, other factors worked their way into the story (including a tie-in to Spock's reunification talks with the Romulans) that excited me and things really started to click. As for how I found out I had won, I'm afraid my initial response to the phone call was rather Vulcan! I had moved on from SNW and started other writing projects. Not only that, but when my phone rang, I was involved at work. So when I answered and heard 'This is Pocket Books . . .' I thought, 'Pocket Books? Why are they calling me?' Then I knew. After being told 'The Smallest Choices' had been accepted, I have to admit I was so involved in other writing projects that I couldn't remember which story that was! After thanking her and asking one or two questions, we said good-bye. It was about a minute later it really hit me. I leaped out of my chair and called my wife to gush my excitement. (After which, I looked up the story to see which one had been accepted!) So ironically, my reaction was the reversal of Spock's at the end of 'Amok Time,' when he shows emotion and then composes himself. I wish I'd have shown some emotion on the phone, but it really blindsided me and served as a pleasant shock."

"Staying the Course"
(STAR TREK: THE NEXT GENERATION)
PAUL C. TSENG

To save a world, Worf must make the ultimate sacrifice.

When asked about his story, Paul remarked, "I have to say that the Gospel according to St. Luke has been an inspiration. Theological themes of the sacrifice of one innocent to save a world have always been a very powerful and personal theme to me. The moral dilemma in 'Staying the Course' plays out on several levels—political, moral, and familial. But what spoke most powerfully to me was the story of the Olympic marathon runner Derek Redmond who tore a muscle in the Barcelona Olympics, mid-race. While the other runners past him by, he refused to stop. He limped, hopped, and tried his best to finish his course. In the end, his father pushed passed security guards and slung his arm around his shoulder helping him to the finish line. Though he came in last, he was a winner on a much deeper level and his father played an important role in that victory. That sparked the idea for the relationship between a future Worf and his mature adult son Alexander."

The story was one of twenty-one submissions for the contest. He commented, "I tend to force myself to write with deadlines and goals, actual and self-imposed. I had to do some research into the history of the Barcelona Olympics and Derek Redmond to properly cite the event in my story. Finding out I had won was a challenge because I was out of town and I didn't get to check my messages. Elisa called an old cell phone number, which I had never officially updated with her. I did state my actual cell number on my manuscripts and cover letters, but I suppose since they already had my contact info from SNW 8 they left messages there. So you can imagine how nervous I was when no one called that cell number. So instead, I called home and had someone play my answering machine messages over the phone. When I heard, I nearly did a backflip!"

"Home Soil"
(STAR TREK: THE NEXT GENERATION)
JIM JOHNSON

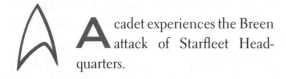

A cadet experiences the Breen attack of Starfleet Headquarters.

Jim said, "My wife and I live in Virginia, where a significant portion of the American Civil War battles played out. We took a day trip to the New Market battlefield, which was the site of a relatively minor battle that featured a significant event—cadets from Virginia Military Institute (VMI) took the field, saw action, and helped turn the tide of the battle for the Confederates. On the drive home, I thought about the battle and (having just recently returned from last year's Shore Leave) thought about how I could somehow turn it into a *Star Trek* story. I remembered that the Breen had attacked San Francisco during the Dominion War, and the concept of the story fell into

place. Like the VMI cadets during the Civil War, the Starfleet cadets would be called upon to help carry the day against the Breen defending the academy's home soil, Earth. That was the concept going in, but the story changed itself as I wrote it. I knew I had to add a *Star Trek* regular to the mix somehow, so I figured one of the officers familiar to us had to be at the academy for some reason. I thought Data would make a good choice, and him paired up with the cadet I created worked out somehow. Story evolution is a wonderful thing. The cadet revealed all kinds of interesting things about herself, and she pretty much carried me along for the ride. Once the basic concept was in place, I started writing it. I went through a couple of false starts, but then found the main character, how she related to Data, and how she worked her way through the Breen attack. Once I had written the first draft (I think it took me three days), I gave it to my wife (also my first reader) and to the members of the Paneranormal Society (a group of SNW and *Star Trek* writers in the northern Virginia area—myself, Kim Sheard, Kevin Summers, Kevin Lauderdale, Gerri Leen, Susan McCrackin, and John Coffren). The feedback I got from everyone was specific and helpful, and I incorporated many of their comments into the story. I revised it and mailed it off to Dean shortly thereafter."

"Terra Tonight"
(STAR TREK: THE NEXT GENERATION)
SCOTT PEARSON

 news service interviews Captain Montgomery Scott.

Scott remembered, "After the death of Jimmy Doohan, I really wanted to write another Scotty story in his honor. I wanted to come up with an idea that would only have a few characters in it, so that it would stay focused on Scotty, and that would have a retrospective feel to it—even though Scotty still has the rest of his life before him. It also seemed natural to do it as a follow-up to 'Full Circle,' which gave me the timeframe for the story. I also sent in a DS9 story and a *Next Generation* story. I liked both of them, but I was hoping that if I won again it would be 'Terra Tonight.' Not only was it my fond farewell to Jimmy Doohan, but I named the cadet character after my eight-year-old daughter, who has become such a *Trek* fan that she asked to have her room redecorated with a *Star Trek* theme. It's a really cool room! The writing went fairly smoothly. The novels *Articles of the Federation* and *Vanguard: Harbinger* inspired the setting of the story on a news program—both of them had the news media as a major presence. The idea about Scotty giving advice about really whacking something, I've had in my head for probably ten years! I just never came up with a story to go around it until now."

"Solace in Bloom"
(STAR TREK: THE NEXT GENERATION)
JEFF D. JACQUES

 friend of Jean Luc's is captured by the Jem'Hadar.

Jeff commented, " 'Solace in Bloom' was the second of only two stories I sent this year, the other being a light-hearted Naomi story for VGR. The idea for the story came about as I wanted to visit a minor character that no one had really explored before in print. After mulling the pantheon of *Trek* characters, I came up with Louis, the old friend of Picard's that we met briefly in the fourth season episode 'family.' I wondered what this guy had been up to since we last saw him. More specifically, I wondered what he was up to during the Dominion War, and from there the story developed. I wanted to see this kind, likable fellow in a truly harrowing, life-changing situation that keeps getting worse and worse for him as the story progresses. I also interweaved flashbacks to his younger days, hanging out with his old friend Jean-Luc. These reflections, while lighter, do vaguely connect with the horror he's facing back in the 'present day,' at least in a transitional way, if not thematically. These interludes also give us some insight into Picard's younger self as the two friends relate to one another. I studied the Louis portions of 'Family' and weaved in most of the details we learn about him in the story, including the Bloom sisters, who figure to some extent in the flashbacks (hence the Bloom in the title, which also works on another level, too). And that's pretty much how the story came about. I finished the story in August and mailed it shortly thereafter. I'm quite happy with how it turned out, and I told myself at the time that if I was going to win SNW this year, I hoped it would be for 'Solace in Bloom.' And lo and behold, that's what happened!"

"Shadowed Allies"
(STAR TREK: DEEP SPACE NINE)
EMILY P. BLOCH

 Is Kira experiencing flashbacks from her life?

Emily remarked, "I heard about SNW from another *Trek* fan. I've been writing *Deep Space Nine* stories for about three years, since I fell madly in love with the series, and once I found out there was a possibility of having one of my stories published, I worked on 'Shadowed Allies' for a year. It's the first story I've submitted to a *Star Trek* writing contest, and my only submission to SNW 9. Many of my stories feature Kira Nerys as the main character, as I'm a huge fan of both her individual storyline and the relationship between her and Odo. After watching the entire television series and reading all of the DS9 relaunch books, I began to write about certain storylines that I've wanted to know more about: Kira's reaction to Odo leaving for the Great Link and their process of saying good-bye; Odo's return and temporary reunion with Kira in *Unity* by S. D. Perry; Kira's loyalty to those she cares about. From

there, the story developed into 'Shadowed Allies' and I kept reworking it until everything felt right. When I found out I was one of the contest winners, I was ecstatic. I'm an aspiring writer and actress, and have respected the creators, writers, and actors of the *Star Trek* universe for many years. Having 'Shadowed Allies' be my first published work has exceeded my wildest dreams."

"Living on the Edge of Existence"
(STAR TREK: DEEP SPACE NINE)
GERRI LEEN

 Sisko's life among the Prophets.

When asked about her story in SNW 9, Gerri said, "I wanted to do a post-'What You Leave Behind' story that centered on Sisko in the Wormhole/Celestial Temple. I wanted it to be trippy—the way the show depicted any interaction with the Prophets—so it was a challenge to get that feel into a story that still had enough cohesion to make sense. And it had to be true to Sisko, who ties with Kirk as my favorite captain, and who was so well developed in the series."

She submitted ten stories for the contest covering all of the series except *Enterprise*. One of the stories was an alternate for SNW 8, three were reworked stories and six were new. "I was very lucky to get into SNW VII on my first attempt. I didn't get into SNW 8, and that was a hard experience, but it was probably a good one. It made me examine how much I want to write, and how hard I'm willing to work. And it made me more open to trying new things. I have two friends who take first crack at my stuff, so I owe them a huge thank you for reading, proofing, and making suggestions on three-years-worth of submissions. Last year, I also joined a writing group with fellow *Star Trek* writers in the Northern Virginia/Baltimore area. That's been enormously helpful, just getting reactions and criticism—as well as having more sets of eyes to find problems or typos. We also share news about other *Star Trek* opportunities and/or sci-fi/fantasy writing in general, which is invaluable. As far as finding out I'd won, when I got into SNW VII, my notification went astray somehow, and I found out when the list was released online—one of the aforementioned friends sent it to me. So for SNW 9, it was still an adventure, because the phone call from Elisa was shiny and new. It was thrilling to hear I'd made it in. Especially coming off a year where I hadn't made it in—that made me appreciate it all the more."

"The Last Tree on Ferenginar: A Ferengi Fable From the Future"
(STAR TREK: DEEP SPACE NINE)
MIKE MCDEVITT

A story set in Rom's reign as Grand Nagus where Ogger wants to cut down the last tree on Ferenginar.

Mike remembered, "I heard about *Strange New Worlds* a few years ago, working in Chapters Bookstore and borrowing books all the time. I submitted a story about three to four years ago called 'Family Reunion,' which took place mostly inside the comatose mind of Data. Then nothing for a few years and this year I submitted three: 'Last Tree on Ferenginar,' 'Uncaged' (about how a Talosian dealt with the death of Pike), and 'I Only Have Eyes for You' (about a hologram on a quest for true love across time and space). I was delighted to hear from Elisa when one made it! I guess I had the idea when I watched my new Jim Henson 'The Storyteller' DVD and I was thinking about myth and fairy tales and thought I'd try my hand at one in a *Star Trek* setting. I've loved *Trek* in all its forms, since watching my uncle's tapes of the classic series at age six. *Star Trek* and *Doctor Who* at my uncle Clifford's house inspired a lifelong love of sci-fi. I wrote my first *Trek* fiction over the summer vacation in 1990 because I was going crazy wondering how 'Best of Both Worlds' would turn out. I wrote my own ending, and as I recall, I saved Picard but killed Shelby. In Grade 11 and 12, I entertained my fellow *Trek* nerds between classes by writing 'Space *Trek*' and 'Space Trek II: The Wrath of Montalkhan': parody novellas which indulged my affection for crossovers and dumb jokes. My evil villain was Dr. Pulaski. For the three stories I submitted this summer, I scrawled the ideas in a notebook on the bus to work, then typed them on my home computer in the evenings while listening to a cassette of the soundtrack to *Star Trek IV*. I owe *Star Trek* big time, not to mention my friends and girlfriend, and now Elisa and Pocket Books, for the chance to share my humor and whatnot. Plus my uncle and aunt and their VCR."

"The Tribbles' Pagh"
(STAR TREK: DEEP SPACE NINE)
RYAN M. WILLIAMS

 Will the tribbles multiply enough to engulf the planet Bajor?

Ryan learned about *Strange New Worlds* by finding the books in the store. "I've always been a fan of *Star Trek* but hadn't read much of the *Trek* fiction. A few years ago I met Julia Ecklar and Karen Rose Cercone at Seton Hill University. I was in the Masters of Arts Writing Popular Fiction program. Talking with them encouraged me to explore *Trek* fiction. I started reading more *Trek* novels and found that I really enjoyed the stories. Although I've mostly focused on writing my own original work I de-

cided I'd really like to write professional *Star Trek* stories as well."

He submitted stories to SNW VII and 8 but didn't win until now. He submitted one other story to SNW 9, but he wasn't as happy with it as he was with the winning story. " 'Tribbles' Pagh' has had a bit of history. The title was actually the first thing that came to me for this story. After I had the title I started asking myself questions. What was the tribbles' pagh? What is the purpose for tribbles? The DS9 episode 'Trials and Tribble-ations' left the crew with a wonderful problem. What were they going to do with the tribbles? What if the tribbles got to Bajor? I gave the story a good shot and sent it off to SNW VII. Dean rejected it and sent it back with some comments about the ending. I looked at what he said and decided he had a good point. I threw out the last two thirds of the story and gave it more thought. While I considered what to do, the fifth season came out on DVD and I rewatched the episode. Watching the episode again helped. I reworked the first third of the story and wrote the rest from scratch. Kathleen, my wife, is my first editor and she had some suggestions for that draft. I made some more revisions based on her feedback and sent the story off for SNW 8. I'd also written one other original series story for SNW 8. Once again the stories came back. I don't remember what Dean said about the other story, but he commented again that he liked the 'Tribbles Pagh.' This time, however, it simply didn't 'fit' with the SNW 8 mix of stories. I held onto the story and sent it back for SNW 9. I found out I'd won while I was at work. Elisa had called my home and talked to Kathleen. Kathleen gave her my work number. I'm the circulation supervisor in a public library so it was a surprise to get a call from Pocket Books instead of a call to renew books. I think my response was pretty calm. Since Elisa asked that I not post the news or make announcements until Pocket issued the news I just kept working. But I think I was smiling more the rest of the day."

"Choices"
(SECOND PRIZE)
(STAR TREK: VOYAGER)
SUSAN S. McCRACKIN

 Seven of Nine finds herself paralyzed.

Susan remarked, "The inspiration for 'Choices' came as a result of visiting my uncle last January. He had been in a bicycle accident the year before and, as a result, is now a quadriplegic. January was my first visit with him. I guess 'Choices' came of our conversations during my first visit. The writing process, once started, was extremely painful and emotionally wrenching. There were a number of nights I could only move the story forward by enough words to make a sentence. Then, I'd shut down the computer and go to bed. It was that hard. And it took a while and the feedback of some great friends to get the final version right. I knew what I was trying to say, but it took some time and a little distance to get my message out. I wasn't sure it was right when I sent it out, but I guess it was! The story is very much in honor of my uncle and I hope it is a message of

hope and of having the courage to make the right choice, even when it is at great personal cost. I sent in two stories this year—'Choices' and 'The Gift,' which had been an alternate for the last two volumes. I was at work when Elisa called. Needless to say I was thrilled, both that I got in and that the winning story was 'Choices.' But I was not expecting for it to be a second place winner! I think I went to sleep that night thinking 'second place' and I definitely woke up the next morning with that thought in my head! What a thrill! And definitely the best Christmas present I got, even if it did arrive a few days after Christmas."

"Unconventional Cures"
(STAR TREK: VOYAGER)
RUSS CROSSLEY

 The doctor tries to save Naomi Wildman.

Russ commented, "This story came about from a work-for-hire workshop taught by Dean Wesley Smith and Loren Coleman in the summer of 2004. We were challenged to write a tribble story and I wrote this one. The genesis of the story came from the line, 'Take two tribbles and call me in the morning,' which struck me as pretty funny. From there I set the story on *Voyager* and the rest just came naturally. I submitted this story for SNW 8 and it made the cut, but for some reason Paula rejected it. Dean suggested I resubmit it this year, and the others that made the alternate list, which I did, and I wrote two new stories that I also submitted. I found out I'd won when Elisa left a message on my answering machine. I must say, while I am no longer eligible for SNW, I am extremely proud to be in three volumes of this anthology because, while I do write other things, it's waaay fun for me to write *Star Trek* stories."

"Maturation"
(STAR TREK: VOYAGER)
CATHERINE E. PIKE

 A young Annika Hansen is assimilated.

Cathy was inspired for her story in an unusual way. "My mother had gotten encephalitis in 1997, and lost her hearing. She died this past August, but had often said she would rather have lost her hearing than her sight (she was an avid reader). I began to wonder what it would be like to be aware, but to not have your sight or your hearing at all, and then I thought, hey, wouldn't that be like a Borg maturation chamber. So I thought I would take Annika Hansen from her abduction at the hands of the Borg to her becoming, when fully grown, Seven of Nine. 'Maturation' pretty much wrote itself after that, with only minor tweaking needed. I submitted 'Maturation' for SNW VII and SNW 8. Of course, in VII, my story 'The Little Captain' was published, but 'Maturation' made it on the alternate list. Last year, it made the alternate list *again*, and Dean asked me to submit it 'one more time.' So I did. Unchanged. And it won. 'Maturation' was my only submission this year. Last year I had also sub-

mitted a Tasha Yar story that didn't make it in. The call that I had been selected came while I was away for Christmas. I had gone out of state actually, came home, listened to my messages, and there it was. I jumped around and hooted and hollered a bit, then, realizing I was now no longer eligible to participate in further contests, felt bummed for about a second. I'm in a very elite group of three-timers, and I'm proud to be there!"

"Rounding a Corner Already Turned"
(STAR TREK ENTERPRISE)
ALLISON CAIN

 Malcolm ends up needing more than just a simple rescue.

Allison heard about *Strange New Worlds* when her parents bought the first book. "I thought it'd be great to enter, and I was already writing back then . . . but nothing really worth reading, so I dropped the idea. A few years down the road, I stumbled across the contest rules for SNW 9 while browsing online and thought I'd give it another shot (and I'm glad I did). The only writing I've submitted to contests previously were requirements in grade school—I think one was a haiku."

This story was her only submission. She continued, "Lt. Reed is my favorite character from *Enterprise*, and when we were little, my sisters and I loved to imagine what it would be like to be able to do all the things animals could do — run fast, hear better, and so forth. As I got older, I realized that being an animal with a human brain would be much more of a hindrance than an advantage — think of all the things you couldn't do: talk, write, use the computer. Because of Reed's rather stoic personality, it amused me greatly to imagine him trapped in Porthos' body — and I also saw him as being the one crew member best equipped to deal with such a situation. I tried the first few pages out on my sister and she thought it was funny (and also demanded a conclusion), so I decided it might be worth a shot, finished it off, and sent it out. For the record, the story is intended to be a comedy. I won't be offended if you laugh (quite the opposite!), because I laughed writing it. Poor Malcolm! (And poor Porthos — although, honestly, he had more fun.)"

"Mother Nature's Little Reminders"
(STAR TREK ENTERPRISE)
A. RHEA KING

 rcher and crew fight some "bad weather."

This story was one of eleven she submitted this year. "My family is from western Kansas and eastern Colorado and tales of twisters have been passed down to me. It was my own brush with one that prompted the story. So I combined elements of tornado stories from across the generations and wove the story into Trip's

past. I wrote this a couple of years ago and I remember I did a lot of research about tornadoes and attended an exhibit at the Denver Natural History Museum about the phenomenon. I was absolutely thrilled to win again."

"Mestral" (THIRD PRIZE)
(STAR TREK ENTERPRISE)
BEN GUILFOY

 he Vulcan left behind in the *Enterprise* episode 'Carbon Creek' watches the world radically change.

Ben remarked, "I've known about SNW for quite some time, probably first saw the anthology on the shelves maybe the fourth year that they'd done it and thought that I'd love to try it. Unfortunately, I fell prey to that beast that usually strikes wannabe writers — making excuses like 'Oh, I don't have the time this year' or whatever, when really it's just that ill-defined fear that keeps you from entering. This year, I'm out of college and told myself as I saw the deadline was approaching that if I was really serious about being a writer (and I am) that I had to *get* serious about it and try. So this was my first (and only) entry into the contest . . . imagine my surprise that I did so well on my first attempt! I'm not entirely certain what gave me the idea for the story because, frankly, I had it a long time ago and I just don't remember. I started writing the story probably two or three years ago and the original version of it was really, really different. And even though I never finished it because I didn't like the way it was turning out, I liked the idea and it stuck with me. So this year I tried again, and wrote it very quickly. I think I started it maybe a week before the deadline, wrote *most* of it, and then dropped it for a few days and almost didn't turn it in at all. I mailed it Friday and the deadline was Saturday. I wasn't even sure the story even made it in on time! Finding out I won was a strange experience, too. I basically just stuttered into the phone, 'I . . . uh . . . are . . . are you serious?' I imagine it was pretty comical. But I was excited. A lot. I tried once or twice earlier in the year, but this is my first actual sale of a story. And I'm hoping, not the last."

"Remembering the Future"
(SPECULATIONS)
RANDY TATANO

irk is offered a chance to tamper with fate.

Randy has entered one or two stories every single year and has made the alternate list the last three. This year, in addition to his winning story, he also submitted the story, "What's a Nice Girl Like You Doing In a Holodeck Like This?" which was an alternate last year. Dean requested he resubmit it. "Someone asked me, 'If you had to do it all over again, would you have been a television reporter?' I've always wondered about that, and thought people should get a 'do-over' at some point during

their lives. Who among us, given the chance, wouldn't go back and change something? So when I was trying to come up with a story this summer, I put myself in Captain Kirk's shoes and asked the same question. What would Kirk change if he could change one thing? The answer hit me immediately. He had to save Edith Keeler from 'City on the Edge of Forever' without changing history. Writing this story was like figuring out a giant puzzle. I knew the ending but had no idea how to get there, so in effect I was writing the story backwards. I also knew I was basing this story on perhaps the best *Star Trek* episode ever conceived, so I had to be extremely careful how I handled it. 'City' is like a priceless heirloom to Trekkers, and I had to treat it as such. After weeks of trying to figure out this story, it hit me when I was watching *Wrath of Khan*. The Kobayashi Maru. Kirk would have to cheat in some way to save Edith Keeler. I picked up the story at Kirk's death in *Generations*, created an afterlife scenario in which he is given the chance for a 'do-over,' and then let him 'remember the future' so that he could trick the Guardian and save Edith."

When asked about the phone call, Randy remarked, "I'm a former television reporter who has had a great many thrills in my career. I've interviewed Jay Leno at his home and he gave me a personal tour of his car collection. I've stood on the floor of the Republican National Convention and turned to watch Ronald Reagan pass by. At the Baseball Hall of Fame I had Ernie Banks playfully steal my microphone while I was doing a stand-up. I got a hug from Vanna White. None of this compares to getting 'the phone call' for the first time. Hands down, it is the thrill of a lifetime. Funny, writers often use the term 'tears of joy,' but this is the first time I literally experienced it. I actually cried when I found out I'd won. That night the left-over Christmas turkey tasted better than lobster. There's a big difference between writing a television news story and getting something published. A TV story is gone to Pluto the minute it airs. Gone forever. Having your work published is something permanent. This has been a long time coming, so it was really special. In 1998 I left TV reporting and started my first novel. I sent it out without showing it to anyone, and of course it didn't sell. A friend put me in touch with two local authors who taught me about the importance of conflict and how to 'show, don't tell.' I got a writing critique partner and attended a few seminars. I read tons of best sellers to try and figure out the common denominator. I wrote two more novels (not sci-fi) and I think the third one has a chance. I was truly a babe in the woods when it came to the publishing business. Writing a television news story and writing fiction aren't even remotely related. But the reason I kept entering this particular contest was Dean Wesley Smith. I didn't realize you should include a SASE for a contest entry; I never expected those who lost to hear anything. Dean sent me a handwritten critique with some suggestions, and used his own postage. I figured: I must be getting close; and Dean must be a great guy to spend his own money on postage to help aspiring writers. The last five years I've gotten handwritten notes from him. They have really inspired me and kept me going. One other note of interest. When I was a student at the University of Connecticut, I signed up for several writing classes. One day about two weeks into one such class the professor arrived and called me out into the hall. He told me, 'Don't come to class any-

more. You have no writing talent.' He handed me the writing I'd submitted. It contained a really nasty note, which belittled my writing and me. I was devastated but had two other professors who believed in me and told me to forget it. But being a New York-area Sicilian, I never did."

"Rocket Man"
(SPECULATIONS)
KENNETH E. CARPER

Gary Seven needs the help of Agent K.

Kenneth commented, "I heard about SNW from reading the *Star Trek Communicator* back when the contest was first announced. I refrained from writing for the contest for many years until this last summer when I finally worked up the sufficient nerve to put my work out there for scrutiny. Luckily Dean, in his great wisdom, enjoyed 'Rocket Man.' I of course am eternally grateful."

He continued, 'Rocket Man' was my third entry in the contest and as they say, 'Third time's the charm.' Funnily I wasn't going to submit it because I thought an action/adventure story wouldn't go over well. Generally the stories in SNW are more character-based whereas mine has a heavy-action element to it. Originally the story was set a few years after the prologue to *Generations*. It featured Chekov and was to show his growth from brash young ensign to hardened captain. In it he would constantly ask himself, 'Vhat vould Keptin Kirk do?' In the end it would turn out to be a holodeck simulation. An initiation into Section 31. The problem was that as I wrote it I discovered a few things:

1. I could in no way see Chekov doing any of these things. Kirk, yeah, but not Chekov.
2. A holodeck simulation? Blaaargh! What a cheat!
3. Section 31 is widely regarded as the bad guys even if there is a necessity for their help. Having Chekov join them would probably not play well.

"So I sat back and asked myself who this story would work with and there was only one answer, Kirk. But I obviously couldn't set it a few years after the prologue as Kirk was in the Nexus. I couldn't set it before *Generations* as he was never a member of Section 31 and I don't think he would join if he were offered the chance. So I asked myself how I could work Kirk into the story. I mean he died at the end of *Generations*, didn't he? Everybody but William Shatner says yes. Well, I never liked that they killed him in the first place and I had to admit that the idea of bringing him back was appealing—but how? I mean Section 31 can keep the Federation secure but they can't bring back the dead. Who could bring back the dead? I flashed on that great episode 'Assignment Earth' and all the advanced technology in it. I doubted that even Seven's benefactors could conquer death, but delay it, maybe. It also helped me with the Section 31 quandary I had. I doubt Kirk would join Section 31 because they're so sinister but Seven is a good guy and he does what Kirk does. He makes a difference. So with Kirk and Seven in place I crafted

my story and I feel it works really well. I certainly wouldn't be against a novelist picking up the threads of my story and running with it. The more Captain Kirk the better. As for how I reacted to finding out I won . . . I reacted like a little girl. Elisa told me I was in and I stood there giggling. She must have thought me quite the prat. I was in a daze for the next day or two. I just couldn't believe it. I still have a hard time believing it. I've got a professional writing credit and a credit for *Star Trek* no less. I grew up on *Trek*. Captain Kirk was my hero. And now not only have I written a *Star Trek* story but also I'm the guy who brought back Kirk. . . . Well, that's quite an honor. No doubt about it. I'm proud of my little contribution to the *Star Trek* literary universe."

"The Rules of War"
(SPECULATIONS)
KEVIN LAUDERDALE

 Nathan Archer, Jonathan's great grandfather, fights in the Eugenics War.

Kevin remarked, "I'm a big fan of the animated *Star Trek* series, and I've always liked Dr. Keniclius (from 'The Infinite Vulcan'—written by Walter Koenig!). I'd been thinking about ways to do a story involving him for a while. Then in the third season of *Enterprise*, in the episode 'The Hatchery,' Archer mentions how his grandfather was in the Eugenics Wars, and we hear the basics of the plot of my story in five sentences, but none of the real details. Instantly, I had my story. It was the perfect setting for Keniclius, and provided a great opportunity for some Eugenics Wars-centered dialog. There's also an I-hope-not-too-lame science fiction writer joke embedded in the story. (I'll leave that to the reader to find.) This story is about a military engagement, on Earth, in the 1990s, so I felt that it needed to be as realistic as possible. I did a lot of research into armaments, ranks, and so on. I hope the details I scattered make it seem like it could have happened. I've been trying for SNW since volume I. Now that I'm no longer eligible for it, I don't feel that I have to turn every idea I get into a story—unless I get an idea for a novel."

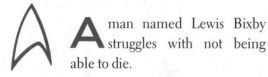

"The Immortality Blues"
(SPECULATIONS)
MARC CARLSON

A man named Lewis Bixby struggles with not being able to die.

Marc answered, "I've seen the previous SNW publications and have been thinking for several years that I should probably write something as well. This was the first time I'd entered this contest (for that matter, except for some other, local writing-group contests, I haven't really entered any of my writing in competitions)."

It never dawned on Marc that he could submit more than one story. He continued, "I used to do a lot of fiction writing until the late 80s when I set it aside. A few years ago my wife

started dragging me to a local SF writing group, and I've managed a few short stories since then—mostly what I would consider unpublishable since I tend to write what I want to read and not what publishers are looking for. This one was intended to be just another one of those. I've always had some difficulties with how the character of Flint has been interpreted in the published fiction, and so I decided to try to demonstrate how I felt an immortal might think and act. I was also curious to see if it would be possible to write a story set in the *Trek* universe without all the self-referential bits that seem to populate so much of the fiction. Arguably I failed miserably at this last bit, although I think I did manage at least one reference to each of the series. I set myself some specific limits and goals; one was to not actually contradict any of the recent novels as well as the established aired continuity. I also wanted to try to explain some otherwise inexplicable aspects of the mid-twenty-first century history because bluntly the history as described is improbable (a war that will destroy 'all the major cities' is unlikely to only kill 600 million). So I chose to look in on the years between the Third World War and First Contact, and view it from Flint's perspective. Because I tend to be a somewhat stylistic writer, I chose to try a teaser plus a four-act episode format. The story went through several major drafts, including one that was just too depressing for the average reader, but explained everything much better, and exceeded the word limit for the contest by half again. Several people read it at this point and were clear that it wasn't going to work, which allowed me to tighten it up. I sent it off expecting it to get bounced fairly early in the process, since there is very little that is blatantly *Star Trek* and I'm told has a definitely non-*Trek* feel to it. I should probably mention that this is the first *Star Trek* story I've written to completion. So I have to say that when Elisa got hold of me to tell me that it had been selected for inclusion, I was really surprised. Delighted, but surprised."

"Orphans" (GRAND PRIZE) (SPECULATIONS)
R. S. Belcher

Admiral Pressman and Dr. Bashir recruit an unlikely ally to protect a top-secret project from the Dominion.

Rod stumbled across SNW while reading the TrekNation Web site and 'Orphans' was his first and only submission to the contest. He commented, "I had always thought Roga Danar, the genetically engineered super solider who ran rings around Picard and the *Enterprise*-D, was an interesting character. Later when the DS9 writers decided to make Juliann Bashir a genetic 'superman,' too, I began to have a germ of an idea for the story. Harlan Ellison's 'City on the Edge of Forever' was one of my favorite TOS shows and concepts. Like a lot of fans, I wondered what became of the Guardian and it became the final metaphorical 'orphan' for my story. I think most fans mix and match characters, villains, and plot devices in their minds and come up

with really cool ideas for stories that never were. Comics' fans do it, and most other genre fans do it, too. Fan fiction is, I think, one of the most sincere forms of flattery to a series or a franchise. We love the mythology so much, we just have to keep asking 'well, what would have happened if. . . .' I wrote this wanting to find a dark corner of the *Star Trek* universe. One of the facets of *Trek* that I think DS9 was really good at exploring was how lofty ideals, like the Federation, have to contend with a universe full of selfish, unenlightened, and mercurial ideologies and people. 'Orphans' is kind of dark, it's supposed to be. But at its core is the idea of determination and perseverance overcoming self-destruction, that it's what you do that, in the end, defines you."

Rod continued, "I wrote it at a very chaotic time in my life—I was separating from my wife. It became a kind of catharsis for me, a way to get out my feelings of being out of control of events for a long time in my life and about trying to make hard choices about my future and my children's future. To be honest, the day I learned I had won, I was putting the story away in my file cabinet and figuring I hadn't even placed in the contest. When I got the call, I was so excited and out-of-my-mind happy in shock that my four-year-old daughter, Emily, had to look at me very wisely and say, 'Daddy, calm down.' It was, and still is a very surreal experience. I've been telling stories to people for a long time. *Trek* was always a huge part of my formative years and encouraged me to write. To get the chance to be a part of that mythology is a dream come true and I feel very grateful for this recognition."

THE LIVES OF DAX
(STAR TREK: DEEP SPACE NINE)
Marco Palmieri, editor

December 1999   (347pp)

**ORIGINALLY PUBLISHED
IN TRADE PAPERBACK**

▲ **M**arco remarked, *"The Lives of Dax* holds a special place in my heart. It wasn't the first *Star Trek* project I worked on after joining Pocket, but it was the first one I'd originated. To me, the idea for it was the perfect synthesis of character and format: Joined Trills are serial beings—living anthologies—and it seemed only natural that their biographies would be anthological. Add to that the fact that Dax is literally almost as old as all of *Star Trek*'s entire future history, which gave us a single point-of-view (albeit an evolving one) through which to experience that history. It's one of the projects I'm most proud of."

"Second Star to the Right . . ."
(THE LIVES OF DAX)
Judith and Garfield Reeves-Stevens

▲ **S**hortly after the Dominion War, Ezri relates to Vic Fontaine the scope of her past lives and how she came to be joined.

The authors declined to be interviewed for this book, but Marco recalls, "Judy and Gar loved the idea of the book, and I think they signed on for the sheer joy of it. Originally they pitched an Audrid story, but that idea wasn't coming together, so I told them my notion for a two-pronged Ezri story: It would be the framing piece for the anthology, and it would tell the tale of exactly how she reluctantly came to inherit a legacy she never aspired to. They were all over it."

Marco added, "Judy and Gar are very intuitive authors. I never mentioned this to them, but one of the inspirations for *The Lives of Dax* was the Ray Bradbury anthology, *The Illustrated Man*, which uses a framing device similar to the one I proposed to Judy and Gar. They grasped that immediately, and observant readers may recognize allusions to Bradbury's short story 'The Veldt' in 'Second star to the right . . .' when Ezri is recalling a childhood holodeck program.

"First Steps"
(THE LIVES OF DAX)
KRISTINE KATHRYN RUSCH

In the late twenty-first century, a ship appears above the planet Trill, and Lela, a councilwoman, must make a life-changing choice.

The author declined to be interviewed. Marco explained, "Jill Sherwin pitched an idea, but wasn't yet ready to turn it into a story. I suggested we allow a more experienced author to develop it. Jill agreed, and Kris just ran with it."

"Dead Man's Hand"
(THE LIVES OF DAX)
JEFFREY LANG

During the Romulan War, Tobin, an engineer and passanger aboard a pre-Federation Earth transport, must help keep the vessel out of Romulan hands.

Jeffrey remembered, "I'll never forget the phone call that I got from Marco about this. I was working on *Immortal Coil* (this is pre-*Abyss*) and he said, 'You want to write a story for this anthology?' And I said, 'Sure.' And that was it. I felt like such a grown-up writerly fellow. He said, 'Go read your *Star Trek Encyclopedia*, figure out which Dax you want to write about and

get back to me.' Two things about Tobin stood out for me: 1) He was alive during the Romulan War and I thought that would be a good era in which to set a story; 2) He was kind of a nebbishy guy. I think in my outline, I wrote something like, 'He's the Woody Allen of the Dax incarnations.'"

Marco said, "That hooked me. Not because I'm a big Woody Allen fan, but because it vividly conveyed a personality type that I wasn't expecting."

Jeff went on, "From there it was just a matter of figuring out what the heck he was doing out in space and why the Romulans would want his ship. Fortunately, *Enterprise* hadn't come on yet and ruined my chance to write the origin and first use of the transporter. I forget who decided the ship would have Vulcans on it, but I know I immediately jumped at the idea of putting Spock's grandfather on board. It's pretty understated. At the time of the story, Sarek hadn't even been born yet, and the only onscreen reference to Skon was a quick mention in *Star Trek III: The Search for Spock*. So there's no obvious connection to Spock unless you recognize the character's name. Again, there are a couple Marco-isms in the story, the notable one being the bit near the end where Skon suggests the idea of a modular design for future spaceships, so they can separate if need be. I love that bit."

"Old Souls"
(THE LIVES OF DAX)
MICHAEL JAN FRIEDMAN

Young Leonard McCoy finds himself in love with a Trill gymnast.

Mike remembered that Marco approached him for the Emony story because of his obvious affection for McCoy, who had been established in "Trials and Tribble-ations" as part of Emony's backstory. "It was a challenge because all these other incarnations of Dax had some interesting things going on—one had been a pilot, another had been an ambassador, another had become a murderer—and I thought Emony was the least interesting because she was a gymnast. A gymnast!"

In the episode, the implied dalliance between the characters was said to have occurred at Ole Miss (the University of Mississippi), suggesting that McCoy may have been college-age at the time. "I was thinking of the movie *Splendor in the Grass.* I wanted to have a very kind of young and impressionable McCoy with Emony as an older woman and make it memorable. It was difficult but it was also fun to have McCoy in there and all the little ironies—Oh, *this* is where he decided to become a doctor!"

"Sins of the Mother"
(THE LIVES OF DAX)
S. D. PERRY

Audrid writes a letter to her estranged daughter, Neema, to explain the truth behind the death of Neema's father.

This was Danelle's first work of *Star Trek* fiction. She remarked, "Marco asked if I would be willing to write a story of Audrid. He mentioned that she and her daughter were estranged for a while. I took that suggestion and ran with it."

Marco recalls, " 'Sins of the Mother' was what earned Danelle the *Avatar* gig. Her subtlety, strength of characterization, and pacing really shine in this story. I loved the idea of doing it as an epistolary."

This tale, together with "Allegro Ouroboros in D Minor" and "Reflections," eventually became integral to the post-TV DS9 fiction.

"Infinity"
(THE LIVES OF DAX)
SUSAN WRIGHT

Test pilot Torias takes out a shuttle with an experimental drive system.

• • •

Marco noted, "In the episode 'Rejoined,' audiences learned that the short, passionate marriage of Torias and Neilani was so powerful an experience that their later incarnations, Jadzia and Lenara, were strongly tempted to renew that relationship in defiance of the Trill taboo against reassociation. That became the emotional core of 'Infinity.'

Susan said, "I wanted to give some backstory as to why Dax was willing to break with Trill tradition. I wanted to write a story that was passionately on-edge, infused with danger as Torias underwent the test flight that killed him."

"Allegro Ouroboros in D Minor"
(THE LIVES OF DAX)
S. D. PERRY AND ROBERT SIMPSON

Musician Joran's killing spree, and how he was finally stopped.

Robert commented, "I wanted to write a Jadzia story. I thought about it for a couple of weeks, but nothing was coming together, so I went back to Marco and asked if any of the other hosts were still available, and he said Joran was. I've always had a fascination with killers in general and serial killers in particular, but for some reason I hadn't initially really thought about Joran. Marco and I batted some ideas around and eventually came up with an idea that we both thought would show an interesting side to Joran's personality. From there I worked out a

really tight plot and started writing the story. And started and started and started—it'd been a while since I'd done any prose writing and I found that I couldn't get the story done. With the deadline racing down on us Marco suggested that I turn over the plot and the small amount of what I'd gotten done to Danelle. So Stephani wrote the story itself, and they were both nice enough to leave my name on it. It was a lot of fun, but here and now I'd like to publicly thank Danelle. She's an amazing writer."

This tale, together with "Sins of the Mother" and "Reflections," eventually became integral to the post-TV DS9 fiction.

"The Music Between the Notes"
(THE LIVES OF DAX)
STEVEN BARNES

A young Benjamin Sisko works with the Curzon, an ambassador involved in a delicate first contact.

Steven said, " 'The Music Between the Notes' was a reworking of a story I'd written in college, and always wanted to publish. Bless *Star Trek* for giving me that chance! The saga of Sabbath Nile, her wondrous talent and somewhat sad end, needed to be told."

Marco remembered, "One of the things I love most about this story is how it shows the other side of Curzon—not the boisterous Klingonophile and party-animal everyone talked about, but the learned diplomat who could have mentored and inspired a young Benjamin Sisko."

"Reflections"
(THE LIVES OF DAX)
L. A. GRAF

Jadzia returns to Trill to help her sister.

"Julia wrote this story on her own, after being invited to participate in the collection. It might seem like a lot less work to do a short story than a novel, but she found out that the plotting and outlining took almost as long! Writing was much easier, of course."

Marco notes, "The TV series talked a lot about Dax's past lives, but said very little about Jadzia's personal history. (We learned more about Ezri in one season than we did about Jadzia in six!) She did, however, once mention that she had an unjoined sister. That became the starting point for 'Reflections.'"

". . . and straight on 'til morning."
(THE LIVES OF DAX)
JUDITH AND GARFIELD REEVES-STEVENS

Ezri concludes her tales, and receives some insight from Vic.

The authors declined to be interviewed for this book. Marco remarked, "Judy and Gar closed out the anthology as they are wont to do in their *Star Trek* fiction, on a note of hope and optimism. I thought it was the perfect ending."

ENTERPRISE LOGS
CAROL GREENBURG, EDITOR

JUNE 2000   **(291 PP)**

TRADE PAPERBACK

"The Veil at Valcour"
(ENTERPRISE LOGS)
DIANE CAREY

 The epic Revolutionary War battle at Valcour Island.

Diane has the distinction of writing two stories in this anthology that dealt with *Enterprises* that actually existed. A requested story, she said, " 'The Veil at Valcour' is about the Sloop of War *Enterprise* at the Battle of Valcour Island, a true story. The captain and ship's doctor in the story were both real people. I used the story to illustrate this critical battle and that without Benedict Arnold's determination and his valor at this battle; there would be no United States. Who'd have thought? I wanted to keep us, if possible, in the science fiction realm with this story, using a hint of mysticism to show that acceptance of old ways can actually lead to the future."

"World of Strangers"
(ENTERPRISE LOGS)
DIANE CAREY

The aircraft carrier that served with distinction in the Pacific during World War II, led to a man named Roddenberry naming his imaginary starship, *Enterprise*.

. . .

Diane said, " 'World of Strangers' is set in the period of the Battle of Santa Cruz in World War II, aboard the Aircraft Carrier *Enterprise*. The captain and some officers were real people. I cast the captain's role as if played by John Wayne, in tribute to all the old war movies my dad and I used to watch. Interestingly, after this book was published I received a surprise e-mail from the grandson of the captain! He liked the story and was very proud of his grandfather's being memorialized. I was very gratified to have given back a little of what those men gave us."

"Through Hell Should Bar the Way"
(ENTERPRISE LOGS)
GREG COX

On a rescue mission to save the inhabitants of Tarsus IV, Captain April and the crew of the *Enterprise* encounter a trigger-happy Klingon.

When asked about this short story, Greg remarked, "Ah, my Diane Carey pastiche. As you doubtless know, Diane had already fleshed out April and his crew in two previous novels. She was the logical person to write the April story for *Enterprise Logs*, except that she already had two other stories in that anthology! My version of April and his crew are based entirely on Diane's work. Plotting the story was fairly easy.

I cracked open my copy of the official *Star Trek Chronology* and looked to see what important *Trek* events took place during April's stint aboard the *Enterprise*. The massacre on Tarsus IV just leaped out at me, as did the idea of dragging in a young Commander Kor. (An aside: Since Koloth appears in the *Eugenics Wars* books, I've managed to work my way through two of the three classic TOS Klingons. Now I just have to write a Kang story!)"

Greg continued, "One last memory: I remember I had to walk all over Manhattan before I finally found a copy of 'The Counter-Clock Incident' on videotape. In the end, it wasn't very useful, since it only featured a much older April, many years after he was captain of the *Enterprise*. The Diane Carey books were my primary source of information."

"Conflicting Natures"
(ENTERPRISE LOGS)
JERRY OLTION

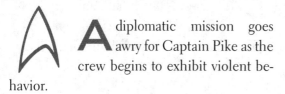 diplomatic mission goes awry for Captain Pike as the crew begins to exhibit violent behavior.

Jerry reflected on writing the story for *Enterprise Logs*. He said, "I've always loved that awkward romance between Pike and his Yeoman, and when I got the opportunity to write a short story about Captain Pike, I had to write about that. The *Enterprise Logs* project was originally conceived as a *Captain's Table* idea, so I had to fit my love story into a framework with enough

derring-do in it to make a good tale for a bar, but I did my best to make the whole thing revolve around love and the obstacles that can get in the way of it. Then the editors decided to drop the *Captain's Table* concept and just let the authors write stand-alone stories, but by then I had outlined the story already and was pretty happy with the hard-hitting action parts, too."

The writing wasn't totally smooth. Jerry said, "I had a lot of trouble with Paula Block, the continuity person at Paramount, who didn't like the characters' motivations and what it said about the state of readiness of the *Enterprise*'s crew, but I fought for a more human level of competence and emotion. We finally compromised by having the alien's psychic ability be responsible for amplifying the well-trained crew's baser instincts, and I got to tell my love story."

"The Avenger"
(ENTERPRISE LOGS)
MICHAEL JAN FRIEDMAN

 aptain Kirk plays detective with a former love to solve a string of murders.

"This follows the principle that nothing goes to waste. While DS9 was still on the air I pitched a story to Ron Moore. It was a murder mystery-type thing involving Kira. Ron said he liked the idea, but it was a little too close to an episode they were already working on." The episode was 'The Darkness and the Light.' I still liked my version of the idea, but obviously I couldn't do it as a DS9 story anymore. But here came this anthology, and I thought substituting recasting Kirk in Kira's role might be interesting. And, I mean, hell; I only had to change one letter. It's true! I really liked the idea of putting Kirk in an unfamiliar situation. He's not the captain here, he's a detective. I think fans are sometimes taken aback when you try to stretch the character. But I like doing that. And I think we owe it to them to try different things."

"Night Whispers"
(ENTERPRISE LOGS)
DIANE DUANE

During the refit of the *Enterprise* in spacedock, Captain Will Decker uses his keen intuition to save the ship.

While Diane doesn't remember where the idea for the story originated, she said, "I chose Will Decker on purpose, for the sake of the challenge. After all, here's a man who was in command of his ship only when it was in spacedock: then in comes James Kirk and pulls it out from under him! I felt for poor Will. After that he *deserved* some hot transcendent alien/robot action, if you ask me."

"Just Another Little Training Cruise"
(ENTERPRISE LOGS)
A. C. CRISPIN

Captain Spock must use cadets on their first space run to solve a mysterious illness that has plagued the crew.

Ann said, "My friend Bob Greenberger asked me if I would write the 'Captain Spock' story for *Enterprise Logs*, and I said sure."

She enjoyed writing this particular short story. "I got to invent a new race of aliens for that story, which is always fun."

"Shakedown"
(ENTERPRISE LOGS)
PETER DAVID

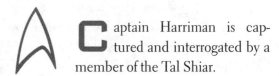

Captain Harriman is captured and interrogated by a member of the Tal Shiar.

Peter commented, "Harriman was almost a reclamation project for me. It's nothing against the character. Alan Ruck did everything he could. They put this guy in charge of the *Enterprise* and you had to wonder, 'Who in the hell is this idiot?' He is on the *Enterprise* ten minutes and he loses Kirk! Kirk spent years on the *Enterprise* going through everything, and Harriman barely gets out of the solar system and Kirk dies! John Harriman was an idiot. Certainly it is a depressing concept when you consider the proud lineage of captains that the *Enterprise* has had. That was the second part of my endeavor, to restore some luster to the captain of the *Enterprise*-B as portrayed by Alan Ruck. I really felt the movie, *Star Trek Generations*, did not do the position of captain of the *Enterprise* any great service. Not only did Kirk get killed in the movie, it made his successor look like a complete idiot, so I tried to help the guy."

Peter continued, "The story of 'Shakedown' was inspired by a movie. The concept being the inquisitor thinks the entire balance of power is one way and discovers to his shock it's a different way."

"Hour of Fire"
(ENTERPRISE LOGS)
ROBERT GREENBERGER

How did Captain Rachel Garrett develop such loyalty in her crew that they would follow her to their deaths?

"I conceived the notion for the *Enterprise Logs* anthology but DC would not let me freelance edit it given Time Warner's Conflict of Interest policies. John then invited me to write the intro and do a story. I picked Garrett because I gravitate towards women characters and she had the most space to explore. Since we saw her at the end of her career, I wanted to go towards the beginning and study how her crew came to be so loyal. With that in mind, I told a story that was the first true test of her career, six months after assuming command. I drew bio notes from her character description from S&S's interactive games, since I continue to believe it all should integrate when possible. Most of the crew I killed early on were DC colleagues at the time."

"The Captain and The King"
(ENTERPRISE LOGS)
JOHN VORNHOLT

Captain Picard has a rousing tale for the folks at the Captain's Table.

John commented, "Back in the early 1970s, I was working as a stuntman in Spain when the Spanish dictator Francisco Franco died. This brought a turning point in Spanish history, when the young king, Juan Carlos, was asked to assume the vacant dictatorship, with the army's blessing. The Spanish parliament wanted a modern democracy or something in between, and the army sent tanks to take over the government. Juan Carlos stood up to the army and encouraged the Spanish legislature to go with democracy, thus turning Spain into a modern country and himself into a figurehead with no real power. For 'The Captain and The King' I basically retold that impressive true story, with savage Andorians and Captain Picard."

THE AMAZING STORIES
Various

A U G U S T   2 0 0 2   (1 5 1 P P)

Reprinting seven stories that were originally published in *Amazing Stories* magazine.

"Last Words"
(STAR TREK: THE NEXT GENERATION)
A. C. Crispin

After Sarek passes away, Captain Picard finds himself dreaming of being the Vulcan Ambassador.

Ann said, " 'Last Words' sprang to mind naturally as story ideas that were either prequels or sequels to other books that I had done in the *Star Trek* universe."

She wrote the story when the magazine con-tacted her. "*Amazing Stories* needed a *Star Trek* story for the launch of their new magazine, so they called and asked me if I would like to write it. I said, sure. I always love writing in the *Star Trek* universe."

"Bedside Manners"
(STAR TREK: THE NEXT GENERATION)
Greg Cox

An alien ambassador falls ill and requires immediate surgery, though he refuses, since the doctor is not one of his species! Greg commented, "Not much to report here. The folks at *Amazing Stories* magazine, who specifically asked for a humorous *Next Generation* story, approached me. Looking about for aspects of TNG that might lend themselves to comedy, I quickly seized on Data and his cat. Bringing in the EMH from *Voyager* was a bit of a cheat, since *Amazing* had requested a TNG story, but since *First Contact* established that the *Enterprise* had an EMH, too, I figured I could get away with it. . . .

"Incidentally, Spot's reaction to the phrase 'herding cats' was something my own cat, Alex, did once. . . ."

"On the Scent of Trouble"
(STAR TREK: THE NEXT GENERATION)
John Gregory Betancourt

First contact is made with the telepathic race, the Pelavians.

"When *Amazing Stories* magazine was switching over to a more media-fiction-oriented format, the editor didn't really know any *Star Trek* authors, so he asked me to write a story. I also recommended some other writers to him, such as A. C. Crispin, who I knew would do good work. My story was an attempt to write a story about an alien race who communicated through scent . . . something the universal translator couldn't deal with quite so easily."

"Life Itself Is Reason Enough"
(STAR TREK: THE NEXT GENERATION)
M. Shayne Bell

Helping with the evacuation of Nunanavik, an arctic world that is now engulfed in a dust cloud, Worf and Deanna must survive now that their shuttle has crashed.

The author was unavailable for an interview.

"A Night at Sandrine's"
(STAR TREK: VOYAGER)
Christie Golden

While traveling through the Nekrit Expanse, Paris convinces Janeway to have a costume party on the holodeck.

Christie said, "I was contacted by *Amazing Stories* and I had quite a few ideas. I floated them past the editor and we eventually decided on a Tom Paris story. The holodeck character Ricki intrigued me when in an episode Paris said, 'She's in all my holodeck programs.' Why? What hold did she have on him? And poof, there was the story. It was also a way to affectionately spoof *Casablanca*—there are a lot of direct quotes from the movie in there, which some astute readers have spotted."

"When Push Comes to Shove"
(STAR TREK: VOYAGER)
Josepha Sherman and Susan Shwartz

The crew of the *Voyager* rescues several members of the nomadic T'kari from a disabled vessel.

Both Josepha and Susan forget where the story idea came from. Josepha said, "we played with the idea of a kid who was a natural teleporter."

Susan said, "We were approached at Worldcon to write for *Amazing,* and we said yes. There's another story, contracted for, paid for, but never published because someone forgot to do the due diligence with Paramount. I think the story came of a few pitches we tried with Brannon Braga."

The pitches didn't work. Susan said, "Much as I'd love to see my name on a TV show or a film, the level of collaboration is a little more hands-on than I feel like doing. I like the medium of fiction. I like the budget for special effects contained within my disk drive—that is to say, unlimited. I don't like people mucking with plots I've invested a great deal of emotion in just because they can. Like most writers, I'm a screaming control freak."

"The Space Vortex of Doom"
(STAR TREK: VOYAGER)
D. W. "Prof" Smith

 Clouds of Minions, which are tiny ant-like creatures, surround Captain Proton's ship with the capability of destroying his vessel!

Dean remembered, "Someone saw my Captain Proton book and wanted me to do one for *Amazing,* I think. I jumped at the chance of doing another Captain Proton story."

PROPHECY AND CHANGE
(STAR TREK: DEEP SPACE NINE)
Marco Palmieri, editor

SEPTEMBER 2003 (434 pp)

TRADE PAPERBACK

"Revisited, Part One"
(PROPHECY AND CHANGE)
Anonymous

The elderly writer Jake Sisko has a guest on a very rainy night.

Marco remembers, "The framing story for the anthology was a new spin on the DS9 episode, 'The Visitor.' The author wished to remain anonymous."

"Ha'mara"
(PROPHECY AND CHANGE)
KEVIN G. SUMMERS

 S et a few days after the pilot episode, Kira and Sisko lock horns on Bajor.

When remembering how he placed the story in this anthology, Kevin said, "I sent a novel pitch to Marco Palmieri after reading *Avatar*. He didn't buy the story, but asked me to pitch for his upcoming *Prophecy and Change* anthology. I sent him a bunch of pitches, and the one he liked was a Sisko/Kira/Opaka story. I sent him an outline, which went through [several] revisions, after which I was off and running. I took a couple of days off work and knocked the story out. It was pretty stressful working under a deadline, but when I was done and I realized that I could do it, I think I improved drastically as a writer. In the end, I was glad the first outline was rejected, as the second version of the story was far, far superior. Marco made several helpful suggestions of ways to improve the story, and I have to say that working with him taught me as much about the mechanics of writing as I ever got in school."

The idea of "Ha'Mara" came, according to Kevin, as follows: "When we first met Kira, she resented Sisko. Then, a couple of episodes later, she was calling him Emissary and trusting him as her leader. I wanted to know what brought about that change. I knew it had to be something major. Also, there was a major event implied in the episode 'Emissary' that we never

got to see, which was Opaka telling the people of Bajor that this Starfleet officer, a person a lot of people might feel is the new prefect, is actually the Emissary of the Prophets. There was something there, and I wanted to explore it."

Kevin remembers why the story was set in the Bajoran catacombs. "It came from the Roman catacombs, and the underground lake is actually a real place. There is a cave I've visited several times in Sweetwater, Tennessee called The Lost Sea. It was, for a time at least, the home of the largest underground body of water in the world. I was fascinated by the place as a kid, and I always wanted to use it in a story. The experts at The Lost Sea also answered a bunch of my questions about spelunking. I called them up one day and posed this interesting, hypothetical question: If a person were trapped in a cave and *knew* there was another exit somewhere, if they had a source of light, what would they do to try and find their way out. Several of the techniques they suggested made it into the story."

"Orb of Opportunity"
(PROPHECY AND CHANGE)
MICHAEL A. MARTIN AND ANDY MANGELS

 T he unlikely pairing of Nog and Kai Winn to recover a Tear of the Prophets.

Mike remarked, "Because of our respective schedules, this story was done in a flaming hurry, though I hope that doesn't show. Marco presented us with the central concept, which was that Nog and Kai Winn were forced by circumstances to collaborate in recovering one of the Bajoran Orbs. This idea also enabled us to show just how Nog did the math that made him arrive at the decision to approach Sisko requesting his sponsorship to Starfleet Academy."

"Broken Oaths"
(PROPHECY AND CHANGE)
KEITH R. A. DeCANDIDO

The story of Bashir and O'Brien's reconciliation, following the events of "Hippocratic Oath."

Keith remembered, "God, I'd wanted to write this story since 1996 or so. I was always stunned that they never picked up on the ending of 'Hippocratic Oath.' Bashir and O'Brien's friendship was sundered at the end of that episode, and then we never saw any kind of resolution to it; before long they were back to throwing darts together. That was one of the biggest danglers from DS9—a show that had very few of them—and when Marco Palmieri started casting about for pitches for *Prophecy and Change*, I threw that in the ring right away."

"... Loved I Not Honor More"
(PROPHECY AND CHANGE)
CHRISTOPHER L. BENNETT

Grilka, Quark's Klingon lover, returns to the station seeking Quark's help.

Christopher noted, "In 'Looking for *par'Mach* in All the Wrong Places,' Quark went to great lengths to win Grilka's affections, and it seemed to be more than a casual fling. Yet we never saw her again, and a year later Quark was pining for Dax. That discontinuity in a show with generally strong continuity always bugged me—I always wondered what happened to Grilka. So as soon as Marco invited me to pitch a story to an anthology meant to fill in such continuity gaps, the very first thing that occurred to me was a story exploring how the Quark-Grilka relationship ended. The specific storyline, in which Quark loses track of his identity under the influence of a domineering lover, was cribbed from something that really happened to a friend of mine. (Though in that case it was the other way around: He was a hippie-at-heart who got too caught up in a world where people only valued money and property.) The comparison of Ferengi and Klingon cultures appealed to me because both followed clearly defined rules of behavior. As a student of world history, I found it interesting to compare different cultures' value systems, and it seemed to me that Ferengi had their own very strong sense of honor, in their own distinctive terms. I wanted to show that. This led to one of my favorite scenes in the story, where Quark argues that he's actually more law-abiding than Odo."

Christopher continued, "The plotting and writing were fairly straightforward, with only a couple of adjustments along the way. I considered exploring Ferengi marriage customs, but when the story became about Quark becoming subsumed into Klingon culture, that fell by the wayside. Another change (for the better) came from Paula Block: In my original proposal, Odo morphed a *mek'leth* and sparred with Quark in the holosuite scene, but Paula pointed out that Odo wouldn't use even a virtual weapon. The revised version of their confrontation is a more interesting dynamic. Also, I wasn't sure where to set the final Quark/D'Ghor confrontation; it was Marco who suggested setting it in the bar. The sequence where Quark jumps on Odo and tries futilely to knock him down is also taken from life—a time in high school when I jumped on a bully to try to stop him from stealing my friend's ball. I actually handled myself a bit better than Quark did, though."

"Three Sides to Every Story"
(PROPHECY AND CHANGE)
Terri Osborne

During the Dominion takeover of the station, Jake Sisko befriends Tora Ziyal.

Terri recalled, "When Marco and I were talking about the story ideas, one of the things he mentioned was the idea of doing character pairings we'd never seen onscreen. One of the pairings he mentioned was Jake Sisko and Tora Ziyal. I admit that I wasn't sure that combination was going to work at first. However, the more I looked at it and let it roll around in my head, the more I saw a story I could really get behind. When we settled on having it take place during the Dominion occupation of the station at the start of season six, suddenly there was a chance there to add a wonderful layer of depth to Ziyal's life (and death) that was impossible to pass up. Marco approached me via e-mail with the opportunity to pitch ideas to him on November 20, 2002. The finished proposal for 'Three Sides' was sent to Paramount for approval about a week before Christmas. In this business, it's not wise to start writing without an approved proposal. You never know what Paramount is going to want changed. I learned that the hard way on 'Q'uandary later. However, the final approval on the proposal didn't come down until about the second week of January 2003, and the story was due on January 31, 2003. Mind you, this was my first professional work, and because I'd been rejected from *Strange New Worlds* on every single attempt to get in, I felt as though there was a tremendous amount of pressure on me to prove that I'd deserved the chance Marco had given me, since I couldn't crack SNW to save my life. So, about a week before the final approval on the proposal came from Paramount, I started writing. Fortunately, I got extremely lucky, and the first change Paramount wanted was on the scene I was in the middle of writing when Marco called me to say it was approved. I spent the rest of January 2003 finishing 'Three Sides,' while Keith finished *Art of the Impossi-*

ble at the same time. It was a little stressed in our house that month. Yeah, I like nervous breakdowns," she said with a grin.

Terri continued, "Marco's the best. I can't say enough good things about him. He has the patience of a saint, and the ability to listen to an opposing viewpoint. I disagreed with him on a couple of things he wanted to do on the final manuscript. I made my case for keeping them as they were, and was able to convince him to keep them. Of course, a couple of other things he wanted to change were things I agreed with him completely on. One thing I learned very quickly in this business is that you learn to pick your battles. On a side note: for everyone that knows my fanfic writing who is thinking that the title is a *Babylon 5* reference, it isn't. It's a very overt and intentional homage to one of my favorite rock bands ever, Extreme. It's also a title that fit the story well."

"The Devil You Know"
(PROPHECY AND CHANGE)
HEATHER JARMAN

Romulan Subcommander T'Rul returns to the station and joins Jadzia in undertaking some questionable research.

Heather remarked, "I was wrestling with my country's stance on the War on Terrorism while I was working on this story; I think my philosophical struggles bled into the creation of the story. Ultimately, I concluded that peace isn't the absence of war, that there are times

and places when war is justified and moral. But I did wonder about whether or not there's a 'moral' way to conduct a war or whether the ends did justify the means when it came to confronting an enemy. If the enemy was ruthless, were you justified in being equally ruthless? At what point do you become your enemy and lose the moral high ground? This story is also the closest thing to a 'song fic' that I've written professionally. I bought Coldplay's *A Rush of Blood To The Head* about the time I started work on this project. The lyrics and rhythms of that CD infused the story—specifically the song Clocks. I also felt that Jadzia was a character who was often shortchanged when it came to portraying her serious side. Here she had all these hundreds of years of life experience and yet we mostly saw her as this party girl who happened to be a science genius. She would have to have gained so much wisdom from Dax that I felt that I wanted to explore that aspect of her personality."

She continued, "Believe it or not, this was the most difficult project I ever tackled for Pocket. The specifics aren't important except to say that I almost quit writing *Star Trek* because the process frustrated me so much. The writing, revision, the creative aspects of it resembled the hobbits' trek through the Midgewater Marshes in *The Fellowship of the Ring*: pure misery. However, once it was published and done, I felt better about the completed work. I was particularly flattered when I heard that Andrew Robinson, whose work in *A Stitch in Time* is the penultimate ST fiction, listed my story as one of his favorites in the anthology. That little piece of flattery has given this project a special 'glow' in my mind. I don't hate it nearly as much as I did when I was writing it."

"Foundlings"
(PROPHECY AND CHANGE)
JEFFREY LANG

 do joins forces with the station's previous chief of security, the Cardassian Thrax.

Jeffrey remarked, "This one is pretty straightforward, too. Marco asked if I wanted to do a story for the anniversary anthology and I said, 'Omygodyes!' I dibbed Odo, who is one of my all-time favorite *Trek* characters. Unlike a lot of people (like my buddy Heather Jarman), I *like* the idea of Kira and Odo as a couple, so I knew I wanted to do a story where that was the case. I also knew I wanted to do a mystery story, or, more accurately, a procedural. Though Odo's abilities as a policeman were often referred to, we rarely saw him exercise them, so I was keen to do that. Then, Marco called and said, 'Hey, you know what would be neat?' And I got my pen and wrote down, 'Bring back Odo's predecessor, Thrax.' I had no idea who this guy was so Marco sent me the tape where he 'appeared' and I immediately glommed onto him. I think Marco suggested the idea of the underground railroad and then it was just a matter of working out the mechanics of the detection, which is fairly easy when you know the ending. My favorite scene is the last one with Odo and Kira because I think it actually gets to the emotional center of those two characters: two very lonely, very isolated individuals who somehow found each other."

"Chiaroscuro"
(PROPHECY AND CHANGE)
GEOFFREY THORNE

 zri must undertake a mission left for her by Jadzia.

Geoffrey remembered, "I asked the ubiquitous Dayton Ward if it was allowed for somebody like me to hit up *Trek* editors for work. He gave me some good advice—'Don't bug. Expect long response times. Be polite. Be succinct.'—and I e-mailed Marco for permission to flood his mailbox which he gave and which I did. I pitched everything I had and he gave them all the thumbs down. Something like twenty-five to thirty stories. All rejected. Then, out of nowhere, he offered me a slot in *Prophecy and Change*. Provided I could come up with something good for Ezri Dax. Something like twenty-five pitches later, he and Paula signed off on 'Chiaroscuro.' Bad news for me, since I had almost no time to actually write the thing. I'd worked for weeks, sometimes months on my earlier SNW subs. On 'Chiaroscuro' I had something like five days. Plenty of time for a pro. For me? I was scared shitless. Marco held my hand through the whole process."

"Face Value"
(PROPHECY AND CHANGE)
Una McCormack

Set during the penultimate episode of the series, Garak, Damar, and Kira are roaming Cardassia, attempting to put an end to Dominion rule. Instead of large battles with high body counts, the story focuses on the three of them and how they learn to trust each other.

Una commented, "Back at the start of 2002, I was quietly getting on with finishing up my PhD, when I got an e-mail out of the blue from Marco Palmieri, whose name I recognized from several of my DS9 mailing lists as an editor at Pocket Books. I had no idea why he wanted to contact me. Well, it turned out that someone had recommended my writing to him, and he was wondering whether I would like to pitch a story for a forthcoming anthology celebrating the tenth anniversary of DS9. We'll pass swiftly over the bit where I fell off my chair (!) and cut straight back to the e-mail I sent back saying how much I would love to pitch. My favorite episode of DS9 is 'In the Pale Moonlight,' so I pitched a story about Sisko and Garak set just after that, looking at some of the ramifications of the events of that episode. Marco liked it, but thought that it had enough material in it to make a novel-length story, so he asked me to pitch another idea. I had really loved the storyline in the final arc of episodes about the civilian rebellion on Cardassia Prime (perhaps it reminded me a bit of *Blake's*

7, which is also about a small groups of rebels fighting against the odds), but I had always wanted to know more about how Garak, Kira, and Damar managed to get on with each other while they were stuck in that cellar. It's a classic set-up for drama, I guess—putting people who don't like each other very much in a small space and seeing how they cope. There seemed so many unanswered questions about the dynamic, particularly how Garak and Kira were able to put aside the fact that Damar was Ziyal's killer. I had always wanted more of it when I watched the episodes, so that's why I picked this time and place. Individually, they are such an interesting set of characters. Damar's particular story had fascinated me—how a brutal and unsympathetic character turns into a hero and a legend. Kira, of course, has many aspects to her character, but the one that was most relevant here was her changing perceptions of Cardassians, which had taken all the run of the show: how she moves from hating them to being able to treat them as individuals. Her experiences in 'Second Skin' seemed very relevant here. As for Garak—I could happily write about him all day, but his particular story here seemed to be about coming back to Cardassia after all this time, and perhaps knowing in his heart that it can't stay how it was before he had left; that it has changed already under the Dominion occupation, and will keep on changing. Also, perhaps, how he has changed during his exile. In terms of the narrative (in which Kira has to choose between an old friend and the people she's currently working with), I was thinking of Damar's similar choice, about his friend Rusot, in 'Tacking Into the Wind,' and how it would be interesting to give Kira a parallel choice, i.e. to put her in a situation where new loyalties come into conflict with old loyalties. I tend to write a lot about situations where people are faced with difficult moral choices. The pitch suited the mix of stories (times, places, characters) that Marco was trying to go for in the anthology, so we went with it. I signed the contract, wrote it over the space of three or four weeks, Marco liked it, we did a few tweaks here and there, and next thing I knew it was published!"

"The Calling"
(PROPHECY AND CHANGE)
ANDREW J. ROBINSON

nother peek into Garak's life after he left DS9.

Andy commented, " 'The Calling' came from Marco's idea of having a collection of DS9 stories. We discussed what my Garak story would be and both of us thought that continuing from where 'Stitch' left off was the way to go. We were both interested in what form his continued quest for healing, both planetary and personal, would take. Marco was quite supportive of Garak's spiritual awakening while he's on Earth (in Paris!) looking for Bashir."

"Revisited, Part Two"
(PROPHECY AND CHANGE)
ANONYMOUS

 major thank you and encouraging words to a wannabe writer ends this anthology.

NO LIMITS
(STAR TREK: NEW FRONTIER)
PETER DAVID, EDITOR

OCTOBER 2003;   (386PP)

TRADE PAPERBACK

eter David lets other authors play with *The New Frontier* universe.

"Loose Ends"
(NO LIMITS)
Dayton Ward

Admiral Nechayev bails out a former Starfleet officer and to repay her hospitality, Calhoun begins to engage in covert activities for her.

Dayton remembers the background of this story well. "Ah, yes, the 'Dayton dares to be David' story." Dayton said, "I think it was mid-April 2003 when Keith DeCandido wrote to me and a few other people, including several alums of various SNW contests, that he and Peter David were putting together an anthology that would, for the first time, invite other writers to write stories featuring characters from the ongoing *Star Trek: New Frontier* series. As you know, the ongoing series was and has been written exclusively by Peter since its beginning in 1997, so this was a pretty big deal, if you ask me."

Authors were invited to submit ideas for the stories and Peter would decide which ideas he liked. "I submitted an idea for what I thought would make a fun story featuring Calhoun in his days as an operative for Starfleet Intelligence, before he became captain of the *Excalibur*. It was just a quick thing, really, probably only three or four sentences. Given the time constraints Keith was working under to pull the anthology together, coupled with the limited number of slots and the fact that several of the A-list *Trek* novelists had already pitched their ideas, I really didn't expect my idea to pass muster."

Dayton was a little overwhelmed to say the least. He said, "I felt that I was stepping right into traffic by submitting a Calhoun story idea. First, I figured that somebody, *anybody*, had to have sent in a Calhoun pitch before me, or else Peter was reserving that story for himself. In fact, I remember thinking; 'No way in hell is Peter David going to let me write this story. In fact, he's probably asking Keith, "Who the hell is Dayton Ward?" Keep that knucklehead away from my characters.' And so far as I was concerned, he would have been justified in feeling that way. With all of this in mind, I didn't even really figure out how the story would go, should it be picked. I had no idea what I might write."

Dayton remembers how he found out his story would be included in the anthology. He said, "Didn't I feel like the total bonehead when Keith e-mailed me with the note, 'Hey, Peter digs your idea! You've got two weeks.'

'What do you mean?' I'm saying. 'Nobody else submitted a Calhoun story?'

'Nobody else is that stupid.'

'Oh. Whoops.'

Summing up the experience, Dayton said, "Seriously, Peter was very supportive toward everyone working on the project, and the suggestions he made for my story once I turned in the manuscript absolutely made it a better finished product. It was huge fun for me to work on that project, as I've enjoyed Peter's writing for years."

"All That Glisters . . ."
(NO LIMITS)
Loren L. Coleman

Before Shelby was first officer on the *Excalibur* and about nine months before her attempts to assist the *Enterprise*-D fight the Borg, she was an engineer on the *U.S.S. Yosemite*.

"Keith asked me if I'd be interested in the anthology. Of course, yes. Then I did some history review on the different characters and settled on Shelby. I wondered what got her to the *Enterprise* in *Next Generation*, and the story started to gel. Then I put in the 'quest for the red command uniform' story, tripped over the original Shakespearan quote 'All that glisters is not gold . . .' and dug up that old Borg incident. Simmer and stir: A very fun story to write."

"Waiting for G'Doh, or, How I Learned to Stop Moving and Hate People"
(NO LIMITS)
David Mack

After graduating from the Academy, the first Brikar in Starfleet finds a security post on the *U.S.S. Ranger*.

David Mack said, "Sometimes a story just comes to me. This was one of those. John Ordover put out a call for *New Frontier* short stories one day, and he made it clear that they needed to be written right away—as in, now. The original request was for each author to submit two short ideas (no more than a paragraph each), about a different *New Frontier* character, set in the time before they were part of the *Excalibur*'s crew. I could only come up with one idea, and that was Zak Kebron going undercover as a park statue."

In terms of writing the story, David said, "I wrote the story very quickly, and the only major editorial change was that, originally, Kebron was to be stuck there in the statue for several days. I was asked to shorten the time. My solution was to have him there only one day and one night—but to make that single day last 61 Federation standard hours. As for the entire story's little 'touches,' I just threw in whatever amused me. The first part of the title, obviously, is an homage to the famous Samuel Beckett play 'Waiting for Godot.' (I'm sure most readers noticed that the fish in the koi pond are named for Beckett and his play's principal characters.) The second part of the title is a play on the subtitle of *Dr. Strangelove, or, How I Learned to Stop Worrying and Love the Bomb.*"

"Lefler's Logs"
(NO LIMITS)
ROBERT GREENBERGER

efler kept her notorious logs even growing up as a child.

"At a lunch filled with *Star Trek* authors, John Ordover announced he and Peter were talking about a *New Frontier* anthology and we would all contribute. Immediately, I grabbed on to Robin Lefler. Why? Well, she was an appealing character on TNG and was getting criticized among readers for how she was behaving. So, I figured I'd explore her background a bit. I also clicked on the notion that the story had to deal with the origin of her laws. Years passed and John assured me this was still happening. Finally, one day in early 2003, Keith says he was now helping Peter assemble the book. Am I still interested? Sure. I quickly wrote up an outline, sent it to Keith and Peter and had it rejected. Peter felt it wasn't a good origin and felt familiar. We spoke one day on the phone and he riffed about something that clicked and we came up with Harriet the Spy kind of observations that would help form not only who she was but how the laws came to be. As I was writing the story, Keith informed me that Ilsa Bick was covering the same territory in her Morgan Lefler tale. I read Ilsa's story and we struck up a friendship which continues to this day. I caught a timing error which we tweaked along the way and then our stories were approved."

"Alice, On the Edge of Night"
(NO LIMITS)
ILSA J. BICK

organ, Robin's mother, contemplates her life prior to her supposed death.

"This story was a total fluke. I got an e-mail from Keith DeCandido, who I'd never met. He sent around a blanket invite for the anthology to all published *Trek* writers, regardless of venue. A lot of characters were already taken, though that didn't matter because I didn't know diddly about *New Frontier*. Had seen the books, hadn't ever read them. So, anyway, the e-mail came, and I went online, figured out who was who (Psiphi.org was a lifesaver), and then went on out to the library, leafed through a couple books while standing in the aisle, and stumbled on Morgan Primus, upon whom I'd had my eye anyway. I read the sections where Morgan re-appears and then she and Robin kind of have it out—and I thought: 'That's not right.' See, being a shrink, I deal with a lot of depressed women. A lot of suicidal depressed women, and I couldn't imagine any of them a) leaving their kids or b) telling their kids that they thought it was OK because the kids could fend for themselves and 'get over it.' Most depressed, suicidal mothers worry about what will happen to their children afterward, and when they do kill their children, it's done out of love. It's their way of not leaving their children alone in what they perceive to be a cruel, heartless universe. So I wondered what it would be like to think about killing yourself over and over again—and then, suddenly, not really wanting to let it all go. Worrying about your children and what would happen. I figured that Morgan had lived long enough to see two, three shrinks; heck, maybe Freud for all I knew. And I wanted to explore a crisis in her life, and a parallel crisis in the shrink's life, with both of them being selfishly destructive without truly understanding why and then discovering that so long as there's love, there's hope. Something like that. I wrote the proposal; Keith liked it and he passed it by Peter David who also liked it. Then I wrote it and sent it to Keith who was an absolute gem and honorary mensch. Again, he liked it; Peter David liked it; and then Keith told me that he'd forwarded it to Bob Greenberger who wrote 'Lefler's Laws' to make sure we meshed. I didn't change a word, but it turned out that both Bob and I had pretty much the same vision."

When asked about the story being published, Ilsa commented, "All I can say is I know that Keith did a great job pulling this all together and in record time. For me, it was thoroughly enjoyable."

"Revelations"
(NO LIMITS)
KEITH R. A. DECANDIDO

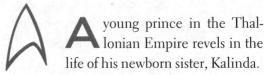

After graduation, Soleta finds herself assigned to the U.S.S. *Aldrin* alongside a fellow graduate named Worf.

• • •

"Soleta is my favorite of the *New Frontier* characters, and I was hot for the chance to write her learning of her Romulan heritage. It was also fun to write Tania Tobias—the one character from the YA books Peter David wrote that he hadn't yet mined for NF—and a much younger Worf."

"Turning Point"
(NO LIMITS)
JOSEPHA SHERMAN

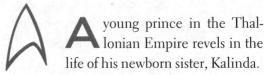

A young prince in the Thallonian Empire revels in the life of his newborn sister, Kalinda.

Josepha loved the character of Si Cwan. She said, "I wanted to show how he started to become a good guy rather than just like the rest of the aristocracy."

"'Q'uandary"
(NO LIMITS)
TERRI OSBORNE

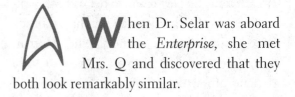

When Dr. Selar was aboard the *Enterprise*, she met Mrs. Q and discovered that they both look remarkably similar.

Terri commented, "You know that story Peter David mentions in the introduction to *No Limits*? That 'wouldn't it be cool if . . . ?' story?

That's 'Q'uandary.' The rest of Peter's sentence was something like, 'Wouldn't it be cool if we had a story with every *Trek* character Suzie Plakson's ever played?' Both Peter David and Keith DeCandido (the assistant editor on *No Limits*) know I'm a longtime fan of Suzie Plakson's. After Peter rejected my initial proposal for a Selar story, he, Keith, and John Ordover all agreed that they would offer me the chance to develop Peter's initial seed of a concept. I came up with the idea of using the Q Civil War almost immediately, and it was initially going to be Selar and K'Ehleyr that the Female Q borrowed to try to put a stop to things.

"Paramount requested that K'Ehleyr be cut, which was fine, because this was another 'down to the wire' story that I started writing before it was approved, and I'd discovered that K'Ehleyr wasn't working in the prose nearly as well as she'd worked in the proposal. Like 'Three Sides' before it, this was another situation where I came to the proverbial party late, and ended up having an insanely short period of time to finish the story. I don't have the dates on this one, but I think I had about two weeks, maybe less, from final approval to manuscript deadline. I still don't know how, but I managed to turn the story in on the deadline. Peter didn't ask for any changes, and Paramount approved it with no changes requested whatsoever. (Mind you, I don't think anybody was more surprised by that than I was.) From there, it went very smoothly."

"Oil and Water"
(NO LIMITS)
ROBERT T. JESCHONEK

The Hermat's posting as an engineer aboard the *U.S.S. Livingston.*

Robert remembered, "I thought it would be fun and interesting to team dual-gendered Burgoyne with an androgynous J'Naii, a member of the species explored in the TNG episode 'The Outcast.' In my first draft of the pitch, Burgoyne and the J'Naii worked to reverse the effects of a device that altered a planet's population, creating thousands of incompatible genders. At the editor's suggestion, I narrowed the gender conflict to that between Burgoyne and the J'Naii . . . then changed the root of the conflict to focus not on gender, but on the friction between Burgoyne's violent nature and the J'Naii's pacifism. Instead of the gender bomb menace from the original pitch, I introduced the Starfly probe, which I envisioned as sort of a sentient, scaled-down starship. I wanted to answer the question, 'What if an artificial lifeform possessed all the capabilities of a starship . . . and went on a rampage?' I thought it was logical that Starfleet might use highly intelligent and fully enabled probes like Starfly for ultra-deep space exploration."

"Singularity"
(NO LIMITS)
CHRISTINA F. YORK

A look at Mark as he begins to learn about his extraordinary abilities shortly after graduating from the academy.

" 'Singularity' was a once-in-a-blue-moon stroke of luck. There were openings in the anthology, and the editor agreed to allow the SNW winners the chance to pitch stories. Opportunities like this are rare, and I couldn't pass up the chance to write in yet another *Trek* universe. It didn't matter that I had only about a week, and I had never read any of the *New Frontier* series. I knew Peter David's work from other venues, and knew I liked him. I hoped he would like me. We live in a very small town. There are no superstores or even chain bookstores within an hour of us. Fortunately, we have a couple great used bookstores. I called one the next morning, they found four volumes and set them aside for me. That night I read most of those four books, and did a lot of online research. I picked out characters that I thought would be interesting to explore, and started pitching ideas. My favorite was bounced immediately with the comment, 'You obviously haven't gotten to #12 yet.' An express shipment of the remaining books arrived the next day, and, of course, I read #12. And I found out why the original pitch didn't work. But I was able to rework it, along with another batch of ideas. All told, I think there were about a dozen ideas in the course of that week. 'Singularity' was my reworked favorite. I didn't have a lot of time to write, because there was a short deadline. Steve (my husband) read the story, told me what needed fixing, and it went off right away. There were, as so often happens, continuity flubs that we had to fix, but it was a pretty smooth process."

"The Road to Edos"
(NO LIMITS)
KEVIN DILMORE

A rex travels with a new officer to his homeworld to attempt to make amends and transition himself into his new life eighty years later.

When asked why he wrote a story without his usual writing partner, Dayton, he said, "Why by myself? I decided to shake that troublemaker Ward for once! OK, not quite." Looking back, Kevin said, "This process still makes me laugh. I got an e-mail from Keith asking whether I'd be interested in pitching a tight-deadline story to a *New Frontier* anthology with the caveats that the story had to center on a specific NF character but take place outside of any NF continuity (or at least in a timeframe before a given character entered Peter David's domain). I jumped at it because that offered me a golden opportunity to try and write a story about one or both of the characters from my beloved *Star Trek* cartoons and make it work in the context of ST fiction continuity. So I pitched 'The Road to Edos' featuring Lt. Arex after about thirty minutes of chucking ideas around. I didn't mention it to Dayton because Keith's letter was sent to me with the recipient's list suppressed, and we always respect each other's separate projects, so I just kind of dropped it . . . for about three days, I think. We were talking and he says he made a pitch to it, so I say I made a pitch to it and we had a big laugh. Since surely Peter and Keith wouldn't bite on both pitches, we agreed to tag-team on whichever one sold. Then Keith fires back with a note saying *both* pitches made the cut. Dayton called me up and said, 'You're on your *own*, homeboy.' So I bit the bullet and wrote the story by myself over the course of about a week less than a month before I got married. Yikes!"

For inspiration, Kevin said, "I wanted to write something light and fun with a bit of a Hope-and-Crosby-esque 'Road to' picture feel to it. I tried to fit dialogue to the DTI agent Stewart Peart with Hugh Grant playing the guy in my mind. I named the character after two of my favorite rock drummers, Stewart Copeland and Neil Peart—but little did I know that Dave Mack also named a *Star Trek* fiction character of his after Neil Peart. We'll have to team them up sometime!"

"A Lady of Xenex"
(NO LIMITS)
PEG ROBINSON

After her servicing by M"k'n'zy, a widow contemplates her future while trying to discourage potential suitors.

"How did I land a spot? Am I the victim of a series of accidents, as are we all? No, more seriously, that's something I only sort of understand. Far too much happened backstage at Pocket Books for me to comprehend how people were called upon. I know Keith DeCandido had found himself assisting Peter David on the project, and they needed authors who had proven out in short fiction to write for the new anthology. Keith had worked with some of the SNWs alumni on other projects. Somehow he and Peter David chose to follow that lead and I ended up with an e-mail I honestly thought was spam and deleted. But the next hour or so I got this rush of e-mail from other SNWs writers who were all mail-listing each other frantically about the offer, so I went and undeleted the mysterious spam and discovered an invitation. The timing was awful in some ways, and while my kid sister is a *New Frontier* worshipper from way back, I hadn't had time to get familiar with the series. On the other hand I love a challenge, and I really wanted to prove to myself that I could go from a dead cold start to submission on an invitational project, so I decided to see what I could do. My husband was out of town and my mom was visiting, both circumstances designed to throw me off my stride, and I not only did not own any of the original series but the local stores were not carrying much. Somehow I scarfed together the majority of the set, read them in a matter of days, started taking notes, called my sister to see what she really loved in the series, put together a set of thumbnail descriptions of stories I thought I could write that would fit usefully but non-disruptively into Peter David's canon. I tossed them off in an e-mail, expecting to lose/be turned down (as seems to always be the case with my Pocket Books experiences). Peter David liked the thumbnail for Lady, and he and Keith DeCandido requested a proper outline. They liked that, too, and the next thing I knew I was writing frantically, and occasionally shooting Keith e-mails screaming, 'It's gonna be too long if I keep the frame and the secondary plot, can I please cut them or will you kill me?' In the end I got the story in by the deadline, they liked it, and for weeks afterward I was insufferable because I had made it from 'Huh?' to 'We'll be sending you a contract' in — I think it was something like a month and a half. And remember, I was entertaining my mother at the time! I am still proud of that. I enjoyed it, too: There's a sense of adrenaline rush going from a cold start and total ignorance to a finished work in limited time, while hitting all the in-between marks. I think in a former life I was a firehouse dalmatian: I love it when the bell rings and there's a new fire to get to at a gallop."

Peg continued, "The story came out of my sense that poor old D'ndai had better reasons for his bad behavior towards Calhoun than the canonical novels could establish. Oh, and my usual female aversion to the whole 'supporting babe' sort of thing. Peter David is, quite de-

lightfully, writing Calhoun's story. But I figured that the whole idea of the anthology allowed me to write D'ndai and Catrine's story, and explore the logic of the planet Calhoun's post-liberation development while I was at it. Remember that I am a History Teacher's Daughter. It's sort of like playing a history teacher on television: it develops certain sensitivities and obsessions without the framed degree to justify them."

"Making a Difference"
(NO LIMITS)
Mary Scott-Wiecek

 The historic vessel's run-in with the second Borg incursion into our solar system.

Mary commented, "*No Limits* is an interesting story. When SNW V came out, all of the winners got to talking via e-mail, and we sort of clicked. Someone jokingly suggested that we pitch our own anthology, and suddenly we were seriously considering it. We contacted the winners from all of the other volumes, and put together a mailing list. Eventually, we contacted Pocket Books with an idea for an anthology, and had pitches for individual stories ready if they were interested. They weren't, because I think they already had something similar in the pipeline. At the time, they were working on gathering writers for the *No Limits* anthology, and I guess they decided to give us a shot. We had one week to send in pitches. I hadn't read any of the *New Frontier* series, so it was quite a challenge to come up with something. I skimmed through some of the books, and looked at all of the timeline and summary information available online. Eventually I settled on writing about the previous captain of *Excalibur*, Morgan Korsmo. He died before *New Frontier* even started, so my lack of knowledge about the series wouldn't hurt me too much. Korsmo had been killed in the battle to defend Earth from the Borg in *First Contact*. I thought it would be interesting to explore what the battle was like for one of the ships we saw briefly on the screen in the film. I pitched the idea, and it was tentatively accepted, but they still needed approval from Paramount. That took a very long time—almost a month, I think—so by the time I had final approval, I only had three weeks to write the story. Three weeks is not a lot of time for me. Not only that, but I had also suddenly realized that I had pitched a Borg battle story, and I knew very little about writing the Borg or about writing a battle! It was a crazy month. I actually had to go out and buy a tech manual, too, because you can't fudge your way around that stuff with a *Trek* audience. They pay attention! In the end, I got it done with a couple of days to spare, and I'm fairly pleased with the way it turned out. All in all, it was an interesting experience, and I'm grateful to have had it."

"Performance Appraisal"
(NO LIMITS)
ALLYN GIBSON

Prior to Calhoun's posting aboard the *U.S.S. Grissom*, Kat was the second officer.

Allyn recalled, "The pitch invitation for *No Limits* came as a complete surprise. It was late February 2003, I had been writing *Ring Around the Sky* for a few weeks, and I received late one night an e-mail from Keith DeCandido. There was going to be a *New Frontier* anthology in the fall, he was taking pitches for the 'minor' characters, and pitches needed to be received by Friday. (This was either Monday or Tuesday, as best I can recall.) My first thought was one of incredulity. My second thought was, Who do I want to write for? Keith's e-mail had specified the 'minor' characters as the 'major' characters had been taken. One character stood out— Norman Kenyon, Calhoun's captain aboard the *Grissom*, the story which was related in *Once Burned*. I sent Keith an IM, not really expecting a response, and asked if Kenyon was fair game. *Once Burned* was (and still is) my favorite of the *New Frontier* books, and a big part of that is the tragic fall of Kenyon as everything he loves is taken away from him. Keith's reply was quick—Kenyon on his own wouldn't work, but if I could work up a story set aboard the *Grissom* with Kenyon that focused upon Calhoun and/or Kat Mueller he would be interested in that. I gave the matter some thought.

"No [workable] ideas were forthcoming that

night, so I retired to bed. At two o'clock that morning I woke. I had a vague idea about Kat Mueller, 'Why is she in command?' I jotted a few sentences down on the notepad I keep by my bed, then rolled over and went back to sleep. When I woke in the morning I looked at the notepad, read what I had written during the night while eating breakfast, re-read it as I drank a few cups of coffee. I typed up the idea, expanded it to two paragraphs—the first explained Mueller's character arc, the second presented a basic plot—and sent it to Keith. Later that day he sent back a suggestion—can we fit Calhoun into the story—that I tried but couldn't really work. Then the waiting began. The pitches had to be whittled down by Keith, Peter, and John, then they had to be approved by Paramount. The story's deadline, May 1st, approached but my story pitch hadn't been approved by Paramount, so I continued to work on *Ring Around the Sky*. Round about April 20, I received word that Paramount approved the pitch. I called my supervisor; told him I was taking a few days of vacation, and hammered out the story in three days. The first day I wrote 6,000 words, the second day 5,000, and on the third I cut it back by 4,000. I e-mailed Keith the story on April 29. At the end of June I found a package on my front step. It was from Pocket. I opened it, and it was a line edit of the story. I had never seen a line edit before, I didn't know what to do with the line edit, and a few days later Keith sent out an e-mail to the contributors about looking the edit over and making corrections. Because I had written the story in such a rush as I looked over the edit, besides wanting to put back in every comma Keith had taken out because I have never seen a comma I didn't like, I saw paragraphs, sentences, *words*,

that didn't work for me. I grabbed a red pen, started striking out words, scribbled in other words, and in one case typed up a new page. Keith sent another e-mail reminding all and sundry that he needed the line edit back the next day, and could we e-mail or fax him the changes? E-mailing the changes would have been massive—on a thirty-page manuscript I had thirty pages of changes—so the next morning I took the line edit into work and faxed it to him. He called me at work that afternoon. 'Allyn, have you any idea when my fax machine stopped spitting out paper?' 'No,' I replied. 'You didn't have to rewrite the story,' he said. 'I just wanted you to tell me if the punctuation was okay.'

"Writing the story was great fun. There's one scene toward the end of the story I would love to have another crack at, but I do feel the story hits what I wanted from it. I feel honored to have been asked to participate."

Xant "Redemption"
(NO LIMITS)
GLENN HAUMAN AND LISA SULLIVAN

nsight into the "God" worshipped by the "Redeemers."

According to Lisa, "Peter David actually gave Glenn the idea (for the story), telling him that he was surprised that no one had suggested a Redeemer story for *No Limits*. The religious group had previously appeared as bad guys in several of the novels. After all of his other story ideas were bounced, Glenn decided to pitch a

Redeemers story. He asked me if I would be interested in cowriting it, as I had spent several years of grad school studying early church history and could lend an appropriately religious sensibility to the piece. After asking him if he was crazy (and being assured that he wasn't), I happily accepted the offer. We ultimately had a lot of fun working together."

Not familiar with the *New Frontier*, Lisa did a lot of reading in a short period of time to become conversant with Peter David's language and universe. Lisa said, "Luckily, I found the NF stories very enjoyable."

Glenn had some comments about writing the story with Lisa. "As with many things in my life, I blame Peter David. I've known Peter for about twenty years now, much to my shock and amazement—yes, I knew Peter before he was a god. Peter had announced that there was going to be a *New Frontier* anthology, and that he was looking for submissions. A few days after the announcement, I was down in his basement fixing his computer (again) and rattled off four quick ideas at him—a Si Cwan story, a Kat Mueller story (which may or may not happen), a Meyer and Boyajian story, and oddly enough, a Hauman story—remember the leader of the Makkusians in *New Frontier* #11, *Restoration?* It's a story featuring him, Dr. Hauman from Genesis Wave, Book Ora, Dr. Hauman from the alternate future in Imzadi, and since there's precedent for science fiction authors showing up in *Star Trek* stories, me. Peter liked my ideas (I recall him being surprised by where I would have gone with Kat Mueller) and then he idly mentioned being surprised that nobody had put in a story for the Redeemers. I came up with a story on the ride home, and much to my surprise, that was the story they wanted me to

run with. Great! A story on religious history! Problem: Although I had an idea of where I wanted to go, I knew damn little about religious history in general, and would have had a hard time giving it the ring of truth. However, I knew the wonderful and lovely Lisa Sullivan, who's a friend of many science fiction authors but had never gotten around to writing any herself. I said, 'Wanna do it together?' and she agreed. And thank heavens—she improved the story tremendously, adding story points and tremendous color to the story."

"Out of the Frying Pan"
(NO LIMITS)
Susan Shwartz

 With the help of Spock and Si Cwan, Soleta escapes the dungeons of Thallon.

Susan said, "Soleta reminds me of Saavik in some ways, and I enjoyed the way Spock interceded when she ran into trouble. My guess is that he saw in her a person very much like Saavik, so he logically had to take an interest. I thought that it would be fun to explore that, and the story was indeed fun."

Looking back, she said, "It was one of those stories I wrote in a weekend, chortling all the way, which is something I really enjoy doing from time to time. Poor Keith DeCandido had all he could do with dealing with how rough the manuscript was. (Sorry, Keith.) Ursula LeGuin calls stories like that 'bung-pullers,' because, when you pull the bung out of the beer barrel, the beer froths up. Personally, I prefer the analogy of a champagne bottle opening, but I always did have champagne tastes on a beer budget. I also wanted to try writing a Klingon, rather than my usual Romulans."

"Through the Looking Glass"
(NO LIMITS)
SUSAN WRIGHT

Transferring from the *Grissom*, Burgoyne is now the assistant engineer aboard the *Excalibur*, under Captain Korsmo.

Susan said, "This story is set in Peter David's *New Frontier* series, with Keith DeCandido editing the anthology. They were tough! I had a couple of ideas, but they wanted me to 'push it' with Burgoyne. So I did. I was curious why a herme who always had wild sex with everything that crossed her path suddenly decided to be a monogamous stay-at-home parent. This story shows the first spark for that turning point in Burgoyne."

"A Little Getaway"
(NO LIMITS)
PETER DAVID

After their wonderful wedding, you knew their honeymoon had to go smoothly.

Peter remarked, "It was the honeymoon from hell. Quite simply, it was the notion that the two of them get involved, get married, and she has never met the relatives. This was a demented story in which poor Shelby gets her ass hauled back to Xenex and she meets the family and has to prove herself worthy. It really appeals to her ego because she could have turned to Calhoun and said, 'F . . . this, F . . . them, I'm your wife. You married me, let's get out of here.' Instead, it was a nice little study in the follies of letting your ego get in the way of your better judgment. Poor Shelby got the crap beat out of her. On one hand, it was one of her most shining moments because she didn't back down from the attitudes of the elders of Xenex. By the same token, it was also one of her low points because she was dumb enough to get herself hauled into this. The whole time Calhoun is standing there saying, 'You don't have to do this.' "

TALES OF THE DOMINION WAR
KEITH R. A. DECANDIDO, EDITOR

AUGUST 2004   (374PP)

TRADE PAPERBACK

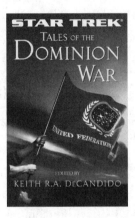

 What was happening in other aspects of the *Star Trek* universe during the Dominion War?

Keith remarked, "I always thought that the anthology format was perfect to show some other stories that happened during the Dominion War. The Breen's attack on Earth, the fall of Betazed. Also, what was the *Enterprise* doing, what were Scotty and McCoy doing, what was Spock doing, what was the *New Frontier* crew doing, what was the SCE doing, what were the surviving members of the *Stargazer* crew doing? All sorts of possibilities opened themselves up. So I pitched the anthology and everybody said yes."

"What Dreams May Come"
(TALES OF THE DOMINION WAR)
MICHAEL JAN FRIEDMAN

The Vorta, Sejeel, discusses a dream with his servant, Draz, who lives on the Dominion controlled planet, Illarh.

Mike commented, "I wanted to do something that was a little slight of hand because I hadn't done that before in a *Star Trek* story. Just a little story to kind of whet people's appetites, nothing too heavy, just a little appetizer. And I was pleased with the way it came out. I think generally people liked it—the criticism has been 'Well, we wanted to see more of these characters. Where are they? And what happened to all these people?' I didn't realize that people were so consumed about what happened to the *Stargazer* cast. My natural inclination was not to give too much away."

"Night of the Vulture"
(TALES OF THE DOMINION WAR)
GREG COX

The entity from the Original Series episode, "Day of the Dove," thrives on the violence and hatred, courtesy of the war.

• • •

Greg confessed, " 'Night of the Vulture' is actually an excised chapter from *The Q Continuum*, which I fleshed out into a Dominion War story. (A smart writer NEVER throws anything away; you never know when you might find a use for it later.) At one point, while writing *The Q Continuum*, I had intended to introduce (*) into the TNG era by showing (*) feeding on a bunch of Jem'Hadar. Later on, though, I decided to confine (*) and Gorgon and The One strictly to the flashback sequences, so the Jem'Hadar scene had to go. Years later, when Keith DeCandido asked me for a Dominion War story, it dawned that I finally had a chance to use that scene, which was still sitting on the hard drive of my computer! On a more artistic level, it also struck me that (*) was the perfect device by which to explore the tensions underlying the whole Cardassia-Dominion alliance. The title, of course, is a deliberate play on 'The Day of the Dove,' the TOS episode in which (*) first appeared."

"The Ceremony of Innocence Is Drowned"
(TALES OF THE DOMINION WAR)
KEITH R. A. DECANDIDO

Laxwana's perspective of the fall of Betazed to Dominion forces.

Keith reflected, "On September 11, 2001, some crazy people flew a couple of planes into a couple of buildings in my hometown. 'Ceremony' was my 9/11-catharsis story, for all that,

it was written a couple of years later. It was a story I needed to write."

"Blood Sacrifice"
(TALES OF THE DOMINION WAR)
JOSEPHA SHERMAN AND SUSAN SHWARTZ

The Romulan government considers an alliance with the Dominion, and an emperor is assassinated.

Susan was very eager to work with DS9, even though she admits, "I came late to the party, and I love that show! Predictably, I especially love the Romulan-centric episodes, and I'm enough of an armchair strategist to know that the Romulans' entry into the Dominion War was critical to the victory."

Spock remained on Romulus in the TNG episode 'Face of the Enemy.' Susan said, "It's illogical to think he wouldn't be politicking for all he was worth, along with his mission to unify Vulcan and Romulus: He is as he is, and one of those things is a profoundly loyal member of the Federation and a Vulcan Ambassador. And he's half-human: he'd wage peace aggressively. As Clausewitz says, war is politics by other means. On Romulus, politics is war by other means."

The character of Ruanek appears again. Josepha said, "Ruanek seemed like the perfect avenger for the murder." Susan said, "it occurred to us that it would be fun to see how Ruanek, a character we created for *Vulcan's Forge* and used in *Vulcan's Heart*, would react to returning to the Homeworld after thirty years or so on Vulcan. Besides, what's the point of having a Firefalls if you don't use it? I'd done all this research at one point on volcanoes, so it was fun to finally get to work with it."

"Mirror Eyes"
(TALES OF THE DOMINION WAR)
HEATHER JARMAN AND JEFFREY LANG

A Romulan spy, disguised as a Vulcan, helps Bashir deal with a genetically designed virus that kills Vulcans.

Heather commented, "Why write with Jeff? Jeff is one of my dearest friends and writing peers. He is like my honorary big brother and one of the main reasons I'm working for Marco. We've worked on each other's projects for years. To collaborate was a natural outgrowth of our friendship. I think we balance each other artistically. Jeff has a dry, almost cynical sense of humor—I tend to be a serious angst girl. While Jeff reads Terry Pratchett or Neil Gaiman, I'll be buried in J. R. R. Tolkien and Jane Austen. He is an earthier fanboy in his T-shirts and jeans; I'm kind of a proper Anglophile in Fair Isle sweaters and khakis. We have complimentary interests and styles. I think we mesh. There are few people who can be totally blunt with me and I can take it without initially getting all girly and overly sensitive: Jeff is one of them. Jeff and I were asked to tell the Dominion War M*A*S*H story. Since Jeff was in the middle of 'Left Hand of Destiny,' I sat down and watched M*A*S*H on DVD and conveyed to Jeff what episodes I thought would be our best inspirations. One of my favorite episode formats from M*A*S*H were the epistle episodes like 'Dear Dad' and 'Dear Sigmund' where a main character narrated the day to day life of life in the 4077th. Also, there was an episode where a North Korean soldier ended up in the 4077th for a period of time and was never caught—they just thought he was a South Korean. I loved this idea of telling a story about a misfit spy in enemy territory caught in an absurd situation. Jeff and I settled on the 'first person' journal format after first entertaining the notion of having Seret's letters to her Romulan handler be the structure of the story. Jeff wrote the first few pages, sent them to me. I overwrote his section, pushed the story forward, then sent it back to Jeff. This process continued until we finished the whole story—it was a true collaboration. Jeff is one of the easiest people I've ever had the opportunity to work with. Did I mention that he's funny?"

Jeffrey commented, " 'Mirror Eyes' grew out of a comment I made at a panel at a Shore Leave convention where someone asked, 'Is there some kind of a story that you haven't been able to do yet?' and I said I'd like to do some kind of medical mystery involving several of the doctors. Someone made the obligatory 'Five Doctors' comment and we went on from there, but sharp-eared Keith DeCandido made a mental note and, a few months later, wrote me a note asking if I'd like to do a medicine-centric story for his Dominion War anthology. By that time, Heather Jarman and I were already talking about collaborating on something and this seemed like a good test bed, especially since HJ is a biology geek. All the stuff in the story about the mechanisms of cells, blah, blah, blah—that's all hers. The actual writing was amazingly easy. I think I did the first couple of sections, then sent them to Heather, who tweaked what I wrote, then added a couple of scenes. We went back and forth like that until we got to the end. The whole thing gelled beautifully, from outline to final edit."

"Twilight's Wrath"
(TALES OF THE DOMINION WAR)
DAVID MACK

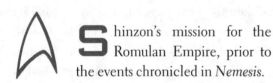hinzon's mission for the Romulan Empire, prior to the events chronicled in *Nemesis*.

David said, "This story was 'sparked' by *Tales of the Dominion War* anthology editor Keith R. A. DeCandido sending me an e-mail telling me that he wanted a Shinzon story for the anthology and asking whether I could go see the movie and write him a story as soon as possible. I said, 'Sure.' "

After seeing "*Nemesis*," he said, "I realized there was a great story waiting to be told in explaining how Shinzon went from abandoned child to slave to evil mastermind with the empire in his icy grasp. Not to mention the fact that I sat there mumbling, 'How the hell did he find B-4?' I put those two unexplored bits of backstory together and the result is 'Twilight's Wrath.'

"Eleven Hours Out"
(TALES OF THE DOMINION WAR)
DAVE GALANTER

With Captain Picard trapped in a ravaged Starfleet Command, courtesy of a Breen attack, the *Enterprise* finds itself eleven hours away from being able to render aid.

When Dave was asked about the story, he said, "I forget if Keith DeCandido asked me to develop something about the Breen attack on Earth or if I suggested it, but from the moment I was on the project I was very excited about the idea of it. Unfortunately it was also the first thing I had to work on after my mother passed away, and it took me a little bit to get back into the swing of things. I had been scheduled to work on the *A Time To . . .* series, but had to turn down the chance because my mother was ill with cancer and I knew her time was limited. I didn't want to waste what time she had left, or not be there for my father after she passed, because I was busy writing books. Having passed on that, 'Eleven Hours Out' was my next project and sitting down to write after that loss was a bit of a task."

Elaborating further, Dave said, "I wrote the first paragraph to 'Eleven Hours Out,' and then nothing for a week or two, because I'd decided my mental state was still a bit morose. If you read that first paragraph, Picard is feeling what I felt, so maybe it worked for the story and me. To then have to have Picard discuss losing his brother and nephew in the first few pages (this was in the outline long before my mother passed away) was actually easier than I thought, if a bit emotional. I let some of my feelings come out through him, and the experience was cathartic."

In terms of the story, Dave said, "I don't know how many people will notice, but 'Eleven Hours Out' pulls less inspiration from the attacks on the U.S. on September 11, 2001 and is more akin to the 1941 sneak attack by the Japanese on our fleet at Pearl Harbor.

"When I was in college I worked at a newspaper where the head of security was a retired police and military man. He'd actually been an aerial gunner on the aircraft carrier *U.S.S. Enterprise* on December 7, 1941. I asked him where *Enterprise* was when Pearl was attacked, and he'd told me, 'We were eleven hours out of port.'

"After a little research, I'd found out that the *Enterprise* was expected to be in port at Pearl, but had been delayed by a storm. I put that in the story as well. I mentioned the *U.S.S. Lexington* close by Earth in the story, escorting ships to Starbase Midway and in 1941 the *Lexington* was escorting navy ships to Midway Island. So all those little bits that most people will probably never notice (and a few I'm forgetting) were taken from some Pearl Harbor research."

Another piece in the story is an homage to the crew of the Space Shuttle *Columbia*. He said, "I just wanted to say something about how brave these people were, and write them into *Star Trek* if I could."

Summing up his feelings, he said, "Overall I enjoyed writing 'Eleven Hours Out' probably more than any other *Trek* project I've done, despite it only being a short story. It was nice to visit Earth a bit, and to see a warmer side of

Picard. And it was fun to use some of my journalism schooling to write news copy for twenty-fourth-century reporters. The news reporting was the only thing I grabbed from 9/11 events. The news media can be a very divisive influence on us as a nation, but in a time of disaster or tragedy they can also bring us together and help hold us together. I wanted to make that point as well."

"Safe Harbors"
(TALES OF THE DOMINION WAR)
HOWARD WEINSTEIN

Scotty and McCoy find their runabout, the *Hudson*, desperately needs repairs.

Howard hadn't written a *Star Trek* novel in a while, so he was flattered to be invited to submit story ideas to this anthology. He said, "There's nothing glorious about war, but it does bring out the best in writers."

Reflecting on where the idea for the story originated, Howard said, "This idea came from a little-known true story: During World War II, the town and farm folks in North Platte, Nebraska made it their business to greet every troop train that briefly stopped at their depot out on the plains, and treat young soldiers to a few minutes of hospitality, warmth, good home-cooked food and fresh-baked cakes and pies, and even a little dancing on their way to and from war. This began when they heard the news that a train carrying local boys would be coming through, but when the train pulled in, the hometown boys weren't on it. So they shrugged and said, 'These boys are from somebody's hometown, so let's treat them like they're our own.' Which they did, over and over, for the duration of the war."

Some years earlier, Howard saw Charles Kuralt do one of his "On the Road" reports about North Platte's spirit, and he never forgot it and neither did the young men who received those gifts of kindness. He thought, "A story set during the Dominion War seemed like the perfect time to use that true tale. I also called up harrowing images of 9/11, and even though I'm far from the first to use the Statue of Liberty in science fiction, Lady Liberty's cameo in this story is much more hopeful than her appearance in *Planet of the Apes*. We live in perilous times, and I wanted to echo that peril in a way that encourages readers to think about the consequences not only of what we do to protect ourselves and our way of life, but *how* we do it. I also knew I wanted to use the elderly McCoy and Scotty, not only because they're a classic pairing, but also to contrast their experience with the inexperience of the kids who usually do most of the fighting in any war. I'm really proud of this story. I don't think I've ever written anything better."

"Field Expediency"
(TALES OF THE DOMINION WAR)
DAYTON WARD AND KEVIN DILMORE

A mission traps several crew members of the *da Vinci* during a Dominion attack, and the ship above must survive intact to achieve a rescue.

Kevin said, "This story was much more Dayton's baby than mine, as he's the military writer. I enjoyed this one chiefly because it allowed us to write Duffy and Stevens (the Hawkeye and Trapper of S.C.E.) again. I think it's a good action-packed *Star Trek* story and it seems to have gotten some good response."

Dayton remembers what Keith DeCandido asked for the two of them. "He also wanted to have at least one story that had what he described as 'kick-ass ground combat scenes' in it, and thought I'd be good for that. Those were the only instructions we had, and the rest was up to us. So, Kevin and I met up one Saturday afternoon at (you guessed it) a local bar and plotted out the storyline, which has the S.C.E. gang traveling behind enemy lines to retrieve a piece of top secret Breen technology. Things go bad during the mission and the team is forced to improvise several things on the fly, coming up with 'field expedient' solutions to their various problems."

Summing it up, Dayton said, "This was a fun story to write, for several reasons. First, both Kevin and I really enjoy writing stories with the S.C.E. characters. It was an action-oriented story, set on the ground in a combat situation, which I definitely like to write. Also, it was the first time an S.C.E. story would premiere in a printed format before first being offered exclusively in eBook form. Finally, it was the first time we were invited to share the stage with writers like Peter David, Michael Jan Friedman, Bob Greenberger, Howie Weinstein, Greg Cox, Susan Shwartz and Josepha Sherman—people whose work I'd been reading and enjoying for years—as well as newer voices like Heather Jarman, Jeff Lang, Andy Mangels and Mike Martin, Dave Mack, Dave Galanter, and Keith (his name keeps popping up a lot here, in case you've not noticed). That by itself was worth the price of admission."

"A Song Well Sung"
(TALES OF THE DOMINION WAR)
ROBERT GREENBERGER

Klag regains consciousness to discover the battered remains of his ship, his dead crew, and his missing arm.

"Keith contacted me, inviting me to write the true story of how Klag lost his arm in the battle of Marcan V. He'd been referring to the incident since re-introducing Klag in his *Diplomatic Implausibility* novel. Since he really wanted to write the story about the fall of Betazed for the anthology, he entrusted me to bring his story to life. To this day he continues to say it turned out well and I hope he's right. The fan reaction has been fairly positive."

"Stone Cold Truths"
(TALES OF THE DOMINION WAR)
PETER DAVID

Zak Kebron tells his interested son the events that transpired on the *Excalibur* during the Dominion War.

Peter remarked, "Keith DeCandido wanted me to do a *New Frontier* story about the Dominion War. The problem was I had only been watching DS9 on and off. I didn't know all of the beats of the war and I wasn't entirely sure of who was fighting over what. Keith knew the Dominion War stone cold, no relation to my title. How much did I want to go out of my way to learn about this whole damn thing to write a short story? If they wanted me to write a Dominion War novel, that would be one thing. I would suck it up and go watch all of the DS9 episodes and get in the loop. Being a short story, I decided to dodge the entire thing by placing it one hundred years later and having it be essentially, 'What did you do during the war, Daddy?' It enabled me to dodge all of the problems because Kebron's entire story was to all intents and purposes bull. So if I got something wrong it didn't matter. Rather than mix the *Excalibur* into the heart of the Dominion War, I just decided to pull back from the whole thing and tell a story that would be a coda to the utter futility of war. War should always be the last resort and we should never forget that it's a tragedy we have to fight in the first place."

"Requital"
(TALES OF THE DOMINION WAR)
MICHAEL A. MARTIN AND ANDY MANGELS

On the threshold of peace between the Federation and the Dominion, an assassin sets his sights on the female shapeshifter, now in custody.

Mike commented, "Ever since DS9's series finale, 'What You Leave Behind,' I had wanted to do a story about a revenge-obsessed Starfleet soldier. Reese seemed like a natural choice for a study on revenge, and how anybody—even someone like Sisko who knows better—might succumb to the base urge for revenge under certain circumstances."

TALES FROM THE CAPTAIN'S TABLE
KEITH DeCANDIDO, EDITOR

JULY 2005   (337PP)

TRADE PAPERBACK

Keith remarked, "I pitched something that had been in the back of my mind for a while and I finally just wrote it down and sent it in. It was the follow-up to the *Captain's Table* anthology. The original books were a really nifty concept and it opened up some real good storytelling possibilities. It gave Peter David the opportunity to tell one of the best ST stories ever told, which was Calhoun's story as First Officer of the *Grissom*. That was a really powerful story and that probably wouldn't have come about if not for that mini-series and I thought the format was a really good opportunity to really get into the heads of some of the Captain characters. Between those books and the *Enterprise Logs* anthologies, a ton of captains have been added to the pantheon. You get Archer obviously on television; since then Shelby, Riker, and Chakotay have all been elevated to the captaincy. Shelby in the *New Frontier* novels, Riker in *Nemesis*, Chakotay in the post-*Voyager* novels. A total of nine new captains—well, eight new captains and one sort of new captain in Picard, in as much as the *Stargazer* series had started since then."

"Improvisations on the Opal Sea: A Tale of Dubious Credibility"
(TALES FROM THE CAPTAIN'S TABLE)
ANDY MANGELS AND MICHAEL A. MARTIN

 iker and Troi have a rather exciting honeymoon.

Andy commented, "It was a complete kick to write, as it's so full of blarney that you just know Riker is making it up . . . and yet, we also tried to make each element completely defensible and true. In the end, as with the people hearing the story in the bar, the reader should be unclear how much truth Riker was telling, but they should know they were entertained."

Mike remembered, "As I recall it, it all started with the idea of putting Riker in a silly costume, based on his remark in 'Angel One' about having had to wear feathers to a diplomatic conference. We had hoped to use that image in conjunction with the untold tale of the Riker-Troi honeymoon, but we couldn't quite make it work. We also both liked the idea of doing a pirate story, and had made various allusions to pirates over the years with Ranul Keru (whom we also wanted to include, as a

way of transitioning him from his duties as a Trill Guardian in *Worlds of Star Trek: Deep Space Nine* to one of *Titan*'s senior staff). We also wanted to do something a little lighter in tone than what we had just done in WoDS9, as a change of pace."

"Darkness"
(TALES FROM THE CAPTAIN'S TABLE)
MICHAEL JAN FRIEDMAN

 icard contemplates his life after the destruction of the *Stargazer*.

Mike commented, "Originally, I was asked to write a *Stargazer*-era story, but I wanted to show a different Picard from the one we had seen—just as I had shown a different Guinan in *Oblivion*. It occurred to me that after Picard had lost his ship and part of his crew to the Ferengi, he would be something less than the man we knew him to be. He would be disturbed, tortured, in doubt about his worth and his future. Of course, it turned out to be a *Stargazer* story in many ways. And as I was on the verge of turning fifty when I wrote it, it was therapeutic to write about a man who had come to a crossroads in his life at the age of fifty."

"Pain Management"
(TALES FROM THE CAPTAIN'S TABLE)
PETER DAVID

Soleta and Shelby run into some Orions.

Peter had no recollections to share about this story.

"loDnI'pu' vavpu'je"
(TALES FROM THE CAPTAIN'S TABLE)
KEITH R.A. DeCANDIDO

Klag tells a tale of his brother.

"The Officers' Club"
(TALES FROM THE CAPTAIN'S TABLE)
HEATHER JARMAN

During the Cardassian occupation of Bajor, Kira discovers treachery close to home.

Heather commented, "Keith gave me the assignment after he heard that I envied him the chance to write 'Horn and Ivory.' I love Kira—I've made no secret of that. Personality-wise, she is the closest thing to an alter ego that I have in *Star Trek*. When this new anthology came up and I was given the chance to write Kira's tale, I accepted eagerly even though I had two assignments I was working on for Marco. Paramount rejected the first idea I had for 'The Officer's Club' as being 'not Kira.' It had to do with Kira having a crisis of faith—kind of her Mel Gibson *Signs* story. According to Paramount, however, Kira never had a crisis of faith. To which I say (as a person of faith), 'Ummmm . . . yeah. Whatever.' (Translation: not possible—every thinking person questions his or her faith at some point, otherwise the faith tends to wither during the bad times)." With this idea rejected, Heather went back to the drawing board, eventually deciding to try a more lighthearted approach. "I also looked to caper movies like *Oceans 11* and *The Sting* for ideas. Once I came up with a few rudimentary ideas, I bounced them off my daughters who all have watched *Deep Space Nine*. I recall driving to Provo, Utah to visit my friend who is a Brigham Young University professor. We stopped in Wal-

Mart to pick up some miscellany and discussed the story while walking up and down the aisles of the store. I'm sure people thought we were very odd discussing genetic doubles and characters posing as hookers."

Heather continued, "One of my goals was to show that I had a sense of humor in the story. As it turns out, I might have a sense of humor but Kira really doesn't. I rewatched lots of DS9 and discovered that Kira doesn't really bring the funny. She's not Jadzia or Quark, nor is she the butt of jokes like Worf can be. So I tried to lighten up the story a bit by creating some outlandish scenarios, but in the end it was still pretty depressing. The writing process was interesting because it was the only assignment I almost had to walk away from because of 'real life' issues. Back when I needed to start writing, I was asked to be a court-appointed supervisor for a couple entangled in a massive visitation fight. One was accused of abuse, the other of neglect and so on. Suffice it to say I was in hell. Every day. For almost two months. At one point, I had to travel with the family. I was verbally attacked. I was threatened with lawsuits. When the judge dragged me into another round of court appointed misery, I called Keith and told him I'd have to drop out. Combined with this was the fact that my mother was going in for a surgical biopsy for a potential cancer and my younger sister was two steps away from eloping with a total loser. Since I was traveling, I sat in front of my computer every night watching hours of A&E's *Pride and Prejudice* completely relying on the merits of Colin Firth and crying myself to sleep to get me through each day. How can a person write under those circumstances? In the end, Keith and Pocket were very patient and allowed me to finish the project on my own time. I will be forever grateful! I did learn that I didn't want to be a lawyer when I grow up and that I have the nicest editors in the world."

Heather had some final thoughts. "I had no idea how the fans would receive the story. For me, it was more a triumph of will than it was a writing triumph. I did try and write from my gut and tell a story in Kira's words. Writing in first person was tough and took time to get used to. I used a lot of phraseology and made stylistic choices that are very different from my own way of speaking. Hopefully it worked."

"Have Beagle, Will Travel: The Legend of Porthos"
(TALES FROM THE CAPTAIN'S TABLE)
LOUISA M. SWANN

Archer tells the story of Porthos the Great, aka Double-0 One.

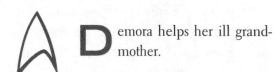

"Iron and Sacrifice"
(TALES FROM THE CAPTAIN'S TABLE)
DAVID R. GEORGE III

Demora helps her ill grandmother.

David remarked, "I began thinking about the story for "Iron and Sacrifice" after Keith De-Candido called me, told me about the *Tales from the Captain's Table* project, and asked if I'd be interested in penning a Demora Sulu piece. Having utilized Demora as a major character in my own *Serpents Among the Ruins,* and having developed her quite a bit in that novel, I felt almost proprietary towards her, and definitely wanted to be the one to write her *Captain's Table* entry. Once I accepted the gig, I asked myself the question I always ask when beginning a new writing project: What do I want to say? I had an immediate desire to tell more than just a simple short story, and I decided almost at once to try to integrate the tale of Demora finding and entering the bar into the larger tale that she would end up telling. I also had a notion that perhaps I could follow up on the Devron II mission that Captain Harriman and Commander Sulu alluded to in *Serpents.* But that still didn't tell me what issues or themes I wanted to address, and that's generally the point where I start my writing process. And so it happened that a couple of days later, my wife Karen and I were driving somewhere, and I brought up my *Captain's Table* story. I told Karen that I was trying to figure out what I wanted to talk about in my story, and after

some thought, she mentioned the issue of a younger person having to care for an older relative. That was an issue that seemed to me worthy of exploration, and pretty quickly, a story started to take shape for me. I then spent time working out the tale of Demora and her grandmother, and entwining with it the bar story and the Devron II story."

David continued, "As I wrote 'Iron and Sacrifice,' the character of Shimizu Hana, Demora's paternal grandmother, took on a life of her own (as characters are sometimes wont to do). When I started out, Hana did not have this reticent, ultimately haunted personality and history, but that's where the tale took me. When I finished it, I realized that along with the three stories I'd told—Demora and Strolt in the bar, Demora and her grandmother, Demora and Iron Mike Paris—a fourth story had been born, namely that of Shimizu Hana's past (which is now pretty well laid out in my mind). Perhaps one day I'll get to go back and flesh out the details of the life of Demora's grandmother, Hikaru's mother. One particularly fulfilling thing that happened during the writing of this story was that, partway through, I stumbled upon another theme, namely that of gay marriage. Although perhaps subtle, I was able to weave that thread through the tale. As *Star Trek* has always been to me about the societal concepts of acceptance and inclusion, I found this particularly satisfying. In the end, the writing proceeded smoothly, although the transitions among the three sub-stories took some time to formulate. I'm very pleased with the end result, although I realize that it might not be to every reader's liking, as it is not what I would consider a 'normal' *Star Trek* story. That is, this is not a tale that unfolds aboard a starship or a space station, and the main tale of Demora's grandmother is not one with any real galactic repercussions. It is rather a simple character piece that seeks to illuminate a couple of issues."

"Seduced"
(TALES FROM THE CAPTAIN'S TABLE)
Christie Golden

A young Chakotay discovers Starfleet.

Christie recalled, "I had a lot of fun getting to create some of Chakotay's past for the two *Spirit Walk* books. It was a real pleasure to revisit the young Chakotay and Sekaya and Blue Water Boy. The Chakotay we have seen has always been completely comfortable with women in positions of power and I often wondered how that came about. Ideally, of course, it shouldn't matter, but people are people and even in the *Star Trek* world there is racism and sexism. Keith wanted the 'Sulu' mentioned in the episode 'Tattoo' to be Demora, and I thought that was great and that it would tie in well with things I wanted to pursue. All was terrific . . . until I rewatched the episode and Chakotay's father clearly said 'he' when referring to Captain Sulu. I chose to use that to my advantage in the story. I also have great respect for Indian traditions (contrary to most PC thought, in my experience the actual indigenous people seem more comfortable with that term than Native American) and, while Chakotay's tribe is completely fictitious, I was able to use my knowledge to fabricate a tribe that I hope felt real to my readers. I do not use first person often, but it came quite naturally for this story, and I think there's a lot of character-based humor in it, which I don't often get to dabble with. Sekaya in particular came quite fully into herself and sometimes cracked me up. Another layer that I liked was the innocence and hope and warmth between these three that, of course, is lying under the shadow of the future and the terrible things that will happen to them. Chakotay is also of course a somewhat romantic figure due to his attraction to Janeway. I thought I would play on readers' expectations and have the great 'love affair' of his life not be with a woman, but with Starfleet."

"An Easy Fast"
(TALES FROM THE CAPTAIN'S TABLE)
John J. Ordover

Gold tells a story during the Jewish holiday of Yom Kippur.

John remarked, "I knew I wanted to do a story set around Yom Kippur, and about atonement and forgiveness. I like the story structure of the 'three confrontations,' which is a standard format, and I went from there."

DISTANT SHORES
(STAR TREK: VOYAGER)
MARCO PALMIERI, EDITOR

NOVEMBER 2005 (389PP)

TRADE PAPERBACK

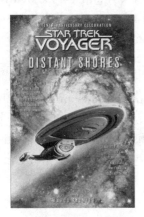

"Da Capo al Fine, Parts I and II
(DISTANT SHORES)
HEATHER JARMAN

Admiral Janeway contemplates her life as she dies at the hands of the Borg Queen in the last episode, 'Endgame.'

"The credit for this is owed to my oldest daughter, Sara. She came up with the idea. She will kill me for saying this, but when she was in elementary school, she was the original Janeway fangirl. She even had a Janeway costume she wore in fourth grade. I think she was the only one writing *Voyager* poetry in her class. I believe a lot of her fearlessness in pursuing her goals came from having Janeway as a role model, from earning a black belt in taekwondo, playing lacrosse, and working in politics to potentially applying for admission to the United States Naval Academy. Sara has an unnatural ability to recall insignificant facts, one of them being obscure pieces of television episodes. While she has advanced out of *Voyager* land in terms of her primary passions, at age sixteen she still remembers *Voyager* episodes from elementary school. When I asked her about what untold story she wanted revisited she said, 'How about that alien guy from "Coda"? He said he was going to come back and he never did.' I talked with my good friend Kirsten and we realized that Janeway did actually die in the series—in 'Endgame.' We put 'Coda' and 'Endgame' together and came up with 'Da Capo al Fine,' which is a music term that means repeat (the entire piece of music), from beginning up to the word *fine* (which means end). Since the first half of the story begins at the end of the *Voyager* series then goes backwards to the beginning, the motif of 'repeat again' works. The second half of the story advances from where the first half leaves off and proceeds to the series finale, 'Endgame,' where we started. Get it? The story follows the *da capo al fine* pattern. The whole Italian music word symmetry was fun to play with. Savvy *Voyager* fans will get the title tie-in pretty quick."

Heather continued, "The writing process was short and, for me, very linear. I typically write on my laptop in my kitchen or in my husband's office. This time, I sat on my bed with the 'Endgame' video in my VCR. I would watch the relevant sections over and over again, transcribing them and then filling in the blanks with my thoughts about what Janeway was thinking or feeling. Once I was done with the 'Endgame' sections, I went back to two of my favorite *Voyager* episodes, 'Sacred Ground' and 'The Year of Hell,' to yank two more 'near death' scenes for Janeway. I rewatched those over and over again, too. Trying to differentiate between the younger Janeway and the older, bitter, cynical Janeway was intriguing. I liked her voice.

"Of all my short stories, I think this was my favorite to write. It wasn't complicated. It just was. I enjoyed being able to write a story that my daughters could not only read, but that they liked. Sara enjoyed the end result and she was the one I was trying to please."

"Command Code"
(DISTANT SHORES)
Bob Greenberger

Shortly after the events of *Caretaker*, Tuvok finds himself at odds with Chakotay, who is in command during a crisis.

Bob commented, "Marco invited me to pitch to the anthology and at first I wanted to tell a story about an ex-Maquis crew member after the ship returned to Earth. Then Marco defined the anthology as set during the seven years lost in space. I then struggled with trying to find a good Janeway story but failed. At that point, I had given up. Marco called a few weeks later to see where my pitch was. I admitted to being stumped and he said he was still looking for stories emphasizing Paris or Tuvok. I gave it some thought and sparked to the notion of a test of wills between Tuvok, who had infiltrated Chakotay's Maquis cell, and Chakotay who was now first officer. As I considered that, I recalled the confrontation between Gene Hackman and Denzel Washington in *Crimson Tide* and that locked things for me. Setting it in the days immediately following the pilot gave me the tension I needed. I rewatched the pilot and some of the other first-season episodes to see how they dealt with one another and then got to work. Marco liked the notion, Paramount approved it, and I wrote the story pretty quickly. After submitting it, my keen-sighted editor noted the tone, entirely from Tuvok's point-of-view, felt stiff. I then reworked the story, shifting between Tuvok and Chakotay which actually helped heighten some of the moments so it's a superior work as a result."

"Winds of Change"
(DISTANT SHORES)
KIM SHEARD

After the events in the episode 'Warlord,' Kes seeks B'Ellanna's help to handle her conflicting aggressive emotions.

Kim commented, "It's a story focusing on Kes and B'Elanna and I got the idea for that combination of characters when Marco told me that the anthology would consist of stories based on opportunities the series failed to exploit, including combining characters that we didn't usually see together. Kes and B'Elanna certainly fit in that category, as they had very little to do with each other in the series. Once I had the idea to put those two characters together I had to come up with a story for them, and I decided to focus on the repercussions of the episode 'Warlord.' Kes went through a lot of changes in season three, and I think 'Warlord' started them off. Kieran showed her aggression and anger, and who better to help her deal with that new side than B'Elanna? I started with a pitch of a couple of sentences. (Actually sent Marco four ideas, and this was the last, thought up at the last minute.) He liked this one the best, so I went on to a six-ish-page proposal, which went through Marco to Paramount and was accepted with a minor caution. Then I wrote the story. Got two pages of notes from Marco. Rewrote the story. It was much better and a little longer, I think."

Kim had some final thoughts. "This has been an interesting process for me because it is the first time the process has been collaborative with an editor. It was a little nervewracking at first, but Marco's great and the story did turn out for the better, so now I'm all for it!"

"Talent Night"
(DISTANT SHORES)
JEFFREY LANG

While Tom Paris works hard to make a talent show be a successful distraction for the crew, B'Elanna begins to realize her true feelings for him.

Jeffrey commented, " 'Talent Night' was written with very specific parameters in mind. Marco and his team had been working on the *Voyager* anthology for several months. They had their line-up and came to the conclusion that 1) They didn't have enough stories set in the early seasons; 2) They didn't have any stories that focused on Tom Paris; and 3) Most of the stories were pretty serious. So, having just finished *Cohesion*, and having a modest reputation for being able to write lighter stuff (and enjoying Tom's character), Marco said, 'Can you write a Tom Paris story set in the early seasons that's not too grim?' I said, 'Uh, okay. When do you need it?' 'In about two weeks.' 'Oh. Uh. Let me get back to you.' Kirsten Beyer (who knows the early seasons really well) helped me hone in on a timeframe that would work and then, reading the episode synopses for season three, I saw the mention of the discussion between Neelix and Janeway about the talent show from the night before. It was all pretty easy after that. Laying down a little groundwork for the Tom/B'Elanna relationship was fun. And, yes, I finished it in about ten days."

"Letting Go"
(DISTANT SHORES)
KEITH R. A. DECANDIDO

Mark struggles with life without Kathryn Janeway by his side.

"My story was inspired by an old *M*A*S*H** episode when B.J. organized a 'reunion' among their loved ones back home in the States, where Hawkeye's dad, B.J.'s wife, Mulcahy's sister, Klinger's mother, etc., all gathered in New York to engage in some support. 'Letting Go' has Samantha Wildman's husband doing something similar for the people left behind when *Voyager* disappeared. The story deals with several of the families of the characters, but the main character is Mark Johnson, Janeway's lover seen in 'Caretaker' taking care of her dog, and who is later revealed to have met someone else and married her. The story takes place over a span of time, starting eleven months after 'Caretaker' and ending shortly after 'Message in a Bottle' (which is when the Alpha Quadrant learns of *Voyager*'s fate)."

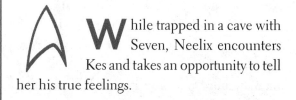

"Closure"
(DISTANT SHORES)
JAMES SWALLOW

While trapped in a cave with Seven, Neelix encounters Kes and takes an opportunity to tell her his true feelings.

James remarked, "I've loved science fiction since I was a kid and I absorbed every bit of science fiction I could get my hands on, from books, movies, comics and of course television. *Star Trek* was always part of my TV landscape growing up, but I think it was in the 1980s when BBC2 re-ran the original series that I really keyed into the themes and characters of the show. I got into *Trek* fandom about the same time I decided I wanted to write for a living, and cut my teeth on fanzines, which in turn led me to writing for professional magazines—including a whole bunch of licensed *Star Trek* publications. That got me onto the Paramount lot . . . and eventually, it got me the chance to pitch for *Star Trek: Voyager*. You can't look at characters you enjoy without thinking 'Hey, wouldn't it be cool if you could do a story where. . . .' I'd already had the chance to come up with stories for the *Voyager* crew when I wrote the story concepts for the episodes 'One' and 'Memorial,' but the TV process is very different from writing prose. There's more creative teamwork but less direct control over the narrative, and I've always nursed the desire to tell a *Star Trek* story single-handedly."

Regarding his story in the anthology, " 'Closure' is an 'end of the affair' coda to the Neelix/Kes romance, and the germ of an idea came from a comment that actor Ethan Phillips made, where he said that he had never been fully satisfied with the way Neelix and Kes broke up. I was always fascinated by that relationship—this goofy guy and this elfin girl, what seems at first glance to be a real mismatch—and the more I thought about it, the more I wanted to explore it. I liked the idea that Neelix had let Kes go but never stopped loving her, that he carried this hurt around with him even though he outwardly was still the same happy-go-lucky chappie. The story came together quickly once Marco gave me the green light; the emotional beats of the narrative flowed smoothly out of the scenes with Neelix and Kes and no obstacles arose during the writing. I think I had to change two tiny things–the placing of the story in the show's chronology and an off-hand reference to the eating habits of Efrosians–and that was that."

James wanted to add, "I guess I would say that I like to fly the flag for non-North American *Star Trek* writers! I always brag that I'm the only British writer to have worked on a *Star Trek* TV show, and I'm pleased to join people like Una McCormack in showing the Union Jack on the Final Frontier. . . ."

"The Secret Heart of Zolaluz"
(DISTANT SHORES)
Robert T. Jeschonek

 Seven must rescue Janeway and she needs the help of a woman shunned by her society.

Robert commented, "This story was inspired by a college student from Central America, a young woman who had a disability which limited the use of her legs. She faced a multitude of struggles in her daily life, and she eventually had to return home to a dangerous and economically depressed homeland, yet she remained perpetually upbeat and succeeded in all the challenges that she faced. I always wanted to explore the motivation of someone like her in a work of fiction, and I found the perfect counterpoint in the character of *Voyager*'s Seven of Nine. By aligning Zolaluz and Seven, I was able to shine a light on the struggle with depression and the human will to triumph over all limitations from within and without. The theme for *Distant Shores* was the exploitation of opportunities missed in the TV series. In that vein, 'The Secret Heart of Zolaluz' unearthed the source of at least some of the motivation that enabled Seven of Nine to rise above her horrific past. Editor Marco Palmieri agreed that this story hit the mark, and he found a place for it in the *Distant Shores* anthology."

"Isabo's Shirt"
(DISTANT SHORES)
KIRSTEN BEYER

 unique birthday gift allows Chakotay to embrace his love for a fellow crew member.

Kirsten recalled, "I sent Marco four or five ideas and the one he liked was the one that answered the question . . . why did Janeway and Chakotay never develop a more intimate relationship? I mean it was always there . . . hinted at. Of course, from the producer's point of view, I could understand their reluctance to pursue it. But I always felt that they could have given us something . . . anything . . . that would allow us to set it aside completely and just move on in our heads. I get that they tried in 'Fair Haven' or 'Spirit Folk' (I've blocked it out to be honest) . . . but . . . well . . . it didn't work for me at all. The only parameters Marco offered were keep it simple. Give me a simple gesture, or a simple misunderstanding that leads to what we always called 'the conversation.' I kept thinking of O. Henry's *The Gift of the Magi* which is where the idea of the birthday present came from. That, and the great moment in 'Year of Hell' when Chakotay tries to give Janeway her birthday present, that silver watch, and she tells him to recycle it, then ends up keeping it until the bitter end. (Can I just say here and now that before I wrote the scene in which we see that Janeway still has the watch I worked through the math in my head. It's one of those details that I expect *Trek* fans to scratch their heads about and wonder, but 'Year of Hell' never happened so how can Janeway have the watch? My feeling was that despite the fact that 'Year of Hell' never happened, her birthday was still coming up in the re-set timeline, Chakotay would still be planning to give her the gift, so why wouldn't it be the same gift? In 'Year of Hell' he tells her he replicated it long before they entered Crenim space, so I took that and ran with it—or justified it—you make the call)."

Kirsten continued, "I didn't have a title for it for the longest time. I refuse to reveal any of the working titles. Then, near the end of my fifth draft or so, I was re-watching 'Resolutions' and kept watching that scene where Chakotay tries to tell Kathryn how he feels by using the made-up legend from his tribe. What can I say . . . I'm a sucker at times. Most of 'the conversation' was already in place, but I was looking for a way to end it for both of them and it dawned on me that he might actually know a real legend that would somehow shed some light on their predicament. I went searching through my mythology collections and found a story similar to the legend he tells Janeway about Isabo and the warrior. Since we're talking about mythology anyway, it didn't seem too much of a stretch that a similar legend would exist among Chakotay's people, slightly modified to make sense in their cultural context."

"Brief Candle"
(DISTANT SHORES)
CHRISTOPHER L. BENNETT

A Lieutenant Marika Willkarah, disconnected from the Borg collective, embraces life in the short time she has left to live.

"Marco invited me to pitch for the VGR anthology, with the brief being to explore missed opportunities, aspects of shipboard life or relationships that warranted more exploration, that sort of thing. I went through the various story ideas I'd come up with in my attempts to pitch for the show, and came up with several proposals for Marco, including an encounter with a colony of Cardassians abducted by the Caretaker, a follow-up on the Doctor's memory loss in 'The Swarm,' and a reworking of an unsuccessful *Strange New Worlds* submission called 'Spirit of the Hunt,' which would later become the basis for *Orion's Hounds*. The only one that wasn't reworked from an earlier VGR idea, and something of an afterthought, was 'Brief Candle.' I came up with this by going through the *Voyager Companion* and looking for dangling story threads. The story of Marika Willkarah's unseen last few weeks of life (following 'Survival Instinct') interested me because it was thematically similar to an original science fiction story that I've been trying to sell for years. I think it's one of the best things I've ever written, and the magazine editors keep telling me it's wonderful and poignant and moving but just doesn't quite work for them. I figured 'Brief Candle' could be a chance to tell a similar story just in case the original story never sold. (However, in the wake of writing 'Candle' I thought about ways to revise the other story to make it distinct, and I may be able to give it a new lease on life.)"

Christopher continued, "Anyway, Marco picked 'Candle,' and I got to work on the outline. The timeframe of the story let me include several other underdeveloped threads from the series, including a subplot about the *Equinox* crew members and some added background on 'Barge of the Dead.' The presence of extras wearing Voth makeup in 'Survival Instinct' gave me an excuse to call back some ideas from 'Distant Origins,' one of my very favorite episodes (and one you can expect me to follow up on again in a future project). Marco asked me to drop the *Equinox* crew subplot since he had two other stories dealing with them. The story premise also gave me an opportunity to work in Kes, another favorite of mine, though length limitations forced me to abandon the flashback scene I originally wrote in favor of a recollection described by Neelix. One thing I decided to do here as well as in 'Loved I Not Honor More' was to overlap the story with an episode of the series. 'Honor' took place before and during DS9's 'Soldiers of the Empire,' while 'Brief Candle' begins between the last two scenes of 'Survival Instinct' and incorporates the events of 'Barge of the Dead.' (I considered leading into 'Tinker, Tenor, Doctor, Spy' as well, but couldn't work it in without it feeling contrived.) I like to do this because I find the chronology of a twenty-six-episode season to be cluttered enough as it is; it can be hard to fit new adventures in, and I don't want to add to the cramping, so I like it when I can have a story overlap an existing episode. Also I think it adds more dimension to the universe, creates a sense that there's more going on than just what's on camera."

"Eighteen Minutes"
(DISTANT SHORES)
TERRI OSBORNE

On the planet in the episode 'Blink of an Eye,' where time runs much faster than on *Voyager*, the Doctor lives three years with the natives while being gone only eighteen minutes from the ship.

"The story chronicles, via the doctor's personal and CMO logs, some of his experiences on the surface those three years (or, to the *Voyager* crew, eighteen minutes) during the episode 'Blink of an Eye.' Yes, how a hologram came to have a biological son will be dealt with. Marco Palmieri specifically asked me to look at how fatherhood affects the doctor. If I've done my job right, it'll also lays a subtle groundwork for the doctor's efforts toward holographic rights in the later seasons. Yes, I am aware of the story in SNW VII. Unfortunately, while I'd love to take it into continuity if I could, I'm forced to ignore it. Taking it into continuity would invalidate the work I've done when we found out about the SNW story's existence, and I was in discussions to do this story before the winners of SNW VII were even chosen. It's an instance of spontaneous story development. There are a few obvious similarities between the stories;

however, I think anyone who looks at the specific details of the time the doctor spent on the planet that we were given in the episode would come up with very similar concepts. I really wish I could have used the SNW VII story, though, because I'm one of those people that likes to include as much as possible into continuity. I tried to contact G. Wood to apprise him of the situation, but the e-mails bounced."

"Or the Tiger"
(DISTANT SHORES)
GEOFFREY THORNE

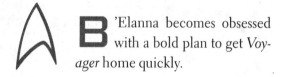

B'Elanna becomes obsessed with a bold plan to get *Voyager* home quickly.

Geoffrey remembered, "The story focuses on B'Elanna Torres and Noah Lessing (of the *Equinox*). Essentially it's a character piece because, though the characters don't know it, the get-home-fast scheme I set up for them can't possibly work. The audience knows they can't possibly get home so they're free to focus on the other things the story is about. What's at the center of the story is how easy it would be for any person to sacrifice big fat chunks of their own morality in order to attain some beneficial goal. The title comes from a Frank Stockton story called 'The Lady Or The Tiger,' which basically sets up a really ugly choice for its protagonist. I do the same with my story, giving B'Elanna the choice of essentially killing an entire crew of aliens or getting *Voyager* home in a week. Who helps her make the right choice? Noah Lessing, who himself was part of a crew, the *Equinox*, who made the wrong choice, first with an alien species and then with *Voyager*. There's a new alien species, the Moyani, a new technology, a whole bunch of character development and B'Elanna even gets to beat the hell out of somebody, old school Klingon style (barehanded). I really like it."

"Bottomless"
(DISTANT SHORES)
ILSA J. BICK

arla, one of the *Equinox* crew, tries to win Janeway's respect.

Ilsa commented, "Oh, my; I wish I could say something brilliant here, but I can't. Marco wanted us to explore things left dangling and I sent in five proposals. 'Bottomless' was the one he picked; a good choice in retrospect because I ended up liking this story. Actually, after Marla and the rest of the *Equinox* folks came aboard, you never saw or heard of them again. They just evaporated. So I decided to take Marla—the one who got the most play, I thought—and do something with her to show her frustration at never fitting in. Janeway's reaction to them and almost all challenges to her authority always seemed to me to be too rigid. Usually, when people are rigid, they're afraid of something, and they're nervous about any change. I think Chakotay pegs it: Janeway's treatment of the *Equinox* folks reflects her own inadequacies, not theirs."

She continued, "This is a story that I did not think out very well in advance. I just proposed it. Then, after Marco wanted it, I had to think of something to write. Actually, I've done a fair amount of diving, and I'd always wanted to do something underwater with a crew. Diving was sort of out of the question, but then I drew on my own experience to give to Marla, and then put her in a classic no-win scenario where the only thing she can do is atone. Just like the Nimtra, she gives a life for a life—and for her, it's the right thing to do. This isn't about her anymore; it's not even about Janeway. It's about giving back what you've taken, and can barely repay. After that, the story just wrote itself. Marco is also a superb editor; I love working with him because he wants to know everything. Well, the funny thing about this story was that it turned out to be one of the first in the anthology that he read and accepted without change. (I mean, this story is exactly what I wrote, word for word.) Except he didn't tell me. His decision about 'Bottomless' was, apparently, months before he finalized a lot of the other stories, and so when I heard other people got accepted, revised, approved and then got checks, I was kind of bummed. So I finally dropped Marco a nice little line—something like, 'Gee, I guess you didn't want the story?' A long story short: Marco called me, apologized, said that he'd read it again and loved it and already accepted it . . . but wondered if Marla needed to die? I felt that if Marla lived, the whole exercise would be meaningless. She wouldn't really make the ultimate sacrifice, and Janeway wouldn't get put in the hot seat, realizing how much she didn't know and would never know—and what she'd lost. So I pretty much said that I didn't think keeping

Marla alive would work. Marco agreed with me, and that was that."

CONSTELLATIONS
(STAR TREK)
MARCO PALMIERI, EDITOR

SEPTEMBER 2006   (382PP)

"First, Do No Harm"
(CONSTELLATIONS)
DAYTON WARD & KEVIN DILMORE

A Starfleet doctor leaves the service and disguises herself so she can help the natives of the planet Grennai.

Kevin commented, "When Marco invited us to pitch for the anthology, one of his guiding tenets for us was to not offer up a mess of simple story ideas but submit only those that felt to us like quintessential *Star Trek*. Dayton and I then sat down with a guiding tenet of our own: We wanted to tell a story that in our minds could have been produced back in the 1960s as an episode of the show. We set our minds toward thinking about such mundane things as budget (how many guest stars can we afford? Set expenses? Special effects? Stunts?) and the like. We also knew that we wanted our story to have an ethical/moral driver to its plot, just like many of our favorite episodes of the series. As far as the writing process, Dayton is a natural when it comes to Kirk's voice and point of view, so he drafted the Kirk scenes and I drafted the others. That pretty well split the story in two."

"The Landing Party"
(CONSTELLATIONS)
ROBERT GREENBERGER

ulu's first command does not go well.

"I had one idea I really wanted to tell but Marco then gave us the guidelines which insisted the stories be set during the five-year mission. I came up with two ideas, one stronger than the other, and submitted them. Marco got back to me, effectively asking, 'What else ya got?' A few days later, I was driving to Maryland and let my mind wander a bit when the idea struck me.

"Even though Marco wasn't looking for continuity implants for this collection, he liked the notion and the time period covered so I got in. I've always wanted a crack at the original series on my own. While I enjoyed *The Disinherited* collaboration, I wanted a solo opportunity so this may be my one shot and I grabbed it."

"Official Record"
(CONSTELLATIONS)
HOWARD WEINSTEIN

 hekov must decide to follow protocol or keep quiet.

Howard recalled, "As usual for me, I'm either inspired or angered by stuff happening in the real world—in this case, in Iraq. Specifically, what can go wrong when politicians, bureaucrats, and military brass send soldiers to tackle impossible tasks without sufficient troop strength, equipment, or planning to do the job successfully? It strikes me as criminal to send troops into harm's way without providing them with the necessary manpower and tools. The story was initially about how young Ensign Chekov handles his discovery of the cover-up of a friendly-fire incident (sparked by the death of Army Ranger and ex-football star Pat Tillman in Afghanistan). In the final version, it evolved into how Chekov deals with a situation in which a superior officer tortures a prisoner for information needed to try and rescue Dr. McCoy, who's been abducted by a local insurgent force. Chekov has to summon the nerve to buck the chain of command, and find a way to support his account of events. In the end, it's about Chekov learning a tough but important lesson—that truth is more important than blind loyalty."

"Fracture"
(CONSTELLATIONS)
JEFF BOND

 irk meets Commodore Merrill, a man that the captain greatly admires.

Jeff commented, "I majored in Creative Writing at Bowling Green State University and wrote science fiction during my last year or so in high school and through college, and I started a *Star Trek* novel between high school and college but never finished it. I never published any fiction but I moved to Los Angeles in 1997 and since then have written about film, music, and movies for magazines including *The Hollywood Reporter* and *Film Score Monthly*, and I'm currently an editor at *Cinefantastique* magazine."

He continued, " 'Fracture' came out of an idea I had developed for the Tholians that was part of the original *Star Trek* novel idea I was tinkering with many years ago. I met Marco Palmieri at the San Diego Comic-Con last summer when he was on a panel discussion of *Star Trek* with me, Mark Altman, the publisher of *Cinefantastique*, Rob Burnett, who made the movie *Free Enterprise* with Mark, and Bill Hunt, who runs the website The Digital Bits. I actually went to pitch some stories to *Enterprise* shortly before it went on the air, one of which they considered briefly. When they didn't use any of those stories I decided to expand some of them and pitch them to Pocket

Books. In the process I came up with a number of stories, one of which I was particularly fond of, but these never got much traction at Pocket Books either. When I was on the panel with Marco I realized this was a great chance to pitch him an idea face to face so I did pitch him a novel idea which he also considered for a while—and then turned that down, too! But the day he called me to turn it down he mentioned the project that would become *Constellations* and asked me to pitch him an idea for it on the spot. The only thing that came to mind was my early idea about the Tholians and how they functioned as life forms. He asked me to give him an outline for a short story, I gave him one that he liked, and a couple of weeks later he called me with another editor's concerns which led to about twenty minutes of very detailed cross examination about the story and various elements that I had to explain or defend. It was quite challenging and involved changing the tone of the ending I had originally pitched, but finally Marco seemed satisfied and gave me the assignment. I have to say that after that the actual writing was relatively easy. I have watched these episodes so many times and now have written long enough that I have my own voice and the voices of the original *Star Trek* characters and the way they speak are very familiar to me. It was challenging incorporating some of the ideas Marco suggested but ultimately I think they led me to write a better story. Since this was supposed to be something like episodes from an imaginary fourth year of the original *Star Trek*, I tried to write it just like an episode of the original show, with an opening captain's log, a big name guest star, fiery arguments and Spock and McCoy exchanging insults at the end."

"Chaotic Response"
(CONSTELLATIONS)
STUART MOORE

McCoy needs to use unorthodox methods to keep Spock alive.

Looking back on his fandom, Stuart said, "I got totally fascinated with the world-building behind the series; I must have read *The Making Of Star Trek* a hundred times. I bought the original *Enterprise* blueprints in 1975 for five dollars, which was a lot of money for me at the time. I figured this was a chance to finally justify that foolish purchase—to do away with thirty years of buyers' remorse, if you will. Unfortunately, it was too late to write the purchase off on my taxes. Seriously—I've always liked the original characters (*Next Gen*, too). I'm primarily a comics writer these days, but I've also written novels for Games Workshop and my roots are in book publishing. When the opportunity came up, I jumped at it. I got talking with editor Marco Palmieri about possibilities in summer of 2005, and everything fell together from there. I almost had to turn it down because my workload was so full, but Marco came back to me and was able to extend the deadline a little. I'm very glad it worked out."

Stuart continued, "I love *Trek* continuity, but for this story I didn't want to get into it very deeply. I just wanted to present a timeless tale of Kirk, Spock, and McCoy—the kind of story that, if it had turned up as an episode of the series, hopefully you'd have tuned in and thought, 'Wow. They really nailed it that time.' Naturally there are Klingons and mind-rippers and Doctor M'Benga, but it's really just a story of how Kirk and Spock, in particular, save each other in a very difficult situation. Once I got into it, I decided it'd be cool to work some actual logic theory into the Spock sequences. I was slightly hampered by the fact that I know absolutely nothing about logic theory, but you know, life is full of these minor obstacles. I figured it out."

"As Others See Us"
(CONSTELLATIONS)
Christopher Bennett

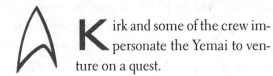

Kirk and some of the crew impersonate the Yemai to venture on a quest.

"I've long been skeptical of the Prime Directive. Its assumption that cultures are 'damaged' by exposure to alien ideas is naive and condescending. Looking at history, you see that the only cases where a less advanced culture has actually been damaged or destroyed by a more advanced one are those where the more advanced culture aggressively tries to destroy or assimilate them. Otherwise, cultures are very robust and adaptable and can adjust to new ideas. (Look at Western Europe. A thousand years ago, it was a primitive, superstitious backwater. Then it was exposed to the new ideas and advanced technology of the East, and rather than being destroyed or assimilated, it

adapted those idea and technology, made them its own, and used them to aggressively spread its own culture.) So I wanted to tell a story that satirized the Prime Directive by having Kirk's landing party encounter a situation that seemed to fit their conventional assumptions about cultural 'contamination,' and then reveal that things weren't as they seemed, turning those assumptions on their head. I also wanted to bring in a different culture with a different philosophy about first contact, one that seems shocking in Prime Directive terms but arguably has its own merits. The Redheri's contact policy in the story is actually an idea I had years before for a non-*Trek* science fiction story that never quite got off the ground. So with several different philosophies of contact and observation involved in the story, I figured I might as well throw in one or two others for comic effect, multiple layers of watchers being watched. The structure of the story as a series of nested scenes moving outward from one observer's perspective to the next was inspired by the opening sequence of the movie *Serenity*. The main difficulty was working out the series of viewpoint shifts, deciding just where to make the switches, and figuring out how to tell a TOS story in which only one scene was actually told from a TOS character's point of view."

"See No Evil"
(CONSTELLATIONS)
JILL SHERWIN

Uhura struggles on the job after her experience with the Nomad probe.

Jill reflected, "I always wanted to write for/about *Trek*. I worked for several seasons as a writers' assistant on the DS9 TV series and pitched stories on many occasions. I got close one or two times, but didn't wind up selling any (though I did sell a story that was produced as an episode of *Gene Roddenberry's Andromeda*). Non-fiction was where I had my first opportunities. While working on DS9, I came up with the idea for *Quotable Star Trek* and that led me to the chance to write other non-fic books. I love writing non-fiction, but my goal has always been to write fiction, too. I came close with my 'story concept' credit in the DS9 anthology *The Lives of Dax*, but this is my first fiction/story sale."

In terms of the story, Jill continued, "A continuity question that's bugged me since I was a kid—in 'The Changeling,' Uhura's memory was wiped by Nomad. By the next episode, she was totally fine—her usual competent officer self. I always wanted to know what happened in between those two stories. How did she get back to herself again? Did she feel any trepidation having to relearn her job and restart her relationships? How did everyone else treat her during the re-learning process? I also wondered how Scotty dealt with having been killed and then revived by Nomad and thought perhaps he and Uhura might have bonded over their related experiences, which might explain what eventually led to their closeness in 'Star Trek V.' And as an anniversary story, I wanted to address Uhura's role and importance in the ship's crew. So 'See No Evil' was a way for me to try to tie those ideas together and answer some questions I'd had for so many years. This story has been in my head for a long time just waiting to be put down on paper, so I was happy to finally get the chance to write it. I did my homework by immersing myself back into TOS—watching multiple episodes daily to get the voices of the characters and the 'feel' of a TOS story. I played TOS soundtrack music as I wrote to stay focused. I've had the pleasure of working with editor Marco Palmieri on other *Trek* books. When I heard this project was being planned, I knew I wanted to be a part of it. I had already mentioned to Marco that I had an idea for a post-'Changeling' Uhura story, so when I had the chance to formally pitch it, I did. It means a lot to me that I've been given the opportunity to contribute to this celebration of the fortieth anniversary of *Star Trek*. For the twentieth anniversary, as a fan I attended the big anniversary convention. For the thirtieth anniversary, I worked on DS9 and spent every spare moment down on the set of 'Trials and Tribble-ations.' And to be able to have my first published story be part of the fortieth anniversary . . . just makes me feel very blessed."

"The Leader"
(CONSTELLATIONS)
DAVE GALANTER

Heading back to the *Enterprise*, the crew of the shuttle *Copernicus* is attacked and they crash on a planet where Kirk and company find a lost colony.

Dave responded, "The idea came from asking myself the question 'What makes Jim Kirk a good leader? Is it instinct? Is it learned?' I decided that some of it was training, and some of it was just his pure force of will and personal charisma. I wanted to write a story where we could see that there were other like individuals who didn't have his training, and maybe didn't even have quite his charisma, but he could look at that leader and say to himself, 'There but for the grace of God go I . . .' and he has that thought about Anders in my story. Anders is a Kirk-like person who has been the force of will who held together his people for years and years. But he doesn't have the wide experience and training of Kirk, and we see that in the end. He ends up doing some things that might well have gotten Kirk killed, but Kirk has nothing but pity for him, because he can see himself, in different circumstances, feeling as Anders did."

Dave remembered how he got into the anthology. "I asked Marco to let me know when he was going to be accepting pitches, and he did. I sent in two ideas (each about two paragraphs long) and he wanted to see more on this one, so I gave him an expanded proposal. It was my first chance to write James Kirk, and to be honest it was easier to write about him from McCoy's point of view than it was to get inside the captain's own thoughts. What can I say—he's our captain—the first one with whom we sought out strange, new worlds, and there's still a bit of awe in attempting to put words in his mouth and thoughts in his head."

"Ambition"
(CONSTELLATIONS)
WILLIAM LEISNER

While Kirk and Spock are left behind, the *Enterprise* rushes to the coordinates of a distress call.

Bill commented, "The initial inspiration for 'Ambition' came from Keith DeCandido's *A Time for War, A Time for Peace*, which had come out at about this same time. In chapter nine of that book, Scotty talks to (a somewhat surprised) La Forge about how he would often be put in command of the *Enterprise* ('sometimes 'twas I, sometimes 'twas Mr. Sulu'), and how he dreaded that duty. Given that it was Sulu who we would eventually see going on to have his own command, I thought to examine how he might have felt about the chief engineer so often being given the role he aspired to, while contrasting that with Scotty's discomfort in the role. So, thanks, Keith!"

Bill continued, "In my initial pitch, the Andorian colony had been hit by an apparent terrorist attack, and when the *Enterprise* eventually catches up with the fleeing suspect, they discover they've been misled, and more complex political machinations were behind the strike. Marco liked the Scotty-Sulu aspects of the story, but asked me to revise the proposal to give the story 'more of a sense of wonder.' Thus the misconstrued 'attack,' the tachyon streamer, and the alien 'turtle eggs' (partly inspired by Carl Hiassen's book *Flush*, in which the pollution of Florida's waters and beaches is a major theme). Marco was very pleased with this new take, and gave me the go-ahead to write the story."

"Devices and Desires"
(CONSTELLATIONS)
KEVIN LAUDERDALE

The *Enterprise* receives a coded message to go to the Yard, a secret Federation Base where alien technology is studied.

Kevin commented, "This story is set at 'The Yard,' a top secret base where all of the alien technology that Starfleet has acquired is studied and stored. It's sort of Starfleet's Area 51. I've been thinking about the concept of The Yard for over a decade, ever since I saw the TNG episode 'Clues,' where at the very end Picard orders Data to keep the existence of the xenophobic Paxans a secret. That got me wondering what other secrets Data might have. Immediately the whole idea of The Yard sprang to my mind. The name is a tribute to the Philadelphia Naval Air Experimental Station (called by most people just 'the Navy Yard') where Robert Heinlein, Isaac Asimov, and L. Sprague de Camp worked during World War II. Before I got invited to pitch to *Constellations*, I had an idea for a TNG novel set there. When Marco invited me I, I found I had Yard-on-the-brain, so one of the ideas I sent him was a sort of prequel to this as-yet-unwritten TNG novel. Marco turned down my original pitch ('It starts off fine, but takes a nose-dive after the first sentence.'), but liked the setting and the idea of Spock there. Originally it was more of an adventure story which just happened to occur while Spock was at The Yard. But when I was forced to look at it from scratch, I decided to make it more about Spock and his past. The story became why he was there and what the antagonist (I won't say villain) wanted from him . . . and I still managed to keep my original pitch's ending. Paramount wanted only one change to my story: Originally the antagonist was nicknamed 'Deacon' (solely for the sake of pulling off a rather dubious tribute to the rock band Steely Dan), but, since that character is a Nasat (insectoid), Paula Block felt that that sounded too much like the bug spray D-CON—not a name you would want to associate with an insect race. I chose 'Bishop' instead. Which, in retrospect, is a better name for a major character, since it's a higher 'rank.' There were also a couple of days of panic on my part when, after I turned in the first draft, Marco called me and pointed out that one of my major plot points had massive logic holes in it. (That's what editors are for.) The camouflage system that The Yard employs in the finished story is a much different one from what I originally envisioned. I actually prefer it because it's much more simple and elegant."

"Where Everybody Knows Your Name"
(CONSTELLATIONS)
JEFFREY LANG

Scott and McCoy wait on the planet Denebia for their fellow crewmen to pick them up.

Jeff commented, "Marco asked me to pitch an idea for the anthology months ago, but, unfortunately, he wasn't much impressed with anything I sent. I think I was trying to come up with something serious, big, revealing . . . I don't know. All I remember about all the ideas was that they were either too ambitious or too grim. Finally, after going 'round and 'round on a couple of ideas, Marco said, 'Maybe you could do something with McCoy and Scotty. Something not so serious.' I think Marco was thinking about my story from the *Voyager* anthology, 'Talent Night,' which was a nice, light, fun piece with lots of character bits. So, we got to thinking and decided the best thing to do was put Bones and Scotty in a bar together, give them a few too many drinks . . . and wait to see what happened. I had one other piece of business that I wanted to cover, which was to address a bit of continuity that I wanted to see; namely, the moment when McCoy decided it was time to leave Starfleet. If you recall, at the beginning of the first movie, he was the only one (besides Spock) who had retired from the service. Why? What chain of events led to it? Or was it anything in particular?"

Jeff continued, "I really wanted to do an original series story since it's the only one of the shows that I haven't written much for. I did my TNG novel, a couple DS9 things, a *Voyager* novel, and a Klingon thing. The only TOS story I did was a comic, which some people might not even count (though I think it's one of the best things I ever wrote), so it was time. I've had these characters' voices in my head since I was about thirteen (a looooonnnggg time ago), so it was fun to finally get them down on paper. The biggest surprise was finding out that I not only enjoyed writing Kirk-and-Spock dialogue, but that it came out sounding so . . . sincere. Bones was always one of my favorite characters, so it was just fun to live inside his head for a few weeks. DeForest Kelley and Jimmy Doohan were wonderful actors, so I was happy to do a story about, as Marco said, 'the ones who aren't with us anymore.' "

"Make-Believe"
(CONSTELLATIONS)
ALLYN GIBSON

Kirk, Spock, and McCoy search for the survivors of a crashed shuttle on a strange planet.

Allyn recalled that he came up with four new ideas for *Constellations* after Marco rejected his original pitch. "If I were to rate the four pitches I made in terms of my own personal interest in developing them and my own sense of their completeness, the one that became 'Make-Believe' was the least developed, least interesting of the bunch. The other three pitches had clearly defined characters, even in the brief sketches I wrote, and clear beginnings and endings. 'Make-Believe' had no clear characters, just a sense of what the story would attempt to say. Indeed, the 'Make-Believe' pitch offered two different approaches to developing the central idea. A reader coming to 'Make-Believe' might think that the story began as a riff on Neil Gaiman's Elric of Melnibone short story, 'One Life' or Rob Shearman's *Doctor Who* audio play *Deadline*. While in retrospect 'Make-Believe' shares some common thematic ground with Gaiman's and Shearman's stories—each focus on real-life characters who fantasize about the stories' respective fandoms and the importance of fandom in dealing with life—'Make-Believe' had a different originating spark: *The Lord of the Rings* films. *Fellowship* opens with Galadriel's recitation of the backstory, and she says of the One Ring that 'history became legend, and legend became myth.' *The Two Towers* closes with Samwise's impassioned speech amidst the ruins of Osgiliath about 'the Great Stories' in which great and terrible things happen to the heroes, but they persevere against the odds because 'there's some good in this world . . . and it's worth fighting for.' 'Make-Believe' arose out of the question, 'What if *Star Trek* were one of the Great Stories, one in which history became legend, legend became myth?' "

Allyn continued, "I offered Marco two approaches to the idea. One involved a child who acts out *Star Trek* fantasies with action figures as a way of coping with a personal tragedy. The other involved a far future setting in which *Star Trek*, though it didn't depict events from the characters' own history, had passed into their mythology much as King Arthur is part of our own mythic past. When Marco replied in September asking for 'Make-Believe' to be developed into a short outline he didn't specify which version of the story to develop, but in my mind there really was no choice—I had to tell the story of the young boy and his action figures. I made that decision partly on the idea of doing something that related events to the Iraq War, something I had suggested in the pitch for no real reason, and partly on the idea of writing a story *about* what *Star Trek* is rather than a story of *Star Trek*. And so, over the course of a week-long business trip to Las Vegas, I developed an outline for 'Make-Believe.' Perhaps my fondest memory of that trip was announcing to my colleagues at dinner one evening that I had been given the 'go' to develop the outline. Unfortunately, the least fond memories of the trip were of trying to work my way through what the story should be—the pitch was a starting point—and little else. In working through the outline, in creating and meeting the characters, I found myself very touched by their plight, very moved by their loss. The ending of the story, at least in the outline, made me cry. The pitch had a sketch of a scene in which Kirk, Spock, and McCoy make their way across a blasted wasteland en route to a vast canyon, and at the end of the scene McCoy flies into the sky and falls lifelessly to the ground as the 'camera' pulls back and reveals that the three *Enterprise* crewmen were not on an adventure at all but were the toys the young boy was using. The outline began with that scene, and with the 'reality' of the situation revealed the story continued as a study of two emotionally damaged characters and the relationship they had to *Star Trek* in their lives. Happy with the outline, I submitted it to Marco, who came back with suggestions. He felt that the outline abandoned the *Enterprise* crewmen too early—what if the *Enterprise* story paralleled the story of the young boy and his toys? The outline was reworked, submitted to Paramount, and prior to Thanksgiving Marco gave me the go-ahead for a manuscript, due December fifteenth."

Allyn was thrilled and terrified at the same time. "Three weeks to produce the manuscript may seem like a great deal of time, but writing a story in the period between Thanksgiving and Christmas seemed like madness for someone who manages a retail store, especially a video game store during the XBox 360 launch and the resulting insanity. Marco asked at one point whether or not writing the story in December was realistic, but that was never a question for me. As I explained to Marco, I *needed* something other than work in December on which to focus, otherwise I'd lose my mind. 'Make-Believe' was written in two marathon writing sessions, approximately a week apart, with three thousand words of the *Enterprise* storyline the first day, twenty-five hundred words of the present day storyline the second. The in-between days I'd revise what I'd written previously and interweaved the two storylines. Because of the way I'd planned out my writing and my job, Marco's deadline of the fifteenth became for me a personal deadline of the twelfth, and I actually finished the final scene and the story itself on the thirteenth. As the story evolved, from pitch to outline to finished story, the focus changed. The pitch suggests a

story that focuses on Breandán, the boy. The outline brought his father Kevin to the front. The finished story, though, focuses on Gabby, almost to the exclusion of her son Breandán. I came to realize that this really was her story— she's not a fan of *Star Trek*, but the people she cares about are, and that becomes a wall in their lives. When asked I find it difficult to summarize 'Make-Believe.' *Ring Around the Sky* and *Performance Appraisal* are straightforward, 'Make-Believe' is not. 'Contemporary fiction, with *Star Trek* elements,' is how I described it to a friend not too long ago."

Allyn continued, "The Kirk scenes were the easiest to write. I tried to put myself in the mind of how an eight-year-old would view *Star Trek*, how mundane objects like Tonka trucks would fit into a *Star Trek* world. I especially enjoyed writing the scene with Kirk and McCoy around the campfire, though at the time I felt that the characterizations were more appropriate to Patrick O'Brian's Jack Aubrey and Stephen Maturin. Given the story's subject matter some may find the story curiously apolitical. While it would have been appropriate, given *Star Trek*'s own criticisms of Vietnam, racism, and other social problems in the 1960s, to criticize the Iraq War and the Bush administration, I felt that criticizing the war didn't fit the story. Instead, I thought that grounding the story in a present-day, even one like the Iraq War, would give the story a sense of immediacy and provide a connection and context for the reader. I needed the war as a catalyst for the story's character drama, nothing more."

Allyn concluded, " 'Make-Believe' may have started as one story—a meditation on an idea from the *Lord of the Rings* films—but it developed into something else, something I was proud to be a part of. In some ways, 'Make-Believe' also humbled me, because I look at the authors lined up for the anthology, authors I've admired and respected for, in some cases, twenty years, and I feel unworthy. But then I look at what I've written, I look at how the story turned out, and I see that I, too, have something to say, and in the end, that's what really matters."

OTHER STAR TREK FICTION

LEGENDS OF THE FERENGI
(STAR TREK: DEEP SPACE NINE)
IRA STEVEN BEHR AND ROBERT HEWITT WOLFE

AUGUST 1997   (157PP)

TRADE PAPERBACK

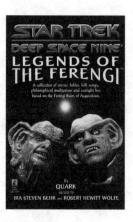

Told by Quark, but written by two *Deep Space Nine* writers, this tells the story behind each Ferengi Rule of Acquisition.

Ira Steven Behr and Robert Hewitt Wolfe were unavailable for interviews.

CAPTAIN PROTON:
DEFENDER OF THE EARTH
D.W. "PROF" SMITH

NOVEMBER 1999   (110PP)

TRADE PAPERBACK

A short story collection designed and laid out like the pulp science fiction magazines of the 1930s. The main novel pits Captain Proton against the evil queen Fems and the comet killers. Chapter two of another story and two other short stories finish the stories. Special Features, including letters to Captain Proton, round out the special "issue."

• • •

Dean remarked, "Since I am a fan of the old Pulp style of writing, and John Ordover knows that, he and I came up with this idea to do a mock pulp magazine using Captain Proton. I wrote all the stories in there, using different styles of old pulp writers like Edmund Hamilton or E. E. Doc Smith."

NEW WORLDS, NEW CIVILIZATIONS
MICHAEL JAN FRIEDMAN

NOVEMBER 1999   (192PP)

HARDCOVER

A Essays, about the various worlds in the Federation. Split over four parts, Fire; Water; Air; and Earth, the stories read like journal entries to the various planets and their societies. The unique and fascinating artwork adds to the mystique of the effort. The mission statement of Starfleet personified in book form.

Mike remarked, "Possibly the best work I've ever done. The book was kind of expensive and probably not seen as an essential buy, so I don't think it got as much play in the marketplace as it might have. But I'm very, very happy with the work I did there. There's stuff on Ferenginar, there's stuff that involves tribbles and Horta and the Q Continuum and I was just in my glory. Little pieces, little vignettes. This stuff to do with Kahless and Martok and stuff that you'll probably see variations on in books that have come out since and I'm sure this had a lot to do with the effort I put out. The artwork in these is spectacular. It would be one thing to have a book with some of their illustrations in it and say 'wow, this is fantastic.' But to have such a wide spectrum of beautiful stuff in there! I think in some ways it transcended the ST market and I think that's why fans didn't latch onto it in the numbers they might have—because they thought it was beautiful and interesting writing but, do I have to buy this? Is this going to tell me what's going on or is this essential? I got to shine a light on every interesting corner of the ST universe. It was a great experience and I think I did my best work there."

He continued, "I asked Margaret Clark, who edited the book, if I contacted the artists do you think they would sell me some of the pieces? She replied, 'I'm sure they've sold other things but they can't.' I said, 'Well, why can't they?' She replied, 'It doesn't exist. Because everything in the book, with one exception (the cover), is a computer-generated image.'"

YOUNG ADULT FICTION

STAR TREK II: SHORT STORIES
WILLIAM ROTSLER

DECEMBER 1982   (159PP)

The Blaze of Glory

Admiral Kirk gets to meet a living legend.

Under Twin Moons

Uhura has an exciting shore leave.

Wild Card

Something Sulu brings on board causes havoc for the *Enterprise*.

The Secret Empire

Spock finds himself kidnapped by giant cockroaches.

Intelligence Test

An away mission led by Chekov encounters resistance.

To Wherever

Scotty discovers the dilithium crystals might have been sabotaged.

STAR TREK III: SHORT STORIES
WILLIAM ROTSLER

JUNE 1984   (126PP)

The Azphari Enigma

The crippled *Enterprise* orbits an unusual world.

The Jungles of Memory

A visit with an old friend might mean death for Uhura.

A Vulcan, A Klingon, and an Angel

Scotty tells a crewman a story to demonstrate how much Spock will be missed.

World's End

Spock has an unusual first contact situation on a world covered with immense abandoned buildings.

As Old As Forever

The *Enterprise* answers a distress call from a seven-year-old girl named Pandora.

William Rotsler was a well-known novelist and cartoonist who won five Hugo awards over his career, two for his art. He passed away in 1997.

STARFLEET ACADEMY

Lisa Clancy edited the *Starfleet Academy* series of books. She became a fan of the original series "Starting with the classic reruns in the mid- to late-70s, watching them after dinner when it was my turn to do the dishes. I came across *The Entropy Effect* novel when it first came out, and then went back and hunted down all the old Bantam titles, while buying the newer Pocket titles as they came out. I don't think I saw the first movie in the theaters, but I definitely saw *The Wrath of Khan* when it came out. And when I attended the *Sit Long and Prosper* movie marathon in Times Square many years back, I knew my fanhood was cemented."

The line got started when she was working for Pocket Books in their Young Adult department. "I met Kevin Ryan and Dave Stern, at the time the two mad scientists behind the whole Trek publishing program in the early 90s. We all loved *Next Gen,* and when we heard that the new show, DS9, was going to have a recurring kid character, we decided that we'd spent enough time saying 'wouldn't it be great?' and 'what if . . . ?' and took the pitch to our then-publisher, Gina Centrello. *Trek* publishing was on an upswing, with multiple title releases every month. Dave and Kevin were very supportive, and hooked me up with Peter David to launch the Next Gen/YA series with a trilogy of Worf titles. After that, I was on my own."

Lisa continued, "Worf was the best character to start with, I thought. Kids would relate to him. He felt different, he knew he looked different, and when he was angry he preferred to hit things. Taking all of the Next Gen characters back to their younger, academy days would allow the readers to experience familiar characters but with relatable problems—how do I survive the class bully? How do I decide what courses to take? What's it going to be like living on my own for the first time? How badly did I screw up my first command? With the introduction of Jake Sisko over on DS9, we had a ready-made teen character in an extraordinary situation. All sorts of new aliens would be coming and going through this station and the only other kid around was a member of an alien race that had quite a few antithetical values to the average human kid. So we spent our time and mapped out a Next Gen/YA series that allowed us to visit every major character, and keep a DS9/YA series that kept up with the growing character of Jake. Eventually we were also able to go back and do titles about a young Jim Kirk, and a young Kathryn Janeway, so at the time we had all the iterations covered."

| # 1 | # 2 |

WORF'S FIRST ADVENTURE
(STAR TREK: THE NEXT GENERATION)
Peter David

AUGUST 1993   (119pp)

LINE OF FIRE
(STAR TREK: THE NEXT GENERATION)
Peter David

OCTOBER 1993   (112pp)

What was Worf's life at Starfleet Academy like? Raised by humans since an early age, Worf doubts his Klingon heritage. But from the moment he arrives at the academy, Klingon prejudices rear their ugly head. A constant struggle to succeed, he can't even rest in his quarters, since his roommate believes that Klingons are the enemy.

Worf and his study mates are considered by the higher ups at the academy a "dream team." The group is asked to accompany Professor Alexander Trump to the planet Dantar, a joint Federation-Klingon colony. From the beginning, the cadets are confronted with the real relationships between the colonists. When the planet is attacked, everyone must put aside his or her petty differences to survive.

3

SURVIVAL
(STAR TREK: THE NEXT GENERATION)
PETER DAVID

DECEMBER 1993 (111 PP)

T he Klingon and Starfleet cadets begrudgingly must work together to survive. The colonists have been evacuated from Dantar, leaving the eight young folks behind. After several weeks of no rescue, it appears that none is forthcoming. Unfortunately, they are not alone, and the intruder into their little habitat is dangerous and responsible for the original attack on the colony.

Peter reflected on writing the first three academy books. "These are now referred to as the *New Frontier* prequels. Who knew? They asked if I would be interested. I created the supporting cast to fill certain slots in various aspects of starship life. When I was working on *New Frontier*, I realized that I had done this already. The characters I created for Worf's young adult books were perfectly good characters and they filled the needs I had for the *Excalibur*. Why did I have to beat my brains out coming up with yet more characters when I have these characters that already exist? I simply brought Soleta, Kebron, and eventually Tania Tobias. I brought Soleta and Kebron forward and did nothing with Tania and got letters from people asking, 'Where is Tania?' She has finally shown up."

4

CAPTURE THE FLAG
(STAR TREK: THE NEXT GENERATION)
JOHN VORNHOLT

JUNE 1994 (114 PP)

G eordi had to overcome a great deal while at the academy. Because of his visor, everyone assumed the worst in him. When he gets the opportunity to lead a team in competition on the planet Saffair, Geordi realizes it's an opportunity. Picking players to participate on his team, he insures he picks the ones always picked last. Now this misfit team has a lot more to prove than its worthiness.

• • •

John reflected, "I loved writing young adult *Trek* books, and I probably wrote more of them than anybody. Most of my own non-*Trek* novels are YA, so I'm comfortable with it. Technically the *Starfleet Academy* books were middle grade digest-sized books, about fifth-grade reading level. One of the continuing mysteries are why YA science fiction novels don't sell to the same huge audience that is buying YA fantasies? In the days of Heinlein and Asimov, science fiction literature for kids was a staple, but no more. We were swimming against the current, but the YA *Trek* publishing program actually lasted for nine years, if you count my movie novelizations. I wrote YA novelizations for all the TNG movies, from *Generations* through *Nemesis*. Lisa Clancy did a great job of editing them. *Capture the Flag* allowed me to replay one of my favorite games from summer camp in a science fiction training atmosphere, and it's one of my personal faves."

5

ATLANTIS STATION
(STAR TREK: THE NEXT GENERATION)
V.E. MITCHELL

AUGUST 1994 (116PP)

Geordi and his fellow cadets travel to Atlantis station, an underwater research base built on the base of a volcano. The students have a hard time getting along, and Geordi feels picked on. When the volcano erupts and the station shakes, stirs, and begins flooding, the cadets must put their petty differences aside if they are going to survive.

Vicki remembered, "Ashley called to tell me that Pocket Books was starting up a Young Adult series of *Star Trek* books built around the idea of what happened to the *Next Generation* characters while they were at Starfleet Academy. He also gave me a list of the characters who already had stories being written about them. I'm sure I must have sent in ideas for most of the characters who weren't on the 'taken' list, but *Atlantis Station* was the one that got picked out of the group. The main idea behind *Atlantis Station* was the statement, 'Geordi goes on a field trip—and everything that can possibly go wrong, does.' I am a geologist by profession, so a geologic field trip was very easy for me to write. Besides, an undersea research station on the flank of an active volcano is an invitation to disaster—and far too tempting a setting for me to ignore. In addition, I have an affinity with Geordi because I have very poor eyesight. Glasses and contact lenses are to me what Geordi's Visor is to him. This book was really a dream to work on. The story was lots of fun to write, and (like all the editors I've worked with on *Trek* projects), Lisa Clancy (the editor on this project) was really great to work with. I like the way the book turned out, and the illustrations are perfect. What more could any writer wish for?"

When asked about her memories, Vicki reflected, "I've been really lucky to work with some great editors on all my *Star Trek* projects. And that I really appreciate the advice and assistance I've had from my agent."

6

MYSTERY OF THE MISSING CREW
(STAR TREK: THE NEXT GENERATION)
MICHAEL JAN FRIEDMAN

FEBRUARY 1995 (119PP)

Data travels to Starfleet Academy on board the science vessel, *Yosemite*. The ship is attacked, and in the aftermath, Data and his fellow cadets realize that all of the adults on board have mysteriously vanished. When an alien vessel attacks and demands surrender, the situation appears hopeless. Can untrained cadets save the day with an untested android?

SECRET OF THE LIZARD PEOPLE
(STAR TREK: THE NEXT GENERATION)
Michael Jan Friedman

April 1995   **(113pp)**

Data and some other cadets are selected to observe a collision of two Jupiter-sized planets, which will result in the formation of a new star. A distress call from an alien space station near the colliding planets forces a hasty rescue effort. With time running out, Data and his crewmates must defeat apparent lizard-like invaders and rescue the aliens before the planets explode.

Mike reflected on his two YA novels. "I actually think it was a good series overall. The reason they didn't do very well is not because of the quality of the writing, and I don't just mean mine, I mean in general. It was the way they were positioned in the bookstores, or not positioned. It was the way they were marketed or not marketed. It sort of went out there. Nobody knew about it. There was no presence in the bookstore and it kind of languished. The stories were actually great stories. They cut to the continuity; I have landmark events in Data's life. I show Data being discovered by Starfleet personnel. That's never been seen in any other book as far as I know. And I think they were good books and should have thrived. That's my opinion anyway. But the Data stuff was fun. I mean out of anybody for the young adult audience I couldn't think of a better character than Data. He shares so much with their demographics. He is learning and young in a lot of ways. He's just like them so I thought he would be a great character and I'm happy with the way these books turned out although I'd probably change the titles. Now that I think about it, the biggest influence on those titles was the *Hardy Boys.* But when I read the *Hardy Boys* it was like in the 60s so titles have come a long way since then. But it was The *House on the Cliff,* the mystery of this and that. Right? So that's what really inspired those titles and I would probably change the titles now."

8

STARFALL
(STAR TREK: THE NEXT GENERATION)
BRAD AND BARBARA STRICKLAND

OCTOBER 1995   (111 PP)

J ean-Luc Picard has failed his Starfleet entrance exams. As a result, his father believes that he will work on the vineyards, and eventually take over the business. His brother wants to study off-world, and Jean-Luc can't get his failure out of his head. He begins to plot to reapply in secret, knowing it will infuriate and alienate most of his family.

Brad and Barbara go back to the original series. Brad remarked, "We both loved the show when we were young, and we've enjoyed every incarnation of it since. Barbara is actually the more devoted Trekker, but both of us are fans."

When asked about writing *Trek*, Brad commented, "It seemed natural. I remember that Paramount sent out a call for SFWA members to pitch story ideas for TNG, and Barbara and I thought of a possible storyline. We pitched it—

but instead of taking it as a show idea, it got passed over to Pocket Books, and they wanted us to write a novel instead. From day one—I just told Barbara that she was doing so much that she was really a co-writer, not just someone who helped me proofread. Barbara helped me refine ideas, worked with me through the outlining process, and read the first draft as fast as I wrote it. Then she revised and rewrote, and I took a final pass through the manuscript to tidy everything up. I'd say Barbara's contribution had always been fifty percent, so adding her credit was really just truth in advertising. We work very well together, especially since I respect Barbara's superior knowledge of ST history and characters."

When asked about *Starfall*, Brad reflected, "The basic idea came from the editors. They wanted a novel in which Jean-Luc Picard's first, failed attempt to enter the academy was detailed. Barbara and I turned in an outline rich with incident—so rich that the editors asked if we would break it into two novels. We did so, and that is how *Nova Command* came about. *Starfall* was an attempt to see Jean-Luc as much more vulnerable and uncertain than he always appeared on the show. We know he must once have been an adolescent, with all the angst that implies, and the book gave us a chance to see that up close. Both Barbara and I, by the way, sharply regret [Ron Moore and Brannon Braga's] decision to kill off Jean-Luc's brother in the movie series. We felt close to that family while working on our book."

#9

NOVA COMMAND
(STAR TREK: THE NEXT GENERATION)
BRAD AND BARBARA STRICKLAND

DECEMBER 1995   (116PP)

Jean-Luc starts his first year at the academy with a bitter rival named Roger. As the two of them continually compete against each other, they are surprised to discover they are both assigned to a special team designed for the top cadets. *Nova Command* places Roger as his superior officer, and Jean-Luc is not happy. When the captain falls ill and the vessel picks up a distress call, can the two rivals work together to survive?

Brad answered, "Again, *Nova Command* split off from *Starfall* early on. We played around with the notion that Picard's nemesis at the academy was a remote descendant of the Wellesley family—that he counted the Duke of Wellington as one of his ancestors and that their rivalry echoed the Napoleonic wars. That was amusing to us, but the editors decided to change a lot of that because kids wouldn't be interested. We wanted to show two strong personalities, each one with good and bad points, and show how Picard became a success because he was adaptable and could learn from his own mistakes and from the actions of others. We saw him as a positive personality, one who built rather than destroyed, and we wanted to show how that trait developed."

#10

LOYALTIES
(STAR TREK: THE NEXT GENERATION)
PATRICIA BARNES-SVARNEY

APRIL 1996   (116PP)

Cadet Beverly Howard gets talked into skipping class, and is caught by one of her instructors. On probation, she must risk being thrown out of Starfleet when her roommate is injured during a holodeck simulation. Beverly must unravel the mystery and steer clear of her instructor in the process. When in doubt, ask Data!

• • •

Patricia commented, "When TOS first started in 1966, I already knew I wanted to be a scientist when the show first started; geology and astronomy have been my favorite subjects since I could pick up a rock and look at the stars. (In fact, I eventually did become a geologist.) And there they were: scientists, engineers, and explorers out in space, with women in important positions onboard—and even a science officer (even if he was a Vulcan). I was hooked, and remain so."

Patricia was already established as a writer of young adult and adult science fiction. "So when I saw the first *Starfleet Academy* book (*Worf's First Adventure* by Peter David), I knew I'd found a fit. I especially liked the idea of writing such a book for "middle readers"—about the age I started enjoying *Star Trek*. And I think almost all of us who wrote for the series wanted to attract younger readers to the *Star Trek* world. I always liked Dr. Beverly Crusher (nee Howard) and Data—and I determined that they went to the academy around the same time. So I approached the series editor, Lisa Clancy, with a story. In a nutshell: Beverly wants to find the person who seems to be framing her roommate at the academy; Data offers his expertise to help—and Beverly uncovers the true culprit. The plot workings were fun to put together, but I loved the research for the book. I had to know the backgrounds of the characters (not hard since I've seen every TNG episode at least two times), keep everyone in the correct time period, and know a bit about the Presidio region of San Francisco (the location of Starfleet Academy where the story takes place; my father helped—he was at the Presidio after World War II). And of course, I also had to throw in some of the angst of being in college again. I used a mix of science and TNG episodes to tell the story, too. For example, I took an idea from *The Arsenal of Freedom*. Beverly and Picard are trapped in an underground pit—she with a broken and cut leg, Picard searching for herbs to treat her wounds. When he asks her how she knows about herbs, she mentions her grandmother and Arvada III—to which Picard says, 'Such a tragedy.' Well, I'm not one to let a good throwaway line go. With my usual bulldog tenacity, I took that line and expanded it to what I thought happened on the Federation colony at Arvada III. Using my knowledge of asteroids (I had just finished an adult science book on the subject), I decided on a tragedy: Beverly and her grandmother would be survivors of a huge impact on Arvada III—not of an asteroid, but of a mile-wide fragment from a deeply fractured, orbiting moon. I also took some ideas from my own experiences: The earthquake archaeological dig site was from my geology background; the grandmotherly figure of Mrs. Oner was a composite of my own grandmother (a great cook) and a tip-of-the-hat to women who ran the homestyle family restaurants I enjoyed when I went to college in North Carolina. Mrs. Oner's name is even a story: One day, I was searching for the character's name when my mother-in-law called, saying she was traveling to Reno the next week . . . Reno = Oner. And the list goes on. . . ."

#11

CROSSFIRE
(STAR TREK: THE NEXT GENERATION)
JOHN VORNHOLT

DECEMBER 1996   (103PP)

Will Riker joins the Starfleet Academy Band, playing trombone. A competition on the planet Pacifica brings glory and unwanted fame, though Riker does have an opportunity to check out the ladies. When an Orion vessel kidnaps the band and demands they play for war-weary troops, the group will play for their very lives!

"Starfleet Academy was essentially school, so it lent itself to school-related activities such as an away trip for the school band. I figured Riker would be playing the trombone, and Geordi would be one of the tech/roadies for the band. They ended up in the wrong place at the wrong time."

#12

BREAKAWAY
(STAR TREK: THE NEXT GENERATION)
BOBBI JG WEISS AND DAVID CODY WEISS

APRIL 1997   (113PP)

Deanna escapes from her domineering mother and enrolls in Starfleet Academy. Misconceptions among her fellow cadets force her to strive harder to prove she isn't cheating by just reading minds. When her mother shows up to teach one of her classes, Deanna almost quits. A "filtering" test will require her to work alongside others, eventually revealing her true destiny.

The authors were unavailable for an interview.

#13

THE HAUNTED STARSHIP
(STAR TREK: THE NEXT GENERATION)
BRAD AND KATHI FERGUSON

DECEMBER 1997   **(115PP)**

Geordi ends up on the training vessel *Benjamin Franklin* (outstanding!) as an assistant engineer. A chance of a lifetime, he will not blow this chance to shine. Near the asteroid belt, mysterious events make it appear that the ship is haunted. Then Geordi sees a ghost of a former commander. If Geordi tells everyone the truth, it could mean his career is over before it even starts!

Brad remarked, "I got married. I wanted to collaborate with my wife on a book and it was a short thing. It actually started as *Haunted Spaceship* and they told me I had to change it to 'starship' and that was fine. I thought spaceship was more suited for kids but it was their party. My editor was Lisa Clancy and I liked her."

He continued, "One of the problems I had with that one was I had these aliens and I kind of liked everybody but sometimes you don't get critical mass and it's just not happening and you don't know why. I stared at this thing for two to three months and I realized my Andorian had to be a girl. That wasn't in the proposal but once the character became a girl the whole thing worked. Lisa never noticed that I had changed the sex of the Andorian. I told her about it afterwards and she thought it was funny."

Brad continued, "My wife's name is Kathi. First they left her name off the cover. Lisa called and asked if I minded. I told her that it was Kathi's first book so Lisa relented. Then they spelled her name with a 'Y.' That is not unreasonable but I had given them the proper spelling. It must have annoyed them but they did it and they have my love and respect forever. I'm very happy with the way the book turned out but whomever they got to do the drawings, he was brilliant. I never met the guy but I want to. He came up with people the way I imagined them."

Brad and Kathi were going to do another Geordi and Riker YA novel but the line was discontinued, ending that possibility.

#14

DECEPTIONS
(STAR TREK: THE NEXT GENERATION)
BOBBI JF WEISS AND DAVID CODY WEISS

APRIL 1998   (117PP)

#1

CRISIS ON VULCAN
(STAR TREK)
BRAD & BARBARA STRICKLAND

AUGUST 1996   (116PP)

Data finds himself still struggling at Starfleet Academy. When asked to join a research team on the planet Arunu, he accepts. The relics of the ancient society are still functioning, and Data's fellow cadets start feeling the effects. When sabotage occurs, Data must figure out the mystery if he wants to keep himself and his fellow cadets alive.

The authors were unavailable for an interview.

A young Spock watches his father negotiate a treaty with the planet Marath. After the signing of the historic document, factions on the planet appear enraged, and begin to sabotage the peace. When Spock's mother is attacked in front of her home, Spock realizes he must help his father solve the mystery, while choosing life at the Vulcan Science Academy, or Starfleet Academy.

Brad remembered, "The editor called one day and spoke to Barbara. 'How would you like to write the first *Starfleet Academy* book about Spock?' she asked. And my darling wife replied, 'How much do we have to pay you?' I had to point out that that was not the writerly approach. We really loved that project, though. Pocket did ask that we delay Spock's admission to the academy and concentrate on the tension between Spock and his father, and if I have any regret, it's just that we never really get to see Spock as a cadet in that novel. It was great fun writing it, though, and seeing Spock as a young man whose Vulcan training has not yet become as strong as it was in the show."

Brad had some final thoughts. "Barbara and I loved our association with ST. Because of it, we were able to meet a good many actors: Leonard Nimoy and James Doohan among others. We heard some wonderful stories from them and the experience deepened our appreciation for the optimism and daring inherent in the ST universe."

2

AFTERSHOCK
(STAR TREK)
JOHN VORNHOLT

SEPTEMBER 1996   (116PP)

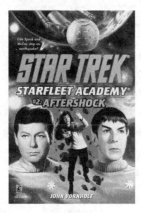

Leonard McCoy is looking forward to taking some time off from his studies and visiting his family. When a touch football game gets out of hand, he is forced to "volunteer" for the Disaster Relief Service Club, which has a training ses-

sion set for the time he planned on going home. Paired with a strange Vulcan named Spock, McCoy contemplates leaving the academy!

"I jumped at the chance to write a Starfleet Academy book about Dr. McCoy's experiences at Starfleet Academy. Yes, there is some controversy over whether McCoy actually went to the academy, but the references are inconclusive. Spock has a major part in the book, and Kirk has a cameo as an incoming freshman. So I got to write the scenes where McCoy meets both Spock and Kirk for the first time! That sent a chill down my spine, and I don't care if the books are in an alternate universe. I wrote the scenes where the three of them met."

3

CADET KIRK
(STAR TREK)
DIANE CAREY

OCTOBER 1996   (126PP)

A youthful cadet earns the opportunity to shuttle computer genius Richard Daystrom to a conference. When Kirk's orders change, he is furious, much to the contempt of his two passengers, McCoy and Spock. On the flight, space pirates hijack the vessel, believing that Daystrom is on board. Now the three of them will have to work together and ignore the usual protocols to survive.

Diane said, "A Young Adult novel is obviously geared toward kids, yet of course the tough part is making sure all the characters are in there to interact with each other before they actually meet as adults. I spun off *Best Destiny*, using the once-juvenile delinquent James Kirk now as a Star Fleet Academy Cadet. Of course, everything else has to be 'downsized' to fit the template of a shorter novel with a linear plot and an audience of kids, without treating the readers as if they're immature. *Cadet Kirk* was the only YA I wrote for *Star Trek*, and I only did it because they asked me. I had no intention of writing any more books for the YA line."

1

THE STAR GHOST
(STAR TREK: DEEP SPACE NINE)
BRAD STRICKLAND

FEBRUARY 1994   (118PP)

Jake and Nog are friends, but that still doesn't make Jake believe his Ferengi associate when Nog claims to have seen a Ferengest, an ancestral spirit. Jake knows that ghosts don't exist, but when he sees it as well, he decides to follow it and figure out what it wants. With the lives of everyone aboard the station at risk, can Jake contact this apparition and save the day?

Brad remembered, "I did my graduate work in folklore, and it seemed to me that all sentient species would have some kind of folklore about ghosts, spirits, and so on. I thought a haunt with, let us say, negative fiduciary powers would be terrifying for Ferengi! Everything went very smoothly. Barbara actually worked on that book (without credit) and with her help and knowledge, I managed to turn in a book that Paramount liked so well they asked for only one small change. My editor called, absolutely thrilled at that—but that was Barbara keeping everything on *Trek* track!"

 # 2

STOWAWAYS
(STAR TREK: DEEP SPACE NINE)
BRAD STRICKLAND

APRIL 1994   **(112PP)**

Doctor Bashir is planning a little vacation on Bajor. Unknown to him, Jake and Nog decide to hitch a ride. When Bashir vanishes and appears to have been kidnapped, the two enlist the help of a Bajoran girl, Sesana, to find their friend. Can Jake and Nog dodge assassins to rescue Bashir and avoid punishment for sneaking away from the station?

Brad remarked, "I thought Dr. Bashir needed some extra dimensions. For some reason or other, it struck me that a very serious doctor might want to unwind by pretending to be a secret agent—and that was the genesis of the storyline. I was delighted later on when show

---

writers picked up on that aspect of Bashir's personality and incorporated it into a couple of scripts. Again, the writing went very smoothly, and again Barbara helped."

 # 3

PRISONERS OF PEACE
(STAR TREK: DEEP SPACE NINE)
JOHN PEEL

OCTOBER 1994   **(112PP)**

A young Bajoran student named Riv hates all Cardassians, because they murdered his parents. Some mysterious incidents on the station lead Jake to a Cardassian stowaway named Kam, who is the daughter of a Gul. When her father arrives with an armada demanding her release, Riv takes advantage and kidnaps Kam. Can Jake save the day?

According to John, "As a writer, there are some editors I love, and will work with at any time. Lisa Clancy is one of them. She's wonderfully efficient and perceptive, and a nice person. She was given the younger *Star Trek* books, and asked me if I was interested. Of course I was, so I set to work on ideas. *Prisoners of Peace* was an unusually serious theme for me—it always seemed to me that sometimes surviving peace could be harder than surviving war. Accepting either victory or defeat can really be a ruinous process and I wanted to talk about that. Plus, I'm not a big believer in the idea that 'all Cardassians are evil' (it smacks of thinly-disguised prejudice, even if Cardassians aren't real), so I wanted a sympathetic Cardassian character."

4

THE PET
(STAR TREK: DEEP SPACE NINE)
MEL GILDEN AND TED PEDERSEN

DECEMBER 1994   (112PP)

When the ship *Ulysses* docks at the station, an animal escapes and lands in Jake's lap. The supposed owner clashes with Odo and Ben Sisko, so Jake is allowed to keep this new animal as a pet. When a vessel arrives and demands the release of the Crown Prince or they will destroy the station, Jake must balance helping his father save the station, or save his pet from an evil plot!

Mel remembered, "Ted had the idea for *The Pet*, but had no track record as a novel writer. He asked me to come on board to sort of legitimize the project. Ted and I had been friends for years, so I had no problem helping him out. He did most of the work because he wanted the experience, and I went over his text, making editorial remarks and changes. I don't really enjoy collaboration. So even though Ted and I didn't kill each other while writing the book, I have never collaborated again."

Ted was a *Trek* fan from the beginning. "I had been a sci fi fan since grade school and so it was only natural to be attracted to Gene Roddenberry's wonderful adventures in the twenty-fourth century, with Bill Shatner as a reincarnation of Flash Gordon and Buck Rogers. I loved the *Next Generation*, but my personal favorite remains *Deep Space Nine*."

Ted moved to L.A. in the 1970s to try his hand at writing for television. "I did several live Saturday morning *Space Academy* shows which led to me being hired on staff at Filmation Studios. They had the rights to *Flash Gordon* and I got to develop and story edit the show as an animated Saturday morning series. That was heaven. The TV animation market started slowing down. I'd always wanted to write a book but the thought of a six hundred-page manuscript frightened me. Young adult books are shorter, usually around one hundred thirty pages. When I heard they were starting a *Star Trek* YA series and being a fan of the series, it was a natural jump. And I thought Jake and Nog would be the perfect protagonists for a series. The idea for *The Pet* came from my all-time favorite author, Robert Heinlein. Years ago I read his novel *Star Lummox* in the *Magazine of Fantasy and Science Fiction* (it was later a book, *Star Beast*) about a creature brought to Earth who turns out to be an heir to a powerful alien race. Mel and I had been friends for a long time. He wrote for my TV series, *Centurions*, and when Lisa Clancy of Pocket Books listened to the pitch for *The Pet* it became a joint effort. Because Mel was busy with another book project, I wrote the first draft and he edited it. On another series we wrote, *Cybersurfers*, we wrote alternate chapters."

 # 5

ARCADE
(STAR TREK: DEEP SPACE NINE)
DIANA G. GALLAGHER

JUNE 1994   **(101 PP)**

riends of Jake, including Nog, are found in deep comas. A Ferengi named Bokat runs an arcade on the station and offers Jake the opportunity to play a game called the Zhodran Crystal Quest. Unknown to Jake, his friends have already played the game, and are trapped inside the virtual reality world. If Jake fails, his mind will become trapped as well! With no one having won the game in over two hundred years, the odds are not in his favor!

Diana remarked, "I started watching the original *Star Trek* when it first went into reruns and loved it. After *Star Wars* in 1977, ST made a comeback on TV and on the big screen. I haven't missed a movie or an episode since. I had an original science fiction novel published in 1990 (*The Alien Dark*, TSR), and I was working on another (unpublished) novel as well as working a 'real' job when Pocket decided to publish YA *Trek* four years later. On my agent's advice, I called Lisa Clancy, the editor, and offered a couple of ideas over the phone. I loved *Trek* and didn't want to pass up a chance to become part of it."

When she started working on *Arcade*, "I wanted to write something that would appeal to today's kids. A twentieth-century quest-type game seemed ideal. I simply expanded on the basic concept by having the 'players' mentally captured by the game. The entire writing and publishing process for *Arcade* was fun and basically glitchless for everyone concerned. That was ten years ago and I'm still writing TV-based books for Simon & Schuster."

6

FIELD TRIP
(STAR TREK: DEEP SPACE NINE)
JOHN PEEL

AUGUST 1995   **(111PP)**

Keiko O'Brien convinces Ben Sisko to let his son and his classmates take a field trip to the planet Cetus Beta in the Gamma Quadrant. Supposedly safe and having no animal life, the shuttle is attacked by the Cardassians, causing a crash landing on the surface. With damaged equipment, an injured pilot, and the appearance of a unique life form, the young people are in way over their heads.

John said, "*Field Trip* came about because Keiko was shown (very rarely!) running the school on DS9, and I thought it would be fun to think about what school there would be like. Where, for example, would they go on field trips? The wormhole is right there, so. . . . The Trofars were another of my aliens who do bad things (in this case stealing) for what they consider good reasons. I just thought they were a whole lot of fun. The Screaming Mimis was a tribute to one of my favorite authors, Fredric Brown (who wrote the short story that the original series' 'Arena' episode was based on). He wrote a number of superb mysteries, including *The Screaming Mimi*."

7

GYPSY WORLD
(STAR TREK: DEEP SPACE NINE)
TED PEDERSON

FEBRUARY 1996   **(114PP)**

The Fjori are a gypsy-like race that lives such a secretive life that nobody knows where their actual homeworld resides. When Nog takes Jake and tries to "borrow" the star maps from the Fjori ship, the two of them are taken from DS9 and sent to the Fjori homeworld for judgement. The decision from the Council of Elders forces Jake and Nog to undertake a Rite of Passage, or never leave the planet for the remainder of their natural lives. Jake is studly in this one—you go, dude!

• • •

Ted remembered, "This was actually my first sale. I submitted an outline and two chapters and it was accepted, but *The Pet* was completed and published first. I've always been curious about gypsies, who were usually social outcasts, and wondered if it would be like the same in the future."

8

HIGHEST SCORE
(STAR TREK: DEEP SPACE NINE)
KEM ANTILLES

JUNE 1996   (118PP)

Jake and Nog are champs in the arcade and a mysterious alien recruits them for a job. Using their gaming skills, the two of them help other kids from around the galaxy mine ore from a remote site. To make it more interesting, the aliens throw in various targets to eliminate, saving the machinery to continue to mine. When Jake figures out that the game is horrifyingly real, he ends up on the planet and a target in the "game."

• • •

Kem Antilles is a pseudonym of the writing team of Kevin J. Anderson and his wife, Rebecca Moesta. Kevin and Rebecca commented, "Both of us watched original *Trek* when it was first on TV; Rebecca used to stay up and watch it with her father on first-run. Kevin really got into it during after-school reruns when he was in high school (around 1977). Kevin skipped college classes to see the first showing of *ST: The Motion Picture*. We have since watched every single episode (and movie) of every single incarnation of the show. Yeah, we're still fans."

They continued, "Because we were writing a lot of YA fiction (especially the *Star Wars: Young Jedi Knights* series) we also wanted to contribute to the *Trek* universe. We knew the editor of the young adult DS9 line and asked if we could do one of the books. However, because of the sheer number of books we had coming out under our own names (fourteen *Young Jedi* in the course of a couple of years, plus Kevin had dozens of his own novels) we didn't want to overload the shelves. Also, we had a few other writer friends help us with *Highest Score* and so it really wasn't a book that we could take full credit for. The idea came from Rebecca's son who (like many kids) was hooked on videogames to the detriment of all other aspects of his life. Like many parents, we thought, 'If only there was a way those videogame skills could be useful for a job!' So we created the scenario."

Kevin and Rebecca also wrote the TNG graphic novel, *The Gorn Crisis,* "Which brings back the Gorn and pits them against Picard, Riker, Data, and a bunch of Klingons. Big muscular Gorns facing off with Klingons and batleths—what's not to love?"

Kevin reflected, "It just occurred to me a few weeks ago, when I was writing the fifth volume in my original science fiction series, *The Saga of Seven Suns,* just how much *Star Trek* has influenced our assumptions of what a big spacecraft would look like, functionally. While describing my large alien space battleships, and large human vessels, I thought, 'Well, of course there's a bridge, and on the bridge the captain sits in a command chair in the middle of the room, surrounded by separate stations for communications, weapons, navigation, etc., and there's got to be a viewscreen on the main wall.' Everybody assumes this will be the way a ship works, and it's all because of *Star Trek.*"

9

CARDASSIAN IMPS
(STAR TREK: DEEP SPACE NINE)
MEL GILDEN

FEBRUARY 1997   **(114 PP)**

Jake and Nog are bored, so they do a horrible thing and actually listen to Garak. On level forty-five, the two discover a toy that appears to be a Cardassian with wings. Activating several of the toys, the creatures multiply on a huge scale and proceed to cause havoc on the entire station. Add a mysterious power loss and a ticked off Odo, and let the mayhem begin.

"DS9 is one of my favorite incarnations of *Trek. Cardassian Imps* is another instance of writing a story it would have been difficult or impossible to show on the screen. And, of course, the big scene at the end occurs in the dark—certainly a problem on TV or in the movies. The scene I enjoyed writing most was the one between Quark and Odo. What wonderful characters they are!"

#10

SPACE CAMP
(STAR TREK: DEEP SPACE NINE)
TED PEDERSEN

JUNE 1997 (116PP)

Commander Sisko compels Jake to enroll in a Starfleet Academy Summer Space Camp on the planet Rijar. Jake agrees only if Nog can join him, so Benjamin reluctantly agrees. On the planet, rigorous training awaits the two of them. When a pretty girl shows interest in both of them, can their friendship survive? A life-changing mission in the catacombs under the base will reveal to Jake and Nog their true destinies.

"NASA has a space camp for kids in, I believe, Houston, so it was natural to think Starfleet would sponsor something similar. At the time of the story Nog wasn't interested in a Starfleet career, so maybe this was the spark that started him on his career path. At least I like to think so."

#11

DAY OF HONOR: HONOR BOUND
(STAR TREK: DEEP SPACE NINE)
DIANA G. GALLAGHER

OCTOBER 1997 (109PP)

Alexander is having trouble in Earth school. His temper keeps escalating, and he finds himself wanting to use violence to solve even simple problems. When Worf visits, Alexander is forced to take an oath that he will learn to control himself. But some of his classmates will do anything to see him break his oath and be expelled. To make matters worse, the Klingon Holiday is just around the corner.

Diana commented, "Again, although *Trek* is set centuries in the future, I wanted a story and a problem kids in the present could relate to. We all encounter bullies and prejudice of some sort in school, and we all have our own faults to conquer. In order to preserve his honor, Alexander chose gymnastics so the fight with his human rivals would be fair."

#12

TRAPPED IN TIME
(STAR TREK: DEEP SPACE NINE)
TED PEDERSEN

FEBRUARY 1998 (111PP)

Professor Jonathan Vance has developed a time travel device and Jake, Nog, and Chief O'Brien visit him to check it out. A changeling obtains the device and jumps in the portal. Before it closes, our DS9 folks follow to stop the potential changing of history. The three of them find themselves in Normandy, France, in 1944, just days before the D-Day invasion!

Ted remarked, "At the time of the story the Changlings were on Earth. I thought what they might do to defeat us. Given access to time travel, where would they go to change our future. What better place than to prevent D-Day. Normandy on the eve before the allied invasion seemed perfect. So Jake and Nog have to stop them. An added bonus was that Picard's ancestors were in France at the time."

Ted had a drastic life-changing moment occur in the summer of 2002 while attending BookExpo in New York City. "I had a much too close encounter of the wrong kind with a transit bus. Immediate brain surgery and they sent me home three weeks later. As I continued to not get better I came home last year and the wonderful doctors at the VA diagnosed me as having Parkinson's, a result of the accident. Happy to say I'm much better, on medication, and I'm walking again, without a cane. And I'm back to writing again."

#1

LIFELINE
(STAR TREK: VOYAGER)
BOBBI JG WEISS AND DAVID CODY WEISS

AUGUST 1997 (116PP)

Cadet Kathryn Janeway finds herself disappointed on the first day of classes, when her father reneges on taking her to the academy grounds. Bizarre roommates and an ambitious commander who demands perfection force her to the breaking point. As the stress mounts,

Janeway isolates herself from the people who could help her. A difficult puzzle will convince her to change her outlook on life as a Starfleet cadet.

The authors were unavailable for an interview.

2

THE CHANCE FACTOR
(STAR TREK: VOYAGER)
DIANA G. GALLAGHER AND MARTIN R. BURKE

SEPTEMBER 1997   (115PP)

To prove her worth, Cadet Janeway joins a group of alien animals and their handlers to a wilderness planet. She doesn't want to be a zookeeper, and her fellow classmates don't want to even talk to her. When the mission becomes an act of self-preservation, the cadets must pool together their resources and let go of their petty differences if they want to survive another year at the academy.

• • •

Diana replied, "As before, the story had to have twentieth-century kid appeal, and I wanted to write a *Star Trek* book using a horse. My husband and I are both animal lovers (ten pets in the house currently: dogs, cats, rodent, and bird!) and we thought it would be fun to use animals that were either mentioned or depicted in all four ST series. Funny story: We wanted to use a three-headed Aldebaran serpent as a riding animal, but couldn't because they don't have a body. The show people suggested that we just use a made-up, one-headed dinosaur. We did, but no one told the cover artist! Consequently, Pocket had a cover painting with a three-headed creature and asked us to change the manuscript to fit. This is why writing science fiction is so much fun. Originally, we were going to give the serpent three individual personalities, but that was too complex a fix for a revision of a completed manuscript. Instead, we gave our dinosaur one brain at the base of his neck and three heads that operated like arms. That way, we just had to add head actions. Fooz the spider was our favorite animal character. My husband, Marty, wanted to try writing and this project seemed like a good one to use as a launch pad to see how it went. Unfortunately, he developed a rare condition that affected his balance, speech, and fine motor skills, leaving him permanently disabled and in a wheelchair a few months after we finished this book. He keeps busy now editing and contributing to a newsletter for people with Ataxia."

Diana has written over fifty novels based on television shows since writing her first YA *Trek* novel.

3

QUARANTINE
(STAR TREK: VOYAGER)
PATRICIA BARNES-SVARNEY

OCTOBER 1997   (114PP)

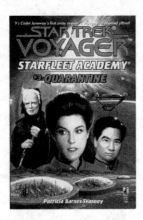

Cadet Janeway is hand-picked, along with four others, to help bring medical supplies to the planet Chatoob. The mission appears wonky from the start, as analysis of the supposed poisonous atmosphere reveals no toxins of any kind. Suddenly, the cadets find themselves in quarantine and exposed to a plague, with no hope of survival or the possibility of contacting Starfleet. Can they escape and solve the bizarre mystery of this strange new plague?

Patricia commented, "*Quarantine* was one of a trilogy of stories about Captain Janeway; the last in the series. Again, I watched all the shows, so I knew her character. This time, too, I could add another familiar face: Geordi LaForge. Jeri Taylor already established the nuts and bolts behind Captain Janeway's personality (in her book *Mosaic*); I just added a few complications. In this story, a group of Starfleet cadets travel to a planet whose people have to live in huge domes. There's a political struggle that ensues, along with a plague in between—and the cadets are caught in the middle. I've always been intrigued by how people can live on inhospitable planets (naturally or artificially inhospitable), and even wrote a few magazine articles on the subject. And aren't all of us intrigued as to whether or not the government is telling us everything? (Ah, the old "Area 51" question. . . .)"

Lisa Clancy remembers the YA series coming to an end. "Once DS9 went off the air, there was no recurring young character for the TV shows to pull in younger viewers. Without that sort of on-air support, it was hard for us to argue for more titles, especially as the more sophisticated young reader would gravitate toward the older titles anyway. Sales flatlined while other genres in the middle-grade and YA market took off, specifically horror. Of course, now there's plenty of fantasy in the marketplace, but not as much pure science fiction. I'd like to think we carved out some shelf space for that genre for a while. And hopefully introduced readers to both a great brand and some new authors."

When asked if she had any particular memories of editing the *Trek* novels, she commented, "Peter David was spinning out Worf story ideas from a hotel room somewhere while he was writing a movie screenplay. Diane Carey was writing the young Kirk story and telling me about her adventures at sea. I had authors give birth, move, get bigger deals, etc. And yet they were all totally psyched to work on this series. It was a labor of love for all of us, and that was fun. O.K., maybe that doesn't count as unusual, but it's certainly the strongest memory of the series I have. I met a bunch of terrific authors, many of whom continued to work with me on other series ten years later. The illustra-tors had a blast; the licenser was totally on board with the concept of retro-history for these characters. Sure there were snags, there are in any tie-in series. But I think we were all pleased with the result!"

THE STAR TREK FICTION TIMELINE

CREATED BY DAVID BOWLING, JOHAN CIAMAGLIA,
RYAN J. CORNELIUS, JAMES R. MCCAIN, ALEX ROSENZWEIG,
PAUL T. SEMONES, AND COREY W. TACKER

THIRD REVISION COMPILED IN COLLABORATION WITH
JASON BARNEY, DAVID HENDERSON, LEE JAMILKOWSKI,
AND GEOFF TROWBRIDGE

WITH SPECIAL THANKS TO KEITH R. A. DECANDIDO,
JAMES E. GOEDERS, ROBERT GREENBERGER,
BOB MANOJLOVICH, JOHN J. ORDOVER,
BILL WILLIAMS AND DAVID YOUNG.

FOREWORD

The genesis of this Fiction Timeline was a discussion thread at the Simon & Schuster *Star Trek* Books bulletin board on www.startrekbooks.com in early 1998. A question, now lost to the mists of time, about when certain books took place in the overall *Star Trek* chronology led to a discussion among a number of the regular posters about timelines and chronologies in Trek and where the various Pocket novels fit in. There were a lot of creative ideas!

Then *Star Trek* editor John Ordover stepped in and made us an offer that we couldn't refuse. He was working on a special publication that was scheduled to be released in the summer of 1999, called *Star Trek: Adventures in Time and Space*. It was intended to be a look at the *Star Trek* books, in celebration of the 20 years that Pocket had held the *Star Trek* publishing license. John thought that a timeline of all the novels would be a great addition to that book, and told us that if those of us who were interested could put together a timeline that was of sufficient quality, he would have it added to the book. Seven of us took on that challenge and the Pocket Books *Star Trek* Timeline came into being, ultimately seeing publication, as promised.

Since that time we have kept the timeline updated, with a second edition being published in *Gateways: What Lay Beyond*, and now a third in the publication you have in front of you. Along the way, we added new members to the group—members who have brought new ideas and enthusiasm and kept the project energized. The construction of this timeline has involved many hours of research and discussion, and a lot of hard work by quite a few folks over the past eight years. We hope you enjoy reading it as much as we did putting it together.

—ALEX ROSENZWEIG AND JIM MCCAIN

This is a complete timeline to the Pocket Books *Star Trek* novels, short stories, eBooks, novelizations, Simon & Schuster Audio original audio books, Minstrel Books young adult books, and classic novels from Bantam and Ballentine Books, published through October 2006. We have also included the collection of Wildstorm comics and graphic novels due to specific ways some of them have tied into the novels, and vice versa. The framework for this timeline was established in *The Star Trek Chronology* by Michael Okuda and Denise Okuda. Individual stories have been placed according to the author's intent at time of writing, internal references to other stories or to canonically established events, and/or external references that suggest the best possible fit with the overall continuity.

Much of the *Timeline* is speculative. Only events established on-screen should be considered definitive. The actual placement of these stories is subject to change as "further evidence" is uncovered, or as the canonical *Star Trek* universe continues to evolve. When known, dates are given in both Earth calendar dates as well as stardates, and often such dates have been altered for the sake of consistency.

Please note that dates marked with a bullet represent portions of a story that occur at a time other than the timeframe of the central portion of the story (for example, backstories, flashbacks, time-travel segments, and so on). These secondary entries are also found in their respective chronological locations, in normal (non-bold) type.

⋀ LEGEND ⋀

TREK SERIES :			
CHA	STAR TREK: CHALLENGER	EL	ENTERPRISE LOGS anthology
DS9	STAR TREK: DEEP SPACE NINE	NL	NEW FRONTIER: NO LIMITS anthology
ENT	STAR TREK: ENTERPRISE		
NF	STAR TREK: NEW FRONTIER	P&C	DEEP SPACE NINE: PROPHECY AND CHANGE anthology
SCE	STAR TREK: STARFLEET CORPS OF ENGINEERS	SNW	STRANGE NEW WORLDS anthology
SGZ	STAR TREK: STARGAZER		
ST	STAR TREK (ALL-SERIES/ CROSSOVER)	TFTCT	TALES FROM THE CAPTAIN'S TABLE anthology
TAS	STAR TREK: THE ANIMATED SERIES	TLOD	THE LIVES OF DAX anthology
		TNV	THE NEW VOYAGES anthology
TLE	STAR TREK: THE LOST ERA	TNV2	THE NEW VOYAGES 2 anthology
TNG	STAR TREK: THE NEXT GENERATION		
		TODW	TALES OF THE DOMINION WAR anthology
TOS	STAR TREK: THE ORIGINAL SERIES	WLB	GATEWAYS: WHAT LAY BEYOND anthology
VGR	STAR TREK: VOYAGER	YA	YOUNG ADULT BOOK
		§ (OR §§)	SECTION(S) OR "SCENE(S)" WITHIN A CHAPTER
OTHER ABBREVIATIONS :			
CON	STAR TREK: CONSTELLATIONS ANTHOLOGY	DATES ARE GIVEN ACCORDING TO EARTH'S "COMMON-ERA" GREGORIAN CALENDAR.	
DS	VOYAGER: DISTANT SHORES ANTHOLOGY		

5 BILLION YEARS AGO

THE Q CONTINUUM: Q-SPACE (TNG #47)

—*Chapter 11* (see primary entry in 2374)

SPOCK'S WORLD (TOS HARDCOVER)[1]

—*Vulcan: One* (see primary entry in 2275)

4 BILLION YEARS AGO

"RECIPROCITY" (TNG SHORT STORY, SNW II)

—*sections 1, 4, 8, 10* (see primary entry in 2374)

3.5 BILLION YEARS AGO

ALL GOOD THINGS . . . (TNG EPISODE NOVELIZATION)

—*Chapter 20§5* (see primary entry in 2370)

2.5 BILLION YEARS AGO

THE Q CONTINUUM: Q-SPACE (TNG #47)

—*Chapter 13* (see primary entry in 2374)

1 BILLION YEARS AGO

THE Q CONTINUUM: Q-ZONE (TNG #48)

—*Chapter 2* (see primary entry in 2374)

C.444,800,000 BC

THE ESCAPE (VGR #2)

—*Chapters 12§2; 17§1; 19§2; 23§2* (see primary entry in 2371)

64,018,143 BC

FIRST FRONTIER (TOS #75)

—*Chapters 23–38* (see primary entry in 2268)

C.500,000 BC

SPOCK'S WORLD (TOS HARDCOVER)

—*Vulcan: Two* (see primary entry in 2275)

C.307,600 BC

THE ESCAPE (VGR #2)

—*Chapters 4§2; 5–7; 23§1* (see primary entry in 2371)

C.27,600 BC

"HORN AND IVORY" (DS9 STORY, WLB)

—*Chapters 1–9* (see primary entry in 2376)

C.10,000 BC

SPOCK'S WORLD (TOS HARDCOVER)

—*Vulcan: Three* (see primary entry in 2275)

7954 BC

EX MACHINA (TOS)

—*Chapter 18* (see primary entry in 2273)

C.3000 BC

SPOCK'S WORLD (TOS HARDCOVER)

—*Vulcan: Four* (see primary entry in 2275)

2703 BC

YESTERDAY'S SON (TOS #11)

—*Chapters 5–6* (see primary entry in 2270)

2683 BC

TIME FOR YESTERDAY (TOS #39)

—*Prologue; Chapters 5§3; 6–10; 14–15* (see primary entry in 2285)

C.2000 BC

"THE BEGINNING" (ST SHORT STORY, SNW VI)[2]

"FORGOTTEN LIGHT" (ST SHORT STORY, SNW VII)

—*sections 1, 4, 6, 8, 10, 12* (see primary entry in 2373)

235 BC

UHURA'S SONG (TOS #21)

—*Chapter 11§5* (see primary entry in 2268)

30 BC

SPOCK'S WORLD (TOS HARDCOVER)

—*Vulcan: Five* (see primary entry in 2275)

193 AD

SPOCK'S WORLD (TOS HARDCOVER)[3]

—*Vulcan: Six* (see primary entry in 2275)

---

[1] This chapter chronicles the period from the formation of the 40-Eridani system to the beginnings of life on the planet Vulcan about two billion years ago.

[2] The time and manner of Borg origins are entirely speculative. Both "The Beginning" (SNW VI) and "Forgotten Light" (SNW VII) each offer unique interpretations.

[3] This chapter chronicles the period from Surak's birth until his death sometime after 300 AD

200 AD

THE DEVIL'S HEART (TNG HARDCOVER)[4]

—*Chapter 13* (see primary entry in 2268)

249

RIHANNSU #2: THE ROMULAN WAY (TOS #35)[5]

—*Chapter 2* (see primary entry in 2276)

280

VULCAN'S SOUL #1: EXODUS (ST)[6]

—*Chapter 2§2; 4; 6–7; 9–10; 12–13; 15–16; 18* (see primary entry in 2377)

281

VULCAN'S SOUL #1: EXODUS (ST)

—*Chapter 19* (see primary entry in 2377)

285

RIHANNSU #2: THE ROMULAN WAY (TOS #35)[7]

—*Chapter 4* (see primary entry in 2276)

300

{VULCAN OLD DATE 140005} THE LOST YEARS (TOS HARDCOVER)

—*Prologue* (see primary entry in 2371)

VULCAN'S SOUL #1: EXODUS (ST)

—*Chapters 21; 23; 25* (see primary entry in 2377)

RIHANNSU #2: THE ROMULAN WAY (TOS #35)[8]

—*Chapter 6* (see primary entry in 2276)

326

VULCAN'S SOUL #2: EXILES (ST)[9]

—*"Memory"* (see primary entry in 2377)

380

VULCAN'S SOUL #1: EXODUS (ST)

—*Chapter 2, §1* (see primary entry in 2377)

750

RIHANNSU #2: THE ROMULAN WAY (TOS #35)[10]

—*Chapter 8* (see primary entry in 2276)

C. 800

KAHLESS (TNG HARDCOVER)

—*Chapters 2; 4; 6; 8; 10; 12; 14; 16; 18; 20; 22; 24; 26; 28; 30; 32; 34; 36* (see primary entry in 2371)

846

RIHANNSU #2: THE ROMULAN WAY (TOS #35)[11]

—*Chapter 10* (see primary entry in 2276)

1571

THE LONG NIGHT (DS9 #14)

—*Prologue* (see primary entry in 2371)

1594

"IF I LOSE THEE . . ." (TOS SHORT STORY, SNW III)

—*London sections* (see primary entry in 2269)

1600

{SEPTEMBER} HOME IS THE HUNTER (TOS #52)

—*Chapters 1; 7; 14; 19; 28; 33; 35; 41; 45; 48* (see primary entry in 2273)

1746

{APRIL} HOME IS THE HUNTER (TOS #52)

—*Chapters 3; 8; 11; 16; 21; 25; 29; 36; 39; 42; 46; 49* (see primary entry in 2273)

[4] As a vision, this may be historically unreliable. The events contradict *Spock's World* regarding the death of Surak's father.

[5] This chapter chronicles the period from the Ahkh War (against the Orions) until the Sundering in 300 AD. The date given in the text as 22 BC was disregarded.

[6] The date of the Awakening is around 2000 years prior to "The Savage Curtain" (TOS), while T'Pol places Surak's death about 1,800 years prior to "Awakening" (ENT). Assuming Surak's death was not long after the Sundering, the Awakening occurred between 254 and 339 AD. A line dropped from the script to "Awakening" claims the event occurred 1,874 years prior to the episode, in 280 AD.

[7] This chapter chronicles the period from S'task's Declaration until the Sundering.

[8] This chapter chronicles the journey of the Rihannsu Travelers until planetfall in 750.

[9] These chapters chronicle the period beginning 25.86 real-time years after the Sundering until the subjugation of the Reman settlers in 753.

[10] This chapter chronicles the period from the Settlement until the fall of the Ruling Queen in 846.

[11] This chapter chronicles the Golden Age, from the establishment of the Senate until first contact with a Starfleet vessel in 2153.

1776

{OCTOBER 11} "THE VEIL AT VALCOUR"
(EL SHORT STORY)

1863

{SEPTEMBER 14} "SHANGHAIED" (TOS SHORT STORY,
SNW VIII)
—*sections 1–4* (see primary entry in 2267)

1864

"A Q TO SWEAR BY" (TNG SHORT STORY, SNW III)
— *"Pine Mountain" section* (see primary entry in 2371)

1867

ISHMAEL (TOS #23)
—*Chapters 2–3; 5–6; 8; 10; 12–14; 16–18* (see primary
entry in 2267)

1874

MARTYR (NF #5)
—*"Five hundred years earlier . . ."* (see primary entry in
2374)

1889

{JULY 21–24} "THE PEACEMAKERS" (TNG SHORT STORY,
SNW V)
—*sections 1, 3* (see primary entry in 2371)

1929

{JUNE 19} "THE PEACEMAKERS" (TNG SHORT STORY, SNW V)
—*section 6* (see primary entry in 2371)

1930

"TRIPTYCH" (TOS SHORT STORY, SNW II)
—*Chapters 1§§1–5; 2; 3§§1–8* (see primary entry in
2267)
"REMEMBERING THE FUTURE"
(ST SHORT STORY, SNW 9)
—*sections 2–7* (see primary entry in 2371)
"DISAPPEARANCE ON 21ST STREET"
(TOS SHORT STORY, SNW V)

1938

{OCTOBER 28} "CAPTAIN PROTON AND
THE ORB OF BAJOR" (DS9 SHORT STORY,
SNW IV)[12]

1939

"THE ADVENTURES OF CAPTAIN PROTON:
CHAPTER 1: THE SPACE VORTEX OF
DOOM" (VGR SHORT STORY, AMAZING
STORIES #598)
CAPTAIN PROTON: DEFENDER OF THE
EARTH (VGR SPECIAL)
"THE DIFFICULTIES OF BEING EVIL"
(VGR SHORT STORY, SNW V)

1940

{JULY} FAR BEYOND THE STARS (DS9 EPISODE
NOVELIZATION)[13]
—*Chapters 10; 13; 16–17; 24; 26; 32–35* (see primary
entry in 2374)

1942

{OCTOBER} HOME IS THE HUNTER
(TOS #52)
—*Chapters 5; 9; 12; 17; 23; 26; 31; 37; 40* (see primary
entry in 2273)
{OCTOBER 26} "WORLD OF STRANGERS"
(EL SHORT STORY)
{NOVEMBER} HOME IS THE HUNTER (TOS #52)
—*Chapters 43; 47; 50* (see primary entry in 2273)

1944

{JUNE 1–3} TRAPPED IN TIME (DS9-YA #12)
—*Chapters 4–11* (see primary entry in 2372)

[12] This story is a Captain Proton radio drama script written by
"Benny Russell" and incorporating elements of *Deep Space
Nine*. Given his age in *Far Beyond the Stars*, this might not be the
same Benny Russell who will later write for the magazine *Incredible Tales of Scientific Wonder*.

[13] The childhood of Benny Russell is seen in the visions of Benjamin Sisko.

1953

WHEN THE STARS COME A-CALLING (DS9 WILDSTORM GRAPHIC)

{OCTOBER} FAR BEYOND THE STARS (DS9 EPISODE NOVELIZATION) [14]

—*Chapters 5; 8–9; 11–12; 14–15; 18–19; 21; 23; 27–29; 31; 36–37* (see primary entry in 2374)

{DECEMBER 14, 1953 TO APRIL 2, 1954} "ISOLATION WARD 4" (DS9 SHORT STORY, SNW IV)

* *1968—[final entry]*

1968

"VISIT TO A WEIRD PLANET REVISITED" (TOS SHORT STORY, TNV) [15]

—*"studio" sections* (see primary entry in 2268)

{APRIL 4} "ISOLATION WARD 4" (DS9 SHORT STORY, SNW IV)

—*Final entry* (see primary entry in 1953)

1969

"THE ALIENS ARE COMING!" (TOS SHORT STORY, SNW III)

{JULY 19–20} ASSIGNMENT: ETERNITY (TOS #84)

—*Chapters 1; 22* (see primary entry in 2269)

1974

{MARCH 13 TO MAY 19} THE EUGENICS WARS: THE RISE AND FALL OF KHAN NOONIEN SINGH, BOOK ONE

—*Chapters 1–23* (see primary entry in 2270)

1984

{NOVEMBER 1 TO DECEMBER 3} THE EUGENICS WARS: THE RISE AND FALL OF KHAN NOONIEN SINGH, BOOK ONE

—*Chapters 26–30* (see primary entry in 2270)

1986

STAR TREK IV: THE VOYAGE HOME (ST MOVIE NOVELIZATION)

—*Chapters 5–12* (see primary entry in 2286)

"WHALES WEEP NOT" (TOS SHORT STORY, SNW VI)

{JULY 5 TO OCTOBER 10} THE EUGENICS WARS: THE RISE AND FALL OF KHAN NOONIEN SINGH, BOOK ONE

—*Chapters 31–33* (see primary entry in 2270)

1989

{NOVEMBER 9} THE EUGENICS WARS: THE RISE AND FALL OF KHAN NOONIEN SINGH, BOOK ONE

—*Chapter 34* (see primary entry in 2270)

1991

"THE MAN WHO SOLD THE SKY" (SHORT STORY, SNW) [16]

1992

{JUNE 14 TO NOVEMBER 6} THE EUGENICS WARS: THE RISE AND FALL OF KHAN NOONIEN SINGH, BOOK TWO

—*Chapters 1–4* (see primary entry in 2270)

1993

{MARCH 15 TO OCTOBER 1} THE EUGENICS WARS: THE RISE AND FALL OF KHAN NOONIEN SINGH, BOOK TWO

—*Chapters 5–6; 8–11* (see primary entry in 2270)

1994

{FEBRUARY 7 TO NOVEMBER 14} THE EUGENICS WARS: THE RISE AND FALL OF KHAN NOONIEN SINGH, BOOK TWO

—*Chapters 12–20* (see primary entry in 2270)

"THE RULES OF WAR" (ST SHORT STORY, SNW 9)

1995

{MARCH 17} THE EUGENICS WARS: THE RISE AND FALL OF KHAN NOONIEN SINGH, BOOK TWO

—*Chapters 21* (see primary entry in 2270)

{APRIL 24} GHOST SHIP (TNG #1)

—*Chapters 1* (see primary entry in 2364)

{SEPTEMBER 7} THE EUGENICS WARS: THE RISE AND FALL OF KHAN NOONIEN SINGH, BOOK TWO

—*Chapters 22–23* (see primary entry in 2270)

[14] Sisko's visions chronicle Benny Russell's career as a science-fiction writer. Whether Russell actually existed in the past of Sisko's reality is unknown.

[15] Takes place in an alternate reality where *Star Trek* is merely a television series broadcast in the 1960s.

[16] A tribute to Gene Roddenberry, who existed in a reality wherein *Star Trek* was his own fictional creation.

1996

{January 5 to February 2} The Eugenics Wars: The Rise
  and Fall of Khan Noonien Singh, Book Two
  —*Chapters 24–27* (see primary entry in 2270)
"Almost . . . But Not Quite" (VGR short story, SNW II)
  —*sections 3–5* (see primary entry in 2373)

1998

"Research" (DS9 short story,
  SNW II) [17]

1999

Spock vs. Q: Armageddon Tonight
  (TOS/TNG audio)
Spock vs. Q: The Sequel (TOS/TNG
  audio)

2001

{September 10–11} "Assignment: One"
  (TOS short story, SNW 8)

2003

{June 21–22} "Project Blue Book"
  (TOS short story, SNW VII) [18]
  —*sections 1–4*
  • *November 30, 2892—[section 5]*
{October} "Make-Believe" (TOS short
  story, CON)

2045

{October} Strangers from the Sky (TOS giant)
  —*Book One: Chapters 1§§1–6; 2§§1–10; 3§§1–5;
  4§§1–5; 5§§1–12. Book Two: Chapters 3–10;
  11§§1–7* (see primary entry in 2284)

2053

{May 1} The Sundered (TLE)
  —*Chapter 6* (see primary entry in 2298)
"Mestral" (ENT short story, SNW 9)
"The Immortality Blues" (ST short
  story, SNW 9)

—*section 1*
  • *2056—[section 2]*
  • *2058—[section 3]*
  • *2063—[section 4]*

2056

"The Immortality Blues" (ST short story, SNW 9)
  —*section 2* (see primary entry in 2053)

2058

"The Immortality Blues" (ST short story, SNW 9)
  —*section 3* (see primary entry in 2053)
{August 9 to September 2} The Sundered (TLE)
  —*Chapters 7–8* (see primary entry in 2298)

2063

{April 4–5} Star Trek: First Contact (TNG movie
  novelization)
  —*Chapters 4–10* (see primary entry in 2373)
The Sundered (TLE) [19]
  —*Chapter 12* (see primary entry in 2298)
Star Trek: First Contact (TNG movie novelization)
  —*Chapters 11–12* (see primary entry in 2373)
"A Private Victory" (TNG short story,
  SNW III) [20]
Star Trek: First Contact (TNG movie novelization)
  —*Chapters 13–15* (see primary entry in 2373)
"The Immortality Blues" (ST short story, SNW 9) [21]
  —*section 4* (see primary entry in 2053)
"Almost . . . But Not Quite" (VGR short story, SNW II)
  —*section 1* (see primary entry in 2373)
Preserver (TNG hardcover)
  —*Chapter 39* (see primary entry in 2375)

2065

{March 19} Federation (TOS/TNG hardcover) [22]
  —*Part One: Chapter 1; Part Four: Chapter 1*
  (see primary entry in 2366)

---

[17] Takes place in a reality where *Star Trek: Deep Space Nine* is a
television series.
[18] These events occur in an alternate history.

[19] Takes place during *Star Trek: First Contact.*
[20] Ibid.
[21] Ibid.
[22] The March 2061 date in the novel contradicts *Star Trek: First
Contact* and has been adjusted to March 2065.

2069

{December 30} The *Valiant* (TNG hardcover) [23]

—*Book One* (see primary entry in 2333)

2070

The *Valiant* (TNG hardcover)

—*Book Three* (see primary entry in 2333)

2075

"First Steps" (TLOD short story)

2078

{June 21} Federation (TOS/TNG hardcover) [24]

—*Part One: Chapters 4; 7; 10* (see primary entry in 2366)

2079

Encounter at Farpoint (TNG episode novelization)

—*Chapter 3* (see primary entry in 2364)

All Good Things . . . (TNG episode novelization)

—*Chapters 11§6; 12§1; 25§1* (see primary entry in 2370)

2093

Surak's Soul (ENT)

—*Chapter 2§4* (see primary entry in 2152)

2098

Surak's Soul (ENT)

—*Chapter 2§5* (see primary entry in 2152)

2119

{April} Federation (TOS/TNG hardcover) [25]

—*Part One: Chapter 13; Part Two: Chapter 1* (see primary entry in 2366)

2121

"A Girl for Every Star" (ENT short story, SNW V) [26]

Broken Bow (ENT episode novelization)

—*Prologue* (see primary entry in 2151)

2135

"Preconceptions" (ENT short story, SNW VI)

2139

Daedalus (ENT)

—*Chapter 1§§2, 5* (see primary entry in 2153)

2140

{October 5} Daedalus (ENT)

—*Chapter 2§2* (see primary entry in 2153)

2149

"Egg Drop Soup" (ENT short story, SNW 8)

2151

{April 9} Shockwave (ENT episode novelization)

—*Chapter 6* (see primary entry in 2152)

{April 10–21} Broken Bow (ENT episode novelization)

• *2121—[Prologue]*

{April 23} What Price Honor? (ENT)

—*Prologue section 2* (see primary entry, below)

"Cabin E-14" (ENT short story, SNW VI)

—*sections 8–10* (see primary entry in 2152)

"Hoshi's Gift" (ENT short story, SNW V)

(ENT) *"Fight or Flight"—May 2–6, 2151*

"Remnant" (ENT short story, SNW V)

(ENT) *"Strange New World"*

(ENT) *"Unexpected"*

By the Book (ENT)

(ENT) *"Terra Nova"*

(ENT) *"The Andorian Incident"—June 16–17*

[23] *The Star Trek Chronology* places the destruction of the *Valiant* the same year that it leaves on its mission in 2065. The author has placed the destruction in 2069 to allow time for the Starship to reach the edge of the galaxy.

[24] Colonel Thorsen's war appears to be a conflict separate from Colonel Green's "World War III," which ended in 2053.

[25] The 2117 date in the novel has been adjusted to a time shortly after Cochrane's speech at the Warp 5 Complex in "Broken Bow" (ENT).

[26] Story is set just before the flashback in "Broken Bow" (ENT), in which the script gives Archer's age as nine and three-quarters; in this story his age is eleven.

DISCOVERY (THE BRAVE AND THE BOLD, ENT STORY)

A TIME TO SOW (TNG)

—*Chapter 1* (see primary entry in 2378)

(ENT) *"Breaking the Ice"*

A TIME TO SOW (TNG)

—*Chapter 2* (see primary entry in 2378)

(ENT) *"Civilization"*—*July 27–31*

(ENT) *"Fortunate Son"*

(ENT) *"Silent Enemy"*—*August 30 to September 2*

(ENT) *"Cold Front"*—*September 9–10*

{SEPTEMBER 10} SHOCKWAVE (ENT EPISODE NOVELIZATION) [27]

—*Chapter 7* (see primary entry in 2152)

(ENT) *"Dear Doctor"*

(ENT) *"Sleeping Dogs"*

(ENT) *"Shadows of P'Jem"*

(ENT) *"Shuttlepod One"*—*November 9–12*

(ENT) *"Fusion"*

(ENT) *"Rogue Planet"*

(ENT) *"Acquisition"*

(ENT) *"Oasis"*

{DECEMBER 31, 2151 TO JANUARY 5, 2152} WHAT PRICE HONOR? (ENT) [28]

—*Chapters 2; 4; 6; 8*

• *April 23, 2151*—*[Prologue section 2]*

• *2152*—*[Chapters 10, 12, 14, 16, 18, 20, 22, 24, 1, 3, 5, 7, 9, 11, 13, 15, 17, 19, 21, 23, 25, Epilogue]*

2152

(ENT) *"Detained"*

{JANUARY} SHOCKWAVE (ENT EPISODE NOVELIZATION)

—*Chapter 16* (see primary entry in 2152) [29]

(ENT) *"Vox Sola"*

(ENT) *"Fallen Hero"*—*February 9, 2152*

(ENT) *"Desert Crossing"*—*February 12–13, 2152*

(ENT) *"Two Days and Two Nights"*—*February 18–20, 2152*

WHAT PRICE HONOR? (ENT) [30]

—*Chapters 10; 12; 14; 16; 18; 20; 22; 24; 1; 3; 5; 7; 9; 11; 13; 15; 17; 19; 21; 23; 25; Epilogue* (see primary entry in 2151)

"CABIN E-14" (ENT SHORT STORY, SNW VI)

—*sections 1–7, 13–14*

• *late April, 2151*—*[sections 8–10]*

• *unknown future*—*[sections 11–12]*

SHOCKWAVE (ENT EPISODE NOVELIZATION)

—*Prologue; Chapters 1–5; 8–11; 12§§1–2; 13§1; 14; 15§1; 16; 17§§1,4–5; 18§§1,3; 19–23; Epilogue*

• *April 9, 2151*—*[Chapter 6]*

• *September 10, 2151*—*[Chapter 7]*

• *January, 2152*—*[Chapter 16]*

• *c.3000*—*[Chapters 12§3; 13§2; 15§2; 17§§2–3; 18§2]*

(ENT) *"Carbon Creek"*—*April, 2152*

(ENT) *"Minefield"*

(ENT) *"Dead Stop"*

(ENT) *"A Night in Sickbay"*

"THE SHOULDERS OF GIANTS" (ST SHORT STORY, SNW V)

—*Prologue* (see primary entry in 2465)

"ROUNDING A CORNER ALREADY TURNED" (ENT SHORT STORY, SNW 9)

(ENT) *"Marauders"*

(ENT) *"The Seventh"*

(ENT) *"The Communicator"*

SURAK'S SOUL (ENT)

• *2093*—*[Chapter 2§4]*

• *2098*—*[Chapter 2§5]*

(ENT) *"Singularity"*—*August 14, 2152*

(ENT) *"Vanishing Point"*

(ENT) *"Precious Cargo"*—*September 12, 2152*

(ENT) *"The Catwalk"*—*September 18, 2152*

(ENT) *"Dawn"*

(ENT) *"Stigma"*

"INSANITY" (ENT SHORT STORY, SNW 8)

(ENT) *"Cease Fire"*

(ENT) *"Future Tense"*

(ENT) *"Canamar"*

(ENT) *"The Crossing"*

---

[27] This chapter narrates portions of "Cold Front" (ENT).

[28] Presumably due to an editing error, the dates in the chapter headings are all off by one year. However, the dates given in Ensign Hart's service record are correct.

[29] This chapter narrates portions of "Detained" (ENT).

[30] Because of references to "Detained" (ENT) and "Desert Crossing" (ENT), the January 13–18 sections have been moved to late February.

"Savior" (ENT short story, SNW VI)

(ENT) *"Judgment"*

"Have Beagle, Will Travel" (Archer short story, TFTCT) [31]

2153

(ENT) *"Horizon"—January 10, 2153*

Rihannsu #2: The Romulan Way (TOS #35) [32]

—*Chapter 12 (see primary entry in 2276)*

(ENT) *"The Breach"*

(ENT) *"Cogenitor"*

(ENT) *"Regeneration"—March 1, 2153*

(ENT) *"First Flight"*

Daedalus (ENT)

- 2139—[*Chapter 1§§2, 5*]
- *October 5, 2140—[Chapter 2§2]*

Daedalus's Children (ENT)

(ENT) *"Bounty"—March 21, 2153*

{April 24} The Expanse (ENT episodes novelization) [33]

Last Full Measure (ENT)

(ENT) *"Anomaly"*

- *August 12, 2238—[Prologue; Epilogue]*

"Earthquake Weather" (ENT short story, SNW VII)

(ENT) *"Extinction"*

"Hero" (ENT short story, SNW 8)

(ENT) *"Raijin"*

(ENT) *"Impulse"*

(ENT) *"Exile"*

(ENT) *"The Shipment"*

(ENT) *"Twilight"*

(ENT) *"North Star"*

(ENT) *"Similitude"*

(ENT) *"Carpenter Street"*

(ENT) *"Chosen Realm"*

(ENT) *"Proving Ground"—December 6, 2153*

(ENT) *"Stratagem"—December 12, 2153*

(ENT) *"Harbinger"—December 27, 2153*

(ENT) *"Doctor's Orders"*

2154

(ENT) *"Hatchery"—January 8, 2154*

(ENT) *"Azati Prime"*

(ENT) *"Damage"*

(ENT) *"The Forgotten"*

(ENT) *"E²"*

(ENT) *"The Council"*

(ENT) *"Countdown"—February 13, 2154*

(ENT) *"Zero Hour"—February 14, 2154*

(ENT) *"Storm Front"*

(ENT) *"Storm Front, part II"*

(ENT) *"Home"*

(ENT) *"Borderland"—May 17, 2154*

(ENT) *"Cold Station 12"*

(ENT) *"The Augments"—May 27, 2154*

"Mother Nature's Little Reminders" (ENT short story, SNW 9)

(ENT) *"The Forge"*

(ENT) *"Awakening"*

(ENT) *"Kir'Shara"*

(ENT) *"Daedalus"*

(ENT) *"Observer Effect"*

(ENT) *"Babel One"—November 12, 2154*

(ENT) *"United"*

(ENT) *"The Aenar"*

(ENT) *"Affliction"—November 27, 2154*

(ENT) *"Divergence"*

(ENT) *"Bound"—December 27, 2154*

2155

Rosetta (ENT)

(ENT) *"In A Mirror, Darkly"—January 13, 2155*

(ENT) *"In A Mirror, Darkly, part II"*

(ENT) *"Demons"—January 19, 2155*

(ENT) *"Terra Prime"—January 22, 2155*

{August 9} The Sundered (TLE)

—*Chapter 15 (see primary entry in 2298)*

2158

The Great Starship Race (TOS #67)

—*Prologue §1 (see primary entry in 2269)*

2159

"Dead Man's Hand" (TLOD short story) [34]

---

[31] Archer's narrated story is entirely apocryphal.

[32] This chapter chronicles the period from the first encounter with a Starfleet vessel until the time of the framing story in 2276. References to the duration of the war and to Sarek's position as Vulcan Ambassador have been disregarded.

[33] This book novelizes ENT episodes "The Expanse" and "The Xindi."

[34] Story is set during the third year of the Romulan War.

2161

STARFLEET: YEAR ONE (SERIAL NOVEL)[35]
KILLING TIME (TOS #24)[36]
—*Chapters 22§§5–6; 23* (see primary entry in 2269)
(ENT) *"These Are the Voyages . . ."*[37]

2169

THE SUNDERED (TLE)
—*Chapter 18* (see primary entry in 2298)

2191

SPOCK'S WORLD (TOS HARDCOVER)[38]
—*Vulcan: Seven* (see primary entry in 2275)

2204

THE SUNDERED (TLE)
—*Chapter 19* (see primary entry in 2298)

2228

BURNING DREAMS (TOS)
—*Chapters 2, 3 §§5–6* (see primary entry in 2320)

2229

STAR TREK V: THE FINAL FRONTIER (ST MOVIE NOVELIZATION)
—*Prologue* (see primary entry in 2287)
BURNING DREAMS (TOS)
—*Chapters 3§7; 4§§1–7* (see primary entry in 2320)
DEMONS (TOS #30)
—*Chapter 1§§5–6* (see primary entry in 2270)
{JUNE 14} **SAREK (TOS HARDCOVER)**
—*Chapter 2, journal entry* (see primary entry in 2293)
{SEPTEMBER 16} **SAREK (TOS HARDCOVER)**
—*Chapter 5, first and second journal entries* (see primary entry in 2293)

---

[35] This story chronicles the end of the Romulan War, but does not explicitly support events from the television series *Star Trek: Enterprise.*
[36] Takes place during the conference in San Francisco which "lays out the groundwork" for the U.F.P. The given date of 2097 was disregarded.
[37] The holodeck scenes in this episode (which chronicle the events of 2161) are supported by a framing story set in 2370, during the events of "The *Pegasus*" (TNG).
[38] This chapter chronicles the period from Sarek's relocation to Earth until Spock's birth in 2230. The year 2212, given for Sarek's appointment as Ambassador to Earth, has been disregarded.

2230

BURNING DREAMS (TOS)
—*Chapters 4§8; 5§§2–10* (see primary entry in 2320)
STAR TREK V: THE FINAL FRONTIER (ST MOVIE NOVELIZATION)
—*Chapter 14, Spock flashback* (see primary entry in 2287)
{NOVEMBER 12} **SAREK (TOS HARDCOVER)**[39]
—*Chapter 5, third journal entry* (see primary entry in 2293)

2231

BURNING DREAMS (TOS)
—*Chapters 6§§6–7; 7§§1–5,7–8, 12; 8§§1–2,4–7* (see primary entry in 2320)
"BUM RADISH: FIVE SPINS ON A TURQUOISE REINDEER" (TOS SHORT STORY, SNW VI)

2233

THE FINAL REFLECTION (TOS #16)
—*Part One* (see primary entry in 2270)

2236

BURNING DREAMS (TOS)
—*Chapters 9; 15§§6–9* (see primary entry in 2320)
THE BETTER MAN (TOS #72)
—*Chapter 1§4* (see primary entry in 2275)

2237

"YESTERYEAR" (TAS NOVELIZATION, STAR TREK LOG ONE)
—*Chapters 7§3; 8§§1–12* (see primary entry in 2269)
{DECEMBER 7} **SAREK (TOS HARDCOVER)**
—*Chapter 6, journal entry* (see primary entry in 2293)

2238

{AUGUST 12} **LAST FULL MEASURE (ENT)**
—*Prologue; Epilogue* (see primary entry in 2153)

2239

THE FINAL REFLECTION (TOS #16)[40]
—*Part Two* (see primary entry in 2270)

---

[39] The given year of 2231 was changed to match *The Star Trek Chronology.*
[40] Takes place six years after Part One. Spock's age is eight. The story mentions that twenty-two years have passed since "first contact" between the Klingons and the Federation, which is very close to *The Star Trek Chronology's* date of 2218, though this assumption was supplanted by *Star Trek: Enterprise.*

2243

THE FINAL REFLECTION (TOS #16)[41]

—*Part Three* (see primary entry in 2270)

2244

SEEDS OF RAGE (TOS, ERRAND OF FURY #1)[42]

—*Chapters 7; 9; 12; 14; 18; 21* (see primary entry in 2267)

"THE COUNTER-CLOCK INCIDENT" (TAS NOVELIZATION, STAR TREK LOG SEVEN)

—*Chapter 1§1* (see primary entry in 2270)

THE BETTER MAN (TOS #72)

—*Chapter 1§6* (see primary entry in 2275)

THE *KOBAYASHI MARU* (TOS #47)

—*Chapter 8* (see primary entry in 2273)

FINAL FRONTIER (TOS GIANT)[43]

—*Chapters 1–24* (see primary entry in 2267)

2245

"OLD SOULS" (TLOD SHORT STORY)

"THE COUNTER-CLOCK INCIDENT" (TAS NOVELIZATION, STAR TREK LOG SEVEN)

—*Chapter 1§§2–5* (see primary entry in 2270)

2246

BURNING DREAMS (TOS)

—*Chapters 11–12; 13§§1–2,4; 10§8; 13§§5–8* (see primary entry in 2320)

{OCTOBER 10} "THOUGH HELL SHOULD BAR THE WAY" (EL SHORT STORY)[44]

A FLAG FULL OF STARS (TOS #54)[45]

—*Chapter 6§5* (see primary entry in 2272)

AVENGER (TNG HARDCOVER)[46]

—*Chapter 1* (see primary entry in 2373)

2247

PAST PROLOGUE (TOS, THE JANUS GATE #3)

—*Chapters 1§1; 2§1; 4§§3–5; 5§2; 6§1; 7§1; 8§2; 9§3* (see primary entry in 2266)

VULCAN'S FORGE (ST HARDCOVER)

—*Chapters 3; 6; 9; 11; 13; 15; 17; 19; 21; 23* (see primary entry in 2296)

2248

"DON'T CALL ME TINY" (TOS SHORT STORY, SNW 8)[47]

"CHAOTIC RESPONSE" (TOS SHORT STORY, CON)

—*section 1* (see primary entry in 2267)

STARFLEET ACADEMY: CRISIS ON VULCAN (ST-YA #1)[48]

2249

SAREK (TOS HARDCOVER)

—*Chapter 7§5* (see primary entry in 2293)

BEST DESTINY (TOS HARDCOVER)

—*Chapters 2–5; 7–8; 10–15; 17–26; 28–31; 37* (see primary entry in 2293)

2250

{APRIL 5} SAREK (TOS HARDCOVER)[49]

—*Chapter 12, first journal entry* (see primary entry in 2293)

THE ENTROPY EFFECT (TOS #2)

—*Chapter 1§12* (see primary entry in 2270)

VOYAGE TO ADVENTURE (TOS, WHICH WAY BOOKS)[50]

—*Time travel* (see primary entry in 2270)

STARFLEET ACADEMY: AFTERSHOCK (ST-YA #2)[51]

---

[41] Takes place four years after Part Two. References which claim that ninety years have passed since the incorporation of the U.F.P. have been ignored.

[42] The story's date of 2242 for the battle at Donatu V was based upon an error in the first edition of *The Star Trek Chronology*. The battle actually takes place 23 years prior to "The Trouble with Tribbles," so we have adjusted the year accordingly.

[43] The letter from George Kirk Sr. to his children, dated May 10, 2183, has been disregarded.

[44] Story is set simultaneously with the Tarsus IV incident.

[45] Ibid.

[46] Ibid.

[47] Story continues throughout Sulu's sixth-grade school year.

[48] Story is set before Spock joins Starfleet Academy in 2249.

[49] The given year of 2249 was changed to a date about a year after Spock entered the Academy.

[50] The time jump of forty years was adjusted to twenty. The presence of Spock aboard April's *Enterprise* can be explained if he was on a training mission as a cadet.

[51] Story is set soon before Starfleet Academy's winter break in Kirk's freshman year, 2250.

2251

Final Frontier (TOS Giant)[52]

—"*Hope and a Common Future*" (see primary entry in 2267)

Starfleet Academy: Cadet Kirk (ST-YA #3)[53]

My Brother's Keeper: *Republic* (TOS #85)

—*Chapters 5–20* (see primary entry in 2265)

2252

"Chaotic Response" (TOS short story, CON)

—*sections 5, 7* (see primary entry in 2267)

Vulcan's Glory (TOS #44)[54]

2253

Shadows on the Sun (TOS hardcover)

—*Book Two* (see primary entry in 2293)

2254

Star Trek V: The Final Frontier (ST movie novelization)

—*Chapter 14, McCoy flashback* (see primary entry in 2287)

(TOS) "The Cage"

Burning Dreams (TOS)[55]

—*Chapters 15§§10–12; 7§10; 15§13* (see primary entry in 2320)

The Rift (TOS #57)

—*Chapter 1–7* (see primary entry in 2287)

Burning Dreams (TOS)

—*Chapters 10§2; 15§§1–5* (see primary entry in 2320)

"Conflicting Natures" (ST short story, EL)[56]

The Captain's Table #6: Where Sea Meets Sky (ST)

—*Chapters 2–30* (see primary entry in 2266)

The Better Man (TOS #72)[57]

—*Chapters 3§§2, 4, 5; 7§4; 13§3; 15§§3, 5–6* (see primary entry in 2275)

[52] April's letter claims he captained the *Enterprise* for nine years, which contradicts *The Star Trek Chronology*.
[53] Spock mentions meeting Pike a "few years ago," which occurred in *Starfleet Academy: Crisis on Vulcan (ST-YA #1)*.
[54] Spock's somewhat lengthy service record conflicts with *The Star Trek Chronology*, which claims he was posted to the *Enterprise* while still a cadet.
[55] These scenes are set during "The Cage" (TOS).
[56] Story is set nine years after the launch of the *Enterprise*.
[57] Said to be eighteen years prior to the main story, but is actually twenty-one years.

"A Test of Character" (TOS short story, SNW VII)

[December] The *Kobayashi Maru* (TOS #47)[58]

—*Chapter 2* (see primary entry in 2273)

2255

Legacy (TOS #56)

—*Chapters 5§5; 10§§2–6; 13§§2–6* (see primary entry in 2268)

"A Private Anecdote" (TOS short story, SNW)

—*Recollections* (see primary entry in 2266)

2256

Crisis on Centaurus (TOS #28)

—*Chapter 3* (see primary entry in 2270)

Burning Dreams (TOS)

—*Chapters 16§2* (see primary entry in 2320)

2257

My Brother's Keeper: *Constitution* (TOS #86)

—*Chapters 4§4; 5–16* (see primary entry in 2265)

2258

The Great Starship Race (TOS #67)[59]

—*Prologue §2* (see primary entry in 2269)

The Covenant of the Crown (TOS #4)[60]

—*Chapter 2§§2–5* (see primary entry in 2276)

2259

The *Kobayashi Maru* (TOS #47)

—*Chapter 6* (see primary entry in 2273)

2260

Burning Dreams (TOS)

—*Chapters 16§§4–11; 10§5; 16§§1,3; 17§§2–9, 11–12,14; 18§§1–11,13; 19§§1–6* (see primary entry in 2320)

[58] This chapter offers a differing interpretation of Kirk's "Kobayashi Maru" test from that found in "A Test of Character" (SNW VII).
[59] The time lapse of seventy-four years was changed to one hundred.
[60] Kirk is a lieutenant commander, set eighteen years before the rest of the story. This allows him to be a lieutenant during the events on the *Farragut* as established in "Obsession" (TOS), and then be promoted after that.

2261

IMMORTAL COIL (TNG)

—*Chapter 19* (see primary entry in 2374)

BURNING DREAMS (TOS)

—*Chapters 17§§1, 10, 13; 18§12; 19§§7–9* (see primary entry in 2320)

2262

BURNING DREAMS (TOS)

—*Chapter 20§1* (see primary entry in 2320)

THE ASHES OF EDEN (ST HARDCOVER)[61]

—*Chapter 35, Carol Marcus flashback* (see primary entry in 2293)

2263

HARBINGER (VANGUARD #1)

—*Prologue* (see primary entry in 2265)

{STARDATE 1197.6} FOUNDATIONS BOOK ONE (SCE EBOOK #17)

—*Chapters 2–7* (see primary entry in 2376)

2264

ENTERPRISE: THE FIRST ADVENTURE (TOS GIANT)[62]

{STARDATE 1305.4} STRANGERS FROM THE SKY (TOS GIANT)[63]

—*Book Two: Chapters 1–2; 11§8* (see primary entry in 2284)

MY BROTHER'S KEEPER: ENTERPRISE (TOS #87)

—*Chapter 5§§1–2* (see primary entry in 2265)

CAPTAIN'S PERIL (ST HARDCOVER)[64]

—*Chapters 4–5; 7; 9; 13; 15; 19; 21–22; 24; 26; 32* (see primary entry in 2378)

---

[61] This scene features Kirk with his infant son. However, other stories claim Kirk was unaware of David's birth at this time. As a dream sequence, this may be historically unreliable.

[62] The story claims Kirk took command of the *Enterprise* shortly after his thirtieth birthday, but this contradicts *The Star Trek Chronology*. Chekov has low watch on the bridge but is assumed to still be an Academy student. Sulu is a recent "graduate," presumed to be some sort of advanced degree.

[63] The story offers a brief explanation for McCoy's departure and replacement by Dr. Mark Piper following *Enterprise: The First Adventure*.

[64] Takes place while Gary Mitchell is recovering at starbase from his poisoning on Dimorus.

2265

{STARDATE 1256.9} DISTANT EARLY WARNING (SCE EBOOK #64)

MY BROTHER'S KEEPER: ENTERPRISE (TOS #87)

—*Chapters 5§§3–4; 6–20* (see primary entry, below)

THE SUNDERED (TLE)

—*Chapter 20* (see primary entry in 2298)

MERE ANARCHY #1: THINGS FALL APART (TOS EBOOK)

"SINS OF THE MOTHER" (TLOD SHORT STORY)

—*section 2* (see primary entry in 2280)

(TOS) *"Where No Man Has Gone Before"*—*Stardate 1312.4 to 1313.8*

Q-SQUARED (TNG HARDCOVER)[65]

—*Track A: Chapter 12* (see primary entry in 2370)

{STARDATE 1313.8} MY BROTHER'S KEEPER: REPUBLIC (TOS #85)[66]

—*Chapters 1–4; 21*

• 2251—[*Chapters 5–20*]

MY BROTHER'S KEEPER: CONSTITUTION (TOS #86)

—*Chapters 1–3; 4§§1–3; 17*

• 2257—[*Chapters 4§4; 5–16*]

"THE LANDING PARTY" (TOS SHORT STORY, CON)

—*Sulu flashback* (see primary entry in 2266)

HARBINGER (VANGUARD #1)

—*Chapters 1–20*

• 2263—[*Prologue*]

MY BROTHER'S KEEPER: ENTERPRISE (TOS #87)[67]

—*Chapters 1–4; 21*

• early 2265—[*Chapters 5–20*]

{STARDATE 1298.9} THE CAPTAIN'S TABLE #1. WAR DRAGONS (TOS)

—*Chapters 1§2; 3; 5; 7; 9; 11; 13; 15* (see primary entry in 2293)

---

[65] Occurs during "Where No Man Has Gone Before."

[66] Ibid.

[67] This novel describes the changes to crew postings which set up the main body of stories in the obligatory "five-year mission," though some of the changes contradict *Enterprise: The First Adventure*. *The Star Trek Chronology* placed the five-year mission in the period from 2264–69, but this assumption was supplanted by "Q2" (VGR) which fixes the end of the mission in 2270. Note that the episode "Where No Man Has Gone Before" (TOS) does not include an opening monologue describing a five-year mission.

SUMMON THE THUNDER (VANGUARD #2)

THE BETTER MAN (TOS #72)[68]

—*Chapter 7§2 (see primary entry in 2275)*

2266

THE *KOBAYASHI MARU* (TOS #47)

—*Chapter 4 (see primary entry in 2273)*

—*Episodes (not*

(TOS) *"Corbomite Maneuver"—Stardate 1512.2*

"THE LANDING PARTY" (TOS SHORT STORY, CON)

- 2265—[*Sulu flashback*]

(TOS) *"Mudd's Women"—Stardate 1329.8*

(TOS) *"The Enemy Within"—Stardate 1672.1*

(TOS) *"The Man Trap"—Stardate 1513.1*

(TOS) *"The Naked Time"—Stardate 1704.2*

PRESENT TENSE (TOS, THE JANUS GATE #1)

FUTURE IMPERFECT (TOS, THE JANUS GATE #2)

—*Chapter 1§2; 2§1; 3§§1,3; 4; 5§2; 6§§1,3; 7§2; 8§§1,3; 9§2; 10§1; 11§§2–3*

- 2284—[*Chapter 1§1; 2§2; 3§2; 5§1; 6§2; 7§1; 8§2; 9§§1,3; 10§§2–4; 11§1*]

PAST PROLOGUE (TOS, THE JANUS GATE #3)

—*Chapter 1§2; 2§2; 3; 4§§1–2; 5§§1,3; 6§2; 7§2; 8§§1,3; 9§§1–2, 4; 10*

- 2247—[*Chapter 1§1; 2§1; 4§§3–5; 5§2; 6§1; 7§1; 8§2; 9§3*]

THE CAPTAIN'S TABLE #6: WHERE SEA MEETS SKY (ST)

—*Chapters 1; 31§§2–3*

- 2254—[*Chapters 2–30*]

(TOS) *"Charlie X"—Stardate 1533.6 to 1535.8, November 29*

"ELEGY FOR CHARLIE" (TOS SHORT STORY, TNV2)

{STARDATE 1699} "THE FIRST ARTIFACT" (THE BRAVE AND THE BOLD, TOS STORY)

- 2267—[*First Interlude*]

{STARDATE 1709.2} BURNING DREAMS (TOS)

—*Chapters 20§§2–7; 21§§1–3 (see primary entry in 2320)*

{STARDATE 1709.2} THE SUNDERED (TLE)

—*Chapter 17 (see primary entry in 2298)*

(TOS) *"Balance of Terror"—Stardate 1709.2*

{STARDATE 1831.5} SHADOW LORD (TOS #22)

THE EDGE OF THE SWORD (TOS, ERRAND OF VENGEANCE #1)

(TOS) *"What Are Little Girls Made Of?"—Stardate 2714.4*

KILLING BLOW (TOS, ERRAND OF VENGEANCE #2)

RIVER OF BLOOD (TOS, ERRAND OF VENGEANCE #3)

SEEDS OF RAGE (TOS, ERRAND OF FURY #1)

—*Prologue (see primary entry in 2267)*

(TOS) *"Dagger of the Mind"—Stardate 2715.1*

(TOS) *"Miri"—Stardate 2713.5*

"YEOMAN FIGGS" (TOS SHORT STORY, SNW V)

(TOS) *"The Conscience of the King"—Stardate 2817.7*

2267

BURNING DREAMS (TOS)

—*Chapter 1§§1–2 (see primary entry in 2320)*

(TOS) *"The Galileo Seven"—Stardate 2821.5*

{STARDATE 2822.5} "A PRIVATE ANECDOTE" (TOS SHORT STORY, SNW)

- 2255—[*recollections*]

(TOS) *"Court Martial"—Stardate 2947.3*

"OFFICIAL RECORD" (TOS SHORT STORY, CON)

(TOS) *"The Menagerie, Part I"—Stardate 3012.4*

BURNING DREAMS (TOS)

—*Chapter 10§3 (see primary entry in 2320)*

(TOS) *"The Menagerie, Part II"—Stardate 3012.4*

{STARDATE 3014.7} BURNING DREAMS (TOS)

—*Chapter 21§§4–10; 1§§3–6; 3§§1–4; 5§1; 6§§1–5; 7§§6, 9, 11; 8§3; 13§§3, 9; 14 (see primary entry in 2320)*

(TOS) *"Shore Leave"—Stardate 3025.3*

---

[68] Said to occur near the end of the five-year mission. However, this is incompatible with Joanna McCoy's age and her relationship to her father in *Crisis on Centaurus.*

HEART OF THE SUN (TOS #83)[69]

(TOS) *"The Squire of Gothos"—Stardate 2124.5*

REQUIEM (TNG #32)

—*Chapters 3§§1, 3, 5; 4§§1, 3; 5§§3–4; 6§§1, 3; 7§§1, 3; 8§§1, 3, 6; 9§2; 10§§1, 3 (see primary entry in 2369)*

(TOS) *"Arena"—Stardate 3045.6*

"A VULCAN, A KLINGON AND AN ANGEL" (TOS, STAR TREK III SHORT STORIES)

—*Narrated backstory (see primary entry in 2285)*

(TOS) *"The Alternative Factor"—Stardate 3087.6 to 3088.7*

(TOS) *"Tomorrow Is Yesterday"—Stardate 3113.2*

{STARDATE 3125.3 TO 3130.4} WEB OF THE ROMULANS (TOS #10)[70]

(TOS) *"Return of the Archons"—Stardate 3156.2 to 3158.7*

{STARDATE 3176.9} FOUNDATIONS BOOK TWO (SCE eBOOK #18)[71]

—*Chapters 2–8 (see primary entry in 2376)*

"THE AVENGER" (ST SHORT STORY, EL)

(TOS) *"A Taste of Armageddon"—Stardate 3192.1 to 3193.0*

(TOS) *"Space Seed"—Stardate 3141.9 to 3143.3*

TO REIGN IN HELL: THE EXILE OF KHAN NOONIEN SINGH (TOS HARDCOVER)[72]

—*Chapters 3–6 (see primary entry in 2287)*

THE JOY MACHINE (TOS #80)

SEEDS OF RAGE (TOS, ERRAND OF FURY #1)

—*Chapters 1; 2§1 (see primary entry, below)*

(TOS) *"This Side of Paradise"—Stardate 3417.3 to 3417.7*

"SONNET FROM THE VULCAN: OMICRON CETI THREE" (TOS SHORT STORY, TNV)

(TOS) *"The Devil in the Dark"—Stardate 3196.1*

SEEDS OF RAGE (TOS, ERRAND OF FURY #1)

—*Chapters 2§2; 3–6; 8; 10–11; 13; 15–17; 19–20; First Epilogue; Second Epilogue*

- *late 2266—[Prologue]*
- *early 2267—[Chapters 1; 2§1]*
- *2242—[Chapters 7; 9; 12; 14; 18; 21]*

(TOS) *"Errand of Mercy"—Stardate 3198.4 to 3201.7*

(TOS) *"The City on the Edge of Forever"*

"TRIPTYCH" (TOS SHORT STORY, SNW II)[73]

—*Chapters 1§6; 3§9*

- *1930—[Chapters 1§§1–5; 2; 3§§1–8]*

"REMEMBERING THE FUTURE" (ST SHORT STORY, SNW 9)

—*sections 8–9 (see primary entry in 2371)*

"MARKING TIME" (TOS SHORT STORY, SNW VI)

FINAL FRONTIER (TOS GIANT)[74]

—*Prologue; Chapter 25*

- *2244—[Chapters 1–24]*
- *2251—["Hope and a Common Future"]*

(TOS) *"Operation—Annihilate!"—Stardate 3287.2 to 3289.8*

"THE WINGED DREAMERS" (TOS SHORT STORY, TNV)

"THE LEADER" (TOS SHORT STORY, CON)

"INDOMITABLE" (TOS SHORT STORY, SNW VII)[75]

ISHMAEL (TOS #23)[76]

—*Chapters 1; 4; 7; 9; 11; 15; 19*

- *1867—[Chapters 2–3; 5–6; 8; 10; 12–14; 16–18]*

(TOS) *"Catspaw"—Stardate 3018.2*

{STARDATE 3163.2} "SHANGHAIED" (TOS SHORT STORY, SNW 8)

—*sections 5–15*

- *1863—[sections 1–4]*

"AMBITION" (TOS SHORT STORY, CON)

(TOS) *"Metamorphosis"—Stardate 3219.4 to 3220.3*

---

[69] Story is set not long after "Court Martial" (TOS).
[70] Story is set shortly after "Tomorrow is Yesterday" (TOS). A footnote that refers to "All Our Yesterdays" (TOS) contradicts the computer malfunction subplot of the story.
[71] These chapters are numbered 10–16 in the paperback edition.
[72] Takes place immediately after "Space Seed" (TOS).

[73] Framing story takes place during "City on the Edge of Forever" (TOS).
[74] Framing story takes place immediately after "City on the Edge of Forever" (TOS).
[75] Takes place immediately before Chekov is assigned to the bridge crew.
[76] Framing story takes place after "The City on the Edge of Forever" (TOS).

"Chaotic Response" (TOS short story, CON)

—sections 2–4, 6, 8

- 2248—[section 1]
- 2252—[sections 5–7]

(TOS) "Friday's Child"—Stardate 3497.2

Invasion! #1: First Strike (TOS #79)[77]

(TOS) "Who Mourns for Adonais?"—Stardate 3468.1

(TOS) "Amok Time"—Stardate 3372.1 to 3372.7

Mere Anarchy #2: The Centre Cannot Hold (TOS eBook)

"Soliloquy" (TOS short story, TNV2)

{Stardate 3375.3} Gemini (TOS)[78]

To Reign in Hell: The Exile of Khan Noonien Singh (TOS hardcover)

—Chapters 7–11 (see primary entry in 2287)

(TOS) "The Doomsday Machine"

"The First Artifact" (The Brave and the Bold, TOS story)

—First Interlude (see primary entry in 2266)

(TOS) "Wolf in the Fold"—Stardate 3614.9

Across the Universe (TOS #88)[79]

(TOS) "The Changeling"—Stardate 3451.9

"See No Evil" (TOS short story, CON)

(TOS) "The Apple"—Stardate 3715.0 to 3715.3

(TOS) "Mirror, Mirror"

(TOS) "The Deadly Years"—Stardate 3478.2 to 3479.4

(TOS) "I, Mudd"—Stardate 4513.3

{Stardate 4521.7} The Case of the Colonist's Corpse: A Sam Cogley Mystery (TOS)[80]

{Stardate 4496.1} Galactic Whirlpool (TOS Bantam PB)[81]

(TOS) "The Trouble with Tribbles"—Stardate 4523.3 to 4525.6

{Stardate 4523.7} Trials and Tribble-ations (DS9 episode novelization)[82]

—Chapters 3–14 (see primary entry in 2373)

"The Trouble with Tribals" (TOS short story, SNW VII)

{Stardate 4524.2} In the Name of Honor (TOS #97)

—Chapter 5§3 (see primary entry in 2287)

"A Bad Day for Koloth" (TOS short story, SNW 9)

"Missed" (TOS short story, SNW IV)[83]

(TOS) "Bread and Circuses"—Stardate 4040.7

{Stardate 3475.3} Mission to Horatius (YA, the first Star Trek novel)[84]

Battlestations! (TOS #31)

—Chapter 6§2 (see primary entry in 2270)

"First Star I See Tonight" (TOS short story, SNW IV)

Twilight's End (TOS #77)[85]

"Cave-In" (TOS short story, TNV2)

(TOS) "Journey to Babel"—Stardate 3842.3

{November, Stardates 3849.8 to 3858.7} Federation (TOS/TNG hardcover)

—Part One: Chapters 2; 5; 8; 11; 14. Part Two: Chapters 2; 4–5; 7–8; 10–11. Part Three: Chapter 7 (see primary entry in 2366)

To Reign in Hell: The Exile of Khan Noonien Singh (TOS hardcover)

—Chapters 12–13 (see primary entry in 2287)

The Vulcan Academy Murders (TOS #20)[86]

The IDIC Epidemic (TOS #38)[87]

"First, Do No Harm" (TOS short story, CON)

(TOS) "A Private Little War"—Stardate 4211.4

[77] Story is set immediately after "Friday's Child" (TOS).
[78] Chapter three references recent events of "Amok Time" (TOS).
[79] Chapter three sets the story soon after "The Doomsday Machine" (TOS).
[80] Continues concurrently through "The Trouble with Tribbles" (TOS). The story's December date is difficult to reconcile and was disregarded.
[81] According to the author, the story is set immediately before "The Trouble with Tribbles." The presence of Arex and M'Ress in the lounge suggests that they were "lower decks" officers at this time. Gods Above (NF) suggests they came aboard sometime after "Who Mourns for Adonais?" (TOS).

[82] Takes place during "The Trouble with Tribbles" (TOS).
[83] This story takes place immediately after "The Trouble with Tribbles" (TOS).
[84] Story is set after "The Trouble with Tribbles" (TOS).
[85] Story is set sometime after "A Taste of Armageddon" (TOS).
[86] Story is set immediately before The IDIC Epidemic (TOS #38). The claim that Spock had not been to Vulcan in two years was disregarded.
[87] The arrival of Dr. M'Benga aboard the Enterprise signals placement prior to "A Private Little War" (TOS).

2268

"Ni Var" (TOS short story, TNV)

"The Trouble with Borg Tribbles"
(TOS short story, SNW V)

To Reign in Hell: The Exile of Khan Noonien Singh
(TOS hardcover)

—*Chapters 14–15* (see primary entry in 2287)

The Disinherited (TOS #59)[88]

(TOS) *"The Gamesters of Triskelion"—Stardate 3211.7*

(TOS) *"Obsession"—Stardate 3619.2*

{Stardate 3629} Day of Honor #4:
Treaty's Law (TOS)[89]

—*Chapters 1–24*

- 2288—[Prologue/Epilogue]

{Stardate 3871.6} The Rings of Tautee
(TOS #78)

(TOS) *"The Immunity Syndrome"—Stardate 4307.1*

"The Enchanted Pool" (TOS short
story, TNV)

"Marginal Existence" (TOS short
story, TNV2)

(TOS) *"A Piece of the Action"*

(TOS) *"By Any Other Name"—Stardate 4657.5*

{Stardate 4720.1 to 4744.8} The
Klingon Gambit (TOS #3)

{Stardate 4769.1 to 5012.5} Mutiny
on the Enterprise (TOS #12)[90]

(TOS) *"Return to Tomorrow"—Stardate 4768.3*

(TOS) *"Patterns of Force"*

{Stardate 2950.3 to 2962.3} Uhura's
Song (TOS #21)[91]

- 235 BO—[Chapter 11§5]

(TOS) *"The Ultimate Computer"—Stardate 4729.4*

"Visit To a Weird Planet Revisited"
(TOS short story, TNV)

- 1968—["studio" sections]

(TOS) *"The Omega Glory"*

(TOS) *"Assignment: Earth"*

(TOS) *"Spectre of the Gun"—Stardate 4385.3*

(TOS) *"Elaan of Troyius"—Stardate 4372.5*

(TOS) *"The Paradise Syndrome"—Stardate 4842.6*

{Stardate 4925.2} Double, Double
(TOS #45)

(TOS) *"The Enterprise Incident"—Stardate 5027.3*

(TOS) *"And the Children Shall Lead"—Stardate 5029.5*

{Stardate 5302.1 to 5321.12} Dreams of the Raven
(TOS #34)[92]

(TOS) *"Spock's Brain"—Stardate 5431.4*

How Much for Just the Planet?
(TOS #36)[93]

(TOS) *"Is There in Truth No Beauty"—Stardate 5630.7*

Ghost Walker (TOS #53)[94]

(TOS) *"The Empath"—Stardate 5121.5*

{Stardate 5258.7} Legacy (TOS #56)

- 2255—[Chapters 5§5; 10§§2–6; 13§§2–6]

(TOS) *"The Tholian Web"—Stardate 5693.2*

The Sundered (TLE)

—*Chapter 24* (see primary entry in 2298)

"Devices and Desires" (TOS short
story, CON)

The Starship Trap (TOS #64)[95]

{Stardate 5419.4} Windows on a Lost
World (TOS #65)

{Stardate 5462.1 to 5465.4} Section
31: Cloak (TOS)[96]

- *late 2268*—[Epilogue]

(TOS) *"For the World Is Hollow and I Have Touched the
Sky"—Stardate 5476.3*

{Stardate 5650.1} The Badlands
(Book 1, TOS story)[97]

(TOS) *"Day of the Dove"*

(TOS) *"Plato's Stepchildren"—Stardate 5784.2*

---

[88] Story is set just before "Gamesters of Triskelion" (TOS).
[89] Story is set after "Errand of Mercy" (TOS). Stardate for the story is from *Day of Honor #2: Armageddon Sky* (DS9).
[90] Story is set immediately after *The Klingon Gambit* (TOS #3).
[91] Story is set after "Private Little War" (TOS).

[92] Using McCoy's age for chronology is problematic, so the stardate was used.
[93] Story is set after "The Omega Glory" (TOS).
[94] Story is set during fourth year of Kirk's first five-year mission.
[95] Story is set after "The Immunity Syndrome" (TOS).
[96] Story is set several months after "The Enterprise Incident" (TOS), and very shortly before "For the World is Hollow and I Have Touched the Sky" (TOS).
[97] Story is set several months after "The Enterprise Incident" (TOS).

FIRST FRONTIER (TOS #75)[98]

—*Prologue; Chapters 1–22; 39–40; Epilogue*

- 64, 018, 143 BC—[*Chapters 23–38*]

(TOS) *"Wink of an Eye"*—Stardate 5710.5

"THE HUNTING" (TOS SHORT STORY, TNV)

(TOS) *"That Which Survives"*

SECTION 31: CLOAK (TOS)

—*Epilogue* (see primary entry, above)

GATEWAYS #1: ONE SMALL STEP (TOS)

"ONE GIANT LEAP" (TOS STORY, WLB)

MUDD IN YOUR EYE (TOS #81)[99]

"A SUCKER BORN" (TOS SHORT STORY, SNW VII)[100]

(TOS) *"Let That Be Your Last Battlefield"*—Stardate 5730.2

(TOS) *"Whom Gods Destroy"*—Stardate 5718.3

SANCTUARY (TOS #61)[101]

"THE SHOULDERS OF GIANTS" (ST SHORT STORY, SNW V)[102]

—*"One: Fiffick"* (see primary entry in 2465)

(TOS) *"The Mark of Gideon"*—Stardate 5423.4

2269

(TOS) *"The Lights of Zetar"*—Stardate 5725.3

(TOS) *"The Cloud Minders"*—Stardate 5818.4

{STARDATE 7513.2 TO 7521.6} CRISIS ON CENTAURUS (TOS #28)

- 2256—[*Chapter 3*]

"THE SLEEPING GOD" (TOS SHORT STORY, TNV2)

(TOS) *"The Way to Eden"*—Stardate 5832.3

"THE QUICK AND THE DEAD" (TOS SHORT STORY, SNW II)

(TOS) *"Requiem for Methuselah"*—Stardate 5843.7

(TOS) *"The Savage Curtain"*—Stardate 5906.4

(TOS) *"All Our Yesterdays"*—Stardate 5943.7

"SURPRISE!" (TOS SHORT STORY, TNV2)

TO REIGN IN HELL: THE EXILE OF KHAN NOONIEN SINGH (TOS HARDCOVER)

—*Chapters 16–18* (see primary entry in 2287)

"IN THE MAZE" (TOS SHORT STORY, TNV2)

{STARDATE 3998.6} FACES OF FIRE (TOS #58)[103]

(TOS) *"Turnabout Intruder"*—Stardate 5928.5

{STARDATE 6021.4 TO 6021.6} ASSIGNMENT: ETERNITY (TOS #84)[104]

—*Chapters 2–18; 20–21*

- July 19–20, 1969—[*Chapters 1; 22*]
- 2293—[*Prologue; Chapter 19; Epilogue*]

"AS OTHERS SEE US" (TOS SHORT STORY, CON)

"MIND SIFTER" (TOS SHORT STORY, TNV)[105]

"IF I LOSE THEE . . ." (TOS SHORT STORY, SNW III)

- 1594—[*London sections*]

"THE FACE ON THE BARROOM FLOOR" (TOS SHORT STORY, TNV)

"SNAKE PIT!" (TOS SHORT STORY, TNV2)

"BOOK OF FULFILLMENT" (TOS SHORT STORY, SNW 9)

{STARDATE 4011.9} SPOCK MUST DIE! (TOS BANTAM PB)[106]

{STARDATE 6720.8} SPOCK, MESSIAH! (TOS BANTAM PB)

{STARDATE 6132.8} PLANET OF JUDGMENT (TOS BANTAM PB)

{STARDATE 6451.3} VULCAN! (TOS BANTAM PB)

{STARDATE 6527.5} THE STARLESS WORLD (TOS BANTAM PB)

{STARDATE 6188.4} TREK TO MADWORLD (TOS BANTAM PB)

{STARDATE 7502.9} WORLD WITHOUT END (TOS BANTAM PB)

---

[98] Story is set after "The Omega Glory" (TOS).

[99] Story is set after "I, Mudd" (TOS).

[100] This story suggests an alternate possibility for the first meeting with Harry Mudd since "I, Mudd" (TOS).

[101] Story is set after "Let That Be Your Last Battlefield" (TOS).

[102] Story continues several weeks past "The Mark of Gideon" (TOS).

[103] Placement represents a compromise between the Historian's Note, which puts the story about halfway through Kirk's first five-year mission, and David's age, which is supposed to be ten. We assume that the planet "Alpha Maluria Seven" is not part of the system destroyed in "The Changeling" (TOS).

[104] Story is set one week after "Turnabout Intruder" (TOS).

[105] Requires about two years of story time. Reconciling this is left to the reader.

[106] Requires several months of story time and ends with the Organians depriving the Klingons of spaceflight capability for a thousand years. Reconciling this is left to the reader.

{Stardate 4231.2} Devil World
(TOS Bantam PB)

{Stardate 6827.3} Perry's Planet
(TOS Bantam PB)

{Stardate 6914.6} Death's Angel (TOS
Bantam PB)

{Stardate 7521.6 to 7532.8} The
Trellisane Confrontation (TOS #14)

Killing Time (TOS #24)[107]

—Chapters 1–21; 22§§1–4; 24–25; Epilogue
  • 2161—[Chapters 22§§5–6; 23]

The Three-Minute Universe (TOS #41)[108]

{Stardate 6118.2 to 6119.2} The Cry
of the Onlies (TOS #46)

Renegade (TOS #55)[109]

{Stardate 3223.1} The Great Starship
Race (TOS #67)[110]

—Chapters 1–24
  • 2158—[Prologue §1]
  • 2258—[Prologue §2]

{Stardate 6453.4} "Fracture"
(TOS short story, CON)

{Stardate 6618.4} All of Me
(TOS Wildstorm graphic)

{Stardate 6769.4} The Patrian
Transgression (TOS #69)

Memory Prime (TOS #42)[111]

{Stardate 4842.6 to 6987.31}
Prime Directive (TOS giant)[112]

» From The Star Trek Chronology, 1996 ed., editors' note
(page 78): "Although this chronology does not use
material from the animated Star Trek series, Dorothy
Fontana suggests that she would place those stories after
the end of the third season, but prior to the end of the
five-year mission." The episode order and stardates are
derived from Alan Dean Foster's novelizations.

{Stardate 5321.3} "Beyond the
Farthest Star" (TAS novelization,
Star Trek Log One)

{Stardate 5373.4} "Yesteryear" (TAS
novelization, Star Trek Log One)

—Chapters 6; 7§§1–2; 8§13
  • 2237—[Chapters 7§3; 8§§1–12]

{Stardate 5380} "One of Our Planets
is Missing" (TAS novelization, Star
Trek Log One)

{Stardate 5402.7} "The Survivor"
(TAS novelization, Star Trek
Log Two)[113]

{Stardate 5483.7} "The Lorelei
Signal" (TAS novelization, Star Trek
Log Two)

2270

{Stardate 5503.1} "The Infinite
Vulcan" (TAS novelization, Star Trek
Log Two)

{Stardate 5510.1} "Once Upon a
Planet" (TAS novelization, Star Trek
Log Three)

{Stardate 5514.0} "Mudd's Passion"
(TAS novelization, Star Trek Log
Three)

{Stardate 5524.5} "The Magicks of
Megas-Tu" (TAS novelization, Star
Trek Log Three)

{Stardate 5525.3} "The Terratin
Incident" (TAS novelization, Star
Trek Log Four)

"The Time Trap" (TAS novelization, Star
Trek Log Four)

Where Time Stands Still (SCE
eBook #44)[114]

—Delta Triangle backstory

{Stardate 5526.2} "More Tribbles,
More Troubles" (TAS novelization,
Star Trek Log Four)

---

[107] Story is set after "The Enterprise Incident" (TOS). Chapters
2–23 occur in an alternate timeline.
[108] Story is set after "Plato's Stepchildren" (TOS).
[109] Story is set two years after "A Private Little War" (TOS).
[110] Story is set after "Taste of Armageddon" (TOS).
[111] Story is set after "The Lights of Zetar" (TOS).
[112] *Prime Directive* requires several months of story time, and
makes a convenient transition point between the live action
episodes (TOS) and the animated episodes (TAS).

[113] Takes place at Christmastime.
[114] The given year of 2268 was adjusted to 2270.

{STARDATE 5527.0} "THE AMBERGRIS
ELEMENT" (TAS NOVELIZATION, STAR
TREK LOG FIVE)

{STARDATE 5527.3} "THE PIRATES OF
ORION" (TAS NOVELIZATION, STAR TREK
LOG FIVE)

{STARDATE 5527.4} "THE JIHAD" (TAS
NOVELIZATION, STAR TREK LOG FIVE)

{STARDATE 5532.8} "ALBATROSS" (TAS
NOVELIZATION, STAR TREK LOG SIX)

"THE PRACTICAL JOKER" (TAS
NOVELIZATION, STAR TREK LOG SIX)

{STARDATE 5535.2} "HOW SHARPER THAN
A SERPENT'S TOOTH" (TAS
NOVELIZATION, STAR TREK LOG SIX)

{STARDATE 5536.3} "THE COUNTER-
CLOCK INCIDENT" (TAS NOVELIZATION,
STAR TREK LOG SEVEN)

—Chapters 1§6; 2–11
• 2244—[Chapter 1§1]
• 2245—[Chapter 1§§2–5]

{STARDATE 5537.1} "THE EYE OF THE
BEHOLDER" (TAS NOVELIZATION, STAR
TREK LOG EIGHT)

{STARDATE 5537.3} "BEM" (TAS
NOVELIZATION, STAR TREK LOG NINE)

{STARDATE 5538.6} "SLAVER WEAPON"
(TAS NOVELIZATION, STAR TREK LOG TEN)

{STARDATE 5459.4} "THE PATIENT
PARASITES" (TOS SHORT STORY, TNV2)

"INTERSECTION POINT" (TOS SHORT
STORY, TNV)

"THE PROCRUSTEAN PETARD" (TOS SHORT
STORY, TNV2)

{STARDATE 6273.6} MUDD'S ANGELS,
"THE BUSINESS, AS USUAL, DURING
ALTERCATIONS" (TOS BANTAM PB)

{STARDATE 3126.7 TO 3127.1} TEARS
OF THE SINGERS (TOS #19)[115]

FROM THE DEPTHS (TOS #66)[116]

"THE GIRL WHO CONTROLLED GENE
KELLY'S FEET" (TOS SHORT STORY,
SNW)[117]

{STARDATE 6251.1} CROSSROAD
(TOS #71)[118]

{STARDATE 7004.1} THE EUGENICS WARS:
THE RISE AND FALL OF KHAN NOONIEN
SINGH, BOOK ONE

—Prologue; Chapters 24–25; 28; 35
• March 13–14, 1974—[Chapters 1–2]
• May 14–19, 1974—[Chapters 3–23]
• November 1, 1984—[Chapters 26–27]
• December 2–3, 1984—[Chapters 29–30]
• July 5, 1986—[Chapter 31]
• October 10, 1986—[Chapters 32–33]
• November 9, 1989—[Chapter 34]

{STARDATE 7004.1–7004.2} THE
EUGENICS WARS: THE RISE AND FALL OF
KHAN NOONIEN SINGH, BOOK TWO

—Prologue; Chapter 7; Epilogue
• June 14, 1992—[Chapter 1]
• July 10, 1992—[Chapter 2]
• November 5–6, 1992—[Chapters 3–4]
• March 15, 1993—[Chapter 5]
• June 14, 1993—[Chapters 6, 8]
• September 10, 1993—[Chapter 9]
• September 30–October 1, 1993—[Chapters 10–11]
• February 7, 1994—[Chapters 12–13]
• April 21, 1994—[Chapter 14]
• August 16–29, 1994—[Chapters 15–17]
• October 2, 1994—[Chapter 18]
• November 14, 1994—[Chapters 19–20]
• March 17, 1995—[Chapter 21]
• September 5–7, 1995—[Chapter 22–23]
• January 5 to February 2, 1996—[Chapters 24–27]

THE PRICE OF THE PHOENIX (TOS
BANTAM PB)

{STARDATE 9722.4} THE FATE OF THE
PHOENIX (TOS BANTAM PB)

---

[115] Story takes place after "Day of the Dove" (TOS) and "Time Trap" (TAS).

[116] Chapter nine sets the story 207 years after Cochrane's first warp flight. The opening at Starbase 23 suggests placement immediately after *Tears of the Singers* (TOS #19).

[117] Story is set after "Once Upon a Planet" (TAS).

[118] Christine Chapel begins pursuit of her doctorate.

{STARDATE 6101.1 TO 6205.7} BLACK
FIRE (TOS #8)[119]

{STARDATE 5064.4 TO 5099.5} THE
ABODE OF LIFE (TOS #6)

"DEMON" (TOS SHORT STORY, SNW 8)

{STARDATE 4380.4 TO 4997.5} CORONA
(TOS #15)[120]

{STARDATE 7003.4 TO 7008.4}
MINDSHADOW (TOS #27)[121]

DEMONS (TOS #30)[122]

• 2229—[Chapter 1§§5–6]

CHAIN OF ATTACK (TOS #32)[123]

BLOODTHIRST (TOS #37)[124]

THE FINAL NEXUS (TOS #43)[125]

{STARDATE 5001.1} THE ENTROPY EFFECT
(TOS #2)

• 2250—[Chapter 1 section 12]

{STARDATE 8405.15} THE FINAL
REFLECTION (TOS #16)

—Prologue; Epilogue
• 2233—[Part One]
• 2239—[Part Two]
• 2244—[Part Three]

GARTH OF IZAR (TOS)[126]

VOYAGE TO ADVENTURE (TOS, WHICH WAY
BOOKS)

• 2250—[Time travel]

PHASER FIGHT (TOS, WHICH WAY BOOKS)

{STARDATE 6324.09 TO 6381.7}
YESTERDAY'S SON (TOS #11)[127]

—Prologue; Chapters 1–4; 7–19; Epilogue
• circa 2703 BC—[Chapters 5–6]

{STARDATE 7881.2 TO 8180.2}
DREADNOUGHT! (TOS #29)

{STARDATE 3301.1 TO 4720.2}
BATTLESTATIONS! (TOS #31)

• 2267—[Chapters 6§2]

". . . AS GOOD AS A VACATION"
(TOS SHORT STORY, CON)

» Kirk's first five-year mission ends and the Starship
Enterprise returns to spacedock.

{STARDATE 6987.31} THE LOST YEARS (TOS HARDCOVER)[128]

—Chapters 1–2 (see primary entry in 2271)

"THE END OF NIGHT" (VGR SHORT STORY,
SNW VI)[129]

—first and last sections (see primary entry in 2374)

THE CAPTAIN'S DAUGHTER (TOS #76)

—Chapters 5–12 (see primary entry in 2294)

2271

{VULCAN OLD DATE 155622} THE LOST
YEARS (TOS HARDCOVER)[130]

—Chapters 3–23; Epilogue
• AD 300—[Prologue]
• 2270—[Chapters 1–2]

119 Prior to the publication of The Star Trek Chronology, many circles within fandom believed that Kirk commanded a second five-year mission prior to Star Trek: The Motion Picture. Stories set in this period typically featured promotions for the bridge crew, the return of Janice Rand, the movie-era uniforms, upgrades to the Enterprise, and so on. Black Fire marks the transition point to this era, the scope of which we have greatly reduced to fit within the final six months of the five-year mission. Reconciling the time constraints is left to the reader.

120 Story is set years after "Devil in the Dark" (TOS). Kirk is said to be in his forties yet the crew ranks and uniforms are from the pre-TMP era. Chekov is temporarily in charge of security.

121 Story is purportedly set three years after "The Enterprise Incident," thus presupposing the second five-year mission prior to ST:TMP. This story introduces the character of Ingrit Tomson, who is featured in several subsequent novels.

122 Story is set after Mindshadow (TOS #27). Spock's age is suggested to be thirty-six, which is incorrect.

123 Story is set after The Abode of Life (TOS #6).

124 Story is set after Demons (TOS #30). References to Halloween are problematic.

125 Story is set after Chain of Attack (TOS #32).

126 Story takes place about two years after "Whom Gods Destroy."

127 The span of "two years" since "All Our Yesterdays" (TOS) has been reduced to about eighteen months. Commodore Wesley has returned to Starfleet since his stint as Governor of Mantilles in 2269.

128 The placement for the end of the Enterprise's five-year mission is drawn from "Q2" (VGR). We assume that this event occurred roughly in mid-to-late 2270.

129 This timeline is eliminated at the end of the story.

130 The bulk of The Lost Years takes place in early 2271 (The Star Trek Chronology has Spock returning to Vulcan to undergo Kohlinar in 2270). Spock's age is established to be forty-one, but Kirk's age thirty-six is incorrect. References to Tomson having served with Kirk for four years and the season being autumn are problematic.

TRAITOR WINDS (TOS #70)[131]

MERE ANARCHY #3: SHADOWS OF THE INDIGNANT (TOS eBOOK)

2272

{MARCH 19} FEDERATION (TOS/TNG HARDCOVER)[132]

—Part Four: Chapter 3 (see primary entry in 2366)

{JULY 4–20} A FLAG FULL OF STARS (TOS #54)[133]

• 2246—[Chapter 6§5]

RECOVERY (TOS #73)[134]

2273

"NIGHT WHISPERS" (ST SHORT STORY, EL)[135]

{STARDATE 7412.3 TO 7414.1} STAR TREK: THE MOTION PICTURE (ST MOVIE NOVELIZATION)[136]

"A & Ω" (ST SHORT STORY, SNW 8)[137]

—section 8 (see primary entry in 2385)

{STARDATE 7435.5} EX MACHINA (TOS)[138]

—Prologue; Chapters 1–17; 19

• 7954 BC—[Chapter 18]

{STARDATE 5960.2 TO 6100.0} PAWNS AND SYMBOLS (TOS #26)[139]

—Chapters 1–4

• late 2273—[Chapters 5–7]
• February 2274—[Chapter 8]
• mid-2274—[Chapters 9–14; Epilogue]

THE KOBAYASHI MARU (TOS #47)[140]

—Chapters 1; 3; 5; 7; 9

• 2244—[Chapter 8]
• 2254—[Chapter 2]
• 2259—[Chapter 6]
• 2266—[Chapter 4]

HOME IS THE HUNTER (TOS #52)[141]

—Chapters 2; 4; 6; 10; 13; 15; 18; 20; 22; 24; 27; 30; 32; 34; 38; 44; 51–52

• 1600—[Chapters 1; 7; 14; 19; 28; 33; 35; 41; 45; 48]
• 1746—[Chapters 3; 8; 11; 16; 21; 25; 29; 36; 39; 42; 46; 49]
• 1942—[Chapters 5; 9; 12; 17; 23; 26; 31; 37; 40; 43; 47; 50]

{STARDATE 8036.2} ENEMY UNSEEN (TOS #51)[142]

PAWNS AND SYMBOLS (TOS #26)

—Chapters 5–7 (see primary entry, above)

FIRESTORM (TOS #68)[143]

2274

TO REIGN IN HELL: THE EXILE OF KHAN NOONIEN SINGH (TOS HARDCOVER)

—Chapters 19–21 (see primary entry in 2287)

{FEBRUARY 8} PAWNS AND SYMBOLS (TOS #26)[144]

—Chapter 8 (see primary entry in 2273)

---

[131] Story is set "shortly after the end of the Enterprise's five-year mission, immediately following the events chronicled in The Lost Years." This occurs after Spock decides to pursue Kohlinar, contradicting the December 2269 date on page 1.

[132] The 2270 date in the novel has been adjusted to 2272, following the first two Lost Years novels.

[133] Story is set "shortly before the events chronicled in Star Trek: The Motion Picture." Since dates placing this novel during the Apollo 11 tricentenial contradict The Star Trek Chronology, we assumed the story to be centered around the tricentennial of the Apollo space program (1969–1972) instead.

[134] Story is set weeks before Star Trek: The Motion Picture. Several references to Kirk having been Chief of Operations for approximately a year, suggest a late 2272 time period for this novel, some four months after A Flag Full of Stars (TOS #54).

[135] Story is set immediately before Star Trek: The Motion Picture.

[136] Spock has been pursuing the Kolinahr disciplines for 2.8 years. This establishes the event in mid-2273.

[137] Reprises the end of Star Trek: The Motion Picture.

[138] Story is set immediately after Star Trek: The Motion Picture.

[139] Story is set after "More Troubles, More Tribbles" (TAS) and "some years" after "Day of the Dove" (TOS). Despite descriptions of the colored uniforms of the first five-year mission, the story must occur after TMP, given that Chapel is a doctor, and Kang's unknown son with Mara is about five years old.

[140] Story is set shortly after Star Trek: The Motion Picture.

[141] Ibid.

[142] Ibid.

[143] Takes place five years after "Elaan of Troyius" (TOS). Uniform details within this and the subsequent novels by L. A. Graf are inconsistent for this period.

[144] Takes place in the weeks leading up to the lunar (Asian) new year, thirty years after the Battle of Donatu V.

ICE TRAP (TOS #60)[145]
SHELL GAME (TOS #63)
DEATH COUNT (TOS #62)[146]
THE PROMETHEUS DESIGN (TOS #5)
TRIANGLE (TOS #9)[147]
PAWNS AND SYMBOLS (TOS #26)
—Chapters 9–14; Epilogue (see primary entry in 2273)
THE PANDORA PRINCIPLE (TOS #49)[148]
—Chapter 1 (see primary entry in 2281)

2275

TO REIGN IN HELL: THE EXILE OF KHAN NOONIEN SINGH (TOS HARDCOVER)
—Chapter 22 (see primary entry in 2287)
{STARDATE 9250.0} THE WOUNDED SKY (TOS #13)
{SEPTEMBER} RIHANNSU #1: MY ENEMY, MY ALLY (TOS #18)[149]
DOCTOR'S ORDERS (TOS #50)
{STARDATE 7412.1 TO 7468.5} SPOCK'S WORLD (TOS HARDCOVER)[150]
—Prologue; Enterprise: One-Eight; Epilogue
- c. 5 to 2 Billion BC—[Vulcan: One]
- c. 500,000 BC—[Vulcan: Two]
- c. 10,000 BC—[Vulcan: Three]
- c. 3000 BC—[Vulcan: Four]
- c. 30 BC—[Vulcan: Five]
- c. AD 193 to AD 330—[Vulcan: Six]
- 2191 to 2230—[Vulcan: Seven]

{STARDATE 7591.4 TO 7598.5} THE BETTER MAN (TOS #72)
- 2236—[Chapter 1§4]
- 2244—[Chapter 1§6]
- 2254—[Chapter 3§§2, 4, 5; 7§4; 13§3; 15§§3, 5–6]
- 2265—[Chapter 7§2]

2276

{STARDATE 7815.3} THE COVENANT OF THE CROWN (TOS #4)
- 2258—[Chapter 2§§2–5]
TIMETRAP (TOS #40)
{SEPTEMBER} RIHANNSU #2: THE ROMULAN WAY (TOS #35)[151]
—Chapters 1; 3; 5; 7; 9; 11; 13–15; Epilogue
- 249–300—[Chapter 2]
- 285–300—[Chapter 4]
- 300–750—[Chapter 6]
- 750–846—[Chapter 8]
- 846–2153—[Chapter 10]
- 2153–2270—[Chapter 12]
{NOVEMBER} RIHANNSU #3: SWORDHUNT (TOS #95)[152]
RIHANNSU #4: HONOR BLADE (TOS #96)

2277

"THE BLAZE OF GLORY" (TOS, STAR TREK II SHORT STORIES)
"UNDER TWIN MOONS" (TOS, STAR TREK II SHORT STORIES)
"WILD CARD" (TOS, STAR TREK II SHORT STORIES)
"THE SECRET EMPIRE" (TOS, STAR TREK II SHORT STORIES)
"INTELLIGENCE TEST" (TOS, STAR TREK II SHORT STORIES)
"TO WHEREVER" (TOS, STAR TREK II SHORT STORIES)
STAR TREK II: DISTRESS CALL (TOS PLOT-YOUR-OWN-ADVENTURE)

---

[145] Chapter 2 establishes that Uhura and Chekov had known each other for eight years. Chapter 3 establishes that Uhura had been in Starfleet for twelve years.
[146] The severe damage incurred by the USS Kongo demands placement after Shell Game (TOS), which also features the ship. Kirk's age is said to be "just over forty" (i.e., perhaps forty-one).
[147] Story is set seven years after "Amok Time" (TOS).
[148] After rescuing Saavik from Hellguard, Spock takes a one-year leave to help her acclimate into Vulcan society. He will return sometime in late summer of 2275, prior to The Wounded Sky.
[149] Story is set immediately after The Wounded Sky and one "standard year" prior to The Romulan Way. Note that the setting originally intended for Duane's novels was a purported second five-year mission prior to Star Trek: The Motion Picture—an idea since discarded. Therefore, crew ranks and Chapel's pursuit of her doctorate are incorrect for this period. These discrepancies will be corrected in the forthcoming Rihannsu omnibus edition.
[150] Story is set two years after Star Trek: The Motion Picture.

[151] Story is set eight years after "The Enterprise Incident" (TOS), when McCoy is age forty-nine, not fifty as stated in the text.
[152] Story is set two months after The Romulan Way.

2278

**STAR TREK III: THE VULCAN TREASURE
(TOS PLOT-IT-YOURSELF ADVENTURE)**

**"WORLD'S END" (TOS, STAR TREK III
SHORT STORIES)**

**"AS OLD AS FOREVER" (TOS, STAR TREK III
SHORT STORIES)**

{STARDATE 7818.1} RULES OF
ENGAGEMENT (TOS #48)[153]

**"THE NAME OF THE CAT" (TOS SHORT
STORY, SNW IV)**

—*section 1*

- *2371*—[*sections 2–3*]

{STARDATE 7823.6 TO 7835.8} DEEP
DOMAIN (TOS #33)[154]

» *The Starship Enterprise returns to spacedock and is
recommissioned as a training vessel. Spock is promoted
to Captain.*

THE CAPTAIN'S DAUGHTER (TOS #76)

—*Chapters 15–17* (see primary entry in 2294)

NEW EARTH #1: WAGON TRAIN TO THE STARS (TOS #89)

— *"Three Months Earlier"* (see primary entry in 2279)

SHIP OF THE LINE (TNG HARDCOVER)

—*Chapters 1–5* (see primary entry in 2372)

**"FAMILY MATTERS" (TOS SHORT STORY,
SNW III)**

{OCTOBER 31} NEW EARTH #1: WAGON TRAIN TO THE STARS
(TOS #89)[155]

— *"The Captains' Meeting"* (see primary entry in 2279)

2279

{APRIL} NEW EARTH #1: WAGON TRAIN TO
THE STARS (TOS #89)[156]

- *2278*—["*Three Months Earlier*"]
- *October 31, 2278*—["*The Captains' Meeting*"]

{JULY} NEW EARTH #2: BELLE TERRE (TOS
#90)

{STARDATE 7952.4} IN THE NAME OF HONOR (TOS #97)

—*Chapters 1–2* (see primary entry in 2287)

TO REIGN IN HELL: THE EXILE OF KHAN NOONIEN SINGH
(TOS HARDCOVER)

—*Chapters 23–25* (see primary entry in 2287)

{DECEMBER} NEW EARTH #3: ROUGH
TRAILS (TOS #91)[157]

2280

NEW EARTH #4: THE FLAMING ARROW
(TOS #92)

NEW EARTH #5: THIN AIR (TOS #93)

NEW EARTH #6: *CHALLENGER* (TOS #94)

GATEWAYS #2: CHAINMAIL (CHA)

"EXODUS" (CHA STORY, WLB)

**"SINS OF THE MOTHER" (TLOD SHORT
STORY)**

—*sections 1, 3–4*

- *2265*—[*section 2*]

**"A LITTLE MORE ACTION" (TOS SHORT
STORY, SNW IV)[158]**

{STARDATE 7981.3} FOUNDATIONS BOOK THREE
(SCE EBOOK #19)[159]

—*Chapters 2–7* (see primary entry in 2376)

2281

THE PANDORA PRINCIPLE (TOS #49)[160]

—*Chapters 2–13*

- *2274*—[*Chapter 1*]

DWELLERS IN THE CRUCIBLE (TOS #25)[161]

**"A PIECE OF THE PIE" (TOS SHORT STORY,
SNW VI)[162]**

—*letters #1–4*

- *2282*—[*letter #5*]

[153] The 2213.5 stardate given in the book is too low since it would
put the story during Kirk's first five-year mission.

[154] This story marks the end of Kirk's conjectural second five-year
mission following *Star Trek: The Motion Picture*.

[155] The year, given as 2272, has been adjusted to 2278, after
Spock has assumed command of the *Enterprise*.

[156] The main story begins five months after departure of the *Belle
Terre* mission, and continues through three additional months.

[157] Story is set six months after *New Earth #2: Belle Terre (TOS
#90)*. Chekov is transferred to the *U.S.S. Reliant*.

[158] At least ten years after "A Piece of the Action." Spock is a "former
captain" and has (temporarily) become a civilian, though
the reason is unclear.

[159] Takes place after the destruction of the *Gagarin* in *In the
Name of Honor* (2279). These chapters are numbered 19–24 in
the paperback edition.

[160] Story is set just after Saavik enters the Academy.

[161] Story is set after Saavik enters the Academy.

[162] At least twelve years after "A Piece of the Action" (TOS).

2282

"A Piece of the Pie" (TOS short story, SNW VI)

—*letter #5* (see primary entry in 2281)

"Just another Little Training Cruise" (TOS short story, EL)[163]

2284

Pathways (VGR hardcover)

—*Chapter 14§1* (see primary entry in 2374)

The Captain's Daughter (TOS #76)

—*Chapters 18–19* (see primary entry in 2294)

Future Imperfect (TOS, The Janus Gate #2)[164]

—*Chapters 1§1; 2§2; 3§2; 5§1; 6§2; 7§1; 8§2; 9§§1,3; 10§§2–4; 11§1* (see primary entry in 2266)

{Stardate 8083.6 to 8097.4} Strangers from the Sky (TOS giant)

—*Book One: Chapters 1§7; 2§§11–12; 3§§6–12; 4§§6–16; 5§§13–24. Book Two: Chapter 11§§9–10; Epilogue*

• *2045*—[*Book One: Chapters 1§§1–6; 2§§1–10; 3§§1–5; 4§§1–5; 5§§1–12. Book Two: Chapters 3–10; 11§§1–7*]

• *2265*—[*Book Two: Chapters 1–2; 11§8*]

2285

Time for Yesterday (TOS #39)[165]

—*Chapters 1–4; 5§1–2; 11–13; Epilogue*

• *2683 BC*—[*Prologue; Chapters 5§3; 6–10; 14–15*]

"Infinity" (TLOD short story)[166]

"The Last Tribble" (TOS short story, SNW)

{Stardate 8130.3 to 8141.6} Star Trek II: The Wrath of Khan (ST movie novelization)[167]

To Reign in Hell: The Exile of Khan Noonien Singh (TOS hardcover)

—*Chapter 26* (see primary entry in 2287)[168]

"Prodigal Father" (TOS short story, SNW IV)[169]

{March 14} Sarek (TOS hardcover)

—*Chapter 12, second journal entry* (see primary entry in 2293)

"The Azphari Enigma" (TOS, Star Trek III Short Stories)[170]

{Stardate 8201.3} Star Trek III: The Search for Spock (ST movie novelization)

"A Vulcan, a Klingon and an Angel" (TOS, Star Trek III Short Stories)[171]

• *2267*—[*Narrated backstory*]

"Jungles of Memory" (TOS, Star Trek III Short Stories)[172]

"Countdown" (TOS short story, SNW IV)[173]

"Trek" (DS9 short story, SNW 8)

"Allegro Ouroboros in D Minor" (TLOD short story)

The Captain's Daughter (TOS #76)

—*Chapters 20–21* (see primary entry in 2294)

2286

{Stardate 8390.0} Star Trek IV: The Voyage Home (ST movie novelization)

—*Chapters 1–4, 13, Epilogue*

• *1986*—[*Chapters 5–12*]

"Scotty's Song" (TOS short story, SNW IV)[174]

---

[163] Story is set in Saavik's second year at the Academy.

[164] Time travel sections are set in an alternate future where the Federation is at war with the Gorn Hegemony.

[165] Story is set 14.5 years after *Yesterday's Son* (TOS) and one month before *Star Trek II: The Wrath of Khan.*

[166] Story is set shortly before *Star Trek II: The Wrath of Khan.*

[167] Story is set during Kirk's birthday, traditionally held by fandom to be in March. However, *The Star Trek Chronology* places *The Voyage Home* (which occurs just a few months later) in 2286.

[168] Takes place during *Star Trek II: The Wrath of Khan.*

[169] Takes place during the final battle in *Star Trek II: The Wrath of Khan.*

[170] Story is set immediately after *Star Trek II: The Wrath of Khan.*

[171] Story is set during *Star Trek III: The Search for Spock.*

[172] Ibid.

[173] Ibid.

[174] Takes place one month after *Star Trek IV: The Voyage Home.* However, the events of *Star Trek V: The Final Frontier* are implied to be just one week away, which contradicts *The Star Trek Chronology.*

2287

{Stardate 8415.9} To Reign in Hell: The Exile of Khan Noonien Singh (TOS hardcover)[175]

—*Chapters 1–2; Interlude; 27–28; Epilogue*

- 2267—[*Chapters 3–6*]
- 2267—[*Chapters 7–11*]
- 2267—[*Chapters 12–13*]
- 2268—[*Chapters 14–15*]
- 2269—[*Chapters 16–18*]
- 2274—[*Chapters 19–21*]
- 2275—[*Chapter 22*]
- 2279—[*Chapters 23–25*]
- 2285—[*Chapter 26*]

{Stardate 8454.1} Star Trek V: The Final Frontier (ST movie novelization)

- 2229—[*Prologue*]
- 2230—[*Chapter 14, Spock flashback*]
- 2254—[*Chapter 14, McCoy flashback*]

{Stardate 8461.7} In the Name of Honor (TOS #97)

—*Chapters 3–4; 5§§1–2; 6–38*

- 2267—[*Chapter 5§3*]
- 2279—[*Chapter 1–2*]

{Stardate 8475.3 to 8501.2} Probe (TOS hardcover)[176]

Pathways (VGR hardcover)

—*Chapter 14§2 (see primary entry in 2374)*

The Rift (TOS #57)

—*Chapters 8–26; Epilogue*

- 2254—[*Chapters 1–7*]

2288

Pathways (VGR hardcover)

—*Chapter 14§3 (see primary entry in 2374)*

"Legal Action" (TOS short story, SNW V)

Starfleet Academy (ST computer game novelization)[177]

Day of Honor #4: Treaty's Law (TOS)

—*Prologue, Epilogue (see primary entry in 2268)*

2290

The Captain's Table #1: War Dragons (TOS)

—*Chapters 2§2; 4; 6; 8; 10; 12; 14; 16 (see primary entry in 2293)*

2291

"JubHa' " (short story, SNW III)

{Stardate 8764.3 to 8774.8} Cacophony (ST audio)

{Stardate 9029.1 to 9029.4} Envoy (ST audio)

2292

{Stardate 9498.3} Bloodline (TOS Wildstorm graphic)

2293

{Stardate 9521.6 to 9529.1} Star Trek VI: The Undiscovered Country (ST movie novelization)

Flashback (VGR episode novelization)[178]

—*Chapters 7§2; 8–9; 11; 13§§1,3; 14§3; 16§1; 18; 20–21 (see primary entry in 2373)*

Assignment: Eternity (TOS #84)[179]

—*Prologue; Chapter 19; Epilogue (see primary entry in 2269)*

"One Last Adventure" (TOS short story, SNW VI)[180]

—*sections 2–17*

- *c. 2500—[section 1]*

---

[175] The "planetary" years on Ceti Alpha V are roughly equivalent to 1.2 Earth years.
[176] Story is set after *Star Trek V: The Final Frontier* yet just "weeks" after *Star Trek IV: The Voyage Home*. This is difficult to reconcile with the implied passage of time in *The Star Trek Chronology*.
[177] Story is set two years before Captain Hikaru Sulu takes command of the *Excelsior* in 2290.
[178] Takes place concurrently with *Star Trek VI: The Undiscovered Country.*
[179] Takes place concurrently with the end of *Star Trek VI: The Undiscovered Country.* The prologue is set in an alternate timeline.
[180] Takes place immediately after *Star Trek VI: The Undiscovered Country.* The story creates an alternate timeline.

"ALL FALL DOWN" (TOS SHORT STORY, SNW VII)[181]

BEST DESTINY (TOS HARDCOVER)[182]

—Prologue; 1; 6; 9; 16; 27; 32–36; Epilogue

• 2249—[Chapters 2–5; 7–8; 10–15; 17–26; 28–31; 37]

{STARDATE 9544.6} SAREK (TOS HARDCOVER)[183]

• June 14, 2229—[Chapter 2, Amanda's journal entry]

• September 16, 2229—[Chapter 5, first and second journal entries]

• November 12, 2230—[Chapter 5, third journal entry]

• December 7, 2237—[Chapter 6, journal entry]

• 2249—[Chapter 7§5]

• April 5, 2250—[Chapter 12, first journal entry]

• March 14, 2285—[Chapter 12, second journal entry]

MIND MELD (TOS #82)

—Chapters 1–15

• 2314—[Chapter 16]

{STARDATE 9582.1 TO 9587.2} SHADOWS ON THE SUN (TOS HARDCOVER)[184]

—Books One, Three

• 2253—[Book Two, McCoy backstory]

STAR TREK: GENERATIONS (TNG MOVIE NOVELIZATION)

—Chapter 1 (see primary entry in 2371)

THE LAST ROUNDUP (TOS HARDCOVER)

• late 2293—[Epilogue]

THE ASHES OF EDEN (ST HARDCOVER)[185]

• 2371—[Prologue; Epilogue]

• 2262—[Chapter 35, Carol Marcus flashback]

{STARDATE 9621.8 TO 9625.10} THE FEARFUL SUMMONS (TOS #74)[186]

THE CAPTAIN'S TABLE #1: WAR DRAGONS (TOS)

—Chapters 1§1; 2§1; 17§1

• 2265—[Chapters 1§2; 3; 5; 7; 9; 11; 13; 15]

• 2290—[Chapters 2§2; 4; 6; 8; 10; 12; 14; 16]

{STARDATE 9910.1} FEDERATION (TOS/TNG HARDCOVER)[187]

—Prologue; Epilogue (see primary entry in 2366)

THE LAST ROUNDUP (TOS HARDCOVER)

—Epilogue (see primary entry, above)

"THE LIGHTS IN THE SKY" (TOS SHORT STORY, SNW)[188]

{STARDATE 9715.5} STAR TREK: GENERATIONS (TNG MOVIE NOVELIZATION)[189]

—Chapters 2–5 (see primary entry in 2371)

» Kirk is believed killed when he disappears into the Nexus during the launch of the Enterprise-B (The Star Trek Chronology).

"ONE OF FORTY-SEVEN" (TNG SHORT STORY, SNW III)[190]

ENGINES OF DESTINY (ST)[191]

—CHAPTERS 1; 8–28 (SEE PRIMARY ENTRY IN 2370)

"THE FIRST LAW OF METAPHYSICS" (TOS SHORT STORY, SNW II)[192]

"OBLIGATIONS DISCHARGED" (TOS SHORT STORY, SNW VII)

2294

THE SUNDERED (TLE)

—Chapter 25 (see primary entry in 2298)

---

[181] Occurs as the Enterprise is returning to spacedock following Star Trek VI: The Undiscovered Country.

[182] The story begins very soon after Star Trek VI: The Undiscovered Country and ends with the Enterprise gaining a reprieve from retirement. This would explain why the Enterprise is still active for Sarek, Mind Meld and Shadows on the Sun.

[183] The given month of September must be ignored to allow enough time for additional stories prior to the launch of the Enterprise-B in late 2293.

[184] The story takes place three months after Star Trek VI: The Undiscovered Country and ends with the Enterprise arriving back at Earth for decommissioning.

[185] Story is set after the Enterprise-A has been decommissioned and features Kirk's retirement from Starfleet.

[186] The story has a retired Kirk and no Enterprise, but the claim that Kirk had been retired for six months must be disregarded. The spring 2294 date contradicts The Star Trek Chronology.

[187] The 2295 date in the novel has been adjusted to a time prior to Kirk's disappearance in Generations.

[188] Story is set just before the TOS-era portion of Star Trek: Generations.

[189] Some authors place the launch of the Enterprise-B in 2294 or 2295, which allows more time for stories set in this period but contradicts The Star Trek Chronology.

[190] Takes place during Star Trek: Generations.

[191] Most of this section takes place in an alternate history, in which the Enterprise failed to repel the Borg invasion of Earth in 2063.

[192] Story is set the same day as Kirk's presumed death.

The Captain's Daughter (TOS #76)

—*Chapters 1–4; 13–14; 22–32*
- 2271—[*Chapters 5–12*]
- 2278—[*Chapters 15–17*]
- 2284—[*Chapters 18–19*]
- 2285—[*Chapters 20–21*]

Engines of Destiny (ST)

—*Chapter 2 (see primary entry in 2370)*

{Stardate 9619.9 to 9622.4} Transformations (ST audio)

—*Sulu backstory (see primary entry in 2314)*

Relics (TNG episode novelization)

—*Prologue (see primary entry in 2369)*

2295

The Sundered (TLE)

—*Chapter 26 (see primary entry in 2298)*

2296

{Stardate 9814.3 to 9835.7} Vulcan's Forge (ST hardcover)[193]

—*Chapters 1–2; 4–5; 7–8; 10; 12; 14; 16; 18; 20; 22; 24–29*
- 2247—[*Chapters 3; 6; 9; 11; 13; 15; 17; 19; 21; 23*]

"Shakedown" (ST short story, EL)[194]

2297

"Guardians" (ST short story, SNW VII)

—"*49970 Years Ago*" *(see primary entry in 52267)*

2298

The Sundered (TLE)

—*Chapters 1–5; 9–11; 14–16; 21–23; 27–35*
- *May 1, 2053*—[*Chapter 6*]
- *2058*—[*Chapters 7–8*]
- *April 5, 2063*—[*Chapter 12*]
- *August 9, 2155*—[*Chapter 13*]
- *2169*—[*Chapter 18*]
- *2204*—[*Chapter 19*]
- *2265*—[*Chapter 20*]
- *2266*—[*Chapter 17*]
- *2268*—[*Chapter 24*]

- 2294—[*Chapter 25*]
- 2295—[*Chapter 26*]

Pathways (VGR hardcover)[195]

—*Chapter 14§4 (see primary entry in 2374)*

2301

"The Hero of My Own Life" (TOS short story, SNW II)[196]

2304

Pathways (VGR hardcover)

—*Chapter 14§5 (see primary entry in 2374)*

Immortal Coil (TNG)

—"*Seventy Years Ago*," *Parts One-Three (see primary entry in 2374)*

2310

"Iron and Sacrifice" (Demora Sulu short story, TFTCT)

—*sections 8; 12–13; 16–18 (see primary entry in 2317)*

2311

Serpents among the Ruins (TLE)

2314

{Stardate 11611.8 to 11618.2} Transformations (ST audio)

- 2294—[*Sulu backstory*]

Mind Meld (TOS #82)

—*Chapter 16 (see primary entry in 2293)*

2315

"Iron and Sacrifice" (Demora Sulu short story, TFTCT)

—*sections 2; 4–5; 7; 9–11; 14–15; 19–21 (see primary entry in 2317)*

2316

"Uninvited Admirals" (VGR short story, SNW IV)

—*first flashback (see primary entry in 2376)*

---

[193] The references setting the story "about a year after Kirk's disappearance" are inaccurate.
[194] Story is set after *The Capain's Daughter* (TOS #76).
[195] This is purportedly six years since Tuvok's "graduation," but we are also told that that he had pursued advanced degrees, so he may have spent up to eight years at the Academy.
[196] If we suppose Gillian Taylor was the same age as actress Catherine Hicks in *Star Trek IV: The Voyage Home*, she was thirty-five when she arrived in the twenty-third century with Kirk and crew. In this story, she is in her fifties; hence this story's placement in 2301.

2317

"Iron and Sacrifice" (Demora Sulu short story, TFTCT)

—*sections 1; 3; 6; 22*

- 2315—*[sections 2; 4–5; 7; 9–11; 14–15; 19–21]*
- 2310—*[sections 8; 12–13; 16–18]*

2319

"Solace in Bloom" (TNG short story, SNW 9)

—*section 1* (see primary entry in 2375)

2320

Burning Dreams (TOS)

—*Prologue; Chapters 10§§1, 4, 6–7; 19§10; Epilogue*

- 2228—*[Chapters 2; 3§§5–6]*
- 2229—*[Chapters 3§7; 4§§1–7]*
- 2230—*[Chapters 4§8; 5§§2–10]*
- 2231—*[Chapters 6§§6–7; 7§§1–5, 7–8, 12; 8§§1–2, 4–7]*
- 2236—*[Chapters 9; 15§§6–9]*
- 2246—*[Chapters 11–12; 13§§1–2, 4; 10§8; 12§§5–8]*
- 2254—*[Chapters 15§§10–12; 7§10; 15§13; 10§2; 15§§1–5]*
- 2256—*[Chapter 16§2]*
- 2260—*[Chapters 16§§4–11; 10§5; 16§§1,3; 17§§2–9, 11–12, 14; 18§§1–11, 13; 19§§1–6]*
- 2261—*[Chapters 17§§1, 10, 13; 18§12; 19§§7–9]*
- 2262—*[Chapter 20§1]*
- 2266—*[Chapters 20§§2–7; 21§§1–3]*
- 2267—*[Chapters 1§§1–2; 10§3; 21§§4–10; 1§§3–6; 3§§1–4; 5§1; 6§§1–5; 7§§6, 9, 11; 8§3; 13§§3, 9; 14]*

2321

"Solace in Bloom" (TNG short story, SNW 9)

—*section 3* (see primary entry in 2375)

2322

Starfleet Academy: Starfall (TNG-YA #8)[197]

2323

Starfleet Academy: Nova Command (TNG-YA #9)[198]

2324

"An Easy Fast" (Gold short story, TFTCT)

—*section 2* (see primary entry in 2373)

2326

Vendetta (TNG giant)

—*Chapter 1* (see primary entry in 2367)

2327

{Stardate 14089.9} Enter the Wolves (TOS Wildstorm graphic)

"An Easy Fast" (Gold short story, TFTCT)

—*sections 4, 6* (see primary entry in 2373)

2328

"The Human Factor" (TNG short story, SNW VI)

—*Ian Troi section* (see primary entry in 2375)

The Art of the Impossible (TLE)

—*Chapters 1–14*

- 2333—*[Chapter 15]*
- 2334—*[Chapters 16–18]*
- 2343—*[Chapters 19–26]*
- 2344—*[Chapters 27–29]*
- 2346—*[Chapters 30–40]*

2329

Vulcan's Heart (ST hardcover)

—*Chapter 1* (see primary entry in 2344)

"Uninvited Admirals" (VGR short story, SNW IV)

—*second flashback* (see primary entry in 2376)

2330

"Solace in Bloom" (TNG short story, SNW 9)

—*section 5* (see primary entry in 2375)

2332

"Hour of Fire" (ST short story, EL)[199]

---

[197] Story spans the period from the fall of 2322 to the fall of 2323.

[198] Story starts at the beginning of Picard's freshman year at Starfleet Academy.

[199] Six months after the launch of the *Enterprise*-C.

2333

"An Easy Fast" (Gold short story, TFTCT)

—sections 8, 10 (see primary entry in 2373)

The Valiant (TNG hardcover)

—Book Two

- December 30, 2069—[Book 1]
- 2070—[Book 3]

Gauntlet (SGZ #1)

Progenitor (SGZ #2)[200]

Three (SGZ #3)

The Art of the Impossible (TLE)

—Chapter 15 (see primary entry in 2328)

Oblivion (SGZ #4)

"Together Again, for the First Time"
(TNG short story, SNW)[201]

Enigma (SGZ #5)

Maker (SGZ #6)

2334

The Art of the Impossible (TLE)

—Chapters 16–18 (see primary entry in 2328)

2336

Well of Souls (TLE)

2338

Starfleet Academy: Mystery of the Missing Crew
(TNG-YA #6)

—Prologue (see primary entry in 2341)

2339

Pathways (VGR hardcover)

—Chapter 14§6 (see primary entry in 2374)

Death in Winter (TNG hardcover)

—"Arvada III" (see primary entry in 2379)

Wildfire Book Two (SCE eBook #24)

—Chapter 8§2 (see primary entry in 2376)

Mosaic (VGR hardcover)

—Chapter 2 (see primary entry in 2372)

2341

Wildfire Book Two (SCE eBook #24)

—Chapter 8§4 (see primary entry in 2376)

Starfleet Academy: Mystery of the
Missing Crew (TNG-YA #6)[202]

- 2338—[Prologue]

Starfleet Academy: Secret of the
Lizard People (TNG-YA #7)[203]

Starfleet Academy: Deceptions
(TNG-YA #14)[204]

2342

Starfleet Academy: Loyalties
(TNG-YA #10)[205]

2343

Rebels: The Conquered (DS9 #24)

—Prologue (see primary entry in 2373)

Rebels: The Courageous (DS9 #25)

—Chapters 1; 6–8; 12§1 (see primary entry in 2373)

Rebels: The Liberated (DS9 #26)

—Chapters 4§3; 9§1; 12§2; 15§1 (see primary entry in 2373)

"The Shoulders of Giants" (ST short story, SNW V)

—"Two: Rayvis" (see primary entry in 2465)

The Art of the Impossible (TLE)

—Chapters 19–26 (see primary entry in 2328)

2344

"An Easy Fast" (Gold short story, TFTCT)

—sections 12, 14 (see primary entry in 2373)

{Stardate 21012.1-21203.6}
Vulcan's Heart (ST hardcover)

—Chapters 2–38

- 2329—[Chapter 1]

"The Fourth Toast" (TNG short story, SNW III)[206]

—sections 2; 4–5; 10 (see primary entry in 2368)

---

[202] Story is set in the Earth year 2341, when Data entered Starfleet Academy.

[203] Data has been a cadet at Starfleet Academy for three weeks at the beginning of this story.

[204] Data has been a cadet at Starfleet Academy for three months at the beginning of this story.

[205] Story is set during Beverly (née Howard) Crusher's first year at Starfleet Academy Medical School.

[206] Concurrent with the time-travel portion of "Yesterday's Enterprise" (TNG).

---

[200] The Commander Rachel Garrett in this story apparently is not the same person who at that time was Captain of the Enterprise-C.

[201] Both this story and Oblivion each tell alternate versions of Picard's first meeting with Guinan.

THE ART OF THE IMPOSSIBLE (TLE)[207]

—*Chapters 27–29* (see primary entry in 2328)

"SEDUCED" (CHAKOTAY SHORT STORY, TFTCT)

—*sections 1–10* (see primary entry in 2378)

PATHWAYS (VGR HARDCOVER)[208]

—*Chapter 2§§1–3* (see primary entry in 2374)

"SEDUCED" (CHAKOTAY SHORT STORY, TFTCT)

—*section 11* (see primary entry in 2378)

MOSAIC (VGR HARDCOVER)

—*Chapter 4* (see primary entry in 2372)

2345

{STARDATE 16175.4} REQUIEM (TNG #32)

—*Prologue* (see primary entry in 2369)

{MID-AUGUST} "ALICE, ON THE EDGE OF NIGHT" (NF SHORT STORY, NL)

—*section 6, "Then"* (see primary entry in 2363)

2346

THE ART OF THE IMPOSSIBLE (TLE)

—*Chapters 30–40* (see primary entry in 2328)

PATHWAYS (VGR HARDCOVER)

—*Chapter 2§§4–7* (see primary entry in 2374)

2347

PATHWAYS (VGR HARDCOVER)

—*Chapter 2§8* (see primary entry in 2374)

"FLASH POINT" (TNG SHORT STORY, SNW IV)

—*"Flashback," refugee camp* (see primary entry in 2367)

MOSAIC (VGR HARDCOVER)

—*Chapter 6* (see primary entry in 2372)

2348

DEATH IN WINTER (TNG HARDCOVER)

—*"San Francisco"* (see primary entry in 2379)

CAPTAIN'S PERIL (ST HARDCOVER)

—*Prologue* (see primary entry in 2378)

WILDFIRE BOOK TWO (SCE EBOOK #24)

—*Chapter 8§3* (see primary entry in 2376)

BEING HUMAN (NF #12)

—*"Then . . ."* (see primary entry in 2376)

THE CAPTAIN'S TABLE #5: ONCE BURNED (NF)[209]

—*"First Encounter"* (see primary entry in 2374)

2349

MOSAIC (VGR HARDCOVER)

—*Chapter 8* (see primary entry in 2372)

DARK ALLIES (NF #8)

—*"Twenty years earlier . . ."* (see primary entry in 2376)

DOUBLE HELIX #6: THE FIRST VIRTUE (TNG #56)

A STITCH IN TIME (DS9 #27)

—*Part One: Chapters 2; 4; 6; 8; 10; 12–13; 15–16; 18–19* (see primary entry in 2376)

{OCTOBER 18} THE RED KING (TITAN #2)

—*Chapter 4* (see primary entry in 2380)

PATHWAYS (VGR HARDCOVER)

—*Chapter 14§§7–11* (see primary entry in 2374)

2350

PATHWAYS (VGR HARDCOVER)

—*Chapters 4§1; 2§9* (see primary entry in 2374)

2351

DARK MATTERS: CLOAK AND DAGGER (VGR #19)

—*Chapters 3§1; 4§2; 15§§2, 4; Epilogue* (see primary entry in 2376)

DARK MATTERS: GHOST DANCE (VGR #20)

—*Chapters 3; 6; 9; 13; 16; Epilogue* (see primary entry in 2376)

DARK MATTERS: SHADOW OF HEAVEN (VGR #21)

—*Chapters 3; 6; 9; 12; 19§1* (see primary entry in 2376)

WILDFIRE BOOK TWO (SCE EBOOK #24)

—*Chapter 8§6* (see primary entry in 2376)

2352

A STITCH IN TIME (DS9 #27)

—*Part One: Chapters 21; 23. Part Two: Chapters 2; 4; 6; 8* (see primary entry in 2376)

"loDnI'pu' vavpu' je" (KLAG SHORT STORY, TFTCT)[210]

—*first story, third story* (see primary entry in 2376)

---

[207] Ibid.

[208] Chakotay's age is fifteen. His birthyear was established to be 2329 in "Endgame" (VGR).

[209] Spans about a year.

[210] The third story chronicles Klag's life, up to the time of the primary entry.

PATHWAYS (VGR HARDCOVER)

—*Chapter 10§1* (see primary entry in 2374)

SURVIVORS (TNG #4)

—*Chapter 1* (see primary entry in 2364)

"REFLECTIONS" (TLOD SHORT STORY)

—*section 2* (see primary entry in 2372)

2353

DAY OF HONOR (VGR EPISODE NOVELIZATION)[211]

—*"Then: Nineteen years ago . . ."* (see primary entry in 2374)

PATHWAYS (VGR HARDCOVER)

—*Chapters 2§10; 6§1* (see primary entry in 2374)

MOSAIC (VGR HARDCOVER)

—*Chapters 10; 12* (see primary entry in 2372)

{JUNE 17} "FINAL ENTRY" (VGR SHORT STORY, SNW V)[212]

—*first entry*

- *February 23, 2354—second entry*
- *March 5, 2356—third entry*
- *March 9, 2356—fourth entry*
- *December 27, 2366—fifth entry*
- *January 2, 2367—sixth entry*
- *January 7, 2367—seventh entry*
- *March 2, 2367—eighth entry*
- *July 15, 2368—ninth entry*
- *July 16, 2368—tenth entry*
- *July 24, 2368—eleventh entry*
- *July 29, 2368—twelfth entry*
- *June 7, 2371—thirteenth entry*
- *June 19, 2371—fourteenth entry*
- *April 9, 2373—fifteenth entry*
- *August 21, 2373—sixteenth entry*
- *May 2, 2373—seventeenth entry*
- *October 23, 2375—eighteenth entry*
- *June 6, 2374—nineteenth entry*
- *April 4, 2376—twentieth entry*
- *September 29, 2377—twenty-first entry*
- *September 30, 2377—twenty-second entry*
- *February 17, 2378—final entry*

[211] The timespan has been adjusted to twenty-one years to remain consistent with *Pathways*.

[212] The story's initial date of June 17, 2355 has been adjusted to a period one year prior to the *Raven's* disappearance in 2354.

MOSAIC (VGR HARDCOVER)

—*Chapter 14§1* (see primary entry in 2372)

"A RIBBON FOR ROSIE" (VGR SHORT STORY, SNW II)[213]

DOUBLE TIME (NF WILDSTORM GRAPHIC)

—*M'k'n'zy flashback* (see primary entry in 2374)

HOUSE OF CARDS (NF #1)

—*"Twenty years earlier: M'k'n'zy"* (see primary entry in 2373)

STARFLEET ACADEMY: LIFELINE (VGR-YA #1)[214]

STARFLEET ACADEMY: CAPTURE THE FLAG (TNG-YA #4)[215]

STARFLEET ACADEMY: THE CHANCE FACTOR (VGR-YA #2)[216]

STARFLEET ACADEMY: QUARANTINE (VGR-YA #3)[217]

STARFLEET ACADEMY: ATLANTIS STATION (TNG-YA #5)[218]

STARFLEET ACADEMY: CROSSFIRE (TNG-YA #11)[219]

DOUBLE HELIX #3: RED SECTOR (TNG #53)

—*Chapters 1–6* (see primary entry in 2369)

2354

"THE MUSIC BETWEEN THE NOTES" (TLOD SHORT STORY)

"MATURATION" (VGR SHORT STORY, SNW 9)

—*sections 1–5*

- *2366—[section 6]*

[213] Story claims Annika left Earth twenty-seven years before "Scorpion, Part II" (VGR), which would be in 2347. However, Annika was abducted by the Borg in 2354 at the age of six.

[214] Story is set as Janeway begins at Starfleet Academy in 2353, according to the "Starfleet Timeline" in this book.

[215] La Forge has been a cadet at Starfleet Academy for three weeks at the beginning of this story.

[216] Conversation in this story indicates it takes place in the same year as *Starfleet Academy: Lifeline* (VGR-YA #1).

[217] La Forge is mentioned as being a first-year cadet in this story.

[218] La Forge is a first-year cadet at Starfleet Academy in this story.

[219] La Forge and Riker are first-year cadets at Starfleet Academy in this story.

{February 23} "Final Entry" (VGR short story, SNW V)[220]

—*second entry* (see primary entry in 2353)

Starfleet Academy: The Haunted Starship (TNG-YA #13)[221]

Pathways (VGR hardcover)

—*Chapter 4§2* (see primary entry in 2374)

Martyr (NF #5)

—*"Nineteen years earlier . . ."* (see primary entry in 2374)

"A Lady of Xenex" (NF short story, NL)

{Stardate 31345.3 to 31610.7}

"Lefler's Logs" (NF short story, NL)

—*first-eighth entries*

- 2355—[*ninth entry*]
- 2356—[*tenth entry*]
- 2358—[*eleventh entry*]
- 2360—[*twelfth entry*]
- 2361—[*thirteenth entry*]
- 2363—[*fourteenth-seventeenth entries*]
- 2364—[*eighteenth entry*]

Stone and Anvil (NF #14)

—*"Then": Chapters 1–13* (see primary entry in 2376)

Starfleet Academy: Breakaway (TNG-YA #12)[222]

2355

"The Human Factor" (TNG short story, SNW VI)[223]

—*Jack Crusher section* (see primary entry in 2375)

{Stardate 32318.5} Home Fires (SCE eBook #25)

—*Chapters 4–9* (see primary entry in 2376)

{June} Deny Thy Father (TLE)

—*Part One*

- *February 2356*—[*Part Two*]
- *March 2357*—[*Part Three*]

"Darkness" (Picard short story, TFTCT)

Mosaic (VGR hardcover)

—*Chapter 14§2* (see primary entry in 2372)

{Stardate 32854.6} "Lefler's Logs" (NF short story, NL)

—*ninth entry* (see primary entry in 2354)

2356

{February} Deny Thy Father (TLE)

—*Part Two* (see primary entry in 2355)

{March 5–9} "Final Entry" (VGR short story, SNW V)[224]

—*third, fourth entries* (see primary entry in 2353)

A Stitch In Time (DS9 #27)

—*Part Two: Chapters 10; 12; 14* (see primary entry in 2376)

"Turning Point" (NF short story, NL)

{Stardate 33678.2} "Lefler's Logs" (NF short story, NL)

—*tenth entry* (see primary entry in 2354)

Pathways (VGR hardcover)[225]

—*Chapters 6§2; 10§§2–3* (see primary entry in 2374)

2357

{March} Deny Thy Father (TLE)

—*Part Three* (see primary entry in 2355)

Mosaic (VGR hardcover)

—*Chapter 16* (see primary entry in 2372)

Starfleet Academy: Worf's First Adventure (TNG-YA #1)

Starfleet Academy: Line of Fire (TNG-YA #2)

Starfleet Academy: Survival (TNG-YA #3)[226]

Survivors (TNG #4)

—*Chapter 3* (see primary entry in 2364)

Double Helix #3: Red Sector (TNG #53)

—*Chapters 7–10* (see primary entry in 2369)

[220] The year, given as 2356, has been adjusted to a time shortly after the *Raven's* disappearance.
[221] Story is set during the spring semester of La Forge's first year at Starfleet Academy.
[222] Story is set during Troi's first year at Starfleet Academy in 2354, according to the "Starfleet Timeline" in this book.
[223] Jack Crusher died one year earlier. His presence at the battle of Maxia Zeta is a hypothetical scenario created by the Traveler.

[224] The year, given as 2358, has been adjusted to a time two years after the *Raven's* disappearance.
[225] The destruction of Rinax in chapter 10 is fifteen years prior to the episode "Jetrel" (VGR), although this was later contradicted by the episode "Mortal Coil" (VGR).
[226] These three stories are set during Worf's first year at Starfleet Academy.

2358

STONE AND ANVIL (NF #14)

—*"Then": Chapters 14–20* (see primary entry in 2376)

MOSAIC (VGR HARDCOVER)[227]

—*Chapter 18* (see primary entry in 2372)

"UNINVITED ADMIRALS" (VGR SHORT STORY, SNW IV)

—*third flashback* (see primary entry in 2376)

THE BATTLE OF BETAZED (TNG)

—*Chapter 3 §§3–4* (see primary entry in 2375)

PATHWAYS (VGR HARDCOVER)

—*Chapters 6§3; 10§§4–5* (see primary entry in 2374)

{STARDATE 35948.1} "LEFLER'S LOGS" (NF SHORT STORY, NL)

—*eleventh entry* (see primary entry in 2354)

2359

MOSAIC (VGR HARDCOVER)

—*Chapter 20* (see primary entry in 2372)

SURVIVORS (TNG #4)

—*Chapter 5* (see primary entry in 2364)

IMZADI (TNG HARDCOVER)

—*Chapters 11–31* (see primary entry in 2368)

2360

CATALYST OF SORROWS (TLE)

{STARDATE 37592.4} "LEFLER'S LOGS" (NF SHORT STORY, NL)

—*twelfth entry* (see primary entry in 2354)

A STITCH IN TIME (DS9 #27)

—*Part Two: Chapter 16* (see primary entry in 2376)

2361

{STARDATE 38548.3} "LEFLER'S LOGS" (NF SHORT STORY, NL)

—*thirteenth entry* (see primary entry in 2354)

PATHWAYS (VGR HARDCOVER)

—*Chapter 8§1* (see primary entry in 2374)

"WAITING FOR G'DOH" (NF SHORT STORY, NL)

2362

{STARDATE 39022.5} "REVELATIONS" (NF SHORT STORY, NL)

DOUBLE TIME (NF WILDSTORM GRAPHIC)

—*Calhoun & Shelby flashback* (see primary entry in 2374)

PATHWAYS (VGR HARDCOVER)

—*Chapters 8§§2–4; 4§3; 6§4* (see primary entry in 2374)

2363

{JANUARY 1} PATHWAYS (VGR HARDCOVER)

—*Chapter 8§5* (see primary entry in 2374)

{MAY 24} "ALICE, ON THE EDGE OF NIGHT" (NF SHORT STORY, NL)

—*section 3, "Then: Memorial Day Weekend"* (see primary entry, below)

HOUSE OF CARDS (NF #1)

—*"Ten years earlier: Soleta"* (see primary entry in 2373)

"OUT OF THE FRYING PAN" (NF SHORT STORY, NL)

{AUGUST 27, 29} "ALICE, ON THE EDGE OF NIGHT" (NF SHORT STORY, NL)

—*sections 7, 9* (see primary entry, below)

{STARDATE 40777.4} "LEFLER'S LOGS" (NF SHORT STORY, NL)

—*fourteenth entry* (see primary entry in 2354)

{SEPTEMBER 2} "ALICE, ON THE EDGE OF NIGHT" (NF SHORT STORY, NL)

—*sections 1–2,4–5,8,10–11*

- *May 24, 2363—[section 3, "Then: Memorial Day Weekend"]*
- *mid-August 2345—[section 6, "Then"]*
- *August 27, 2363—[section 7, "Tuesday"]*
- *August 29, 2363—[section 9, "Thursday"]*
- *October 15, 2363—[section 12, "Tuesday"]*

{STARDATE 40778.4–40879.4} "LEFLER'S LOGS" (NF SHORT STORY, NL)

—*fifteenth-sixteenth entries* (see primary entry in 2354)

{OCTOBER 15} "ALICE, ON THE EDGE OF NIGHT" (NF SHORT STORY, NL)

—*section 12* (see primary entry, above)

{STARDATE 40910.6} "LEFLER'S LOGS" (NF SHORT STORY, NL)

—*seventeenth entry* (see primary entry in 2354)

---

[227] Phoebe's age (twenty-three) is incorrect for this period.

2364

{Stardate 41150.7 to 41254.7}
Encounter at Farpoint (TNG episode novelization)

- 2079—[Chapter 3]

{Stardate 41148 to 41153.7} All Good Things . . . (TNG episode novelization)[228]

—Chapters 3§3; 6§2; 7; 8§§1–3; 11§5; 15§§2–5; 16§4; 18§3; 20§6; 21§§1–2; 23§§3, 5; 24§§1, 4, 7, 10, 13 (see primary entry in 2370)

Imzadi (TNG hardcover)[229]

—Chapter 32 (see primary entry in 2368)

Q-Squared (TNG hardcover)[230]

—Track A (see primary entry in 2370)

{Stardate 41153.7} "Lefler's Logs" (NF short story, NL)

—eighteenth entry (see primary entry in 2354)

Pathways (VGR hardcover)

—Chapter 8§6 (see primary entry in 2374)

(TNG) "The Naked Now"—Stardate 41209.2 to 41209.3

{Stardate 41211 to 41260.1}
Double Helix #1: Infection (TNG #51)

(TNG) "Code of Honor"—Stardate 41235.25 to 41235.32

(TNG) "Haven"—Stardate 41294.5 to 41294.6

(TNG) "Where No One Has Gone Before"—Stardate 41263.1 to 41263.4

Ghost Ship (TNG #1)

—Chapters 2–13

- 1995—[Chapter 1]

(TNG) "The Last Outpost"—Stardate 41368.4 to 41368.5

(TNG) "Lonely Among Us"—Stardate 41249.3 to 41249.4

(TNG) "Justice"—Stardate 41255.6 to 41255.9

(TNG) "The Battle"—Stardate 41723.9

(TNG) "Hide And Q"—Stardate 41590.5 to 41591.4

The Peacekeepers (TNG #2)[231]

(TNG) "Too Short A Season"—Stardate 41309.5

" 'Q'uandry" (NF short story, NL)[232]

—section 1 (see primary entry in 2369)

(TNG) "The Big Goodbye"—Stardate 41997.7

"loDnI'pu' vavpu' je" (Klag short story, TFTCT)

—second story (see primary entry in 2376)

(TNG) "Datalore"—Stardate 41242.4 to 41292.5

(TNG) "Angel One"—Stardate 41636.9

"Flash Point" (TNG short story, SNW IV)

—"Flashthen," Garon II (see primary entry in 2367)

A Stitch In Time (DS9 #27)

—Part Two, Chapter 18 (see primary entry in 2376)

(TNG) "11001001"—Stardate 41365.9

(TNG) "Home Soil"—Stardate 41463.9 to 41484.8

(TNG) "When the Bough Breaks"—Stardate 41509.1 to 41512.4

(TNG) "Coming of Age"—Stardate 41416.2

(TNG) "Heart of Glory"—Stardate 41503.7

(TNG) "The Arsenal of Freedom"—Stardate 41798.2

Survivors (TNG #4)[233]

—Chapters 2; 4; 6–11

- 2352—[Chapter 1]
- 2357—[Chapter 3]
- 2359—[Chapter 5]
- 2364—[Chapter 12]

Pathways (VGR hardcover)[234]

—Chapter 6§5 (see primary entry in 2374)

(TNG) "Symbiosis"

The Children of Hamlin (TNG #3)[235]

(TNG) "Skin of Evil"—Stardate 41601.3 to 41602.1

Survivors (TNG #4)

—Chapter 12 (see primary entry, above)

---

[228] This "anti-time" portion of the story is an alternate past in which the Enterprise does not go to Farpoint Station.

[229] Takes place concurrently with "Encounter at Farpoint" (TNG). The stardate of 42372.5 given in the book is a mismatch with the episode.

[230] This "track" is set in an alternate timeline where Jack Crusher is the Enterprise captain.

[231] Takes place after "Hide and Q" (TNG).

[232] Takes place concurrently with the episode "Too Short a Season" (TNG).

[233] Story is set immediately after "Arsenal of Freedom" (TNG).

[234] Elsewhere in Pathways we learn that Torres and Paris spent at least one year at the Academy at the same time. Therefore, Torres must have entered the Academy no later than 2364.

[235] Set two weeks after "The Arsenal of Freedom" (TNG) and immediately before "Skin of Evil" (TNG).

{STARDATE 41800.9} THE CAPTAIN'S
    HONOR (TNG #8)[236]

(TNG) "We'll Always Have Paris"—Stardate 41697.9

(TNG) "Conspiracy"—Stardate 41775.5 to 41780.2

(TNG) "The Neutral Zone"—Stardate 41986.0

VULCAN'S SOUL #1: EXODUS (ST)[237]

—Chapter 1 (see primary entry in 2377)

2365

(TNG) "The Child"—Stardate 42073.1

STRIKE ZONE (TNG #5)

(TNG) "Where Silence Has Lease"—Stardate 42193.6
    to 42194.7

(TNG) "Elementary, Dear Data"—Stardate 42286.3

{STARDATE 42315.5} THE LEGACY OF
    ELEANOR DAIN (TNG WILDSTORM
    GRAPHIC)

(TNG) "The Outrageous Okona"—Stardate 42402.7

{STARDATE 42422.5} POWER HUNGRY
    (TNG #6)

(TNG) "The Schizoid Man"—Stardate 42437.5 to
    42507.8

PATHWAYS (VGR HARDCOVER)

—Chapter 8§§7–9 (see primary entry in 2374)

(TNG) "Loud As a Whisper"—Stardate 42477.2 to
    42479.3

PATHWAYS (VGR HARDCOVER)

—Chapter 8§§10–11 (see primary entry in 2374)

MOSAIC (VGR HARDCOVER)

—Chapter 22 (see primary entry in 2372)

PATHWAYS (VGR HARDCOVER)[238]

—Chapter 14§12 (see primary entry in 2374)

(TNG) "Unnatural Selection"—Stardate 42494.8

(TNG) "A Matter of Honor"—Stardate 42506.5

(TNG) "The Measure of a Man"—Stardate 42523.7

MANY SPLENDORS (SCE EBOOK #66)[239]

• 2376—[Epilogue]

{STARDATE 42528.6} METAMORPHOSIS
    (TNG GIANT)

(TNG) "The Dauphin"—Stardate 42568.8

MASKS (TNG #7)

(TNG) "Contagion"—Stardate 42609.1

(TNG) "The Royale"—Stardate 42625.4

(TNG) "Time Squared"—Stardate 42679.2

(TNG) "The Icarus Factor"—Stardate 42686.4

(TNG) "Pen Pals"—Stardate 42695.3 to 42741.3

"THE CAPTAIN AND THE KING"
    (EL SHORT STORY)

—Andorian story (see primary entry in 2372)

(TNG) "Q Who?"—Stardate 42761.3 to 42761.9

(TNG) "Samaritan Snare"—Stardate 42779.1 to
    42779.5

(TNG) "Up The Long Ladder"—Stardate 42823.2
    to 42827.3

(TNG) "Manhunt"—Stardate 42859.2

(TNG) "The Emissary"—Stardate 42901.3

{STARDATE 42908.6} A CALL TO
    DARKNESS (TNG #9)

(TNG) "Peak Performance"—Stardate 42923.4

(TNG) "Shades of Gray"—Stardate 42976.1

2366

DOUBLE HELIX #2: VECTORS (TNG #52)[240]

"LIFE'S WORK" (TNG SHORT STORY,
    SNW VII)

{STARDATE 43095.1} "ALL THAT
    GLISTERS" (NF SHORT STORY, NL)

A ROCK AND A HARD PLACE (TNG #10)

(TNG) "Evolution"—Stardate 43125.8

(TNG) "The Ensigns of Command"

GULLIVER'S FUGITIVES (TNG #11)

(TNG) "The Survivors"—Stardate 43142.4 to 43153.7

PATHWAYS (VGR HARDCOVER)[241]

—Chapters 4§4; 6§§6–7; 14§13 (see primary entry in
    2374)

---

[236] Story is set shortly after "Skin of Evil" (TNG).

[237] Takes place immediately after "The Neutral Zone" (TNG).

[238] Janeway meets Tuvok on the same day as Tom Paris's accident. Tuvok is an ensign here, but earlier in Catalyst of Sorrows he was a lieutenant.

[239] Begins simultaneous with "The Measure of a Man" (TNG) and continues throughout Sonya Gomez's tour on the Enterprise-D.

[240] Doctor Pulaski is leaving the Enterprise and Doctor Crusher is returning.

[241] Near the end of chapter 14, Janeway informs Tuvok that she will soon take command of the Intrepid-class U.S.S. Voyager, even though the events of "Caretaker" are still years away. One might presume that these plans were delayed substantially following the debacle at Wolf 359.

(TNG) "Who Watches the Watchers"—*Stardate 43173.5 to 43174.2*

{Stardate 43197.5} Doomsday World (TNG #12)

(TNG) "The Bonding"—*Stardate 43198.7*

(TNG) "Booby Trap"—*Stardate 43205.6*

Wildfire Book Two (SCE eBook #24)

—*Chapter 8§9 (see primary entry in 2376)*

"I Am Become Death" (TNG short story, SNW II)

—*sections 2–5 (see primary entry in 4367)*

Security (SCE eBook #54)

—*Chapters 7–8; 10 (see primary entry in 2376)*

Pathways (VGR hardcover)

—*Chapters 4§§5–6; 8§§12–14 (see primary entry in 2374)*

(TNG) "The Enemy"—*Stardate 43349.2*

(TNG) "The Price"—*Stardate 43385.6*

"Beginnings" (TNG short story, SNW VII)

"Maturation" (VGR short story, SNW 9)

—*section 6 (see primary entry in 2354)*

(TNG) "The Vengeance Factor"—*Stardate 43421.9*

{Stardate 43429.1} Exiles (TNG #14)[242]

(TNG) "The Defector"—*Stardate 43462.5 to 43465.2*

(TNG) "The Hunted"—*Stardate 43489.2*

Buying Time (SCE eBook #32)

—*Chapters 4§1; 5; 6§3 (see primary entry in 2376)*

(TNG) "The High Ground"—*Stardate 43510.7*

(TNG) "Déjà Q"—*Stardate 43539.1*

Pathways (VGR hardcover)

—*Chapter 2§11 (see primary entry in 2374)*

(TNG) "A Matter of Perspective"—*Stardate 43610.4 to 43611.6*

"Performance Appraisal" (NF short story, NL)

(TNG) "Yesterday's Enterprise"—*Stardate 43625.2*

Q-Squared (TNG hardcover)

—*Track C (see primary entry in 2370)*

Q-In-Law (TNG #18)

(TNG) "The Offspring"—*Stardate 43657.0*

Fortune's Light (TNG #15)

(TNG) "Sins of the Father"—*Stardate 43685.2 to 43689.0*

{September 16} The Eyes of the Beholders (TNG #13)[243]

(TNG) "Allegiance"—*Stardate 43714.1*

(TNG) "Captain's Holiday"—*Stardate 43745.2*

{Stardate 43747.3} Boogeymen (TNG #17)

(TNG) "Tin Man"—*Stardate 43779.3*

(TNG) "Hollow Pursuits"—*Stardate 43807.4 to 43808.2*

(TNG) "The Most Toys"—*Stardate 43872.2*

(TNG) "Sarek"—*Stardate 43917.4 to 43920.7*

{Stardates 43920.6 to 43924.1} Federation (TOS/TNG hardcover)[244]

—*Part One: Chapters 3; 6; 9; 12; 15. Part Two: Chapters 3; 6; 9; 12. Part Three: Chapters 6; 8*

- 2065—*[Part One: Chapter 1. Part Four: Chapter 1]*
- 2078—*[Part One: Chapters 4; 7; 10]*
- 2119—*[Part One: Chapter 13. Part Two: Chapter 1]*
- 2267—*[Part One: Chapters 2; 5; 8; 11; 14. Part Two: Chapters 2; 4–5; 7–8; 10–11. Part Three: Chapter 7]*
- 2272—*[Part Four: Chapter 2]*
- 2293—*[Prologue, Epilogue]*
- 2371—*[Part Four: Chapter 3]*
- $t = \infty$ —*[Part Three: Chapters 1–5]*
- New Stardate γ 2143.21.3—*[Part Four: The Artifact]*

(TNG) "Ménage à Troi"—*Stardate 43930.7*

{Stardate 43945.4} "What Went through Data's Mind 0.68 Seconds Before the Satellite Hit" (TNG short story, SNW)[245]

{Stardate 43951.6} Contamination (TNG #16)[246]

(TNG) "Transfigurations"—*Stardate 43957.2 to 43960.6*

(TNG) "The Best of Both Worlds"—*Stardate 43989.1 to 43993.5*

---

[242] Data's thoughts in chapter 11 suggest that Pulaski has left the ship only recently.

[243] Takes place twenty-six years after Geordi first received his VISOR; not twenty-seven as claimed in the text.

[244] The May calendar date was ignored in favor of the stardate.

[245] The 42945.4 stardate given in the book was adjusted to fit a timeframe shortly after "Ménage à Troi" (TNG).

[246] The 44261.6 stardate given in the book was adjusted to fit a timeframe shortly after "Ménage à Troi" (TNG).

{December 27} "Final Entry" (VGR short story, SNW V)[247]

—*fifth entry* (see primary entry in 2353)

2367

(TNG) *"The Best of Both Worlds" Part II*—Stardate 44001.4

STAR TREK: BORG (TNG INTERACTIVE MOVIE AUDIO ADAPTATION)[248]

—*Wolf 359 backstory* (see primary entry in 2377)

{Stardate 44002.3} Emissary (DS9 episode novelization)[249]

—*Chapter 1* (see primary entry in 2369)

{January 2–7} "Final Entry" (VGR short story, SNW V)[250]

—*sixth, seventh entries* (see primary entry in 2353)

"Civil Disobedience" (TNG short story, SNW)

(TNG) *"Family"*—Stardate 44012.3

(TNG) *"Brothers"*—Stardate 44085.7 to 44091.1

(TNG) *"Suddenly Human"*—Stardate 44143.7

Reunion (TNG hardcover)

(TNG) *"Remember Me"*—Stardate 44161.2 to 44162.8

{March 2} "Final Entry" (VGR short story, SNW V)[251]

—*eighth entry* (see primary entry in 2353)

(TNG) *"Legacy"*—Stardate 44215.2 to 44225.3

Spartacus (TNG #20)

(TNG) *"Reunion"*—Stardate 44246.3

"The Officers' Club" (Kira short story, TFTCT)

—*Kira's story* (see primary entry in 2376)

(TNG) *"Future Imperfect"*—Stardate 44286.5

{Stardate 44295.7} Perchance to Dream (TNG #19)[252]

"See Spot Run" (TNG short story, SNW)

(TNG) *"Final Mission"*—Stardate 44307.3 to 44307.6

(TNG) *"The Loss"*—Stardate 44356.9

"Prodigal Son" (TNG short story, SNW IV)[253]

"Flash Point" (TNG short story, SNW IV)

—*"Flashnow," Jaros II*

- 2347—[*"Flashback"*]
- 2364—[*"Flashthen"*]

(TNG) *"Data's Day"*—Stardate 44390.1

{Stardate 44410.2} Dark Mirror (TNG giant)[254]

Vendetta (TNG giant)[255]

—*Chapters 2–30*

- 2326—[*Chapter 1*]

"Of Cabbages and Kings" (TNG short story, SNW)

"The Monkey Puzzle Box" (TNG short story, SNW V)

(TNG) *"The Wounded"*—Stardate 44429.6

(TNG) *"Devil's Due"*—Stardate 44474.5

(TNG) *"Clues"*—Stardate 44502.7

(TNG) *"First Contact"*

{July 15–29} "Final Entry" (VGR short story, SNW V)

—*ninth–twelfth entries* (see primary entry in 2353)

(TNG) *"Galaxy's Child"*—Stardate 44614.6

(TNG) *"Night Terrors"*—Stardate 44631.2 to 44642.1

Chains of Command (TNG #21)

(TNG) *"Identity Crisis"*—Stardate 44664.5 to 44668.1

Pathways (VGR hardcover)

—*Chapter 4§§7–10* (see primary entry in 2374)

(TNG) *"The Nth Degree"*—Stardate 44704.2 to 44705.3

(TNG) *"Qpid"*—Stardate 44741.9

The Forgotten War (TNG #57)

(TNG) *"The Drumhead"*—Stardate 44769.2

(TNG) *"Half a Life"*—Stardate 44805.3 to 44812.6

(TNG) *"The Host"*—Stardate 44821.3 to 44824.4

{Stardate 44839.2} Imbalance (TNG #22)

---

[247] The year, given as 2367, has been adjusted to a time during "The Best of Both Worlds" (TNG).

[248] Takes place during "The Best of Both Worlds" Part II.

[249] Ibid.

[250] The year, given as 2368, has been adjusted to a time just after "The Best of Both Worlds" (TNG).

[251] The year, given as 2368, has been adjusted to a time shortly after the Borg attack on Earth.

[252] The 45195.7 stardate given in the book was adjusted to fit a timeframe between "Reunion" (TNG) and "Final Mission" (TNG).

[253] This story is concurrent with "The Loss" (TNG).

[254] Given that Keiko's last name is now "O'Brien," the 44010.2 stardate given in the book was adjusted to fit a timeframe after "Data's Day" (TNG).

[255] References to O'Brien's wedding in chapter six suggest placement soon after "Data's Day" (TNG).

"Reflections" (TLOD short story)

—*section 5 (see primary entry in 2372)*

(TNG) *"The Mind's Eye"—Stardate 44885.5 to 44896.9*

(TNG) *"In Theory"—Stardate 44923.3 to 44935.6*

(TNG) *"Redemption"—Stardate 44995.3 to 44998.3*

2368

(TNG) *"Redemption, Part II"—Stardate 45020.4 to 45025.4*

"The Fourth Toast" (TNG short story, SNW III)[256]

—*sections 1, 3, 6–9, 11*

- *2344—[sections 2, 4–5, 10]*

(TNG) *"Darmok"—Stardate 45047.2 to 45048.8*

(TNG) *"Ensign Ro"—Stardate 45076.3 to 45077.8*

{Stardate 45091.4} The Badlands (Book 1, TNG story)[257]

(TNG) *"Silicon Avatar"—Stardate 45122.3 to 45129.2*

(TNG) *"Disaster"—Stardate 45156.1*

Wildfire Book Two (SCE eBook #24)

—*Chapter 8§11 (see primary entry in 2376)*

"Oil and Water" (NF short story, NL)

"Singularity" (NF short story, NL)

(TNG) *"The Game"—Stardate 45208.2 to 45212.1*

"Dementia in D Minor" (TNG short story, SNW V)

{Stardate 45233.1 to 45245.8} Unification (TNG episodes novelization)[258]

"Last Words" (TNG short story, Amazing Stories #593)

Pathways (VGR hardcover)

—*Chapter 4§11 (see primary entry in 2374)*

(TNG) *"A Matter of Time"—Stardate 45349.1 to 45351.9*

(TNG) *"New Ground"—Stardate 45376.3*

(TNG) *"Hero Worship"—Stardate 45397.3*

(TNG) *"Violations"—Stardate 45429.3 to 45435.8*

Star Trek: Klingon (TNG/DS9 game novelization)

—*Chapters 2§§2, 4; 5§§2, 4; 6§§2, 4, 6; 7§3; 9§§3, 5, 7, 9; 10§§3, 5; 11§§3, 5, 7, 9; 13§§3, 5; 19§§2, 4 (see primary entry in 2370)*

(TNG) *"The Masterpiece Society"—Stardate 45470.1*

(TNG) *"Conundrum"—Stardate 45494.2*

"Kristin's Conundrum" (TNG short story, SNW V)[259]

"Efflorescence" (TNG short story, SNW V)

Imzadi (TNG hardcover)

—*Chapters 7–10; 33; 37–43*

- *2359—[Chapters 11–31]*
- *2364—[Chapter 32]*
- *2408—[Chapters 1–6; Epilogue; 34–36; 44]*

{Stardate 45523.6} The Last Stand (TNG #37)

(TNG) *"Power Play"—Stardate 45571.2 to 45572.1*

(TNG) *"Ethics"—Stardate 45587.3*

(TNG) *"The Outcast"—Stardate 45614.6 to 45620.4*

War Drums (TNG #23)[260]

Nightshade (TNG #24)

A Stitch in Time (DS9 #27)

—*Part Two: Chapter 20. Part Three: Chapter 1 (see primary entry in 2376)*

(TNG) *"Cause and Effect"—Stardate 45652.1*

Ship of the Line (TNG hardcover)

—*Chapters 6–7 (see primary entry in 2372)*

(TNG) *"The First Duty"—Stardate 45703.9*

(TNG) *"Cost Of Living"—Stardate 45733.6*

{September 24} "Future Shock" (TNG short story, SNW VII)[261]

—*first entry*

- *March 3, 2369—second entry*
- *March 10, 2369—third entry*
- *March 17, 2369—fourth entry*
- *March 24, 2369—fifth entry*
- *March 30, 2369—sixth entry*
- *April 6, 2369—seventh entry*
- *April 13, 2369—eighth entry*
- *April 20, 2369—ninth entry*
- *April 27, 2369—tenth entry*
- *May 3, 2369—eleventh entry*
- *May 10, 2369—twelfth entry*

---

[256] Takes place soon after "Redemption, Part II" (TNG).

[257] Story is set immediately after "Ensign Ro" (TNG).

[258] This book novelizes parts I and II of the episode, and takes place concurrently with "Dementia in D Minor."

[259] Takes place during the episode "Conundrum" (TNG).

[260] Molly is cutting her first tooth, thus we assume this occurs about six months after "Disaster" (TNG).

[261] Date adjusted from February to a time shortly after "Cause and Effect."

- *May 27, 2369—thirteenth entry*
- *June 10, 2369—fourteenth entry*
- *January 24, 2370—fifteenth entry*
- *May 7, 2370—final entry*

SINS OF COMMISSION (TNG #29)[262]

(TNG) *"The Perfect Mate"—Stardate 45761.3 to 45766.1*

(TNG) *"Imaginary Friend"—Stardate 45852.1*

(TNG) *"I, Borg"—Stardate 45854.2*

"THE SHOULDERS OF GIANTS" (ST SHORT STORY, SNW V)

— *"Three: Nyda"* (see primary entry in 2465)

{STARDATE 45873.3 TO 45873.6} THE DEVIL'S HEART (TNG HARDCOVER)

- *c. AD 200—[Chapter 13]*

(TNG) *"The Next Phase"*

THE ROMULAN PRIZE (TNG #26)

{STARDATE 45923.4} GROUNDED (TNG #25)[263]

(TNG) *"The Inner Light"—Stardate 45944.1*

"THE PROMISE" (TNG SHORT STORY, SNW IV)[264]

(TNG) *"Time's Arrow"—Stardate 45959.1 to 45965.3*

2369

(TNG) *"Time's Arrow, Part II"—Stardate 46001.3*

THE BEST AND THE BRIGHTEST (TNG)

— *"Year One," Chapters 1–3*

- *2370—["Year Two," Chapters 4–6]*
- *2371—["Year Three," Chapters 7–9]*
- *2371—["Summer," Prologue, Chapters 10–11]*
- *2371—["Year Four," Chapter 12, Epilogue]*

(TNG) *"Realm of Fear"—Stardate 46041.1 to 46043.6*

(TNG) *"Man of the People"—Stardate 46071.6 to 46075.1*

"CALCULATED RISK" (TNG SHORT STORY, SNW II)

{STARDATE 46125.3} RELICS (TNG EPISODE NOVELIZATION)

- *2294—[Prologue]*

ENGINES OF DESTINY (ST)[265]

— *Chapter 3* (see primary entry in 2370)

(TNG) *"Schisms"—Stardate 46154.2 to 46191.2*

HERE THERE BE DRAGONS (TNG #28)

{MARCH 3–10} "FUTURE SHOCK" (TNG SHORT STORY, SNW VII)[266]

— *second, third entries* (see primary entry in 2368)

(TNG) *"True Q"—Stardate 46192.3 to 46193.8*

{MARCH 17–24} "FUTURE SHOCK" (TNG SHORT STORY, SNW VII)[267]

— *fourth, fifth entries* (see primary entry in 2368)

(TNG) *"Rascals"—Stardate 46235.7 to 46236.3*

{MARCH 30 TO APRIL 6} "FUTURE SHOCK" (TNG SHORT STORY, SNW VII)[268]

— *sixth, seventh entries* (see primary entry in 2368)

(TNG) *"A Fistful of Datas"—Stardate 46271.5 to 46278.3*

"ON THE SCENT OF TROUBLE" (TNG SHORT STORY, AMAZING STORIES #593)

{APRIL 13–20} "FUTURE SHOCK" (TNG SHORT STORY, SNW VII)[269]

— *eighth, ninth entries* (see primary entry in 2368)

{STARDATE 46300.6} A FURY SCORNED (TNG #43)

(TNG) *"The Quality of Life"—Stardate 46307.2 to 46317.8*

{APRIL 27–MAY 10} "FUTURE SHOCK" (TNG SHORT STORY, SNW VII)[270]

— *tenth-twelfth entries* (see primary entry in 2368)

A STITCH IN TIME (DS9 #27)

— *Part Three: Chapters 3; 5* (see primary entry in 2376)

MILLENNIUM BOOK THREE: INFERNO (DS9)[271]

— *Chapters 9§2; 10§2; 12§1; 13§1; 14§2; 15; 17§1; 18§1; 19§2; 21§1; 22§1; 23§1; 24§1; 25; 26§1* (see primary entry in 2374)

MILLENNIUM BOOK ONE: THE FALL OF TEROK NOR (DS9)

— *Chapter 1* (see primary entry in 2374)

---

[262] Story is set over a year after "The Drumhead" (TNG), but not long after "New Ground" (TNG).

[263] The 45223.4 stardate given in the book was adjusted to fit a timeframe shortly after "The Next Phase" (TNG).

[264] Story is set within Picard's vision of life as Kamin in "The Inner Light" (TNG).

[265] Takes place concurrently with "Relics" (TNG).

[266] The year, given in the journal as 2368, was adjusted to 2369, a few months after "Cause and Effect" (TNG).

[267] Ibid.

[268] Ibid.

[269] Ibid.

[270] Ibid.

[271] The timeshifts cover the period from two weeks before to two weeks after the Cardassian withdrawal in *Book One*.

DEBTORS' PLANET (TNG #30)[272]

(TNG) *"Chain of Command, Part I"*—*Stardate 46357.4 to 46358.2*

(TNG) *"Chain of Command, Part II"*—*Stardate 46360.8*

THE CAPTAIN'S TABLE #5: ONCE BURNED (NF)[273]

—*"The Interview"* to *"The Hearing"* (see primary entry in 2374)

{STARDATE 46379.1 TO 46393.1} EMISSARY (DS9 EPISODE NOVELIZATION)

—*Chapters 2–12*

- 2367—[Chapter 1]

"HA'MARA" (DS9 SHORT STORY, P&C)[274]

"FABRICATIONS" (DS9 SHORT STORY, SNW VI)

(DS9) *"Past Prologue"*

{MAY 27} "FUTURE SHOCK" (TNG SHORT STORY, SNW VII)[275]

—*thirteenth entry* (see primary entry in 2368)

PATHWAYS (VGR HARDCOVER)

—*Chapter 2§12* (see primary entry in 2374)

{STARDATE 46401.9} GUISES OF THE MIND (TNG #27)[276]

- *Late 2369*—[Epilogue]

(DS9) *"A Man Alone"*—*Stardate 46384.0 to 46421.5*

PATHWAYS (VGR HARDCOVER)

—*Chapter 2§§13–14* (see primary entry in 2374)

(TNG) *"Ship in a Bottle"*—*Stardate 46424.1*

(DS9) *"Babel"*—*Stardate 46423.7 to 46425.8*

{JUNE 10} "FUTURE SHOCK" (TNG SHORT STORY, SNW VII)[277]

—*fourteenth entry* (see primary entry in 2368)

(TNG) *"Aquiel"*—*Stardate 46461.3*

(DS9) *"Captive Pursuit"*

THE SIEGE (DS9 #2)[278]

PATHWAYS (VGR HARDCOVER)

—*Chapters 8§15; 10§§6–8* (see primary entry in 2374)

(TNG) *"Face of the Enemy"*—*Stardate 46519.1*

(DS9) *"Q-Less"*—*Stardate 46531.2 to 46532.3*

(TNG) *"Tapestry"*

" 'Q'UANDRY" (NF SHORT STORY, NL)[279]

—*sections 2–4*

- 2364—[section 1]

(DS9) *"Dax"*—*Stardate 46910.1*

SEVEN OF NINE (VGR #16)

—*Prologue* (see primary entry in 2375)

(TNG) *"Birthright, Part I"*—*Stardate 46578.4*

(DS9) *"The Passenger"*

(TNG) *"Birthright, Part II"*—*Stardate 46579.2*

THE STAR GHOST (DS9-YA #1)

(DS9) *"Move Along Home"*

BUYING TIME (SCE EBOOK #32)

—*Chapters 6§3; 7§2* (see primary entry in 2376)

(DS9) *"The Nagus"*

(TNG) *"Starship Mine"*—*Stardate 46682.4*

THE DEATH OF PRINCES (TNG #44)[280]

(TNG) *"Lessons"*—*Stardate 46693.1 to 46697.2*

(DS9) *"Vortex"*

DOUBLE HELIX #3: RED SECTOR (TNG #53)

—*Chapters 11–25*

- 2353—[Chapters 1–6]
- 2357—[Chapters 7–10]

(TNG) *"The Chase"*—*Stardate 46731.5 to 46735.2*

BLOODLETTER (DS9 #3)[281]

(DS9) *"Battle Lines"*

(TNG) *"Frame of Mind"*—*Stardate 46778.1*

TO STORM HEAVEN (TNG #46)

---

[272] Story is set after "First Duty" (TNG).

[273] Story spans about three months. The book says this portion of the story takes place six years before the framing story, which would place it in 2368. However, we placed it in 2369 after "Chain of Command" (TNG), when Jellico was a captain, due to the fact that Jellico is an admiral in this story.

[274] This story is set a few days after the events of "Emissary," the pilot episode of *Star Trek: Deep Space Nine.*

[275] The year, given in the journal as 2368, was adjusted to 2369.

[276] The 45741.9 stardate given in the book was adjusted to fit the post "Emissary" (DS9) timeframe.

[277] The year, given in the journal as 2368, was adjusted to 2369.

[278] Takes place after the Aphasia virus outbreak in "Babel" (DS9) and about a month after "A Man Alone" (DS9). References to Molly's age (3) and the years since the O'Briens' wedding (4) are incorrect.

[279] Takes place concurrently with the episode "Tapestry." The year 2367 given in the story is an editing oversight.

[280] Story is set before "Timescape" (TNG).

[281] Story is set before the episode "Battle Lines" (DS9).

{Stardate 46722.4} Dark Passions (ST duology)[282]

(DS9) *"The Storyteller"*—Stardate 46729.1

(TNG) *"Suspicions"*—Stardate 46830.1 to 46831.2

Double Helix #5: Double or Nothing (TNG #55)

—*"Seven Years Earlier"* (see primary entry in 2375)

(DS9) *"Progress"*—Stardate 46844.3

(TNG) *"Rightful Heir"*—Stardate 46852.2

Warped (DS9 hardcover)[283]

(DS9) *"If Wishes Were Horses"*—Stardate 46853.2

Pathways (VGR hardcover)

—*Chapter 2§§15–17* (see primary entry in 2374)

{Stardate 46892.6} The Romulan Stratagem (TNG #35)

Guises of the Mind (TNG #27)

—*Epilogue* (see primary entry, above)

(TNG) *"Second Chances"*—Stardate 46915.2 to 46920.1

{Stardate 46918.6} A Rolling Stone Gathers No Nanoprobes (TNG Wildstorm graphic)

{Stardate 46921.3} Foreign Foes (TNG #31)[284]

(DS9) *"The Forsaken"*—Stardate 46925.1

Stowaways (DS9-YA #2)

(DS9) *"Dramatis Personae"*—Stardate 46922.3 to 46924.5

{Stardate 46931.2} Requiem (TNG #32)[285]

—*Chapters 1–2; 3§§2, 4; 4§2; 5§§1–2; 6§§2, 4; 7§§2, 4; 8§§2, 4–5; 9§§1–3; 10§§2–4; Epilogue*

• 2267—[*Chapters 3§§1, 3, 5; 4§§1, 3; 5§§3–4; 6§§1, 3; 7§§1, 3; 8§§1, 3, 6; 9§2; 10§§1, 3*]

• 2345—[*Prologue*]

(TNG) *"Timescape"*—Stardate 46944.2 to 46945.3

(DS9) *"Duet"*

Progress (SCE eBook #61)

—*Main story* (see primary entry in 2377)

"The Farewell Gift" (TNG short story, SNW V)

{Stardate 46982.1 to 47025.4} Descent (TNG episodes novelization)[286]

(DS9) *"In the Hands of the Prophets"*

2370

Warchild (DS9 #7)[287]

Valhalla (DS9 #10)[288]

Engines of Destiny (ST)

—*Chapters 4–7; 29*

• 2293—[*Chapter 1*]

• 2294—[*Chapter 2*]

• 2369—[*Chapter 3*]

• 2293—[*Chapters 8–28*]

Betrayal (DS9 #6)

{January 24} "Future Shock" (TNG short story, SNW VII)

—*fifteenth entry* (see primary entry in 2368)

(TNG) *"Liaisons"*

(DS9) *"The Homecoming"*

(TNG) *"Interface"*—Stardate 47215.5

Blaze of Glory (TNG #34)[289]

(DS9) *"The Circle"*

The Big Game (DS9 #4)[290]

(TNG) *"Gambit, Part I"*—Stardate 47135.2

(DS9) *"The Siege"*

(TNG) *"Gambit, Part II"*—Stardate 47160.1 to 47169.2

(DS9) *"Invasive Procedures"*—Stardate 47182.1

Prisoners of Peace (DS9-YA #3)

(TNG) *"Phantasms"*—Stardate 47225.7

---

[282] These two books take place over the course of several months in the Mirror Universe of "Mirror, Mirror" (TOS), and ends before "Crossover" (DS9).

[283] Story is set after "Battle Lines" (DS9) and before "The Homecoming" (DS9).

[284] The 47511.3 stardate given in the book was adjusted to fit a timeframe shortly after "Second Chances" (TNG).

[285] The 47821.2 stardate given in the book was adjusted to fit a late 2369 timeframe prior to the departure of Ensign Ro.

[286] This book novelizes part I of the episode, which is set in late 2369, and part II, which is set at the beginning of 2370.

[287] Story is set between the first and second seasons of *Star Trek: Deep Space Nine*.

[288] Most references in this book would place it between the first and second seasons of *Star Trek: Deep Space Nine*. A reference to the *Defiant* was accidentally added during editing, since the book was published after the *Defiant* was introduced at the beginning of the third season.

[289] Story is set before "Force of Nature" (TNG).

[290] Describes the events of "A Matter of Time" (TNG) as occurring "a few years ago." This is the final appearance of George Primmin.

PATHWAYS (VGR HARDCOVER)

—*Chapter 6§§8–10 (see primary entry in 2374)*

(DS9) *"Cardassians"*—Stardate 47177.2 to 47178.3

(TNG) *"Dark Page"*—Stardate 47254.1

(DS9) *"Melora"*—Stardate 47229.1

STAR TREK: KLINGON (TNG/DS9 GAME NOVELIZATION)[291]

- 2368—*[Chapters 2§§2, 4; 5§§2, 4; 6§§2, 4, 6; 7§3; 9§§3, 5, 7, 9; 10§§3, 5; 11§§3, 5, 7, 9; 13§§ 3, 5; 19§§ 2, 4]*

(TNG) *"Attached"*—Stardate 47304.2

POSSESSION (TNG #40)

(DS9) *"Rules of Acquisition"*

{STARDATE 47237.8} FALLEN HEROES (DS9 #5)[292]

(TNG) *"Force of Nature"*—Stardate 47310.2 to 47314.5

EMBRACE THE WOLF (TNG WILDSTORM GRAPHIC)

{STARDATE 47321.6} DYSON SPHERE (TNG #50)

(DS9) *"Necessary Evil"*—Stardate 47252.5 to 47284.1

{STARDATE 47358.1} INFILTRATOR (TNG #42)

(TNG) *"Inheritance"*—Stardate 47410.2

PATHWAYS (VGR HARDCOVER)

—*Chapter 12§1 (see primary entry in 2374)*

(DS9) *"Second Sight"*—Stardate 47329.4

INTO THE NEBULA (TNG #36)[293]

THE PET (DS9-YA #4)[294]

{STARDATE 47384.1} DEVIL IN THE SKY (DS9 #11)[295]

(TNG) *"Parallels"*—Stardate 47391.2

(DS9) *"Sanctuary"*—Stardate 47391.2

"LIFE ITSELF IS REASON ENOUGH" (TNG SHORT STORY, AMAZING STORIES #598)

(DS9) *"Rivals"*

ARCADE (DS9-YA #5)[296]

(TNG) *"The Pegasus"*—Stardate 47457.1[297]

"LOOSE ENDS" (NF SHORT STORY, NL)

(DS9) *"The Alternate"*—Stardate 47391.7

(TNG) *"Homeward"*—Stardate 47423.9 to 47427.2

Q-SQUARED (TNG HARDCOVER)[298]

—*Track B*

- 2364—*[Track A]*
- 2366—*[Track C]*
- 2265—*[Track A: Chapter 12]*

(TNG) *"Sub Rosa"*

(DS9) *"Armageddon Game"*—Stardate 47529.4

(TNG) *"Lower Decks"*—Stardate 47566.7

FIELD TRIP (DS9-YA #6)

(DS9) *"Whispers"*—Stardate 47569.4 to 47581.2

(TNG) *"Thine Own Self"*—Stardate 47611.2

BALANCE OF POWER (TNG #33)[299]

(DS9) *"Paradise"*—Stardate 47573.1

GYPSY WORLD (DS9-YA #7)[300]

(TNG) *"Masks"*—Stardate 47615.2 to 47618.4

(DS9) *"Shadowplay"*—Stardate 47603.3

{STARDATE 47616.2} DRAGON'S HONOR (TNG #38)[301]

(TNG) *"Eye of the Beholder"*—Stardate 47622.1 to 47623.2

PATHWAYS (VGR HARDCOVER)

—*Chapters 8§§16–17; 6§11; 2§18 (see primary entry in 2374)*

(DS9) *"Playing God"*

HIGHEST SCORE (DS9-YA #8)

(TNG) *"Genesis"*—Stardate 47653.2

(DS9) *"Profit and Loss"*

---

[291] Story is set one year before "Defiant" (DS9).
[292] Chapter 2 references the poker tournament from *The Big Game* (DS9 #4).
[293] Story is set after "Force of Nature" (TNG).
[294] Story is set during the first anniversary of the discovery of the Bajoran Wormhole on stardate 46379.1.
[295] An historians' note places this story in the second season of *Star Trek: Deep Space Nine*. The 46384.1 stardate given in the book was adjusted to fit the specified timeframe.
[296] Story is set three years after the Borg attack at Wolf 359 in 2367.
[297] Additionally, this is the timeframe of the non-holodeck portions of (ENT) "These are the Voyages . . ."
[298] Worf mentions he encountered a similar type of dislocation before. Hence, the story is set some time after "Parallels" (TNG).
[299] Story is set shortly after "Thine Own Self" (TNG).
[300] Story is set in the first or second season of *Star Trek: Deep Space Nine*.
[301] The 47146.2 stardate given in the book was adjusted to fit a timeframe shortly before "Eye of the Beholder" (TNG).

"WHATEVER YOU DO, DON'T READ THIS STORY" (TNG SHORT STORY, SNW III)

THE BEST AND THE BRIGHTEST (TNG)

—*"Year Two," Chapters 4–6 (see primary entry in 2369)*

(TNG) "Journey's End"—Stardate 47751.2 to 47755.3

(DS9) "Blood Oath"

"ANCIENT HISTORY" (ST SHORT STORY, SNW VI)[302]

"I AM KLINGON" (TNG SHORT STORY, SNW II)

(TNG) "Firstborn"—Stardate 47779.4

(DS9) "The Maquis, Part I"

(TNG) "Bloodlines"—Stardate 47829.1 to 47831.8

(DS9) "The Maquis, Part II"

PATHWAYS (VGR HARDCOVER)

—*Chapters 10§9; 6§12; 8§18 (see primary entry in 2374)*

CARDASSIAN IMPS (DS9-YA #9)

(TNG) "Emergence"—Stardate 47869.2

(DS9) "The Wire"

ANTIMATTER (DS9 #8)[303]

"THE NAKED TRUTH" (TNG SHORT STORY, SNW)

(TNG) "Preemptive Strike"—Stardate 47941.7 to 47943.2

ROGUE SAUCER (TNG #39)[304]

(DS9) "Crossover"—Stardate 47879.2

{STARDATE 47581.2} "DAWN" (ST SHORT STORY, SNW 8)[305]

{STARDATE 47988.1} ALL GOOD THINGS . . . (TNG EPISODE NOVELIZATION)

—*Chapters 1–2; 3§§1, 4; 4; 5§1; 8§4; 9; 10§1; 12§2; 13; 14§1; 15§6; 16§§1–3; 17§§3–4; 18§§1–2; 20§§2–4; 21§3; 23§2; 24§§2, 5, 8, 11, 14; 25§2; 26*

- *3.5 billion years ago—Chapter 20§5*
- *2079—[Chapter 11§6; 12§1; 25§1]*

• *2364—[Chapters 3§3; 6§2; 7; 8§§1–3; 11§5; 15§§2–5; 16§4; 18§3; 20§6; 21§§1–2; 23§§3, 5; 24§§1, 4, 7, 10, 13]*

• *2395—[Chapters 3§2; 5§§2–3; 6§1; 10§§2–3; 11§§1–4; 14§§2–3; 15§1; 16§5; 17§§1–2; 18§4; 19; 20§1; 21§4; 22; 23§§1, 4; 24§§3, 6, 9, 12; 15]*

(DS9) "The Collaborator"

SPACE CAMP (DS9-YA #10)

(DS9) "Tribunal"—Stardate 47944.2

"THE SECOND ARTIFACT" (THE BRAVE AND THE BOLD, DS9 STORY)

• *2370—[Second Interlude]*

(DS9) "The Jem'Hadar"

2371

"THE SECOND ARTIFACT" (THE BRAVE AND THE BOLD, DS9 STORY)

—*Second Interlude (see primary entry in 2370)*

"THE NAME OF THE CAT" (TOS SHORT STORY, SNW IV)

—*sections 2–3 (see primary entry in 2278)*

"DOCTORS THREE" (ST SHORT STORY, SNW II)[306]

{STARDATE 48022.5} INTELLIVORE (TNG #45)

{STARDATE 48212.4} THE SEARCH (DS9 EPISODES NOVELIZATION)[307]

THE BEST AND THE BRIGHTEST (TNG)

—*"Year Three," Chapters 7–9 (see primary entry in 2369)*

PATHWAYS (VGR HARDCOVER)

—*Chapter 12§§2–5 (see primary entry in 2374)*

"THE PEACEMAKERS" (TNG SHORT STORY, SNW V)

—*sections 2, 4–5, 7*

- *July 21, 1889—[section one]*
- *July 24, 1889—[section three]*
- *June 19, 1929—[section six]*

PROUD HELIOS (DS9 #9)[308]

---

[302] Over two years after "Cause and Effect" (TNG).

[303] Story is set late in the second season of *Star Trek: Deep Space Nine* when the runabout *Mekong* was in use by DS9 personnel.

[304] Story is set shortly after "Preemptive Strike" (TNG).

[305] Story is set shortly after "Crossover" (DS9). The given date of March 15, 2368 may be an error, or may be a result of the corrupted timestream.

[306] Story is set prior to *Voyager's* launch.

[307] This book novelizes parts I and II of the episode.

[308] The *Defiant* is undergoing repairs, which would be consistent with the damage inflicted during "The Search" (DS9).

DAY OF HONOR #1: ANCIENT BLOOD (TNG)[309]

(DS9) *"The House of Quark"*

"TEARS FOR ETERNITY" (TOS SHORT STORY, SNW IV)[310]

—*sections 1, 2*

- *c. 52,267*—[*final section*]

"THE THIRD ARTIFACT" (THE BRAVE AND THE BOLD, VGR STORY)

- *(after "Caretaker")*—[*Third Interlude*]

"A Q TO SWEAR BY" (TNG SHORT STORY, SNW III)[311]

- *1864*—[*"Pine Mountain"*]

DOUBLE HELIX #4: QUARANTINE (TNG #54)[312]

CROSSOVER (TNG HARDCOVER)[313]

(DS9) *"Equilibrium"*

PATHWAYS (VGR HARDCOVER)

—*Chapter 12§§6–8 (see primary entry in 2374)*

KAHLESS (TNG HARDCOVER)

—*Prologue, Chapters 1; 3; 5; 7; 9; 11; 13; 15; 17; 19; 21; 23; 25; 27; 29; 31; 33; 35; 37; Epilogue*

- *circa AD 800*—[*Chapters 2; 4; 6; 8; 10; 12; 14; 16; 18; 20; 22; 24; 26; 28; 30; 32; 34; 36*]

THE CAPTAIN'S TABLE #2: DUJONIAN'S HOARD (TNG)

—*"The Tale" (see primary entry, below)*

(DS9) *"The Abandoned"*

"FLIGHT 19" (TNG SHORT STORY, SNW IV)

HOUSE OF CARDS (NF #1)

—*"Two years earlier: Selar" (see primary entry in 2373)*

DO COMETS DREAM? (TNG)

(DS9) *"Second Skin"*

TOOTH AND CLAW (TNG #60)

{STARDATE 48501.9} PERCHANCE TO DREAM (TNG WILDSTORM GRAPHIC)

"MORNING BELLS ARE RINGING" (TNG SHORT STORY, SNW 8)

(DS9) *"Civil Defense"*

THE CAPTAIN'S TABLE #2: DUJONIAN'S HOARD (TNG)[314]

—*"Madigoor"*

- *2371*—[*"The Tale"*]

(DS9) *"Meridian"—Stardate 48423.2*

"PASSAGES OF DECEIT" (TNG SHORT STORY, SNW 8)

PATHWAYS (VGR HARDCOVER)

—*Chapter 12§§9–10 (see primary entry in 2374)*

INVASION! #2: THE SOLDIERS OF FEAR (TNG #41)

{STARDATE 48632.4 TO 48650.1} STAR TREK: GENERATIONS (TNG MOVIE NOVELIZATION)[315]

—*Chapters 6–16*

- *2293*—[*Chapters 1–5*]

THE BEST AND THE BRIGHTEST (TNG)[316]

—*"Summer," Chapter 10 (see primary entry in 2369)*

"TRIBBLE IN PARADISE" (TNG SHORT STORY, SNW VI)[317]

{STARDATE 48649.7} "REFLECTIONS" (TOS SHORT STORY, SNW)[318]

"REMEMBERING THE FUTURE" (ST SHORT STORY, SNW 9)[319]

—*section 1*

- *1930*—[*sections 2–7*]
- *2267*—[*sections 8–9*]

---

[309] A reference to Alexander as being twelve years old is inconsistent with *The Star Trek Chronology*.

[310] This story takes place over 100 years after "The Devil in the Dark" (TOS), between "Doctors Three" (*SNW II*) and *Star Trek: Generations*.

[311] Story takes place on Riker's birthday (around Stardate xx286.5) but after Deanna and Worf have begun courting. Therefore, the year was adjusted to 2371.

[312] *The Star Trek Chronology* mentions Tom Riker was on the *Gandhi* for about a year before joining the Maquis. Two statements in this novel that indicate that he was on the *Gandhi* for two years have been disregarded.

[313] Story is set during Picard's eighth year of command of the *Enterprise*-D.

[314] Picard's gray uniform on the cover is not indicative of the uniform in use in the story.

[315] There is also a Young Adult novelization available. Note that the hardcover edition gives a differing account of Kirk's death.

[316] Occurs simultaneously with *Star Trek: Generations*.

[317] Takes place during *Star Trek: Generations*.

[318] Takes place at the time of Kirk's death during *Star Trek: Generations*.

[319] Occurs during and immediately following Kirk's death in *Star Trek: Generations*.

"Rocket Man" (ST short story, SNW 9)[320]

—*section 2*

 • *2372*—[*sections 3, 5, 7, 9, 11, 1, 4, 6, 8, 10, 12–13*]

"Full Circle" (TNG short story, SNW VII)[321]

"Solemn Duty" (TNG short story, SNW VII)

The Best and the Brightest (TNG)

—*Prologue; Chapter 11* (see primary entry in 2369)

"The Change of Seasons" (TNG short story, SNW III)

(DS9) "Defiant"—*Stardate 48467.3*

The Wake (TOS Wildstorm graphic)

Triangle: Imzadi II (TNG hardcover)

—*"Then . . ."*

 • *2374*—[*"Now . . ."*]

{May 7} "Future Shock" (TNG short story, SNW VII)[322]

—*final entry* (see primary entry in 2368)

(DS9) "Fascination"

Pathways (VGR hardcover)

—*Chapter 12§11* (see primary entry in 2374)

(DS9) "Past Tense, Part I"

(DS9) "Past Tense, Part II"—*Stardate 48481.2*

{May 28} Federation (TOS/TNG hardcover)

—*Part Four: Chapter 3* (see primary entry in 2366)

The Ashes of Eden (ST hardcover)

—*Prologue; Epilogue* (see primary entry in 2293)

The Return (TOS/TNG hardcover)[323]

Avenger (TNG hardcover)

—*Prologue* (see primary entry in 2373)

Pathways (VGR hardcover)

—*Chapter 6§13* (see primary entry in 2374)

{Stardate 48305.8} The Badlands (Book 2, VGR story)[324]

{Stardate 48315.6} Caretaker (VGR episode novelization)

Pathways (VGR hardcover)[325]

—*Chapters 8§19; 12§12; 6§14* (see primary entry in 2374)

"The Third Artifact" (The Brave and the Bold, VGR story)

—*Third Interlude* (see primary entry, above)

{June 7} "Final Entry" (VGR short story, SNW V)[326]

—*thirteenth entry* (see primary entry in 2353)

"Command Code" (VGR short story, DS)

(VGR) "Parallax"—*Stardate 48439.7*

The Escape (VGR #2)

—*Chapters 1–3; 4§1; 8–11; 12§1; 13–16; 17§2; 18; 19§1; 20–22; 24*

 • *circa 307,600 BC*—[*Chapters 4§2; 5–7; 23§1*]

 • *circa 444,800,000 BC*—[*Chapters 12§2; 17§1; 19§2; 23§2*]

"Terra Tonight" (TNG short story, SNW 9)

Ragnarok (VGR #3)[327]

{June} "The Ones Left Behind" (VGR short story, SNW III)[328]

—*first entry*

 • *January, 2372*—[*second entry*]

 • *February, 2373*—[*third entry*]

 • *June, 2374*—[*fourth-fifth entries*]

 • *July, 2374*—[*sixth-seventh entries*]

(VGR) "Time And Again"

Violations (VGR #4)[329]

"Uninvited Admirals" (VGR short story, SNW IV)

—*fourth flashback* (see primary entry in 2376)

{June 19} "Final Entry" (VGR short story, SNW V)

—*fourteenth entry* (see primary entry in 2353)

(DS9) "Life Support"—*Stardate 48498.4*

---

[320] Occurs during *Star Trek: Generations* and offers an account of Kirk's resurrection differing from that in *The Return*.

[321] Takes place during *Generations*, with the last section occurring after "Solemn Duty."

[322] The month, given in the journal as November, was adjusted.

[323] Story is set a month after *Star Trek: Generations*.

[324] Story begins prior to "Caretaker" (VGR) and continues through the beginning of that episode.

[325] These sections take place during "Caretaker" (VGR).

[326] The month, given as March, has been adjusted.

[327] The author suggests this novel takes place during the first half of the first season of *Star Trek: Voyager*.

[328] The month has been adjusted from April.

[329] References in this novel and its publication date suggest a *Star Trek: Voyager* first-season timeframe.

{Stardate 48531.6} Incident at Arbuk (VGR #5)[330]

"The Orb of Opportunity" (DS9 short story, P&C)[331]

(VGR) "Phage"—Stardate 48532.4

(DS9) "Heart of Stone"—Stardate 48521.5

(VGR) "The Cloud"—Stardate 48546.2

(DS9) "Destiny"—Stardate 48543.2

(VGR) "Eye of the Needle"—Stardate 48579.4

(DS9) "Prophet Motive"

(VGR) "Ex Post Facto"

(DS9) "Visionary"

(VGR) "Emanations"—Stardate 48623.5

"Infinite Bureaucracy" (DS9 short story, SNW VII)

(VGR) "Prime Factors"—Stardate 48642.5

(VGR) "State of Flux"—Stardate 48658.2

(DS9) "Distant Voices"

"Touched" (VGR short story, SNW II)

(DS9) "Through the Looking Glass"

(VGR) "Heroes and Demons"—Stardate 48693.2 to 48710.5

(DS9) "Improbable Cause"

(VGR) "Cathexis"—Stardate 48734.2 to 48735.9

(DS9) "The Die Is Cast"

The Best and the Brightest (TNG)

—"Year Four," Chapter 12; Epilogue (see primary entry in 2369)

(VGR) "Faces"—Stardate 48784.2

(DS9) "Explorers"

(VGR) "Jetrel"—Stardate 48832.1 to 48840.5

The Laertian Gamble (DS9 #12)[332]

(DS9) "Family Business"

(VGR) "Learning Curve"—Stardate 48846.5 to 48859.3

(DS9) "Shakaar"

{Stardate 48897.1} The Murdered Sun (VGR #6)[333]

(DS9) "Facets"

"Through the Looking Glass" (NF short story, NL)

The Long Night (DS9 #14)

—Chapters 1–27; Epilogue

• 1571—[Prologue]

(DS9) "The Adversary"—Stardate 48959.1 to 48962.5

Station Rage (DS9 #13)[334]

(VGR) "Projections"—Stardate 48892.1

Objective: Bajor (DS9 #15)[335]

(VGR) "Elogium"—Stardate 48921.3

Invasion! #3: Time's Enemy (DS9 #16)[336]

Invasion! #4: The Final Fury (VGR #9)[337]

(VGR) "Twisted"

(VGR) "The 37's"—Stardate 48975.1

2372

Saratoga (DS9 #18)[338]

"Good Night, Voyager" (VGR short story, SNW)

(VGR) "Initiations"—Stardate 49005.3

Wrath of the Prophets (DS9 #20)[339]

(VGR) "Non Sequitur"—Stardate 49011

{Stardate 49011.4} The Way of the Warrior (DS9 episode novelization)

{January} "The Ones Left Behind" (VGR short story, SNW III)

—second entry (see primary entry in 2371)

Ghost of a Chance (VGR #7)

(DS9) "The Visitor"

(VGR) "Parturition"—Stardate 49068.5

Cybersong (VGR #8)

(DS9) "Hippocratic Oath"—Stardate 49066.5

---

[330] The story's stardate of 48135.6 was adjusted to a time after "Caretaker" (VGR).

[331] This story is set between the third-season episodes "Life Support" and "Heart of Stone."

[332] Takes place prior to the station's defensive upgrades in "The Way of the Warrior" (DS9), but Sisko is incorrectly addressed as "Captain."

[333] The 43897.1 stardate given in the book was adjusted to fit a Star Trek: Voyager first-season timeframe.

[334] Story is set between "The Adversary" (DS9) and "The Way of the Warrior" (DS9).

[335] Ibid.

[336] Ibid.

[337] Story is set after "Learning Curve" (VGR), roughly around the same time as Invasion! #3: Time's Enemy (DS9 #16).

[338] Story is set between the third and fourth seasons of Star Trek: Deep Space Nine.

[339] Ibid.

BLESS THE BEASTS (VGR #10)

(DS9) "Indiscretion"

THE TEMPEST (DS9 #19)[340]

(DS9) "Rejoined"—Stardate 49195.5

(VGR) "Persistence of Vision"

(DS9) "Little Green Men"

(VGR) "Tattoo"

(DS9) "Starship Down"

MOSAIC (VGR HARDCOVER)[341]

—*Chapters 1; 3; 5; 7; 9; 11; 13; 15; 17; 19; 21; 23*

- 2339—[*Chapter 2*]
- 2344—[*Chapter 4*]
- 2347—[*Chapter 6*]
- 2349—[*Chapter 8*]
- 2353—[*Chapters 10; 12*]
- 2353—[*Chapter 14§1*]
- 2355—[*Chapter 14§2*]
- 2357—[*Chapter 16*]
- 2358—[*Chapter 18*]
- 2359—[*Chapter 20*]
- 2365—[*Chapter 22*]

(VGR) "Cold Fire"—Stardate 49164.8

(DS9) "The Sword of Kahless"

(VGR) "Maneuvers"—Stardate 49208.5

{MAY} SHIP OF THE LINE (TNG HARDCOVER)[342]

—*Chapters 8–25*

- 2278—[*Chapters 1–5*]
- 2368—[*Chapters 6–7*]
- 2373—[*Chapter 26*]

"LETTING GO" (VGR SHORT STORY, DS)

—*section 1 (see primary entry in 2374)*

(VGR) "Resistance"

(DS9) "Our Man Bashir"

"BROKEN OATHS" (DS9 SHORT STORY, P&C)[343]

(DS9) "Homefront"—Stardate 49170.65

(DS9) "Paradise Lost"

"REFLECTIONS" (TLOD SHORT STORY)

—*sections 1; 3–4; 6–8*

- 2352—[*section 2*]
- 2367—[*section 5*]

TRAPPED IN TIME (DS9-YA #12)[344]

—*Chapters 1–3; 12–13*

- *June 1–3, 1944*—[*Chapters 4–11*]

THE GARDEN (VGR #11)

(VGR) "Prototype"

"LETTING GO" (VGR SHORT STORY, DS)

—*section 2 (see primary entry in 2374)*

(VGR) "Alliances"—Stardate 49337.4

(DS9) "Crossfire"

(VGR) "Threshold"—Stardate 49373.4

"ON THE ROCKS" (VGR SHORT STORY, SNW V)

DAY OF HONOR #2: ARMAGEDDON SKY (DS9)[345]

{STARDATE 49588.4} DAY OF HONOR #3: HER KLINGON SOUL (VGR)

(DS9) "Return to Grace"

(VGR) "Meld"

THE HEART OF THE WARRIOR (DS9 #17)[346]

(DS9) "The Sons of Mogh"—Stardate 49556.2

(VGR) "Dreadnought"—Stardate 49447

(VGR) "Death Wish"—Stardate 49301.2

(DS9) "Bar Association"

THE 34TH RULE (DS9 #23)[347]

---

[340] Chapter 5 sets the story shortly after Cassidy Yates moved to the station in "Indiscretion" (DS9). Molly's age six in chapter 2 is incorrect.

[341] Framing story is set during the second season of *Star Trek: Voyager*.

[342] Since the *Enterprise*-E must have been launched after the events of "The Way of the Warrior" (DS9), some of the references in this book to Klingon/Federation/Cardassian relations are problematic. We suspect that a second major Klingon invasion of Cardassia space was in the works during the events of this book. The storyline continues through September. References to *Generations* having occurred 4–5 months earlier have been disregarded.

[343] This story is set shortly after the fourth-season episode "Our Man Bashir."

[344] Story is set immediately after "Paradise Lost" (DS9). The historians' note placing this book in the first or second season of *Star Trek: Deep Space Nine* is incorrect. This story presents the first meeting between Sisko and the Temporal Investigators, Dulmer and Lucsly, even though they appear to never have met each other in "Trials and Tribble-Ations" (DS9).

[345] Story is set three months after dissolution of Khitomer accords, right before *Day of Honor #3: Her Klingon Soul* (VGR). The story is unclear as to whether the stardate of 3962 is a colloquial shortening of a current stardate, or whether it a reference to the TOS-era stardate for *Day of Honor #4: Treaty's Law* (TOS).

[346] Story is set in the fourth season of *Star Trek: Deep Space Nine*.

[347] Set just after "Bar Association" (DS9).

CHRYSALIS (VGR #12)

(DS9) "Accession"

(VGR) "Lifesigns"—Stardate 49504.3

"THE SMALLEST CHOICES" (TOS SHORT STORY, SNW 9)

(VGR) "Investigations"—Stardate 49485.2

"THE CAPTAIN AND THE KING" (EL SHORT STORY)[348]

- 2365—[*Andorian story*]

(VGR) "Deadlock"—Stardate 49548.7

(DS9) "Rules of Engagement"—Stardate 49648.0 to 49665.3

"ROCKET MAN" (ST SHORT STORY, SNW 9)[349]

—*sections 3, 5, 7, 9, 11, 1, 4, 6, 8, 10, 12–13* (see primary entry in 2371)

(VGR) "Innocence"—Stardate 49578.2

(DS9) "Hard Time"

(DS9) "Shattered Mirror"

TRIAL BY ERROR (DS9 #21)[350]

"BEST TOOLS AVAILABLE" (DS9 SHORT STORY, SNW VI)

"THE BOTTOM LINE" (DS9 SHORT STORY, SNW III)[351]

(DS9) "The Muse"

(VGR) "The Thaw"

"PROMISE MADE" (DS9 SHORT STORY, SNW VIII)

(DS9) "For the Cause"

"ADVENTURES IN JAZZ AND TIME" (TNG SHORT STORY, SNW VII)[352]

(VGR) "Tuvix"—Stardate 49655.2 to 49678.4

(VGR) "Resolutions"—Stardate 49690.1 to 49694.2

"OUT OF THE BOX, THINKING" (TNG SHORT STORY, SNW III)[353]

{STARDATE 50368.0 TO 50454.1} SECTION 31: ROGUE (TNG)[354]

- 2373—[*Epilogue, Prologue*]

(DS9) "To the Death"—Stardate 49904.2

(DS9) "The Quickening"

(DS9) "Body Parts"

(DS9) "Broken Link"—Stardate 49962.4

"LETTING GO" (VGR SHORT STORY, DS)

—sections 3–5 (see primary entry in 2374)

(VGR) "Basics, Part I"

» *The second edition of The Star Trek Chronology ends with 2372. Subsequent sequencing is based on air date.*

2373

(VGR) "Basics, Part II"—Stardate 50023.4

"WHERE I FELL BEFORE MY ENEMY" (DS9 SHORT STORY, SNW)[355]

DAY OF HONOR (VGR EPISODE NOVELIZATION)

—*"Then: One year ago . . ."* (see primary entry in 2374)

{STARDATE 50126.4} FLASHBACK (VGR EPISODE NOVELIZATION)

- 2293—[*Chapters 7§2; 8–9; 11; 13§§1, 3; 14§3; 16§1; 18; 20–21*]

THE BLACK SHORE (VGR #13)[356]

(VGR) "The Chute"—Stardate 50156.2

(VGR) "The Swarm"—Stardate 50252.3

(DS9) "Apocalypse Rising"

(VGR) "False Profits"—Stardate 50074.3 to 50074.5

"SEEING FOREVER" (TNG SHORT STORY, SNW IV)

THE KILLING SHADOWS (TNG WILDSTORM GRAPHIC MINI-SERIES)

(DS9) "The Ship"—Stardate 50049.3

[348] The author's notes suggest that Picard tells this story in the Captain's Table bar as the captain of the *Enterprise*-E though the events he describes are several years earlier aboard the *Enterprise*-D.

[349] Takes place seventy-nine years after the launch of the *Enterprise*-B or about a year after Kirk's death in *Generations*.

[350] Story is set after "Bar Association" (DS9).

[351] Story is set between "Little Green Men" (DS9) and "The Ascent" (DS9). Both this story and "Best Tools Available" tell of Nog taking the Kobayashi Maru test.

[352] Story takes place during the period of cooperation between the Federation and Cardassia, about six years prior to Wesley's return in *A Time to Be Born*.

[353] Story is set "years after" "The Nth Degree" (TNG) in late 2367, and after the launch of *Voyager* in early 2371.

[354] Story is set six months prior to *Star Trek: First Contact*.

[355] Story is set after Worf joins the DS9 crew, but before the Dominion War.

[356] 491750.0 was the original stardate for the book, but aside from having too many digits, this book takes place at least a year later than 49175.0.

{February} "The Ones Left Behind" (VGR short story,
SNW III)[357]

—*third entry* (see primary entry in 2371)

(VGR) *"Remember"—Stardate 50203.1 to 50211.4*

"Life's Lessons" (DS9 short story, SNW)

(DS9) *"Looking for par'Mach in All the Wrong Places"*

(DS9) *"Nor the Battle to the Strong"*

(DS9) *"The Assignment"*

Day of Honor: Honor Bound (DS9-YA #11)[358]

(VGR) *"Sacred Ground"—Stardate 50063.2*

Trials and Tribble-ations (DS9 episode novelization)

—*Chapters 1–2; 15*

• *2267—[Chapters 3–14]*

(VGR) *"Future's End"*

{April 9} "Final Entry" (VGR short story, SNW V)

—*fifteenth entry* (see primary entry in 2353)

"The Tribbles' Pagh" (TOS short story, SNW IX)

(DS9) *"Let He Who Is Without Sir . . ."*

(VGR) *"Future's End, Part II"—Stardate 50312.5*

"Letting Go" (VGR short story, DS)

—*section 6* (see primary entry in 2374)

"Ambassador at Large" (VGR short story, SNW)[359]

Vengeance (DS9 #22)[360]

Echoes (VGR #15)[361]

(DS9) *"Things Past"*

"Forgotten Light" (ST short story, SNW VII)

—*sections 2, 3, 5, 7, 9, 11, 13*

• *c.2000 BC—[sections 1, 4, 6, 8, 10, 12]*

(VGR) *"Warlord"—Stardate 50348.1*

"Winds of Change" (VGR short story, DS)

(DS9) *"The Ascent"*

(VGR) *"The Q and the Grey"—Stardate 50384.2*

{Stardate 50893.5} Star Trek: First Contact (TNG movie novelization)[362]

—*Chapters 1–3*

• *2063—[Chapters 4–15]*

Ship of the Line (TNG hardcover)[363]

—*Chapter 26* (see primary entry in 2372)

"Making a Difference" (NF short story, NL)[364]

{Stardate 50907.2 to 50915.5} Section 31: Rogue
(TNG)

—*Prologue; Epilogue* (see primary entry in 2372)

"Protecting Data's Friends" (TNG short story, SNW VI)[365]

"Almost . . . But Not Quite" (VGR short story, SNW II)

—*sections 2, 6*

• *1996—[sections 3–5]*

• *2063—[section 1]*

{May 2} "Final Entry" (VGR short story, SNW V)[366]

—*seventeenth entry* (see primary entry in 2353)

(VGR) *"Macrocosm"—Stardate 50425.1*

(DS9) *"Rapture"*

(DS9) *"The Darkness and the Light"—Stardate 50416.2*

(VGR) *"Fair Trade"*

{Stardate 50446.2} "A Night at Sandrine's" (VGR short story, Amazing Stories #595)[367]

(VGR) *"Alter Ego"—Stardate 50460.3 to 50471.3*

(DS9) *"The Begotten"*

The Captain's Table #3: The Mist (DS9)[368]

—*Chapters 2–20* (see primary entry in 2374)

---

[357] A reference to the Dominion War is erroneous, as the war did not start until very late in 2373.

[358] Story is set one year after *Day of Honor #2: Armageddon Sky* (DS9).

[359] Takes place about two years after "Caretaker" (VGR).

[360] Story is set between "Nor the Battle to the Strong" (DS9) and "the Ascent" (DS9).

[361] References in chapter 31 set the story shortly after "Future's End" (VGR).

[362] There is also a Young Adult novelization available.

[363] Concurrent with the Borg invasion in *Star Trek: First Contact*.

[364] Ibid.

[365] Data can turn off his emotion chip but apparently cannot yet remove it, and Worf is aboard. Therefore, the story must be set immediately after *Star Trek: First Contact*, before Worf returns to DS9.

[366] The month, given as December, has been adjusted.

[367] The 50396.2 stardate given in the story was adjusted to fit a timeframe shortly after "Fair Trade" (VGR).

[368] A reference to the Klingon invasion of Cardassia is inconsistent with the rest of the main story.

"TALENT NIGHT" (VGR SHORT STORY, DS)

(VGR) *"Coda"—Stardate 50518.6*

(DS9) *"For The Uniform"—Stardate 50485.2 to 50488.2*

(VGR) *"Blood Fever"—Stardate 50537.2 to 50541.6*

"THE SECOND STAR" (VGR SHORT STORY, SNW III)

{STARDATE 50502.4} THE BADLANDS (BOOK 2, DS9 STORY)[369]

(DS9) *"In Purgatory's Shadow"*

(VGR) *"Unity"—Stardate 50614.2 to 50622.5*

(DS9) *"By Inferno's Light"—Stardate 50564.2*

"LETTING GO" (VGR SHORT STORY, DS)

—*sections 7–10 (see primary entry in 2374)*

{AUGUST 21} "FINAL ENTRY" (VGR SHORT STORY, SNW V)

—*sixteenth entry (see primary entry in 2353)*

{STARDATE 50564.2} "GODS, FATE, AND FRACTALS" (TNG SHORT STORY, SNW II)

• *Limbo—Wesley, Dulmer, and Lucsly's discussion*

(VGR) *"The Darkling"—Stardate 50693.2*

REBELS: THE CONQUERED (DS9 #24)[370]

• *2343—[Prologue]*

REBELS: THE COURAGEOUS (DS9 #25)

• *2343—[Chapters 1; 6–8; 12§1]*

REBELS: THE LIBERATED (DS9 #26)

• *2343—[Chapters 4§3; 9§1; 12§2; 15§1]*

(DS9) *"Doctor Bashir, I Presume"*

AVENGER (TNG HARDCOVER)[371]

—*Chapters 2–45; Epilogue*

• *2246—[Chapter 1]*

• *2371—[Prologue]*

(VGR) *"Rise"*

{STARDATE 50714.2} "MONTHUGLU" (VGR SHORT STORY, SNW)

(VGR) *"Favorite Son"—Stardate 50732.4*

(DS9) *"A Simple Investigation"*

(DS9) *"Business as Usual"*

(VGR) *"Before and After"—Stardate 50973*

(DS9) *"Ties of Blood and Water"—Stardate 50712.5*

{SEPTEMBER 29} "AN EASY FAST" (GOLD SHORT STORY, TFTCT)

—*sections 1, 3, 5, 7, 9, 11, 13, 15*

• *2324—[section 2]*

• *2327—[sections 4, 6]*

• *2333—[sections 8, 10]*

• *2344—[sections 12, 14]*

(DS9) *"Ferengi Love Songs"*

(VGR) *"Real Life"—Stardate 50836.2*

(DS9) *"Soldiers of the Empire"*

". . . LOVED I NOT HONOR MORE" (DS9 SHORT STORY, P&C)[372]

"FICTION" (VGR SHORT STORY, SNW)[373]

{STARDATE 50573.2} MAROONED (VGR #14)[374]

(VGR) *"Distant Origin"*

(DS9) *"Children of Time"—Stardate 50814.2*

"I, VOYAGER" (VGR SHORT STORY, SNW)

"LETTING GO" (VGR SHORT STORY, DS)

—*section 11 (see primary entry in 2374)*

(VGR) *"Displaced"—Stardate 50912.4*

(DS9) *"Blaze of Glory"*

HOUSE OF CARDS (NF #1)

—*"Now . . ."*

• *2353—["Twenty years earlier: M'k'n'zy"]*

• *2363—["Ten years earlier: Soleta"]*

• *2371—["Two years earlier: Selar"]*

{STARDATE 50923.1} INTO THE VOID (NF #2)

{STARDATE 50926.1} THE TWO-FRONT WAR (NF #3)

{STARDATE 50927.2} END GAME (NF #4)

(VGR) *"Worst Case Scenario"—Stardate 50953.4*

(DS9) *"Empok Nor"*

(VGR) *"Scorpion"—Stardate 50984.3*

(DS9) *"In The Cards"*

"CHANGE OF HEART" (DS9 SHORT STORY, SNW II)

---

[369] Story is set "just prior to the Dominion War," specifically, just before "In Purgatory's Shadow."

[370] The historian's note placing this trilogy in the fourth season is inaccurate. It takes place after "By Inferno's Light" but before "Doctor Bashir, I Presume."

[371] Story is set two years after *The Return*.

[372] This story is set during the fifth-season episode "Soldiers of the Empire."

[373] Story is set after the Doctor gets his mobile emitter in "Future's End" (VGR) but before Seven of Nine joins the *Voyager* crew in "Scorpion, Part II" (VGR).

[374] Takes place after Kes learns of her possible future(s) in "Before and After" (VGR).

{Stardate 51145.3} The Dominion War #2: Call to Arms . . . (DS9 episodes novelization)[375]

"What Dreams May Come" (ST short story, TODW)[376]

Vulcan's Soul #1: Exodus (ST)
—Chapter 11 §2 (see primary entry in 2377)

The Dominion War #1: Behind Enemy Lines (TNG)[377]

2374

(VGR) "Scorpion, Part II"—Stardate 51003.7

The Dominion War #3: Tunnel through the Stars (TNG)[378]

{Stardate 51173.2} The Dominion War #4: . . . Sacrifice of Angels (DS9 episodes novelization)[379]

"This Drone" (VGR short story, SNW 8)[380]

(VGR) "The Gift"—Stardate 51008

"The Healing Arts" (VGR short story, SNW II)

"Witness" (VGR short story, SNW V)[381]

Day of Honor (VGR episode novelization)[382]
—"Now"
  • 2353—["Then: Nineteen years ago"]
  • 2373—["Then: One year ago"]
(VGR) "Nemesis"—Stardate 51082.4

"Night of the Vulture" (ST short story, TODW)[383]

"Three Sides to Every Story" (DS9 short story, P&C)[384]

(VGR) "Revulsion"—Stardate 51186.2

(VGR) "The Raven"

(VGR) "Scientific Method"—Stardate 51244.3

The Captain's Table #4: Fire Ship (VGR)
—Chapters 2–24 (see primary entry, below)

"The First" (TNG short story, SNW)

"Reciprocity" (TNG short story, SNW II)[385]
—sections 2–3, 5–7, 9
  • circa 4 Billion BC—[sections 1, 4, 8, 10]
(VGR) "Year of Hell"—Stardate 51268.4

{Stardate 51246.9} War Stories (SCE eBook duology: #21, #22)
—"U.S.S. Lexington" (see primary entry in 2376)

(DS9) "You Are Cordially Invited"—Stardate 51247.5

The Dominion: "Olympus Descending" (Worlds of DS9, Vol. 3)[386]
—Chapters 2; 4; 6 (see primary entry in 2376)

(VGR) "Year of Hell, Part II"—Stardate 51425.4

Planet X (TNG/X-Men)[387]

(DS9) "Resurrection"

(VGR) "Random Thoughts"—Stardate 51367.2

(DS9) "Statistical Probabilities"

(VGR) "Concerning Flight"—Stardate 51386.4

(VGR) "Mortal Coil"—Stardate 51449.2

(DS9) "The Magnificent Ferengi"

---

[375] The stardate applies to later events in the book. This novelization adapts the DS9 episodes "Call to Arms," "A Time to Stand," "Rocks and Shoals," and the first portion of "Sons and Daughters." The book concludes in early 2374.

[376] Set between the episodes "Call to Arms" and "A Time to Stand."

[377] This novel begins soon after the fall of DS9 to Cardassian control late in 2373, as described in The Dominion War #2: Call to Arms.

[378] This book ends in early 2374, several days after the end of "Sacrifice of Angels" (DS9).

[379] This novelization adapts the second portion of DS9's "Sons and Daughters," plus the episodes "Behind the Lines," "Favor the Bold" and "Sacrifice of Angels," ending shortly after "Three Sides to Every Story" (P&C). The 69923.2 stardate given in the book was adjusted to fit the Dominion War timeframe.

[380] Occurs simultaneously with the beginning of "The Gift" (VGR).

[381] Story continues through a period ending concurrently with "The Killing Game" (VGR).

[382] References to Day of Honor #3: Her Klingon Soul (VGR) occuring one year ago are inaccurate.

[383] Set approximately during the episode "Favor the Bold."

[384] This story spans the sixth-season episodes "Behind the Lines," "Favor the Bold," and "Sacrifice of Angels."

[385] The story is set sometime during the Dominion War.

[386] Set during the episode "You Are Cordially Invited . . ." (DS9).

[387] Story is set shortly after "You Are Cordially Invited . . ." (DS9).

{Stardate 51401.6} "Bedside Matters" (TNG short story, Amazing Stories #601)[388]

(DS9) "Waltz"—Stardate 51408.6 to 51413.6

Martyr (NF #5)

—"Now . . ."

- 1874—["Five hundred years earlier . . ."]
- 2354—["Nineteen years earlier . . ."]

(VGR) "Waking Moments"—Stardate 51471.3

"Who Cries for Prometheus?" (VGR short story, SNW V)

(VGR) "Message in a Bottle"—Stardate 51462

"Uninvited Admirals" (VGR short story, SNW IV)

—fifth flashback (see primary entry in 2376)

"Letting Go" (VGR short story, DS)

—sections 12–13

- 2372—[section 1]
- 2372—[section 2]
- late 2372—[sections 3–5]
- early 2373—[section 6]
- 2373—[sections 7–10]
- late 2373—[section 11]

{June} "The Ones Left Behind" (VGR short story, SNW III)[389]

—fourth, fifth entries (see primary entry in 2371)

(DS9) "Who Mourns For Morn?"

{June 6} "Final Entry" (VGR short story, SNW V)[390]

—nineteenth entry (see primary entry in 2353)

Far Beyond the Stars (DS9 episode novelization)

—Chapters 1–4; 6–7; 20; 22; 38–39

- July 1940—[Chapters 10; 13; 16–17; 24; 26; 32–35]
- October 1953—[Chapters 5; 8–9; 11–12; 14–15; 18–19; 21; 23; 27–29; 31; 36–37]
- nonlinear time—[Chapters 25; 30]

{July} "The Ones Left Behind" (VGR short story, SNW III)[391]

—sixth, seventh entries (see primary entry in 2371)

(VGR) "Hunters"—Stardate 51501.4

"The Soft Room" (TNG short story, SNW VI)

{Stardate 51505.9} Immortal Coil (TNG)

—Chapters 1–18; 20–28; Epilogue

- 2261—[Chapter 19]
- 2304—["Seventy Years Ago," Parts One–Three]

(DS9) "One Little Ship"—Stardate 51474.2

Fire on High (NF #6)

{Stardate 51604.2} The Q Continuum: Q-Space (TNG #47)[392]

- 5 billion years ago—[Chapter 11]
- 2.5 billion years ago—[Chapter 13]

The Q Continuum: Q-Zone (TNG #48)

- 1 million years ago—[Chapter 2]

The Q Continuum: Q-Strike (TNG #49)[393]

(VGR) "Prey"—Stardate 51652.3

(DS9) "Honor among Thieves"

The Captain's Table #3: The Mist (DS9)

—Chapters 1; 21

- 2373—[Chapters 2–20]

The Captain's Table #4: Fire Ship (VGR)

—Chapters 1; 25

- 2374—[Chapters 2–24]

The Captain's Table #5: Once Burned (NF)

—"Second Encounter"; "The End" §1

- 2348—["First Encounter"]
- 2369—["The Interview" to "The Hearing"]

(VGR) "Retrospect"—Stardate 51679.4

(DS9) "Change of Heart"—Stardate 51597.2

---

[388] The 52501.6 stardate given in the story was adjusted to fit a timeframe before "Message in a Bottle" (VGR). Data and Doctor Crusher's uniforms in the story's picture are not indicative of the uniforms in use in the story.

[389] The year was erroneously given as 2375.

[390] The date, given as October 2377, has been adjusted.

[391] The year was erroneously given as 2375. Story continues concurrently with "Hunters" (VGR).

[392] The given stardate of 500146.2 was changed to fit a time shortly after "Message in a Bottle" (VGR).

[393] In chapter 18, Picard reflects on the recent entry of the Romulans to the Dominion War. This is inconsistent with the fact that at the time of this trilogy Betazed has not yet fallen to the Dominion, an event which indirectly led to the Romulan entry to the war ("In the Pale Moonlight" [DS9]). The omnibus edition of this trilogy corrects both this problem and the stardate in Q-Space.

DOUBLE TIME (NF WILDSTORM GRAPHIC)[394]

—"Now . . ."

- 2353—[M'k'n'zy flashback]
- 2362—[Shelby and Calhoun flashback]

{STARDATE 51701.3} THE GORN CRISIS (TNG WILDSTORM GRAPHIC)

(VGR) "The Killing Game"

(VGR) "The Killing Game, Part II"—Stardate 51715.2

10 IS BETTER THAN 01 (SCE EBOOK #65)

(DS9) "Wrongs Darker Than Death or Night"

(DS9) "Inquisition"

SPECTRE (TNG HARDCOVER)[395]

DARK VICTORY (TNG HARDCOVER)[396]

—Part One

- 2375—[Part Two]

(VGR) "Vis à Vis"—Stardate 51762.4

"THE CEREMONY OF INNOCENCE IS DROWNED" (ST SHORT STORY, TODW)

(DS9) "In the Pale Moonlight"—Stardate 51721.3

"BLOOD SACRIFICE" (ST SHORT STORY, TODW)[397]

"THE END OF NIGHT" (VGR SHORT STORY, SNW VI)

—sections 2–7

- 2370—[first and last sections]

(VGR) "The Omega Directive"—Stardate 51871.2

HOLLOW MEN (DS9)

(DS9) "His Way"

(VGR) "Unforgettable"—Stardate 51813.4

(DS9) "The Reckoning"

"SEVENTH HEAVEN" (VGR SHORT STORY, SNW II)[398]

(VGR) "Living Witness"[399]

(DS9) "Valiant"

(VGR) "Demon"

(DS9) "Profit and Lace"

"THE DEVIL YOU KNOW" (DS9 SHORT STORY, P&C)[400]

(VGR) "One"—Stardate 51929.3 to 51932.4

"CONCURRENCE" (ST SHORT STORY, SNW 8)

PATHWAYS (VGR HARDCOVER)[401]

—Chapters 1; 3; 5; 7; 9; 11; 13; 15

- 2344 to 2370—[Chakotay's story: Chapter 2]
- 2350 to 2371—[Kim's story: Chapter 4]
- 2352 to 2371—[Torres' story: Chapter 6]
- 2361 to 2371—[Paris' story: Chapter 8]
- 2352 to 2370—[Neelix's story: Chapter 10]
- 2370 to 2371—[Kes' story: Chapter 12]
- 2284 to 2366—[Tuvok's story: Chapter 14]

(DS9) "Time's Orphan"

(VGR) "Hope and Fear"—Stardate 51978.2 to 51981.6

STRING THEORY, BOOK ONE: COHESION (VGR)

"DORIAN'S DIARY" (DS9 SHORT STORY, SNW III)[402]

(DS9) "The Sound of Her Voice"

MILLENNIUM BOOK ONE: THE FALL OF TEROK NOR (DS9)

—Chapters 2–28

- nonlinear time—[Prologue]
- 2369—[Chapter 1]
- 2400—[Chapter 29]

MILLENNIUM BOOK TWO: THE WAR OF THE PROPHETS (DS9)

- nonlinear time—[Prologue]
- 2400—[Chapters 1–29]
- Limbo—[t= ; Epilogue]

{STARDATE 51884.2} MILLENNIUM BOOK THREE: INFERNO (DS9)[403]

—Chapters 10§1; 11; 12§2; 16§1; 19§1; 20§2; 21§2; 22§2; 23§2; 24§2; 26§§2, 4; 27–29

---

[394] Story starts after the framing sequence of *The Captain's Table #5: Once Burned* (NF) and ends shortly before *Double Helix #5: Double or Nothing* (TNG #55).

[395] Story is set shortly after "Message in a Bottle" (VGR).

[396] Story is a direct sequel to *Spectre*.

[397] Takes place concurrently with "In the Pale Moonlight."

[398] Story is set some time after "The Killing Game, Part II" (VGR).

[399] Only the holographic recreations seen during the episode are set in this timeframe. The framing story is set roughly around the thirtieth century.

[400] This story is set after the events of the sixth-season episode "In the Pale Moonlight," in the days leading up to "Time's Orphan."

[401] The framing sequence for this book takes place a little less than a year after Seven of Nine joins the *Voyager* crew.

[402] The story begins forty-three days after "Valiant" (DS9) and continues for about ten days.

[403] The timeshifts cover the period from five days before to five days after the destruction of the station in *Book One*.

- *nonlinear time*—[Prologue; 26§5]
- *Limbo*—[Chapters 1–8; 9§1; 13§1; 14§1; 16§2; 17§2; 18§§2–3; 20§1; 21§3; 22§3; 23§3; 24§3; 26§3]
- *2369*—[Chapters 9§2; 10§2; 12§1; 13§2; 14§2; 15; 17§1; 18§1; 19§2; 21§1; 22§1; 23§1; 24§1; 25; 26§1]
- *2377*—[Epilogue]

STRING THEORY, BOOK TWO: FUSION (VGR)

(DS9) *"Tears of the Prophets"*

A STITCH IN TIME (DS9 #27)[404]

—*Part One: Chapters 5; 9; 11; 14; 17; 20* (see primary entry in 2376)

TRIANGLE: IMZADI II (TNG HARDCOVER)

—*"Now . . ."* (see primary entry in 2371)

"NINETY-THREE HOURS" (DS9 SHORT STORY, SNW III)[405]

"SECOND STAR TO THE RIGHT . . ." (TLOD SHORT STORY)

—*sections 1, 6* (see primary entry in 2375)

"ORPHANS" (ST SHORT STORY, SNW 9)

{Stardate 51993.8} WAR STORIES (SCE EBOOK DUOLOGY: #21, #22)

—*"U.S.S. Da Vinci"* (see primary entry in 2376)

STRING THEORY, BOOK THREE: EVOLUTION (VGR)

2375

"MIRROR EYES" (ST SHORT STORY, TODW)

THE BATTLE OF BETAZED (TNG)[406]

- *2358*—[Chapter 3(§3–4)]

"TWILIGHT'S WRATH" (ST SHORT STORY, TODW)

SPIRIT WALK #1: OLD WOUNDS (VGR)

—*Prologue* (see primary entry in 2378)

"FOUNDLINGS" (DS9 SHORT STORY, P&C)[407]

(DS9) *"Image in the Sand"*

(DS9) *"Shadows and Symbols"*—Stardate 52152.6

(DS9) *"Afterimage"*

A STITCH IN TIME (DS9 #27)[408]

—*Part Two: Chapters 1; 3; 7* (see primary entry in 2376)

(VGR) *"Night"*—Stardate 52081.2

"CLOSURE" (VGR SHORT STORY, DS)

SEVEN OF NINE (VGR #16)[409]

- *2369*—[Prologue]

"CHIAROSCURO" (DS9 SHORT STORY, P&C)[410]

(DS9) *"Take Me Out to the Holosuite"*

(VGR) *"Drone"*

(DS9) *"Chrysalis"*

(VGR) *"Extreme Risk"*

DEATH OF A NEUTRON STAR (VGR #17)

(DS9) *"Treachery, Faith, and the Great River"*

(VGR) *"In the Flesh"*—Stardate 52136.4

(DS9) *"Once More Unto the Breach"*

"UNCONVENTIONAL CURES" (VGR SHORT STORY, SNW 9)

(VGR) *"Once Upon a Time"*

BATTLE LINES (VGR #18)

(DS9) *"The Siege at AR-558"*

"REQUITAL" (ST SHORT STORY, TODW)[411]

—*sections 1,3* (see primary entry, below)

(VGR) *"Timeless"*—Stardate 52143.6

(DS9) *"Covenant"*

PLANET KILLER (VGR WILDSTORM GRAPHIC MINI-SERIES)

STAR TREK: INSURRECTION (TNG MOVIE NOVELIZATION)[412]

(VGR) *"Infinite Regress"*—Stardate 52356.2

(DS9) *"It's Only a Paper Moon"*

(VGR) *"Nothing Human"*

(DS9) *"Prodigal Daughter"*

(VGR) *"Thirty Days"*—Stardate 52179.4

(DS9) *"The Emperor's New Cloak"*

(VGR) *"Counterpoint"*

---

[404] Takes place during "Tears of the Prophets."

[405] This story retells the same events as "Second Star to the Right . . ." (TLOD short story).

[406] This story takes place about two months after "Tears of the Prophets" (DS9), a month before "Image in the Sand" (DS9), and a few months before *Star Trek: Insurrection.*

[407] This story is set during the three-month period between the sixth and seventh seasons of *Star Trek: Deep Space Nine.*

[408] Takes place during "Afterimage" (DS9).

[409] Takes place "almost a year" after "The Raven" (VGR).

[410] This story is set between the seventh-season episodes "Afterimage" and "Take Me Out to the Holosuite."

[411] Takes place concurrently with "The Siege at AR-558."

[412] There is also a Young Adult novelization available.

ECHOES OF COVENTRY (SCE EBOOK #63)[413]

—*Chapters 2–10* (see primary entry in 2377)

(DS9) *"Field of Fire"*

DARK VICTORY (TNG HARDCOVER)

—*Part Two* (see primary entry in 2374)

PRESERVER (TNG HARDCOVER)[414]

—*Prologue; Chapters 1–4*

  • *two weeks later*—[*Chapters 5–11*]

  • *six weeks later*—[*Chapters 12–18*]

  • *about seven weeks later*—[*Chapters 19–37*]

  • *about nine weeks later*—[*Chapters 38; Epilogue*]

  • *2063*—[*Chapters 39*]

  • *2400*—[*"The Ashes of Eden"*]

(VGR) *"Latent Image"*

(DS9) *"Chimera"*

(VGR) *"Bride of Chaotica!"*

"THE MONSTER HUNTERS" (VGR SHORT STORY, SNW III)[415]

"THE BEST DEFENSE" (DS9 SHORT STORY, SNW III)[416]

"THE SECRET HEART OF ZOLALUZ" (VGR SHORT STORY, DS)

(DS9) *"Badda-Bing, Badda-Bang"*

PRESERVER (TNG HARDCOVER)

—*Chapters 5–11* (see primary entry, above)

(VGR) *"Gravity"*—Stardate 52438.9

(DS9) *"Inter Arma Enim Silent Leges"*

(VGR) *"Bliss"*—Stardate 52542.3

"GIFT OF THE MOURNERS" (VGR SHORT STORY, SNW III)

(DS9) *"Penumbra"*—Stardate 52576.2

"ISABO'S SHIRT" (VGR SHORT STORY, DS)[417]

(VGR) *"Dark Frontier"*—Stardate 52619.2

"WHEN PUSH COMES TO SHOVE" (VGR SHORT STORY, AMAZING STORIES #595)

(DS9) *"'Til Death Do Us Part"*

FORGIVENESS (TNG WILDSTORM GRAPHIC)

(VGR) *"The Disease"*

(DS9) *"Strange Bedfellows"*

A STITCH IN TIME (DS9 #27)[418]

—*Part Two: Chapters 11; 15* (see primary entry in 2376)

(VGR) *"Course: Oblivion"*—Stardate 52586.3

"ELEVEN HOURS OUT" (ST SHORT STORY, TODW)

"HOME SOIL" (TNG SHORT STORY, SNW 9)

"SAFE HARBORS" (ST SHORT STORY, TODW)

(DS9) *"The Changing Face of Evil"*

"SOLACE IN BLOOM" (TNG SHORT STORY, SNW 9)

—*sections 2, 4, 6–7*

  • *2319*—[*section 1*]

  • *2321*—[*section 3*]

  • *2330*—[*section 5*]

"FIELD EXPEDIENCY" (ST SHORT STORY, TODW)

WILDFIRE BOOK TWO (SCE EBOOK #24)

—*Chapter 8§10* (see primary entry in 2376)

(VGR) *"The Fight"*

THE QUIET PLACE (NF #7)

—*"Six months earlier . . ."* (see primary entry in 2376)

(DS9) *"When It Rains . . ."*

A STITCH IN TIME (DS9 #27)[419]

—*Part Two: Chapter 19* (see primary entry in 2376)

THE FUTURE BEGINS (SCE EBOOK #62)

—*"Situational Engineering"* (see primary entry in 2376)

(VGR) *"Think Tank"*

PRESERVER (TNG HARDCOVER)

—*Chapters 12–18* (see primary entry, above)

"A SONG WELL SUNG" (ST SHORT STORY, TODW)

(DS9) *"Tacking into the Wind"*

{STARDATE 52601.6} WAR STORIES (SCE EBOOK DUOLOGY: #21, #22)[420]

—*"Starbase 92"* (see primary entry in 2376)

---

[413] Runs concurrently through "The Changing Face of Evil" (DS9) until two months after the Breen attack on Earth.

[414] Story is set sometime before the siege of Cardassia in "The Changing Face of Evil" (DS9), and immediately follows the second half of *Dark Victory* (TNG hardcover).

[415] Story is set after "Once Upon a Time" (VGR).

[416] Story is set after "It's Only a Paper Moon" (DS9) and before "What You Leave Behind" (DS9).

[417] Story continues through "Dark Frontier" (VGR).

[418] Takes place during "Strange Bedfellows."

[419] Takes place during "When It Rains . . ."

[420] Takes place during "Tacking into the Wind."

"The Human Factor" (TNG short story, SNW VI)

—*final section*

- 2328—[*Ian Troi section*]
- 2355—[*Jack Crusher section*]

"An Errant Breeze" (DS9 short story, SNW III)[421]

(VGR) *"Juggernaut"*

(DS9) *"Extreme Measures"—Stardate 52645.7*

(VGR) *"Someone to Watch over Me"—Stardate 52647*

Preserver (TNG hardcover)

—*Chapters 19–37 (see primary entry, above)*

(DS9) *"The Dogs of War"*

{Stardate 52646.1} War Stories (SCE eBook duology: #21, #22)

—*"U.S.S. Sentinel (see primary entry in 2376)*

"Face Value" (DS9 short story, P&C)[422]

(VGR) *"11:59"*

"Stone Cold Truths" (ST short story, TODW)[423]

—*section 2*

- 2525—[*sections 1,3*]

"Requital" (ST short story, TODW)[424]

- February 2375—[*sections 1,3*]

What You Leave Behind (DS9 episode novelization)

—*Chapters 1–10*

- November 2375—[*Chapters 11–15*]

{October 23} "Final Entry" (VGR short story, SNW V)[425]

—*eighteenth entry (see primary entry in 2353)*

Preserver (TNG hardcover)[426]

—*Chapter 38; Epilogue (see primary entry, above)*

(VGR) *"Relativity"—Stardate 52861.574*

What You Leave Behind (DS9 episode novelization)[427]

—*Chapters 11–15 (see primary entry, above)*

Double Helix #5: Double or Nothing (TNG #55)

- late 2369—[*"Seven Years Earlier"*]

The Left Hand of Destiny (DS9 duology)

- 2376—[*Epilogue*]

"Second Star to the Right . . ." (TLOD short story)

—*sections 2–5*

- 2374—[*sections 1, 6*]

". . . and Straight On 'til Morning" (TLOD short story)

Equinox (VGR episodes novelization)

—*Prologue (see primary entry, below)*

"Fear Itself" (DS9 short story, SNW V)

(VGR) *"Warhead"*

I, Q (TNG hardcover)[428]

Section 31: Shadow (VGR)

"Barclay Program Nine" (DS9 short story, SNW VII)

Gemworld (TNG duology: #58, #59)[429]

Equinox (VGR episodes novelization)[430]

- a month earlier—[*Prologue*]

n-Vector (DS9 Wildstorm graphic mini-series)

» *From this point onward, only one television series remains on the air. The ordering of episodes of Star Trek: Voyager will therefore revert to production sequence.*

2376

"Bluff" (TNG short story, SNW V)[431]

The Left Hand of Destiny (DS9 duology)

—*Epilogue (see primary entry in 2375)*

---

[421] This story spans from the middle of "Tacking Into the Wind" (DS9) through "What You Leave Behind" (DS9).
[422] This story is set during the seventh-season episode "The Dogs of War," the penultimate episode of *Star Trek: Deep Space Nine*.
[423] This is an apocryphal story, told by Zak Kebron to his son 150 years later.
[424] Takes place concurrently with chapters 1–11 of *What You Leave Behind*.
[425] The month, given as September, has been adjusted.
[426] Occurs simultaneously with "What You Leave Behind" (DS9).

[427] Sisko's disappearance occurs around Thanksgiving, according to *Cathedral* (DS9).
[428] Takes place after "The Q and the Grey" (VGR) but before *Voyager* has returned home.
[429] *Gemworld* #1 states Reginald Barclay is on the *Enterprise*, but "Pathfinder" (VGR), set in 2376, mentions Barclay was on Earth for almost two years.
[430] This book novelizes part I of the episode, which is set in late 2375, and part II, which is set at the beginning of 2376.
[431] Takes place ten years after "The Most Toys" (TNG).

DIPLOMATIC IMPLAUSIBILITY (TNG #61)

—*Prologue, Chapters 1–9*

- 2376—[*Epilogue*]

MANY SPLENDORS (SCE eBook #66)

—*Epilogue* (see primary entry in 2365)

MAXIMUM WARP (TNG DUOLOGY: DEAD ZONE (#62), FOREVER DARK (#63))[432]

DIPLOMATIC IMPLAUSIBILITY (TNG #61)

—*Epilogue* (see primary entry, above)

THE QUIET PLACE (NF #7)

—"*Now . . .*"

- 2375—["*Six months earlier . . .*"]

DARK ALLIES (NF #8)[433]

—"*Now . . .*"

- 2349—["*Twenty years earlier . . .*"]

(VGR) "*Survival Instinct*"—Stardate 53049.2

"BRIEF CANDLE" (VGR SHORT STORY, DS)[434]

(VGR) "*Barge of the Dead*"

EXCALIBUR [NF TRILOGY: REQUIEM (#9), RENAISSANCE (#10), RESTORATION (#11 HARDCOVER)][435]

(VGR) "*Tinker Tenor Doctor Spy*"

(VGR) "*Dragon's Teeth*"—Stardate 53167.9

"THE LITTLE CAPTAIN" (VGR SHORT STORY, SNW VII)[436]

(VGR) "*Alice*"

THE FUTURE BEGINS (SCE eBook #62)[437]

— "*Damage Control*" (see primary entry, below)

(VGR) "*Riddles*"—Stardate 53263.2

BELLY OF THE BEAST (SCE eBook #1)[438]

FATAL ERROR (SCE eBook #2)

HARD CRASH (SCE eBook #3)

(VGR) "*One Small Step*"—Stardate 53292.7

"CHOICES" (VGR SHORT STORY, SNW 9)

(VGR) "*The Voyager Conspiracy*"—Stardate 53329

NEW WORLDS, NEW CIVILIZATIONS (ST ANTHOLOGY)[439]

A STITCH IN TIME (DS9 #27)

—*Prologue; Part One: Chapters 1; 3; 7; 22. Part Two: Chapters 5; 9; 13; 17. Part Three: Chapters 2; 4; 6. Epilogue*

- 2349—[*Part One: Chapters 2; 4; 6; 8; 10; 12–13; 15–16; 18–19*]
- 2352—[*Part One: Chapters 21; 23. Part Two: Chapters 2; 4; 6; 8*]
- 2356—[*Part Two: Chapters 10; 12; 14*]
- 2360—[*Part Two: Chapter 16*]
- 2364—[*Part Two: Chapter 18*]
- 2368—[*Part Two: Chapter 20. Part Three: Chapter 1*]
- 2369—[*Part Three: Chapters 3; 5*]
- late 2374—[*Part One: Chapters 5; 9; 11; 14; 17; 20*]
- early 2375—[*Part Two: Chapters 1; 3; 7*]
- mid 2375—[*Part Two: Chapters 11; 15*]
- late 2375—[*Part Two: Chapter 19*]

(VGR) "*Pathfinder*"

"UNINVITED ADMIRALS" (VGR SHORT STORY, SNW IV)

- 2316—[*first flashback*]
- 2329—[*second flashback*]
- 2358—[*third flashback*]
- 2371—[*fourth flashback*]
- 2374—[*fifth flashback*]

{APRIL 4} "FINAL ENTRY" (VGR SHORT STORY, SNW V)[440]

—*twentieth entry* (see primary entry in 2353)

[432] Story is set less than three months since the end of the Dominion War.

[433] The backstory takes place much earlier than the stated twenty years, given Si Cwan's age.

[434] The story continues through "Barge of the Dead" (VGR).

[435] Stories span several months. The three books take place simultaneously.

[436] Takes place eight months after Naomi's first away mission in "Bliss" (VGR).

[437] Concurrent with the *Excalibur* trilogy.

[438] SCE #1–4 were collected into the printed volume *Have Tech, Will Travel (SCE Book One)*.

[439] The entire collection of reports was "published" sometime after the Bajoran celebration of Ha'mara in 2376. The *Voyager*-specific information was obtained following "Message in a Bottle" (VGR). "Ashes, Ashes" and "At Times of Peril" report events that occurred prior to the end of the Dominion War, while "Glories of the Hebitians," "A Warrior's Path" and "Footfalls of Tradition" report events that occurred just after the war's end, around the cusp of 2375/76.

[440] The date, given as January 2378, has been adjusted.

INTERPHASE (SCE eBook duology: #4, #5)[441]

WILDFIRE BOOK TWO (SCE eBook #24)[442]

—*Chapter 8§7 (see primary entry, below)*

(VGR) "Fair Haven"

"LIVING ON THE EDGE OF EXISTENCE" (DS9 short story, SNW 9)

{April} AVATAR, BOOK ONE AND TWO (DS9 duology)[443]

"GUMBO" (DS9 short story, SNW 8)

{Stardate 53267.5} RISING SON (DS9)[444]

—*Chapters 1–7; 8§1*

- *early May—[Chapter 8§2]*
- *mid June—[Chapter 8§§3–4]*
- *late June—[Chapter 8§5]*
- *early July—[Chapter 9]*
- *late July—[Chapter 10]*
- *early August—[Chapters 11–14]*
- *mid August—[Chapter 15]*
- *late August—[Chapters 16–20; Epilogue]*

COLD FUSION (SCE eBook #6)

{Stardate 53270.2 to 53291.5} INVINCIBLE (SCE eBook duology: #7, #8)[445]

(VGR) "Tsunkatse"—Stardate 53447.2

(VGR) "Blink of an Eye"

"EIGHTEEN MINUTES" (VGR short story, DS)

"I HAVE BROKEN THE PRIME DIRECTIVE" (VGR short story, SNW VII)

"URGENT MATTER" (DS9 short story, SNW VI)

SECTION 31: ABYSS (DS9)[446]

(VGR) "Virtuoso"—Stardate 53556.4

"OR THE TIGER" (VGR short story, DS)

(VGR) "Spirit Folk"

THE RIDDLED POST (SCE eBook #9)[447]

(VGR) "Memorial"

"THE ROAD TO EDOS" (NF short story, NL)

"A LITTLE GETAWAY" (NF short story, NL)

(VGR) "Collective"

{early May} RISING SON (DS9)

—*Chapter 8§2 (see primary entry, above)*

GATEWAYS #3: DOORS INTO CHAOS (TNG)

GATEWAYS #4: DEMONS OF AIR AND DARKNESS (DS9)

GATEWAYS #5: NO MAN'S LAND (VGR)

GATEWAYS #6: COLD WARS (NF)[448]

"HORN AND IVORY" (DS9 story, WLB)

—*Chapters 10–12*

- *c. 27,600 BC—[Chapters 1–9]*

"INTO THE QUEUE" (VGR story, WLB)

"DEATH AFTER LIFE" (NF story, WLB)

"THE OTHER SIDE" (TNG story, WLB)[449]

GATEWAYS EPILOGUE: HERE THERE BE MONSTERS (SCE eBook #10)

THE FUTURE BEGINS (SCE eBook #62)

—*Prologue; Interlude; Epilogue*

- *2375—["Situational Engineering"]*
- *early 2376—["Damage Control"]*

AMBUSH (SCE eBook #11)

(VGR) "Ashes to Ashes"—Stardate 53679.4

SOME ASSEMBLY REQUIRED (SCE eBook #12)

{late May} TWILIGHT (DS9, Mission: Gamma #1)

—*Part One*

- *three weeks later—[Part Two]*
- *six days after Part Two—[Parts Three, Four]*

{Stardate 53181.9} DIVIDED WE FALL (DS9/TNG Wildstorm graphic miniseries)

---

[441] SCE #5–8 were collected into the printed volume *Miracle Workers* (SCE Book Two).
[442] Takes place during the events of *Interphase* (SCE).
[443] Story is set three months after "What You Leave Behind" (DS9).
[444] Story runs parallel to DS9 stories *Section 31: Abyss*, *Gateways #4: Demons of Air and Darkness*, and the *Mission: Gamma* miniseries.
[445] *Invincible, Book One* is simultaneous with *Avatar*; and *Invincible, Book Two* is simultaneous with *Cold Fusion*.
[446] Story begins two weeks after *Avatar* (DS9 duology).

[447] SCE #9–12 were collected into the printed volume *Some Assembly Required* (SCE Book Three).
[448] *Gateways* books three through six occur simultaneously.
[449] "Horn and Ivory," "Into the Queue," "Death After Life," and "The Other Side" occur simultaneously.

NO SURRENDER (SCE eBOOK #13)[450]

THE FINAL ARTIFACT (THE BRAVE AND THE BOLD, TNG STORY)

CAVEAT EMPTOR (SCE eBOOK #14)

RISING SON (DS9)

—Chapter 8§§3–4 (see primary entry, above)

{MID-JUNE} TWILIGHT (DS9, MISSION: GAMMA #1)

—Part Two (see primary entry, above)

A GOOD DAY TO DIE (GORKON #1)

—Chapters 1–4

• nine weeks later—[Chapters 5–13]

TWILIGHT (DS9, MISSION: GAMMA #1)

—Parts Three–Four (see primary entry, above)

PAST LIFE (SCE eBOOK #15)

THE GENESIS WAVE: BOOK ONE (TNG HARDCOVER)

—Chapter 1 (see primary entry, below)

(VGR) "Child's Play"

{STARDATE 53661.9 TO 53670.1} OATHS (SCE eBOOK #16)

{LATE JUNE} RISING SON (DS9)

—Chapter 8§5 (see primary entry, above)

{STARDATE 53471.3} THIS GRAY SPIRIT (DS9, MISSION: GAMMA #2)

{EARLY JULY} RISING SON (DS9)

—Chapter 9 (see primary entry, above)

{STARDATE 53675.1–53684.7} FOUNDATIONS (SCE eBOOK TRILOGY: #17, #18, #19)[451]

—Book One: Chapters 1; 8. Book Two: Chapters 1; 9. Book Three: Chapters 1; 8

• 2264—[Book One: Chapters 2–7]

• 2267—[Book Two: Chapters 2–8]

• 2280—[Book Three: Chapters 2–7]

ENIGMA SHIP (SCE eBOOK #20)[452]

WILDFIRE BOOK TWO (SCE eBOOK #24)

—Chapter 8§5 (see primary entry, below)

{STARDATE 53675.1 TO 53678.9} WAR STORIES (SCE eBOOK DUOLOGY: #21, #22)[453]

• 2374—[Book One: "U.S.S. Lexington"]

• 2374—[Book Two: "U.S.S. Da Vinci"]

• 2375—[Book One: "Starbase 92"]

• 2375—[Book One: "U.S.S. Sentinel"]

(VGR) "Good Shepherd"—Stardate 53753.2

(VGR) "Fury"

WILDFIRE BOOK ONE (SCE eBOOK #23)

{STARDATE 53781.1} WILDFIRE BOOK TWO (SCE eBOOK #24)

• 2339—[Chapter 8§2]

• 2348—[Chapter 8§3]

• 2341—[Chapter 8§4]

• 2376—[Chapter 8§5]

• 2351—[Chapter 8§6]

• 2376—[Chapter 8§7]

• 2366—[Chapter 8§9]

• 2675—[Chapter 8§10]

• 2368—[Chapter 8§11]

{LATE JULY} RISING SON (DS9)

—Chapter 10 (see primary entry, above)

BEING HUMAN (NF #12)

—"Now . . ."

• 2348—["Then . . ."]

GODS ABOVE (NF #13)[454]

{STARDATE 53574.3 TO 53581.0} CATHEDRAL (DS9, MISSION: GAMMA #3)[455]

A GOOD DAY TO DIE (GORKON #1)

—Chapters 5–13 (see primary entry, above)

{EARLY AUGUST} RISING SON (DS9)

—Chapters 11–14 (see primary entry, above)

{STARDATE 53704.8–53709.2} HOME FIRES (SCE eBOOK #25)[456]

—Chapters 1–3, 10

• 2355—[Chapters 4–9]

---

[450] SCE #13–16 were collected into the printed volume No Surrender (SCE Book Four).

[451] SCE #17–19 were collected into the printed volume Foundations (SCE Book Five), and the chapters were renumbered to run sequentially.

[452] SCE #20–24 were collected into the printed volume Wildfire (SCE Book Six).

[453] The "current day" portions are simultaneous with Foundations and Enigma Ship.

[454] Story continues concurrently to the beginning of Stone and Anvil (NF #14).

[455] A reference that Sisko went missing 214 days earlier was disregarded in favor of the story's other claims that Sisko disappeared around Thanksgiving whereas the current date is in August.

[456] SCE #25–28 were collected into the printed volume Breakdowns (SCE Book Seven).

AGE OF UNREASON (SCE eBook #26)

BALANCE OF NATURE (SCE eBook #27)

BREAKDOWNS (SCE eBook #28)[457]

(VGR) *"Live Fast and Prosper"*—Stardate 53849.2

STONE AND ANVIL (NF #14)

—*"Now": Chapters 1–21*

- *2354*—[*"Then": Chapters 1–13*]
- *2358*—[*"Then": Chapters 14–20*]

RISING SON (DS9)

—*Chapter 15 (see primary entry, above)*

HONOR BOUND (GORKON #2)

AFTERMATH (SCE eBook #29)[458]

{MID-AUGUST} LESSER EVIL (DS9, MISSION: GAMMA #4)

{LATE AUGUST} RISING SON (DS9)

—*Chapters 16–20; Epilogue (see primary entry, above)*

{STARDATE 53798.2} ISHTAR RISING (SCE eBook duology: #30, #31)

BUYING TIME (SCE eBook #32)

- *2366*—[*Chapters 4§1; 5; 6§3*]
- *2369*—[*Chapters 6§3; 7§2*]

{SEPTEMBER} UNITY (DS9)[459]

"ALWAYS A PRICE" (DS9 SHORT STORY, SNW 8)[460]

{STARDATE 53851.3} COLLECTIVE HINDSIGHT (SCE eBook duology: #33, #34)

{STARDATE 53854.7} ELITE FORCE (VGR WILDSTORM graphic)

THE DEMON (SCE eBook duology: #35, #36)

RING AROUND THE SKY (SCE eBook #37)

ORPHANS (SCE eBook #38)

ENEMY TERRITORY (GORKON #3)

"SHADOWED ALLIES" (DS9 SHORT STORY, SNW 9)

BAJOR: "FRAGMENTS AND OMENS" (WORLDS OF DS9, VOL. 2)[461]

—*Chapters 1–2; 5; 7; 10–12; 15; 18; 21 (see primary entry, below)*

"LODNI'PU' VAVPU' JE" (KLAG SHORT STORY, TFTCT)

- *2352*—[*first story*]
- *2364*—[*second story*]
- *2352-2376*—[*third story*]

GRAND DESIGNS (SCE eBook #39)

{STARDATE 53757.6 TO 53785.4} TRILL: "UNJOINED" (WORLDS OF DS9, VOL. 2)

"THE OFFICERS' CLUB" (KIRA SHORT STORY, TFTCT)

- *2367*—[*Kira's story*]

{OCTOBER 24–25} BAJOR: "FRAGMENTS AND OMENS" (WORLDS OF DS9, VOL. 2)

—*Chapters 3–4; 6; 8–9; 13–14; 16–17; 19–20; Epilogue*

- *early October*—[*1–2; 5; 7; 10–12; 15; 18; 21*]

FAILSAFE (SCE eBook #40)

"BLACK HATS" (VGR SHORT STORY, SNW IV)

(VGR) *"Life Line"*

{STARDATE 54101.9} BITTER MEDICINE (SCE eBook #41)

SARGASSO SECTOR (SCE eBook #42)

AVALON RISING (VGR WILDSTORM graphic)

PARADISE INTERRUPTED (SCE eBook #43)

THE DOMINION: "OLYMPUS DESCENDING" (WORLDS OF DS9, VOL. 3)

—*Preamble (see primary entry, below)*

{NOVEMBER 1–10} ANDOR: "PARADIGM" (WORLDS OF DS9, VOL. 1)

{STARDATE 54200.9} WHERE TIME STANDS STILL (SCE eBook #44)

- *2270*—[*Delta Triangle backstory*]

{STARDATE 54153.6} THE ART OF THE DEAL (SCE eBook #45)

SPIN (SCE eBook #46)

---

[457] *Home Fires, Age of Unreason, Balance of Nature,* and *Breakdowns* take place simultaneously, during the weeks when the *da Vinci* is being repaired.

[458] Takes place immediately before *Mission: Gamma #4: Lesser Evil*. SCE #29–36 were collected into the printed volume *Aftermath (SCE Book Eight)*.

[459] Continues through the beginning of *Enemy Territory*.

[460] Both this story and *Unity* each tell alternate versions of Kira's reunion with Odo.

[461] Continues over the next three weeks, to the time of the primary entry.

{NOVEMBER 17–22} FERENGINAR:
"SATISFACTION IS NOT GUARANTEED"
(WORLDS OF DS9, VOL. 3)

(VGR) "Muse"—Stardate 53896 through 53918

DARK MATTERS: CLOAK AND DAGGER
(VGR #19)

—Chapters 1–2; 3§§2–4; 4§1; 5–14; 15§§1, 3, 5; 16
  • 2351—[Chapters 3§1; 4§2; 15§§2, 4; Epilogue]

DARK MATTERS: GHOST DANCE (VGR #20)

—Chapters 1–2; 4–5; 7–8; 10–12; 14–15; 17–19
  • 2351—[Chapters 3; 6; 9; 13; 16; Epilogue]

DARK MATTERS: SHADOW OF HEAVEN
(VGR #21)

—Chapters 1–2; 4–5; 7–8; 10–11; 13–18; 19§§2–5;
  Epilogue; Coda
  • 2351—[Chapters 3; 6; 9; 12; 19§1]

CREATIVE COUPLINGS (SCE eBOOK
DUOLOGY: #47, #48)

SMALL WORLD (SCE eBOOK #49)

THE GENESIS WAVE: BOOK ONE (TNG
HARDCOVER)

—Chapters 2–27
  • six months earlier—[Chapter 1]

MALEFICTORUM (SCE eBOOK #50)
  • 2376—[Epilogue]

LOST TIME (SCE eBOOK #51)

MALEFICTORUM (SCE eBOOK #50)
—Epilogue (see primary entry, above)

{EARLY DECEMBER} CARDASSIA: "THE
LOTUS FLOWER" (WORLDS OF DS9,
VOL. 1)

GENESIS FORCE (TNG HARDCOVER)
—Part One
  • about a week later—[Part Two]
  • 2377—[Part Three]

IDENTITY CRISIS (SCE eBOOK #52)

SECURITY (SCE eBOOK #54)
—Chapters 1–2 (see primary entry, below)

FABLES OF THE PRIME DIRECTIVE
(SCE eBOOK #53)[462]

SECURITY (SCE eBOOK #54)
—Chapters 3–6; 9; 11–13
  • 2376—[Chapters 1–2]
  • 2366—[Chapters 7–8; 10]

WOUNDS (SCE eBOOK DUOLOGY:
#55, #56)[463]

OUT OF THE COCOON (SCE eBOOK #57)

{DECEMBER 16–31} THE DOMINION:
"OLYMPUS DESCENDING" (WORLDS OF
DS9, VOL. 3)[464]

—Chapters 1; 3; 5; 7; Terminus
  • October 2376—[Preamble]
  • 2374—[Chapters 2; 4; 6]

(VGR) "The Haunting of Deck Twelve"

THE GENESIS WAVE: BOOK TWO (TNG
HARDCOVER)

"REDEMPTION" (NF SHORT STORY, NL)

GENESIS FORCE (TNG HARDCOVER)
—Part Two (see primary entry, above)

(VGR) "Unimatrix Zero" Part I

{DECEMBER 31 TO JANUARY 2} WARPATH
(DS9)

2377

(VGR) "Unimatrix Zero" Part II—Stardate 54014.4

THE GENESIS WAVE: BOOK THREE (TNG
HARDCOVER)[465]

{STARDATE 54002.5} EXERCISE IN
FUTILITY (VGR WILDSTORM GRAPHIC)

HONOR (SCE eBOOK #58)

GENESIS FORCE (TNG HARDCOVER)
—Part Three (see primary entry in 2376)

MILLENNIUM BOOK THREE: INFERNO (DS9)
—Epilogue (see primary entry in 2374)

{JANUARY} VULCAN'S SOUL #1:
EXODUS (ST)

—Chapters 3; 5; 8; 11§§1, 3; 14; 17; 20; 22; 24; 26
  • late 2364—[Chapter 1]
  • c. AD 380—[Chapter 2§1]
  • c. AD 280—[Chapters 2§2; 4; 6–7; 9–10; 12–13;
    15–16; 18]

---

[462] Runs concurrently with chapter 2 of Security.

[463] Runs concurrently with SCE #52–54.
[464] Runs concurrently through the end of 2377.
[465] A reference to Kai Opaka being dead is not easily reconcilable
with Unity.

- *late 2373*—[*Chapter 11§2*]
- *c. AD 281*—[*Chapter 19*]
- *c. AD 300*—[*Chapters 21; 23; 25*]

(VGR) "*Imperfection*"—Stardate 54129.4

Blackout (SCE eBook #59)

The Cleanup (SCE eBook #60)

(VGR) "*Drive*"—Stardate 54058.6

"You May Kiss the Bride" (VGR short story, SNW 8)

(VGR) "*Critical Care*"

"Pain Management" (Shelby short story, TFTCT)

—*backstory w/Soleta* (see primary entry, below)

(VGR) "*Repression*"—Stardate 54090.4 to 54101

Echoes of Coventry (SCE eBook #63)

—*Chapter 1; Epilogue*
- *early 2375*—[*Chapters 2–10*]

"Redux" (VGR short story, SNW VII)

(VGR) "*Inside Man*"—Stardate 54208.3

Vulcan's Soul #2: Exiles (ST)[466]

—"*Earth*"; "*U.S.S. Alliance*"; "*Waraii Homeworld*"
- *326–753*—["*Memory*"]

(VGR) "*Body and Soul*"—Stardate 54238.3

"Welcome Home" (VGR short story, SNW IV)

After the Fall (NF #15)

—"*Before . . .*" (see primary entry in 2379)

(VGR) "*Nightingale*"—Stardate 54274.7 to 54282.5

"Restoration" (VGR short story, SNW V)

(VGR) "*Flesh and Blood*"—Stardate 54337.5

Progress (SCE eBook #61)

—*Prologue, Epilogue*
- *2369*—[*Main story*]

A Hard Rain (TNG)

(VGR) "*Shattered*"

"Transfiguration" (VGR short story, SNW 8)

Star Trek: Borg (TNG interactive movie audio adaptation)[467]

- *2367*—[*Wolf 359 backstory*]
- *Limbo*—[*Q and Furlong's discussion*]

(VGR) "*Lineage*"—Stardate 54452.6

"Return" (VGR short story, SNW IV)

(VGR) "*Repentance*"—Stardate 54474.6

"Pain Management" (Shelby short story, TFTCT)

- *a few months earlier*—[*backstory w/Soleta*]

(VGR) "*Prophecy*"—Stardate 54518.2 to 54529.8

(VGR) "*The Void*"—Stardate 54553.4

(VGR) "*Workforce*"—Stardate 54584.3 to 54608.6

(VGR) "*Workforce, Part II*"—Stardate 54622.4

"The Last Tree on Ferenginar" (DS9 short story, SNW 9)[468]

—*backstory* (see primary entry in 3377)

"Shadows, in the Dark" (VGR short story, SNW IV)

The Nanotech War (VGR)

(VGR) "*Human Error*"

(VGR) "*Q2*"—Stardate 54704.5

{September 29–30} "Final Entry" (VGR short story, SNW V)[469]

—*Twenty-first to twenty-second entries* (see primary entry in 2353)

(VGR) "*Author, Author*"—Stardate 54732.3 to 54748.6

"Hidden" (VGR short story, SNW VI)

(VGR) "*Friendship One*"—Stardate 54775.4

"Iridium-7-Tetrahydroxate Crystals are a Girl's Best Friend" (VGR short story, SNW IV)

(VGR) "*Natural Law*"—Stardate 54814.5 to 54827.7

"Seven and Seven" (VGR short story, SNW VI)[470]

(VGR) "*Homestead*"—Stardate 54868.6

"Bottomless" (VGR short story, DS)

(VGR) "*Renaissance Man*"—Stardate 54890.7 to 54912.4

{Stardate 54968.4–54989.1} Endgame (VGR episode novelization)

—*Chapters 8–18*
- *2403*—[*Chapters 1–7*]

---

[466] Story is set two months after *Vulcan's Soul #1: Exodus*.

[467] Framing story is set ten years after the Battle of Wolf 359 and six months before Stardate 54902.

[468] Occurs eight years after "The Nagus" (DS9) and after Ro's first visit to Ferenginar in *Satisfaction Is Not Guaranteed*. The details of the relationship between Quark and Ro may be apocryphal.

[469] The date, given as February 2378, has been adjusted.

[470] References to "Scorpion" (VGR) being "over four years ago" are inaccurate.

"Da Capo al Fine," parts I and II (VGR short story, DS)[471]

2378

Homecoming (VGR)

—*Chapters 1–3*
- *February 2378—[Chapters 4–20]*

{January} "Widow's Walk" (VGR short story, SNW VI)[472]

—*first entry*
- *March 2378—[second-fourth entries]*

"Fragment" (VGR short story, SNW V)

"Homemade" (VGR short story, SNW VI)

{February 17} "Final Entry" (VGR short story, SNW V)[473]

—*final entry* (see primary entry in 2353)

Homecoming (VGR)

—*Chapters 4–20* (see primary entry, above)

The Farther Shore (VGR)

{March} "Widow's Walk" (VGR short story, SNW VI)[474]

—*second-fourth entries* (see primary entry, above)

"Coffee with a Friend" (VGR short story, SNW 8)

"Seduced" (Chakotay short story, TFTCT)

- *2344—[sections 1–11]*

Spirit Walk #1: Old Wounds (VGR)

- *2375—[Prologue]*

Spirit Walk #2: Enemy of My Enemy (VGR)

{Stardate 55595.4 to 55600.7} Captain's Peril (ST hardcover)

—*Chapters 1–3; 6; 8; 10–12; 14; 16–18; 20; 23; 25; 27–31; 33; Epilogue*
- *2348—[Prologue]*
- *2265—[Chapters 4–5; 7; 9; 13; 15; 19; 21–22; 24; 26; 32]*

A Time to Be Born (TNG)[475]

A Time to Die (TNG)

A Time to Sow (TNG)[476]

—*Chapters 3–31*
- *June 2151—[Chapter 1]*
- *July 2151—[Chapter 2]*

2379

A Time to Harvest (TNG)

A Time to Love (TNG)

A Time to Hate (TNG)

A Time to Kill (TNG)

A Time to Heal (TNG)

After the Fall (NF #15 hardcover)

—*"After..."*
- *2377—["Before..."]*

A Time for War, A Time for Peace (TNG)

—*Chapters 1–15*
- *about two weeks later—[Epilogue sections 1–6]*
- *about seven weeks later—[Epilogue section 7]*

Missing in Action (NF #16 hardcover)[477]

{Stardate 56828.8} Taking Wing (Titan #1)

—*Chapter 1* (see primary entry, below)

{Stardate 56844.9} Star Trek: Nemesis (TNG movie novelization)

—*Prologue; Chapters 1–10; 11§§1–4*
- *about five weeks later—[Chapter 11§§5–8]*

"Final Flight" (TNG short story, SNW 8)[478]

—*Sections 1, 3, 5, 8* (see primary entry, below)

A Time for War, A Time for Peace (TNG)

—*Epilogue §§1–6* (see primary entry, above)

Death in Winter (TNG hardcover)

—*Chapters 1–17*
- *2348—["San Francisco"]*
- *2339—["Arvada III"]*

"Improvisations on the Opal Sea: A Tale of Dubious Credibility" (Riker short story, TFTCT)

"Final Flight" (TNG short story, SNW 8)

—*Sections 2, 4, 6–7*
- *about three weeks earlier—[sections 1,3,5,8]*

---

[471] Occurs during the events of *Endgame*.
[472] The given date of August 2377 has been adjusted.
[473] The month, given as June, has been adjusted.
[474] The given dates of September to October 2377 have been adjusted.
[475] The given month of May was disregarded.

[476] Story carries over into 2379.
[477] Continues through the events of *Nemesis*.
[478] Occurs during the events of *Nemesis*.

{STARDATE 56941.1–56941.4} TAKING WING (TITAN #1)

—*Chapters 2–4 (see primary entry, below)*

STAR TREK: NEMESIS (TNG MOVIE NOVELIZATION)

—*Chapter 11 §§5–8 (see primary entry, above)*

{STARDATE 56944.2} TAKING WING (TITAN #1)

—*Chapter 5 (see primary entry, below)*

A TIME FOR WAR, A TIME FOR PEACE (TNG)

—*Epilogue section 7 (see primary entry, above)*

{STARDATE 56979.5–57023.3} TAKING WING (TITAN #1)

—*Chapters 6–24*

- *six weeks earlier—[Chapter 1]*
- *two weeks earlier—[Chapters 2–4]*
- *less than two weeks earlier—[Chapter 5]*

2380

{STARDATE 57024.0–57080.6} THE RED KING (TITAN #2)

—*Chapters 1–3; 5–22; Coda*

- *2349—[Chapter 4]*

{JANUARY} ARTICLES OF THE FEDERATION (ST)[479]

—*Chapters 1–6*

- *March—[Chapters 7–12]*
- *May—[Chapters 13–17]*
- *August—[Chapters 18–21]*
- *October—[Chapters 22–24]*
- *December—[Chapters 25–28]*

"THE CALLING" (DS9 SHORT STORY, P&C)[480]

{STARDATE 57137.8–57223.6} ORION'S HOUNDS (TITAN #3)

{MARCH, MAY} ARTICLES OF THE FEDERATION (ST)[481]

—*Chapters 7–17 (see primary entry, above)*

{STARDATE 57465.6} CAPTAIN'S BLOOD (ST HARDCOVER)

{AUGUST, OCTOBER, DECEMBER} ARTICLES OF THE FEDERATION (ST)

—*Chapters 18–28 (see primary entry, above)*

CAPTAIN'S GLORY (ST HARDCOVER)

2381

"ONCE UPON A TRIBBLE" (VGR SHORT STORY, SNW 8)

2385

"A & Ω" (ST SHORT STORY, SNW 8)[482]

—*sections 1–6*

- *circa 12385—[section 7]*
- *2273—[section 8]*

2386

"DON'T CRY" (VGR SHORT STORY, SNW VII)

—*Miral's flashback (see primary entry in 2403)*

2395

"STAYING THE COURSE" (TOS SHORT STORY, SNW 9)[483]

ALL GOOD THINGS . . . (TNG EPISODE NOVELIZATION)[484]

—*Chapters 3§2; 5§§2–3; 6§1; 10§§2–3; 11§§1–4; 14§§2–3; 15§1; 16§5; 17§§1–2; 18§4; 19; 20§1; 21§4; 22; 23§§1, 4; 24§§3, 6, 9, 12, 15 (see primary entry in 2370)*

2400

{AUGUST 9} PRESERVER (TNG HARDCOVER)

—*"The Ashes of Eden" (see primary entry in 2375)*

MILLENNIUM BOOK ONE: THE FALL OF TEROK NOR (DS9)

—*Chapter 29 (see primary entry in 2374)*

---

[479] Chapters 1–6 are concurrent with *The Red King*.

[480] This story is set an unspecified number of years after the events of the novel *A Stitch in Time* and the stage play "The Dream Box," both of which follow the story of Garak beyond the events of the television series.

[481] Chapters 7–12 are concurrent with *Orion's Hounds*.

[482] Presumably this timeline is "rebooted" by the V'Ger/Decker/Ilia entity in or about 12385.

[483] Story takes place when Picard is still in his eighties and Alexander has been ambassador to the Klingon Empire for at least fifteen years. Picard and Worf have known each other for thirty-eight years, so we assume they must have met during Worf's freshman year at the academy.

[484] This "anti-time" portion of the story must be regarded as an alternate future that is divergent from the "mainstream" universe.

Millennium Book Two: The War of the Prophets (DS9)[485]

—*Chapters 1–29 (see primary entry in 2374)*

2403

Endgame (VGR episode novelization)[486]

—*Chapters 1–7 (see primary entry in 2377)*

"Don't Cry" (VGR short story, SNW VII)[487]

- 2386—*[Miral's flashback]*

2408

Imzadi (TNG hardcover)[488]

—*Chapters 1–6; Epilogue; 34–36; 44 (see primary entry in 2368)*

2442

"Revisited" (DS9 short story, P&C)[489]

2462

"Guardians" (ST short story, SNW VII)

—*"49805 Years Ago" (see primary entry in 52267)*

2464

"Guardians" (ST short story, SNW VII)

—*"49803 Years Ago" (see primary entry in 52267)*

2465

"The Shoulders of Giants" (ST short story, SNW V)

—*Epilogue*

- 2152—*[Prologue]*
- 2268—*["One: Fiffick"]*
- 2343—*["Two: Rayvis"]*
- 2368—*["Three: Nyda"]*

C.2500

"One Last Adventure" (TOS short story, SNW VI)

—*section 1 (see primary entry in 2293)*

2525

"Stone Cold Truths" (ST short story, TODW)

—*sections 1, 3 (see primary entry in 2375)*

C.2569

"Gone Native" (TOS short story, SNW 9)

2696

"Guardians" (ST short story, SNW VII)

—*"49571 Years Ago" (see primary entry in 52267)*

2867

"Guardians" (ST short story, SNW VII)

—*"49400 Years Ago" (see primary entry in 52267)*

2892

{November 30} "Project Blue Book" (TOS short story, SNW VII)

—*section 5 (see primary entry in 2003)*

C.2948

(VGR) *"Living Witness"*[490]

C.3000

"Personal Log" (VGR short story, SNW IV)[491]

Shockwave (ENT episode novelization)

—*Chapters 12§3; 13§2; 15§2; 17§§2–3; 18§2 (see primary entry in 2152)*

C.3100

"The Law of Averages" (ST short story, SNW VII)

---

[485] These sections of the two *Millennium* novels take place in an alternate future.

[486] This portion of the story must be regarded as an alternate future, based on Admiral Janeway's interference.

[487] Story is set in the alternate future from "Endgame," though apparently in a parallel timeline where Neelix did not leave the ship in 2377.

[488] Except for the final chapter, this portion of the novel, set forty-two years after "The Offspring" (TNG), takes place in an alternate future.

[489] This story takes place in an alternate version of "The Visitor."

[490] The date was calculated from "Personal Log" (SNW IV), which establishes a Kyrian year as .82 standard years.

[491] Story takes place twenty-seven years after the Emergency Medical Hologram Backup Module left Vaskan/Kyrian space, assuming his term as Surgical Chancellor was about twenty-five years. The EMH's claim that the story occurs in the middle of the thirtieth century is incorrect.

C.3377

"THE LAST TREE ON FERENGINAR" (DS9 SHORT STORY, SNW 9)[492]

—*framing story*
- 2377—[*backstory*]

4367

"I AM BECOME DEATH" (TNG SHORT STORY, SNW II)[493]

—*section 1*
- 2366—[*sections 2–5*]

5307

"GUARDIANS" (ST SHORT STORY, SNW VII)
—"*46960 Years Ago*" (see primary entry in 52267)

10141

"GUARDIANS" (ST SHORT STORY, SNW VII)
—"*42126 Years Ago*" (see primary entry in 52267)

C.12385

"A & Ω" (ST SHORT STORY, SNW 8)
—*section 7* (see primary entry in 2385)

17602

"GUARDIANS" (ST SHORT STORY, SNW VII)
—"*34665 Years Ago*" (see primary entry in 52267)

22862

"GUARDIANS" (ST SHORT STORY, SNW VII)
—"*29405 Years Ago*" (see primary entry in 52267)

28397

"GUARDIANS" (ST SHORT STORY, SNW VII)
—"*23870 Years Ago*" (see primary entry in 52267)

36702

"GUARDIANS" (ST SHORT STORY, SNW VII)
—"*15565 Years Ago*" (see primary entry in 52267)

44247

"GUARDIANS" (ST SHORT STORY, SNW VII)
—"*8020 Years Ago*" (see primary entry in 52267)

52266

"GUARDIANS" (ST SHORT STORY, SNW VII)
—"*One Year Ago*" (see primary entry in 52267)

52267

"TEARS FOR ETERNITY" (TOS SHORT STORY, SNW IV)
—*final section* (see primary entry in 2371)

"GUARDIANS" (ST SHORT STORY, SNW VII)

- 2297—[*49970 years ago*]
- 2462—[*49805 years ago*]
- 2464—[*49803 years ago*]
- 2696—[*49571 years ago*]
- 2867—[*49400 years ago*]
- 5307—[*46960 years ago*]
- 10141—[*42126 years ago*]
- 17602—[*34665 years ago*]
- 22862—[*29405 years ago*]
- 28397—[*23870 years ago*]
- 36702—[*15565 years ago*]
- 44247—[*8020 years ago*]
- 52266—[*One year ago*]
- "*The Future*"

1012260

{STARDATE 17613341.4} "OUR MILLION-YEAR MISSION" (SHORT STORY, SNW VI)

---

[492] Over a thousand "fiscal cycles" and/or forty-three generations after the timeframe of the storyteller's legend.
[493] Framing story is set 2,000 years in an alternate future of TNG.